THE TRESPASSERS

OTHER BOOKS AND AUDIOBOOKS

BY STEPHANIE BLACK

Natalie Marsh Mystery Series

Not a Word

Mind Games

To Die, To Sleep

Bound in Shallows

Come, Gentle Night

Megan O'Connor Mystery Series

Fool Me Twice

Played for a Fool

Dystopian Series

The Believer

The Witnesses

Stand-Alone Mysteries

Methods of Madness

Shadowed

Rearview Mirror

Cold as Ice

*Eye for an Eye**

Compilations

Twisted Fate

Entangled

* Novella

THE TRESPASSERS

A TRESPASSERS SUSPENSE NOVEL

STEPHANIE BLACK

Covenant Communications, Inc.

Cover: *Coastal Town* © Jason Leung, *Silhouette of Woman* © Tyler Nix, *Red EKG* © istockphoto.com

Cover design by Kevin Jorgensen
Cover design © 2023 by Covenant Communications, Inc.

Published by Covenant Communications, Inc.
American Fork, Utah

Library of Congress Cataloging-in-Publication Data

Name: Stephanie Black
Title: The Trespassers / Stephanie Black
Description: American Fork, UT : Covenant Communications, Inc. [2023]
Identifiers: Library of Congress Control Number 2023931167 | 9781524424541
LC record available at https://lccn.loc.gov/2023931167

Printed in the United States of America
First Printing: September 2023

30 29 28 27 26 25 24 23 10 9 8 7 6 5 4 3 2 1

PRAISE FOR *THE TRESPASSERS*

"Black (*Come, Gentle Night*) sets a murder mystery against a paranormal backdrop in this gripping series opener. When Rayna Kirkpatrick learns that her father died the day after they had a blowout fight, she worries that she inadvertently killed him. Though friends dismiss her concerns, Rayna has a secret: along with sensing others' heartbeats, she can stop hearts at will. Despite lingering anxieties about her abilities, Rayna returns home to Willet Beach, Calif., where she bonds with her sister Annemarie and revives the pottery business she's neglected since her divorce a year earlier. Unbeknownst to Rayna, the government monitors 'Trespassers' with abilities like hers, and when several unexplained deaths are linked back to Rayna, government agent (and fellow Trespasser) Damon Hale is sent to investigate. Soon afterward, an apparent murder occurs in Willet Beach, and Damon and Rayna must try to work together to find the culprit, while Rayna seeks answers as to whether her powers are a gift from God or a dangerous liability. Black's page-turner is buttressed with sympathetic characters and a smart, fast-moving plot that believably fleshes out the supernatural framework. Readers will eagerly await the next installment."

—*Publishers Weekly*

"A family reunion degenerates into a murder mystery where everyone is a suspect in Stephanie Black's [*The Trespassers*]. Her cast of characters is impressive, as is her opting to keep it simple by creating a story around familial relationships in a close-knit community. This elevates the tale from what I expected to be a mystery novel with a supernatural orientation into an account that is sufficiently grounded in the realities of the present times. Her subplots are well thought out as evidenced by the evolving relationship between Rayna and the mysterious Damon Hale.

"What I love about *The Trespassers* is the way Black uses her style of storytelling to change an unusual mystery into an immersive and exciting adventure that will push readers to their cognitive limits to solve the puzzles hidden within it. This is an absolute gem."

—*Readers' Favorite* five-star review

"There were no dull moments. The characters are terrific."

—Jill Daugs, NetGalley review

"Stephanie Black is so incredibly masterful at writing suspense."

—Shauna Jones, NetGalley review

"The writing is phenomenal, as usual, and the concept so intriguing and original. Lots of action and suspense, growing friendships, escalating insanity and mysteries keep the story going and unputdownable."

—Cindy Whitney, NetGalley review

PRAISE FOR *COME, GENTLE NIGHT*

"The fair but surprising solution is satisfying. Black manages to make her lead's involvement in another whodunit plausible."

—*Publishers Weekly*

"*Come, Gentle Night* is a riveting tale that leaves the reader craving more drama, secrets, and action amidst a roller coaster of emotions caused by a budding romance that is tried and tested in every manner. This amazingly unique story has a very enticing shade thrown into the damsel in distress giving it an overall exotic feel."

—*InD'Tale* Magazine

"*Come, Gentle Night* is an excellent and absorbing mystery that continues Natalie's journey into the world of the detective with a story that will absorb and mystify readers whilst it keeps them on the edge of their seats."

—*Readers' Favorite* five-star review

To Stanford and Kathleen McConkie,
my wonderful parents, who always use their unique gifts to share goodness

ACKNOWLEDGMENTS

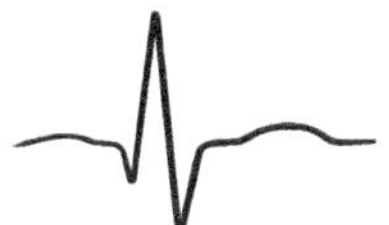

For generously answering my questions and sharing their expertise, thank you to Mikki Helmer, Traci Abramson, Marshall McConkie, Shauna Rasband, Gregg Luke, Monique Hickman, Dianna Hall, Rebecca Hall, Justin Rasband, Nicholas Welch, Shari Phippen, and Gracie Dunster. Thank you to the members of my Facebook Mystery Chat group; you're a great source for helpful and entertaining suggestions. For providing feedback on the manuscript, thank you to Sue McConkie and Ken Reynolds; I greatly appreciate your insights.

Thank you to my editor and dear friend, Samantha Millburn; Sam, you are my hero. Thank you to Kevin Jorgensen for the fantastic cover design, to Shara Meredith and her team for all their marvelous work with marketing and publicity, and to everyone at Covenant Communications. As always, it's a pleasure to work with you, and I'm so grateful for everything you do to bring my books to readers.

CHAPTER 1

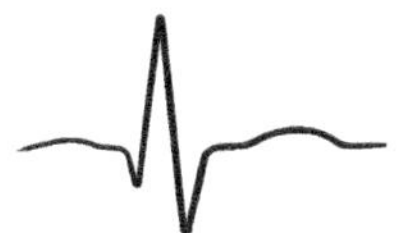

Rayna Kirkpatrick watched dark, metallic-gray waves strike the rocks and froth into foam. A sliver of sun remained on the horizon, dyeing streaky clouds orange. She leaned against the railing of the resort's wraparound balcony and breathed slowly, drawing as much ocean air into her lungs as she could. Muscles that had been taut on the flight from Denver had slackened, and the throbbing anxieties in her head had quieted to ripples. This trip would be fine.

Through the buzz of heartbeats and the sensations of life filling the reception room behind her, Rayna sensed someone stepping away from the others and approaching the door to the balcony. She automatically identified the person about to join her: her sister. She didn't turn toward Annemarie yet. Though Annemarie knew about her ability, pretending she wasn't aware of someone until a normal person would notice them was always the more prudent choice in public.

A normal person. Even Annemarie had no inkling of how frighteningly far from normal Rayna was now.

The door opened, and Annemarie came to stand next to her. "You're going to freeze to death out here."

"I won't freeze to death watching the sunset." After eight years in Colorado, Rayna regarded February on the northern California coast as balmy by comparison, even though the temperature had dropped in the twilight and the wind was brisk.

"In that wet dress, you *might* freeze," Annemarie said. "Come inside and get warm."

"Only the hem is wet." Rayna pushed back strands of hair that the wind had blown loose from what had been a smooth updo an hour ago.

Annemarie reached down and patted the damp fabric over Rayna's knees. "A good eight or ten inches of hem is wet. Good thing the texture of the lace helps camouflage it. You're worse than my kids."

Rayna laughed. After dressing for the party, she hadn't been able to resist one more beach stroll. She'd relished the icy water brushing her bare toes—until she'd settled too deeply into her own thoughts and hadn't noticed a larger wave rolling in.

"You could move back here, you know," Annemarie said. "You could walk the beach every day."

"There's no way I could afford to move here right now." And as much as she loved Willet Beach, she didn't want to live that close to her father. She'd been nervous to attend his sixty-fifth birthday/engagement party, but skipping it would have wreaked havoc on an already dicey relationship. She wanted to strengthen her connections with her family, not stomp on them. So far, so good—when she'd arrived this afternoon, her conversation with her father had been a light, jokey one about shoveling snow and air travel.

"I can't afford to live here at all," Annemarie said, rubbing her arms through her silky sleeves.

The edge in Annemarie's voice stirred Rayna's concern. "Is everything—"

"Yes, the store's fine. I'm just whining. You need a fresh start, Ray. Are you finding that in Denver?"

"More or less."

"Meaning you aren't, but you don't want to talk about it."

"This isn't the time to talk about it. This is a time to celebrate." Rayna smiled at Annemarie. "How do you feel about having Jody Wyeth for a stepmother?"

"I feel like I'm glad Jody planned this whole extravaganza so I didn't have to do a thing." Annemarie linked her arm with Rayna's. "And I feel like if she jokes one more time about Dad marrying the 'girl next door,' I'll vomit. We should go socialize. Have you even had a chance to speak with Jody since you arrived?"

"Not yet." Rayna let Annemarie guide her into the reception room, where the warmth *was* a relief. Her father was standing in the center of the room, ruggedly handsome, all but mobbed by people eager to enjoy the company of Glenn Kirkpatrick and deliver best wishes. Jody was at his side, beaming.

As Annemarie steered her toward the group, Rayna studied her former neighbor. Jody's salt-and-pepper hair was shorter than Rayna had ever seen it and far more chic, stylishly layered and flipped at the ends. The frames of her glasses were new as well, steel instead of the variety of colorful plastic rims she used to wear, and her magenta cocktail dress was stunning.

"My dear, there you are!" Jody stepped forward to embrace Rayna. Her perfume hadn't changed; it was the gardenia scent Rayna remembered from childhood. Rayna and her father didn't hug. They'd exchanged their one obligatory hug of greeting earlier today.

"Thank you *so* much for being with us tonight," Jody said.

"My pleasure," Rayna said. "Congratulations."

"Thank you! My stars, you look lovely. That periwinkle blue is such a flattering color on you, and the same with that green on you, Annemarie. Glenn, your redheads will soon be my little cubs!" Jody squeezed his arm. "Isn't that amazing?"

Annemarie and Rayna glanced at each other. *Redheads* was accurate; Rayna's hair was deep auburn and Annemarie's strawberry blonde, but "little cubs" didn't exactly fit women in their thirties.

"With these two and my beautiful Kaitlyn, imagine what lovely grandchildren we'll have!" Jody exclaimed. "If I can ever get Kaitlyn married off, of course. She's so particular."

Rayna's father looked her over. She hoped he wouldn't notice her damp skirt. "You'll need to marry off Rayna as well, seeing as how the first round didn't take. Good luck with that. I give Evan credit for lasting as long as he did with a woman who spends her time playing with Play-Doh."

Caught off guard, Rayna scrambled inwardly to grab her emotions before a whirlwind of humiliation could blow them loose.

"Dad!" Annemarie said. "Rayna's a skilled potter."

"Making bowls and pots that would be more efficiently produced by machine," he said. "Is that a wise use of time?"

Jody tittered. "Oh, Glenn, you're such a philistine. Rayna is an artist. Her work is unique."

"Art's a fine hobby, my love, but first, you pay the bills."

"I pay my bills." Rayna did her best to sound matter-of-fact. Though most of the people who'd been surrounding her father were now involved in other conversations, there were plenty of people in earshot if they wanted to listen, and Rayna didn't want to draw attention. "I work full-time at a museum."

"What do you do there, dear?" Jody asked.

"I work at the gift shop."

"So, you're a cashier because what else can you do with an art degree?" Her father shook his head. "You need something more practical like Annemarie's business degree. Have you thought of going back to school?"

"Let her be." Annemarie intervened again. "She's an adult."

"An adult who'll never be able to retire. She has to plan for the future."

"I'm sure she'll find a handsome man to help her with that." Jody smiled at Rayna.

Annemarie snorted. "Jody, really? Is this 1950? Rayna's retirement plan is not 'find a man.'"

Jody laughed. "I know I'm old-fashioned. Kaitlyn tells me I'm horribly sexist. But I didn't think I'd marry again, and here I am with Glenn!" She ran her fingers along his sleeve.

He winked at Jody. "Rayna can't count on getting another husband until she figures out the basic functions of pregnancy. Maybe she ought to pursue a degree in biology instead."

This gibe punched so savagely that Rayna all but doubled over. What had happened to this afternoon's lighthearted friendliness? *He thinks he* is *being lighthearted. Look at his grin.*

"*Dad*!" Annemarie's voice was knife sharp.

"Oh, Glenn, you don't mean that." Jody swatted his arm. "You say the worst things sometimes."

"Relax, everyone, I was joking."

"Excuse me." Rayna walked quickly toward the exit that led into the hallway.

Annemarie pursued her but didn't speak until they were out of the reception room. "In here," she said, nudging Rayna in the direction of the women's restroom.

Not sure where else to go, Rayna pushed the door open and discovered a small lounge attached to the restroom—an area for nursing mothers, no doubt, which Rayna would never be. Pain roiling, she sank onto the couch. Annemarie sat beside her.

"I'm done." Rayna spoke under her breath, though she knew no one else was in the restroom to overhear her. "I told myself I could handle him, that it would be okay, but—"

"I'm so sorry." Annemarie took Rayna's hand. "That was an incredibly awful thing for him to say. He can't wrap his head around how devastating your miscarriages have been for you—how much a joke like that would sting."

"And he also doesn't think it will sting when he tells everyone he admires my ex for putting up with Useless Rayna for so long?"

"That was ridiculous." Annemarie's grip on her hand tightened. "He's always had trouble understanding you, but that's no excuse for the things he says. Ignore him."

Rayna *wanted* to ignore him right this moment, but she could sense him so sharply that they might as well have been face-to-face. She pulled her hand free from Annemarie's grasp. "I'm skipping the dinner."

"Rayna. I'm so sorry you have to deal with this garbage, but don't miss the dinner. You didn't fly out here to spend the evening holed up in your hotel room because Dad's being himself."

Rayna didn't respond.

"Don't make it a local scandal, which is what it'll become if you bail out," Annemarie added. "Jody thrives on gossip, and she knows everyone in town. Do you want her jabbering all over the place about how you stomped out of your father's birthday party? Besides, with his heart condition, who knows how many more birthdays he'll have with us?"

"He has a heart condition, all right," Rayna snapped. "But not one his medication can regulate."

"Ray."

Rayna leaned her head against the couch and closed her eyes, trying to lessen her awareness of her father, make him part of the background.

"Take a little time to calm down and we'll go back in," Annemarie said. "Skip the family breakfast tomorrow if you have to. I'll tell them you woke up feeling sick. But you can't miss tonight. Just hang out with Seth and me, and we'll all keep our distance from Dad."

Keep our distance. How would that help when she could constantly sense him? Tuning him out wasn't working. Even with all the other people in the reception room and the rest of the resort, she could feel his heartbeat thudding in her brain. If she wanted to stop obsessing over his presence, she'd have to shut him out completely.

Do it if it will get you through tonight. It'll be a strain, but it might keep you sane. She mentally scanned the ballroom for people unfamiliar to her. Randomly, she selected someone in a group of strangers and focused on that person, concentrating as hard as she could.

"You okay?" Annemarie asked.

Rayna nodded, not explaining what she was doing. She'd cultivated this skill when her relationship with Evan had been at its most excruciating and she'd needed mental distance from him. Fixed her mind on one random person: blurred Evan and everyone else into white noise.

When even Annemarie, right next to her, didn't register as a distinct person and she was sensing only the stranger in the reception room, she opened her eyes and slowly rose to her feet. It would be difficult to hold this level of concentration all evening, but she didn't plan to be chatty anyway, and challenging herself this way would be an effective distraction. "I'm ready to go in," she said. Maybe she didn't have the guts to confront him directly, but to Rayna, at this moment, her father didn't exist, and that was the best she could do.

* * *

Rayna awoke to the sound of her alarm, her neck cramped, her back and shoulders stiff, and her head throbbing. She'd occupied herself all through the party by keeping her father out of her brain, and even after she'd gone to her hotel room, she'd kept up what had become a darkly satisfying game: how long could she erase him? Too wound up to sleep, she'd sat in bed, mindlessly viewing pottery-making videos on YouTube while her brain kept up the fight. By four in the morning, exhaustion had siphoned away bitterness, and she'd tumbled into slumber, letting her control crumble, too weary to care as white noise developed into impressions of the people around her.

She'd won her mind game, and the prize, apparently, was misery. Nauseated, fervently hoping she had ibuprofen in her purse, she went to check. She found the medication, swallowed the maximum dose, and slogged her way into the bathroom.

A prolonged, steaming-hot shower, combined with the ibuprofen kicking in, brought partial relief, but the more she thought about last night's coping strategy, the more sheepish she felt. She should have looked her father in the eyes and called him out on his "jokes" instead of indulging in the mental equivalent of teenage door-slamming and sulking. How old was she?

When have you ever had the courage to call him out?

Maybe it was time to rally that courage. She should pull him aside before the family breakfast. Where was he? She couldn't sense him anywhere within her range. He must have gone on an early-morning walk.

She was making a diligent attempt to hide the shadows under her eyes with makeup when she sensed Annemarie nearing her room. At her sister's knock, she went to answer the door.

"Good morning," Annemarie said. "May I come in?"

"Of course."

Annemarie entered and let the door shut behind her. "You doing okay this morning? You look exhausted."

"I'm tired, but if you're here to persuade me to come to the breakfast, you don't need to. I'm planning on it."

"I'm so glad you didn't let him scare you away." Annemarie gave her a quick hug. "I'm here on a mission from Jody. Dad was supposed to meet her in the lobby this morning at eight so they could go on a walk before the family breakfast, but he didn't show up, and he's not answering his phone. His car's here, but he's not in his hotel room—or at least not answering his door—so she came pounding on my door. I said he probably woke up early and went for a pre-walk walk, but she's getting worried that he got washed out to sea or something. I told her I'd find him, so I'm taking a shortcut by checking with you."

"He's not in the hotel or nearby." Rayna checked her watch. 8:28. He'd left Jody waiting for half an hour? They wouldn't have time left for their romantic stroll. The breakfast was at nine.

"Did you notice him leaving the hotel?" Annemarie asked.

"No, but I've only been up for forty minutes."

"This is weird. You're sure he's not in his room, still asleep maybe, or sick?"

"I'm sure." Stabbing pain in her neck made her wince. She kneaded her neck muscles with both hands. "Should we drive along the coast and search for him? Maybe he really is injured. He could have twisted an ankle, and maybe he doesn't have his phone with him."

"Yeah." Annemarie's phone beeped. She pulled it out of her pocket to check her text. "Seth says he still has the key card Dad gave him last night when he was hauling Dad's luggage to his room. He's asking if we want to check the room, just in case."

"Annie, if he were there, I'd know, unless . . ." Rayna trailed off, the snarky words she'd spoken last night about her father's heart condition now skewering her memory.

For an anxious moment of silence, Annemarie stared at Rayna. "Maybe . . . we should check his room."

Seth met them at the door of their father's room, smelling of the hotel's lemon-rosemary body wash, his sun-bleached hair wet and tousled. "I hope we're about to get yelled at." He rapped loudly on the door. "Glenn? You in there?"

No response.

Seth unlocked the door. Chilled from within, her legs heavy, Rayna followed Seth and Annemarie into the room.

He was there, in bed, lying on his side. His eyes were closed, and his face was a bleak grayish-blue.

"Dad!" Annemarie shrieked. She rushed forward to shake him, to check his pulse, but Rayna didn't need to touch him to know there was no trace of life in him.

Annemarie drew her fingers away from his neck. "He's gone."

Seth's tanned face blanched. "That . . . I can't believe . . . I'm so sorry, babe." He edged toward Annemarie as though wanting to go comfort her but not wanting to get too close to the still body in the bed.

Rayna stared at her father. His shoulder showed above the edge of the bedspread, clad in navy-blue flannel, the same winter pajamas he'd worn for as long as she could remember. Horror twisted around her, immobilizing her. Had she done this? Murdered her own father?

Mechanically, Annemarie picked up the reading glasses that sat on the nightstand—the foldable reading glasses their father had always carried in his pocket. She folded them and tucked them into their case. "At least he had that last celebration," she said hoarsely. "Seth, can you notify the hotel desk and see what we do next?"

"On it." Seth all but sprinted out of the room.

Once the door had shut behind Seth, Annemarie spoke quietly to Rayna, tears flowing down her face. "You never . . . sensed anything wrong with his heart? Everything was normal last night?"

Her words knocked Rayna's tears loose.

"Oh, Ray, I'm so sorry." Annemarie moved to enfold Rayna in a hug. "What a stupid question. Of course you didn't notice anything wrong, or you'd have gotten help for him."

"I should have noticed," she whispered. "But I—"

"Do *not* blame yourself. Do you think you were supposed to sit up all night monitoring him in case his heart decided to go wonky?"

She *had* sat up most of the night, but she'd been blocking him, not monitoring him. *You didn't kill him. You didn't kill him.*

Did you?

At the very least, if she hadn't been playing petty mind games, she might have sensed he was in trouble in time to save his life. At worst, maybe her mind had—

That's not how it works.

"Jody needs to know." Annemarie broke the embrace. "We should—" Her teary eyes widened. "Are you going to faint? You look awful. Sit down."

"Not in here," Rayna rasped.

Hastily, Annemarie steered her toward the door. "Let's get you back to your room. You need to lie down. I'll talk to Jody."

CHAPTER 2

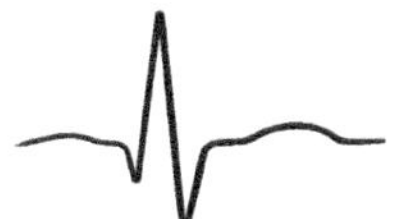

Rayna had brought her flashlight, but the moonlight was bright enough that she didn't need it. Hands in the pockets of her jacket, she wandered along the sand, water splashing her ankles. Her whole body, not only her ears, seemed to hear the swish of the water.

She'd spent the day barely able to function, but no one had expected anything of her anyway. Annemarie had dealt with Jody, with the police and ambulance crew, with condolences from friends and extended family, all while coddling Rayna and lecturing her—via whispers when no one else was around—that she had nothing to feel guilty about.

Rayna hadn't dared admit the depth of her fear. How could she tell Annemarie—or anyone else—about the ability she'd discovered in her twenties, discovered when she'd desperately wanted to end the suffering of an injured animal and had realized . . . weirdly . . . clearly . . . that she could stop its heart? Her far more benign ability to sense people was scary enough. This new ability made her a monster.

Water splashed higher on her legs, drenching the hems of her rolled-up jeans. She retreated to ground the incoming tide wouldn't reach and settled cross-legged on the sand.

You didn't kill your father. She repeated that assurance to herself for the thousandth time as she rolled her jeans down and put on her socks and shoes. *Stopping a heart takes deliberate focus. Being furious with him wouldn't have killed him. Shutting him out wouldn't have killed him.*

She was going to drive herself insane, so terrified and confused by her own mind that she was poised to jump to the worst of conclusions. She'd never even tried to understand herself—never so much as dared to google anything about her condition. Her father's mockery about her "glitchy brain" and her mother's warnings to keep her "quirks" to herself had always pulsed in her head.

"You don't want your friends to think you're scary or strange. You don't want them spreading rumors about you all over social media. You don't want hordes of scientists experimenting on you."

Pointlessly, she gathered sand into a mound in front of her, then flattened it and sat gazing out at the moonlight reflecting off the water. She didn't have to ask questions of anyone or share information, but she could conduct her own private research. Find out if anyone else had discussed this.

Do it. What if there are other people out there like you?

She brushed sand off her hands, reached into her jacket pocket, and took out her phone.

She put the phone back. She didn't want to look into this. She didn't want to think about it at all. It wouldn't help.

But maybe it *would* help. Maybe she needed to stop being so afraid of herself, afraid to ask questions that piercingly reminded her how horrifying she was. *Do it. What if there are answers about what caused this and how it all works?*

She pulled the phone out. Her fingers felt floppy as she slowly typed into the search bar: *ability to kill with your mind.*

* * *

"Rayna?"

A familiar voice taut with worry. Sensing Kaitlyn Wyeth leaning over her, Rayna opened her eyes and hastily sat up, wincing in the glare of a flashlight. Kaitlyn lowered the beam.

"Hi." Rayna groped for the phone she'd mashed into the sand next to her. "I . . . dozed off."

"Dozed off on the beach at ten o'clock at night in February. That's one way to get some sleep. Hang on. I need to tell Annemarie I found you." Kaitlyn started texting.

"Sorry." Rayna peered up at Kaitlyn. Sleek brown hair brushed into a ponytail. Sympathy and humor in her face. A fleece jacket with *Wyeth's Grill* embroidered on the pocket above the logo of flames rising through a metal grate. "I didn't mean to make you come searching for me."

"Oh, we knew you'd be somewhere on the beach." Kaitlyn stuck her phone in her pocket. "Come inside. You're not equipped to camp out here."

"Yes, I am. This is a Colorado-grade jacket."

Kaitlyn laughed and held out her hand to Rayna. "Come on."

Rayna clasped Kaitlyn's hand, and Kaitlyn helped her to her feet. Feeling slightly disoriented, Rayna brushed sand off her jeans, jacket, and the hood she'd pulled up so her head wouldn't lie directly on the cold sand. She hadn't expected to fall asleep when, drained after a long stretch of googling, she'd decided to rest before returning to the resort.

"You okay, more or less?" Kaitlyn asked.

"I think so. Tired." Tired but much less terrified. The flood of search terms she'd poured into the internet had garnered her no answers, but the attempt had been calming and cathartic. Rationality had finally conquered panic. She absolutely hadn't murdered her father. If fury alone were lethal, she'd have inadvertently killed him before now. If shutting people out of her mind were lethal, everyone within a quarter-mile radius—except for the one stranger whom she'd focused on last night—would be dead. And she'd have killed Evan long ago.

Her fleeting desire to seek answers had gone with that one fruitless attempt. She could do what she could do, she didn't need to know why, and that was her life.

They walked in the direction of the stairs that led up to the resort.

"How's your mom doing?" Rayna asked.

"She'll be fine. It's a shock, but you know her. Smile and carry on. And let's be frank, milk the situation for all the sympathy and gossip she can. Her fiancé drops dead the night of his birthday party, and now she gets to play the role of the bereaved pretty-much-a-widow. That's quality drama, especially since she can work my father's death into her conversations, too, and get double sympathy." Kaitlyn sighed. "Was that too crass? I have strange ways of coping with death." She touched Rayna's arm. "We nearly became stepsisters, so I can be candid. Speaking as someone who's known your family forever, I give you permission to admit you have mixed feelings about your father's passing—and part of you is relieved."

Fiery tingling spread through Rayna's cheeks.

"I know that's a hard thing to admit, but you can admit it to me because I get it," Kaitlyn said. "I went through it after my dad passed. In a lot of ways, our dads were two peas in a pod, which explains why my mom fell for your dad. She has lousy taste in men."

"Kaitlyn! My father . . . He had a lot of positive qualities."

"Sure, and he had negative ones. Mom told me what he said to you before dinner last night. Blaming you for your husband ditching you. Mocking your fertility problems. Lucky for him I didn't overhear, or I'd have given him an earful in front of his guests."

"He was . . . joking."

"*Joking.* Yeah, that's how he always tried to play it off when he said cruel things, but that's not joking. That's *trying* to hurt you. I don't know why he picked on you like he did, but if—along with your grief—you're a little relieved he's gone, I don't blame you." Kaitlyn paused at the base of the stairs, where lampposts on either side cast bright light. Rayna tried to continue up the stairs, but Kaitlyn grasped her shoulder. "Look at me."

Rayna forced herself to meet Kaitlyn's keen gaze.

"It's okay to feel that way," Kaitlyn said. "No one else will tell you that because they'll all be jamming misfitting halos on his head like we do when someone dies, but you need to know it's normal and it's okay."

Rayna scoured her mind for something positive to say. "We . . . got along well most of the time. Some of the time, at least. He didn't connect with me as well as with Annemarie."

"No kidding. You're not blaming yourself for his death, are you?"

"No," Rayna said shortly. She still had plenty to regret with the way she'd missed that he was in distress, but none of this was a topic she wanted to discuss.

"Annemarie's worried you think it's your fault. That you should have somehow guessed he was in trouble and checked on him, even though he seemed fine at the party."

Rayna picked up a tiny shell from a heap someone had left near the base of one of the lampposts. "I don't know how he seemed at the party. I was . . . ignoring him."

"Good. He didn't deserve your attention. *None* of us realized he was in trouble, Rayna. Why is that on you? Be honest. You're afraid your walking out on him and then cold-shouldering him during his birthday dinner upset him? You think his anger played a role in tipping his heart into a fatal arrythmia?"

Kaitlyn's candor kindled an urge to respond with at least some degree of honesty. "I don't think I caused it." Rayna's mouth was dry. She swallowed. "But if I hadn't been ignoring him, maybe I would have noticed—"

"There was nothing to notice. He was fine at the party. None of this is your fault. Let me guess. You're used to getting blamed for things."

"I should go find Annemarie," Rayna said, pointlessly examining the purplish shell she held.

"You haven't listened to anything I've told you, have you? That's fine if you can't process it now, but remember it for later in case anyone—including yourself—tries to tell you that the only thing you're allowed to be is sad." Kaitlyn started up the stairs. "At least he did right by you in his will. Annemarie told me it's 50/50 between the two of you. Don't you dare feel like you have to do something *he'd* approve of with that money."

"I don't." She didn't yet know how much money she would inherit, but Annemarie, the executor of her father's estate, had told her it would be a significant amount. Enough to allow her to quit her job at the museum. Enough to allow her to focus on transforming her pottery side hustle into a full-time career. Enough to allow her to leave Denver and everything connected to her life with Evan Novak.

She could imagine what her father would have said to her leaving Denver, a remark in the vein of his comment when he'd found out she was switching back to her maiden name: *"What's the point of that? Changing labels doesn't hide the failure."* Changing her location wouldn't hide it either, but it might help her move beyond it.

And her father wasn't here to criticize her any longer.

Yearning stirred inside her, stronger than the guilt twining around it. She wanted to come home to Willet Beach. Start over.

Maybe . . . finally . . . find peace.

CHAPTER 3

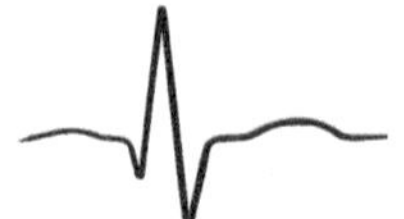

Wind and sleet rendered the walk from the Metro a miserable one. Damon Hale kept his head down and hurried toward a nondescript office building that blended into everything around it on this Washington D.C. street. Eager for the shelter of the lobby, he scanned his access card and waited for verification, his shoes and the legs of his pants getting wetter and his fingers turning to ice inside his gloves. Finally, the lock clicked open.

Gratefully, he stepped inside, stripped off his gloves, and hung his dripping coat on a rack in the corner. A retinal scan allowed him into the corridor that led to Logan Tilburg's office.

"Good morning. Or not a good morning. Rotten morning." Logan took his feet off his desk. "How does a California-beach vacation sound?"

"It sounds like you're spin-doctoring a new assignment." Damon settled in a chair and wiped away melted sleet rolling down his forehead. "What is it this time? Conspiracy theorist, spacey New Ager, or person in need of anti-psychotic medication?"

Logan grinned, a wide smile in a face so boyish that graying hair was the only sign of middle age. "Look who woke up feeling cynical. Just because almost none of these leads are worth anything, that's no reason to get jaded." He scooted a file across the desk. "This one might be the real deal."

"Still paper?" Damon picked up the file. "I thought you were finally going all electronic."

"I like running things through the shredder. And you can't hack a piece of paper."

Damon opened it and studied the photograph of a woman. Oval face with a squarish chin. Angles and straight lines in the features, softness in her brown eyes. Long dark-red hair. The photo was labeled *Rayna Colleen Kirkpatrick (Rayna*

Novak) with a home address in Denver and a birthdate that would make her thirty-one.

"How did she come to our attention?" Damon asked.

"Google ratted her out."

Damon turned a page and scanned the phrases that had snagged in their surveillance net. When he reached the search for *extrasensory abilities miscarriage connection*, he understood Logan's heightened interest. He reviewed the list a second time, noting time stamps and locations.

"Two hours of internet searches last month, all in one sitting, all while she was in Willet Beach, California," Damon said. "There was nothing noted before or after that date?"

"Nothing we caught. Under those circumstances, we'd wonder if the search wasn't about *her*—if she was reacting to information someone confided in her during her visit—but as you can see, she got specific on some of her searches, and all the details match her background. Places she's lived. Parents' birthplaces and occupations. All the chemicals she references are ones used in ceramics. She runs a little Etsy pottery shop."

That explained such searches as *paranormal powers hydrous aluminum silicate* and *thought killing kiln firing fumes* that were located near the end of the list. By that point, she'd really been scrounging to find anything that could explain what her mind could do. "Any evidence that she's ever asked anyone besides Google these questions?"

"Nothing obvious that the initial assessment picked up on, but that's something for you to figure out. And we have a red-flag death. Her reason for being in California was her father's birthday party. He died the night of the party, a death ruled natural causes."

Damon shifted in his chair, feeling even colder in his sleet-dampened clothing. "Do we know if there's a reason to think she killed him—besides the fact that she was in town?"

"That's for you to determine. We know her father was well-to-do, so money might be a motive. After the funeral, she promptly started wrapping things up in Denver. She's moving back to Willet Beach. You're going to beat her there and get your cover established. Go find out if we have a Trespasser. If we do, is it someone we can work with or a killer we need to take care of?"

Damon nodded.

"Damon." Logan's perpetually cheery expression went serious. "It's been a while since we stalked a lion. I know you're still beating yourself up over McCuller, but you shouldn't. You did as well as anyone could, and I trust you to handle this situation no matter what it turns out to be. You have more finesse than the rest of the team put together. Think, but don't overthink. Trust yourself."

Trust yourself. A scorching cramp seized Damon's gut.

If he failed again, how many innocent people would lose their lives this time?

CHAPTER 4

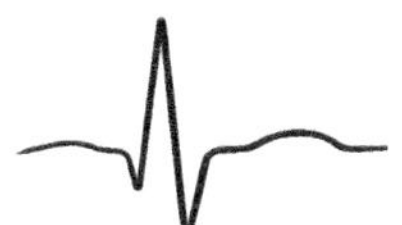

The mildness of the March twilight made Rayna smile as she watched Annemarie fiddle with the padlock on the backyard shed. During the six weeks it had taken her to wrap things up in Denver, she'd managed to shove guilt and regret farther and farther behind her and focus on the future. She hadn't even told Evan she was leaving, though she was sure he'd heard the news from mutual friends. Why would he care? He'd already moved on; she'd heard he was seriously dating a woman from work. Good for him. He could live his life however he wanted. Rayna was moving back to Willet Beach to live *her* life.

"I didn't realize how rusty this lock had gotten." Annemarie jiggled the key. "I don't think anyone has opened the shed since you last used it. Sorry. I planned to clean it out but never got to it. At least I got the painting done in the guesthouse and the yard cleaned up. Seth keeps saying we should hire a yard service now that . . . now that we're more financially secure. But that feels like a waste of money to me. I can take care of the yard. I like working outside . . . when I can find the time, which doesn't happen very often."

"I'd be happy to take over the yard work," Rayna said. "I like your new landscaping. The lupine is beautiful."

"Thanks. A lot of these are native plants. Low water."

"They look a lot easier to care for than Mom's perfect flowerbeds. You should have left the painting for me too. You've already been more than kind, letting me move into the guesthouse."

"*Making* you move into the guesthouse. I want you close. Those cracks in the tile on the kitchen counter . . . Sorry about that. Tiled counters are the worst anyway. I was thinking about replacing the counters, but—"

"Annie, everything is fine. You aren't charging me enough rent to cover redoing countertops."

"I shouldn't charge you rent at all, seeing as how *we* didn't pay for the place."

"The house was a big part of your inheritance, and you absolutely *should* charge me rent."

Annemarie yanked the key out of the lock. "We need some WD-40."

"Let me try." Rayna took the key and grasped the padlock. After a few seconds of wriggling and twisting, she got the key to rotate. The lock popped open.

"Nice!" Annemarie said. "It remembers you."

Rayna laughed and tugged open the door of the prefab fiberglass shed. The air smelled musty. She stepped inside and scanned her studio.

Dust layered her pottery wheel and supply buckets, each bucket marked with the now-faded labels Annemarie had made when Rayna was a teenager: *Rayna's Pottery*, with the *O* in *Pottery* transformed into a sun radiating golden rays across the whole logo. Spiderwebbed shelves held a scattering of pieces Rayna had left behind.

Annemarie hurried to open the windows. "Whew, this place needs air. I hope there aren't mice in here."

"There aren't," Rayna said.

"Right, you'd know that. Thank goodness. Please tell me we don't have them in the house either, because if Fig meets a mouse, she'll surrender."

"She probably would." Rayna focused in the direction of the house, on the sensations of life she found there. Her niece and nephew were together on the second floor, with Fig the cat a yard or so away from them. "There's a mouse nest . . . I think it's in the garage? At the front?"

"Yuck, really? Serves me right. I bought traps last fall but never put them out."

"I'll take care of it."

"I'm not going to make you deal with my vermin. What a horrible welcome."

"I don't mind dealing with mice, and obviously, it's easy for me to stick the traps in the right spots."

"If you honestly don't mind, I'd appreciate it very much. The traps are in the cupboard over the washer."

"I don't mind at all." She didn't need the traps, but she wasn't telling Annemarie that.

Annemarie picked up a red-glazed serving bowl and wiped it with the hem of her The Beach Umbrella: Old and New Treasures T-shirt. "This is beautiful. Why'd you abandon it?"

Rayna shrugged.

Annemarie returned the bowl to the shelf and checked her watch. "We'd better not get into cleaning and sorting yet. We need to head to Cheney's before it gets much later. The kids have been so excited to get ice cream with Aunt Rayna."

Rayna drew a smiley face in the dust on her worktable. "I've been excited too."

"I'll go get them and myself ready. Let's plan to leave in twenty minutes. It'll just be us. Seth's giving a potential buyer a tour of the town." Annemarie paused. "I ought to give *you* a tour. So much has changed here."

"A tour would be great. Especially one that starts at Cheney's."

"Amen." Annemarie scrutinized her, not looking down as she traced a smiley face next to the one Rayna had drawn. "You're looking much better, Ray."

"Thanks, I guess. Or is that a comment about how awful I looked before?"

"It was supposed to be a compliment, but it was an awkward one." Annemarie wiped her dusty fingers on her jeans. "There's something I need to tell you. Ben and Lucy Orozco are living in Willet Beach now."

A shock of old pain flashed through Rayna, but even before she opened her mouth to respond, she was over it. Ben and Lucy were water *so* far under the bridge that they were all the way across the Pacific. "What brought them back here?"

"They bought that old restaurant on Beachcomber Street, the one that used to be the all-you-can-eat Italian place."

"They bought it? Ben's finally living his dream. He always talked about opening his own restaurant."

"They're going to turn it into a seafood/American-classics-type place. Along the lines of Wyeth's Grill but a step up. Not too high-end though. They want it family friendly."

"Good for them."

Annemarie twisted a lock of her hair back and forth. "Are you . . . okay with them being here? I was horrified when Seth told me. Here you are coming home for a fresh start, and . . ."

"I'm totally fine with it. Not a problem at all."

"I'm glad." Annemarie kept playing with her hair. "College was eons ago, right? But ugh, I'm still furious at the way they treated you. I worried you might be raw after your divorce, and that might make it harder to . . . I don't know . . . deal with a blast from the past?"

"No grudges here," Rayna said. "Lucy's parents must be thrilled to have her close again."

"I'm sure they are. Um . . . Seth sold Lucy and Ben the property, the doofus. He'd forgotten there was a history between you, even thought I'd *told* him the whole story."

"I don't expect him to remember the details of my romantic history. He didn't even grow up here. He didn't know Lucy and Ben." Rayna noted the pinkness in Annemarie's cheeks and the increase in her pulse rate. "You don't think I'll hold this against Seth, do you? How dare he do his job and not screen clients for anyone who might have a history with his sister-in-law?"

"Okay, okay. I admit we needed the commission bad. I just worry about you. You've kept to yourself so much these past years. I feel like we don't know each other anymore."

"With me living in your backyard, you'll *really* get to know me."

"I hope so. How's this for nervy? Ben and Lucy stopped by The Beach Umbrella the other day. Seth told them you were moving back, and they wanted to know if you'd be getting your pottery studio going again. I said yes, and they said they want to talk with you about custom designs for their restaurant. They said they've always been impressed by your skill and your style, and they like the idea of using the work of a local artist."

Rayna blinked. "Ben and Lucy want to commission pottery from me?"

"Maybe. They want to talk with you about it. I felt like saying, 'Wow, you two are the most clueless pair on the planet, to think Rayna would even want to see your faces.' But I didn't want to get between you and a commission, so I told Ben to give me his number and I'd pass it on to you. Don't feel obligated to contact that skunk if you don't want to."

"It's fine," Rayna said. "I'd be happy to talk with him. I need all the business I can get."

"Then make sure you soak him on the price." Annemarie took out her phone and texted. "I sent you his info. I'll go get the kids ready."

After Annemarie exited, Rayna picked up the bowl that had drawn her sister's eye. She traced her finger over the whimsical pattern of swirls and circles, remembering the hours she'd worked on the bowl—the perfect gift for her foodie boyfriend's birthday. A gift she'd been excited to give him until two weeks before his birthday, when she'd discovered him and Lucy kissing on the back porch of Rayna and Lucy's student apartment.

She'd thought of smashing the bowl on the concrete steps as a farewell to her now-ex-boyfriend and now-ex-best friend, but she'd kept it, not wanting to waste her work. Why hadn't she sold it instead of leaving it in her shed?

Time to list it on her Etsy shop. She wouldn't offer it to Ben now. Whatever she designed and created for his and Lucy's restaurant, it wouldn't be this.

* * *

"Welcome home!" White-haired Mark "Owl" Cheney stepped from behind the ice-cream counter to hug Rayna. "I was over the moon when your sister told me you were moving home. My little Kirkpatrick gals, together again. And hello to you, Miss Nancy and Mr. Tate." He shook hands with Annemarie's eight-year-old daughter and six-year-old son.

Cheney returned to his spot behind the counter. "What can this wise old owl get for you today?"

Nancy and Tate both giggled, and Rayna smiled. Cheney had always embraced the nickname he'd received both for his habit of giving advice and for his round glasses and round face.

"Who wants a sample of our white-chocolate mango?" Cheney asked.

"Me!" Nancy and Tate shouted together.

"Don't put your nose on the glass." Annemarie drew Tate back from the display case. Cheney handed out sample spoons of ice cream.

While Annemarie and the kids ordered their ice cream, Rayna gazed around the shop. When Annemarie had referred to how much things had changed in town, she plainly hadn't been referring to Cheney's. It looked exactly like Rayna remembered: grayish reclaimed-wood walls filled with framed newspaper articles and awards, a pink-tile floor crowded with orange- and lime-sherbet-colored tables. Customers occupied every table, and a crowd of people filled the entryway, waiting to be served.

"You need bigger digs," Annemarie said as Cheney handed her a waffle cone with a scoop of strawberry-banana. "It'll be insane here this summer."

"So your husband keeps telling me. I'm seriously considering it, but change is hard. Rayna, what can I get for you?"

"What do you recommend?"

"Let's see." Cheney scanned the tubs of ice cream. "Tidal Wave. I've updated my classic. A vanilla base with waves of chocolate and butterscotch caramel, loaded with milk-chocolate fish and dark-chocolate starfish. In a chocolate-dipped cone dusted with graham-cracker crumbs." He scraped up a large curl of ice cream. "This one's on me. A welcome-home gift."

"You don't need to do that," Annemarie said. "I was going to treat her."

"You treat your kids. I'll treat Rayna. Oh, hang on. Excuse me, Mr. Hale!"

Rayna automatically looked where Cheney was looking: at a thirty-something man in a Cheney's Ice Cream Shop sweatshirt who'd approached the trash can near the counter to throw away a napkin. The man gave Cheney a polite, questioning look.

"Here're some gals you'll want to talk to." With his ice-cream scoop, Cheney pointed at Annemarie and Rayna. "Annemarie Bristol and her sister, Rayna . . ."

"Kirkpatrick," Rayna said.

"They grew up here. Ladies, Mr. Hale is a writer. He's doing a book on Willet Beach. He interviewed Vivian and me—he looks good in our sweatshirt, don't you think? He's been interviewing locals, and I told him I'd keep my eyes open for new victims for him."

The man nodded a greeting. "Damon Hale. A pleasure to meet you." He was tall, with enough muscle that a computer keyboard clearly wasn't his only form of exercise. Wavy brown hair, a little shaggy, curled around his ears. "I'd welcome the chance to speak with—"

"Hold on a sec." Annemarie bolted toward a table for two, where the occupants had stood up to leave. Nancy and Tate trailed after her, licking their ice creams. Once the kids were seated, Annemarie returned to the counter, where Cheney was handing Rayna her cone.

"Nice move," Rayna said.

"Thanks," Annemarie said. "Sorry for the rudeness, Mr. Hale."

"Damon. No need to apologize. The competition for seating is fierce." He had a low, mellow voice—pleasant but slightly solemn. It matched his face: handsome but guarded. Not easy to read.

Annemarie opened her purse to pay the teenager working at the cash register.

"No charge for the double on the chocolate-dipped cone," Cheney said to the boy before turning to his next customer.

Annemarie paid, stuffed a few dollars into the tip jar, and turned to Damon. "Come to our standing-room-only table, and you can tell us about your book."

"I don't want to interrupt your night out," Damon said.

"You're not interrupting," Annemarie said. "We'd love to hear about it."

Rayna figured Annemarie hoped getting interviewed by Damon Hale would be free promo for her store. Rayna would've liked free promo for her pottery business, but right now, it hardly existed at all and didn't exist in local form, which is what would interest Damon.

"You're very kind. I'll keep it short." Damon followed them, and they stood around the table where Nancy and Tate were seated. He took business cards from his jeans pocket and handed one to Annemarie and one to Rayna. "The project combines both a broad approach—for instance, the geology of the town, history, economy, and so forth—with a personal and specific one: deep dives into the experiences of some of its residents."

Rayna read the card. *Damon Hale, Freelance Writer.* A graphic of a compass, a local office address, a local phone number, a nonlocal cell phone number, an email address, and a URL for a website called *Hale's Trails.*

"How did you choose Willet Beach?" Annemarie broke off a piece of waffle cone and dunked it into her ice cream. "Are you from the area?"

"No. Virginia. The project is funded by a former Willet Beach resident with a love for her roots. She prefers to remain anonymous. She doesn't want anyone's perspective affected by personal knowledge of her or her family."

"Mysterious," Annemarie said.

"More practical than mysterious. You'll find the details of the project on my website. I'd be grateful for the opportunity to interview both of you, but let me state the disclaimers up front: there's no payment for the interview or for the use of your material. I'll ask you to sign a release that spells all this out in legalese. There's also no guarantee that I'll include any of the material from the interview in the final book. I'm gathering far more information than I'll end up using."

Annemarie wrapped a napkin around the tip of Nancy's dripping cone. "There go my hopes of becoming rich and famous. I'd be happy to let you interview me. I own a gift and consignment shop down the street from here. It's called The Beach Umbrella. We focus on gently used beach-related clothes and gear along with gifts and souvenirs."

Damon took out his phone. "I can work around your schedule, and I can either come to you or you can come to the office I'm renting."

"Why don't you come to my store?" Annemarie passed her ice-cream cone to Rayna and fished in her purse. She took out her own business card and gave it to Damon. "Tomorrow or Friday in the late afternoon or early evening would work for me."

Rayna sneaked a taste of Annemarie's ice cream.

"How about tomorrow at three thirty?" Damon said.

"How about four fifteen? Rayna's arriving at four to help out since my assistant is off at a family event. That'll give me a few minutes to get her set. She can cover the sales floor while you interview me."

"Four fifteen works. I look forward to it." He and Annemarie both entered the appointment in their calendars.

"You should interview Rayna as well," Annemarie said. "She's a local potter who just moved back here after a decade away. We'll be featuring her work at The Beach Umbrella."

"Work I haven't created yet," Rayna said. "I arrived here today."

"She has her own studio and kiln in the backyard of the house where we grew up." Annemarie reclaimed her ice cream. "My husband and I own the house now, and Rayna will be living in the guesthouse on the back of the property."

"I have a shed that I use as a studio." Rayna snatched a napkin and wiped a trickle of ice cream off her hand. "Right now, it's all spiderwebs and dust. I need to get everything cleaned out."

"She might be getting a commission to create custom designs for an upcoming restaurant in town." Annemarie's desire to promote Rayna apparently outweighed her distaste for Ben and Lucy.

"That's a long shot," Rayna said. "Don't oversell me."

"A local artisan returned home and bringing her studio back to life." Damon had taken a stylus out of his pocket and was jotting notes on his phone. "Would you consider letting me take 'before' and 'after' pictures? From dust and spiderwebs to gleaming rows of handmade ceramics?"

Rayna's cheeks went hot. "It's a *shed.* I promise it won't make for interesting visuals." She'd rather be candid now than go through the embarrassment of having Damon show up expecting potentially usable material for his book. "And it never had much of a 'life' in the first place. My parents bought it for me when I was a teenager to get my pottery wheel out of the corner of the dining room. I used it in high school and on breaks during college. Everything I've done since then has been at studios in Denver where I've rented space, and that has been sporadic. My 'business' is currently a bare-bones Etsy shop with inventory that fits in one box."

Annemarie frowned at her. "Will you stop running yourself down? You're extremely talented."

"I'd still be interested in having a look," Damon said. "The story of a childhood hobby turned adult vocation has potential. If you're uncomfortable because you're concerned the 'before' photos won't show your business in the best light, we can sign an agreement that all photographs must be specifically approved by you prior to inclusion in the book or on my website—if that becomes a possibility. Again, at this point, I'm casting the net wide."

"Do it, Ray," Annemarie said. "If it does make the final book, what a boost for you."

Rayna caved. Even though the odds were minuscule that Damon would be interested once he saw the place, she'd be foolish to keep pushing away the possibility of free publicity. "All right. You're welcome to come take pictures, but you'll be underwhelmed. I should have *you* sign a release promising not to sue me for wasting your time."

Damon smiled. "None of my explorations are a waste of time. Even material I don't end up using enlarges my understanding of this area and makes for a better book."

"If you say so, but I warned you," Rayna said.

"Your sister can be your witness that I went into this with my eyes open."

"If you want 'before' pics, you'd better come over in a hurry because I was planning to start cleaning things up tomorrow."

"How about eight o'clock in the morning?"

"That works."

"I'll text you the link to the forms, and you can e-sign them. I'll keep this first visit short. Half an hour max. Also, I've hired an assistant, a local older woman whom I can bring along if you'd like. To make sure everyone is comfortable."

"I can arrange for my husband to be home if your assistant would rather sleep in," Annemarie said. "Who'd you hire?"

"Her name is Jody Wyeth. She owns Wyeth's Grill, but her daughter runs it, and Jody has a lot of free time."

Rayna and Annemarie exchanged wry smiles.

"Jody's our neighbor," Annemarie said. "In fact, she was engaged to our father, but he passed away at the beginning of February."

"I'm sorry to hear that. She did mention she'd lost her fiancé and that was one reason she needed to keep busy. I had no idea he was your father. Her daughter recommended Jody to me."

"Kaitlyn," Annemarie said. "She's a good friend. Welcome to our small town. Here, give Rayna my business card and she can write our home address and her phone number on the back."

* * *

Sitting in his parked car across from Cheney's, Damon jotted down his impressions of his first face-to-face meeting with Rayna Kirkpatrick, adding them to his notes on other Willet Beach residents. Even on the infinitesimal chance that someone cracked the layers of security on his phone, his comments on Rayna wouldn't stand out. Any comments that *would* stand out, he'd record only on the secure laptop he used for classified reports and communication.

Rayna had seemed friendly but content to stay in the background and let her sister take the lead. Not eager for attention. He was grateful Annemarie had stepped in to urge her to allow him to photograph her studio. He needed to create opportunities to observe her, but he wouldn't have dared push her too hard himself. He needed to move cautiously. Showing undue interest could be a dangerous mistake.

He stuck his phone in his jacket pocket and started the engine. Tomorrow's photo shoot would be a prime opportunity both to gain more insights about Rayna and to run his first test on her.

CHAPTER 5

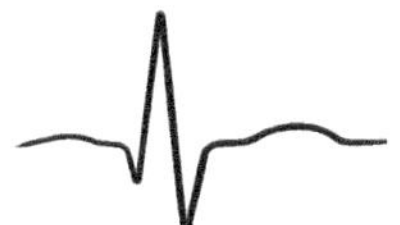

The fluffy comforter was the perfect weight, the sheets were smooth and soft, and the mattress on the guesthouse bed was much more comfortable than it had been when Rayna had stayed here for the week between her father's death and his funeral. Annemarie must have purchased a new one without telling her, indulging in the financial relief that had come with their recent inheritance. Rayna had to hand it to her father—innately organized as well as conscious that his long-standing difficulty with cardiac arrhythmias was likely to get worse and could cut his life short without warning, he'd left his affairs so well planned that there had been remarkably little delay in settling the estate.

Guilt slashed her thoughts.

Stop. You don't know that you could have helped him. Don't think about it. Move forward.

Exhausted from two days of driving and from hauling and unpacking boxes, she'd thought she'd fall asleep quickly, but she kept struggling against the urge to start cleaning out the shed, despite her promising Damon Hale a "before" picture. Not that he'd want to use the picture, or any of the pictures he'd take here tomorrow. *If* he took any once he saw how amateurish her workspace looked. No, he'd take photos. He seemed like a guy who'd tactfully fill his camera's memory card with images of her grimy shed to avoid embarrassing her, then mass-delete them later.

You're not an amateur. Ben Orozco is interested in commissioning pottery for his restaurant.

Or maybe Ben had told that to Annemarie out of pity for Rayna. He'd buy one piece from her and put it in a closet.

If he's not truly interested, he doesn't have to buy anything, but that doesn't mean your work isn't any good. Why don't you go ahead and contact him? Even an appointment to discuss the possibility of a commission will give you more of a professional vibe with Damon than you have now.

Rayna took her phone off the charger and checked the time. Five after midnight. Ben was a night owl. He'd be awake. Unless he'd changed his habits after marrying Lucy, in which case he could answer her text in the morning.

Texting Ben was something she'd never expected to do again, but she could handle this like a professional. She started typing. *Hello, Ben. This is Rayna Kirkpatrick. Annemarie mentioned you might be interested in commissioning pottery for your restaurant. I'd be happy to discuss this with you and Lucy at your convenience.*

She set the phone on the nightstand, already feeling a little less restless.

The screen of her phone lit up with a prompt response. *Thanks for getting back to me! We want to meet with you. Are you free for dinner on either Thursday or Friday?*

She texted back. *Either works.*

Let's say Thursday. Wyeth's Grill at 6:30?

I'll see you there.

Thanks! Looking forward to it.

Smiling, Rayna returned her phone to the charger. *There. Appointment made.* She liked the idea of dealing with Ben and Lucy in a professional capacity, personal feelings no longer an issue. Who cared what Damon thought of her workshop? *She* was excited to get in there and get started.

What else had Damon written? She ought to learn more about him before he showed up. What had she done with his business card? It must be in the pocket of the jeans she'd worn to Cheney's. She got out of bed and retrieved the jeans from the hamper where she'd tossed them due to a Tate-sized ice-cream handprint on the leg.

She took her laptop and got back in bed. Leaning against a stack of pillows, she pulled up the website for Hale's Trails.

* * *

"Good morning," Annemarie greeted Rayna as she walked into the kitchen of the main house. "Did you rearrange everything in the shed to give it that *artful* untouched-for-years look?"

Rayna laughed. "I wanted to, but I made myself stay away. I haven't even opened the door since we were in there yesterday."

"That reminds me." Annemarie pointed to a can of WD-40 on the counter. "For the padlock."

"You should toss the lock and buy a new one," Seth said. He was sitting at the kitchen table, dressed in a long-sleeved rash guard and board shorts and eating a piece of toast. "It'd only be a few bucks."

"I'll try the WD-40 first," she said. "Going surfing?"

"Annie asked if I'd stick around the house while this Hale dude is meeting with you." Seth took another piece of toast. "I'll come straight home after I drop the kids at school."

"Thanks. That's nice of you." Rayna opened the canister of Annemarie's homemade granola. "I was checking out his website last night."

"Yeah, same," Annemarie said. "I couldn't find any other books or articles he's written, which makes me dubious about his ability and experience, but his website was solid. Great photography, and his description of the project was interesting. I couldn't find any social media feeds, either personal or for Hale's Trails, which seems like a promotional shortcoming—time to enter the twenty-first century, Damon—but I like how on his website, he's doing blog updates about interviews and things he's discovered here. Teasers, as it were. We should make a teaser, even if we don't make the final book."

"The question is," Seth said, "Does anyone besides his mother visit his website?"

"He writes well." Rayna sat at the table and used a napkin to blot up a splash of milk no doubt left by her niece or nephew. "Straightforward but vivid."

"I've been hearing buzz about him," Seth said. "Haven't heard anything negative so far. I wonder who's funding his research."

"No one in *our* social circles, obviously," Annemarie said.

"The fact that the person no longer lives here makes guessing harder." Seth reached for the butter. "But they must have piles of money. Do you know how much the rent is for that office where Hale set up shop downtown? Not to mention rent for wherever he's living? You can't tell me a book like this will ever pay for itself, let alone make a profit. How many people will want to read a book about Willet Beach?"

"Tourists and locals, maybe." Annemarie gathered two milky cereal bowls off the table. "If my store or Rayna's pottery gets mentioned in the book, it'll boost business at least a little."

"*Daddy*!" a voice shrieked from the other room along with wild giggles. "Nancy's hitting me with my squid!"

"So bean her with an octopus," Seth yelled back.

"Daddy!" More giggles and yelps.

"Are you two ready for school?" Seth exited the kitchen.

"Thank you for breakfast," Rayna said. "I'll get grocery shopping done today so I don't have to keep mooching off you."

"Mooch anytime." Annemarie checked her watch. "I need to get to the shop. Gotta make sure everything is shipshape for Mr. Hale's Trails this afternoon. You look great, by the way. Love the hair."

Rayna smiled sheepishly and touched her french fishtail braid. "I couldn't decide whether I should go for the 'messy ponytail, no makeup, stained T-shirt' look to match my shed or try to look like a businesswoman. Dressing up felt too weird, so I tried for middle ground." She gestured at her jeans and the colorfully embroidered hoodie their mother had sent her from Cabo San Lucas.

"Perfect. See ya." Annemarie grabbed her purse and headed toward the garage.

Rayna ate her granola and took an apple from the fridge. She kept telling herself there was no need to be nervous about Damon's visit, but apprehension had ramped up again. She stretched her senses as far as they could go in every direction, methodically moving past the neighbors in their houses or out walking dogs as she waited for Damon to come into range.

Wait . . . was that him? It took her an extended moment of concentration to be sure; she didn't know him well enough for a quick ID. He was approaching on foot from the direction of the park.

Monitoring him in the back of her mind, Rayna returned the apple to the fridge, took the WD-40 and a paper towel, and went to spray the rusty shed lock.

An abrupt forward and downward movement from Damon reclaimed her full attention. He was horizontal now . . . on the ground . . . He must have tripped.

One hand on the lock and one finger on the spray trigger, Rayna waited for him to stand. Finally he sat up but didn't rise to his feet. Was he injured? She couldn't sense anyone near enough to help him, but he'd have a phone with him. He could call 911 if he needed to. She couldn't go rushing to check on him with no way to explain how she'd known where he was or that he'd fallen.

She sprayed WD-40 into the lock. *He'll be fine. He'll call for help if he needs it.*

You thought Dad was fine too. You didn't see any need to check on him.

"This is totally different," Rayna whispered to herself. Damon's heartbeat had accelerated when he'd gone down, but it was regular, neither alarmingly fast nor slow. He was capable of dealing with this on his own.

Unless he'd hit his head, dazing himself, and wasn't thinking straight . . .

She couldn't stand here fiddling with a rusty lock, ignoring what might be a serious situation. She dropped the can of WD-40 into the grass and raced past the house, heading toward the street.

At the corner, she turned onto the road that ran alongside the park and looped around the picnic area so she could approach Damon from a direction that would make it appear as though she'd been heading home from a walk.

As she got closer to him, she slowed to a walking pace. He was sitting on the grass near a drainage ditch lined with rocks, massaging his calf. A backpack lay on the grass next to him.

"Damon?" Rayna called his name in a surprised tone and walked to him.

"Rayna! Hi!" He grimaced. "This is mortifying."

"Are . . . you . . . okay?" She should have slowed to a walk sooner; she couldn't hide how winded she was. Quickly, she offered the obvious excuse. "I was . . . out walking longer than . . . I meant to be and was . . . rushing home to meet you."

"And you find me here looking like a fool."

"What happened?"

"About those release forms," he said ruefully. "Before I tell you what happened, I'd like you to sign an addendum agreeing you'll never tell anyone."

Rayna gave a breathless laugh. "I'm not signing it. I might need this experience as blackmail material to keep you from telling the world you were bored stiff visiting my shed-studio."

"I'm never bored on my explorations." Moving tentatively, he stretched his leg out straight. "There's something of interest in every person I talk to and every place I research."

"You're never bored? Challenge accepted. What happened, and have you sprained or broken something?"

"I don't think so. I forgot I wasn't a teenager, tried to jump over this culvert, and misjudged it. Slipped on the rocks. Bruised my knee and aggravated an old injury. Caused a muscle spasm."

"Ouch. What can I do to help?"

He grasped the toe of his shoe and pulled it toward him, stretching his calf muscles. "It's already a lot better."

"Where's your car?"

"I walked from my office. When I have time, I walk as much as I can. It gives me a better feel for the town than driving does."

"I could call Seth—my brother-in-law—to come pick you up and take you to your office. We can reschedule the photo shoot."

Damon bent his legs, braced one hand on the grass, and pushed himself up.

Gingerly, he took a step forward, paused, then took another. "I'm good." He trudged toward the street. "We can do the photo shoot."

"Are you sure? I don't want you to suffer through this."

"I'm fine. Thank you."

Together they headed toward Annemarie's house, Rayna feeling sweaty and awkward. "I was looking at your website," she said. "Which is great, by the way. I noticed you haven't done any Hale's Trails reports anywhere in California. All East Coast and Europe."

"Correct. That's another reason I'm never bored out here. This area is all new to me."

"How did you end up doing this Willet Beach book?"

"Personal connection," he said. "I have a friend who's friends with the former Willet Beach resident sponsoring the book. He found out she was looking for a writer to do a book about her hometown, and he told her about me. Hale's Trails was a side gig. My real job was doing research and writing reports for the Department of the Interior. She liked my writing, we met several times to discuss the project, I did some sample work for her, and the rest is history."

"Or *will* be history, once you get the book written."

He chuckled.

"Here we are." Rayna waved toward the two-story, pale-yellow house with white shutters. "My childhood home." She guided him along the packed-sand path that led to the backyard. "Here is my incredibly interesting shed and the guesthouse, which I now rent from Annemarie and Seth."

Damon pivoted, scanning everything. "How long have your sister and her husband owned your family home?"

"They've lived here for . . . let's see . . . maybe . . . five years? My parents divorced while I was in college, and my mom remarried and moved to Florida. My dad lived here for a few more years until he decided he was done caring for a house. He moved into a condo and rented the place to Annemarie and Seth. When he died, he left them the house in his will."

Damon unzipped his backpack. "I won't record you since this isn't a sit-down interview, but I'll be taking notes here and there, if you don't mind."

"Make me sound good." A sudden touch of croakiness in her voice tainted her effort at nonchalance.

Damon gave her an understanding look. "Don't worry," he said. "As you know, there's no guarantee that I'll use material from any given interview or photo shoot, but I *can* guarantee you this: anything I do publish about your pottery business will be in a positive or, at worst, neutral light. My sponsor wants to honor her hometown and the people here, not embarrass anyone."

At the moment, Rayna was embarrassed by how obvious her nervousness was. "I'll aim for neutral, then."

Damon smiled. "Also bear in mind that I'm not a reviewer. I know you've had a reviewer tear you apart before. In my research on the arts scene here, I ran across an article from a few years back about a crafts fair in which you participated."

The heat in her face would have made the firing temperatures inside her kiln seem lukewarm. "I can't believe you still want to interview me after reading that review."

"Appreciation of handicrafts is subjective. The writer's opinion isn't of interest to me. I form my own opinions."

She fervently hoped he meant that. "I know this will come across as bitterness, but that review was both dishonest and personal." Old anger crackled inside her. "The writer had a . . . beef with me."

"I'm sorry," Damon said. "Lashing out at your work over a personal disagreement is exceedingly unprofessional. Is he still covering the arts scene?"

"He . . . actually died in an accident," Rayna said.

"Ah. That's unfortunate."

Wanting to change this wretched subject, Rayna said, "You're welcome to get started." She picked up the can of WD-40 she'd abandoned. "The padlock is so rusted it was giving me trouble, but I gave it a spritz of this, and I hope it helped."

Damon reached into his backpack and took out a camera. "I'll start with the exterior."

Rayna set the can next to Annemarie's back door and tried both to stay out of Damon's way and remain close enough to answer questions while he took pictures of the shed from multiple angles.

He then approached the kiln next to it. "Did your parents get you the kiln along with the shed?"

"No. When I was sixteen, I worked at Wyeth's Grill after school and then worked two jobs all summer to earn the money for that kiln. I got a decent price on a used one, but the electrical upgrades to get a 240-volt line out here weren't cheap."

Damon rested on one knee to snap a close-up of the kiln. "Was it hard to walk away from this after putting so much money and effort into it?"

"I missed it like crazy when I went off to college, even though they had a craft center there where I could throw pottery. I sort of thought I'd come back to Willet Beach, but that's not how life worked out. Until now."

"What made you decide to come back now?"

Rayna hesitated, trying to decide how thorough of an answer to give. Being too vague might come across as weirdly cagey, but she had no desire to explain how her life in Denver had fallen apart. "My father left me some money that made it possible for me to return here and focus on building my pottery business."

"I'm sure he'd be happy he could make that happen for you."

Rayna said nothing. The truth was he'd be furious, accusing her of wasting his hard-earned money.

"When did you first get interested in making pottery?" Damon crouched, getting a shot of the seaside daisies that grew near the kiln.

"We had a ceramics unit in art class when I was in sixth grade. That started it all."

Damon's camera clicked several more times, then he straightened up, his movements stiff enough that she could tell his leg was hurting. "May I see the interior of the shed now?"

Rayna unlocked the door, which took a lot less jiggling of the key this time. She switched on the light and stepped out of the way so Damon could enter first. "Feel free to sit down if you need to rest your leg," she said.

"Thanks." He took a measured look around the room, scanning everything from the ceiling to underneath the tables. Rayna had forgotten about the smiley faces she and Annemarie had drawn in the dust, but Damon grinned when he saw them and raised his camera.

"You don't need a picture of those," Rayna said.

"Did you draw them?"

"One of them. Annemarie drew the other." She reached to erase them with her palm but too late. The camera had clicked.

"I like them," he said. "Evidence that you're both happy you're here."

CHAPTER 6

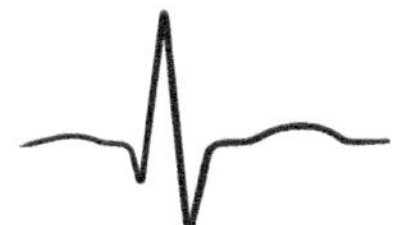

The results of Damon's first test on Rayna had been clear: she had the ability to sense people. He thought of her flushed and out of breath from running, pretending it had been coincidental that she'd found him after his fall—a staged mishap he'd inadvertently made too real; he'd scraped his leg and banged his knee so hard that it still ached. It spoke well for her character that she'd hurried to his rescue, though that didn't prove her innocence. It was more than possible to show compassion for a near-stranger while being guilty of killing a family member. Especially if that near-stranger might provide a financial boost to your and your sister's businesses.

Partway through the photo session, Seth Bristol had wandered into the backyard to introduce himself. As they'd chatted, Damon had casually slipped in a reference to his plans to walk back to his office, drawing an objection from Rayna—he couldn't make that long of a walk on his injured leg. As Damon had anticipated, Seth had immediately offered to give him a ride. This was an excellent opportunity to further assess the Kirkpatrick family dynamics through an in-law's point of view.

"Sorry you don't get the decent car." Seth settled in the driver's seat of an old blue Toyota pickup. "This is the surf-mobile, and I'm meeting a friend at the beach."

"Not a problem," Damon said. The floor mats were coated in sand, and the cab smelled of sunscreen. "I appreciate the ride."

"You surf?"

"Never tried it."

"You gotta let me teach you."

"I might take you up on that."

"Annie can fix you up with the right gear. Talk to her about it when you go interview her this afternoon. If she doesn't have the stuff you need now, she will soon. She's always getting new inventory."

"Thanks for the tip." Damon braced himself as Seth took a corner too fast. "Annemarie must be excited to have her sister back in town."

"Yeah, totally."

"Not just in town but in your backyard," Damon added.

"Ha, yeah." Seth ran his fingers through his hair. "Good thing we have that guesthouse because otherwise, Annie'd probably have hounded Rayna to bunk in our spare bedroom. Doesn't want her too far away. That'd make it hard to boss her around." He laughed. "Kidding."

"Protective older sister?"

"Yeah, totally. Don't run afoul of Annie." He grinned. "But she worries about Rayna."

How deeply could he explore this without making it weird? He decided on a humorous approach. "Like . . . worrying she won't let Annemarie boss her around?"

Seth snickered. "Nah. Rayna's just . . . been through tough stuff, and she keeps her mouth shut about it, you know? She's one of those people who always pretends she's fine."

"I was sorry to hear she and Annemarie lost their father recently."

"Yeah." Seth braked hard at a stoplight, jarring Damon. "It was super sudden. Night of his sixty-fifth birthday party, plus he'd just announced his engagement. How's that for the universe punching you in the face?"

"That must have been devastating for Annemarie and Rayna."

Seth's brow wrinkled, and his amiability drooped into a moment of silence. "Yeah," he said. "Yeah, it hit hard. Hey, so, I'm a real estate agent, and I could give you a rundown on the state of the market, if that's something you'd be interested in for your book."

Quick change of subject, Damon noted. Seth didn't want to talk further about Glenn Kirkpatrick's death. "I'd like to interview you. Thanks for the offer. I don't know what direction I'll go with the book yet, but as I tell people, I'm throwing the net wide. What time would work to meet with you?"

With an appointment set for the following afternoon, Seth dropped Damon in front of his office and sped off.

"Good morning, Mr. Hale," Jody greeted Damon as he entered. She was sitting at her desk, sorting through photographs.

"Good morning." Damon had told her to call him by his first name, but she had declared that "unseemly" since he was her boss.

"I'm organizing these prints of the best photos you've taken so far. It's easier for me to decide how they'll look on the walls if I can tape small versions up there." Jody flapped one hand at the white walls and beige laminate flooring. "I can't believe you didn't notice how bare it looks in here. Men! I'll get this fixed up before you know it, and then I'll start on your inner office."

"You're a treasure." Damon had convinced Logan that hiring Jody to assist him with his alleged book project would make her a valuable—if unwitting—asset to his real project. Not only would her presence in his office shore up his cover, but it would give him regular, natural opportunities to draw on her knowledge of the town and particularly of the Kirkpatrick family.

He picked up a stack of photographs and looked through it, not out of any interest in which photos Jody had chosen but to give her time to initiate a conversation about Rayna, which he knew chatty and curious Jody would do. She'd have seen on his calendar that he was speaking with Rayna this morning.

"How did your interview with Rayna Kirkpatrick go?" Jody asked, fulfilling Damon's prediction. "I saw you added her and Annemarie Bristol to your calendar. You should have let me give you background information on Rayna before the interview. I could have helped you prepare."

"I didn't make the appointment until last night," Damon said. "I didn't want to pester you."

"Oh stars, pester me anytime. I don't mind working after hours. I know the Kirkpatrick girls well. Did you know they were almost my stepdaughters?"

"They told me. I ran into them at Cheney's Ice Cream, and Mr. Cheney recommended them as interview subjects. I could still use any background information you have. I've barely talked to Rayna. Mostly, I took pictures of her pottery studio."

"That shed in the backyard?"

"Yes."

"I remember when her parents bought that for her. She was making such a mess of the house with her pottery. It drove Jeanette—her mother—crazy." Jody gave him a dubious look through her wire-framed glasses. "Goodness, Mr. Hale, I'm not sure that shed will be interesting material for your book."

Damon picked up one of the chairs positioned under the front window, set it in front of Jody's desk, and sat down. "I'm thinking a before-and-after angle, as she gets her business running." He set his camera bag on the floor. "A local business getting off the ground."

"Well . . . yes, that might be interesting, I suppose. You're the expert. I think you'll find Annemarie a more compelling subject though. She's the age of my Kaitlyn, thirty-four. They've been friends since they were little, and they're both such smart girls, remarkable businesswomen. Hard workers. I suppose you know Annemarie owns a consignment shop?"

"Yes." Damon rubbed his bruised knee.

"She started it all by herself," Jody said. "She wanted to make quality swimsuits and wet suits and things like that available to everyone while cutting down on clothing waste. Isn't that brilliant?"

"Great idea."

"She's married to Seth Bristol. Did you meet him?"

"He gave me a ride here from Rayna's this morning. I have an appointment tomorrow to interview him about the Willet Beach real estate market."

"Do you? I suppose it would be rude to cancel it, but I could give you the names of real estate agents much more experienced and competent than Seth."

"I take it you don't think much of Seth."

"He's a nice boy, but Glenn—Rayna and Annemarie's father, my late fiancé—thought he was immature. More interested in surfing than working, letting Annemarie do the heavy lifting when it comes to family finances. Though he *is* a gifted salesman when he decides to pay attention to his job." Jody straightened a pile of photographs. "I always tell my Kaitlyn how important it is that she find a hardworking husband."

"No doubt she appreciates her mother lecturing her about that."

"Oh, she rolls her eyes, but I can tell she agrees with me. I'm a mother bear, always protecting my cub, and she knows it. A happy-go-lucky fellow like Seth Bristol would drive her mad. Men *do* chase Kaitlyn all the time, of course. She's a lovely girl, and so successful. But you know that; you interviewed her. If you need to speak with her again about our restaurant, or about anything else, she'd be happy to meet with you."

"Thank you," Damon said. "I'll keep that in mind."

"She's not a partier," Jody said. "She's never liked late nights. Early to bed and early to rise. She finishes at the Grill, and she's ready to crash after working so hard. Remember that if you're wanting to schedule an appointment with her."

"I'll bear that in mind. What should I know about Rayna before I speak with her again?"

"Rayna is . . . hmm." Jody tapped her fingernails on her desk. "She's a sweet girl, but Glenn always called her an odd duck."

"Odd in what way?"

"The truth is I never quite understood why he felt that way. She's a nice girl. A bit shy. I wouldn't say she's *odd*, but she certainly has a poor track record at life, and Glenn was a demanding father."

"Tell me about her poor track record."

Beaming at Damon's interest, Jody leaned forward. "Well, she's an artist, a potter, and that's a hard way to make a living, isn't it? Glenn couldn't understand why she'd want to make it anything more than a silly hobby. Majoring in art? My stars! But then she married a man with a master's degree in bioengineering, very smart man, and Glenn said, well, she got *something* right."

"Was that his version of 'congratulations'?" Damon asked dryly.

Jody giggled. "I suppose it was. But a year or so ago, Rayna and her husband divorced. None of us know what happened because Rayna wouldn't talk about it, but I think the biggest strain was her infertility, or whatever word you use for not being able to carry a pregnancy to term. She'd get pregnant and miscarry, over and over. Glenn was sure she must be doing something wrong, but I told him these things just happen, that of course Rayna was doing everything she could for her babies."

From what Jody was telling him, Damon would have chosen a harsher description for Glenn Kirkpatrick than *demanding*. "So her relationship with her father was strained?"

"Well, it was uneven. Sometimes they got along fine. Sometimes he was so impatient with her. I do feel bad for the way things ended between them."

"How did things end?"

"The night before he died, at his birthday party, they . . . well . . ." Jody lowered her voice. "He was trying to tease her, I know, but . . . sometimes he was tactless. Rayna took it hard."

Given how eager Jody plainly was to share what she knew, Damon figured he was safe digging deeper. "What did he say?"

"Oh, he cracked a joke about how it was amazing her ex-husband hadn't dumped her sooner since she just spent her time playing with Play-Doh." Jody sighed. "That is rather harsh, isn't it? And then he said she couldn't count on finding another husband until she figured out how pregnancy worked."

With an effort, Damon kept his expression neutral. He didn't want to shut Jody down by revealing his revulsion at her late fiancé's behavior. "How did Rayna react?"

"She walked out," Jody said. "Annemarie finally talked her into rejoining the party, but she didn't speak to her father for the rest of the night or even come near him, and . . . the next morning . . ." Tears welled in Jody's eyes. "He'd planned to go on a walk with me before breakfast, but it got later and later, and he didn't show up . . ." Her voice broke. She opened her purse and took out a tissue.

"I'm sorry for your loss," Damon said.

"Thank you." Jody took off her glasses and dabbed away tears. "At least we ended on happy terms. It was a lovely party, so many friends and family with us. Rayna must have terrible regrets, the poor child. I'm guessing she moved back to Willet Beach hoping to feel closer to him, even though she knows they can never work things out now. But maybe his ghost will speak to her. Is that strange of me to admit I believe in ghosts?"

Whether or not Rayna was responsible for her father's death, Damon couldn't imagine she'd welcome a visit from his ghost. "It's not strange of you." He decided to take the opportunity Jody had created for him. If word reached Rayna that Damon had asked about paranormal experiences, it wouldn't seem suspicious, given the context. "In fact, my sponsor is interested in anything paranormal or unusual. Local ghost stories. People with extrasensory abilities. Odd rumors. Legends. Anything like that. Got anything for me, either in the town's history or happening now?"

"That's a very interesting question." Jody's reddened eyes were thoughtful. She showed no signs of being unsettled by his query. "I can't think of anything off the top of my head, but I'd be happy to read up on any town legends or ghost stories I can find. And, of course, I'll keep my ears open for you."

"I appreciate it." It seemed plain that Jody didn't know what Rayna could do. If any of Glenn Kirkpatrick's "odd duck" comments about his daughter had referred to her abilities, he'd never clarified that for Jody.

"I hope Rayna's happy here," Jody said. "She's overdue for something good in her life. It *is* charitable of you to show interest in her little pottery business."

"It's research," Damon said. "Not charity."

"Then it's lovely of you to be so supportive of budding businesses, no matter how unlikely they are to—Oh stars! That reminds me."

"Reminds you of what?"

"This is straight-up gossip, Mr. Hale, so don't spread it around, but I know you'll be discreet. There's an old restaurant on Beachcomber Avenue that's being renovated. The people who bought it, Ben and Lucy Orozco, are locals who recently moved back to the area, and—would you believe this?—Ben is an ex-boyfriend of Rayna's. Lucy was Rayna's best friend . . . until Rayna caught the two of them sneaking around behind her back. Such a painful betrayal. It was years ago, while they were in college, but after all Rayna's been through since then, don't you think seeing them will be a slap in the face?"

A restaurant being renovated . . . Could that be the same restaurant Annemarie had referred to with the owner who might commission pottery from Rayna? "I imagine she's long since gotten over teenage drama."

"Well, they weren't teenagers. They were in their twenties by then. Rayna and Ben didn't date in high school—he was a couple of years older, between Rayna and Annemarie in age, but they all knew him. Popular boy, very handsome. The girls all had crushes on him. Then Lucy and Rayna were roommates at . . . oh, what was the college? In San Diego, anyway, and Ben was down there as well—I think he'd already graduated and was working there when he and Rayna started dating. They got quite serious from what I heard. Then Rayna found out he was cheating on her with Lucy, and it was devastating, losing her boyfriend and her best friend all at once."

"That's rough," Damon said.

"Ben is a charming boy. Lucy must be so thrilled that she won him."

Ben didn't sound like much of a catch to Damon, but he wasn't going to say so, lest Jody add his commentary when she gossiped to someone else about Ben and Lucy. He rose to his feet. "I'd better get to work. Thanks for the information."

"Of course," Jody said. "I'm always happy to help."

Damon kept a cordial expression on his face until he'd retreated into his office and shut the door. He settled at his desk and took a sober moment to gather his thoughts. This had been a productive morning. After he finished writing his notes, he'd set the stage for the second test he planned to run on Rayna this afternoon.

CHAPTER 7

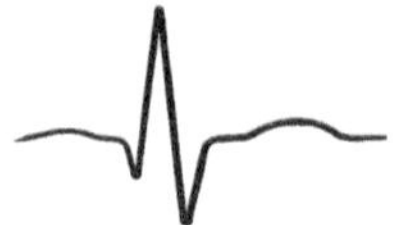

"DOES EVERYTHING LOOK OKAY?" ANNEMARIE paced frenetically between displays of beach cover-ups, sun hats, and swimsuits. "Straighten that red boogie board. It's crooked."

"Relax." Rayna adjusted the foam board on its display hooks. "Your store always looks great. Besides, Damon was taking pictures of my shed this morning, so The Beach Umbrella is the Ritz by comparison."

Annemarie shook out a neon-pink towel and refolded it. "How did that go?"

"Fine, except that he fell when he was walking through the park—tried to jump over that drainage culvert and misjudged it—and he aggravated an old injury in his leg."

"Ouch. What a dork. I'm glad he didn't fall on our property. The last thing we need is to get sued. So, what did he say about your pottery shed?"

"Nothing much. He took pictures, and we chatted a little about how I got interested in pottery. He was probably bored out of his skull, but he didn't show it. He's very nice."

"Nice *and* nice to look at." Annemarie pulled a plastic shovel out of a bucket of sand toys, then stuck it back in. "No wedding ring. Did you notice?"

"I have no interest in his marital status." A tiny life essence skittered several yards away from Rayna. A mouse? Annemarie's head would explode if she knew a mouse had invaded her pristine store right before her interview—two mice, actually. The other was near the front of the store.

Rayna had already sensed Damon nearby. He'd arrived early. Judging by his location and position, he was sitting in his car.

"You know what would serve Ben Orozco right?" Annemarie's oblique reference to Rayna's single status had apparently turned her attention to Rayna's former relationships. "If your pottery gets prominently mentioned in Damon's book, big photo spread, and Ben's restaurant gets ignored. That would drive him batty. He's such a gotta-be-number-one, I'm-everyone's-favorite-person guy."

Rayna mentally tracked the nearest mouse, hoping Annemarie wouldn't see it. "I wish Ben and Lucy the best."

"*I* sure don't. That guy . . . And speaking of betrayal, you know who's been tutoring him in the restaurant business? Kaitlyn!"

"She has?"

"Yeah, she's given him tons of advice."

"I thought Ben got on Kaitlyn's nerves."

"He does, and she said he's an egotistical nuisance, just like he was in high school, but she doesn't mind helping another business owner get things off the ground. I said, 'After what he and Lucy did to Rayna, you're helping them?'"

"Let me guess," Rayna said. "She told you that was ages ago, Rayna's over it, and you need to chill out."

Annemarie scowled. "Did she already tell you about our conversation?"

"No. I just know Kaitlyn's not the type to get petty or stew over the past. You need to loosen up about Ben. If my appointment with him and Lucy goes well tomorrow, my work will be on display in their restaurant. Wish them success for *my* sake, will you?"

"Where are all *my* customers?" Annemarie stomped toward the front window. "Why did we have to get a slow moment now? What will Damon think when he arrives and no one's shopping?"

"He'll know successful businesses aren't crammed with customers every minute of the day. Stop pacing. We don't both need to be out here, and you look fidgety and nervous. Go to your office and watch videos of puppies while you pretend to do something important on your computer. When he gets here, I'll escort him back."

"*Fine*." Annemarie stalked toward the staff-only area.

Rayna focused her full attention on the mouse she'd been monitoring. Paying careful attention to its position relative to her so she could find it once it was dead, she zeroed in on its beating heart and killed it. She located its body underneath a rack of board shorts, scooped it up with an advertising flyer, and dropped it into the trash basket. After dispatching and disposing of the second mouse, she tied the now-verminous trash sack, raced it to the dumpster out back, washed her hands, and returned to the front counter, ready to greet Damon. When she had a chance, she'd take the canister of disinfectant wipes and clean up any souvenirs the mice had left behind, but at least Annemarie wouldn't end up humiliated by a mouse running across the sales floor while she was giving Damon a tour.

Rayna settled on the stool behind the cash register and tried not to dwell on how satisfying it *would* feel to outshine Ben and Lucy in the pages of Damon's book. She truly *did* wish them well.

And tomorrow night, she'd impress them, not only with her pottery but with how content she was in her life.

* * *

The burden of responsibility grew heavier inside Damon as he jotted down the details of Rayna's completion of the second test. He was definitely dealing with a Trespasser. He took his camera, exited his car, and headed into The Beach Umbrella, ready to feign interest in Annemarie's consignment shop while subtly probing for intel on Rayna—particularly regarding Rayna's personal conflict with that local reporter and whether or not she'd been in town when he'd taken a header down the stairs two weeks after savaging Rayna's work.

After forty-five minutes of touring the store, taking pictures, and discussing such things as sales percentages versus flat fees and Annemarie's criteria for what items she'd accept to sell, Damon got a convenient opening for the questions he really wanted to ask.

"How did it go with Rayna's pottery shed this morning?" Annemarie asked, opening a box on her desk. She passed him a chocolate-chip cookie on a napkin—a gift from Kaitlyn, who'd sent Annemarie off with a stack of cookies after the two women had eaten lunch together at Wyeth's Grill.

"It went well," Damon said. "It was gracious of her to allow me to take pictures when it isn't yet what she wants it to be. I hope I didn't offend her though. I put my foot in my mouth when I was trying to reassure her I wouldn't publish anything negative about her work."

"What did you say?"

"That I could understand why she was edgy—that I'd seen an article about a craft fair where the writer criticized—" At Annemarie's wince, Damon stopped.

"You brought up Collin Burgess's review?" she said.

"It was bad judgment."

"Did Rayna tell you the whole story?"

"She said the writer had a personal conflict with her and the review was unfair. That was all."

"She's afraid to tell you the rest, for fear you'll think she's making things up," Annemarie said grimly, folding her arms. "*I'll* tell you. At the crafts fair, Collin swaggered into her booth, pretended to be interested in her pottery, then started hitting on her. She told him she was married and tried to politely brush him off, but he kept pestering her. Personal remarks. Suggestive remarks. Touching her. Hinting that he had a lot of influence in the arts scene and could help advance her career. She finally told him flat-out to get lost. Next thing we know, there's this article about the fair in the paper, where he singles out Rayna's pottery, calling it 'amateurish and unoriginal' and of interest only 'if you miss having your five-year-old show you what she made in kindergarten today.'"

Damon grimaced in disgust. "He sexually harassed her, then wrote a negative review of her work when she rejected him?"

"Yep."

"I hope she reported him."

"She tried. The problem was, there were no witnesses, and Collin was a respected and popular community member. Movie-star face. Influential friends. And reviews are subjective. Rayna certainly wasn't the only artist who'd gotten panned by him at one point or another. There was no way to prove he'd hit on her at all, let alone that it had anything to do with his stated opinion of her pottery."

"I'm so sorry that happened to her."

"Rayna didn't want to push it—she couldn't stand the thought of a public he-said-she-said battle. She said she was only here for a few weeks anyway and no one in Denver would ever read the review. I was livid, but I couldn't force her to pursue it. I hardly had the energy to nag her at all. This was right before Tate—my son—was born."

"Did Rayna stay to help you after the birth?"

"Yes, that was why she'd originally planned to come. Then she'd heard about the fair and had decided to come early and rent a booth. But—this isn't nice of me to say—that sleazeball got his in the end. Not long after that review—a week, maybe? A couple of weeks?—he got drunk, fell down a flight of stairs, and broke his neck. I remember Rayna and me just staring at each other when we heard the news, and I said something snarky like, 'Don't expect me to send flowers,' and she didn't say anything, because she's a better person than I am. Anyway, *that's* the sordid story she was reluctant to tell you." Annemarie's posture had relaxed; she reached for a cookie. "No thanks to Mr. Burgess, Rayna's reputation in the Willet Beach arts scene is fine. Did she tell you that tomorrow night, she's meeting with the new restaurant owners I mentioned to discuss creating unique designs for their restaurant?"

"That's great news," Damon said. "Who are the restaurant owners? I should get them on my interview list."

* * *

"You've picked up a tan." Logan grinned at Damon over the secure video link. "Spending a lot of time splashing around in that California surf?"

"The water temperature is currently around fifty degrees, and the air temperature is only a few degrees warmer," Damon said. "I'll stick to dry land."

"Don't be a coward. Get a wet suit, and go catch a wave. What've you got for me?"

Damon rested his elbows on his kitchen table. "Rayna Kirkpatrick is unquestionably a Trespasser. I'll write up the details of the tests in my report but wanted to let you know immediately."

"Well then," Logan said. "Glad to hear we put taxpayer money to good use sending you out there. What's your estimation of how far word has spread?"

"Not far. She seems to be a very private person. I've heard no gossip about her abilities, including from Jody Wyeth. Rayna's father told Jody that Rayna was—he told Jody that Rayna was 'odd' but never got more specific. I'd say her family knows she can sense people, but I doubt even her sister knows she can link-kill. She waited until Annemarie was out of the room before she killed the mice I slipped in there earlier."

"Wonderful, fine, that's excellent."

"We need to assess what the ex-husband knows."

"I'll send someone to nose around Denver. What's your take on her father's death?"

"Multiple red flags. Their relationship was strained. The night before he died, he was publicly cruel and insulting to Rayna, and she was upset with him."

"Autopsy?"

"None performed. Though the death was unattended, Glenn Kirkpatrick had dealt with atrial fibrillation for several years. He saw his doctor only a week or two before he died and set appointments for some tests—Jody told me his doctor was concerned there might be additional cardiac issues at play. The medical examiner concluded an autopsy wasn't mandatory and the family didn't want one. Glenn was cremated."

"Unfortunate."

"Rayna and her sister both inherited a substantial amount of money upon his death. That inheritance is what made it possible for Rayna to move back to Willet Beach with the hope of building her pottery business. Of course, a financial motive for murder could apply to Annemarie as well as to Rayna."

"But presumably Annemarie doesn't have the ability to kill from a distance and make it look like natural causes."

"Annemarie also had a far better relationship with her father. And there's a second red-flag death connected to Rayna." Damon offered a summary of what he'd learned about reporter Collin Burgess.

Logan leaned closer to the camera, one graying eyebrow arched. "Significant coincidence that Rayna was in town for both deaths when she lived a thousand-something miles away."

"Yes. But the reporter's blood-alcohol level was through the roof when he fell. It could have been an accident—or Rayna could have link-killed him at the top of the stairs. Her father had a worsening heart condition. His death could have been natural or not." Damon stretched his legs under the table and probed at his sore knee. He should have iced it. "Her ex-husband is alive and well, and judging by his social media, he has a new girlfriend who is also alive and well."

"Then at least we know murder isn't Rayna's *only* coping skill."

"She also has an ex-boyfriend who's moved back to town to open a restaurant. Back in their college days, he cheated on Rayna with Rayna's best friend—who is now his wife."

Logan scratched his chin. "Nice soap opera you've discovered."

"This was nearly a decade ago, likely before Rayna's ability to link-kill manifested."

"Lucky for them, the little cheaters. Are you worried about them?"

"I'm wary. Rayna's had a lot of time to get over her anger, and clearly, she hasn't sought lethal revenge before now, but she's recovering from another failed relationship; that might render her more hostile. She's meeting with them tomorrow night to discuss creating pottery for their restaurant, so things are at least surface-level civil. I'll engineer an opportunity to run into her to see if I can get a read on her attitude toward them."

"Good. I'll let you know what the Denver investigation turns up. Keep a close eye on your new Trespasser friend."

CHAPTER 8

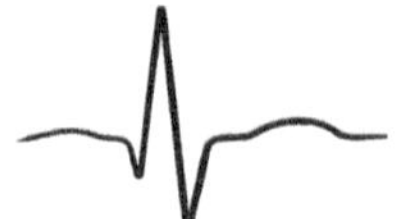

"It's fantastic to see you again." Ben opened his arms for a hug, and Rayna moved easily into his embrace. Of course she'd hug an old friend, and Ben was nothing more than an old friend. He looked the same: the sparkle in his eyes, the energy in his smile, the thick dark hair worn short on the sides and long on top.

Rayna stepped away from Ben and turned toward Lucy. Lucy had changed. She'd gone from cute to gorgeous.

Lucy tucked glossy black hair behind one ear and smiled at Rayna. Unlike Ben, Lucy was nervous. Her heart was racing, the hard beat registering in Rayna's awareness above all the sensations of life from other restaurant patrons. "How are you, Rayna?"

"I'm great." Rayna hugged Lucy. Lucy's embrace went from tentative to tight to abruptly loosened.

"I love your outfit," Rayna said. Lucy was wearing a cantaloupe-colored swing dress and loose-weave ivory sweater with a ruffly hem. Lucy had always had the ability to appear put together under any circumstances. She could roll out of a sleeping bag on a backpacking trip and look ready to pose for an REI ad.

"It's memory lane for me, seeing you two girls together." Kaitlyn approached their group. "Takes me back to high school." She hugged Lucy, then held her hand out to Ben. "How goes the restaurant planning?"

Ben grinned. "It's awesome."

"Kaitlyn has been a huge help to us," Lucy said. "She's been so generous with her time, giving Ben tons of guidance on the local business community and on running a restaurant."

"She's the expert, for sure," Rayna said.

"We're about to become her fiercest competition," Ben said.

Cocky Ben. That hadn't changed either. "You'll have your work cut out for you. You know how iconic Wyeth's Grill is around here."

"We can take 'em," Ben said.

"Your table is ready." Kaitlyn led them to a table next to a window and passed menus around. "Anything to drink?"

"There's only one right answer to that question," Lucy said. "Your house-made fruit punch."

"Same," Rayna said.

"Same," Ben said. "I'm working on reverse-engineering and then outshining the Grill's secret recipe."

Lucy put her hand on his arm. "Will you stop?"

Ben winked at Kaitlyn. "Kaitlyn and I are old hiking and fishing buddies. She doesn't mind my teasing."

"Fishing buddies?" Rayna looked at Kaitlyn. "You actually got interested in fishing?" Kaitlyn had always grumbled about how boring fishing was when their families had gone out together on Elliott Wyeth's fishing boat.

Kaitlyn rolled her eyes. "Fishing, as in discussing the best suppliers for fresh seafood . . . that someone *else* caught."

Rayna laughed.

"Ben, you should show more appreciation for Kaitlyn's help." Lucy put her hand over her mouth, shielding a yawn. "Excuse me. I knew I'd regret it when I let Ben talk me into staying up late last night for a MasterChef marathon."

"Late nights are a pain," Kaitlyn said. "Morning is where it's at."

"Did you get your new fryer-oil filtration system?" Ben asked.

Kaitlyn nodded. "Top of the line."

"We want to drool over it. Come on, Lu." Ben pushed back from the table.

"Not now," Lucy said. "We'll look at it later. We're here to talk business with Rayna."

"I don't mind," Rayna said. "You two go have a look at the fryer thing."

Lucy shook her head. "I'll stay here."

"I'll send a server out with your drinks, and I'll have Ben back in a few minutes." Kaitlyn started toward the kitchen. Ben followed her.

"Sorry about that," Lucy said. "Restaurant equipment is a siren song for him."

"No worries. Kaitlyn is too busy to keep him away for long. I can't believe he's finally opening a restaurant—and in Willet Beach!"

"Right? I'm happy to be near my parents. They live in Monterey now, so not too far. Mom still works at the hospital here a couple days a week. And here *you* are, back home too. That doesn't surprise me though. You always loved the beach so much. I don't know how you endured being inland. Your brother-in-law said you moved from Denver?"

"Yes." Rayna wondered what else Seth had told them. "Where have you and Ben been living?"

"Arizona. Ben missed living on the coast. He'd fly to California multiple times a year to go surfing and deep-sea fishing and jet-skiing."

A server approached with a tray and three huge glasses of fruit punch garnished with strawberries, orange slices, and lime wedges.

Rayna and Lucy sipped.

"This concoction is *so* divine." Lucy picked the lime wedge off the rim of her glass and squeezed it into the drink. "Since we have a moment alone, there's something I want to say. I feel like we never really . . . We didn't . . . I should have . . . It was a long time ago, but—"

"Lucy, we were dumb kids. Don't worry about it. I hope you and Ben are happy."

"You're very kind." Lucy set the lime wedge on her napkin. "When Ben and I realized we had feelings for each other, we should have been up-front with you. We were cowards. We didn't want to hurt you, so it seemed easier to sneak around. That was dishonest and cruel. It's way too late for this, but I want to say it anyway: I've always regretted how I handled that situation. It was an awful way to treat my closest friend, and I'm sorry."

"Thank you. Apology accepted." Lucy's words nudged Rayna into candor. "If you and Ben are 'interested' in my pottery out of pity or guilt, we don't have to go through the charade of a token commission. I don't hold grudges against either of you. We've all moved on with our lives."

"Oh, no, I didn't mean to give you that impression. The interest is genuine. You're a gifted artist, and we both love your work."

Rayna sipped more fruit punch, the tension she'd tried to deny she was experiencing starting to ease. Her relationship with Lucy would never be the close friendship they'd had in high school or as college students pre-Ben-fiasco, but that was fine. Neither of them expected it to be. They'd be pleasant to each other, maybe do business together. Wave if they crossed paths in town.

Lucy glanced at the door to the kitchen, where Ben had gone, and a pinched smile told Rayna she was irritated with her husband. "I'm not going to wait for him to come back. Who knows how long he'll take. I don't want to waste your time." She reached into her bag. "The name of our restaurant is The

Sanddab." Lucy set an iPad on the table and rotated the screen so Rayna could see a photograph of a flatfish. "As in the Pacific sanddab."

"Ooh, I've always loved sanddab."

Lucy swiped the screen so it displayed the name of the restaurant superimposed on a playful drawing of a sanddab with its bulging eyes and feathery fins. "Here's our logo. It'll be a place casual enough that you can bring your children but nice enough for a date. Appealing to both locals and tourists. We're thinking of your pottery in decorative terms. Candleholders for the tables. Some larger vases for the hostess stand. A bowl for business cards, and so forth."

Rayna studied the logo. "Do you have any images of what the interior will look like? I know it's all under construction right now."

"Yes." Lucy swiped to another screen.

A faint, rapid pulsing caught Rayna's attention. Lucy was calm now, and without the distraction of her pounding heart and Rayna's own nerves, Rayna could sense . . . was she imagining . . . with all the background heartbeats she'd been ignoring, apparently, she'd ignored this one too. Within Lucy was another separate life. Tiny, with a soft, fast heartbeat.

Lucy was pregnant.

". . . sand-colored paint with dark-blue accents . . ."

Rayna kept nodding at Lucy's descriptions, but she couldn't concentrate on anything but the fetus inside Lucy. From the size of the baby, Lucy was well into her second trimester, farther than Rayna had ever made it. The loose dress wasn't simply a style choice.

". . . various shades of blue, like the sunlight shining through the waves, or that bright teal when the sky is—Rayna, are you okay?"

"Fine," Rayna said, all but smacking her brain into paying attention to what Lucy was saying. "Are you looking for pieces that incorporate the full logo or just the fish or something more abstract? Or plain pieces?"

"That's what we'd like to brainstorm with you." Lucy swiped to a new screen. "Here are the dimensions of the tables."

The server was back. "Are you ready to place your orders?"

"Yes, we are. My husband is touring the kitchen with Kaitlyn, but I'm starving. I'll order for him, and if he doesn't like it, he shouldn't have wandered off."

"Would you like me to go find him?" the server asked.

"No, don't bother." Lucy opened her menu.

After they'd placed their orders and the server left, Lucy sighed. "Maybe I should go get him."

"Or make all the decisions without him," Rayna suggested, hoping her smile looked believable. She ought to stop focusing on the baby, but she couldn't.

"I would, but he's so particular that he'll want to change everything, and I don't want to waste time doing things he'll undo." The fetus inside Lucy rolled over. Lucy's hand went beneath the table, resting on her belly.

Rayna wondered how the baby's movements felt.

The baby kicked, and Lucy smiled. "Besides, I'll be stepping back from the restaurant for a few months this summer. I'm pregnant. You . . . probably noticed." She tugged at the front of her loose dress.

"Congratulations!" Rayna said brightly.

* * *

Rayna pulled over onto the sandy shoulder of the road and parked. She'd eaten and smiled and talked and made notes as she and Lucy—and finally Ben—had discussed pottery and the Orozcos' plans for The Sanddab, but throughout the dinner, Rayna had been aching for the moment when she could be alone. With dessert eaten and a verbal agreement to create four candleholder designs for the Orozcos to consider, Rayna had at last been able to flee the restaurant.

She stowed her purse and phone in the center console, stuffed her keys in the pocket of her dress pants, and took out the mini flashlight she always left in her car. Moving carefully in her heels, she walked down the wooden stairs that led to the beach. When she reached the sand, she removed her shoes, rolled up her pantlegs, and walked as quickly as she could to the familiar flat rock where she'd sat thousands of times.

No one else was on the beach. Sitting in the darkness, listening to the ocean, Rayna let tears pour down her face. Why had the news of Lucy's pregnancy hit her so hard? *You knew Lucy loves kids. You should have expected kids would be in her and Ben's plans. Why is this a shock? Why are you reacting like it's personal? Are you going to start resenting everyone around you who has a baby?* That *sounds like a joyful way to live.*

The night was getting cold, and her lightweight blazer was almost useless at keeping her insulated. Still, she didn't want to leave until she'd finished crying. She dug her toes into the sand and drew lung-straining breaths of sea air, waiting for the pain to ebb.

The problem wasn't Lucy's pregnancy. It was Lucy's pregnancy plus everything else. The end of her marriage. Her father's death and the mocking words that had been the last things he had said to her. The secrets she couldn't confide in anyone.

What if she *did* try to tell someone what she could do? She imagined calling her mother and spilling the truth. *"Remember how you always thought my ability to sense people was a quirk I should keep hidden? Just wanted to let you know that now I can commit murder with my mind. Nice to chat with you. How are things? What's next on your travel agenda? Dubai? Morocco?"*

A blur of human energy came into her range, approaching from the left, moving along the beach in a steady tread. Someone out for an evening walk. Rayna didn't move. A section of the beach between the intruder and Rayna was too rocky to make it attractive to runners and walkers. This one would probably veer up to the road before . . . Was that Damon Hale?

It was.

He was getting closer to her, not heading for the road, his path weaving—he must be moving over and between rocks. She spotted the glare of his flashlight.

Rayna snatched her shoes and scuttled in front of a tall rock near the water, blocking herself from his view. He'd pass before the tide got too high and she ended up soaked or swimming.

Seawater sped toward her, sloshing around her ankles. Was Damon slowing down? Slowing. Stopping. What was he . . . Oh, stretching. The leg injury he'd aggravated yesterday must be bothering him. *Go away. Go home and put your feet up.*

He started walking. Rayna tracked him, waiting for him to pass her, but when he neared her hiding place, he stopped again and sat down. Was he sitting on the same rock she'd used? Granted, it was the best seat around, but how bad could her luck get that he'd chosen that spot to—

Though she'd been facing the water, she'd been concentrating on Damon and hadn't noticed a bigger wave coming. With an involuntary yelp, she tried to dash out of the way, but the water caught her, splashing her to the waist, sending her stumbling against the rock behind her.

"Ma'am, are you—Rayna!" Damon had rushed toward her, summoned by her cry. The head lamp he wore blinded Rayna. He quickly adjusted the beam. "The tide's coming in. You'd better—Or maybe you noticed it's coming in . . ."

Rayna tried to laugh, wiping tears off her cheeks with the hand not holding heeled pumps dripping with seawater. "I noticed." She must look comically ridiculous, skulking behind a rock in the dark, her dressy business clothes drenched.

"I'm stating the obvious again," he said, "but that's a dangerous place to stand."

"You'd think I'd know that after growing up here."

"Come on." As a smaller wave rushed in, Damon took her by the arm and hurried her around the rock to higher ground. "Seriously, you're going to get hurt. Or drown."

She rubbed the smarting elbow she'd whacked on the rock. "Thanks for the help."

"I owed you a rescue," he said.

With that bright head lamp, there was no way he hadn't noticed what must be tear-blotched skin, smeared makeup, and reddened eyes. "How's your leg?" Rayna asked, hoping they could talk about muscle spasms instead of why she'd been hiding and crying.

"It's fine. I decided to stick with walking tonight instead of running."

"I'm glad. I won't keep you. You'll want to finish your walk before it gets too late. Have a good evening and don't get drenched." She started toward the stairs, clutching her wet shoes.

Damon caught up with her. "I'll walk you to your car," he said. "Quid pro quo, since you accompanied me away from my accident."

She walked faster. With her soaked clothes, she'd gone from cold to freezing. "I'm okay. Just out of practice with the ocean."

"Do you have a towel or a jacket in your car?"

"No, but I'll crank the heater up."

"Rayna." Damon's voice was gentle. "This isn't my business, but can I do anything to help you? This obviously wasn't a planned . . . or enjoyable . . . beach trip."

"It's no big deal." Rayna averted her head. "It was just . . . a stressful evening. I'm fine now."

They reached her car, and she stuck her hand into her soggy pocket for her keys.

They weren't there, and neither was her flashlight. She checked both front pockets, repeatedly. Patted her back pockets and blazer pockets, even though they were fake, stitched shut.

"I lost my keys. And my flashlight." They'd fallen out of her too-shallow pockets, probably when she'd gotten doused. Was there any hope they hadn't been swept out to sea?

"I'll help you find them," he said.

"Thank you." She dropped her shoes next to her car and retraced her path to the beach, Damon at her side, his head lamp illuminating the ground. When they reached the rock where she'd been sitting, she groped through the sand around the base of it. Nothing, and she was starting to shiver.

"Take my sweatshirt." He pulled it over his head. "You're going to get hypothermia."

She should protest that Damon needed the sweatshirt himself, but she was miserably cold, miserably frustrated by the stupidity of losing her keys, and miserably ready to start crying again. "Thank you." She accepted the sweatshirt and pulled it on.

Damon stripped off his shoes and socks and rolled up his pant legs. "Stay here. I'll check the area where you got hit by that wave."

"I can do that," she said, following him. "You don't need to risk getting wet."

"Here." Damon took his own keys, phone, and a stack of business cards out of his pockets and handed them to Rayna. "You keep these dry."

At least it was something useful to do. Rayna watched as Damon darted around the rock, then retreated as a new wave hit. Back and forth, back and forth, until he finally returned to her.

"Sorry. I checked as much of the area as I could. If you dropped them there, they've been pulled farther out."

"Thank you for checking." She handed him his belongings. "That was beyond the call of duty."

"Not a problem. Sorry I couldn't find them. Maybe in the daylight when the tide's out we'll be able to find them wedged in the sand or caught on a rock."

"I'll check the tide charts and come back tomorrow," Rayna said. "Not with much hope though. I'll call my sister to come pick me up." *Great.* She'd been planning to slip into the guesthouse unseen. The last thing she wanted to do was face her sister while disheveled, soaked, and puffy-eyed after having repeatedly assured Annemarie that it wouldn't bother her at all to do business with Ben and Lucy.

"Do you have your phone?" Damon asked.

Rayna paused, then uselessly patted her empty pockets. "No. I locked it in my car with my purse. I'm such a flake."

"You're not a flake. You can use my phone to call Annemarie if you'd like, but may I give you a ride home instead? My car isn't far away."

Not having to call Annemarie for a rescue appealed to her, though she'd still have to face her or Seth to get a spare key to the guesthouse. "Thank you, but I'm a mess. Your car upholstery will pay a high price."

"I don't mind. How do you expect me to understand the residents of a beach town if my car is untouched by seawater and sand?"

"You're welcome, then."

He laughed. They started toward the stairs.

"Do you have another key to your car at home?" he asked.

"Yes."

"After you change into dry clothes, I'll bring you back here so you can get your car."

"I'd appreciate that, but that's a lot of trouble for you."

"I'm happy to do it."

"Just please promise me none of this will show up on your blog or in your book."

"You keep my secrets," he said, "and I'll keep yours."

Uselessly, Rayna brushed sand off her feet, stepped into her wet shoes, and accompanied Damon to his car.

"Tell me about some of the people you've interviewed," she said as Damon drove along the beachside road. With the warmth of Damon's sweatshirt, the heated air flowing from the vents, and Damon's calm, nonjudgmental company, she felt herself relaxing a little. "I'll bet you already know more about Willet Beach than I do."

"I imagine I know different things than you do. Unless you like to graph population growth since the town was founded in 1872 or read census reports."

"I didn't even know it was founded in 1872. How embarrassing."

"You can live in a town for a lifetime and never learn facts like that. Most people don't. How are you adjusting to being back? Does it feel like home, or is it disorienting dealing with how things have changed?"

"Both. But if I feel too disoriented, I can go get ice cream. Mr. Cheney and his store have looked exactly the same my entire life. Seth is trying to persuade him to relocate to a bigger new location, but if he does, I'll lose one of my mental anchors."

"At least the ice cream will taste the same no matter where he is."

"True. You know what else you need to try if you haven't? Dorotea's Bakery. Their olive bread makes the best sandwiches on earth."

"I haven't tried the bread yet, but their chocolate croissants are fantastic. Do you have a lot of old friends who live in the area?"

"Other long-timers you could interview? Not a lot of them. Most people leave for college and don't move back. But . . ." Why not suggest this? "I can think of a pair of friends who'd be interesting interview subjects. Ben and Lucy Orozco. They moved back here not long ago and will be opening a restaurant. I might be doing custom pottery for them—Annemarie mentioned that to you the other night. If you like the before-and-after aspect of a developing business, that's an angle you could pursue with Lucy and Ben. I'm sure they'd love to speak with you."

"Thank you for the tip." Damon glanced at her. "I apologize for bringing this up, but I suspect you'll worry about it, so let me be clear. As I talk to people, I pick up gossip. I'm aware that there's a difficult history between you and Mr. and Mrs. Orozco, and I want you to know that I respect your privacy. No personal incidents from your past will be fodder for the book."

Rayna exhaled and stared at the road, wanting to avoid even momentary eye contact with Damon. He had a disconcerting knack for knocking her off balance with his knowledge of her past even as he attempted to reassure her. "Thanks," she said. "Who blabbed? Never mind. Silly question. Jody Wyeth is your assistant. She told you, didn't she?"

"I'd rather not risk creating tension between you and my sources."

"Do you think I'll go yell at them?" Rayna bent to unroll the legs of her pants as though this topic meant so little to her that she was more interested in dealing with soggy wool. "I've known Jody all my life. I love her, but I'm well aware that she knows everything and tells everything. I'm not upset. This all happened years ago, and everything's fine now. Ben and Lucy and I are friendly business acquaintances. But thanks for being candid with me. I appreciate it."

Damon didn't respond. Rayna straightened up and looked out the windshield just as he drove straight through an intersection where he should have turned right.

"That was the . . . Okay, go to the next light and turn right," Rayna said.

He cleared his throat. "If you appreciate candor, I'd better admit that when I was speaking with Annemarie yesterday, she mentioned that your appointment to discuss your pottery commission was tonight."

Rayna plunged into mortified silence. There was no point in denying she'd been with Ben and Lucy tonight. That lie would only make her look more ludicrous, and she looked ludicrous enough after the way she'd claimed everything was fine. As if her physical appearance weren't enough evidence for how shaken she was, she'd told Damon that she'd had a stressful evening.

"Rayna," he said, "you don't have to pretend everything about returning home is wonderful. I've already given you my word that I won't share in print or online anything you don't give me express permission to share. You don't need to keep up a facade."

Her voice came out low and scratchy. "It's not what you think. I'm not hung up on Ben after all these years or holding a grudge against Lucy." Rayna wasn't sure if she wanted to go on, but if Jody hadn't already told him this, she would eventually. "Tonight, I just . . . My husband—ex-husband—and I wanted children very much and weren't able to have them. Tonight I found out Lucy is pregnant, and it just . . . hit wrong."

"I'm sorry, Rayna."

"It's all right. All I needed was to vent for a while, alone on the beach. I'm fine now, I swear I am. Drenched, but fine. Good grief, that's enough about my personal problems. I'm sure this isn't what you're after in learning about the experiences of Willet Beach locals. Don't worry. You'll find plenty of normal people here to interview. Wholesome stories for your book."

"You don't consider yourself normal?"

"I . . . put on a good show," she said.

CHAPTER 9

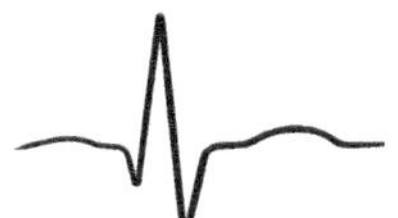

"GUT PUNCH. BRUTAL." LOGAN LEANED partly out of the camera's view and came back into sight holding what Damon recognized as one of Logan's wife's homemade piroshkis. "You'll have to put up with me eating and talking. I'm due in a meeting in twenty minutes, and without lunch first, I won't survive it. Does Rayna's reaction to the backstabbing best friend's pregnancy worry you enough that you recommend pulling her now and finishing your evaluation while we isolate her?"

Damon brushed grains of sand off the corner of his kitchen table. He'd spent a significant portion of last night asking himself that question as he'd repeatedly reviewed every note he'd made on Rayna. He hadn't picked up on anger or hostility from her, but clearly, her meeting with parents-to-be Lucy and Ben had cut deep. "I'm debating that."

"I got word from my Denver agent this morning," Logan said. "It was Evan Novak who filed for divorce, and from what the agent's gathered so far, it sounds like Rayna didn't want it."

That was helpful data. Rayna obviously had the capacity to deal with rejection, so the odds that she'd belatedly lash out at Ben were low. But her pain over Lucy's pregnancy was an unsettling variable. Promptly removing Rayna from Willet Beach to ensure she didn't have the chance to harm anyone appealed to Damon.

Logan swallowed a mouthful of piroshki. "Your report was as scholarly and impartial as always. It's time to wallow in the muck of opinion. What's your take? Are the red-flag deaths and the potential danger to the Orozcos sufficient to justify pulling her now, considering what we'd lose as far as her willingness to work with us? We need her. We want her help. But we have no use for a rogue."

Damon picked up Rayna's keys that he'd set on the table. Last night when he'd reached the rock where she'd been sitting prior to fleeing at his approach, he'd spotted her keys lying in the sand. Lost keys offered a pretext for gaining more one-on-one time to study her. Already, this tactic had earned him last night's conversation as he'd driven her home then back to her vehicle. This morning, the keys would earn him an additional chance to speak with her when he returned them, as well as her gratitude when he claimed to have gone to the beach at dawn to search for them.

Returning the keys would also offer an opportunity to take her into custody, if that was his decision. Which would mean heartbreak for Rayna's family due to the evidence Damon would leave behind that she had drowned, as well as emotional devastation for Rayna at the destruction of her life and critical damage to the possibility that the team would ever be able to recruit her—if she turned out to be innocent after all.

If she was guilty, that scenario had a quicker resolution.

Damon released the keys, letting them clank against the table.

"What's your recommendation?" Logan asked.

"Leave her in place for now," Damon said. "I'm not ready to destroy her life on iffy circumstantial evidence and overdone caution."

"Very well. I'd say that's a wise call. Iffy circumstantial evidence aside, she seems to have high potential. We don't want to wreck that by acting prematurely." Creases formed in Logan's brow. "Off the record, old mentor to old recruit, how are you holding up?"

"Fine."

"Wrong. How long have we known each other?"

Damon did the math. "Sixteen years."

"Sixteen years. Since you were a geeky kid. I can tell when you're putting yourself under too much pressure. You're a good man, Damon. Too good, maybe, too ready to hold yourself accountable for an inability to know the unknowable. We can't always get it right."

Damon picked up Rayna's keys and shoved them into his pocket. "There's a high price for getting it wrong."

"I know, and you've paid it. I'm sorry. But that's the nature of what we do. National security isn't tidy. We do what we can. Now, go show up on Rayna's doorstep, smoldering and heroic and brandishing her keys."

Damon snorted. Smoldering and heroic, returning the keys he'd stolen in the first place.

"Copy the keys first though," Logan said. "Who knows when they'll come in handy?"

"I already have," Damon said.

* * *

The morning sky was sapphire blue as Rayna strode along the side of Annemarie's house, heading for her car. She'd give herself half an hour to search for her keys in the daylight, and if she didn't find them, she'd declare them permanently lost and start the process of replacing them. She didn't want to spend more time on the keys than she had to. After two days of cleaning her shed, doing maintenance on her pottery wheel, organizing the supplies she'd had shipped to Annemarie's house before she'd arrived, and making a run to a ceramics supply store in San Jose, she was antsy to get to work. She'd start off with a few pieces for The Beach Umbrella. While she worked on those, she'd think about designs for The Sanddab candleholders.

Today would be a productive, satisfying day. Last night's emotional turmoil had settled. She was happy for Lucy and Ben's impending parenthood and was no longer humiliated by what Damon had witnessed of her breakdown. In fact, she felt better for having talked with him. He'd been so kind, and she was confident he wouldn't tell anyone about finding her crying on the beach.

Her phone pinged with a text.

Hi it's Damon Hale. I found your keys. They were covered with sand near the foot of the stairs. No flashlight though. I can drop the keys off this morning. Let me know what time works for you.

Smiling, Rayna texted back. *THANK YOU. I didn't expect you to go hunting for them! You don't need to drop them off. The least I can do is come to you. Will you be in your office today?*

Yes from nine to around noon. I'll be out most of the afternoon.

I'll stop by this morning. Thanks again. You are beyond nice.

It wasn't a problem. Any beach exploration is fodder for the book.

I doubt this did much for your book but it's a load off my mind. What's the address?

Damon sent it. Rayna did an about-face and returned to the guesthouse. She would shower, dress in something that wasn't the glaze-stained sweatshirt and faded capris she was wearing now, then stop at Dorotea's Bakery on the way to Damon's office. She definitely owed him a chocolate croissant.

Twenty minutes later, with her wet hair wrapped in a towel, Rayna paused with her lipstick in her hand and frowned at the mirror. She was carefully putting on makeup. She was wearing a boho-style teal dress with a ruffled skirt—a flattering dress that had brought her more compliments than anything else in her closet. She'd already chosen her jewelry: a long silver chain with a starfish-shaped pendant and matching earrings.

Why was she so concerned about her appearance this morning? It wasn't as though Damon was planning to interview her or take pictures, and she certainly wouldn't be wearing this outfit later while throwing pottery. Why hadn't she grabbed a T-shirt and jeans, combed her wet hair into a ponytail, and gone to fetch her keys so she could return and get started on the work she'd been so eager to do prior to Damon's text?

You're dressing up for him. You're interested in him.

"No, I'm *not,*" she said aloud. She didn't want to be romantically interested in *anyone,* and absolutely not in a man who was only in Willet Beach short-term. And Damon had shown no romantic interest in her. He was simply a nice guy, quick to help others. His helping her last night and returning to the beach this morning to search for her keys were things he'd have done for anyone.

Stop panicking. There's nothing happening here. She was taking her time to look her best because it made *her* feel good. She finished applying her lipstick, unwound the towel around her hair, and reached for her blow-dryer.

* * *

"Oh, Rayna, honey, don't you look lovely today?" Jody welcomed her from behind a desk decorated with a pot of tulips, a pencil jar painted with sailboats, and a business-card holder created from an oyster shell. "That bright-blue dress is perfect with your hair."

"Thank you." Rayna could sense Damon to the left of the small reception area, behind a closed door, in what must be his private office. "How are you doing?"

"I'm okay, dear, thank you for asking. I've been helping Mr. Hale get his office put together. These walls won't be bare much longer. I told him no travel writer should have bare walls. I've ordered prints made from his photographs. That's one of my jobs—sorting his photos and deleting the bad ones and organizing the rest of them."

"He's lucky to have you."

"It's been a favor to me to have work to keep me busy. Kaitlyn gets cross if I do too much at the Grill—never mind that I *own* the place—and I need *something.* You understand. Glenn used to fill so much of my time." Jody sighed. "Losing both Elliott *and* Glenn seems so unfair."

"It really does. I'm sorry."

"At least they both died doing things they loved. Glenn after that wonderful party and Elliott out there fishing, alone with the waves and the sea creatures."

Elliott Wyeth had died doing *two* things he loved, Rayna thought—fishing and drinking too much, which had led to his falling overboard and drowning.

"I'll tell you, darling, your father was a sweetheart to me," Jody said. "Elliott meant well, but he had his own ways."

"I'm glad Dad was good to you." Rayna had to agree that her father, flaws included, had been an improvement on Elliott.

"I *am* making new friends," Jody said. "I even have a new pickleball partner. He's a police officer, a sergeant. Isn't that an exciting job? Don't think I'm leaping back into dating so soon—I'm very much mourning your father. Sgt. Fischer and I are only friends. Stars, he must be at least fifteen years younger than I am anyway."

"I'm glad you enjoy his company."

"I've been doing research for Mr. Hale." Jody touched the edge of her computer monitor. "Who'd have thought I'd be a researcher? I'm searching news archives about Willet Beach. He gave me a list of things he's particularly interested in."

"I imagine you're a great source about Willet Beach yourself." *And a source of gossip about my personal life.*

"I do know a lot of people and a lot of town history," Jody said. "He's interviewed me for hours at a time." She lowered her voice. "He's a wonderful listener. I'm afraid I bored him when I got too reminiscent about Glenn, but he's so courteous. He let me talk about your father to my heart's content. I told him stories about when you and Annemarie were children and your parents would bring you to the Grill. Remember that otter statue we had in the waiting area? You'd always sit next to it and pet it."

Damon really must have been bored silly. Between tales of child Rayna petting a brass otter and college Rayna getting dumped by Ben, Jody was ensuring he was more informed on Rayna's history than he could possibly want to be. "I loved that statue."

"I did, too, but after Elliott died, Kaitlyn insisted on getting rid of it. She said it was tacky. How is your pottery studio coming along, dear? I was impressed with how Mr. Hale's skill with a camera could make even a dusty old shed look artistic."

Rayna smiled, grateful that the pictures had apparently turned out as well as they could have. "It's much less dusty now. Everything's ready. I'll be working in there today."

"How delightful! You're so creative. But here I am chatting away, and you're here to see Mr. Hale. He told me you'd be stopping by." Jody crossed the reception area to tap on Damon's door.

"Come in," Damon called.

Jody opened the door a crack. "Rayna's here."

Rayna sensed Damon rising to his feet and walking toward the door. It swung the rest of the way open.

"Good morning," he said. "Come in."

Rayna stepped inside his office. To her surprise, Damon closed the door behind her and gestured to a chair facing his desk. She'd assumed he'd hand over the keys, she'd hand over the bakery box, and she'd go. But she didn't mind taking a moment to chat.

"It was incredibly nice of you to go searching for my keys. Thank you again for all your help last night as well." She sat and placed the white cardboard box on his desk. "This is a little thank-you."

Damon tapped the Dorotea's Bakery sticker sealing the box. "Feel free to lose your keys anytime if this is what it gets me."

"I should bring you a croissant a week after the favors you've done for me."

"It's not a big deal." He sat behind his desk and opened the center drawer. "I was going on a morning walk anyway. It was easy to do it where you lost your keys."

"It's a big deal to me. Thank you."

"You're welcome." He took her keys out and handed them to her. "How are you doing this morning?"

The attentiveness in his expression told her he expected a genuine answer. He had olive-green eyes; she hadn't noticed that before. "I'm much better," she said. "If you could please forget everything that happened last night along with about 85 percent of whatever Jody has told you about me, that would be great."

"You don't need to be embarrassed. We all hit rough patches."

"Okay, but next time, I'd better stick to crying on my living room couch."

"If you're not going to take advantage of the opportunity to cry on the beach, why pay these housing prices? You could cry on a couch in Kansas."

Rayna laughed. "Here's some positive news: my studio shed is clean and stocked and ready to go. Today I'll start working in my own space, which I haven't done for years, and I'm thrilled about it."

"Congratulations! Mind if I stop by tomorrow morning to get a second round of photos?"

Rayna tried to ignore how pleased she was by this request. "You're welcome to do that, but honestly, it's not that visually interesting yet. Just cleaner than it was last time you saw it."

"How does ten o'clock sound?" he asked.

* * *

"She's certainly looking breathtaking today." Jody spoke as Damon reentered the reception area after walking Rayna to her car. "She's a beautiful girl." Jody winked at him. "And you're the knight in shining armor."

Jody was worse than Logan with his crack about smoldering. "I poked around in the sand and picked up her keys. That's not a feat of bravery."

"But it was a feat of kindness, and she's so grateful. She likes you. A lot."

"What makes you say that?"

"Oh stars, Mr. Hale, don't be a dunce. Didn't you notice how fixed up she was? That dress. Jewelry. Lipstick. Her hair brushed so elegantly with the front pulled back and the back loose. Like Princess Buttercup at her wedding. Rayna's always been so clever with that long auburn hair."

"Princess Buttercup?"

"*The Princess Bride*! Oh, for heaven's sake. Just take my word for it. Rayna took some time on herself this morning, and it wasn't for the benefit of her pottery wheel."

"You're jumping to conclusions. Uh . . . would you put an appointment on my calendar? Tomorrow morning, ten o'clock, for photos of the progress on Rayna's studio."

Jody smirked and typed. "I'm sure the exceptional depth of interest you have in *this* local business has nothing to do with the business owner herself."

It had everything to do with the business owner herself. Yes, he'd noticed how classy she looked today. He'd also noticed how beautiful she'd looked last night, half-drenched in seawater, wearing his sweatshirt, her eyes swollen from crying. He'd noticed her kindness, her sense of humor, the way she tried to avoid admitting to pain, her lack of close friends, her devotion to her sister. He'd noticed a lot of things, most of which had gone into his reports worded as objectively as possible. He couldn't afford any degree of personal attachment to Rayna Kirkpatrick.

Could she possibly be interested in him? Guilt roiled. He didn't want to manipulate her emotions to create opportunities to see her, but at the same time, he needed to keep close tabs on her. This would be a fine line to walk.

"There," Jody said. "Your appointment is set. Should I order flowers and have them sent to her in your name?"

"Absolutely not."

"Well, if you're going to deny interest in Rayna, you should get to know my Kaitlyn better. She's a beautiful girl as well and so smart. You'll have lots of time to chat with her at the fishing hut on Saturday. You'll love our cozy little oceanside place."

Damon started regretting that he'd accepted Jody's invitation to visit their vacation property twenty minutes from Willet Beach for lunch and a trip on her late husband's fishing boat. He liked Kaitlyn but wasn't interested in a relationship with her—or with anyone right now. "Enough with the matchmaker schtick. I'm in Willet Beach to do a job. That's all."

CHAPTER 10

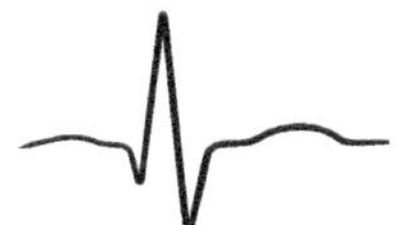

WITH THE METICULOUSLY CUSHIONED SAMPLE candleholders in a box on the backseat, Rayna drove toward The Sanddab, eager to present her work to Ben and Lucy. They'd chosen these styles from the designs she'd sent them, and tonight she'd show them the completed pieces so they could make their decision. She'd created four very different options—a whimsical sand-and-turquoise-colored piece embossed with the bulgy-eyed sanddab from their logo, a round style with fish-shaped cutouts, a cylindrical piece with an ombre glaze in shades of blue, and an asymmetrical piece with a ruffled edge that resembled a breaking wave. In Rayna's opinion, the candleholders were some of her best work, and she was confident Ben and Lucy would be pleased.

In the three weeks since she'd first sat down at her own pottery wheel again, the flow of peace and productivity had increased in her life day by day. She'd filled her sketchbook with design ideas. She'd filled the shelves in her shed with pieces in different stages of drying, waiting for the kiln, or waiting for glazing. The muscle soreness from a level of physical labor she hadn't reached in ages had disappeared. And free time spent hanging out with Annemarie and Seth or helping at The Beach Umbrella was a delight. With a life like this, she might have to reinstate the word *tranquility* in her vocabulary.

If she could just block out the nightmares.

Damon had returned twice to take photographs and to interview her about her creative process, and she'd run into him in town several times at places like Wyeth's Grill and Cheney's or while walking on the beach. The more she got to know him, the more she enjoyed his company. She didn't pretend to herself that she wasn't attracted to him, but she had no plans to act on it—no matter how much Annemarie teased her. Her interaction with Damon remained comfortable and businesslike, veering toward friendship. He'd conducted additional interviews with Annemarie as well, and Annemarie had high hopes that both her consignment shop and Rayna's pottery would make the cut for his book. Annemarie had invited him for dinner last Sunday, and it had been a relaxed evening involving Annemarie's children giving him detailed reports on all the neighborhood cats, comparing them to Fig, and insisting Damon come for a walk to see how many he could spot. He'd turned out to be skilled at spotting cats.

Traffic was heavy on Beachcomber Avenue. It must be spring break somewhere, bringing tourists to town. Rayna didn't mind inching along. She'd left herself plenty of time to get to her appointment, and tourists were people who might buy her pottery. The pieces Annemarie had displayed in her store had sold quickly. Along with selling at The Beach Umbrella and building up the inventory on her Etsy shop, Rayna was in the process of contacting gift shops, coffee shops, and any other brick-and-mortar locations that might be interested in selling her work. Someday, she'd have a studio/shop location where she could both work and sell her pottery, but she needed to get much better established before she poured money into renting retail space.

The old restaurant that the Orozcos were transforming into The Sanddab came into sight. Waiting for a group of teenagers to cross the street, Rayna idly reached past the life sensations of the numerous people between her and her destination and searched for Ben and Lucy.

There Ben was, above ground level. The office was upstairs, he'd told her . . . Rayna went rigid. What was wrong with . . . his heartbeat . . . It was slow, so slow, the rhythm irregular. He was lying down . . . Something was horribly wrong.

The blare of a horn made her jump. She hadn't noticed the crosswalk was clear. Automatically, she drove forward, her mind scouring the rest of The Sanddab, and got caught by a red light.

Lucy wasn't anywhere near Ben; Rayna couldn't find her at all. No one else was close enough to him to be inside the building. She snatched her phone out of her purse and called 911.

"911, what's your emergency?"

"My friend is sick. He's at The Sanddab Restaurant—or what will be The Sanddab. It's that old Italian restaurant on Beachcomber Avenue. I can't remember the address. He needs an ambulance. He's upstairs."

"Ma'am, what are his symptoms?"

"He . . . collapsed. His heart is beating very slowly and unevenly."

Another horn beeped; the light had changed. Rayna drove through the intersection and got stopped fifty feet later behind backed-up traffic. This was absurd. She twisted the steering wheel, pulling into a parking lot.

"Ma'am? Can you hear me?"

Rayna sprang out of her car and sprinted along the sidewalk toward The Sanddab. "What did you say?"

"Is he conscious?"

"I don't think so . . . Hang on . . . I found him like this, just got here . . ." Gasping, she wrenched open the front door that Ben had said he'd leave unlocked for her and raced through the empty dining room and up the stairs that led to his office. Ben was sprawled on the floor, facedown.

"Ben!" She knelt next to him. "*Ben*!"

No response. She set her phone down, grabbed his shoulders, and heaved him onto his back. His eyes were glassy, his face ashen and sweaty. "Ben, it's Rayna. Can you hear me?"

No response. Just a shallow quiver from his heart. Another weak quiver.

"His heart's not beating!" Rayna shouted the update in the direction of her phone as her brain groped for the first-aid training the employees had all taken when she'd worked at the museum. Thirty compressions, two breaths. "I'll start CPR." She tilted Ben's head back, pinched his nose shut, and breathed into his mouth. Once. Twice.

She positioned her hands on his sternum and pressed down hard, counting each beat.

Sirens became audible from outside, but with the heavy traffic, how long would it take for help to arrive? *Hurry, please hurry.* She forced two more breaths into Ben's lungs and resumed chest compressions.

She could sense no response from him.

Another round of compressions; two more breaths. Another round. Another.

No stirring of an independent heartbeat. Only her own brute force pushing oxygen into his blood and blood to his brain. "Ben." Sweat rolled down her sides. "*Ben.* Lucy needs you. Your baby needs you."

More compressions. She gritted her teeth, watching his chest sink and rise beneath her hands. Two more breaths. Her arms shook with fatigue as she repositioned her hands on his chest and pressed down.

"*Ben*! You . . . can't . . . die!" She gasped out the plea, momentarily losing track of the number of compressions. "You're going to be a *father.* You have to come back. Can you hear me?"

Nothing. Rayna's tears splattered onto Ben's face as she bent to offer two more rescue breaths. "Ben, Lucy loves you. Don't leave her. Please don't leave her. Don't leave your child."

The sirens stopped. Rayna shifted her attention from Ben barely long enough to sense two people running toward them, then returned her full focus to the search for any sensation of life within the man whose ribs she'd felt crack under the pressure of her hands.

Footsteps thumped on the stairs, and two EMTs rushed into the room. "Keep going, ma'am." One of them spoke as they knelt on either side of Ben. "Finish this round, and we'll switch on my signal."

Rayna couldn't nod. She didn't have muscle control for anything beyond the motion of her arms. When she reached thirty compressions and moved to deliver two breaths, the EMT scooted into her place. "Give the breaths and move back. We've got it now."

With all the strength she had left, Rayna breathed air into Ben's lungs, then crawled backward to give the EMTs the room they needed. As soon as she was out of the way, she dropped to the floor on her stomach, closing her eyes. Her whole body trembled, and her shoulders burned.

Ben, don't die. Don't die. Please don't die.

But he was already dead. Nothing the EMTs were doing was changing that.

She couldn't sense him at all.

* * *

"I'm Detective Claire Stafford." A middle-aged woman with blonde curls, laugh lines around her eyes, and a lemon-yellow pantsuit slid onto the opposite bench of the booth where Rayna sat in The Sanddab's empty dining area. "I'm sorry we've kept you waiting so long."

"It doesn't matter." Rayna had no idea how long it had been. After she'd answered the questions asked by one of the responding officers, he'd escorted her here and asked her to wait. She'd texted Annemarie to tell her what had happened, had insisted Annemarie *not* come downtown to meet her, and had fallen into a fog, unable to do anything except relentlessly scan for Lucy. Where *was* Lucy? She was supposed to be here tonight for their meeting.

Had the police told her Ben was dead?

"Would you like more water, hon?" Stafford asked. She had a strong Southern accent.

Rayna looked dully at the half-empty cup of water in front of her. "No, thank you."

"Now, be patient with me. I know you already answered many of these questions for Sgt. Fischer, but I'd like to go through them with you as well."

Rayna nodded, Fischer's name finally clicking. Jody's new pickleball partner. Rayna had been too rattled to realize that was whom she was speaking to.

"Could you tell me what happened?" Stafford asked.

Rayna repeated the version of the story she'd given Fischer, accurate except for the omission of how she'd initially realized Ben was in trouble. Her strange abilities were irrelevant. Let the police think she'd witnessed his distress like a normal person.

"Thank you," Stafford said. "I know it's difficult for you to talk about this. You mentioned you were old friends with Mr. and Mrs. Orozco?"

"Yes. We all grew up together here. Lucy and I were close friends. Ben was a little older."

"How nice that you were helping them with the decor for their restaurant. Where are these sample candleholders you brought to show them tonight? I'd love to see them."

The question zapped Rayna's brain. She'd forgotten about leaving the candleholders in her car when she'd rushed to Ben's aid, hadn't considered how to explain why she didn't have them with her now. Could she claim she'd returned the box to the car while she'd been waiting for Detective Stafford to question her? No. The officers on the scene could tell Stafford they'd never seen her with the box, never seen her leave the building.

"They're in my car," Rayna admitted. "Ben was going to give me a tour of the place, and then I planned to bring them inside for the . . . dramatic unveiling."

"How fun." Stafford smiled as though she hadn't noticed Rayna's hesitation in answering the question. "Who doesn't like to dress up an exciting moment with a bit of theatrics? Where's your car parked, hon?"

Another zap of dismay. "It's . . . down the street. Traffic was so backed up that I got impatient and ditched my car."

"Were you running late for your appointment with the Orozcos?"

Rayna wanted to claim she had been, but she'd already told Stafford the appointment was set for seven and the timing of the 911 call would show she'd been early. "No. I was just restless. Do you . . . know what killed Ben?"

"I don't know. I'm sorry. That's for the medical experts to determine. Tell me more about your relationship with the Orozcos. I understand you dated Mr. Orozco in college and your breakup was a painful one, resulting from his relationship with the now-Mrs. Orozco."

The warmth in her face made her feel like she was under a spotlight. She should have stated that information up front. Jody had probably shared it with Sgt. Fischer, who'd told Stafford. Or for all Rayna knew, Stafford could be in a quilting club with Jody Wyeth. Or one of the cops could be surfing buddies with Ben or friends with Lucy. No, Lucy wouldn't be the source. She would have kept their history to herself. Ben might have shared it though . . .

"Miss Rayna?"

"Sorry. I'm having trouble concentrating. The situation with Ben and Lucy was a long time ago. Everything is—was—fine among us."

"I'm happy to hear that. Betrayal *does* sting for a very long time though." Stafford patted Rayna's arm. "My ex couldn't resist parading his pageant-queen mistress in my face."

"I'm so sorry."

"It's what brought me to California. As soon as our youngest daughter was off to college, I wanted to get as far away as possible from the ex and Miss Have-I-Shown-You-My-Rhinestone-Crown-Collection." Stafford tapped one pink-painted fingernail on the table in a repetitive click.

Rayna drew a deep breath. "Does Lucy Orozco know about . . . what happened? She was supposed to be here tonight. I don't know why she wasn't."

"She's been informed," Stafford said. "She was delayed when she got caught in traffic driving back from Sunnyvale. Her parents are with her now."

Rayna's eyes stung. She closed them, fighting tears. She didn't want to bawl in front of Stafford.

"It's hard, isn't it?" Stafford said. "Coming home? The pressure to convince everyone who knew you as a kid that your life is marvelous, that you're thriving after your divorce? That you're thrilled to be home, living in your sister's backyard?"

Rayna quickly wiped her eyelashes and opened her eyes. "I *am* happy to be home. There's good and bad in everyone's life."

"How did you feel when Ben and Lucy Orozco approached you about commissioning pottery for their restaurant? That's bold of them, thinking you'd want to do work for them after the way they treated you."

"I was honored," Rayna said. "It would be a much-needed boost for my business. I don't know what rumors you've heard, but there was no conflict between Ben and Lucy and me, and I love being in Willet Beach."

"I'm happy to hear that. In that case, hon, let's review your report and see if there are any mistakes you need to correct."

The dining room had felt chilly when Rayna had entered it, but now she was drenched in sweat. "Can you please tell me what happened to Ben? The EMTs must have some idea."

"How about we do this?" Stafford set her phone on the table. "I have the recording of your 911 call. Let's listen to it and focus on the background noises. Traffic. A horn honking. A car door slamming. Running footsteps. A door opening. And so forth. Almost as though you hadn't yet arrived at Mr. Orozco's office when you made the call. But you already knew he was dying."

Frozen, Rayna stared at the phone.

Stafford moved to tap the screen.

"*No,* don't play it. Please don't play it." She'd been an idiot, thinking a police detective wouldn't catch the inconsistencies in her story. Stafford must think she'd . . . she'd what? Hit Ben over the head? Stabbed him? She hadn't noticed any blood or injuries. Done *something* lethal to him, anyway—poison?—then left the restaurant, regretted her actions, and returned in a panic, calling for help.

"I understand it would be hard for you to hear the call," Stafford said, sympathy in her voice. "How about you tell me what happened instead?"

Rayna gulped water, dripping it down her chin. She couldn't think of any other way to convince Stafford she hadn't killed Ben except to tell her the truth. After a lifetime of never speaking of this outside her family, she was about to confide in a police detective. Then what? Tests? News articles? Reporters, scientists, conspiracy theorists all streaming to her front door? Researchers examining her to determine what else she could do?

Rayna wiped her chin on her sleeve. "Could I . . . could I speak with you privately?"

"Sure, hon." Stafford glanced at the two uniformed officers in the room, one near the hostess stand and the other near the exit. "Gentlemen," she called, "would y'all mind stepping outside for a moment? Right outside the doors would be fine. Keep an eye on us from there."

Both officers exited the restaurant. Through the glass door and front windows, they'd be able to observe the conversation but not overhear it.

"Thank you." Rayna's voice shook. "This . . . this is going to sound weird. *Extremely* weird."

"I promise you, nothing shocks me."

"You'll think I'm insane though." Rayna gripped the edge of the table, pressing her thumbs hard against the tabletop. "Could you keep what I tell you as confidential as possible? I understand that if it's relevant to the . . . to whatever happened to Ben, to your work, you'll be discussing it with your colleagues, but if you could tell as few people as possible and ask them not to share it . . ."

"Of course. We'd never plunk our backsides on bar stools and ramble your secrets to whoever sits next to us."

"If possible, I'd particularly appreciate it if you wouldn't share it with Sgt. Fischer. He is . . . socially acquainted with a very talkative friend of mine."

"I know about Jody Wyeth. I'll be discreet. Don't worry: none of our department would gossip about a case."

"Thank you." Rayna met Stafford's keen eyes and spoke quietly. "I have . . . as long as I can remember . . . I've had the ability to . . . sense people, even when I can't see them."

"Sense them?"

"Yes. I can sense heartbeats and . . . basically, the . . . sensation of life. If the person is someone I know, I'll recognize their . . . essence . . . like you'd recognize a face or a voice. I can get a sense of whether they're sitting, standing, walking, and so on."

"That's fascinating." Stafford didn't sound skeptical, though Rayna assumed she was. "From how far away can you sense someone?"

"My range is just under a quarter of a mile. Beyond that, I can pick up a fuzzy sense of life being present for a little farther, then it fades out completely. When I was driving here tonight, I got stuck in traffic a block or so away. Sitting in my car, I zeroed in mentally on this location and found Ben. I knew something was seriously wrong with him. His heartbeat was slow and irregular, and he was lying down. That's when I called 911. I pulled into the nearest parking area and ran here. I went upstairs to where I'd sensed Ben, started CPR, and the rest of the story is what you already know."

Elbows on the table, fingers interlaced, Stafford studied her. Rayna still couldn't discern any disdain or disbelief in her face.

"I know it sounds like I'm a liar or crazy," Rayna said, "but I've been able to do this all my life. My parents and my sister know, but we've never told anyone else."

"You never told *anyone* else? Not your doctor? Not your ex-husband?"

"No. I was always afraid people would think I was a . . . paranormal freak or an alien or whatever." Now that she'd gotten the explanation out and Stafford seemed to be taking her seriously, her anxiety eased slightly. "I thought it wouldn't matter if I left it out of my report, but that was a mistake. I apologize for holding back. I *can* prove what I can do if you need me to. I don't want you to get the wrong idea about what happened."

"What would the wrong idea be?"

"That I . . . that the reason I knew before I got inside . . ." Rayna floundered, afraid elaborating would sound like a confession. "I have no idea how Ben died, but if there are any questions about it . . ."

"What kind of questions, hon?"

"Any . . . questions about it being natural causes. I don't know if there *are* questions. I can't imagine why anyone would want to hurt him. It must have been a stroke or something like that."

"Couldn't you tell what it was? With your ability to sense vital signs?" There was no sarcasm in Stafford's tone.

"I'm not a doctor." Under the table, Rayna gripped her clammy hands together. "I knew he was in trouble. I didn't know why."

"Thank you for sharing this with me," Stafford said. "We'd better let you get home. You've had a traumatic evening." She passed a business card to Rayna. "If you think of anything else you want to share with me, day or night, you call me, all right? I'm always ready to listen."

Startled, Rayna nodded. Stafford wasn't going to press her about her abilities? Ask for proof?

No, because she thought Rayna was a nut. But she was letting her go.

Stafford scooted off the bench and stood up. "Would you like an officer to walk you to your car?"

"No, thank you." Rayna rose on shaky legs and stumbled toward the exit at the fastest pace she could manage.

CHAPTER 11

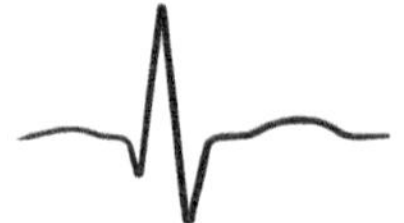

After giving Annemarie a long hug and an abridged version of what had happened with the police, Rayna had insisted she was too exhausted to talk further and had fled to the guesthouse. Now it was two o'clock in the morning, and after hours of tossing and turning, consumed by memories of Ben's lifeless body, her own awkward lies and confession, and her grief for widowed Lucy, Rayna was ready to lose her mind. The only thing that might make her less likely to somersault into madness was a walk on the beach.

She dressed in sweatpants, a heavy sweatshirt, and hiking boots that could handle water-worn chunks of granite. She was lacing the boots when she sensed Annemarie descending the stairs in her house. She hadn't realized Annemarie was awake. In areas where she didn't want to intrude—such as Annemarie's bedroom—she'd trained herself to keep her awareness at a background level, as minimal as possible without the strain of total numbing like she'd done at her father's party.

Annemarie was heading toward the guesthouse. She must have seen Rayna's bedroom light turn on, which meant she'd been watching out the window. Rayna went to open the door.

"Hi." Annemarie was dressed in her bathrobe and flip-flops. She scanned Rayna's warm clothing. "Going to the beach? May I come?"

"You . . . seriously want to come?" Annemarie had never approved of her late-night de-stressing walks, despite Willet Beach's low crime rate and Rayna's repeated, *"It's not like anyone could sneak up on me."*

"Give me five minutes to get dressed and I'll meet you in the front yard." Without waiting for Rayna to agree, Annemarie retreated toward the house.

Rayna shut the door. Holing up alone in the guesthouse had only made her feel worse; she might as well talk with Annemarie. It might be a relief to give Annemarie the details of what had happened. She brushed her hair into a ponytail, grabbed her new flashlight and a windbreaker to put over her sweatshirt, and headed for the front yard.

Annemarie stepped out of the house, carrying a tote bag, two fleece blankets, and a beach blanket. "I'll drive," she said.

Rayna nodded. It was only half a mile to the nearest beach, but she was fine getting there as quickly as possible. Neither of them spoke as Annemarie drove to the beach and parked by the side of the road.

"If you want to walk by the water, I'm good with that," Annemarie said. "If you want to sit, I have blankets and this awesome camping heater we gave Seth for Father's Day last year."

Cozy warmth juxtaposed with the chilly, ocean-scented wind abruptly sounded more appealing than trudging through sand and over rocks. "Let's sit." Rayna led the way along the beach until they reached a cluster of rocks far enough from the surf that the sand was dry.

Annemarie spread the beach blanket over the sand, lit the portable heater, and set it on the blanket. She shook out one of the fleece blankets, handed it to Rayna, and wrapped the other around herself. They both switched their flashlights off and sat together, the glow from the heater providing illumination.

For a long stretch, the only noise was the rumble of the waves.

"The police don't have any idea what happened to him?" Annemarie asked at last.

"Not that they told me." Rayna moved so she could lean against the rock behind her. "But if there's anything questionable about it, I'm going to get arrested."

"That's ridiculous. You're the one who tried to save his life."

"I'm also the one who knew he was in distress when I was a block away from him." Rayna described in detail what had happened and what she'd told Stafford.

"You *told* her what you can do?" Annemarie gaped at her. "I can't believe you actually told someone. Well done!"

"Well . . . done?"

"You've spent your life thinking your gift is freakish, something to be ashamed of. It's not. I'm proud of you for telling her."

"She didn't believe me though," Rayna said. "She thought I was a kook. Had no interest in having me prove what I can do. She just smiled and let me walk out. I don't get it."

"She didn't have any justification for holding you. There probably wasn't any evidence of foul play except for the presence of Ben's jilted ex-girlfriend with big holes in her story. So while you're shaken up, she pounces and tries to get you to admit you did something to him."

Rayna brushed wisps of hair off her face. "Instead, I got *real* weird."

"You surprised her, anyway. And she thinks, okay, this isn't going anywhere useful, I'm not going to waste time playing along. I'll send her home until we have evidence Ben didn't die of natural causes and then we'll talk again. But I doubt you'll hear from her again, because I'm sure Ben died of a heart attack or a stroke or an aneurysm or something like that. There was no crime."

"She'll add my name to her list of local weirdos and forget about me," Rayna muttered. "I hope."

"Maybe Damon should do a 'local weirdos' chapter in his book," Annemarie said. "Which reminds me . . . Kaitlyn told me that Damon told Jody . . . wow, what a gossip chain . . . Anyway, Kaitlyn said Damon's sponsor is interested in paranormal things like ghost sightings or ESP. Has he mentioned that to you?"

"No, thank heavens. And I'm certainly not mentioning it to him." She imagined Damon showing up to grill her about her mutant brain instead of her pottery.

"I can't believe you never told Evan," Annemarie said. "No . . . I *can* believe it. Our parents drummed it into you that this was shameful, something to keep hidden."

"They were concerned for me. They didn't want me treated like a circus act or a lab rat."

"And they spooked you to the point that you thought you needed to keep it from your husband. Besides, their concerns for you were only part of it. The older I get, the more I can see it. Dad liked being in control, being the smartest guy in the room. Your ability was something he couldn't comprehend, and he had trouble dealing with that. Mom was caught up in her perfectionism, her worrying what everyone else would think. She didn't want our family to be different."

Rayna closed her eyes and braced her head against the rough surface of the rock.

"If you could stop treating this like a skeleton you have to keep hidden in your closet . . ." Annemarie trailed off.

"Maybe I'd be able to maintain a romantic relationship? A marriage?"

"I didn't say that."

"It's what you meant."

"I just wish you didn't think you're . . . monstrous somehow. It says volumes that you didn't feel you could even tell your husband. You can only tell a police detective, and *that's* because you're afraid she'll arrest you if you don't."

"If I'd told her everything I can do, she'd have hauled me to the ER for a psych evaluation." Rayna snapped the words out and regretted them. Her filters were too thin tonight.

"What do you mean 'everything'?"

Rayna opened her eyes. The night was clear, and between the moonlight and the glow from the heater, she could easily see the concern in Annemarie's face.

Grief, shock, and deep loneliness gouged at her self-control. Part of her *wanted* Annemarie to know . . . yearned for her to know, to truly understand. No matter how horrible the full truth was.

"Ray? What's going on in your head right now?"

"Not homicide," Rayna said, and giggles rushed from her throat, bobbling with hysteria.

"Oh goodness. You're exhausted. Here." Annemarie drew the blanket off her own shoulders, folded it into a bundle, and put it on her lap. "Lie down." She patted the makeshift pillow.

"No, I'm . . . I'm good." Tears trickled down Rayna's cheeks. "Perfectly rational. Perfectly normal. Definitely *not* committing murder."

"Lie down."

Rayna slid, stretching her body to the side. She rested her head on Annemarie's lap, facing the water, her feet sticking over the edge of the blanket. Annemarie tugged the scrunchie off Rayna's ponytail and massaged her scalp.

Calmness and weariness began to trickle through Rayna. After a long spell of silence, she murmured, "Remember how you used to play with my hair when we were kids?"

"I learned to french braid on you. Ray, talk to me."

"You *will* think I'm a monster."

"No, I won't. Your ability is beautiful, not scary."

"Sensing people isn't all I can do, Annie. And what I can do *is* scary, I promise you."

"What can you do?"

"I can kill." Rayna made the words solid. Certain. She didn't want Annemarie to think this was dark humor. "I can kill people with my mind. Should I let police and doctors and scientists dig into *that* part of me?"

Annemarie's heart rate increased, but she kept rubbing Rayna's scalp. "All right," she said, motherly composure in her voice. "Tell me about that."

"I didn't kill Ben. Let's establish that first. But if I had, I wouldn't have been near him at the time. I can kill from anywhere in my range. If I can sense someone, I can stop their heart."

"Did you . . . ever tell Mom and Dad?"

"No. Can you imagine how they'd have reacted?"

Annemarie rubbed the back of Rayna's neck. Her hands were getting clumsy, her fingernails occasionally scratching Rayna. "Have you always been able to do this?"

"No. And no, I've never killed a person. Only animals, but I assume it would be the same with humans. I was in my early twenties when I realized I could do this."

"How did you figure it out?" Annemarie's thudding heart belied her composure. She was scared. Scared of Rayna herself? Scared of where Rayna's confession would go next? Both probably.

"It was after Evan and I first moved to Colorado," Rayna said. "We were on a back road one night and came across a pickup truck that had hit an elk. The driver . . . young guy . . . was shaken up, but he was okay. His truck looked totaled. The elk was . . . It was badly injured and in agony. The driver felt horrible. He was trying to call the police but couldn't get a cell connection. Evan offered to drive him into town, and he asked us to drive on and call the police for him. He didn't want to leave the elk to suffer alone. If any of us had had a gun, we would have put the elk out of its misery."

"What did you do?" Annemarie asked, her hands now motionless.

"It was strange. While Evan and the driver were talking, I was standing there feeling the way the elk's heart was racing . . . I was so focused on it, and it was like something . . . clicked into place? Like I . . . connected with him?" Rayna watched the bluish flames flickering in the camping heater. "I've never explained this to anyone. I don't know how to describe it."

"So . . . it was different from how you usually sense people?"

"Yes." Rayna wished Annemarie would let herself sound *less* calm. Her serene composure seemed more and more phony. "It was like . . . not only could I sense him, but I sensed I could affect him too. I was . . . mentally . . . surrounding his heart. I wanted so much for him to stop suffering, for his heart to stop beating. I instinctively . . . I . . . tightened my grip, as it were? That's not quite it. The electrical impulses passing through his heart . . . I could zero in on where they began. I realized I could block them. It was . . . like putting up a dam, like I could stop the impulses before they could trigger heartbeats. And then I couldn't feel anything from him. He was gone. Dead."

"And Evan and the driver assumed he'd succumbed to his injuries."

"Yes. I was stunned by what I'd done. I felt light-headed, almost disoriented, like I wasn't sure where I was. Evan had to help me back to our car."

"And you let him think you were just shaken up by witnessing a suffering animal and its death."

"Can you imagine how it would have sounded if I'd tried to explain? 'I felt bad for this dying creature so I thought about it really hard and stopped its heart with my mind.'"

"Yeah . . . that . . . sounds strange."

"Later, I questioned what had happened—if I'd caused it or if I only thought I had because I'd been intently focused on the elk when it died. I . . . decided to try again. Our apartment complex was having trouble with mice . . ."

"And?"

"Once I got to work, the complex no longer had a mouse problem. I hadn't misinterpreted or imagined what had happened with the elk."

Annemarie began stroking Rayna's hair again. "Was it easier with mice? Took less effort, I mean?"

"The size of the animal made no difference. It took the same level of concentration, but I did get better at it. Faster. I no longer got dizzy. Do you think it's . . . warped . . . that I kept doing it?"

"Listen," Annemarie said. "If I could dispatch rodents with my mind, there's no way I'd ignore the germy vermin nesting in my garage or waste money on traps and poisons that would cause them a lot more pain before killing them."

"That's how I felt about it. I didn't go wiping out animals to, I don't know, flex my mental prowess, but I didn't feel guilty about doing my own pest control. Then when we were visiting Evan's brother in Arizona, he told us their cat had been injured by a coyote. A couple of other pets in the neighborhood had been killed."

"By the time you left, that coyote was no longer a problem?"

"Yes." Rayna rolled onto her back and looked up at Annemarie. "Don't worry that this is something that could happen by accident—like I was feeling a surge of bitterness toward Ben and next thing I knew, he was dead. It doesn't work like that. It's deliberate. It takes sustained concentration. Intentionality."

"Do you think you've had this ability since childhood, like your ability to sense people, but only discovered it as an adult?"

"I don't think so. Like I said, it felt different when I connected with the elk. It was a sensation I'd never felt before, no matter how intently I'd focused on another person or animal. Maybe it's something my brain grew into? I don't know."

"It sure doesn't sound like an ability that belongs in a child's brain."

"It doesn't belong in anyone's brain. *Now* do you believe I'm a monster?"

"You are not a monster. Ray . . . you've been through so much . . ."

Rayna rolled onto her side and gazed at the moonlit water. "Do you see why I never told Evan? I *was* planning to tell him about my ability to sense people, but then I discovered this new ability and . . ."

"If you couldn't trust him enough to share hard things, no wonder your marriage fell apart."

Annemarie's curt words caught Rayna off guard. She sat up and looked at her sister.

"I'm sorry." Annemarie averted her head. "I'm sorry. That was a harsh thing to say."

"It's true though," Rayna said. "I was scared the truth would freak him out. And after I started having miscarriages, I was even more afraid to confide in him. What if . . . what if our fertility problems were linked to my weird abilities?"

"That's ridiculous. It's not your reproductive system that's . . . unique."

"Doctors never found anything to explain why I couldn't carry a pregnancy to term."

"Doctors can't always find answers."

"I know. But Evan was fixated on diagnosing the problem, always hunting for different experts, more tests . . . He can't stand questions without answers, problems with no possible solution. He was already pushing me into every doctor's office and lab on the planet. If I'd told him how . . . abnormal . . . I actually was, what would have been the solution for *that*? A psych hospital? A government research lab? I . . . couldn't face it."

"Oh, Ray." Annemarie squeezed her shoulder. "That must have been so hard. You'd better not be taking all the blame for the divorce."

"I'm not. But I was pushing him away, and I can't blame him for getting fed up and leaving me. I hope he's happier now. You're not going to throw me out of the guesthouse, are you?"

"Not as long as you keep the rodents in check." Annemarie ruffled Rayna's hair. "But will you consider letting me tell Seth? Not about the . . . what you told me tonight. Just about the way you sense people."

"Annie, no, I—"

"Give it some thought. He can keep secrets. If I asked him not to share private information about you, he wouldn't. And if he did," she added dryly, "you could kill him for me and we could make a profit since he finally got a life insurance policy. The police would never suspect a thing."

A remnant of a giggle slipped out. "We'll keep that as a financial backup plan. But I'm not ready for anyone else to know."

"I don't like hiding things from him. It wasn't a huge deal when you and I only saw each other a couple of times a year, but now that we're nearly in the same household, it's uncomfortable pretending I don't know what you can do."

Rayna's relief from confiding in Annemarie tangled into knots.

"You can't know how far what you told that detective will travel, no matter how discreet she claimed she'd be," Annemarie said. "Ben's death is going to be big news. If rumors spread, do you want Seth learning this about you through the grapevine—realizing you didn't trust him enough to confide in him?"

Rayna *didn't* want Seth—or Annemarie—thinking Rayna didn't trust his ability to keep confidences. She'd wrecked her marriage by shutting Evan out. Did she want to damage her relationship with her sister and brother-in-law?

Trust them. If you can talk to a police detective about it, you can talk to Seth.

"Don't tell him," Rayna said. "I'll talk to him myself. Tomorrow night—I mean tonight—after the kids are in bed."

"Thank you." Annemarie wrapped an arm around her. "The more you let us in, the more we can support you. You need support after what you've been through."

Not to mention what's coming. What *would* happen when news of Ben's death and the fact that he'd died with Rayna at his side began to spread?

"I need to check in with Lucy," Rayna murmured. "I'll call her tomorrow."

CHAPTER 12

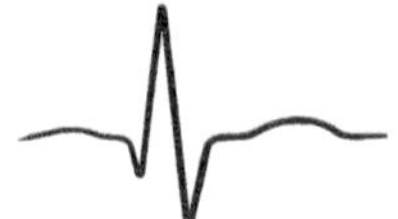

No jovial grin showed on Logan's face, and no trace of humor warmed his voice. His gaze was so intense through the video feed that Damon could almost feel Logan's hand settle on his shoulder, gripping hard. "You okay?" Logan asked.

Damon shook his head. He was seething with rage at himself. He'd screwed up again. He'd given Rayna Kirkpatrick a chance despite the evidence against her, and Bennett Orozco had paid for that misjudgment with his life.

"Stop beating yourself up," Logan said. "I told you before, we do the best we can."

The best we can. A man was dead. His wife was a widow. His unborn child would grow up without a father. "I'm pulling Rayna as fast as I can stage her death."

"Don't stage her death."

Damon stared at Logan. "You don't want to question her? Test her? Learn whatever we can from her before we—"

"I don't mean execute her now. I mean don't burn the bridges yet. Our information on what happened is incomplete. All we know is what was on the news: Orozco is dead, Rayna had an appointment with him last night and was on the scene, she claims she found him unconscious, she did CPR, and he died. The police are investigating. Consider this: if she murdered him, why did she insert herself into the situation at all? Why didn't she sit in a café the next block over and do him in from there, safe from suspicion?"

"I don't know. Maybe she wanted a bigger thrill, to get a kick out of knowing they'll suspect her but when they do an autopsy they'll find no evidence that his death wasn't from natural causes, so they'll never be able to prove anything. A bonus slap in the face to his wife."

Logan gave him a speculative look, one eyebrow raised.

Silence wasn't a typical response from Logan, and it prompted Damon to review and analyze his own words. "Theatrics and thrill-seeking don't sound anything like the profile I've written on her," he admitted.

"No," Logan said. "They don't. Which is why I don't want you to burn bridges."

"We cannot assume Orozco's death was coincidental and leave her in place."

"No, no, we can't put the wife and baby at risk. But rather than staging Rayna's death and making this permanent, here's what I want you to do: leave a message 'from' her telling her sister she's leaving town for a while to get away from the gossip after Orozco's death. You take Rayna and hold her at the cabin until we know more about what happened to him. If it looks like she's responsible, we make her disappearance permanent. If it looks like she isn't, we evaluate what remains of the possibility of building a productive alliance with her."

"Fine," Damon said. "As long as Rayna's not free to kill anyone else, I can hold off. But let me go to the police and get their direct cooperation—"

"No. You know full well that every time we spread the word, we further compromise security. At this point, there's no need to inform them of your investigation. Maintain your cover story in town as best you can, keep your ear to the ground, and draw on your sources to figure out what's going on."

"Understood."

"I'm putting Maggie on a plane. She'll join you tonight to assist you with the particulars of keeping Rayna detained and to start on that questioning and testing you mentioned. Keep Maggie safe."

"I will," Damon said coldly.

* * *

Rayna's right hand drizzled water over the clay spinning on her wheel while her left hand remained curved around it. Her conscious mind kept disengaging, leaving the creative process to muscle memory. All she could think about was the text she'd sent Lucy an hour ago saying she wanted to speak with her whenever she felt up to it. She hadn't dared call Lucy directly. That seemed too intrusive.

What if Lucy—like Detective Stafford—suspected Rayna of killing Ben?

The clay began to wobble beneath Rayna's hands. It was off-center—again. Rather than adjusting it, she lifted her foot from the pedal. Maybe she should dump this blob back in the bucket and go on a walk.

Her phone rang. Rayna seized a towel, wiped her hands, and snatched the phone. Lucy. "Hi."

"Rayna." Lucy's voice was hoarse. "They told me how you did CPR. Thank you for trying to save him."

"I'm sorry it didn't help." Relieved that there was no accusation in Lucy's tone, Rayna rolled her tight shoulders. She was sore from her frantic attempt to revive Ben. "Lucy, I'm so sorry."

"I don't know what to do. I keep telling myself, 'Be strong. You can deal with this,' but I don't think I can." Lucy talked fast, drawing sobbing breaths between phrases. "I keep asking my mom, 'What was it? What do you think happened?' and she keeps saying, 'He wasn't my patient; I didn't examine him; I have no idea.'"

Tears filled Rayna's eyes. "I'm so sorry."

"She said we'll have to wait for the results of the autopsy, but that might take weeks. Autopsy! I can't believe I'm saying that word connected to Ben. He was absolutely fine yesterday. I don't understand."

"Neither do I. I'm so sorry."

"I should have been there last night. I was planning to be there, we both wanted to see your samples, but I went to a restaurant supply warehouse in Sunnyvale, and it took me longer than I planned to find things, and then I got stuck in traffic, and I told Ben to go ahead and meet with you on his own . . . If I hadn't been so slow, I would have been there when he collapsed. I could have gotten help for him earlier. Maybe that would have made a difference."

"I don't think it would have. If something was that . . . severe, that sudden . . ." Rayna knew she was speaking in ignorance. She had no idea if earlier intervention would have saved Ben, but she hated that Lucy was blaming herself.

Like Rayna blamed herself for missing the signs of her father's distress.

"They told me he was unconscious when you arrived," Lucy said. "He wasn't able to say anything at all?"

"No, he didn't say anything. I'm sorry. He was . . . in the office, lying on the floor. When I first checked, he had a faint pulse, but . . . it stopped."

"How does . . . how does . . . something like this even happen?" Lucy's voice shook so much that she was plainly fighting to speak. "He was only thirty-three! He was healthy! And he just . . . he just . . . drops *dead*?"

"I don't know, Lu. Is there anything I can do to help you?"

"No. I'm with my parents. They're taking care of me."

"Can I notify friends for you? Or deal with anything related to the restaurant?"

"The restaurant . . ." Lucy sniffled. "Right now, I hate the thought of that place."

"If you want someone to temporarily take over managing the construction and whatever else, let me talk to my brother-in-law, Seth Bristol. He'd be happy to do that."

"I thought of Seth. He was so helpful when we bought it. I'll probably contact him. Or maybe I won't. Maybe I'll do it all myself because what else am I going to do? Sit and cry? Rayna, what am I supposed to do? The Sanddab was a job to me. It was Ben's passion, not mine . . . and I'm having a baby . . . and Ben was *so* thrilled to be a father . . ."

Tears flowed down Rayna's cheeks. "He'd have been a wonderful father."

"I have *no* desire to run a restaurant on my own, thinking of him the whole time, how he should be there, how he would have loved it." She groaned. "I don't know what to do."

"You don't have to make any decisions about the business right now."

"May I see the sample candleholders? That sounds weird, doesn't it? That I'd care? I don't even know if I'll be continuing with the restaurant plans. I'm certainly not ordering any pottery right now, but it's . . . it was the last thing Ben and I talked about. How we were excited to see what you'd created for us."

"Of course you can see them. You can have them. I'll bring them to you this afternoon."

"You don't have to drive all the way to Monterey. I'll come to you."

"No. I want to bring them to you."

"You went to a lot of work, thinking we'd put in a big order from you. I'll pay for the sample—"

"No, Lucy. I don't want money. Let me do this tiny thing for you."

"Thank you. You've always been so generous. I should . . ." She hesitated. "I should tell you that a police detective asked me about you. Detective . . . hang on; I have her card . . . Detective Claire Stafford. She'd heard there was a history between you and Ben and me, and she asked me what you were doing at the restaurant last night. I told her about the pottery commission and the samples and that I was supposed to be there too."

It didn't surprise Rayna that Detective Stafford had checked with Lucy to see if Rayna's story matched hers. "What else did she say?"

"That was about it. I asked her if there was any reason to suspect Ben's death wasn't . . . natural. She said it was standard procedure to check into unexplained deaths and I didn't need to worry that it meant anything. I wanted to give you the heads-up in case she asks you embarrassing questions."

"Thank you for the warning." Rayna scraped her thumbnail down the side of the clay she'd abandoned on her wheel. It didn't sound like Stafford had mentioned Rayna's kooky explanation for knowing Ben was in trouble before she'd seen him. "She talked to me last night, asking those same questions. She didn't say anything about signs of foul play."

"I'm sure there aren't any. Thank you for everything. You've always been a far better friend to me than I was to you."

"That's not true. You were a huge support to me. High school would have been a nightmare without you. Text me your parents' address. I'll drop the candle-holders off this afternoon. If no one's home, I can leave them on the porch."

"I'll be here." Lucy's voice caught and shifted back into weeping. "I can't do this. How do people . . . get through . . . things like this? You've been through hard things. How did you handle them?"

"One minute at a time," Rayna said. "Right now, you don't have to think past the next minute. Forget everything else. Let other people deal with things you can't deal with. Let your parents help. Let me help."

"You're right." Lucy drew a ragged breath. "I need to go. I'll see you soon." She hung up.

Rayna began cleaning her workspace. She'd eat lunch, then head to Monterey. What else could she bring Lucy along with the sample candleholders? Wildflowers. Lucy loved wildflowers.

When her studio was in order, Rayna hung up her apron and texted Annemarie. *Is it okay if I raid some flowers from the backyard? I want to take them to Lucy. Wildflowers are her favorite.*

Annemarie replied. *Help yourself. Did you talk to her? How is she?*

In shock.

Let me know if there's anything Seth or I can do for her.

Thanks. I'll tell her you offered.

From her shelf of newly finished pieces, Rayna selected a medium-sized vase with a lilac and deep-purple glaze. From Annemarie's garage, she took pruning shears. It would be tricky to balance a vase of flowers while she drove. She'd better stow the vase in the backseat, transport the flowers in a bucket with a few inches of water, and create the bouquet in front of Lucy's parents' house.

She was snipping crimson Indian paintbrush blooms when she sensed Damon approaching at a brisk pace. She didn't have an appointment with him, and neither Seth nor Annemarie was home. Did he have another destination nearby? Not Jody's house; she wasn't home. Or had he heard about Ben's death and was coming to check on Rayna? Of course he'd heard about Ben's death;

he paid attention to everything going on in town. What if rumors had already seeped out about her claim that she could sense people? If he asked her about that, what would she say?

She'd tell him to go away, that she didn't have the emotional stamina to deal with nonsense. And she'd hope his source wasn't credible.

Fingers rubbery, Rayna clipped a sprig of yellow lupine. Damon's footsteps scratched along the packed-sand path. As he entered the backyard, Rayna looked up. "Oh, hi," she said.

"Sorry to drop by without notice." He gave her a fleeting smile. "I came to see how you're doing."

"You heard about Ben Orozco."

"Yes." He crossed the yard and stood next to her. "I'm sorry. That must have been traumatic for you."

Rayna clipped another sprig of lupine. "Lucy is devastated."

"You've spoken to her?"

"Yes." She'd never found Damon's face easy to read, but today his eyes were giving away nothing at all. "She wants the sample candleholders I was going to show them last night. It's the last thing she and Ben talked about, so it means a lot to her to have them. I thought I'd take her some wildflowers as well. She loves them. She's with her parents in Monterey."

"You're driving up there today?"

"Yes, this afternoon."

"With Annemarie?"

"No, by myself. Annemarie's at her store, and she doesn't know Lucy well." Rayna held up the yellow blossoms she'd cut from the bush. "She was happy to provide the flowers though. I wish I could think of something more to do for Lucy."

"I'm sure she'll appreciate the flowers."

"I have a vase in her favorite color. Just finished the glaze firing yesterday." Yesterday, when Ben had been alive. Rayna swallowed. She didn't want to break down in front of Damon, especially when she had no idea what rumors he'd heard about her. He didn't seem in the mood to volunteer anything. If she wanted to know what he'd heard, she'd have to ask.

"What's her favorite color?" he asked.

"Purple. Any shade of purple. Actually . . . that was her favorite color back when we were in school. I hope she still likes it. Not that it matters. Not that a vase or flowers or candleholders or anything matters." The tears were going to fall; she couldn't stop them.

"It matters that she knows people care about her. May I see the vase?" He held up his hands. "No photos, no book mentions. I understand this is a deeply private situation."

"It's on my kitchen counter." She led the way toward the guesthouse, glad for an excuse to walk ahead of Damon so she could wipe her eyes.

In the house, she laid the flowers on the counter and picked up the vase to hand it to Damon.

He rotated it, examining it. "This is beautiful work."

"Thank you."

"That was fortuitous timing." He set the vase down. "That you'd have the ideal piece to hold a sympathy bouquet for Lucy."

The remark felt strange—a little cold, maybe? Was she overthinking it? "I wish I didn't need it as a sympathy gift. May I ask an awkward question?"

"Go ahead."

"What have you heard about Ben's death?"

"Only what's been in the news." Damon's expression remained unreadable. "Did you want to tell me anything else?"

"There's nothing to tell." Thank heavens he hadn't heard weird rumors about her. "Did you ever have the chance to interview Ben and Lucy?"

"Just Ben, informally. I stopped by The Sanddab and introduced myself. He took me on a tour of the place, and I had a sit-down interview with him and Lucy scheduled for next week."

Rayna wished she could stop herself from picturing Ben grinning and radiating enthusiasm as he guided Damon through his construction-zone restaurant. Blithely setting an appointment he'd never have the chance to keep. "I'm glad you had the chance to meet him. I'm sorry to rush you out, but I need to finish putting this bouquet together and get ready to head to Monterey."

"Thank you for showing me the vase. Could I impose on you for a glass of water before I go?"

"Sure, and thanks for checking in on me." Rayna walked toward the cupboard where she kept glasses. She was thirsty herself and tired and headachy.

She took a glass. Damon came up behind her. "Here, I can do that."

"I've got it." Rayna turned toward the fridge. "Let me get you some filtered—"

In a lightning flash of motion, he seized her, one arm curling around her body, pinning her against him. The glass fell from her hand and shattered against the tile. Stinging pressure spread through her shoulder, and she glimpsed a hypodermic syringe in his hand. With a light click, the empty syringe hit the floor.

What was he doing? What had he given her? Struggling to free herself, she threw her head backward in hopes of breaking his nose or his jaw, but her head struck his shoulder. She gasped in air for a scream. Damon's hand clamped over her mouth.

Rayna thrashed, fighting with all her strength, yanking at his arms, kicking at his legs, trying to stomp on his feet. *I don't want to kill him. I don't want to kill him.* The thought whirled in her head but savage realization stamped another message into her brain. Whatever he'd injected into her was either going to knock her out entirely or make her too woozy to resist him. Once it took effect—minutes from now? Seconds from now?—she'd lose her chance to defend herself. Damon could do whatever he wanted, including kill her, and she couldn't stop him, unless she stopped him *now.*

She stopped writhing, letting her muscles go lax. All her focus was mental now as she zeroed in on his heart, on the electricity spreading through it in regular impulses. She closed her senses around it.

A sensation like a collision with solid stone struck Rayna. She couldn't see; she couldn't draw a breath. An avalanche of pain thundered through her skull, down her neck, all the way to her feet.

Dim awareness stirred. She was no longer standing. Damon was carrying her, Damon undamaged and deadly. Her body shook as she struggled to control her mind. Her senses skidded, latching onto his heart, losing it, latching, losing.

Panic growing, Rayna fumbled again to take control, but she couldn't connect at all. Her thoughts were sinking; her body was sinking; she felt something soft beneath her, then heavy, overwhelming oblivion.

CHAPTER 13

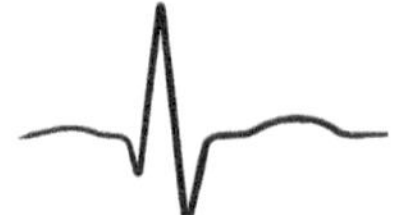

Flexing what was going to be a bruised shoulder to match a bruised leg, Damon stepped painfully back from Rayna, who now lay unconscious on her living-room sectional. Her face was relaxed but still flushed from exertion. She'd hesitated before trying to kill him. He hadn't expected that. He'd expected his attack to bring an instant attempt on his life, but she'd put up a fierce physical struggle first, only resorting to her Trespasser abilities when it had become obvious she couldn't escape him. Maybe he'd caught her so off guard that there had been a lag as she'd processed a situation she hadn't faced before: the need to kill in self-defense.

He pushed up his sleeves to check the damage to his forearms and found deep-red marks that would likely turn purple. Not much in the way of scratches. Rayna's fingernails were clipped short, and his jacket sleeves had given some protection. At least all his injuries were minor and concealable.

He had to get moving. The less time he was here, the better. He slid his hand beneath Rayna, pulled her phone out of her hip pocket, and turned it off. He found her keys on a hook near the fridge and went to move her car into her sister's currently empty garage. On the way back to the guesthouse, he checked her studio shed. She'd already padlocked it. The kiln was running, but it would switch off automatically when it finished whatever program Rayna had set.

In the guesthouse, he capped and pocketed the empty syringe, swept up the broken glass, and tossed the cut flowers into the trash. In Rayna's bedroom, he snatched clothes from the closet and dresser and heaped them into a suitcase he'd found in her hall closet. From her bathroom he grabbed whatever looked like it might be a necessity and packed that as well. He stowed the suitcase in the trunk of Rayna's car, then lifted Rayna off the sectional and carried her to the car, every new bruise aching. With Rayna in the passenger seat, seat belt fastened and the seat tilted back, he made a final pass through the guesthouse to verify that nothing indicated she hadn't left voluntarily. He locked the guesthouse door, locked the side door to the garage, and backed out of the garage, closing the rolling door with the remote in Rayna's car. Helpful of Annemarie to give her a remote, though he hadn't seen Rayna park in the garage.

An hour later, he was on a narrow dirt road surrounded by redwoods, oaks, and sycamores, approaching a cabin that was the only building for at least a mile in every direction. The road was bumpy enough that he reached over and rested his hand on Rayna's head to keep it from flopping around.

He parked on a gravel-covered patch to the side of the single-story, wood-sided cabin. Rayna squirmed slightly, one hand lifting toward the seat belt, then falling into her lap. She'd be awake soon.

He took her suitcase inside, then returned to the car and unfastened her seat belt.

"Rayna? Can you hear me?"

Her head tipped toward him. Her eyes opened halfway, then closed.

He adjusted her seat so she was sitting up straight. She sagged forward. He grasped her under the arms and hauled her out of the car. Her feet scuffed the gravel, and she clutched his jacket for stability as she tried to stand. The attempt failed; her legs buckled, and her head fell against his chest. Damon lifted her into his arms.

In the cabin, he laid her on the couch and removed her shoes. Rubbing his sore shoulder, he glanced around the living room, trying to remember where he'd seen blankets. There they were, folded in a willow basket next to the couch. He draped a blanket over Rayna. She was asleep again, her body limp and her breathing regular.

After sending Logan a quick update, he took Rayna's phone, powered it up, and held it above her to unlock it with face ID. Sitting at the kitchen table, he linked her phone to the satellite connector on the counter and skimmed her recent text exchange with Annemarie.

Doing his best to phrase his message in a semblance of Rayna's style, he texted Annemarie from her phone: *I changed my mind about going to Monterey. I was way too optimistic thinking I could handle facing Lucy. I need time alone. I'm not sure where I'm headed. I'll drive along the coast until I feel like stopping. Please don't worry about me. I'm fine.*

Rayna's most recent text from Lucy contained Lucy's parents' address in Monterey and a *Thanks. See you soon* from Rayna. Damon texted Lucy: *I'm so sorry. I realized I'm not up to bringing you those candleholders today. I'm sorry to flake out. I can't even think straight. I'll get them to you as soon as I can.*

The thought of what might have happened if Rayna had made that trip to Monterey drove fresh, bitter-cold spikes of anger into Damon's gut. He doubted she would have taken Lucy's life today—or possibly not ever. More likely, she would have targeted Lucy's unborn baby. Rayna had lost Ben, and she'd lost the children she'd tried to bear. Would she have retaliated by taking the same from Lucy?

He glanced at Rayna, and the wrath inside him dulled slightly. His goal was to protect the innocent and learn the truth of what Rayna had done, not to jump to premature condemnation—no matter how warranted that condemnation felt to him right now.

Rayna's phone beeped. A reply from Annemarie. *Wait no don't go yet. I'll come with you. Give me a little time to arrange things with Seth. We can leave tonight. We'll do a sister getaway.*

Damon typed a response. *Thanks but you have a ton of responsibilities at home. I don't want to interfere with that. We'll do the sister getaway soon. Right now I need to work through things on my own.*

Annemarie's reply came fast. *Forget my responsibilities. I'll come with you. You're all shaken up. Did you sleep at all last night?*

I'm fine. Not tired. Stop worrying.

Can we at least talk about it before you go?

I already left.

Rayna! Where are you? What if the detective wants to speak with you again and she finds out you've left town? How's that going to look?

What had transpired between Rayna and the police? Annemarie's *How's that going to look?* implied that they were treating Rayna as a person of interest. He'd have to find out.

If she wants to talk she can call me, Damon texted. *I promise I'll be fine. Alone time is healing for me. I'll talk to you soon.*

Is this your way of dodging your promise to talk to Seth tonight?

Damon's interest in the conversation shot even higher. Talk to Seth about what? *I'm too overwhelmed to deal with it right now.*

Seth isn't going to wig out. Trust him. Trust me.

It was unrealistic to hope Annemarie would say something confirming Rayna had killed Ben, her father, or the reporter, but it would certainly be convenient. *I'm afraid of what he'll think of me,* Damon typed.

You should be. He'll be terrified of your freakish power and go arm a mob with torches and pitchforks to destroy you.

Presumably, that was sarcasm. *Funny*, Damon responded. *Seriously what will he think?*

He'll think you're the same sister-in-law he's always known and loved. If you aren't here to tell him tonight then I'll tell him myself.

Loquacious Seth Bristol with secrets? Bad idea. *Please don't. I'll tell him myself soon. I just need a little more time.*

Forget it. You said tonight and I'm not letting you chicken out. I'm not keeping this from my husband any longer. Seth needs to hear it from his family not from gossip.

Give me one more day. Please.

No. Tonight.

This wasn't an argument he could win in a text conversation. *What exactly will you tell him?*

Only what we agreed on last night. I know you're not ready to share it all. I won't push you on that.

On the couch, Rayna stirred. He'd do better getting details from her than trying to coax them out of Annemarie without revealing he wasn't Rayna. *Let me think on it.*

Think all you want but I'm telling him tonight. I want you to be here.

I'll think about it.

Stop hiding from us. You're not a monster.

Damon paused, then typed, *I hope not.*

* * *

Blearily, Rayna noted the faint scents of wood smoke and evergreens, the life sensations of small animals, the heartbeat of another person nearby. Yawning, she rolled over and bumped into a padded barrier.

She squinted at the barrier and drew her head back so she could focus on it. Orange-and-brown-flowered upholstery. The back of a couch. She was lying on a strange couch, a blanket covering her.

The other person in the room. Damon.

Damon in the backyard with her while she picked flowers for Lucy.

His sudden attack. The needle stabbing her shoulder.

Rayna thrashed, trying to sit up. He was towering over her, looking down, a stone-hard face and olive-green eyes. For a split second, she was falling; she'd flailed halfway over the edge of the couch.

Damon caught her and heaved her onto the cushions. "Calm down," he said. "I'm not going to hurt you unless I have no choice."

"What are you going to—Why did you . . . ?"

She'd tried to kill him. Self-defense . . . but it hadn't worked. That sensation of striking an unbreakable barrier . . . torrents of pain . . . What had happened?

She *couldn't* kill another human being after all. At any other time, that realization would have evoked vast relief. Now it terrified her. She was at Damon's mercy. Desperately, she scanned for any other people within her range. No one. No one to help her.

She pushed up on her elbows. "What are you going to . . . do to me?"

"Lie back. You're still woozy."

She was too light-headed to do anything else. She sank onto the cushions. Damon draped the blanket over her. Past him, she glimpsed tall, triangular windows and sunlit trees.

Eyes closed, she repeated the search for any other people, but her thoughts kept blurring. She sensed Damon moving away from her. Sitting down.

She drifted toward sleep. Sloshed back to alertness. Drifted. *Wake up. You need to wake up.*

"Where are we?" she mumbled.

He didn't respond.

She opened her eyes and skimmed the room. A scarred hardwood floor. A shaggy brown area rug. A basket of logs on a stone hearth. Damon in a wing chair next to the fireplace. Watching her.

"Why did you . . . bring me here?" she asked.

"To isolate you."

Isolate her. Keep her away from anyone who might hear her screaming.

Tentatively, Rayna sat up and lowered her feet to the floor. The wood was cold beneath her sock-covered feet. Her shoes were next to her suitcase at the edge of the rug. The bright turquoise case she'd bought for her honeymoon.

Damon was backlit by the sun shining through the windows behind him, light edging the hair curling around his ears. His face was shadowy.

"Annemarie will panic when she realizes I'm missing," Rayna said. "She'll call the police."

"What will the police think?" Damon asked. "The evidence indicates that you left home voluntarily."

"She'll know I wouldn't run off without telling her. She'll know something's wrong."

Damon took Rayna's phone out of his pocket and brought it to her. "Don't try to contact anyone. Just read your conversation with Annemarie."

Rayna scrolled through it. "Did I . . . tell her these things?" What *had* she done while she was drugged?

"No," Damon said. "I did." He held out his hand for the phone.

For an instant, Rayna measured the odds that she could bolt past him, phone in hand, and either reach an exit or lock herself in another room long enough to dial 911. *So they can send a team to pick up your body? You'll be dead before help can get here. And you're too sluggish to move quickly anyway.*

Damon removed the jacket he wore, exposing a gun stowed in a shoulder holster. He tossed the jacket onto a nearby chair.

Taking the hint, Rayna handed him her phone. What had he made of Annemarie's talk of her "freakish powers" and her secrets?

"What's your passcode?" he asked.

Refusing to tell him would be a pointless reason to get shot. He'd obviously already been unlocking the phone using her face ID. She gave him the numbers.

"Thank you," he said.

Thank you. How polite. If she treated him as if he were still kind, reasonable Damon, might she be able to persuade him not to hurt her? "May I have a glass of water?" she asked.

"Yes," he said. "But you should know that all doors and windows are locked and alarmed. If you try to escape, you won't make it, and I'll handcuff you to a chair to make sure you don't try again. Is that clear?"

Rayna nodded. So much for kind, reasonable Damon.

He went into the kitchen area adjoining the living room. Rayna braced her head against the back of the couch and watched him take a glass from a cupboard. His heart thumped, steady and firm but seemingly vulnerable in her reach. Maybe she was wrong about her inability to stop his heart. Maybe her attempt had been hampered by the drug already taking effect. Maybe she *could* kill him if she had to.

She still didn't want to do it. She didn't want to kill anyone, and the thought of watching Damon collapse lifeless under the force of her mind made her shrink inside. But she *wouldn't* passively let him harm her. If killing him was what it took to protect herself, she'd do it.

She wouldn't kill him now, not until there wasn't a sliver of a chance left that she could talk him out of whatever his plans were. But she could test the connection. Build it, hold it, drop it. If and when it became necessary, she'd be ready to complete the full process.

She concentrated on his pounding heart, connecting with it, curving her awareness to envelope—

"Rayna, don't." He turned from the sink, a full glass in his hand. "It won't work this time either."

She froze, holding her connection but not strengthening it. How did he know what she was doing?

"Drop the link," he said. "*Now.* Are you too doped to remember how much it hurt when you tried it before?"

She drew a shallow breath and let her concentration dissipate.

"Thank you," he said. "Don't try it again."

More shallow breaths as she fought panic now turbulent with confusion. He sat on the couch, leaving the width of a cushion between them, and held out the glass of water. Not until she took it did she realize how severely her hands were trembling, but she was too thirsty to care that she was spilling water down her shirt as she drank.

Damon took the empty glass before she could assess the possibility of breaking it and using it as a weapon. "More?" he asked.

She shook her head. "How did you know what I . . . that I was . . . ?"

"Because I'm a Trespasser like you," he said. "That's why you can't kill me."

CHAPTER 14

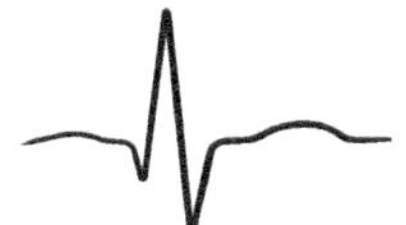

Dazed, Rayna stared at Damon's inscrutable face. "You're a . . . what?"

"A Trespasser," he said. "I didn't choose the term, but it's what people like us got labeled. Trespassing in territory that should be off-limits to our minds."

She wanted to ask him to repeat himself even though she'd heard every word. "You have the . . . same abilities I do?"

"Near as I can tell. Obviously, we haven't examined you directly yet to find out if there are any variations."

For several foggy seconds, Rayna processed that. "It's because of Ben's death, isn't it—how you figured this out about me? You heard what I did."

"What did you do?"

"I called 911 before I should have known Ben was . . ." She trailed off. Damon had abilities like hers . . . He'd spent hours interviewing her, remarkably interested in her measly pottery business . . . His sponsor was interested in paranormal things . . . "Did you suspect I was a . . . Trespasser . . . all along?"

"Yes."

"You've been researching me?"

"Yes."

"For a book project, you drug and kidnap people?"

"It's not a book project."

"What is it? You said *we* haven't examined you. Who is *we*? You and your sponsor?"

"Yes."

"Who is your sponsor?"

"The United States government."

The government? Maybe this was a bad dream. She'd had so many nightmares of herself trapped on the wrong end of endless tests and experiments.

You didn't get any sleep last night. You must have dozed off after Damon stopped by to check on you. That's how he ended up starring in your nightmare.

If it was a dream, could she jar herself out of it? Make a break for the door, and at the moment of crisis, she'd wake up at home . . . *Stop it. You know this isn't a dream.*

"Is your kidnapping me . . . official, then?"

"As official as anything I do."

Rayna managed to draw a steady breath and relax her fingers that she'd clenched around the edge of the couch cushion. As nightmarish as this scenario was, it was better than her original fears that she'd been abducted by a serial killer. "You're what, then? CIA?"

"No. We're our own group. Oversight agency is the FBI, but we have a lot of leeway."

"Show me your badge or your ID or whatever you carry."

"I don't carry ID undercover."

Rayna's fears split in two, half of them veering back in the direction of her serial-killer theory. "That's handy."

He shrugged. "How many people are aware of your Trespasser abilities?"

"My parents—well, my mother now. Annemarie. And a police detective named Claire Stafford, whom I talked to last night. I've never told anyone else."

"Do they know everything you can do?"

"Until last night, only that I could sense people. Last night, I told Annemarie how I could . . . Wait. You said I couldn't kill you because you were a Trespasser. Does that mean if you *weren't* a Trespasser, I could have killed you?"

He studied her, his expression stoic.

Rayna struggled to keep her churning emotions under control. Here was someone who could understand and explain, and instead of answering her question, he was assessing her like she was a lab rat. Maybe he thought the answer was obvious. Maybe it was. Someone with the same abilities could block her; a normal person couldn't. "I didn't *want* to kill you. I just didn't want to die. I thought you were going to kill me."

"What precisely did you tell the police last night when they interviewed you after Bennett Orozco's death?"

"Why precisely did you drug me and kidnap me instead of questioning me at my house?"

"We're taking precautions."

"Precautions against what?"

"Against the possibility of your harming anyone."

"Harming anyone? Like Ben? Do you think I killed him?"

"Did you?"

"*No.*" Rayna's voice rose. "Kidnapping me is a lot more than a precaution. It's an outrage. This can't be legal no matter who you work for. I want a lawyer."

"A lawyer couldn't do anything for you. Because of the unique threat you pose to national security, we have a lot of latitude."

"What does that mean?"

"It means we can hold you as long as we deem it necessary."

"Hours? Days? Years?"

"The more you cooperate, the more quickly things will resolve. What did you tell the police?"

Holding Damon's piercing gaze, she recapped her interview with Detective Stafford and Stafford's blasé reaction to her explanation of how she'd known Ben was in distress. "I assume she thought I was a nut and she's waiting to see if there's evidence of foul play before she wastes more time interrogating me. But I can't imagine she'll find evidence. Why would anyone want to kill—" Rayna stopped. If Ben's death appeared to be from natural causes, that would convince Stafford she was innocent, but would it convince Damon of the opposite? He knew she could have killed Ben without leaving evidence.

"I didn't kill him." Rayna wedged herself in her corner of the couch and pulled the blanket up to her chin. "I swear I didn't kill him. Do you think I've been nursing a murderous grudge over a college romance for the past decade?"

No change in his flinty expression. "What did you discuss with Annemarie last night?"

Panic returned, striking from so many directions that she couldn't fight it off. How was she supposed to convince Damon she was innocent when no proof at all was the same as damning proof? If he had the authority to drug and kidnap her as a "precaution," what did he have the authority to do if he concluded she was a murderer? Assuming he was accountable to any authority at all. Rayna looked frantically around the room, not knowing what she was searching for. Did she think she'd spot an escape hatch that Damon hadn't noticed?

"Rayna. Answer my question."

"I forgot what you asked me."

"What did you discuss with your sister last night?"

The room was cold, though she doubted that was why she kept experiencing spasms of shivering as she told him about her conversation with Annemarie—a disjointed report full of repetitions and tangents that Damon kept having to pull back on track.

"So all she plans to tell Seth tonight is that you have the ability to sense people," Damon said. "Nothing else."

"Yes, that's all. She's good at keeping secrets. Damon, please, I—Is Damon Hale your real name?"

"Yes."

"Not your secret-spy alias?"

"I'm not a spy." He rose to his feet, took a blanket from a basket next to the couch, and layered it on top of the blanket already covering Rayna.

"Thank you." He'd noticed her shivering. The gesture reminded her of his handing her his sweatshirt after she'd gotten soaked on the beach the night she'd learned Lucy was pregnant. He'd seemed so thoughtful, so concerned about her. But Ben had been alive then. Damon hadn't suspected her of murder.

He suspected her now, but he'd still bring her a blanket if she needed it.

"Are you working with the police?" she asked, then realized that was a silly question. If he was working with the police, he wouldn't have needed to ask her what she'd told Detective Stafford. And he wouldn't have told her that if Annemarie reported her missing, the police would think she'd run off. "You're not working with the police. Why not?"

"Information involving Trespassers is extremely sensitive." He reseated himself on the couch. "We don't tell anyone—including local law enforcement—anything we don't absolutely have to."

"So, no one knows I'm here. You can hold me as long as you want, and nobody but your . . . group . . . will ever know anything about it."

"That's correct."

"If Annemarie does convince the police I've been kidnapped, they could track my cell phone."

"Your phone was off while we were in transit. There's no cell service here, and the satellite connection I'm using isn't one your local detective could access."

Rayna tried to sound calm and harmless. "May I please at least talk to Annemarie? I hate that she thinks I ran out without even speaking with her. I'll stick with the story you texted her, that I took off on a drive because I needed to be alone. I won't mention you or who you work for."

"If you speak with her, do you think you could convince her not to tell Seth about any of your abilities?"

"Why?" Again, Rayna realized she was asking a question he'd already answered: they tried to keep publicity about Trespassers to a minimum.

"Judging by how private you've kept your abilities, I think you have some sense of the issues that the spread of information could cause," he said.

"'Researchers' like you were one of the main things I was afraid of. But I can try to talk her out of telling him."

"Do you think you'll succeed?"

Rayna paused, contemplating whether or not Annemarie would bend on this. "I don't know. Let me try."

"I'll think about it."

Rayna leaned against the back of the couch and closed her eyes. Dizziness fluttered through her head, and the weight of both blankets was warming and relaxing her muscles. "How many Trespassers are there?"

"Not many."

"Was a hunt for Trespassers why you came to Willet Beach? Are we a hot spot for them or something?" Rayna imagined learning that friends and neighbors shared her abilities while all this time she'd assumed she was a lone freak.

"We've never found a hot spot," he said. "You were why I came to Willet Beach. You came to our attention a few months ago when you were doing research of your own."

Research. Those Google searches after her father's death, when desperation had finally driven her to ask questions she'd always been too afraid to confront. She wanted to scream, *I told you so*, at herself. She should have stayed paranoid. "What do you want with me? Or what *did* you want with me before you decided I murdered Ben?"

"Two things," he said. "We're working to understand what creates these unusual abilities and how to handle them. The more people we can research, the more we'll learn. And we need to know if you're someone we can trust. As I said, Trespassers pose a unique threat."

"You don't trust me." She opened her eyes. "Obviously."

"We're taking precautions."

She glanced at the straps of his shoulder holster, dark against the heather-gray T-shirt he wore. "Do those precautions include shooting me?"

"Not unless you make it necessary. Do what I ask. Don't try to escape. If anyone comes into range, do not link with them."

"Can you tell if I link with someone besides you?" She shouldn't have asked that—it made it sound like she planned to kill any random hiker who approached the cabin—but she wanted to know.

"I'll show you." He gestured toward the triangular windows that covered the upper half of one wall. "You sense the birds in those nearest redwoods?"

"Yes."

"High up, to the left, not moving, is a large one—I'm guessing it's an owl."

Rayna mentally scanned the trees and focused on the bird Damon was referring to. "You're not going to kill it, are you? Please don't kill it."

"I'll drop the link before I cause it any harm. I'm linking now. Sense that?"

"Yes." It was as though the life she sensed in Damon had created a path connecting him with the life essence of the bird.

The link disappeared. "All right," he said. "Link with anyone and I will immediately put a bullet in your head."

Rayna flinched. "Okay, then. Please don't worry about giving me information delicately."

"You need to understand. I won't warn you, and I won't wait to see how serious you are about completing a link-kill. I'm not risking innocent lives."

"I won't link with anyone. I don't *want* to kill anyone. The only reason I linked with *you* was because I thought you were planning to torture and murder me."

"I understand. Would you like something to eat? You must be hungry."

"No, thank you." She wasn't sure if eating on top of the empty queasiness inside her would fill her up or make her sick. "All your Willet Beach research for your alleged book. Setting up your office. Hiring Jody. That's all a cover. My tax dollars at work."

"It's partly a cover. We don't care about the history of Willet Beach, per se, or plan to publish a book to sell in gift shops, but we *are* interested in the history and environment of the area in which you grew up."

"You're searching for anything that might have affected the development of my abilities?"

"Yes. And searching for any commonalities with the backgrounds of other Trespassers."

"You don't know what causes this weirdness?"

"We're working on that."

"If you came to Willet Beach to research me, why didn't you *ask* me about my abilities?"

"We prefer to be discreet and gather information before directly approaching a Trespasser."

"Because you're *taking precautions*." Anger surged through Rayna. "I don't see how your 'precautions' help now, even if you do think I killed Ben. He's already dead. I can't do anything to him, and you can't possibly think I'm prone to randomly slaughtering . . . Oh." She was overlooking the obvious. "You think I'm going to kill Lucy Orozco next. Or kill her baby."

Damon said nothing.

"Who will I kill after that?" Humiliation and horror at what Damon thought of her rendered her words acrid. "Detective Stafford because she's suspicious of me? Jody Wyeth because she's a gossip? Annemarie because she has a husband and kids and I don't? Mr. Cheney because I despise black-licorice ice cream but he won't stop selling it? Forget those famous serial killers who got a dozen or two dozen people. I'll take out the whole *town*. I'm sure you know the population of Willet Beach, so you know the number I'm aiming for."

Damon watched her in silence, no doubt evaluating her rant.

Overheated now, Rayna shoved the blankets to the floor. She wanted to scream at him, but she dragged the volume of her voice lower. "I was going to Monterey to give Lucy the candleholders and the vase of wildflowers. That's all. And I *told* her I was coming, and now she thinks I flaked out on her. She's grieving her husband and asks me for one tiny thing and I stand her up. Thanks for that."

Damon took Rayna's phone out of his pocket, tapped the screen, and handed it to her. It displayed a text conversation between her and Lucy, or rather, between Damon and Lucy, with Rayna apologizing and begging off on the appointment and Lucy assuring her that she understood.

"Thanks for letting her know," Rayna said tiredly as Damon reclaimed the phone. The irony of the whole situation made her want to sob-laugh. She'd worried all her life about normal people thinking she was a monster. She'd finally met someone like her, and *he* was the one who thought she was a monster. "Do you think I've killed other people besides Ben, or was he the first?"

"Tell me about Collin Burgess's death," Damon said.

"Collin Burgess! Where did *that* come from?"

"Tell me about his death."

"He fell down a flight of stairs and broke his neck." It annoyed Rayna how hard her heart was pounding, a response Damon would take note of and interpret as guilt. "You don't think I mind-killed him over a bad review, do you? That's ludicrous. All artists get bad reviews sometimes."

"He sexually harassed you, then struck back with a negative review when you rejected him. You complained about him, but no action was taken. You were in town when he died."

Damon had learned a lot more about Burgess than she'd told him. When he'd brought up Burgess while taking pictures of her pottery shed, had that been a test to see how she'd react? "I stayed in town after the fair to help Annemarie. That's when Tate was born. Ask her, or maybe you already have. Is she the one who told you all this?"

"The night before Burgess died, you saw him in the parking lot at Wyeth's Grill. You had a brief conversation with him that caused you to stalk back to your car and leave without going inside the restaurant."

That startled Rayna. She'd never even mentioned that encounter to Annemarie. Annemarie had been furious enough with Collin, and Rayna hadn't wanted to stir her up. Had Jody noticed her? Or Kaitlyn? It didn't matter. "Did your source overhear what he said to me, or should I fill in those blanks for you?"

"Go ahead."

"He said—this is a direct quote—'Rayna! Nice to see you! What are you up to now? I presume you quit making pottery since it's clearly not your forte.' I didn't want to deal with him or even be in the same building with him, so I left and texted Seth, asking him to stop by Wyeth's to pick up the takeout I'd been planning to collect. That's the end of the story. I didn't kill him, but how am I supposed to prove that when all you need in order to blame me is a possible motive and me in the same town?"

"Just tell me the truth."

"I didn't kill him! I haven't killed anyone!" Mortified by her sudden screeching, Rayna shrank back into her corner of the couch. The last timbers of her self-control were cracking, and she did *not* want that to happen in front of Damon.

"Tell me about your father's death," Damon said.

The timbers splintered, and tears flooded from her eyes. "That's none of your business. I don't have to talk about it. It's none of your business."

"What about it is none of my business?"

"All of it!"

"Kaitlyn Wyeth told her mother you blame yourself for your father's death. Why is that?"

Her grief-and-guilt-twisted conversation on the beach with Kaitlyn thumped into her mind. "Not because I killed him. You've asked me enough questions. Go make lunch or dinner or whatever meal matches whatever time of day it is and leave me alone."

"You had a difficult relationship with your father."

Hunching forward, elbows on her knees, Rayna pressed her fingertips against her closed eyelids. *Stop crying. Stop crying. You need to handle this rationally.*

Like she needed to handle Ben's death rationally, handle the experience of him dying in front of her, of sensing his last heartbeat. Like she needed to handle being a suspect in his murder rationally, where either Stafford or Damon was going to declare her guilty no matter what evidence did or didn't come out. Like she needed to handle being a prisoner rationally, with Damon accusing her of killing creepy, drunken Collin and matter-of-factly threatening to shoot her.

"Jody told me what happened between you and your father the night he died." Damon's voice was level. "The vicious things he said to you."

Rayna pressed her fingertips harder against her eyes. The tears kept leaking out, dripping between her fingers. "I didn't kill him, but it's my fault he's dead. Is that enough of a confession for you?"

"Why is it your fault he's dead?"

Rayna lifted her head. There was no point in hiding her face. Damon was fully aware she was crying. "If the story is good enough," she said icily, "do you think it'll make your final book?"

"Rayna."

Her vision was so muddled from tears and the pressure of her fingertips that his face was a blur. "You want the story? It's all yours. I'd . . . flown out for the party, hoping I could . . . that things could get better between us. That we could improve our relationship." Couldn't she stop her voice from shaking? She drew a deep breath.

"Go on," Damon said.

"At first . . . it was going well. I was hopeful. Then . . ." She gathered knife-sharp memories and flung them toward him, wanting to hold them as briefly as possible. "It was in the same vein as always. Criticizing me, lecturing me, but making it half joking . . . Let the listeners tell themselves he wasn't as cruel as he sounded. But when he cracked a joke . . . or not a joke . . . blaming my miscarriages on my incompetence and ignorance, I was done."

"What did you do?" Damon asked quietly.

"I walked out. I was going to skip the dinner and program, but Annemarie talked me into going back in. But I . . . His presence was so *loud* in my head . . . I wanted to get away from him, and I couldn't, not if he was within my range. So I . . . shut him out."

"Shut him out how?"

"It's something I figured out how to do when it was . . . too painful to be anywhere near my soon-to-be ex. If I picked one person—I'd choose a stranger—and concentrated as hard as I could on sensing that person, I could numb my awareness of everyone else. Like only that person had a distinct identity. Everyone else was a blur. Is that something you can do?"

"Yes."

"That's what I did that night." Goose bumps pricked her arms. "I did it for the entire dinner, then kept it up when I went back to my room. Kept it up until I was so tired my brain basically crumbled into sleep."

"You kept it up for multiple hours? That takes incredible concentration."

"I was very motivated. It became a challenge . . . a spiteful game. How long could I keep it up? I had a splitting headache the next day, and my whole body was sore, but congratulations on winning your childish game, Rayna, and while you were shutting him out, he *died*." More tears gushed, and she prodded senselessly at the bare ring finger on her left hand. "If I hadn't been so intent on pretending he didn't exist, I could have sensed he was in distress."

Damon leaned over, picked up the blankets she'd shoved to the floor, and laid them over her lap.

She pulled the blankets up to her shoulders. "That's my story. I've never even told Annemarie all those details." Weary, raw inside, Rayna drew her legs up and curled under the blankets with her wet cheek resting on the arm of the couch. "Maybe I could have saved him, and I didn't because that night, I hated him too much to care. Write that up in your book or your government report or whatever records you're keeping."

CHAPTER 15

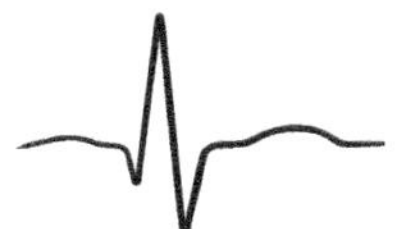

Under the circumstances, the scene struck Damon as incongruously cozy. He'd lit a fire in the fireplace. In the early evening darkness, the only other light in the room came from the floor lamp next to the chair where he sat impersonating Rayna as he texted Annemarie in another effort to get her to keep Rayna's secrets. He'd switched off the overhead light for Rayna's sake. With her initial waves of terror out of the way, physical and emotional exhaustion had augmented the sleepiness lingering from the sedative he'd given her earlier. She'd barely finished the dinner he'd offered before she'd shuffled back to the couch and collapsed.

Making it through dinner had strained his own self-possession: maintaining stoicism while looking at her swollen, red eyes; the strands of auburn hair straggling loose from a casual topknot and sticking to her tear-blotched face; the hunched, defensive set of her shoulders. He despised what he'd done to her, but all of it had been necessary and too-long delayed already. Letting his guard down now because she appeared so vulnerable would be the worst mistake.

His wish that she'd make his decision straightforward by confessing to murder jumbled with deep relief that she *hadn't* confessed to murder—a contradictory mix that made it difficult to concentrate. At least Maggie would be here soon. He'd appreciate her help and her objectivity.

A text from Annemarie appeared on the screen. *Our parents really messed with your head. You think if people learn you have ESP your whole life will implode. It won't. I'll be talking to Seth at around eight as soon as we get the kids to bed. I don't know how far away you've driven but if you can get home in time I really want you here.*

Damon texted back. *I'm too far away to make it. Could you please wait for a day or two? Why does it have to be tonight?*

You won't want to do it any more tomorrow night or the next or weeks from now.

Damon debated how to respond. In order to intervene directly, he'd have to allow Annemarie at least a scrap of information about who he was—which might lead her to figure out that Rayna was in his custody, which would be a far bigger problem than letting her tell her husband that Rayna could sense people's heartbeats. It was surprising Annemarie hadn't told Seth years ago. She *was* good at keeping secrets, as Rayna had claimed.

But it was worth Damon's continued efforts as "Rayna" to avert that conversation. *Annie, please. I'm begging you. When I said I'd tell him, I honestly planned to do it, but everything's caved in on me. I can't deal with it right now.*

You don't trust us at all do you?

I do trust you.

When are you coming home?

Not sure yet.

You're making me crazy. I'm worried about you.

I'm sorry. I just need time.

You don't need time. You need help. Please come back.

A flicker of energy caught his attention. Maggie was approaching.

Abruptly, Rayna sat up. She must have been awake enough to sense Maggie as well.

Damon stood and stuck Rayna's phone in his pocket. "She's working with me. Don't link with her and we won't have a problem."

Rayna tugged loose the hair tie holding the strands that hadn't already escaped. Her hair uncoiled, and she ran her fingers through it in a puzzled way, as though not certain where this avalanche of hair had come from.

"Did you hear me?" Damon asked.

"Yes. I hope your friend is coming to get me out of here. Is she a Trespasser too?"

"No." He switched on the overhead light. Under bright illumination, Rayna's face was ashen. "She's a doctor and researcher."

Rayna recoiled. "What's she going to do to me?"

"She's not going to hurt you. You don't need to be afraid of her." At the noise of a car door slamming, Damon moved toward Rayna. "Come with me."

Rayna pushed the blankets back and rose slowly to her feet. Not sure how steady she was, Damon took her by the arm and led her to the front door. He used his phone to disconnect the security system and twisted the dead bolt.

Standing on the porch was a tall Black woman with a curly afro shot with silver. "Damon," she said. "Nice to see you again."

"Thanks for coming," Damon said.

"Like I'd miss *this* party." Maggie stepped inside carrying a briefcase and pulling a large roller bag. Her gaze fixed on Rayna. "So, you're Rayna Kirkpatrick. You look like you've had a hard day."

Rayna didn't respond. Her posture was tight, and Damon could sense her heart hammering.

"Hungry, Maggie?" Damon asked. "Or do you want to crash? You must be exhausted."

"It'll hit, but it hasn't yet. Traveling leaves me wired. I'm not hungry. I grabbed dinner at the airport. I want to talk to this girl. We'll keep it short tonight. Where can I set up shop?"

"There's a library off the living room," Damon said. "That should give you space."

"A library, eh? Elegant. Is there a conservatory as well? This is quite the entryway." She waved toward the warped parquet squares arranged in an elaborate pattern. "Is this house a Clue board? And, Rayna, let's establish this up front: if you're an innocent young woman who's been unfairly detained, I'm sorry for what you're going through. If you're a conscienceless killer and you try anything on me, that'll be your last act on earth, and I'm sure that hell has reserved a room for you." She extended her hand. "Dr. Margaret Latimer. Call me Maggie."

Bewilderment on her face, Rayna mechanically shook Maggie's hand.

Maggie held on for a long squeeze. "I'm skilled at listening, and I'm skilled at talking," she said. "I'm sure you have a lot of questions. Some things I can't tell you, of course. But I'll tell you what I can." She released Rayna's hand. "Here's what's going to happen. While I speak with Damon, you're going to get ready for bed. Take a shower if you want, get your PJs on, do yoga, read a book, whatever helps you unwind. You have thirty minutes. Then we'll chat."

A trace of hope showed in Rayna's face. She glanced at Damon, clearly wondering if he'd allow her this half hour of solitude. Thus far, the only time he'd let her out of his sight had been a trip to the bathroom.

"Fine," Damon said. "Rayna, if you value your privacy and your freedom of movement—"

"Such as it is," Maggie interjected.

"Then don't touch the window or the door or do anything else stupid," Damon finished. "Remember, every exit is alarmed."

Rayna nodded.

Damon retrieved Rayna's suitcase from the living room and escorted her to the bedroom he'd prepped with external locks on the windows and a reversed doorknob he could lock from outside. He locked Rayna in the room, activated the portable alarm he'd attached to the door, and joined Maggie in the library.

Maggie had seated herself behind a scratched laminate-topped desk that took up half the room. "Frightful decor, eh?" she remarked as she typed on her laptop. "My grandmother's kitchen appliances were the color of these ghastly yellow drapes. On the plus side, if you need to look something up in the 1974 *Encyclopedia Britannica*, you're in luck."

Damon eyed the bookshelf covering one wall. "We didn't have a lot of options for a safe location."

"Sit down and give me one second here." Maggie kept typing. He sank into an overstuffed chair with a fringed base.

She closed her laptop and squinted at him. "Did you know that when you're under pressure, you look chiseled out of stone? They could stick you in the National Statuary Hall and you'd blend right in."

"Do you want an update, or do you want to hound me?"

"Both. What's wrong with your shoulder?"

Damon realized he'd been fidgeting with the strap of his holster where it pressed against his bruised shoulder. "Nothing. Just a bruise. Rayna put up a fierce fight before the sedative took effect."

"After she realized link-killing wouldn't work on you?"

"No. She didn't link until after she'd tried to fight me off."

"Is that so?" Lines deepened between Maggie's eyes. "You must have done a superb job gaining her trust if she was willing to seek a nonlethal escape route."

"It surprised me."

Maggie tilted backward, causing her vinyl chair to creak. "Doesn't this rustic marvel of a cabin have central heating? It's cold in here."

"Something's wrong with the furnace, unfortunately. I'll see what I can do with it after you put Rayna to bed."

"Here I was imagining the California coast as a tropical paradise. Do you want me to have a look at your shoulder? Where else are you hurting?"

"It's all just bruises. No medical care needed."

"Then, let's hear the update. I've read your reports. What haven't you written up yet?"

Damon reviewed the day's events.

"Yikes." Maggie picked up a pen and tapped it on the legal pad next to her computer. "Plans to visit the pregnant widow?"

"Yes."

"Do you think Rayna told you the truth about her father's death?"

"I don't know. She was certainly upset while she was talking about it, but that could mean anything. Committing murder and regretting it could be a pattern with her. Take the way she dealt with Ben Orozco's death."

"She zaps him from down the street, gets hit with remorse, and races to his side to try to resuscitate him?"

"Maybe."

"Or maybe she's never killed anyone."

"Also possible."

"I want to meet with her alone."

Damon frowned.

"You can hang out in the living room and monitor us from there," Maggie said. "Nothing's more off-putting when it comes to opening up to your doctor than an armed man glowering next to you. Are you afraid you wouldn't be able to intervene in time if she links with me?"

"No. I'd have more than enough time. But there are other ways she could hurt you, as my bruises bear witness. If I'm in the other room, I wouldn't be able to intervene in time to prevent her from breaking your jaw. If you want to be alone with her, I'm zip-tying her to a chair." He tilted his head toward the chair next to him, upholstered with the same striped fabric and fringe as Damon's chair but with wooden arms and legs.

"Don't do that either," Maggie said. "I want her relaxed enough to talk to me, not terrified I'm going to rip her fingernails out. Take her Trespasser abilities out of the equation, which you can do from the living room, and I promise you, I can handle her. If you sense anything that worries you, feel free to come barging in, and if you're not in time, the broken jaw is my own fault. I got the impression from your reports that she's more rational and self-contained than to punch me when it would only make her situation worse."

"I wrote those reports before I drugged and kidnapped her. She might not be so rational now."

"I'll risk it."

Damon rubbed his temples. Why was he suddenly twice as tired as he'd been before Maggie had arrived?

Because Maggie was astute and capable and he could let her carry part of the burden of dealing with Rayna. Which was giving his exhaustion too much space. "Maggie, your safety is my responsibility. Here's my compromise. I won't fully restrain her, but I'll handcuff one wrist to the arm of her chair. That way she won't be afraid you're about to torture her, but she won't be able to tackle you either, and you'll only have one fist to dodge."

"That works," Maggie said. "Tell me: is your gut impression of her worse after dealing with her today?"

"No."

"Better? This is off the record. Say whatever you want and it won't leave this room."

Damon ran his thumb over a frayed spot on the arm of his chair. "I don't know."

"You mean your gut impression of her is positive, which clashes with the circumstantial evidence."

"If someone else dies because I was biased in her favor, that blood is on my hands. I have enough blood on my hands."

"Damon," Maggie said, "here's my two cents. You're afraid of being biased in her favor because she comes across as a sympathetic, likable person. Not to put too fine a point on it, but she's also an attractive, single woman."

"Maggie."

"Not saying that's a factor. Just saying it could be. Make sure you aren't biased *against* her as an overcompensation. More importantly, remember Rayna is not Tristan McCuller. Let her stand on her own. Make sure you aren't biased against her because you feel compelled to punish her—and yourself—for Tristan's crimes and for a decision you wish you'd made differently."

Damon couldn't hold Maggie's thoughtful gaze. "Thanks for your input," he said.

* * *

Even knowing Damon would sense what she was doing, Rayna searched the bedroom where he'd taken her, opening every drawer and closet and peering underneath a queen-sized bed covered with a patchwork quilt. He hadn't told her she couldn't look around, and she wanted to know if there was anything she could possibly use as a weapon or a quick, efficient tool to break a window.

There was nothing under the bed. The dresser drawers were empty. The closet contained extra blankets, two pillows, and an electric fan. The drawers in the en suite bathroom were empty. The cupboard under the sink contained only toilet paper, Kleenex, and hand soap. A laminated sign decorated with hand-drawn butterflies hung next to the mirror, asking guests to please conserve water, noting that extra towels could be found in the hallway linen closet, and giving a detailed list of what not to flush down the toilet.

She doubted Damon's Trespasser team would have posted notices decorated with butterflies. This was a rental cabin, which explained why the alarm on her door had been one she'd sensed him placing there after he'd locked her in, not an alarm built into the house. Why hadn't he taken her somewhere more secure? Maybe he hadn't had time? Maybe his group was underfunded, so instead of secret compounds, they had to use Airbnb?

Or maybe there was no Trespasser group, no government agency overseeing any of this. Maybe it was only Damon and his doctor friend hunting and imprisoning Trespassers for their own purposes. What purposes might those be? Experimentation? Forcing Rayna to use her powers in terrorist schemes? Did they consider her a rival, a threat they'd eliminate when they finished using her?

Rayna walked to the window and pulled back one side of the curtains, careful not to touch the glass or window frame. Whatever alarm or external locking mechanisms were in place, she couldn't see them, but whether they were there or not didn't make much difference. If she tried to escape the cabin, she couldn't get away fast enough. Damon could effortlessly track her and outpace her. Even if she *could* escape, where would she go? To the police? She imagined herself racing through the woods, reaching a town, babbling to an officer about fleeing from a kidnapper who could kill with his mind. The officer would think she was insane and, meanwhile, Damon could close in, murder everyone around her without their ever seeing him, then recapture or kill her.

How about you stop inventing even worse alternatives to an already awful situation? What Damon claims to be is bad enough news for you. You don't have to get creative about the threat he poses.

Rayna pivoted away from the window. She was too drained to stand here wallowing in fear, struggling to think of a way to fix a problem she had no idea how to fix.

Fix the problem. Fix the problem. Evan's voice played in her memory. *"There's a solution, Rayna. We have to keep searching for it. The doctors haven't found any medical reason why your body can't carry a baby to term. This is fixable."*

It hadn't been fixable.

Stop it. How is this type of thinking helping you now?

Rayna checked her watch. She had twenty minutes left, and she wanted to take that shower Maggie had suggested.

She unzipped her suitcase. It was crammed with T-shirts, other shirts, jeans, lounge pants, socks, underwear, pajamas, and what appeared to be everything that had been in her shower stall and bathroom cabinet.

Irritation at Damon's intrusiveness in going through her personal items quickly ebbed. It was plain he'd tried hard to gather what she'd need. If she had to be a prisoner, she'd rather be a prisoner with clean clothes and a toothbrush.

And something to read. He'd included the pottery magazines and both books that had been on her nightstand. That was a strangely thoughtful thing to do—not strange for the Damon she'd thought she knew but strange for the Damon who was holding her captive. Or maybe it wasn't strange. Even as her guard, he'd been respectful, attending to her needs. Maybe he *was* who he claimed to be, attempting to manage what he perceived as a serious threat to national security. He didn't want to hurt her; he didn't even want her to be uncomfortable. He only wanted to keep her from hurting anyone else.

Maybe he'll be strangely thoughtful when he shoots you. How can you convince him you're innocent? You can't. What happens then? Do you think there's a special Trespasser prison on an island in the middle of the ocean where you'll be locked up by yourself because otherwise, you could kill your jailers?

The far more likely option was execution.

She snatched her pajamas out of the suitcase and stalked into the bathroom. There had to be a way for her to legally defend herself. She must have options.

Maybe Maggie Latimer could help her.

CHAPTER 16

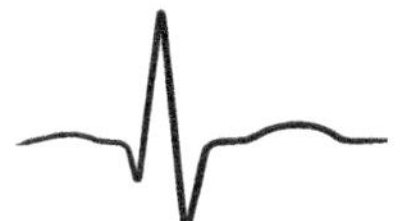

WHILE MAGGIE CHECKED RAYNA'S BLOOD pressure, listened to her heart and lungs, and asked a slew of questions about her health history, Rayna tracked Maggie's pulse and tried not to tug nervously against the handcuffs shackling her right wrist to the arm of the chair. Maggie didn't seem at all bothered to be alone with her, which struck Rayna as a positive sign. Damon had instructed Rayna to do whatever Maggie told her and to make no sudden moves, after which he'd exited, closed the door, and stationed himself directly outside it. Rayna was determined to keep herself as calm and cooperative as possible. She didn't want Damon crashing into the room, interrupting Rayna's hopes of gaining Maggie as an ally.

"Any allergies?" Maggie asked as she checked Rayna's eyes with a penlight.

"No."

"Surgeries?"

"Two D&Cs after incomplete miscarriages."

"How many pregnancies?"

"Seven. All miscarried."

"I'm sorry, Rayna. What was the range for how long you were able to carry the fetuses?"

"The farthest along I ever got was fifteen weeks. All the miscarriages were between ten and fifteen weeks."

"Any trouble conceiving?"

"No." Rayna spilled the question she'd never thought she'd have the courage to ask a doctor. "Do you know if my problems carrying a pregnancy to term have any connection to my being a Trespasser?"

"I assume you had fertility workups? Recurrent miscarriage tests?"

"Yes. Every test they could think of."

"No issues showed up? For either you or your partner or partners?"

"My ex-husband. None of the tests showed anything wrong at all."

"Then, I'd say yes, the problem is related to your being a Trespasser." Maggie picked up her briefcase. She slid a chair across the floor until it directly faced Rayna's chair and sat down, placing her briefcase next to her. "I'm sorry to tell you this, but so far, we haven't seen a case where a fetus with either a Trespasser mother or father has reached the age of viability."

Sorrow slapped Rayna, sorrow she hadn't anticipated. She thought she'd accepted that she'd never be able to bear children; she'd told herself that even if she married again, she'd never attempt another pregnancy. Apparently, she'd been lying to herself. She'd still been hoping.

"I'm sorry," Maggie said gently. "I wish I had better news for you."

Rayna's heart was beating so wildly that she felt sick to her stomach as she gathered the courage for her next question.

The door opened, and Damon leaned in, no doubt drawn by her frenetic heartbeat. "Everything okay?" he asked.

"We're fine, Damon. Go away," Maggie said.

He obediently shut the door.

Rayna drew a croaky breath and forced her question out. "Am I . . . Is it my mind? Am I . . . killing the babies myself? Without meaning to?"

"No, sweetie." Maggie grasped both of Rayna's hands, her grip warm and firm. "This isn't some type of inadvertent link-killing. We do know that."

"How can you be sure?"

"As I said, the same pattern holds whether the Trespasser parent is the mother or the father. We even have a case where a Trespasser father was killed before his wife even knew she was pregnant. She was nowhere in proximity to any Trespassers when she miscarried eleven weeks later. It's not your mind doing this."

A thread of relief twined around Rayna's guilt and grief. "Then, what is it about these weird abilities that affects pregnancy? Do Trespassers pass on some kind of . . . fatal gene?"

"The issue is likely genetic, but we simply don't know any more than we know what causes Trespasser abilities at all." Maggie released Rayna's hands. "We haven't yet been able to nail down any genetic explanations for what you can do, but the research is ongoing. We're also exploring your personal histories for any experiences or environmental factors that might be common among you."

"Like whether we were all bitten by radioactive spiders?"

"Something like that."

"Have you found anything we all share?"

"There are countless things you all share, but so do millions or billions of other people. What we haven't found is anything relevant. But you'll be undergoing a lot of interviews and tests." She yawned. "Not tonight, of course, and don't worry. None of the tests will be painful, aside from the occasional needle stick."

"How many Trespassers are there?"

"We have no idea."

"How many have you found?"

"That's not an answer I'm free to give you, but let me put it this way: our sample size is sorely limited, so every shred of data we can collect from you is valuable."

"Are the rest of them . . . living regular lives?"

"What's your definition of regular?"

"Not being locked up." Rayna rattled the handcuffs. "Not being shadowed by government operatives. What's the best-case scenario for me . . . if you decide I'm innocent?"

"I don't know. But you'll need to keep your Trespasser status confidential. This information is considered very sensitive. You can assume the government will be keeping an eye on you for the rest of your life."

"What do you mean keeping an eye on me?"

"Where you are, what you're up to, who you're close to. You'll need permission to do certain things, such as travel internationally."

"Why?"

"Because think what a superb assassin you could be. The last thing they want is for, say, terrorist groups or enemy nations to come recruiting."

"I sit in a shed in my sister's backyard and make pottery. I love that life. I have no desire whatsoever to become an international assassin. Or a local one, or whatever the career tracks are for assassins."

Maggie smiled, the assessment in her eyes making Rayna realize every word she spoke was already getting analyzed and stored in Maggie's mind as research data. "On the flight out here, I was poking around your Etsy site. You do remarkable work. I've always had a weakness for handmade pottery."

"Thank you," Rayna said, disconcerted by this compliment.

"Speaking of flights and jet lag and such, I'm officially wiped out, and I suspect Damon's in far worse shape, so let me tell you what happens now." Maggie yawned again and unlatched her briefcase. "Damon needs to sleep, which means you get to sleep too. To make sure you're asleep when we need you to be, I'm going to administer medication via an IV drip. That will give me maximum control over when you fall asleep and when you wake up."

Rayna concentrated on keeping her breathing even and her muscles relaxed. She didn't want another interruption from Damon. "It isn't necessary to knock me out. I'll be locked in my bedroom. Do you think I'm so bloodthirsty that I'd murder you even though I'd still be trapped and it would get me shot?"

"I think we all need a good night's rest, and this is how we'll get it. I'll be monitoring your respirations and heart rate to make sure you stay healthy through all of this."

"How are you going to monitor me if you're asleep?"

"Wirelessly, with a device that will set off an alarm if it detects any issues. Which arm would you prefer I use for the IV?"

"Wait. Please. I know Damon is convinced I've killed multiple people, but what do *you* think?"

"Damon isn't convinced you've killed anyone. He's convinced it's *possible*. Three people with whom you were in conflict have died near you since you were old enough for your full Trespasser abilities to have manifested. Obviously, that's something we can't ignore."

Rayna dug her fingers into the striped arms of her chair. "I wasn't in conflict with Ben Orozco. We resolved that conflict years ago."

"Did you? Because from what Damon reported, it sounds like the only 'resolution' was you avoiding each other until you all moved back to Willet Beach and suddenly you're face-to-face with the past. Evidence indicates that reunion was difficult for you."

"There were things I needed to work through, but we weren't in conflict. I get why you're all suspicious of me. I get that a Trespasser willing to kill anyone who offends her would be an extraordinarily dangerous person and you have to take 'precautions,' as Damon puts it. But if I'm locked up and drugged, how am I supposed to prove my innocence? I can't communicate with anyone. Damon said a lawyer wouldn't do me any good. How can I be stuck like this? How is this justice?"

"I'm sorry," Maggie said. "It's not fair, but this is how it is. You're in a unique position as far as the law is concerned. Due process doesn't apply to Trespassers. You're too much of a threat, and it's impossible to deal with you through the criminal justice system. Your best option is to fully cooperate with us. If you have killed someone, tell us. We won't be shocked. You wouldn't be the first to give in to the temptation to use your abilities to deal with a problem."

"How about giving into temptation to deal with three problems? Would that shock you?"

"It wouldn't shock me."

"But it would lead you to assume I'm too dangerous to ever go free. What's the worst-case scenario for me if you decide I'm guilty?"

"How about we don't assume the worst?"

"I'll tell you what I assume. I assume there are two groups of Trespassers: ones your group trusts, like Damon, and ones who are dead. I can't imagine you try to hold us long-term. Does Damon have the authority to execute me?"

"It's far too early to worry about worst-case scenarios."

She'd dodged the question. That meant the answer was yes. Rayna shifted in her chair, metal digging into her wrist.

"We won't be making any decisions until we have all available information about you and about the deaths in question," Maggie said. "We'll do everything we can to be certain of the truth before we make any recommendations about what happens to you. Now, left arm or right?"

Icy waves of panic and confusion slammed into Rayna, leaving her struggling to find her mental footing, struggling to breathe. The door opened.

"Hi, Damon," Maggie said. "Do me a favor and bring me that little table by the window—minus the abominable silk plant. That'll give me a place to set my stuff."

Damon crossed the room, put the silk plant on the floor, and brought the table to Maggie.

"Thanks." Maggie took several items wrapped in plastic packaging out of her briefcase and set them on the table. "Rayna, let's try your left arm. Rest it on the arm of the chair, please."

Shrinking into the soft upholstery behind her, Rayna looked from Maggie to Damon. "I have no proof that either of you are who you say you are. How do I know what you're planning to do once you knock me out?"

"Who do you think we are?" Damon asked.

"I don't *know.* Terrorists? Serial killers who kidnap and torture people who have strange powers? Rogue scientists conducting unethical experiments?"

Maggie fished in an outer pocket of her briefcase. "This won't reassure you that I'm none of the above, but at least it'll confirm that evil schemes aren't my only job." She passed Rayna an ID badge on a lanyard; it was for the NIH Clinical Center. "That's a research hospital in Bethesda, Maryland," Maggie said. "I do some work there." She pulled out a second badge and traded it for the first one. It was a faculty badge for the University of Maryland. "I do some work there too. Let's see; what else? I could show you my access card to our Trespasser team headquarters, but since it's nothing but a blank card with my name on it, that won't help. I could show you photos of my grandchildren, which won't prove anything either, but they're very cute, and I like to show them off."

Damon took the badge out of Rayna's hand and gave it back to Maggie. "How would it benefit us to lie about who we are? It's not as though we've earned your trust and willing cooperation by telling you we work for the government."

"True," Maggie said. "That statement has never earned *anyone's* trust."

A compulsion to laugh warned Rayna she was on the verge of falling apart entirely. No matter who these people were, they had control over her, and she couldn't do anything about it.

"Annemarie called," Damon said. "She left you a voice mail."

Rayna looked up at him. "What did she say?"

"She's worried about you and wants to speak with you. She said if you'll call her back—not text—that she'll hold off on telling Seth about your ESP tonight."

That roused a fragment of hope. "May I call her?"

"Yes, if you'll stick with the story. We'll call when Maggie's done with you."

"Let's finish up, then." Maggie patted the arm of the chair.

Rayna's arm felt so heavy that moving it into position seemed to strain her shoulder joint. Maggie donned gloves, rolled up Rayna's long pajama sleeve, and tightened a tourniquet around her upper arm. "You'll be glad to know I'm better at starting an IV than most MDs."

Rayna would have been gladder if Maggie had been incapable of starting an IV at all.

Maggie rotated her arm, probing it in various spots in search of a vein, finally tearing open an alcohol wipe to scrub the chosen spot on her forearm. Rayna focused on Maggie's intermingled silver and black curls, needing to focus on anything that wasn't the needle Maggie was sliding into her vein.

"If Annemarie asks where I am now, what do I tell her?" she asked.

"Tell her you stopped somewhere south of Morro Bay."

"Is that where we really are?"

"No."

"Where *are* we?" How far from Willet Beach had he taken her?

"Tell her you're staying in a little beachside hotel." Damon ignored her question. "If she asks the name of it, don't give her one—say you need to be alone and don't want her coming down."

Maggie pressed a clear dressing over the short, capped-off tube now extending from Rayna's arm. "You're set. Do not mess with my handiwork in any way. That will annoy me, which you don't want. I won't hurt you—let's keep that clear, because obviously, you're worried about it—but I will restrain you so you can't pull the tube out again. Got it?"

"Yes."

Maggie took a small red-plastic sharps container from her briefcase. "Damon, find me a trash can."

Damon fetched the wire trash basket from next to the desk. Maggie disposed of her materials and stood. "Make your phone call. When you're done, we'll get you in bed and hook up the drip." Briefcase in hand, she exited the room.

Damon unlocked the handcuffs, stuck them in his pocket, and settled in Maggie's empty chair. Grim weariness dulled his eyes as he gave Rayna an assessing look, and she had the feeling he wasn't enjoying any of this.

"Annemarie will want to know when I'm coming home," she said. "What do I tell her?"

"Tell her you're not sure. Keep everything vague. You have two goals: to reassure her that you're okay so she doesn't panic and take steps to try to find you, and to get her to continue holding off on telling Seth anything about your abilities. The call will be on speaker, and I'll keep hold of the phone. If you try to say anything you shouldn't—"

"You can stop there," Rayna said. "I've heard enough dire warnings today. I understand."

Damon unlocked her phone and tapped the screen to call Annemarie. Rayna wiped her hands on the knees of her pajamas and breathed as steadily as she could. She needed to keep herself under control no matter how much she wanted to scream, *Help me!*

"*Ray*. Thank heavens. Thank you for calling me back. I've been worried sick. Are you okay?"

"Yes." Rayna's voice shook slightly. "I'm sorry. I didn't mean to scare you. I just . . . couldn't deal."

"Where are you?"

"I'm not exactly sure. Somewhere past Morro Bay."

"Oh, Ray, did you have to go that far?"

"I didn't plan it. I drove until I was too tired to go farther and stopped for the night. I'm in a hotel near the beach. I needed a place to decompress. Away from home."

"You don't sound okay."

"I'm exhausted." Rayna rolled her left arm from one side to the other, hyperaware of the slight tenderness where Maggie had inserted the tube. "I'm going to bed right after we talk."

"You being alone right now is a bad idea. I'll join you. Give me the name of the hotel where you're staying."

"You don't need to drive for hours tonight to come to me. I *need* to be alone."

"You need to hide, you mean."

"I'm not hiding."

"You definitely are. When are you coming home? It'd better be tomorrow."

"I'm too tired to think right now. Can I take things one step at a time?"

Annemarie's voice sharpened. "That's a weaselly answer."

"I'm not trying to be weaselly. I'm trying to cope. Thank you for holding off on talking to Seth. I'm sorry for backtracking. I shouldn't have told you I'd do it . . . should have realized I wouldn't be up to it."

"I shouldn't have pressured you like I did. You tell him when you're comfortable with it . . . keeping in mind that he might hear it through the grapevine first."

Rayna glanced at Damon. He'd be pleased with Annemarie's concession. "Thank you for being patient with me."

"I'm not being patient with you. You don't have to tell Seth anything you don't want to, but the same doesn't hold for me. I'm your sister. You can't handle this situation on your own. You need to trust me. You need to let me help you."

"I know you're there for me."

"I'm *not* there for you because you won't even tell me where you are. You ran off."

"I'm sorry. I wasn't thinking straight. I didn't handle it well."

"If you're sorry, start handling it well now. Tell me the whole truth. You think I don't know you're hiding things?"

"I'm not hiding things. After what I told you last night, how can you think I'm holding back?"

"Because you are. Give me the name of where you're staying."

"I'm at the Stop Nagging Me Beach Hotel."

"*Rayna.* Listen to me. No matter what mistakes you've made, I can help you. I won't condemn you for anything. I won't judge you. But you can't hide like this. It's going to tear you to pieces."

Stinging apprehension enveloped Rayna. Was her "mistake" her flight from Willet Beach? Or was Annemarie referring to Ben's death? Her own sister couldn't possibly think she'd murdered Ben. Could she?

Rayna stared across the room at a row of old paperbacks bookended by two huge ceramic frogs. She didn't have the guts to meet Damon's eyes. "Annie,

I'm sorry. My brain isn't working. I didn't sleep at all last night. I need to go to bed. I'll be more clear-headed tomorrow."

"All right." Annemarie softened her tone. "Go to bed. But call me tomorrow. Promise?"

"I'll try."

"You'll try? If you don't forget how to pick up your phone and tap my name?"

Rayna shot Damon a questioning look. He nodded.

"I'll call you," Rayna said.

"I love you, Ray. Please trust me."

"I love you too, and I do trust you," Rayna said. "I'll talk to you tomorrow."

"Good night."

Damon tapped the screen to end the call. "You handled that well."

"Thank you," Rayna said bleakly. "To be clear, I'm not hiding things from her except for what you're forcing me to hide from her. The only reason she thinks I am is because of the way I left today without telling her, which you know very well was not my choice."

Without comment, Damon rose to his feet. "Come on," he said. "Maggie's waiting for you."

CHAPTER 17

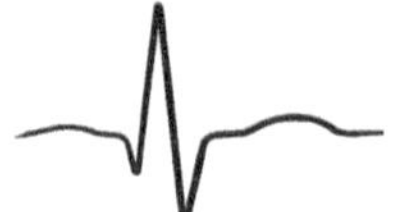

After a much-appreciated night's sleep, Damon left Rayna in Maggie's care and drove the hour back to Willet Beach. Maggie would keep Rayna safely sedated while Damon kept up his cover and gathered all the information he could that might have bearing on Rayna's guilt or innocence. High on his list of people to speak with was Annemarie, but for that, he'd have to wait until The Beach Umbrella opened for business at nine. Contacting her earlier than that would make her wonder why he was so eager. Meanwhile, he'd find out what Jody Wyeth had to say. After his absence from his office yesterday, Jody must be so full of rumors that she'd erupt like Old Faithful at his first question.

After a stop at the bakery, he headed to his office. Leaving the door between his office and the reception area open, he sat at his desk to study the local news and wait for Jody.

Jody burst into the reception area at ten minutes to nine and made a beeline into his office. "Oh, Mr. Hale, I was so glad to see your car."

Damon had driven Maggie's rental to town, parked it at his apartment complex, and picked up his own vehicle. "Good morning, Jody."

"I can't believe you chose yesterday to do out-of-town exploring when so much was happening *in* town."

"Have a seat and tell me what's going on."

Jody settled herself into one of the chairs facing his desk. "You must have heard about Ben Orozco's death."

"Yes. What an unexpected tragedy."

"And with his wife pregnant! Lucy Yin is a tough cookie though. She'll get through it. I was able to bounce back after my Elliott drowned, though when I got the news, I was so destroyed that I didn't know what to do. I was so alone. My Kaitlyn wasn't in town when he died; she was on a business trip—she's such a smart girl—and when the Coast Guard told me they'd found his body, my goodness, it was terrible. But once Kaitlyn was home to help me, I got my feet on the ground. Then losing Glenn on top of that! My stars! Kaitlyn tells me, 'See, Mom, I'd rather not fall in love at all than go through that heartbreak.' She won't believe me that it's worth it. I know you enjoyed her company when you were over to our fishing hut. You should get to know her better. You're lonely, too, and you're such a nice man and so handsome. After all that's happened, I can't imagine you're interested in Rayna Kirkpatrick anymore, no matter how the girl flirts with you."

Damon couldn't think of a single instance in which Rayna had flirted with him, even before he'd transformed into her enemy, but he didn't correct Jody. "Why wouldn't I have any interest in Rayna?"

"Mercy, you're usually so on top of things. Where were you yesterday? At the top of a mountain? You remember what I told you about the history between Rayna and Ben and Lucy Orozco, don't you? The way they betrayed her?"

"Yes." Damon passed Jody a napkin holding the pastry he'd picked up for her at Dorotea's. "This is for you."

"Well, thank you! You're so thoughtful, and you have such an excellent memory, remembering that apple turnovers are my favorite. I'm quite a pastry chef myself, not to brag." She took a bite, swallowed it, and set the turnover on the desk. "*This* will interest you. Guess who called 911 to report Ben was dead? Rayna did. She had an appointment with him the night he died, you see, to show him pottery he was interested in buying for his restaurant. Isn't that a coincidence, that it would be Rayna who found him?"

"How so?"

"Let's face facts, shall we?" Jody leaned toward him. "Ben hurt Rayna so deeply. I'll wager there were many times she wished that man were dead, and then she actually found him dead. Eerie, isn't it?"

"Did you ever hear Rayna express the wish that Ben was dead or express a desire to harm him?"

Jody's forehead creased. "Goodness, I wouldn't expect her to say things like that out loud. But don't you think she would have felt that way?"

"Did her father ever say anything about her wanting to hurt Ben?"

"No, no. The only thing I remember him saying was that he couldn't blame Ben for dumping Rayna in favor of Lucy, that Lucy was a real catch, a stunning woman who had her life together."

Damon added this insult to Rayna's reasons to want her father dead—and his own reasons for wanting to punch Glenn Kirkpatrick. "What's the word on how Ben died? Was it natural causes?"

"They haven't figured that out yet. I have a friend at the police department, you know, so I have a bit of an in on the investigation. We're *only* friends, no matter what Kaitlyn says. I taught him how to make clam chowder, which annoyed Kaitlyn because it's a *secret recipe.* I said, 'Dear, people don't come to the Grill because that's the only way they can get *secret chowder*; they come because they don't want to go to the trouble of cooking for themselves.' She said, 'Mom, you don't understand the restaurant business.' I said, 'Dear, I understand I own the Grill and could fire you if I wanted to.' And she rolled her eyes because, stars, I'd never fire her in a million years no matter how cheeky she gets, and she knows it."

Damon chuckled. "What did Sgt. Fischer tell you about Ben?"

"You understand that he can't rattle on about the case or tell me anything confidential, but he can confirm what was in the papers and give me a more personal perspective. He interviewed Rayna at the scene."

"Oh? What did he say about that?"

"That she was very shaken, so upset it was hard for her to even talk at first. She told him she'd found Ben collapsed and tried CPR, but it didn't help. He confided in me that there's an investigation going on, and there are questions about Ben's death, but that's all he could say. There will be an autopsy, of course." Jody leaned closer. "He knows how connected I am in town, and he asked me if I knew of anyone who might have had a grudge against Ben. That's not the sort of question you ask when someone dies of natural causes, is it?"

"Probably not."

"I had to be honest with him, so I told him about Rayna's history with Ben and Lucy. He wanted to know everything I could tell him about Rayna. I was objective, of course, only giving him facts."

"Do you know of anyone else who might have had issues with Ben?"

"I keep thinking about that, but nothing has occurred to me yet. He hasn't lived here for years, you see, though he'd visit periodically. In fact, before he showed up last month to get Kaitlyn's counsel on running a restaurant, the last time I'd seen him personally was three years earlier when he was out for a visit and attended Elliott's funeral. Wasn't that sweet of him to attend the funeral when he could have been out kayaking or whatever he liked to do?"

"Very thoughtful of him. Did Sgt. Fischer say anything about clues indicating there might have been foul play?"

"No, he just told me they were investigating." She winked at Damon. "But I'll pump him for information when I get the chance. I *knew* you'd be interested."

"I am," Damon said. "Thank you."

Jody heaved a loud sigh. "I do hope Rayna is innocent."

Damon doubted Jody hoped that at all. She would hope for the most thrilling outcome, whatever that was.

"She's an odd girl though. Glenn always told me that. What shall I focus on today? If you like, I can gather more information about what happened to Ben and if Rayna was involved. I know so many people in town. In fact, I know Grace Yin, Lucy's mother. She's a doctor. Lives in Monterey but works some days at the hospital here."

More information was what Damon wanted, and no one would be suspicious if gossipy Jody was curious about Ben's death. "I'd appreciate that," he said. "But be discreet. I don't want people to know I'm paying you to learn about this."

"Of course. No one will know about this special assignment at all. It's natural for me to act interested since I've been neighbors with Rayna all her life and she was almost my stepdaughter. What are you up to today?"

"I'm playing it by ear," he said. "There are a couple people I'm hoping to catch—not formal interviews; no need to put them on my calendar. Later this afternoon, I'll be heading out of town again. You don't need to stay in the office at all today unless you want to."

"I'll be in and out. It's such a convenient place to sit and make notes. I want to plan this out carefully so I can get you the most information possible."

"Go ahead and get started on that. Thanks, Jody."

Jody stood and took the apple turnover. "Of course. My pleasure."

* * *

"Hey, Writer Man." A twenty-something guy with wild blond hair that reached his shoulders paused in rearranging a display of Willet Beach magnets. "How's our sweet town shaping up in your book?"

Mike Taylor, Annemarie's assistant.

"As a more complicated place than I thought," Damon said.

"Yeah, I'll bet. What can I help you with today?"

"I'm looking for a quality rash guard. Long-sleeved."

"Right over here." Mike led the way. "Got a couple of O'Neills that'd fit you. Black for the classic look or lime green if you want to glow like the deep-sea fishies. Quiksilver's a solid brand too. Got one in red."

Damon pulled the black shirt off the rack to look at it. "Is Annemarie around? I wanted to talk with her." He knew she was around; he could sense her in the back office with . . . Who was that? Someone he hadn't met before.

"She's in her office," Mike said. "She's talking with the woman whose husband died a couple days ago in that restaurant they're renovating on Beachcomber."

He spoke under his breath, clearly not wanting the father and daughter who were exploring the sand toys on the other side of the store to overhear him. "Real sad thing. Did you hear about it?"

"Yes." Lucy Orozco was speaking with Annemarie?

"Annemarie's sister is the one who found the dude. You know Rayna."

"That's why I wanted to talk with Annemarie, actually, to see how the family is doing."

"Hey, that's nice of you to check in. Annemarie said Rayna left town, needed to get away, but Annemarie's losing it, she's so worried about the little sis. Me, I can't blame Rayna for finding a hidey hole. I'd take off too. So, that shirt you're holding is a tight one, form-fitting, good to wear under a wet suit. If you want a looser fit—Ah, here comes the boss."

Annemarie entered from the staff-only area. Lucy wasn't with her. Damon sensed Lucy heading in the opposite direction. Annemarie must have sent her out the staff entrance. That was unfortunate; he'd have liked to meet her.

"Damon, hello." Annemarie offered him a customer-service smile.

"Writer Man wants a chat," Mike said. "Got a moment?"

"Sure. Come on back."

Damon hung the shirt on the rack and followed Annemarie. In her office, she gestured him into a chair and closed the door. "What can I do for you?"

"How are you and Rayna doing?" he asked. "I heard about Ben Orozco."

Annemarie groaned and leaned against the door. "I do not want to be interviewed about that. I don't want to talk about it at all."

"My apologies," Damon said. "I didn't mean to give the impression that this was an interview. I'm here as a friend. I was speaking to Rayna last night and was concerned—"

Annemarie sprang across the office and plunked into the chair next to Damon. "You saw Rayna last night?"

"No, I spoke with her on the phone."

"When?"

"I don't remember the time exactly. Late evening. She hadn't answered the text I sent earlier, so I called her."

"She answered? You got her to respond after *one* text and *one* call? She really must trust you."

Searing guilt at Annemarie's words caught Damon by surprise. Whatever trust Rayna had had in him was gone. "I don't know about that."

"It's true. She's a lot more comfortable with you than with most people. It took *me* a lot more tries than that to get her to respond. Did she tell you she left town?"

"Yes. She didn't say where she was though. She didn't say much."

"That's Rayna." The remainder of Annemarie's businesslike expression crumbled, leaving exhaustion and anxiety exposed. "Let me guess. She told you she's fine."

"She did say that."

"Have you seen her at all since Ben's death?"

"No," he said.

"This situation . . . She *cannot* handle this by herself, but what is she doing? Hiding. Literally hiding. She needs help but she doesn't know how to ask for it."

"Annemarie, you don't have to say anything you don't want to say, and I'll keep anything you do say confidential, but is there any way I can help? I plan to call her again today to check in. Is there anything particular you'd like me to ask her? Any messages you'd like me to give her in case she's . . . reluctant to respond to you?"

"Because she knows I'll chew her out and try to track her down?" Annemarie massaged her forehead. "Anything you can do to persuade her to come home would be much appreciated. She did promise to call me today, and when she does, I'll try not to nag. I hope I'm overreacting, worrying this much. Seth keeps telling me I'm not her mother, to back off, but . . . she . . . I don't know. She's scaring me."

Damon spoke gently. "Scaring you how?"

"Oh . . . you don't want to hear this. I'm saying too much. She's always been good at closing me out when she's struggling, but now she's . . . it's like she's opening up to me but in . . . strange ways."

"Strange ways?"

"Like telling me crazy stories that can't be true. That's *not* like her."

"What kinds of crazy stories?"

Annemarie shook her head. "It doesn't matter. Just do what you can to urge her to come home."

"I will."

"You can also tell her Lucy Orozco is worried about her. Ben's widow. She stopped by here right before you came."

"Lucy is worried about Rayna?"

"She's concerned that Rayna will blame herself because she couldn't save Ben."

"That's kind of her to worry about that when she just lost her husband."

"I know, right? Lucy said they haven't yet determined how Ben died, that it could take a while. But the police are asking her things like, 'Did Ben have any enemies?' and they even asked questions about the state of her marriage and why she wasn't there that night. She says nobody, including her, had any reason to hurt Ben and questions like that are salt in the wound."

"I'm sorry she has to deal with that."

"She stopped by here to get my opinion—business owner to business owner—about what she should do with The Sanddab. She's probably going to have Seth sell it for her. She's made an appointment to meet with him tomorrow."

"She's going to sell it?"

"She doesn't want to run it on her own. She admitted to me that she never really wanted to run it at all."

"Oh?"

"The Sanddab was a compromise between Ben and her. He'd always wanted to own a restaurant in the San Diego area, but he's a dream-big-and-hope-it-all-works-out guy—no wonder he and Seth got along so well when Seth sold them the place. Lucy is the one with the business expertise. She was reluctant but finally agreed to the restaurant plan if they could move here instead of to southern California so she could be near her family. Without Ben, she just wants The Sanddab out of her life. I'm amazed she can think about business at all at this point, but she said doing practical stuff helps her cope. Honestly, she's spot-on about Rayna blaming herself. I worry she blames herself for our dad's death. Which goes back to this whole mess being too much for Rayna to handle. She hasn't even worked through Dad's death, and now this?" Annemarie stood. "I'm sorry to kick you out, but I have work to do and I'm already behind."

Damon stood. "Thank you for speaking with me."

"Let me know when you talk to Rayna. Thanks for being such a support to her. She needs a friend."

Damon couldn't think of a response that wouldn't either blow his cover or make him a hypocrite, so he turned silently toward the door.

"Damon, wait."

He turned back. Annemarie was standing with her arms folded, her gaze fierce. "As her bossy older sister, I'm going to be frank. If you're hoping for more than friendship from her, and I suspect you are, be *very* careful. She has a lot of healing to do. Obviously she likes you, but the last thing she needs is to fall for a man who only wants a fling while he's in town for a few months and who'll then walk away from her."

Instant sweatiness at the nape of his neck informed Damon that he'd flushed a starkly visible scarlet. "That's not what I want."

"Good," Annemarie said. "Because if you hurt her, the police really will have a murder to investigate."

CHAPTER 18

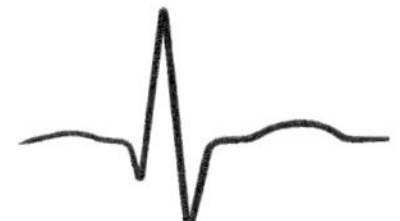

After purchasing the lime-green rash guard—the least he could do was give Annemarie's shop a sale, though what he wanted at that point was to flee from her as fast as he could—Damon walked toward Wyeth's Grill for an early lunch. Kaitlyn always made a point of greeting him when he went there, and he wanted to speak with her. She was the pragmatic opposite of her mother as well as an old friend of Ben's, and Damon wanted her perspective.

"Hi, Mr. Hale." The lithe, tanned girl at the hostess station smiled at him. She'd cornered him the last time he'd eaten here, told him about her experience as a model, and tried to convince him she'd make a great "face of Willet Beach" for the cover of his book. "Table for one?"

"I'll take him, Shelly." Kaitlyn marched up and snatched a menu from the holder on the side of the hostess stand. "He doesn't need you talking his ear off again." She led Damon away. "Do you want to sit inside or outside?"

"Outside, thanks," Damon said. "How are things?"

"Buzzing." Kaitlyn guided him to a table on the patio. The temperature was on the line between pleasant and too cool, and only two other patrons had chosen outdoor seating. "Buzzing, but not for happy reasons. I assume my mother has filled you in on Ben Orozco's death. We're all in shock, and everyone in town wants to chatter about it."

Including Damon. "Devastating tragedy." He sat and set the paper bag from The Beach Umbrella next to his chair.

"I can't imagine how awful this is for Lucy." Kaitlyn handed him the menu. "Have you spoken to Rayna?"

"Briefly."

"How's she doing?"

"Hard to say." Damon waved toward an empty chair at his table. "Sit if you have a moment."

Kaitlyn pulled out the chair and sat across from him. He wasn't concerned that Kaitlyn would misinterpret his desire for her company as flirtatious. During his visit to the Wyeths' fishing hut, she'd made it clear she didn't endorse her mother's matchmaking.

"Annemarie told me Rayna has gone on a trip down south to get away from here," Kaitlyn said. "I don't blame her. I know my mother has been gossiping away about her, and so have a lot of other people. I hope you're not taking anything Mom says about Rayna as accurate. Put anything in print based on what Mom tells you and you'll be following it up with retractions and apologies. Or dealing with a lawsuit."

"I'm not planning to write about any of this."

"Unless your sponsor hears the news and decides she wants you to write a true crime story."

"*Is* there a crime? Have they found any evidence that he didn't die of natural causes?"

"I have no idea." Kaitlyn lowered her voice. "But my head cook is friends with Owl Cheney's daughter, and the daughter told him Owl's been flapping his wings and hooting about the police questioning his employees."

"About Ben's death?"

"Not sure, but that was his impression. I haven't had time to find out what Owl was on about."

Damon made a mental note to visit Cheney's Ice Cream as soon as he finished his lunch.

A server approached the table. Damon hadn't looked at the menu yet. "Order for me," he said to Kaitlyn. "What should I try today?"

"How hungry are you?"

"Very."

"Bring him the mushroom-bacon burger and herb-cheese fries."

"Yes, ma'am. Anything to drink?"

"Just water, please," Damon said.

"And a strawberry-rhubarb slush," Kaitlyn said. "The drink is on the house. We're testing a new flavor, and I want to know what you think of it."

"I'm happy to be your guinea pig."

When the server had reentered the restaurant, Kaitlyn resumed speaking at a low volume. "Try to discourage my mother from gossiping about Rayna, will you? It's infuriating. A decade ago, Ben cheats on her, so she must still be *so* angry at him that she'd murder him? Because how could she ever move on from such a heartthrob of a guy, especially now that she's divorced and lonely?" Kaitlyn rolled her eyes. "Ben's death is a tragedy, but how patronizing to assume

Rayna would have had anything to do with it. She was there on *business*. What murderer would be dumb enough to make an appointment to show up and kill someone? Rayna's a smart woman, no matter what her father used to tell her. If the cops find out Ben's death was from natural causes, I hope there are a lot of people in town feeling like the idiots they are. Don't tell anyone I said that. It'll be bad for business."

"I suspect," Damon said, "that you'll tell them yourself."

Kaitlyn laughed.

"You knew Ben and Lucy well?" Damon asked.

"Ben and I were casual friends in high school. Didn't hang around with the same crowd much, but we knew each other. He was a lot of fun, but kind of . . . oblivious."

"Oblivious?"

"Not great at empathy. On the self-centered side. I only knew Lucy as Rayna's friend. But I saw quite a bit of Ben after he bought his restaurant here. He was full of questions about the restaurant business. It's a shame he never got to see The Sanddab open. He was so excited about it. Had some great ideas. I don't know if Lucy is planning to go through with opening the restaurant or not."

"Hey, you two look familiar." Seth Bristol, who'd approached from the parking lot, deftly hoisted himself onto the edge of the raised patio and climbed over the railing.

"That's not the entrance, Seth," Kaitlyn said.

"Sure it is." Seth pulled out the chair next to Kaitlyn's and sat down. His hair was damp, and he smelled of sunscreen and seawater, but he was wearing a button-down shirt and khakis.

"Meeting a client this afternoon?" Kaitlyn asked.

"Yep, if they don't run away because they heard there's a murderer in town." Seth's characteristic grin looked shallow today, like his facial muscles had shaped it out of habit but his emotions weren't supporting it. "First, that's an idiotic rumor. Second, it's not exactly a draw for home buyers."

"Kaitlyn and I were talking about Ben's death," Damon said. "Have you heard any actual indications that the police think it's murder?"

"All I've heard is drivel," Seth said. "People are ghouls, jumping on news of an unexplained death as an excuse to talk smack about the victim—or anyone connected to the victim—while feeling like smug armchair detectives. Nobody killed Ben. It was just one of those sad, crazy things. Heart attack or stroke or whatever."

"What kind of smack are people talking about Ben?" Kaitlyn asked.

Seth finally erased his phony smile. "Cliché stuff. Haven't people been whispering questions to you about it? You two were friends. Like, was he an addict, could it have been related to a drug deal, or was he up to some other illegal business, or was he having an affair, or whatever other scandal they can invent."

"Like, an affair with Rayna?" Kaitlyn asked.

Seth shrugged, fiddling with the salt and pepper shakers on the table. "That's one of the rumors, that they started up again, then Ben ditched her a second time, and she snapped. Or that Lucy found out and killed him. It's all stupid."

"Seth, you were friends with Ben?" Damon asked.

"Yeah, we'd go surfing, biking, whatever, but don't tell Annemarie because she despised Ben. Couldn't get past the whole 'you hurt my sister's feelings a million years ago' thing."

Kaitlyn stood. "Enjoy your lunch, Damon, and let me know what you think of the drink. Seth, take it easy. Rumors will blow over."

"Yeah, I hope so," Seth said. "How about people shut up with the drama? Here's what I think: if you have any dirt on Ben, you keep it to yourself and let the widow mourn in peace."

"Unless it turns out Ben *was* murdered, in which case the dirt might be evidence," Damon said.

"Yeah, well, he wasn't murdered."

"I'll see you guys later." Kaitlyn headed inside the restaurant.

Seth checked his watch and started to push back from the table.

Damon wanted to—as tactfully as possible—learn anything else he could from Seth. "Join me for lunch?"

"Nah, can't. I'm meeting my client here in five minutes. Thanks though." Seth followed Kaitlyn inside.

Damon ate quickly, paid, and walked over to Cheney's. A dozen or so people were sitting at tables in the ice-cream parlor. Cheney was behind the counter, wiping down equipment. No one was in line.

"Damon, my friend." Cheney welcomed him, his affable smile flatter than usual. "What can I get for you?"

Damon had no room whatsoever in his stomach after that massive burger and what must have been a double portion of fries, but he had to buy something from Cheney. "A shake. Small. You pick the flavor. Impress me."

"I can do that."

"How's your day been?" Damon asked as Cheney scooped ice cream.

"Okay," Cheney muttered. "Yours?"

"Uncomfortable," Damon said. How best could he maneuver the conversation to get Cheney to tell him why the police had spoken with his staff? "I'm out of my depth, what with the tragedy of Ben Orozco's death. As an outsider, I don't know what to say to anyone."

"I've known both him and his wife since they were babies. Heartbreaking thing, young guy like him dying. Don't worry, people will still want to talk to you." There was an edge to Cheney's voice. "Drop his name into an interview and locals will yammer until your ears wilt. You'll wish they'd shut their traps, but, hoo boy, they won't."

"From what I've heard, nobody knows what happened," Damon said.

"That's right." Cheney dumped a scoop of chocolate chunks on top of the ice cream. "And they'd better not spread gossip that taints the life's work of innocent people."

Life's work didn't sound like a reference to Rayna. "What gossip is getting spread?"

Cheney jammed the metal cup into place on the shake mixer. "I know you'll hear lies and nonsense from someone, so I want you to hear the truth from me: my ice cream is the highest quality. My standards are flawless. I have a Gold Seal from the Health Department. Never had a bad inspection."

"Did someone question the quality or safety of your ice cream?"

"The cops were here," he said. "Detective woman—Stafford was her name—asked me if I had a new flavor of ice cream, a chile-lime-coconut. I said I'd never tried that combo, that chile's a chancy ingredient when it comes to ice cream; a lot of people don't like it. She asked if I'd given any cups of sample ice cream to Ben Orozco, that she'd heard he was trying desserts from vendors all over town, hoping to feature some of them in his restaurant. I said, 'Sure, I gave him half a dozen the other week.' She asked what flavors, and I told her." Cheney paused while he blended the shake. "She wanted to know where we kept our individual-serving-size takeout cups and where I keep my business cards, and she wanted to talk to all my people."

Cheney poured the shake into a cup, tucked a straw and a spoon into it, and handed it to Damon. "That's a butterscotch shake with toasted pecans and chocolate chunks."

"Sounds fantastic. Thanks. Did Detective Stafford explain why she was asking these questions?"

"Nope." Cheney moved to the register to ring up the shake. "She said they were 'looking into things.' What could my ice cream have to do with Ben's death? Do they think he died of an allergic reaction? I'd told him where to find a list of my ingredients for every flavor. He wouldn't have eaten anything by accident. Or was he poisoned? Did someone taint a chile-lime-coconut concoction and put it in one of *my* cups? Why else would the cops be asking about the cups? Was someone imitating my ice cream? They could do it if they wanted to. I told Detective Stafford that. I teach ice-cream classes, give people recipes for some standard bases. Anybody could have made something and tried to pass it off as mine. All I can say is the police better make it clear that honest-to-goodness Cheney's ice cream had nothing to do with anyone's death, or I'll get me a lawyer. That'll be five-fifty for the shake."

Damon handed him a ten-dollar bill. "I haven't seen anything in the news about a connection between your ice cream and Ben's death."

"It better never show up in the news." Cheney handed him his change. "I can imagine it—people whispering about my new flavor being *death*."

Damon dropped his change into the tip jar. "That might bring you more business. Especially around Halloween."

"Sounds like a spin Seth Bristol would give it. I was about to tell him I was interested in leasing bigger premises, but now I think I'd better hold off."

"Anything I can do for you?" Damon asked.

"Just keep buying my ice cream, son. You have visibility in town. You talk to a lot of people. Let them see that you trust it."

"That," Damon said, "is the best assignment I've ever been given."

Cheney grinned. Damon moved away from the counter so Cheney could help three new customers. He walked out of the ice-cream parlor, the steel-hard fear inside him starting to soften.

If the police were asking questions about tainted ice cream, that was the beginning of evidence that Ben's death might not be Rayna's doing.

* * *

Rayna awakened feeling relaxed and spacey. Maggie had disconnected the IV line and pushed the stand into the corner of the room. The IV cannula itself remained in her arm, capped off, ready for reuse. Rayna wondered vaguely how long it would be until Maggie drugged her again, what time of day it was now, what had happened while she'd been unconscious, but she didn't care enough about any of those questions to ask them out loud. She could sense Damon elsewhere in the cabin, moving around but not approaching her room. She lay in bed, staring at the overhead light and marveling that someone had created that ruffly orange-glass fixture on purpose.

"No rush," Maggie said, "but as soon as you're ready, we'll get you some dinner."

Dinner? How long had she been asleep? All night . . . all day . . . ?

Maggie was sitting in an armchair near the bed with a book on her lap that served as a makeshift desk. A square of what looked like Styrofoam lay on top of the book. On top of the foam was a pile of yellow fluff that Maggie was stabbing repeatedly with a thick needle.

Mesmerized, Rayna watched her hands move. "That's not . . . practice for a medical procedure you're going to perform on me, is it?"

Maggie smiled. "This is called felting. I'm making a chicken."

"A chicken?"

"It's part of a Noah's Ark set I'm making for my grandson." Maggie reached into a tote bag by the side of her chair and pulled out a round, pink something. "This is one of the pigs." She held it up.

"*Oh my gosh.* That is *adorable.*"

Maggie reached into the bag again and pulled out a fluffy white sheep. "Here's a sheep."

"May I pet it?" Rayna sat up and stretched her hand toward Maggie. Maggie rose and set the sheep in Rayna's palm.

"It's *so cute.*" Rayna ran her index finger along its back. "I need a flock of these. I'd make a bowl for them. Green, like grass. A grass bowl filled with sheep."

Damon approached the room, his pace rapid. He stopped in the doorway.

"Isn't this adorable?" Rayna held up the sheep.

"Yes," he said.

"You should pet it."

"No, thank you."

"You should definitely pet it. It's like . . . it's like . . . petting a *very small* sheep."

His gaze shifted to Maggie. "Not quite with it yet, I see."

Maggie chuckled. "Give her a little time."

"You said I could call Annemarie today," Rayna said. "I need to call her."

"You can," Damon said, "once you're not loopy."

"I'm not loopy."

"You're talking about a grass bowl of sheep and trying to get Damon to pet my craft project," Maggie said. "You're loopy."

Rayna handed the sheep to Maggie, flopped onto her pillow, and closed her eyes.

When she awoke the second time, it was to a touch on her shoulder and Damon's voice. "Rayna, you need to get up. We need to talk."

"All right." She sat up. Maggie had left the room. Rayna sensed her in the area of the library where she'd examined Rayna last night. "What time is it?"

"Six," he said. "Six p.m. Come get some food."

"May I get dressed first?" Rayna tried not to sound scared, but anxiety was stirring again.

"Go ahead, but don't take too long. I won't lock or alarm your door. Come out as soon as you're ready." He exited and closed the door behind him.

Rayna shuffled into the bathroom. The mirror over the sink reflected wide, glazed eyes, a chalky-pale face, and a mane of tangled hair. She hoped her mind was in better shape than her appearance, or she wouldn't be able to handle anything tonight. But she was alive, unharmed, and still lacking any indication that Damon and Maggie weren't what they claimed to be. That was as hopeful of circumstances as she could expect at the moment.

Ten minutes later, dressed in a T-shirt, hoodie, and jeans, with her hair brushed and twisted into a knot at the nape of her neck, she sat at the kitchen table to eat the grilled sandwich and soup that Damon offered.

When she was nearly finished, he sat across the table from her. "I went to Willet Beach today and talked with several people," he said. "Including Annemarie."

"What did she say?"

"She's worried about you. She said you need help but don't know how to ask for it."

"I assume you didn't tell her I'd love to ask for help but my kidnapper won't let me."

"I didn't bring that up."

"Because you didn't want to get strangled on the spot?" Rayna asked. Damon's demeanor seemed less stone-like than it had been yesterday. More like it had been prekidnapping—though the gun he carried didn't allow for much increase in her comfort level.

"She said you were telling her 'crazy stories that can't be true,' which wasn't like you," Damon said.

"Crazy stories?" Rayna set her spoon in her empty soup bowl. "What crazy stories? Does she mean my lies about why I left town?"

"I don't think so."

"Then I don't know what . . ." The obvious meaning clicked. *Oh no. Annie, no.* "She . . . she must be talking about what I told her the other night about my . . . mind-killing ability. Link-killing. Whatever you call it."

"You said she believed you."

"I thought she did!" She knew Annemarie had been rattled by her confession, but she'd been so supportive, so accepting, and Rayna had been grateful not to be hauling that secret around by herself. But Annemarie hadn't believed her after all. She didn't think Rayna was a monster, but she thought Rayna was a liar or psychotic. "Did she say anything else about my 'crazy stories'?"

"No."

"At least she kept my insanity confidential," Rayna said caustically. "Why didn't she *tell* me she didn't believe me? Don't answer that. I know why she didn't. She was scared, like I was always afraid she would be. Because it's too freakish to handle. *I'm* too freakish to handle. She tells herself I'm having a nervous breakdown, pats me on the head, and hopes I'll snap out of it."

Damon picked up Rayna's empty bowl and plate. "It's better for you and for her if she doesn't believe you."

"I need to talk to her. Has she tried to call me?"

"Yes." He set the dishes in the sink and returned to the table. "She's left you a voice mail and multiple texts. I'd like you to call her before she gets even more upset, but when you do, I want you to confirm to her that you lied about your ability to link-kill."

"No." It took Rayna a moment to comprehend her own knee-jerk refusal. "No. It took me years to work up the nerve to confide in her. I'm not denying it now. I'm telling her it's true, and she needs to deal with that."

"Rayna. This is a foolish thing to get stubborn over."

"Do you have family?"

His eyes were getting flintier. "I have a brother and a sister."

"Do they know you're a Trespasser?"

"They don't know the term, they don't know what I do for a living, and they don't know I can link-kill. They know I can sense people."

"Have you ever wanted to tell them the rest of it?"

"No." He spoke the word so curtly that Rayna wondered what experiences had built that reticence. "The fewer people who know the extent of our abilities, the easier it is to keep the information secure. It's better for national security, it's safer for you, and it's safer for your family. With Annemarie, you have a second chance to conceal this from her. Take it."

"She'll keep the information secure. She's kept my weirdness a secret for most of her life. Besides, how am I supposed to retract it? 'Just kidding! Sorry about the little white lie! I think it's funny to claim I can think people to death!'"

"Tell her you aren't sure why you made up a story so bizarre but you were reeling after Ben's death. You didn't mean to stretch the story as far as you did. You thought she'd challenge you right away, but when she didn't, you kept inventing more details until you were too embarrassed to retract it. Make her promise not to mention it to anyone. Tell her you don't know what you were thinking. She'll be glad to have it resolved."

"Wow. You have the whole script written. What happens if I refuse to do it?"

He rested his elbows on the table, interlinking his fingers. At least he wasn't reaching for his gun, but his expression was so guarded that she had no idea what he was thinking. "Here's a compromise. You don't have to bring up the subject of link-killing with Annemarie. If she doesn't mention it, you don't have to mention it either. If she does mention it, either tell her you lied or, if you can't stomach that, be evasive. Tell her you don't want to talk about it right now. Promise you'll talk about it later. I imagine you have abundant experience being evasive with her."

New humiliation added to the crushing dismay inside Rayna. He was right about her evasiveness. And *he'd* been evasive when she'd asked about the consequences of refusing, and that wasn't a question she wanted answered via a practical demonstration. This *was* a foolish thing to get stubborn over. "Fine," she said. "I agree. Let me call her."

He stood and moved his chair so he was sitting next to her. "Read her texts first and listen to the voice mail." He handed her the phone.

All the messages had the same theme: *Detective Stafford visited me this afternoon, and unless you're on the road driving home this second, you'd better call me* NOW.

"This can't be good," Rayna murmured.

CHAPTER 19

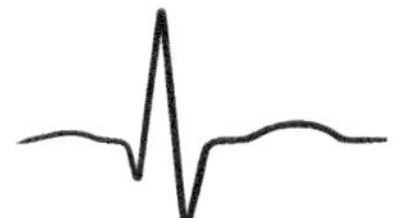

"SET THE PHONE ON THE table and don't touch it while you're talking to her," Damon said.

Rayna laid the phone on the table, positioning it between the two of them. "After urgent messages like that, what excuse do I give for ignoring her for hours?"

"Tell her you were out on a walk without your phone."

"She's going to hunt me down and eat me alive."

"Apologize. Calm her down. Find out what Detective Stafford said to her."

"What do I say when she pressures me to come home?"

"You say unless Stafford has a warrant for your arrest, you'll come home when you're ready. If you get stumped and don't know what to say, tell her you need to grab a glass of water. I'll mute the phone and give you guidance."

Calm her down. Rayna repeated the words to herself. Calming *herself* down would be difficult enough, let alone soothing Annemarie. *Calm down. Whatever happened between Annemarie and Stafford can't be worse news than the situation you're already in with Damon's group.*

"Ready?" Damon asked.

"Yes."

He tapped the phone to call Annemarie.

Annemarie's voice erupted from the speaker. "At *last.* You are making me *crazy.* Was the police questioning me about you not enough motivation to get you to return my call right away?"

"I'm sorry. I was on a walk on the beach without my phone."

"How far did you walk? To San Diego and back? I called you hours ago."

"I'm sorry. I didn't mean to worry you. I'm coping the best I can."

"I'm happy *you're* coping by reveling in nature, but *I'm* here dealing with the cops. Are you in your car? You're not in your car. Get in your car. You need to *come home*, because this is getting worse and worse. Do you know how it felt trying to handle Southern-belle Stafford when she was drilling into me about why you took off and where you are? I was all, 'Oh, that's Rayna. When she's had a shock, she needs solitude, haha. It's fine, I'm sure she'll be back soon.' And Stafford's giving me this sympathetic, knowing look, and I'm wanting to *scream* at you."

The rush of heat now radiating off Rayna's skin made her regret the long-sleeved hoodie. "Why didn't she call me instead of hounding you? I don't have any missed calls or messages from her."

"I asked her that, and she said, 'It's helpful to get multiple perspectives, isn't it, hon?' I swear, if she calls me hon one more time—"

"What else did she ask you, besides where I was?"

"She—Hang on— " Rattling noises sounded, followed by thuds. "Whoever that is, *knock it off.* The door's locked because I don't want anyone in here. Go ask Dad for whatever you need."

"But, *Mom*," Nancy's muffled voice responded. "Daddy said to ask *you*. He's playing his new game."

"Tell him I'm on the phone with Aunt Rayna."

"But, *Mom*—"

"*Ask Dad*!" Annemarie yelled. "*I don't care about his game*!"

Damon pressed the button on the side of the phone to lower the volume.

"Sorry," Annemarie said. "I shouldn't have screamed at her. It's you and Seth who are driving me nuts, not the kids."

"What's Seth doing?"

"He won't take any of this seriously. Says Stafford is bored because nothing major happens in Willet Beach and she's making a case out of nothing. I said, 'Whether or not she is, Rayna's in her cross hairs, and that *is* serious.'"

Rayna peeled off her hoodie. "What else did Stafford ask you?"

"She wanted to know about you and Ben and Lucy. And she asked me about your claim to ESP, and I said, 'Yes, it's true; she can sense people.'"

"What did she say to that?"

"Something vague, like, 'How interesting.' I could tell she thought I was lying. She also asked questions about you and Evan and you in general. And questions about Dad."

A chill splashed over Rayna. "About Dad?"

"About you and Dad. Your relationship. Did you get along? Was it hard on you when he died?"

Clutching the hoodie she now wished she hadn't removed, Rayna tried to keep her voice steady. "What did you tell her?"

"That your relationship was rocky, that you'd never been close, that you had trouble understanding each other, but you both tried. She asked me about his birthday party, said she'd heard there was an ugly scene between the two of you that night. I said, 'Whatever you heard, you must have heard from Jody Wyeth, so take it with a grain of salt.' She said, 'Tell me the un-salted version.' I told her what happened and said you handled the whole thing fine, that we were all used to Dad's tactlessness. That you were devastated when he died."

Rayna's neck muscles had stiffened as though to keep her from looking toward Damon and seeing condemnation in his face. "She knows his death was ruled natural causes, right?"

"Yes. But she asked a lot of questions about what happened the day he died. Had he been sick at all? Showed any symptoms? Were you and I together the whole evening? How much money did we inherit when he died? Even if she thinks you killed him—I'm betting that's Jody's wackadoodle theory—there's no way to prove it now with his ashes at the bottom of the ocean. I think she was implying there's a pattern, that both Ben and Dad had hurt you and both died suddenly. She was trying to shake me into saying something she can use to pin Ben's death on you."

No way to prove it. Stafford couldn't arrest her for her father's death, but Damon would take Stafford's suspicions as validation that he was correct in thinking Rayna had killed him. He wouldn't need courtroom-grade proof to condemn her for that. With her wadded-up hoodie, she mopped cold sweat off her neck, battling an impulse to dash toward the door. "What does she think caused Ben's death?"

"I don't know, but she was asking questions about ice cream."

"About *ice cream*?"

"Yes. Did you ever make homemade ice cream? Had you made it lately? I said you knew how to make it—we both took Owl Cheney's ice-cream class when we were teenagers, but if you'd made any lately, you hadn't shared it with me."

"I'm lost," Rayna said. "Did Ben die from eating ice cream?"

"I told you, I don't *know*. Stafford didn't give context for her questions or answer *my* questions. But it must be connected, or why would she care? Maybe he was poisoned? Or had an allergic reaction?"

"Ben didn't have any allergies." Rayna wiped her hands on her hoodie. "I'm sorry you got caught in the middle of this. I wish she'd called me."

"So you could've ignored her calls along with mine?"

"I didn't mean to ignore you. I didn't know you'd called."

"Yes, you did. You were avoiding me, and now you're lying to me. *Lying.* What's going on with you? Give me the address of where you're staying because I'm coming. We need to talk, face-to-face."

"Don't come yet. I need a little more—"

"No, you do not need more alone time or whatever cliché you were going to throw at me. You need help. You *cannot* hide from this mess with Ben's death, and you can't deal with it alone. Not this time, Rayna."

"I'm not *hiding.*" Rayna wanted to grab the phone and yell as much of the truth as she could before Damon yanked the phone away and ended the call. "It's easier to think things through when I don't have to worry that everyone who sees me has been briefed by Jody. I'm not hiding from Detective Stafford either. If she does call me, I'll talk to her."

"What exactly do you need to think through? What decisions are you trying to make?"

"I mean . . . process things. Get my head on straight."

"Lying to me is part of getting your head on straight?"

Rayna didn't realize she was picking at the transparent film protecting the tube in her arm until Damon reached over and lifted her hand away from it. She dropped her hands into her lap. "I'm not lying to you."

"Rayna, listen to me. No matter what you've done, I'll help you, but you have to tell me the truth. *Did* you kill Ben?"

"Annie! *No.*"

"Just *tell* me! I'll understand if you did. I'll still love you. But I need the truth. Don't give me some bizarre half-confession by making up stories about killing with your mind."

The tension in Rayna's chest snapped into a thousand flailing threads of pain. *That* was how Annemarie had interpreted her explanation of her abilities—as a confession to murder? "No—that has nothing to do with—"

"How gullible do you think I am? You can't *kill* someone by thinking about it. No one can do that. You can sense people in a way most of us can't, but there have always been stories about people with ESP. But not *this.* Good grief, Rayna. That was *sick.*"

The threads of pain knotted together, cinching around her throat. "I don't want to talk about it."

"I don't care if you don't want to talk about it. If you're making up stories like that, you're *losing* it. Just tell me the truth so I can *help* you."

"I . . . I need some water," Rayna rasped. "Give me a second."

"Hang up on me now and I'll call Detective Stafford and tell her what you told me the night Ben died."

"I won't hang up. I need a drink. I'll be right back."

Damon touched the mute button.

Trembling, Rayna faced him. "What am I supposed to tell her now? If I confirm I was making things up, she'll think that's a confession that I killed Ben. I *didn't*, and I'm not going to tell her I did."

"Do you think she'll actually call Stafford?"

"Not unless she's so scared for me that she thinks the police need to bring me in for my own safety."

Taking the phone with him, Damon went to the kitchen, filled a glass with water, and brought it to Rayna. Either he'd decided to take the code phrase seriously, or he'd noticed she kept swallowing, trying to wet her dry mouth.

"Thank you." Rayna gulped the water and set the glass down. "Please let me tell her I wasn't lying about my abilities. I can do better with that than fumbling around trying to convince her I was lying but it wasn't out of guilt over Ben."

Damon set the muted phone on the table. "You don't have to confess to murder. Go back to the excuses I gave you earlier. You were so shaken after having Ben die in front of you that you don't know what you were thinking; you didn't mean to take it that far. I think your admission of lying will do a lot to calm her down."

My admission of lying? I'll be lying about lying. She wiped her face with her hoodie and drew a deep breath, but before she could speak, Damon reclaimed the phone.

"She hung up," he said. "And sent a text." He showed the message to Rayna: *I have to go. Stafford's here with a search warrant.*

"A *search warrant*?" Rayna pushed back from the table and jumped to her feet. "I need to go home. How far away are we?"

"You don't have to be there. Annemarie's already dealing with it."

"Are you *kidding* me? She shouldn't have to deal with this! Do you want to push her over the edge? Even if I can't get there until Stafford is gone, I need to get there tonight."

"I'll go to Willet Beach and check on things," Damon said.

"I'm coming too."

"You need to stay here."

"No, I do *not*." Rayna yanked her hoodie over her head and poked her arms through the sleeves. "If the police have enough evidence to get a search warrant, they must have evidence that Ben was murdered, and that means it *wasn't me.* If I'd killed him, there wouldn't *be* evidence. You have no right to keep me here."

Creases between Damon's eyes made his expression a shade less stoic. "Maggie!" he called.

The door to the library opened, and Maggie stepped out.

"I'm heading back to Willet Beach," he said. "We need to get Rayna settled."

Fury boiled inside Rayna. She was not going to meekly let Maggie knock her out again, leaving Annemarie convinced that Rayna was a murderer, a liar, and a coward. If evidence that Ben had been murdered but *not* via link-killing wasn't enough to reassure Damon that Rayna wasn't guilty, what would be? Nothing. Had releasing her ever been an actual option?

His eyes were on her, narrowed, alert. He was ready to intercept her if she made a break for the door.

Maggie walked toward her. "All right," she said cheerfully. "Let's—"

Rayna whirled around and shot past Maggie, heading not toward an exit but toward the library. She sensed both Maggie and Damon in pursuit, but they were a beat too late; her direction had surprised both of them.

She slammed the library door and fumbled to lock it . . . to lock it . . . Where was . . . ? There was no lock. Just an old-fashioned crystal doorknob, which Damon was now turning from outside. Bracing her shoulder against the door, Rayna clutched the doorknob with both hands, fighting to keep it from rotating while she looked desperately around for any makeshift weapons she could use to hold Damon and Maggie off long enough for her to go out the window. *Weapons better than Damon's gun?*

The knob rotated, digging into her palms, and the door swung inward with enough force to throw her backward. Staggering, she tried to pivot toward the window. Damon seized her and twisted, taking both of them to the floor.

A scream burst from her throat, a release of air so violent that it hurt. Rayna thrashed, the energy of panic blazing in her muscles.

Maggie's voice came from above her. "Whoa, girl, you are not up for this kind of a smackdown."

"*Don't touch me!*" Rayna screeched the words into the rug beneath her face. Damon was kneeling over her now, pinning both of her arms against her back. "*Stay away from me.*"

"Rayna." Damon's voice was low and calm. "You're going to hurt yourself. Stop fighting us and let Maggie do her job."

"You have . . . no right . . . to do this to me." The battle had become absurd. She couldn't win it, yet she continued writhing against Damon's grip.

"*Rayna*," he said. "You're not doing yourself any good. If you got out of here, you couldn't head to Annemarie's, or I'd pick you up on the way. Did you have a plan other than that? Somewhere else to go?"

A plan? No plan at all. Damon was pointing out that this had been the dumbest escape attempt ever, and he was right, starting with her choice of a room with no lock. Abruptly, her chest contracted with laughter at her own ridiculousness, laughter which transformed to sobs. Annemarie was right too: Rayna was losing her mind.

"Maggie, give her something now to calm her down," Damon said. "Then we'll get her to bed and set up the drip."

"*No*," Rayna sobbed. "Maggie—please—"

"Easy, kiddo," Maggie said.

Rayna heard the click of latches—Maggie opening her briefcase. She tried to look up at Maggie, but everything in her line of vision blurred and tilted in odd contortions.

Rayna rested her cheek against the carpet. Her limbs were slack now, all remaining energy diverted to swimming through an emotional tidal wave. Gradually, Damon relaxed his hold, allowing Rayna's arms to flop to the floor at her sides.

"Stay where you are," he said.

Tears streamed sideways across her face. "There will never be enough evidence to convince you, will there? You'll never let me go. It doesn't matter what you learn."

"Not true," Maggie said. "He'll do everything possible to discover the truth and act on it. I've known Damon since he was a kid. To say he tries to do the right thing is an understatement. Damon, if you could roll her onto her right side . . . Yes, that's good . . . Rayna, just lie still . . ."

Damon gripped Rayna's wrists. Maggie rolled up the sleeve of Rayna's hoodie to expose the IV site. "Straighten her left arm a little more," Maggie said. "Thank you . . . Rayna, all I'm doing now is disinfecting the injection port . . ."

Rayna shut her eyes and tried to steady her uneven breaths, but the urge to scream was growing again.

"This first injection is saline. I'm making sure nothing got dislodged in that wrestling match . . . Good . . . very good . . . This next injection is going to burn a bit . . ."

A stinging sensation spread up Rayna's arm. Stars swirled through her brain, scattering over her last thought: *Scream all you want. Who cares? No one can help you.*

CHAPTER 20

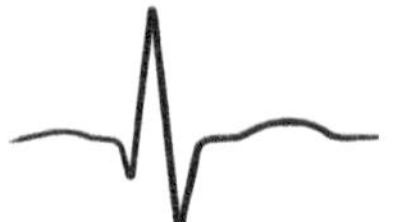

It took Damon the full length of the drive to Willet Beach before the tension in his spine and shoulders loosened and the queasiness in his gut settled. He'd hoped more physical confrontation with Rayna wouldn't be necessary, and maybe he *could* have avoided this explosion of resistance if he hadn't done such a clumsy job of ordering her to lie to her sister about her ability to link-kill. Annemarie's doubt was fortuitous, an opportunity to reduce the danger that word would spread about Rayna's complete abilities, but he hadn't expected his demand to shake Rayna so acutely, nor had he expected Annemarie to accuse her of murdering Ben. Annemarie's belief that her sister might be capable of murder was troubling data, but given her frustration with Rayna, the accusation might have been more of an effort to scare Rayna into cooperating than an honest suspicion.

The granting of a search warrant was positive news for Rayna. She'd been correct that Stafford would have needed significant evidence to get a judge to sign the warrant. But bringing Rayna back to Willet Beach tonight would have been premature. The risks of letting her loose were too high. He couldn't allow that until he had as much evidence as possible.

Rayna's despairing words replayed in his mind. "*There will never be enough evidence to convince you, will there?*"

There would be. But with her father's and Collin Burgess's deaths mostly beyond investigation, disproportionate weight rested on Ben Orozco's death. Damon couldn't leap to trusting Rayna simply because the police were exploring the possibility of homicide via tainted ice cream.

Maggie's words grated across his memory. "*Remember that Rayna is not Tristan McCuller. Make sure you aren't biased against her because you feel compelled to punish her—and yourself—for Tristan's crimes.*"

He wasn't biased against Rayna. Was he?

Would Maggie's warning smart like this if he didn't recognize it as valid?

Stop stewing. Go find the evidence you need. Without blowing his cover, he needed to learn what was going on with the search warrant. He hoped Annemarie or Seth could tell him, but knocking on their door and asking would be too blunt of a strategy. He parked in the lot next to his office and sent Annemarie a text from his own phone. *I spoke to Rayna this evening. Call me when you get a chance.*

Fifteen minutes later, when he was sitting at his desk, typing up a report, his phone rang.

"When did you talk to her?" Annemarie barked the question at him.

"An hour or so ago," Damon said. "It was a short conversation. She sounded upset. She said you were angry with her and that the police were talking to you. She wouldn't give me any details. She said she was trying to figure out what to do. I wanted to pass that along to you."

"I *am* upset with her, and the police are more than talking to me. They're searching the guesthouse and my kitchen. Detective Stafford wants to talk to you. Where are you?"

He'd welcome a chance to speak with Stafford. "I'm at my office, but I can go to her."

"She'll come to you. Give her about a half hour."

"Does she need the addr—" Damon stopped. Annemarie had hung up.

He finished the report, sent it to Logan, and started reviewing photos that Jody had curated for him so if Stafford asked what he'd been up to in his office this evening, he'd have something to show her.

Within twenty minutes, he sensed two people pulling up to the curb in front of his office, then one person approaching the door. Stafford must be leaving her backup officer in the car. Damon waited for a knock, then went to unlock the door.

A woman with blonde curls, a tailored business suit, and a gold badge on a lanyard smiled at him. "Mr. Damon Hale, the talk of the town. It's an honor to meet you." She offered him her hand. "Detective Claire Stafford, Willet Beach Police."

Damon shook her hand, thinking about the research he'd done on her. Born and raised in Knoxville, Tennessee. Worked as a receptionist at the police department. In her thirties, following a divorce, she'd gone to the police academy to become an officer and had rapidly excelled in that career. Two young-adult daughters. Relocated to Willet Beach two years ago. "Come in, Detective."

"It's gracious of you to let me interrupt your evening." Stafford breezed into the reception area and strolled around the room, peering at the photographs Jody had hung on the wall. "Your work?"

"Yes. Chosen and arranged by my assistant, Jody Wyeth."

"I heard Mrs. Wyeth is working for you. She's a busy bee, isn't she?"

"She's very capable."

"I've heard a lot about you," Stafford said. "Everyone is interested in your book project."

"Willet Beach is a great community."

"I do love it." Stafford settled into one of the chairs near the wall.

Damon went to sit next to her. "What can I do for you?"

She smiled at him. Her teeth could have been featured on an ad for teeth-whitening strips. "You're friends with Rayna Kirkpatrick."

"Yes. I've only known her a short time, but I consider her a friend."

"Do you know where she is now?"

"I'm afraid not. I've spoken to her a couple of times, but she won't tell me where she's staying. She needs some solitude after the trauma of Ben Orozco's death."

"When was the last time you saw her?"

"Last Sunday. Her sister, Annemarie Bristol, invited me over for dinner. Rayna was there."

"How gracious of Mrs. Bristol. People are so friendly here, aren't they?"

"They are."

"Are you sure you haven't seen Miss Rayna since last Sunday?"

This repetition triggered Damon's wariness. "I believe so. I don't recall running into her in town, and I didn't interview her this week."

"You didn't see her yesterday?"

"No, ma'am."

"You didn't take her anywhere yesterday?"

Damon kept his affable public-face expression in place. "May I ask why you're pressing this issue?"

"Did you take her anywhere yesterday, Mr. Hale?"

"Did someone tell you I did?"

"That's not an answer, hon."

Was Stafford fishing, or had someone noticed him driving Rayna's car yesterday? If Stafford had a witness and Damon kept denying that he'd seen her, that would get Stafford a lot more interested in him than he wanted her to be. Who might have noticed him? Not Jody. He hadn't sensed her anywhere nearby. There had been a few people home in the neighborhood, but no one in their front yards. The likeliest time for someone to have gotten a good look at him in her car was at a stoplight. He'd hit two of them on his way out of town.

"Don't be shy." Stafford kept smiling at him. "It's not a crime to fall for a pretty girl. I can't imagine a big, handsome hero like you would be able to resist a damsel in distress."

Stafford certainly laid it on thick. He didn't dare deny romantic interest in Rayna. He might need that excuse for his actions, depending on where this conversation went next. "What do you think I've done, Detective?"

"Why don't you tell me?"

"What am I accused of doing?"

"I'm not accusing you of anything. I just have an eyewitness who can testify they saw you driving Miss Rayna's car yesterday afternoon."

Damon thought fast. Had this eyewitness also been able to see Rayna reclining in the passenger seat? He'd better assume so. "All right. Here's what happened. After I heard the news about Ben, I was concerned about Rayna. I stopped by her house yesterday around midday to see how she was doing. She was overwrought and exhausted and said she needed to get out of her house but was too tired to drive. I offered to take her for a drive, but I didn't have my car—I'd stopped by Rayna's while out on a walk. I drove her car along the coast for a while, and she fell asleep in the passenger seat. After she'd had a nap, I brought her home."

"That was sweet of you," Stafford said. "Why did you feel the need to conceal a kind deed?"

Damon shrugged. "Fear of Rayna's sister. On the drive, Rayna told me she was planning to leave town and wouldn't tell anyone until she was gone so Annemarie couldn't stop her. I promised her I wouldn't forewarn Annemarie, and frankly, I was afraid to tell Annemarie later because I knew she'd be furious with me. It seemed simpler to deny seeing Rayna yesterday at all."

"Lies are never simpler, Mr. Hale. They might be more convenient in the moment, but the complications always come."

"I apologize for withholding information from you. I didn't think it was anything the police would care about. Rayna didn't talk about Ben Orozco on the drive. She talked a little about growing up in Willet Beach, then slept the rest of the time. I have no idea where she is now. At the time, I assumed Ben's death was from natural causes. Has it been ruled a homicide?"

"We're sorting through possibilities."

"If you're at the point of getting a search warrant, those possibilities have become evidence-based probabilities. What were you looking for?"

"What should we be looking for?"

"Mark Cheney told me you were questioning him about an ice-cream flavor he doesn't make and asking if he gave any samples to Ben Orozco. Do you suspect Mr. Orozco was poisoned?"

"Are you switching your focus to crime reporting, Mr. Hale?"

"No. Rayna's a friend. Naturally, this is of concern to me. Did Mr. Orozco show signs of having been poisoned?"

Stafford gave him a look of patient sympathy. "Have you spoken with Rayna about her history with the Orozcos?"

"Jody Wyeth told me about it a few weeks back. I let Rayna know I was aware of it and that I would respect her privacy and not share any of the story on my website or in the book."

"Did she ever show anger or bitterness toward Mr. and Mrs. Orozco for the way they treated her?"

"Not in my presence."

"Did she show any distress over the fact that Mrs. Orozco is pregnant?"

"Distress, yes. Not anger or bitterness, though, and she recommended Ben and Lucy to me as local business owners I should interview. I had the sense she was striving to be objective and professional when talking about them."

"But you said she showed distress."

"I ran into her on the beach after she'd found out about Lucy's pregnancy. She was crying."

"That cute gal has had a hard time, hasn't she?"

"She's faced some challenges."

"Mrs. Bristol told me you've conducted several interviews with her."

"About her pottery business, yes."

"I assume she's talked about her personal life. Y'all can't talk plates and pots *all* the time."

Damon suspected Stafford played up her Southern accent to give herself the air of a guileless country girl while beneath the surface, she was setting traps. "She's mentioned things here and there, but it's not her favorite subject. She came to Willet Beach to start over."

"Has Rayna ever claimed to have ESP? Or any type of paranormal abilities?"

Damon looked into Stafford's ingenuous eyes. The pink rims of her eyeglasses had gold hearts in the corners. "No."

"I heard your sponsor is interested in any supernatural manifestations or paranormal abilities found in Willet Beach."

"That's correct."

"Rayna knows this?"

"Yes."

"You told her personally?"

"Yes."

"And she never claimed to have unusual abilities."

"No."

"You interviewed her or otherwise met with her several times, and she never mentioned this."

Damon could guess the conclusion Stafford was reaching: she thought it was Damon's mention of paranormal abilities that had planted the idea in Rayna's mind—Rayna's odd excuse for knowing Ben was in jeopardy before she'd seen him. "Did she tell *you* she had supernatural abilities?"

"She mentioned it," Stafford said.

Damon slid to the edge of his chair, looking intently at Stafford. It would seem strange if he didn't show strong interest in this. "What did she say?"

"She asked me not to blab it around. You'll have to ask her."

"I will." Stafford's discretion pleased him.

Stafford pushed a blonde curl behind her ear. "Mr. Hale, who is your sponsor?"

"She prefers to remain anonymous."

"How did you find each other?"

"We connected through a longtime friend. He told her I had experience with travel writing and referred her to my website so she could get samples of my work. She liked what she saw and contacted me about the Willet Beach project."

"This friend must have given you a marvelous recommendation. An expensive project for the sponsor, I imagine, with little possibility of making back any significant percentage of the money."

"Making a profit on the book is not her goal."

"You said she was impressed enough with your work to hire you. You've published town histories or travel guides before?"

"Not in print. But I've been running a travel website, and there's a lot of material there."

"Detailing your years of travel."

"Yes. It's called Hale's Trails, if you want to look it up."

"I have, hon. Gorgeous website. How long ago did she hire you for this project?"

"A couple of months back. It came together fast."

"Mmm. Was your sponsor aware, when she was taking your website as evidence for your ability to complete this project, that the whole of it came into existence a couple of months back?"

Internally, Damon cursed himself. He hadn't anticipated the police having enough interest in him to delve into the provenance of his website. He could claim the material had been transferred from an earlier website to a nicer one, but then she'd ask the details of that earlier website. "The website is new," he said. "Most of the material isn't. I was keeping records on my computer with thoughts of compiling it into a book someday, but I decided to put it online instead."

"Before or after this potential sponsor contacted you?"

His cover story was warping out of shape. Stafford thought he was a huckster who'd scrambled to deceive a sentimental lady who had too much money and not enough savvy. A huckster who probably hadn't written any of the material on the website himself and who would go through the motions of conducting research while living it up on his sponsor's dime. Until he got bored with Willet Beach. Then he'd ditch the project and disappear.

"I'd put the material on my website before she contacted me," he said. "The new website was why I was on my friend's mind when he was talking with her at a party. I'd discussed it with him not long before that."

"What auspicious timing. What's your friend's name?"

"Logan Tilburg." He had to give Stafford *some* scrap of information. Let Logan field questions about his alleged sponsor and help straighten out Damon's cover. Logan was going to be annoyed at Damon's provoking of Stafford's suspicions, but he'd be far more annoyed if Damon had to resort to telling Stafford the truth to keep himself from getting arrested as an accessory to Ben Orozco's murder. "We worked together in D.C. Department of the Interior. Would you like his number?"

"That'd be sweet of you, hon." She took a business card out of her jacket pocket and handed it to Damon. "Text it to the cell number listed there."

Damon took out his phone and sent her Logan's regular, unsecured number, the one he used in daily life. As soon as Stafford left, he'd warn Logan to expect her call.

"Thank you," Stafford said. "I'll leave you to your evening, but let me tell you this first. Lying to a police officer who is in the performance of her duty, like you did tonight, is a crime. No, I'm not planning to arrest you on the spot for fudging on when you last saw Rayna Kirkpatrick, but I'm guessing that's not the only thing you don't want to share with me. If you know anything about Ben Orozco's death and you conceal that from me—even if it's something you didn't learn until after Ben was gone—I *will* arrest you for that. If you don't want that to happen, now's the time to come clean." Another smile, this one coaxing. "Is there anything you'd like to tell me before I leave?"

"Rayna has not confided anything in me about Ben's death. I know nothing about it. May I ask *you* a very direct question?"

"Fire away."

"Did you find anything significant when you executed your search warrant this evening?"

"It'll take a little time to determine that."

"What are you trying to determine? Did you seize any evidence?"

"That remains to be seen."

Damon sank back in his chair, trying to relax muscles that were tensing up again. "As I'm sure is obvious to you, I'm interested in Rayna as more than a source for my book. It's clear from the nature of your investigation that you have evidence that Ben's death was a homicide and he was likely poisoned. It's also clear Rayna is a suspect. Could you at least tell me if she's the *only* suspect? Is there anyone else you have reason to suspect?"

"The investigation is ongoing."

This was useless. "You're a seasoned officer. What's your gut feeling about Rayna? Can you at least tell me if I'd be wise to keep my distance from her?"

Stafford stood. "That's a judgment call only you can make." She patted his shoulder. "I'll see myself out. Call me if you think of anything else you'd like to tell me."

CHAPTER 21

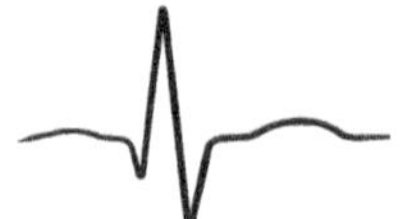

"Fine, yes, I'll feed her some nonsense on how I connected you with your reclusive sponsor and you wowed her with your charm and writing genius." The screen showed Logan sitting in his study at home, wearing one of his collection of Washington Capitals T-shirts. He must use those shirts as pajamas; every time Damon contacted him past midnight, East Coast time, he was wearing one. "Rookie mistake, getting recognized driving Rayna's car."

"I apologize for that." Damon looked away from the computer on his lap, absently focusing on a sunset photo Jody had hung on a wall of the reception area. "I'll see what I can find out regarding the search warrant."

"Let me know, and don't get yourself arrested. I'll be irritated if I have to intervene with your detective friend to spring you."

"Understood."

"Get back to work. I'm going to bed." Logan ended the call.

Damon heaved himself to his feet and went into his office to check Rayna's phone, where he'd left it in a desk drawer. There was a missed call from Annemarie and a text: *Cops are gone now. Call me.*

He texted her back. *What happened? What did they say?*

Annemarie's response: *If you want to know, call me.*

I'm so tired I can't think. I'll call you in the morning. I'm going to bed.

Fine call me in the morning. Be ready to tell me what's going on between you and Damon because the guy's lying and covering for you and Stafford knows it.

Damon grimaced. *I have no idea what you're talking about. I'll call you tomorrow.*

No response from Annemarie.

He set his phone on the desk next to Rayna's and waited. If Annemarie wasn't getting answers from Rayna, frustration would likely propel her to confront

Damon. As he'd expected, a message from Annemarie popped onto his screen. *As soon as Detective Stafford is done with you call me. Immediately.*

He texted back. *Stafford's done with me. I'm coming over to your house. I'd rather talk with you in person. Be there in ten.*

No reply from Annemarie. She was probably too busy sorting through her kitchen knives, choosing one to sink into his heart.

When he reached the neighborhood, he sensed Jody in her home down the street from the Bristols'. She had, without a doubt, kept an eye on the police activity. Tomorrow, he'd seek out her take on things.

The Bristols' front door opened before he'd exited his car, and Annemarie stepped onto the porch. Her heart was beating fast. This conversation was going to be far less civil than the one he'd had with Stafford.

Keeping a conciliatory expression on his face, he approached her. Behind her, Seth hovered in the doorway like a nervous bodyguard who hoped he wouldn't have to spar with anyone.

Damon stopped at the edge of the porch. "Annemarie—"

"What have you done to my sister?"

For an instant, the memory of tackling a panicked Rayna and holding her so Maggie could sedate her made it impossible for Damon to meet Annemarie's gaze. "I don't know what Detective Stafford told you, but let's sit down, and I'll explain."

"You're not coming into our house."

Seth touched her shoulder. "Babe, you're overreacting. Let him in."

Annemarie spun to face Seth. "I'm overreacting? You're *underreacting.* Do you have any idea how serious any of this is? Do you think this disaster is part of your video games?"

Seth's face hardened. "I think this mess will be all over town if you shout about it on the porch. Are you trying to give Jody a front-row seat?"

Annemarie muttered something under her breath and stalked into the house with such speed that Seth had to jump aside.

"*Sorry,*" Seth mouthed at Damon, waving for him to come in.

As soon as Seth had shut the door behind them, Annemarie started to speak, but Seth interrupted her. "Let the guy sit down."

Damon followed the Bristols into the living room. Seth and Annemarie sat on opposite ends of the couch.

Damon took the chair across from them. "I owe you an apol—"

"Where is Rayna?" Annemarie cut in.

"I don't know."

"You told me you hadn't seen her since Ben's death. Detective Stafford told me a witness saw you driving Rayna's car yesterday afternoon. Are you going to deny that?"

"No. I—"

"Where did you take her? Where did you leave her? She wasn't in the car with you unless you'd locked her in the trunk."

"She was in the passenger seat," Damon said. "She'd reclined the seat. The witness must not have been at an angle where he or she could see Rayna."

"She'd reclined the seat," Annemarie echoed. "Uh-huh. What, did you drug her?"

"She was exhausted. She fell asleep on our drive." He fleshed out the story with the same details he'd given Stafford.

"I think you're lying," Annemarie said. "You expect me to believe you stopped by here all helpful and innocent, took her for a nice drive, brought her home, then, *boom*, she disappears?"

"Annie, you've talked to her," Seth pointed out. "You know Damon didn't hurt her."

"Taking advantage of an emotionally vulnerable woman *is* hurting her. Did you scare her into thinking she was about to get arrested so her only option was to run away with you?"

"No," Damon said. "I never—"

"Now she either ignores my messages or acts all cagey and weird when she does respond to me. Refusing to tell me where she is? That's not like her. Is that *your* coaching? 'I'm the only one who can take care of you, baby. Don't tell anyone else where we are because they're all your enemies.'"

"That's a cold accusation." Seth tried again to intervene. "Of course she sounds weird when you talk to her. Most people would sound weird if an ex-boyfriend died in front of them and the cops think they might have murdered him."

"I'll tell you what else sounds weird," Annemarie snapped. "The fact that she'd let Damon 'help' her at all. I can't believe I was dumb enough to think, 'Oh, how nice that she trusts Damon; he must be an unusually great guy.' If she's so closed down that she won't even tell *me* where she is, she wouldn't be responding to contacts from a guy she's known for a month, let alone letting him *drive her car* while she sleeps in the passenger seat. Not unless he's really, really good at mind games and manipulation and she's in such a bad space that she can't recognize the abuse."

"Annemarie," Damon said quietly. "I'd never want to hurt—"

"What will you do if Stafford gets a warrant for her arrest? Panic her into making a run for it so this ends with a manhunt and a shootout?"

Seth gaped at her. "*Geez*, Annie. Enough with the wild accusations."

"I shouldn't have lied to you about seeing her the day after Ben died," Damon said. "That was a bad decision, and I'm sorry. But I don't want to hurt her. I want to help her."

Annemarie's eyes were glacial. "In that case, leave her alone. That will help a lot."

"I understand why you doubt my motives. But if she's willing to reach out to me, I'm not going to ghost her because her sister doesn't trust me."

"Solid point," Seth said. "Give the guy a break."

"Here's what you need to know." Annemarie all but hissed the words. "If you hurt Rayna in any way, I will make sure everyone in Willet Beach knows it. I will destroy your reputation here. People won't want to get interviewed by you—they'll want to burn you in effigy. Good luck on finishing your book. Have fun facing your sponsor and explaining why the project she's dumped piles of money into has disintegrated."

Seth winced. "Uh, Damon, forget she said that, and please don't sue us. Maybe you should go. Annie's not herself tonight."

"I understand." Damon didn't rise from his seat. He didn't want to retreat until he'd pushed for as much information as he could get. "You had your house searched by the police. Of course Annemarie's on edge, and I'm at fault for lying to her. May I ask if the police found anything?"

Annemarie's harsh "None of your business" and Seth's "Not that we know of" crashed against each other.

"We don't have anything to hide." Seth scooted across the couch so he was next to Annemarie and took her hand. "Would you believe they confiscated my ice-cream maker? The warrant said they were looking for evidence of ice cream being made along with substances that can be harmful if ingested. I sat there sweating, hoping they wouldn't find my microwave popcorn stash."

Annemarie yanked her hand away from Seth. "This isn't a joke."

"Yeah, it is, Annie. A stupid farce. I got my *ice-cream maker* taken into custody by the police. Tell me that's not a bad joke." He looked at Damon. "Stafford talked to Owl Cheney about ice cream too. Owl told me she'd asked him about a nonexistent flavor, chile-lime-coconut, and his single-serving cups. Pretty easy to piece things together, right? Someone dropped a sample at Ben's restaurant in one of Cheney's cups. Ben assumed it was legit, ate it, and croaked. Lucky that Lucy wasn't there, or he would've shared, and she'd be gone too."

"That's fortunate," Damon said.

"I'm betting Lucy isn't going to eat samples of desserts from this town ever again." Seth scratched a flake of dried skin off his sunburned nose. "If the killer was targeting her, too, and missed, what if they try again? Good thing she's holing up with her family in Monterey. Heyyyy. I just figured it out. Murder solved! It's been Damon all along."

Damon rolled his bruised shoulder, which ached despite being free from the holster and gun he'd left with Maggie. "I beg your pardon?"

"Yeah, admit it. Rayna sweet-talked you into taking out her enemies. She won't tell us where she is because she's currently in Hawaii while sucker Damon Hale does her dirty work. Who goes down after you get Lucy? Rayna's ex-husband? The ex-husband's new girlfriend? Annie was stalking him on social media, and he's posting all these pics with his new lady. I hope Rayna's paying your travel expenses to Denver."

"Stop it." Annemarie sagged backward on the couch, fatigue muting the anger in her face. "You've made your point. I got carried away on accusing Damon."

"Even if he did help Rayna run off, is that your problem to deal with?" Seth rested his hand on her thigh. "She's an adult. Let her deal with her own life. If it gets to the point of arresting her, the cops will get a warrant for her phone, and they'll GPS their way to her hideout. If Damon is reckless enough to gum up a homicide investigation, he'll end up in the slammer too. You want to go to prison, bro?"

"No," Damon said. "I want this investigation to succeed. I want to know what happened to Ben Orozco."

Annemarie's eyes filled with tears. "Do you think Rayna killed him?"

"I very much hope not. Do you?"

"No. That's not Rayna." Tears streamed down Annemarie's face. "She's . . . *too* kind. Too patient with people. She doesn't strike back. She hunkers down and endures."

"Come clean, bro," Seth said. "You're into this girl."

"I admit it, but I've made no attempts to initiate a relationship beyond friendship. Under current circumstances, that's not something I'd do, and not just because I'm afraid of Annemarie. I respect that this is rotten timing for Rayna on multiple levels."

Seth snickered. "Being afraid of Annemarie would be enough motivation."

Annemarie wiped her face. "I should apologize for threatening you, Damon. But I don't want to."

"You don't have to. I earned your mistrust. Do you know if Stafford has other suspects in Ben's murder? I couldn't get a straight answer out of her."

"Yeah, she doesn't do straight answers." Seth ran his fingers through his sun-bleached hair. "Know what I think? I think Ben died of natural causes and the whole poison angle is wishful imagination on Stafford's part. She's only been in Willet Beach for a year or two. This is the first mysterious death she's had to deal with in town, so she's making the most of it. Blowing things out of proportion."

"She must have more evidence of poisoning than her imagination, or she wouldn't have been able to get a warrant," Damon said.

"Okay, maybe. But the cops had better not damage my ice-cream maker. It belonged to my grandpa."

"Quit grousing about your ice-cream maker," Annemarie said irritably.

"Have you heard *anyone* float the names of people who might have had a beef with Ben?" Damon asked.

"No," Seth said. "Ben's a likable guy. Everybody was happy he was renovating that old restaurant."

"I wasn't," Annemarie said. "Couldn't he and Lucy have gone somewhere else? Rayna shouldn't have had to deal with them being here."

"Babe, they moved back here before she did."

"I don't care!" Annemarie snarled. "After the way they betrayed her, leaving Willet Beach would be the least they could do. And *you* sold them that wretched restaurant."

"It was a business transaction—"

"Mike told me he saw you and Ben out surfing last week. You are—you *were*—hanging around with him, weren't you? Best buds with the guy who treated Rayna like trash?"

Seth stood. "Yeah, so, we're going way off in the weeds here. You'd better clear out, Damon. I think Annie needs to go to bed."

CHAPTER 22

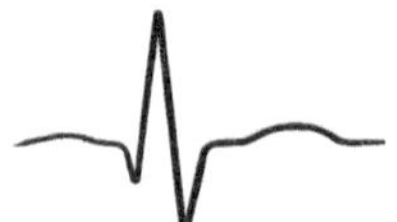

Rayna kept thinking she'd returned to full alertness, but she didn't seem to be getting Maggie's "What is your name?- and "Do you know where you are?"-type questions right. Maggie kept repeating them, or maybe Rayna only thought she was repeating them, or maybe Rayna was repeating her answers, forgetting she'd given them. She kept trying to get out of bed but never seemed to finish the motion; she kept finding herself back on the mattress, her head on her pillow.

"Take it slowly." Maggie rested her hand on Rayna's shoulder firmly enough that it would be too much work to push against it in another attempt to sit up. "There's no rush."

No rush. Yes, there was a rush, but Rayna couldn't think of what it was. Damon was in the room as well, standing near the window.

Window. She'd meant to go out the window of the library. She'd tried to escape. Failed.

Annemarie. The search warrant. "What happened?" Why was her voice so croaky? "The search warrant."

"I'll tell you when you're more coherent," Damon said.

"It's all right if I'm not. Tell me anyway."

"If he does, he'll have to tell you twice." Maggie squeezed her shoulder. "I'm going to scramble some eggs. We all need breakfast. Damon, sit with her, please, and don't let her get out of bed yet."

Damon pulled a chair up to the bed and sat.

Rayna tried to focus on him. "The search warrant," she said. "There was a search warrant."

"Close your eyes and relax while Maggie makes breakfast," Damon said. "After you've eaten, I'll answer your questions."

"Okay." Rayna closed her eyes, her thoughts skidding around on the remnants of the medication that had been dripping into her arm all night. "Wait." She opened her eyes. "Are you going to kill me?"

"No. Relax."

"I tried to escape."

"Under the circumstances, I can't blame you for momentarily losing it. Just don't try it again."

"I'm glad you didn't shoot me." Rayna closed her eyes. A new question bounced into her head, and she opened her eyes again. "If you do decide that I'm a . . . danger to all mankind . . . what happens? Is there an official death sentence pronounced? Or does nobody tell me and Maggie knocks me out like usual, only this time I never wake up?"

The remote expression on his face would have been impossible to read even had her brain been fully functional. "We're a long way from that point."

"I don't think you'd tell me." Rayna lifted her left arm and eyeballed the tube piercing her vein. "Why would you create trouble for yourself when it would be so easy to kill me without warning?" She let her arm fall to the bed. "Nothing's stopping you legally . . . assuming you'd follow any legal requirements. You're not a freelance killer, are you? Or an agent who went rogue? I don't think you are."

"I'm not." Damon scratched his shoulder beneath the strap of his holster. "What I tell you is left to my judgment. Unless being candid with you would put lives in danger, I'll keep you updated on any decisions."

"That's very kind," Rayna said blearily, which felt like the wrong response, though she couldn't analyze why.

"As I said, we're a long way from any decisions you'd need to worry about."

"Are you trying to keep me from panicking, thinking it's the end every time Maggie goes to drug me?"

"I'm being straightforward with you."

She blinked at the ceiling, appreciating the toast-and-cinnamon aroma now wafting from the kitchen. "Have you had to do that before? Execute someone?"

"Rayna, you're doped out of your mind. How about you stop talking and give yourself time to fully wake up?"

He didn't want to answer the question. "The search warrant," she said. "Did you talk to Annemarie?"

"Yes."

"Is she furious with me?"

"No."

"She thinks I'm a monster," Rayna said. "Wait. A liar. She thinks I'm a liar. If I weren't a liar, I'd be a monster. Am I making sense?"

"Barely."

"It's hard for you, isn't it? Executing someone. I think it would be hard for you. You'd care."

For a long moment, he looked at her—looked through her? His expression didn't seem stony to Rayna now. It seemed haunted. "It's hard," he said. "But the consequences of not doing my duty when it's necessary are far harder to live with."

"I'm sorry," she said. "That's not a job I'd want."

"It's not a job I want either, but there aren't a lot of people who can do it."

"Because dealing with Trespassers is too dangerous? Except for another Trespasser?"

"Yes."

"That makes sense." Idly, she tracked Maggie around the kitchen. Switched her focus to Damon. Back to Maggie. Back to Damon. "Did you talk to Annemarie? Did I already ask you that?"

"Yes. I talked with her."

"What happened with the search warrant?"

He sighed and leaned back in his chair. "Seth got his ice-cream maker confiscated."

"His ice-cream maker?"

Damon summarized what he'd learned about the search. Rayna concentrated as hard as she could, determined to follow and retain the report.

"Chile-lime-coconut ice cream," she said. "Strong flavors to mask poison, maybe?"

"Maybe."

"Lucy wouldn't have been in danger from it if she'd been home. She wouldn't have eaten it. She's allergic to coconut."

"She is? That's interesting."

"Has Detective Stafford called me yet?"

"No."

"I wonder why not. She's searching my place and my sister's place, but she's not questioning me directly?"

"She did question you directly, right after Ben died. She thinks you lied to her. She's gathering evidence against you so when she calls you in again, she'll be ready to rip those lies apart."

"And arrest me. But she won't find any evidence. Wait, no, she will find evidence. Not against me though. Or maybe she won't find evidence. Maybe his death was an accident."

"Someone didn't accidentally put a flavor of ice cream that Cheney doesn't make into one of Cheney's cups and drop it off at The Sanddab with Cheney's business card."

"That's how it got delivered?"

"Cheney said Detective Stafford asked him and his staff about his individual-serving takeout cups and his business cards. I'm assuming those items were involved. Can you think of anyone who might have had a motive to kill Ben?"

Was he sincerely considering culprits beyond Rayna? "No."

"Ben cheated and lied in your relationship. A man who'd do that probably wasn't a stellar example of integrity in every other facet of his life—unless he got his act together. Did he?"

"I have no idea. We just talked about pottery. He and Lucy seemed happy. She said he was thrilled to be a dad. He was insanely excited about opening his new restaurant."

Maggie was approaching. Cautiously, Rayna pushed herself to a sitting position. She didn't feel light-headed, so she remained sitting as Maggie entered the room.

"How are you feeling?" Maggie asked.

"Fine." Rayna flipped the covers back. Maggie or Damon had removed her hoodie and her shoes, but she was wearing yesterday's T-shirt, jeans, and socks. "May I take a shower?"

"After breakfast, when I'm sure you're steady on your feet," Maggie said. "I'll wrap your arm to keep the IV site dry. Eggs and toast are ready. Do you feel up to coming to the table?"

"Yes." Rayna swung her legs over the side of the bed. Damon hastily moved to take her by the arm, either out of concern for her balance or out of concern that she'd bolt toward the window. Probably both.

"I owe you an apology," he said as he escorted her to the table. "I'm in hot water with Annemarie, and she's going to hound you about me when you talk with her this morning."

"*You're* in hot water? What did you do?"

"Made a rookie mistake," he said. "I'll explain while we eat."

* * *

After breakfast and a shower, Rayna sat at the kitchen table with Damon and nervously eyed her phone on the table in front of him. Endorsing Damon's tale of why he'd been driving her car wouldn't be difficult, but she dreaded fielding more of Annemarie's accusations that she'd been making up "crazy stories" out of guilt over Ben's death.

"I'm fine *not* talking to Annemarie right now," she said. "If that's an option."

"It's an option that will get her more upset, which we don't want," Damon said. "I know you're concerned about recanting your admission that you can link-kill if Annemarie brings that up. Let me elaborate a little on why I'm asking you to do that. The members of the team I work with aren't the only people aware that Trespassers exist. There are others, some of whom are extremely dangerous, who might attempt to recruit Trespassers for their own purposes."

Rayna pulled the sleeves of her overlarge cardigan down over her icy hands. "You mean, like . . . hiring Trespassers as assassins."

"Or using family members of Trespassers as leverage to pressure Trespassers into cooperation."

"Or eliminating Trespassers they regard as rivals? Or experimenting on them?"

"Those are all possibilities." His words were so measured and calm that he sounded almost robotic. "The less Annemarie knows, the less likely it will be that she'll inadvertently draw attention or react suspiciously if she's ever approached. I know trying to withdraw what you told her is problematic, and if it creates more issues than it solves, we can reevaluate. But please try it."

Thoughts of Annemarie and her family in danger crashed through Rayna's mind like an avalanche. She wasn't sure how much denying her abilities could help now, but if it could help even a minuscule amount, she wasn't going to protest.

"I know you're still questioning if I pose that brand of danger to you and your family," Damon said. "I can't ask for your trust, but I'm asking for your cooperation."

Trust. It was surreal remembering how surprisingly easy it had been for her to trust Damon. To confide in him. To like him. Until the instant he'd seized her and stabbed a needle into her arm and she'd tried to kill him, literally kill him.

His left hand rested next to her phone, a taut hand with fingers arched, fingertips pressing against the table, tendons stretching his skin. A small scar marked the knuckle of his thumb. Mindlessly, she stared at his hand. She'd tried to kill another human being. If he weren't a Trespasser, he'd be dead now.

"Rayna?"

"Yes. Sorry." Rayna refocused her thoughts. "I'll cooperate. I'll try to retract what I told her."

"Thank you. Ready to talk to her?"

Rayna nodded.

Damon tapped the phone, calling Annemarie.

Voice mail, to Rayna's relief. An opportunity to stall a little longer. "Hi, Annie. You're probably swamped with customers, so just call me back when you can. I'm sorry for all the stress I've been causing you. Talk to you soon."

Damon disconnected the call and stood. "I'll stay here at the cabin as long as I can today. Maggie would like to get started on interviewing you. She has an endless string of questions and tests related to your abilities."

"Okay." Rayna's shower-damp hair felt cold and seaweedy against her neck. She should have dried it or put it up, and now, she didn't want to make Damon edgier by asking to leave the room for more grooming. After last night's blundering escape attempt, he was on high alert. He'd already stood in the hallway directly outside her bedroom while she'd gotten ready, warning her that any move toward the window would bring him into the room. She searched the pockets of the flannel lounge pants she'd chosen and was glad to find a hair elastic.

While Rayna secured her hair into a sloppy bun, Maggie rose from the couch in the living room. "Damon, where do you want us?"

"Not the library or anywhere else with a closed door. You can sit here at the table or stay in the living room."

"Living room, then. Those kitchen chairs make my back ache." Maggie beckoned to Rayna. "Let's rearrange the furniture."

Under Maggie's direction, Rayna helped position two faded wood-frame club chairs beneath the windows, with the chairs facing each other and a lamp table between them. On the table, Maggie set her laptop, two glasses of water, and a digital recorder similar to the one Rayna had seen Damon use in interviews.

"Here's the deal," Maggie said as they settled into the chairs. "If you get tired, need a bathroom break, need to get up and stretch . . . if you need a break for any reason, let me know. This isn't meant to be an intimidating or miserable experience for you."

"Okay. Thank you."

"If there are any questions you don't want to answer, please don't give me false information. Tell me you don't want to answer, and I'll set the question aside for now."

"Okay."

"I'll be recording us, but this is for research purposes only and will be held wholly confidential." Maggie activated the digital recorder. "First off, let's dig into the timeline of your Trespasser abilities. What is the first time you recall being aware of your ability to sense people?"

"I don't recall ever *not* being able to do that," Rayna said. "When I was little, I thought everyone could. I remember when I was . . . three or four? . . . we were camping, and my mom got upset with me for not responding when she called me. She kept telling me I'd scared her, that she'd thought I was lost. I'd been sitting behind a tree arranging pine cones I'd found, and I remember being confused. I was close by. How could she not know where I was?"

"Do you recall anyone on either side of your extended family ever mentioning having extrasensory abilities or referring to a relative—living or dead—who had them?"

"No."

"Even in jest? Like, 'Grandma always said Great-Great-Aunt Gertrude had eyes in the back of her head; she always knew what people were up to'?"

"No. I'd remember it, even if it had been a joke. As soon as I was old enough to realize I could do something other people couldn't and that it freaked my parents out, I was always on alert for any hint that I wasn't the only glitchy one."

"You're not glitchy. You have remarkable abilities we don't understand but would like to."

Rayna glanced at Damon, who was sitting at the kitchen table, typing on his computer. "Considering that the government has labeled us 'Trespassers' and I'm currently being held prisoner, I don't think our abilities are viewed as 'remarkable' in a positive way."

"Unfortunately, your remarkable abilities can also be used as a deadly weapon," Maggie said. "That makes things complicated."

"A little," Rayna said dryly.

* * *

Throughout the morning, Damon kept himself in the background while Maggie interviewed Rayna. Not wanting any open interest from him to make Rayna more reticent, he spent most of his time feigning concentration on the laptop in front of him while he listened to the discussion. As the hours passed, Rayna became increasingly relaxed under Maggie's friendly questioning. She talked readily, giving full answers and even volunteering information Maggie hadn't specifically asked for. She smiled. She laughed at Maggie's jokes; she cracked jokes of her own. Even when the questions delved into sensitive areas, such as her miscarriages, she didn't hold back as far as Damon could tell. He suspected she found it a relief to talk openly with someone who didn't find anything about her the slightest bit strange. When a text from Annemarie showed up on Rayna's phone—*Store's crazy today. Spring break crowd. I'll call you tonight and you'd better be ready for a serious conversation*—Damon responded with an *Okay* and didn't pass the message along to Rayna. He'd tell her later. He didn't want to interrupt the rhythm of the interview.

He sent an email to Jody, telling her he wouldn't be in the office today and asking if she'd learned anything relating to her "special assignment." Just before lunchtime, a reply came: Jody wanted him to call her as soon as he was available. She had very important things she wanted to discuss. He questioned how important her information would be, but nonetheless, he didn't want to delay, and that wasn't a conversation he wanted to have in front of Rayna.

He looked over at Rayna and Maggie. He was confident Rayna wouldn't link with Maggie and attempt to kill her. He wasn't as confident that she wouldn't try another reckless dash for freedom. She'd been calm and cooperative all morning, but the stressors that had provoked last night's resistance were still there. If he was out of the room for a significant length of time and distracted by a phone call, he wasn't willing to gamble that Rayna wouldn't jump on that opportunity.

He pushed back from the table and took the handcuffs from his pocket. As he approached the women, Maggie paused in her explanation of an experiment she wanted to run. Rayna stiffened, her gaze on the handcuffs.

"Excuse me for interrupting," he said. "I need to make a call. I'll go into the library to take care of that. Rayna, I apologize for this, but while I'm out of the room, I need to make sure you stay here. Right hand, please."

Avoiding eye contact, Rayna held out her hand. Damon clicked one link of the handcuffs around her wrist and the other around the wooden arm of the chair. "I'll remove the cuffs as soon as I'm done with my call."

"She's going to run away," Maggie said. "As soon as you leave the room, she'll drag that big old chair along with her, go crashing through a window, and scale a redwood to live with the squirrels. While I watch it happen and take notes."

"Take thorough notes, then, because I want to know how she gets the chair up the tree."

"I won't climb the tree," Rayna said, the tension in her face relaxing a little. "You'll find me sitting in the shade, stressing over how much it's going to cost me to replace the broken window."

Maggie laughed. "Go make your call, Damon. We'll be fine."

Damon retreated into the library, closed the door, and called Jody.

CHAPTER 23

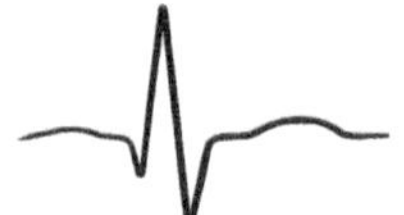

"OH, MR. HALE, I'M *SO* glad you got back to me." Jody answered the phone with enthusiasm. "Where are you today? I was hoping to give you this report in person."

"I have other research I need to work on," Damon said. "What have you learned?"

"First, you probably already know this because I saw your car in front of the Bristols' home last night after the police were there, but in case they didn't tell you everything, here's what I learned from Seth this morning. I caught him when he was returning home after taking the kids to school, and I asked him what the police had been up to. It turns out they had a search warrant to hunt through the kitchens in both the main house and the guesthouse *and* through the garbage cans." Jody rattled on about the search. Damon let her talk, hoping to pick up something he didn't already know.

"Ice cream!" Jody said after detailing the confiscating of Seth's ice-cream maker. "What an absolutely vicious way to administer poison, don't you think?"

"How sure are the police that that's what killed Ben?"

"Well, I can tell you *this*. I met my friend Sgt. Fischer for brunch this morning, and after I told him what *I* knew, he added a bit: they found a two-thirds-empty Cheney's ice-cream container in a minifridge in Ben's office, and preliminary tests on it showed something suspicious. He wouldn't get more specific than that, and he wouldn't tell me if they were sure that's what killed Ben. I asked if they were going to arrest Rayna, and he said he didn't know yet." She moaned. "Why ice cream? Ice cream should always be a delightful experience. The Grill has benefited so much by being next door to Cheney's. We bring each other customers. Kaitlyn calls it a symbiotic relationship."

"I'm sure it is. Both of your establishments are the best of their kind."

"Oh, thank you so much. I said to Seth, 'My stars, this must be so embarrassing for you, having police poking through your things,' and he said it was all ridiculous and they didn't find any evidence that Rayna poisoned Ben, and he doubts anyone poisoned Ben. I said, 'Oh, Seth, you're such a good-natured boy, you don't realize that people around you can do horrible things.' In confidence, Mr. Hale, my Glenn wasn't a big fan of Seth. Did I tell you that?"

"You mentioned he thought Seth was immature."

"Yes. 'You'll have to support that boy'—that's what Glenn kept telling Annemarie. Glenn was too hard on people. But I'd have to say Seth *is* naive, not realizing there might be a murderer close by. This is horrible, and I don't want to say it, but it's getting more and more likely that Rayna is a killer—and a serial killer at that! That darling girl, a murderer! Listen to this. The detective in charge of the case interviewed *me* this morning!"

Damon sat on the edge of the desk. In the living room, the anxious acceleration he'd provoked in Rayna's pulse rate had slowed, and the muted cadence of conversation between Maggie and her sounded amiable. "What did the detective ask you?"

"I thought she was going to ask me about Ben Orozco, of course, and I thought, 'Oh dear, she'll be disappointed because I hardly knew Ben at all.' Kaitlyn was the one who was friends with him in high school and who'd been helping him lately with restaurant advice. She was *so* willing to assist him, so generous. I thought she'd regard him as a competitor, to be honest, and tell him he was on his own!

"But Detective Stafford wanted to know about Glenn Kirkpatrick. She asked me about his daughters' relationships with him and wanted details about the night he died. She wouldn't say so straight out, but I could tell what she was up to: she thinks *Glenn* was murdered! Glenn! We all assumed it was his heart, but maybe he was poisoned like Ben."

"Do you think he was murdered?" Damon asked.

"Well, at first I thought it was silly, but you know, it *does* make sense. He was so thoughtless to Rayna. After everything she'd been through . . . losing all those pregnancies and getting dumped by her husband . . . the way Glenn treated her at his birthday dinner *was* shocking. Would it be that surprising if she cracked and killed him?"

"What do you think?"

"I think there's *something* wrong with her. I told you Glenn always said she was odd, but he would never elaborate. Don't you think that's suspicious that he wouldn't elaborate? When I would ask Jeanette about it—Jeanette is Rayna's mother—she'd say Glenn didn't know how to handle having a shy daughter when Glenn was so outgoing himself. But now I'm thinking it must have been more than that. What if there was something frightening about her? Something sinister? And that got me thinking even more. You know how Elliott, my husband, died in a fishing accident?"

"Yes. I'm sorry."

"Thank you. Or we all *assumed* it was an accident, like we assumed Glenn's death was natural causes. But here's something to consider. Elliott wasn't kind to Rayna either, though I'm sure he meant no harm. Men are so tactless—no offense, Mr. Hale."

"In what way was Elliott tactless?"

"Our families were friends, as I've told you, and he'd heard Glenn describe Rayna as an odd duck. Elliott never passed up a chance to tease someone, so he would quack at Rayna when we'd get together, which I could tell embarrassed her. I'd tell him to stop, but he'd ignore me. He wouldn't do it in front of Jeanette, of course."

Damon frowned at the thought of child Rayna getting mocked by her father's friend. Jody had a pattern of being attracted to domineering jerks.

"The Kirkpatricks went with us on Elliott's fishing boat many times," Jody said. "Rayna was familiar with it. It would have been easy for her to hide somewhere on board when Elliott went out to fish that last day, then, after he'd had *far* too many beers, to push him overboard."

Damon wasn't sure whether to be alarmed by this theory or annoyed with himself for giving drama-loving Jody this assignment. "How long ago did he die?"

"Three years ago," Jody said. "It will be three years in June."

"Was Rayna in town when he died?"

"She must have been. I remember her being at the funeral. Isn't that suspicious that she'd happen to be here when she was living so far away?"

It was definitely worth investigating, Damon thought grimly. "Can you think of any particular reason she'd have gone after Elliott at that time? Anything that might have pushed her too far?"

"No, but something must have occurred in her personal life that made her want to strike out. Maybe that's when her husband told her he was leaving her? I don't know. I plan to call Jeanette to see what I can learn. The police would need to figure out how Rayna got back to shore after pushing him overboard, but that's where my new idea comes in. It might have been a team murder."

"A team murder?"

"Yes. One person hides on the boat and kills Elliott. Then the partner jet skis out, or what have you, to pick her up and get her back to shore."

"Who do you think the partner was?"

"Look at the big picture. Annemarie has always been protective of her little sister. Maybe she and Rayna together decided to take care of the people who'd hurt Rayna. My Elliott. Their father—and both girls inherited money from their father, so they both have another motive there, don't you think? And Ben Orozco—Kaitlyn told me Annemarie was furious at how Ben had treated Rayna, and she was upset about him moving back here. Here was Rayna coming home to make a new life, and there's this nasty reminder of her past! It would make sense, wouldn't it, if the two of them were working together?"

"It's an interesting theory." It could also be applied to journalist Collin Burgess's death. But if Rayna's relationship with her sister included conspiring to commit murders, she would have told Annemarie of her full Trespasser abilities long ago, not shocked her with that revelation the night of Ben's death.

"Be *very* careful around the Kirkpatrick girls," Jody said. "Just because they're lovely, sweet girls doesn't mean they aren't dangerous. I know Elliott would never have fathomed they could lash out. He thought women were weak. He was so foolish at times. Listen to this, Mr. Hale. Seth told me Rayna ran away, left town without telling anyone where she was going. That's suspicious, isn't it? That she'd run off?"

"Maybe she needed time away."

"You're too trusting. Seth said Annemarie is worried to death about her. I wonder if Rayna and Annemarie had a falling-out over Ben's murder. Maybe being there when he died was too much for Rayna."

"Have you found any hints that someone other than the Kirkpatricks might have wanted Ben dead?"

"Of course the spouse is always a suspect, and I did call Lucy's mother to express my sympathy in hopes that I could learn if there were problems in Ben and Lucy's marriage. I ended up leaving a voice mail, and she hasn't called me back yet. I'll try again in a few days. I doubt she'll have anything helpful for us though. Kaitlyn talked a lot with Ben about his restaurant, and she told me he never gave any signs that there was strain in his marriage."

"Thank you for checking. You've been a great help."

"My pleasure, and *be careful.* I don't want you to be the next victim."

"I'll be careful."

"I mean it," Jody said sternly. "I'm afraid you might be gaga over Rayna and you'll let your guard down."

"I won't let my guard down. You be careful too. Please don't tell anyone what we've discussed. Don't do anything that might tip someone off that you're too interested in this case."

"The only thing that would tip people off that something was up would be if I *weren't* interested in the case." Jody giggled. "Don't worry. I won't tell anyone you're paying me to research this. I can keep secrets, and I know you want the scoop."

"Thanks, Jody. Talk to you soon." Damon hung up.

Taking the handcuff key from his pocket, he went to free Rayna. "What do you know about Elliott Wyeth's death?"

She looked up at him, weariness in her eyes. "I know I didn't murder him. He drowned when he was out fishing alone. Got drunk and fell overboard. I was in Denver at the time of his death, and if you need a witness for that, my ex-husband can verify it."

"You attended the funeral?"

"Yes. I wouldn't have, but my mother was concerned that we all show support for Jody. She flew in for the funeral, and she bought me a plane ticket. Will I have to answer for every death that's occurred in Willet Beach since I was born?"

"No," Maggie said. "Just since your ability to link-kill manifested."

"That's all the information I have about Mr. Wyeth's death," Rayna said. "I'm sure Jody will give you any details that . . ." She paused. "Or does Jody think I killed him?"

"Jody has some creative theories." Damon slid the handcuffs into his pocket. "I'm not accusing you of killing him. I'm gathering information."

"She must have found out Detective Stafford is interested in my father's death and decided if I killed him, I killed Elliott, too, because . . . it's a habit of mine?"

"She said he liked to tease you in cruel ways."

"He did, but he treated his own family a lot worse than he treated me."

"Jody suggested you and Annemarie might work in tandem committing murders. Elliott, your father, Ben."

"Seriously? That's a new one. Did you tell her when it comes to murder, I don't need help?"

"No," Damon said. "And don't worry. I'm aware that any information or theories she provides require rigorous sifting. What would you like for lunch? We have ingredients for spaghetti or hamburgers."

* * *

The afternoon was an uneventful continuation of interview questions and tests, but as twilight neared, Rayna's apprehension grew. She'd brushed off Jody's irrational suspicion of Annemarie, but the more she thought about what Damon had said, the more anxious she got. She'd assumed Stafford had attained a warrant to search both the guesthouse and Annemarie's kitchen because Rayna could have used either location to produce poisoned ice cream. But what if Stafford actually suspected Annemarie of killing Ben? What if Stafford thought Rayna had rushed toward Ben's restaurant in a panic because she'd discovered Annemarie had poisoned him and she'd hoped to intervene before it was too late? The more Rayna worried, the more she wanted to speak with Annemarie but also feared it. What if Annemarie got arrested for murder?

With dinner over, Maggie told Rayna to take it easy for a while, an instruction Rayna had trouble following. She sat in the chair near the fireplace, flipping through her pottery magazine without reading it, watching out of the corner of her eye for Damon to reach for her phone. He was working on his laptop, Rayna's phone on the couch cushion next to him. Maggie had gone into the library and closed the door, Rayna assumed to write up reports on the work she'd done with Rayna today.

Damon reached for the phone. Rayna jumped, knocking the magazine off her lap.

He set the phone down. "If you'd like, you can call her instead of waiting for her to call you."

"No." Rayna picked up the magazine. "If she's had a hectic day on top of everything else, I'd rather let her choose the time to call."

"Do you want to text her?"

"No. I'll wait. What I really want is to go for a walk, but I'm guessing that's not an option."

"Unfortunately not. If we get too far from the cabin, we'll lose the link to the satellite connector that's allowing us cell phone service."

Rayna suspected that wasn't the only reason a walk wasn't an option, but it was one she wouldn't protest. "What's your story?" she asked. "How did you end up on this Trespasser team? Did they find you like you found me?"

He brushed a spiderweb away from the lampshade on the table next to him. "Yes, but it was earlier in my life. Midteens."

"What gave you away?"

He rotated the lamp and brushed away another spiderweb. "An article in my local paper. A kid from my high school was hiking and got separated from his friends. This was in late fall, snow was forecast for that night, and the guy only had a sweatshirt. A bunch of people volunteered to help the search-and-rescue team. I was one of them."

"You found him."

"Yes. Turned out he'd been taking pictures of the scenery, got too close to the edge of the trail, and lost his balance—they figured this out from the last pictures on his phone; he couldn't remember it—and he went crashing down a hill. Broke some bones, including his skull. The way he'd fallen, he was in an area very difficult to see, nearly hidden by some rocks."

"Did he survive?"

"Yes. Recovery took a long time, but eventually, he was fine."

"And your role in his rescue made the news."

"Not by my doing. But his parents were intensely, publicly grateful, and next thing I knew, there was a reporter on my doorstep. I tried to play it off as a lucky guess, but my mother wouldn't go for that. She told the reporter the truth."

Yearning flickered in Rayna. "Your parents were proud of your ability."

"They believed we all have gifts from God, and this was one of mine. It was something to be grateful for, not something to be ashamed of. I was a shy kid who didn't want the spotlight, and they respected that, but given circumstances like this, they weren't going to pretend my gift didn't exist, and they were going to thank God for it."

"A gift from God," Rayna murmured. "That sounds a lot nicer than a glitch, which is what my father called it. And he never even knew the dark side of what I can do."

"Any gift can be used for good or evil," Damon said. "Anyone can choose to do harm or not do harm."

"You're still trying to figure out what harm I've done." Rayna averted her eyes; she didn't want to see his expression shift from contemplative to flinty. "I googled you right after we met, before that first interview. I didn't see any news articles about you helping rescue an injured hiker."

"The articles aren't there anymore. They all got deleted."

"By your government people."

"Yes."

"But your community knew. People must think of it every time you go back . . . *Do* you go back?"

"No. A week after that rescue got publicized, a member of the Trespasser team showed up on our doorstep. Interviews, tests, all discreetly conducted. Shortly after that, my family was relocated to the East Coast."

"Did your parents *want* to relocate?"

"They wanted whatever was best for—" Damon picked up Rayna's phone. "It's Annemarie."

Rayna dropped her magazine, sprang to her feet, and came to sit next to him. "I'm ready."

He answered the call and switched it to speaker mode.

"Hi," Rayna said. "Thanks for—"

"I'm . . . at the . . . ER." Annemarie's voice shook, each word nearly fracturing. "Seth is sick, really sick."

Fear slashed through Rayna's chest. "What's wrong with him?"

"I don't know." Annemarie inhaled several ragged breaths before continuing. "I was stuck at the Umbrella—we were closed, but I was so behind on my work. He called and said he felt horrible and had a fever, and I told him to stop whining, take some Tylenol, and lie down. He said, 'No, it's different; something's wrong,' so I went home. I found him lying on the bathroom floor . . . out of his mind, like delirious . . . I called 911, and they brought him in."

"They don't know what's going on with him?"

"I'm not sure . . . They're working on him; I had to step out to give them space. He's in bad shape . . . Ray, with everything that's been happening . . . I think he's been poisoned."

"*What?* Why would—"

"I need you with me," Annemarie sobbed. "I can't handle this on my own. Please come home. I need you. I'm sorry for what I said yesterday. I know you wouldn't have hurt Ben. Please . . . I don't care what—I have to hang up. The doctor's here." The call ended.

Cries formed inside Rayna, a mashup of terror and rage she could barely hold back. She faced Damon, struggling to speak calmly. "Whatever precautions you need to take, whatever you want me to say or not say, I'll cooperate. I won't cause you any trouble. I'll return here with you once she has the support she needs. But please, let me go to her." She couldn't hold her composure; words were already scraping against each other and breaking apart. "*Please*, Damon. I can't leave her to—"

Damon rested his hand on her shoulder, his grasp weighty but gentle. "I'll take you to her," he said. "I'll text her—from your phone—and tell her you'll be there in an hour."

Relief washed through Rayna with such force that she couldn't find words to thank him.

“We’ll work out the details of our story on the way,” Damon said. “But you cannot say anything to anyone—including Annemarie or Detective Stafford—about who I am, who I work for, why you’ve been away from home, or what you’ve learned about Trespassers.”

“I won’t.”

“If you do, that rips this operation out of my hands. No second chances. You’ll be viewed as a dangerous liability, we’ll remove you from Willet Beach immediately, and you won’t return. Everyone there—including your family—will assume you’re dead.”

Will I be *dead?* Rayna didn’t ask the question out loud. The answer seemed obvious, and she didn’t want to hear him say it. “I understand.”

He stood. “Go pack your things, and I’ll get Maggie to take that tube out of your arm.”

CHAPTER 24

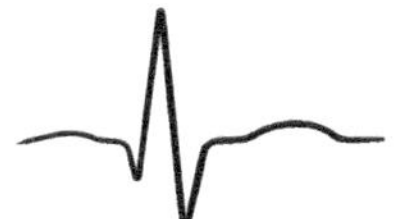

In a far corner of the hospital parking lot, Damon switched off the engine and flexed his surprisingly stiff fingers. He must have spent the drive gripping the steering wheel like it might break loose and fly out the window. "Detective Stafford's here," he said. "I assume you noticed."

"What?" Rayna sounded bewildered. "Oh, right. I was focused on Seth and Annemarie."

It didn't surprise Damon that Rayna had been too preoccupied with Seth's erratic pulse and Annemarie's rapid, panicky one to sense the detective's presence. Stafford was in the parking lot, stationary. She must be sitting in her car. Waiting for what?

"If she's here, does that mean Seth *was* poisoned?" Rayna asked.

"I don't know. But if she sees you, she might want to question you, about Ben *and* Seth."

"I'm ready."

Damon hoped she was. On the drive from the cabin, he'd given her the guidelines he and Logan had agreed upon in an earlier discussion of how to handle things if Damon allowed Rayna to return to Willet Beach to get questioned again by the police. She couldn't say anything about link-killing, but she didn't have to retract what she'd already told Stafford about her extrasensory abilities. If Stafford wanted proof, she could provide it. Refusing to provide proof might well lead to her arrest, which would be more problematic.

He wished Stafford hadn't been here tonight. He'd have liked additional time to fortify Rayna's rickety confidence that he was what he claimed before she had to speak with Stafford. But he'd known bringing her home would toss her into dicey situations and they'd both have to deal with whatever happened.

Seth's illness had been Damon's tipping point. After Annemarie's call, when Rayna had turned to him with raw desperation and pleading in her eyes, he'd known he could either let her go support her sister or he could stage her death and remove her permanently from Willet Beach. The halfway situation she was in was no longer tenable. Her devastation at being kept from her sister while Seth might be dying would shatter any willingness to cooperate and create such strain between her and his team that she'd view them as cold-blooded opponents, people she could never trust.

If she couldn't trust them, they couldn't trust her.

What had happened to Seth added significantly to the evidence that Rayna was not the one causing harm. It was time to loosen his grip—but not loosen it further than he had to. Under his lightweight jacket, he carried his gun, and zipped inside his jacket pocket were two filled syringes. The lives of everyone within Rayna's range were his responsibility, including that of the detective who might be investigating Rayna's sister for murder and attempted murder. But he was much less worried about the low probability that she'd attempt to kill Stafford or anyone else than he was that she'd cling to Stafford with frantic tales of having been kidnapped by a psychopath.

They walked toward the emergency room. Stafford stayed put. She probably hadn't noticed them.

"Do you want to text Annemarie to tell her we're here?" He handed Rayna her phone. In the parking lot lights, she looked colorless and disheveled.

"Yes. Thank you." She typed while she walked.

With one eye on the screen, Damon noted that her fingers were creating more typos than communication. He finally took her by the elbow and stopped her so she'd have a hope of finishing the message.

"Done." She held the phone out to him.

"Keep it."

She gave him a surprised glance and stuck the phone in the pocket of her flannel pants. "Thanks. I guess it would look pretty weird if you're guarding it from me."

"It wouldn't go over well with Annemarie." He'd texted Annemarie from his own phone, telling her he was giving Rayna a ride to the hospital—that earlier that afternoon, he'd managed to coax Rayna into telling him where she was staying. He'd gone to see her and had been with her when she had received news of Seth's illness.

"I won't contact anyone without your agreement," Rayna said. "I know you're taking a huge risk bringing me here. I promise, I'll stick to our plan."

"I appreciate that."

Wind blew a stray lock of hair across her eyes. She stuffed it into the bun on the back of her head. It blew free again, followed by another lock of hair on the other side. She yanked the hair tie out, which Damon didn't see as helpful. The wind now had a full head of hair to snarl.

"Do you need a moment?" he asked.

"No." She grabbed her hair with both hands and looped the hair tie around it, creating a ponytail that looked more controlled but still messy. Her phone pinged. She checked it. "Annemarie will meet us in the ER waiting room."

Damon sensed Annemarie's rapid approach. When the doors to the emergency department slid open, she rushed to throw her arms around Rayna. The sisters clung to each other, blocking the sidewalk and keeping the automatic doors open.

"Let the door close, ladies," a voice called.

Annemarie broke the embrace and hauled Rayna into the waiting room. "*Thank* you for coming, and you look awful. Have you slept at all this week?"

"I haven't done much besides sleep," Rayna said. Damon caught the trace of sarcasm in her voice. She clutched Annemarie's hands. "How is Seth?"

"Not great. But he's holding on." Tears trickled from Annemarie's swollen eyes. "They're getting ready to transfer him to the ICU. He's unconscious now; they gave him medication . . . He's having trouble breathing, so he's on a ventilator. They don't know exactly what they're dealing with. They have to wait for tests to come back. Nothing showed up in the initial tox screening, but that's for common stuff. But after what happened to Ben . . . Ray, this is *insane*."

"Do you have any idea how he . . . what he might have eaten?" Rayna asked.

"Like *ice cream*?" Annemarie drew her hands away from Rayna and wiped her eyes. "I have no idea. By the time I got home, he was too incoherent to answer questions. I can't believe that when he called me, I told him to stop *whining*." New tears spilled. "I need to call Detective Stafford to yell at her about how he's been poisoned and clearly this has nothing to do with you because you weren't even in town . . ."

"She's here," Rayna said. "In the parking lot."

"Did you talk to her?"

"No. I don't think she saw us. What can I do to help you? Where are the kids?"

"They're home. Jody's with them . . . I *know*, news is going to be all over town, but she saw the EMTs arrive, and I was desperate for someone to take care of them so I could go with Seth. Could you go relieve her and send her home? She's sweet with the kids, but I'd feel much better if you were with them instead."

"Yes, I'll do that."

"Are you sure you're up to it?" Annemarie touched Rayna's cheek. "You're having such a rough time. I could call Seth's parents, though they don't like driving at night—"

"I've got it. I'll take care of the kids. You focus on Seth." Rayna tilted her head toward Damon. "I even brought my own chauffeur."

"We're at your service," Damon said.

"Thank you." Annemarie hugged Rayna again. "Thank you, Damon. I'm sorry I was such a jerk to you."

"Don't worry about it."

"I need to get back to Seth. I'll call as soon as I have any updates." Annemarie sped back into the treatment area.

Damon and Rayna started toward the exit. Stafford was walking toward the hospital.

"Here we go," Rayna said, sotto voce.

The doors slid open, and they met Stafford on the sidewalk.

"Miss Rayna, I'm glad to see you're back." Stafford was wearing a flowered scarf over her hair, tied under her chin. "Mr. Hale, we meet again."

"Detective Stafford."

"I was sorry to hear Mr. Bristol is ill," Stafford said. "How is he doing?"

"Not well," Rayna said. "I hope you're working to figure out who did this to him, because it wasn't me, and it wasn't Annemarie."

"Who did what to him, Miss Rayna?"

"Poisoned him. Annemarie said . . . I don't know if . . ." Rayna paused. Damon could tell she was floundering, afraid she'd made Stafford even more suspicious.

"What makes you think he was poisoned, hon?"

"You've been implying Ben was poisoned." Rayna rallied. "You've been searching for poisons. Don't you think it's natural that Annemarie would suspect poisoning when Seth got sick all of a sudden?"

"I wasn't trying to trip you up. I just wondered if there was any news on the cause of his condition."

"Not yet. Annemarie told us they're admitting him to the ICU. I'm on my way to watch her kids for her so her neighbor can go home."

"That's a kind thing to do." Stafford's eyes shifted to Damon. "You're assisting her?"

"I'm the chauffeur," Damon said. "When she got the news about Seth, I was visiting with her, and I offered to drive her to the hospital."

"That's gallant, sir. Rayna, before you go take care of your niece and nephew, I need a moment of your time."

"I should get over there now," Rayna said. "The neighbor helping out is an older woman. She'll need to get to bed soon."

Stafford chuckled. "It's lucky she didn't hear you say that. Jody Wyeth can weather late nights better than the rest of us."

So, Stafford knew the situation. Had she learned it from Annemarie or from Jody? Damon could imagine Jody calling Stafford, eager to inform her of what had happened to Seth and to speculate on how it had occurred.

"I'll be astounded if you're able to persuade her to go home at all," Stafford added. "She'll be more than delighted to remain on duty for a spell. Come into the hospital with me. There's a lounge by the main entrance with plenty of private corners. Mr. Hale, you can mosey along to your car and wait for Rayna there."

Reluctantly, Damon walked toward the parking lot as Rayna and Stafford walked toward the main entrance. What would Rayna tell her when they were alone?

Once the two women were inside, Damon backtracked and sat on a bench under the entrance canopy. He rested his elbows on his knees and concentrated on Rayna and Stafford, grappling with the fear that he was making another catastrophic mistake.

She's not Tristan. If you can't trust her enough to let her have a conversation with Claire Stafford, why did you bring her here?

He closed his eyes, monitoring Rayna's heartbeat, monitoring Stafford's.

* * *

Stafford untied the scarf from around her blonde curls and tucked it into her blazer pocket. "Where would you like to sit?"

Rayna selected a seat in a corner where a grouping of chairs was partly shielded from the rest of the lobby by a tall planter filled with tropical foliage.

"Your sister's been worried about you." Stafford sat in a chair next to her. "Where have you been?"

"An Airbnb in Big Sur. I needed time on my own."

"On your own with Mr. Hale?"

"No. He didn't stay with me. We're just friends. He called me a couple of times, and I finally told him where I was. He came down today and was there when I got Annemarie's call about Seth. He drove me up here. We'll go back later to get my car."

"Just friends?"

"Yes."

"Someone saw him driving your car here in Willet Beach on Wednesday, the day you left town. Were you in the car with him?"

Yes, too drugged to know what was happening. "Yes. He'd walked over to see how I was doing. He took me for a drive—at my request—which turned out to be boring for him because I fell asleep about three minutes into it. He kept driving for a while to let me nap."

"You and Mr. Hale have gotten to know each other well?"

"We're getting to know each other."

"Where is he now?"

Rayna pressed her thumb against a small frayed rip in the knee of her lounge pants. Good grief, could she appear any scruffier? She should have taken thirty seconds to put on decent clothes and brush her hair before leaving the cabin. Stafford must be wondering if she was even a functioning adult. "You told him to wait in his car."

"Yes, hon, but is he there? Last time we spoke, you told me you had the ability to sense people, their heartbeats, their locations, and so forth. Did he go to the car like I asked?"

This hairpin turn into a discussion of her abilities threw Rayna off balance. She gathered her thoughts. "No. He didn't go that far. He's . . . I think he's on those benches we passed on the way in here."

"Nice to know," Stafford said. "Is anyone with him?"

"No."

"You tell me if that changes, all right?"

"All right." Was this a test?

"What did your sister tell you about her husband's condition?" Stafford asked.

"Not much. We only had a few minutes to talk." Rayna related what Annemarie had said. "Have you spoken to her?"

"Not yet. Tell me about your relationship with Seth Bristol. Did you get along well?"

"Yes, we got along great. He's a friendly, easygoing guy. No, I didn't poison him, and Damon can testify I wasn't in Willet Beach when he got sick . . . Okay, someone's with Damon now."

"Oh? Who is it? Can you tell?"

"I've met them before, but . . . Hang on . . . Oh, it's the officer who questioned me after Ben's death." Jody's friend. It took Rayna another moment to remember his name. "Sgt. Fischer."

"Is he standing or sitting?"

"They're both standing. Damon stood when Sgt. Fischer approached."

Stafford gave her a long, assessing look.

"Sgt. Fischer is walking away now," Rayna said. "Heading away from the hospital."

"Thank you. Tell me about your sister and brother-in-law. How is their relationship?"

"Fine," Rayna said. "Absolutely fine."

"No tension?"

There *had* been some tension lately between Seth and Annemarie. Sometimes Rayna worried about their relationship. But Annemarie would never have tried to murder him; that was ridiculous. "Just normal spats."

"Were you aware that earlier this year, Mrs. Bristol's store was on the verge of bankruptcy?"

Rayna goggled at Stafford. "No," she said. Was that true? "Did Annemarie tell you that?"

"That must have been a difficult time for her, thinking she'd have to close down." Stafford sidestepped Rayna's question. "She has a passion for that cute shop, doesn't she?"

"She loves it." Rayna was glad the detective didn't have the ability to sense the increase in her heart rate. Annemarie had been on the verge of having to close The Beach Umbrella? Annemarie fretted about money, but Rayna had had no idea things had been that dire.

"What perfect timing," Stafford said, "receiving an inheritance from your father, may he rest in peace. That money must have been a tremendous help in keeping her business afloat."

"He'd have been proud of her, putting the money to use like that." Rayna's mouth was so dry that it was difficult to enunciate clearly, let alone sound confident. "He was always proud of her business abilities."

"But he wasn't much for helping out, was he? I hear he wasn't one to step in at a time of financial crisis. Thought if his children were struggling, that was their own fault and they needed to learn that lesson."

Rayna wished she could cool the warmth in her face and slow her heartbeat. Stafford wouldn't need Trespasser abilities to recognize that she was upset. Rayna's pulse was pounding so hard that it was probably visible in her neck. "He valued independence, yes."

"Is Sgt. Fischer still here on this hospital campus?"

The way Stafford whipped between topics left Rayna frazzled and confused. Damon had moved closer to the hospital doors, a sign that her agitation was making him nervous.

"Hon?"

Rayna drew a deep breath. "Give me a minute to figure out if he's here. I don't know him well enough to identify him in a quick sweep. I'll need to go slowly."

"Take your time."

Rayna began where she and Stafford sat and scanned outward in circles, carefully searching for Fischer. She'd swept through about a fourth of her range when a familiar sense startled her.

"What is it?" Stafford had noticed her surprise.

"Lucy Orozco is here," Rayna said. "She's with her mother, Dr. Yin. I thought she was in Monterey . . ." Was Lucy all right? Was her baby all right? Heartbeats all seemed strong and regular. "I think they're in Dr. Yin's office. At any rate, they're in the area of the medical office building." Had Lucy been anxious about her child and Dr. Yin had brought her to the office to examine and reassure her? "Sorry . . . you were asking about Sgt. Fischer." Rayna kept sweeping until she zeroed in on an area behind the hospital building. "There he—" She sat up straighter, sliding to the edge of her seat. "Something's wrong. He's on the ground, lying on the ground, and his heart rate is much faster than . . . Wait, he's . . . What is he—"

"He's fine." Stafford tucked her hair behind her ear, revealing an earpiece. "Sgt. Fischer, that's enough push-ups. You're welcome for the workout."

Rayna drooped in her chair. After Ben and Seth, she'd been ready to conclude that Fischer was in trouble. But no. It had been a test for her.

Stafford scrutinized her with a penetrating Maggie-like gaze. "I'm going to ask permission to do something that you have the right to refuse. May I search you for any devices that would allow someone to feed you information?"

"Um—yes, of course."

"Thanks, hon. Stand up, please. Are you carrying anything sharp or anything else I should be aware of?"

"No."

Stafford began with what Rayna assumed was a standard pat-down to make sure Rayna wasn't concealing a weapon. "Mind if I take your phone out of your pocket?"

"Go ahead."

Stafford took the phone. "That's a beautiful photo of your sister's family," she said, referring to the lock-screen photo Rayna had chosen. "Would you be willing to unlock the phone and let me see what apps you currently have running?"

"Yes."

Stafford turned the screen toward Rayna so she could unlock it. After a few seconds of tapping and scrolling, Stafford set the phone aside and took a flashlight out of her purse. "Do you mind if I remove that elastic band from your hair?"

"Go ahead."

Stafford slid the elastic off Rayna's ponytail. With the extra illumination of the flashlight, Stafford checked Rayna's ears. After the visual examination, she switched to a tactile one, probing around Rayna's ears, running her fingers over her scalp and through her hair, patting her neck. Rayna wondered how tiny listening devices had become if Stafford had to check this thoroughly to see if Rayna was wired.

"Would you take off your sweater and let me have a look at it?"

Rayna removed her cardigan and handed it to Stafford, glad no one else was in this part of the lobby to witness what must appear to be a public medical exam. Stafford shook out the sweater, checked the seams, and draped it over the arm of a chair.

"Almost done." She ran her hands down Rayna's back, shoulders, and arms, probing through the thin fabric of her long-sleeved knit shirt. Rayna was glad she'd already peeled off the Band-Aid covering the spot where the IV had been. Stafford would have noticed the Band-Aid and probably asked about it.

Finally, Stafford completed her search with Rayna's shoes. Rayna had no idea what she expected to find there—a device that would allow Rayna's coconspirator to zap her foot with messages in Morse code?

"Thanks, hon," she said as Rayna stepped back into her tennis shoes. "You can sit down."

Rayna and Stafford both settled into their chairs.

"Would you mind telling me what my heart rate is right now?" Stafford asked, looking at her smart watch. "I'll time fifteen seconds for you; give me that count. Go."

Concentrating on Stafford, Rayna counted.

"Time."

"Fourteen, which gives you a pulse rate of . . ." Rayna's brain felt laggy as she tried to multiply the count by four. "You have a slow pulse rate. Fifty-six."

Stafford pursed her lips. "You do have some remarkable abilities, don't you?"

"Yes, but like I mentioned before, I'd appreciate it if you'd keep that to yourself. I do *not* want the attention I'd receive if word gets out."

"I understand. Sgt. Fisher and I will do our best to keep mum. I've heard Mr. Hale's sponsor is interested in paranormal abilities. Does he know what you can do?"

"I haven't told him," Rayna said, the answer Damon had instructed her to give if Stafford asked this question. "The only people I've ever told are my immediate family. Thank you for your discretion. I hope this is enough evidence to show you I could have known Ben was in trouble before I arrived without having poisoned him myself. Or knowing someone else had."

"Who do you think might have poisoned him?" Stafford asked.

"I have no idea."

"You and your sister are close?"

"Yes," Rayna said emphatically.

"I'm glad. Since she didn't confide in you about her financial troubles and you didn't confide in her about where you've been these past couple of days, I wondered if you had some difficulty trusting each other."

Rayna fidgeted with one sleeve of the cardigan hanging over the arm of her chair. "We trust each other. We just . . . aren't always great at reaching out to each other when we're dealing with hard things."

"She wasn't happy about Mr. and Mrs. Orozco returning to town, was she?"

"No," Rayna admitted. "But she certainly wouldn't have poisoned Ben over disliking him."

"She was concerned that having to associate with him would be difficult for you, wasn't she?"

Was Stafford guessing, or had someone told her this? "She worries too much about me, but good grief, she wouldn't have killed him."

Stafford rose to her feet. "Thank you for your help. I know you're anxious to get to your niece and nephew, so I'll let you go now, but please call me if you think of anything else you ought to tell me." She held out a business card.

Rayna took the card, grabbed her sweater and phone, and hurried out of the lobby.

CHAPTER 25

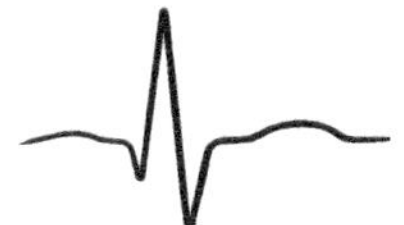

KEEPING HIS EXPRESSION IMPASSIVE TO cover the relief he was feeling, Damon met Rayna at the hospital exit. "Thank you for not getting me arrested," he said as they walked toward the parking lot. "When Sgt. Fischer stopped to talk to me, I thought things were about to get more complicated."

"That was Detective Stafford testing me." Rayna's face was flushed, and she walked so quickly that he had to speed his gait to keep up. As soon as they were in his car, she offered a rapid report of the interview.

"What happens now?" she asked when she finished. "Are you staying with me at Annemarie's to stand guard?"

"I'll stay with you."

"Will Maggie be joining us? Or are *you* going to knock me out tonight? Please don't drug me. I need to be able to respond if Nancy or Tate needs anything. I need to be able to respond if Annemarie calls."

"I'm not planning on drugging you."

"Thank you." Rayna slouched in her seat, closing her eyes. When Damon glanced at her at the next stoplight, tears were pouring down her face, catching glimmers of headlights.

"Rayna," he said softly, "*do* you think Annemarie might be guilty of murder?"

She shook her head, but the acceleration in her heart rate and her fast, shallow breathing didn't indicate confidence.

He remained silent until he'd parked in front of the Bristols' house. Lights were on in the living room, and Jody was visible through half-open blinds, standing at the window, obviously waiting for their arrival.

Rayna groaned. "I cannot cope with Jody tonight. If she starts slamming me with questions about Seth . . . If she *dares* look gleeful—"

"You don't have to cope with her," Damon said. "When we get inside, head straight upstairs like you want to check on the kids. I'll field her questions."

"*Thank* you."

"I apologize," Damon said, "for the personal gossip about us that's going to blanket Willet Beach."

"Oh, let Jody gossip. Who cares anymore?"

He opened his door. "I'll get your suitcase."

Before the two of them reached the front door, Jody swung it open. "My stars, Mr. Hale, Annemarie didn't tell me *you* were coming with Rayna. May I talk to you alone for a minute? Rayna, you go on inside." Jody took Rayna's hand, pulled her over the threshold, then stepped onto the porch with Damon.

"Give us a moment, dear." She closed the door. "It's *cold* out here, isn't it? Well, I'll be fast. Come away from the door. We need privacy." She clutched Damon's arm and hustled him off the porch.

No need for him to shield Rayna from Jody—Jody was taking care of that separation herself. "What can I do for you, Jody?"

Jody clucked her tongue. "What are you thinking? You seem like a smart man, but you're brainless when it comes to women. Didn't I warn you about Rayna?" She poked his shoulder. "Now Seth is down! Another victim! Do you think it's coincidence that he got deathly sick all of a sudden? Rayna poisoned him, like she did Ben Orozco, like she did my Glenn, her own daddy."

"Why would she want to kill Seth?"

"Jealousy! Of course jealousy. Her sister has a darling husband and adorable children, and she has no one, and she couldn't stand it anymore, like she couldn't stand Lucy taking her Ben. And *now* she shows up to take care of the kiddies while Seth is dying and her sister suspects nothing."

"I take it you don't suspect Annemarie anymore."

"No, that was a wrong turn. Annemarie wouldn't hurt Seth. This is Rayna's doing. Someone else must have helped Rayna when she murdered my Elliott. And here *you* are, following her around with your head in the clouds."

"Rayna was out of town today," Damon said.

"Are you sure about that?"

"Yes. She was staying in Big Sur. I went down to visit her and brought her back tonight when she learned about Seth."

"That's where you were all day?" Jody folded her arms. "Oh, Mr. Hale. She's Delilah to your Samson. She'll be the death of you. Even if you were with her today, she could have planted that poison before she left. Poisoned something she knew Seth would eat."

"Other people could have done that as well. Have they found any definitive evidence against her? Have you learned anything new from Sgt. Fischer?"

"Not yet. But you don't want to believe she's guilty, and that makes you blind. Be *careful*, for heaven's sake."

"I'm careful."

"Keep an eye on the kids. I don't think she's far gone enough to hurt children, but you never know."

"I'd better get inside, then. May I walk you home?"

"That would be lovely." Jody rested her hand in the crook of his elbow, and he walked her two doors down.

"Good night, and thank you for the escort," she said, unlocking her door. "Mind yourself. You're too trusting."

"Good night."

Damon returned to Annemarie's house, took the suitcase he'd abandoned on the porch, and carried it inside.

Rayna was in the living room, sprawled on the couch. Shadows were developing under her eyes. "What did Jody want?"

"To warn me my life is in danger from you. She told me I'm too trusting."

Rayna burst into laughter. "Too trusting? Yes, you really should stop treating me like I'm harmless."

* * *

Stretched out on Annemarie's couch in her darkened living room, warm under layers of blankets, mentally and physically depleted, Rayna hoped for a while that she'd be able to sleep, but the best she could manage was relaxing her body, and that took deliberate concentration. The instant she stopped trying to keep her muscles loose, everything would tense up again. The usually comforting presences of Nancy and Tate, asleep in their rooms, brought agonizing thoughts of the pain they would experience if their father died—and their mother was arrested for his murder.

Across the room, Damon was sitting in Seth's usual chair, his phone screen throwing dim light on his face. He must be exhausted, but he wasn't showing it.

Rayna's phone lay on the floor next to the couch, plugged in and charging. She reached for it, wanting—again—to see if Annemarie had sent an update that Rayna had missed, despite leaving the volume of the phone up.

No updates. Too overwrought to even scroll mindlessly, she flung the phone onto the carpet.

"Anything I can do for you?" Damon asked.

"You can answer a question." Rayna sat up. "If Detective Stafford concludes I killed Ben, or Annemarie did and I protected her, I'll get arrested. My abilities would get publicized, since they'd be key to my defense. Trials are public record. Word of what I can do would spread. Would your group let that happen?"

"No." Damon set his phone on the table next to him. "We can't let your abilities get showcased in a trial."

"How would you prevent it?"

"By getting you out of here."

"I'm surprised you let me prove to Detective Stafford I could sense people."

"Word on Claire Stafford indicates she's discreet and careful. Someone we can work with if we need to. Since pulling you out means destroying the life you have here, we're hoping to avoid that if possible."

"Thank you," she said. "I'm grateful for that. It would have been a lot easier for you to toss me on board your government jet and take me to . . . wherever." *Like the cemetery.* Wearily, she sank onto her pillow. He'd let her come help Annemarie tonight. He'd let her be alone with Stafford. Those were both encouraging signs. "Earlier you were talking about when the Trespasser team found you as a teenager. Did you know then about your ability to kill?"

"No. We've never seen that ability manifest in a Trespasser until they're in their twenties, when brain development is nearing completion."

"Did the team tell you what was coming?"

"No. But they told me if I detected any changes in or expansion of my abilities to let them know immediately."

Rayna thought of her experience with the injured elk, the impulse she'd never felt before, to link, to encompass, to affect instead of observe. "Do all Trespassers figure out link-killing on their own?"

"To some degree. They sense they can do something new, that they can interfere with the electrical impulses in the heart. Not everyone follows through and stops a heart, but they all sense that they can."

"Has anyone ever killed another person experimentally, not intending to go that far? And no, I'm not saying I've done that."

"What do you think?"

"I'd guess no," Rayna said. "When I was doing it, I could tell . . . I knew what was happening. It was clear in my mind. I knew what would happen if I didn't release the connection."

"That's consistent with what others have reported."

"Once the team relocated your family out east, what happened to you?"

"They kept tabs on me. I went in for regular interviews and testing, but other than that, I lived a normal life. They wanted me on the Trespasser team eventually, offered to pay my way through college if I'd commit to working for them when I graduated. I've been with them ever since. I'm mostly a researcher. Trespassers are rare, so I'm not often in this type of situation."

"I asked you this morning if you've ever had to execute a Trespasser you were investigating. You didn't answer that question. If you're willing to discuss it, I'd like to know."

Without the light from his phone, his face was all dark shadows. "I've dealt with two Trespassers who we determined were guilty of multiple murders. The first was a clear-cut situation that I quickly took care of. The second was more complex. I handled it poorly, and it cost innocent lives."

"I'm so sorry. Poorly . . . how?"

"I figured out too late that the Trespasser—his name was Tristan McCuller—was investigating me even as I was investigating him. Our team had reached the conclusion that he was a threat, not someone we could work with, but before I acted, he disappeared." Damon's tone went cold and flat. "The next day, I got news that my parents had been found dead in their home. Autopsies couldn't identify a cause of death."

Her throat muscles seemed to be crushing her windpipe, and she had to gasp for air before she could speak at all. "I'm so sorry."

"I got a note in the mail saying it was payback for what I'd intended to do to him and to stay out of his way."

"I'm so sorry." Rayna repeated the words; she could think of nothing else to say. "But you don't blame yourself, do you?"

"It's my fault. I underestimated him. I gave him too much leeway."

"Where is he now?"

"Dead. He was working around the world as a hit man and assassin, raking in cash. A member of our team—not me—was able to track him down."

A thud from upstairs came along with the sense of a sudden downward movement from Tate. Rayna sprang to her feet in sync with Damon as faint crying sounded.

"Tate fell out of bed," Rayna said. "I'll take care of him. You stay here."

"Fine."

She hurried upstairs, glad for a chance to let the tumult inside her settle. Visible in the glow from an octopus night-light, Tate was sitting on the floor. When he saw Rayna, he wailed, "I want *Mommy*."

"Hey, Tate." Rayna leaned over him. "Your mommy is at the doctor's with your daddy. Can I help you get back in bed?"

Tate sniffled. "Lie down with me."

Rayna lifted Tate into bed, drew the covers over him, and lay next to him.

"Sing the pumpkin song."

The pumpkin song. The Halloween song he'd learned in kindergarten and had, by Annemarie's report, demanded every night since October. "I don't know all the words."

"Daddy knows them."

Rayna blinked, trying to keep tears from leaking. "I know a song about puppies. How about that one?"

"I want the *pumpkin song*."

"I'll try it. You help me if I get stuck." Quietly, Rayna started the song, scrounging through her brain for the words and trying her hardest not to think about what Tate would go through if he never heard this song from his father again or what Damon was still going through after the loss of his parents.

CHAPTER 26

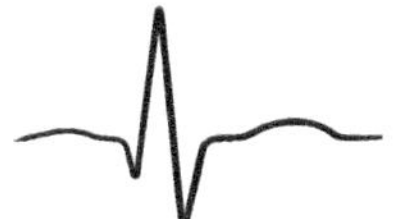

Damon paused, pruning shears in hand, as Annemarie pulled her car into the garage. She parked and walked into the front yard to greet him.

"I'm surprised you're alive," she said. "According to Jody, my sister is going to slaughter you any second now and you're too entranced by her to realize it."

"I appreciate Jody's concern for me." Damon assessed Annemarie. Beyond the family resemblance, her emotional state made her look even more like Rayna today: wan, glassy-eyed, and wary. "How are you holding up?" Damon asked. "We were grateful to hear Seth is awake."

"He's made a lot of improvement, enough that Detective Stafford wanted to interview him, so I got kicked out. I came home to grab a shower and a nap. You didn't need to do my yard work, but thanks. Is this an excuse to stick around? Don't give me any more silly lines about how there's nothing going on between you and Rayna. Jody told me you stayed here last night."

"I stayed to help out," Damon said. "Rayna doesn't have her car here, and I wanted to be available if she needed a ride. Or any other help."

"Uh-huh. If only there were a way for Rayna to contact you if she needed help instead of you having to stay at her side. Where is she?"

"She's in the guesthouse. After we got the kids off to school, she went to take a shower. We took them to McDonald's for breakfast, by the way. We weren't sure if we should be touching anything in the kitchen."

"Or eating any of my poisoned food. I don't think Stafford is coming back to search. She already tore things apart and didn't find anything. I don't think it was anything here that poisoned him. The only meal he ate at home yesterday was breakfast, and we all ate the same thing." She took the pruning shears out of Damon's hand. "Quit it with the yard work and come inside."

Damon followed her into the house. "Have they confirmed that Seth was poisoned?"

"They don't have a final report yet, but the doctor says that's what it looks like." Annemarie dropped the pruning shears on the floor and sank onto the couch. "This is all *nuts.* Who would want to hurt Seth? If you're thinking it's me, it's *not.*"

"I'm not thinking anything." Damon sat in the chair where he'd spent most of the night. "That's up to Detective Stafford."

"Oh, *please*, of course you're thinking 'anything.' You're always asking questions, you're paid to dig up anything interesting about our town, *and* you're chasing Rayna and don't want her arrested for murder. Just the other night you asked us if we had any idea who, besides Rayna, might have had a grudge against Ben. Whoever went after Ben must be the same person who went after Seth, because I doubt there's more than one poisoner in Willet Beach. Do you think it was me? Go on. Say it to my face."

"Annemarie," Damon said, "you've been up all night. Go take that shower and nap. I'll clear out."

"No, you will not clear out. You'll stay right here because I need to talk to you and Rayna."

Rayna was hurrying across the lawn toward the house. She'd be backup for Annemarie, no doubt, and now that he was sitting down, exhaustion was about to swamp him. This wasn't going to go smoothly. "Have you eaten breakfast?" he asked. "I'd be happy to—"

At the sound of the back door opening, Annemarie sprang to her feet. Rayna rushed into the living room, barefoot, her wet hair loose.

"Oh, Annie." She wrapped her arms around her sister. "I'm so, so, so happy that he's improving."

"Me too." Annemarie broke the embrace. "He feels awful, but he's coherent." She pulled Rayna onto the couch so they were side by side. "Damon was about to tell me the truth about what you two have been up to."

"He . . . was?"

"I don't know what you mean, Annemarie," Damon said.

"You knew where Rayna was all along." Her angry gaze shifted to Rayna. "I'm done with this. You're going to tell me exactly what's going on, because this is not like you, trusting someone to this degree this fast and lying to me about it. You're acting weird and scary, and you know what else?" Annemarie spoke faster. "Since Damon showed up in Willet Beach, there's been a murder and an attempted murder. Is that coincidence? I don't think so. What do we actually know about this guy? How is he manipulating you?"

"He's not manipulating me." Rayna wrapped both of her hands around one of Annemarie's. "Let's talk about this later. You need to rest."

"Don't you *dare* try to dodge this!" Annemarie yanked her hand free. "Seth almost *died*, and you're protecting the guy who might have attacked him? Why? Because he's cute?"

"I'm not protecting him," Rayna snapped. "Why would he have attacked Seth?"

"For fun? How do we know?"

"If you think he's a killer, maybe you shouldn't yell that in front of him, or he'll kill us both to hide his crimes."

"I'm not going to kill anyone," Damon said.

Annemarie shot him a scorching look. "Anyone *else*, you mean?"

"*Stop* it," Rayna said. "You don't believe what you're saying. If you thought he was a killer, you wouldn't have let me go off with him last night. You would have told him to get lost and pulled me into the back of the ER, and you'd have left Jody with the kids rather than sending me here with Damon hovering around."

"I wasn't thinking straight!" Annemarie screamed the words. "I was afraid Seth was dying! I'm done with your hiding, I'm done with lies, I'm done with all of this, and now he's *sitting* there staring at us like a . . . like a . . . I don't know, a serial killer—"

"Annie." Rayna grabbed her arm. "Can we do this later? None of us got much sleep last night."

"He has that vibe, you know. A serial-killer vibe. It's his eyes. They're too calm. Like he doesn't see us as people. He's analyzing our vulnerabilities so he can—"

"Excuse us." Rayna stood, pulling Annemarie to her feet. Hauling her sister with her, she exited the room.

Damon braced his head on the back of the chair, closing his apparently too-calm eyes as he tracked the sisters' progress up the stairs and into what he assumed was the master bedroom. It didn't take long before Annemarie's heart rate was dropping. Whatever Rayna was saying was working to soothe her.

Ten minutes later, Rayna returned to the living room. "Come over to the guesthouse," she said. "Annemarie needs to be rid of us for a while. I need to finish getting ready, then we can go wherever you want. Assuming you can keep the serial-killer vibes under control."

"Thank you for not openly agreeing with her evaluation of me."

"You don't have serial-killer vibes. Annemarie says irrational things when she's sleep-deprived, then later apologizes."

If Rayna was referring to that accusation as irrational, that was progress. He accompanied her to the guesthouse. "What did you say to Annemarie while you were upstairs?"

"I repeated our agreed-upon story—several times—and told her you weren't threatening or manipulating me, just trying to help us, and I wasn't going to talk about this anymore until she'd had a nap. We didn't discuss my . . . 'crazy stories.'"

"Did she tell you anything she learned from Seth?"

"No."

"Are the police keeping an eye on him to make sure no one harms him while he's in the hospital?"

"There's an officer stationed at his door, and if there are any visitors, including Annemarie, the officer accompanies them into the room. Getting escorted infuriates Annemarie, and I said, 'Don't get upset about it; they're just taking precautions,' which was a comment I thought you'd appreciate."

"I do," he said, yawning.

"You need to sleep. You didn't sleep at all last night, did you?" She waved toward the sectional in the living room. "If you trust me enough to close your eyes while I'm conscious but you don't want to get too far away, you're welcome to crash here."

"Thank you for the offer." He ran his knuckles along his stubble-covered jaw. He ought to go home, clean up, and sleep, but the more he trusted Rayna, the less he trusted Annemarie. Would she harm Rayna? Unlikely. If she'd killed Ben, that had been *for* Rayna . . . or had it?

"Is that a yes or a no?" Rayna asked, now yawning herself. "I can get you blankets and a pillow."

Shadowing Rayna for the entire course of an investigation until Annemarie was arrested or cleared wasn't feasible. If he wanted to control every move she made, the only option was to take her to the cabin and hold her there. That no longer seemed justified.

"I'll head home," he said.

Rayna gave him a cautious look. "You head home, and I . . . what?"

"Stay here."

"Stay here, not . . . under observation? Are you comfortable with that?"

"I'm not comfortable with any of this, but yes, stay here. Please be careful. I hope your sister is innocent, but we don't know that yet."

"She *wouldn't*—" Rayna cut herself off. "I'll be careful."

"You're connected to everyone who's died. If you're not the killer, it's not paranoid to worry you might become a victim. Please don't eat or drink anything Annemarie gives you today."

"That's ridiculous. But fine, I won't . . . if you'll take the same precaution with Jody."

"With Jody?"

"She's making me nervous. Hasn't she known me long enough to give me the benefit of the doubt? Maybe her accusations are red herrings."

"Red herrings?"

"Maybe she doesn't only gossip about murder. Maybe she produces murders to gossip about. You told me she was recasting her husband's fishing accident as one of my murders. Maybe it was *hers*."

"You think she might have killed her husband?"

"I'm not accusing her. I'm saying she had a motive. He was emotionally and physically abusive. She certainly had reasons to want to get rid of him. And my father . . . He didn't lash out physically, but he was no gem either, as you know."

"What about Ben Orozco? Did she have a motive there?"

"Um . . . okay, I haven't the faintest idea why she'd want to murder Ben. But she doesn't have to be guilty of *everything* to be dangerous, and with you asking questions, she might get nervous that you'll start suspecting her . . ." Rayna trailed off. "This sounds like knee-jerk defensiveness on my part, doesn't it? You're accusing me of murder? I'll accuse *you* of murder!"

"You're presenting a legitimate theory," Damon said.

"Thank you for being polite about my sleep-deprived ranting." Rayna picked up the vase she'd left on the counter—the vase she'd intended to fill with wildflowers to take to Lucy before Damon had intervened. "Anyway, you said I'm connected to all the murders, but so are you because *you're* connected to me, at least in Jody's gossip and in Annemarie's suspicions. So be careful."

"I will be."

"What happens next?" Rayna examined the vase as though checking her work. "Obviously, you've decided you're comfortable giving me some rope. You go take a nap, I take a nap, then what?"

His eyes burned with exhaustion, his head throbbed, and he didn't know the answer to that question. "Truth is, I'm having trouble thinking past the nap."

"Same."

"Stay here for now, please. Unless you go to the hospital with Annemarie to visit Seth."

"That's fine. I'll tell you one thing I'd like us to do post-nap. I want to get this vase and the candleholders to Lucy. I feel bad about delaying when the candleholders were the one thing she wanted from me. I don't know if she's in Willet Beach or in Monterey, but I'll contact her and find out." She set the vase down. "Would you give me a ride to wherever she is, seeing as how my car is on vacation in Big Sur?"

"I'd be happy to do that. Later, we'll head to the cabin to get your car."

"What's Maggie doing now, since we ran out on her? Did she go back home?"

"Not yet. Before she leaves, she wants one more full day with you to finish her preliminary research."

"That was all preliminary?"

"She's warming up."

"I don't want to stay away from Willet Beach for an entire day while Seth's sick."

"I understand. She can divide it up, but we can't keep her waiting too long. She has a family and a slew of responsibilities in D.C. She can't hang around at the cabin for days on end if she isn't needed there."

"Can she come to Willet Beach to interview me?"

"I don't want anyone getting curious about her and trying to figure out who she is and what she's doing here with you."

"What happens after she finishes her preliminary research?"

"Eventually, we'll need to fly you out to our facility so she'll have access to the equipment she needs. But that's not something to worry about now. Let's play this by ear. We'll find a balance, respecting Maggie's time while keeping you available to help your sister when you're needed."

"Thank you." The curve to her mouth was uneasy, but her attempt at a smile softened the anxiety in her eyes. "And thank you for trusting me enough to bring me back here."

He nodded and started for the door. "Get some rest. Call if you need anything. I'll leave my phone on."

"Don't leave your phone on," she said. "The way things have been lately, if anything happens while you're napping, you'd be better off sleeping through it."

* * *

"Well then," Logan said. "Are you confident she won't tell her sister what's been happening to her?"

"Yes," Damon said. "She won't draw Annemarie into this. She won't want to burden her with information that could tear her life apart."

Logan's gaze was keen, no doubt noting every trace of fatigue, stubble, and doubt on Damon's face. It made Damon want to shut the computer. Then, as long as he'd ended the call, he might as well rest his head on his kitchen table and fall asleep right here.

"Sorry to hear about the brother-in-law," Logan said. "Glad to hear the evidence is pointing away from Rayna. Maggie's glad, too, even if she's cross about being left at the cabin twiddling her thumbs. Her impressions of Rayna were positive."

"Good."

"You realize you'll have to play up the impression of a personal relationship between Rayna and you to excuse your attentiveness to her."

Damon grunted. "I'll figure that out."

The smirk on Logan's face was fleeting but clear enough to annoy Damon. "Go take a nap," Logan said. "And watch your back. I don't want you getting poisoned."

CHAPTER 27

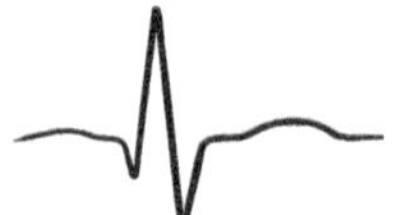

Back in her own home. Alone. Rayna had feared she'd never have this privilege again, but Damon was gone, and she was completely unguarded. After three days of imprisonment, this change was disorienting. The only signs of what she'd experienced were the red mark on her arm where Maggie had inserted the IV, a few minor bruises, and the fact that her car was parked an hour away at a remote cabin.

Considering the risks Damon had taken in bringing her back to Willet Beach, then leaving her here alone—all in light of the horrific actions of that Trespasser who'd eluded him—he must be on edge, wondering if he'd made the right call. She'd do whatever she could to ease his mind. It wouldn't be difficult to keep her word to stay here unless she was at the hospital visiting Seth. All she wanted was to collapse in her own bed.

When she awoke two hours later, there were no messages from Damon. She hoped he was sound asleep. She messaged Lucy about the candleholders and got an instant response: *I'm here in town. I'll come pick them up. Are you home now?*

Yes, Rayna responded. *But you don't have to come to me. I can bring them to you later this afternoon.*

I want to come to you. Be there in fifteen minutes?

Would Damon be troubled by her meeting with Lucy on her own? He wouldn't have a chance to worry about it—he wouldn't even find out until the meeting was over and Lucy and her baby were clearly fine. *Come around to the guesthouse in back.*

She got herself ready, debating if she should pick wildflowers to fill the vase or if she should wait and take the vase and flowers to Lucy later.

It would be a hassle for Lucy to transport the flowers and vase. Rayna would drop the filled vase at her house, or at her parents' house, another time. She stowed the vase in a kitchen cupboard.

Hungry, Rayna scanned the contents of her fridge, wanting a snack before Lucy arrived. Everything, including sealed cups of yogurt and an unopened carton of orange juice, seemed marked with invisible skull-and-crossbones warnings. She was poking through a cupboard, pondering if she should throw away every food item in her kitchen or if that would be wastefully paranoid, when she sensed Lucy approaching. She closed the cupboard and waited for the doorbell to ring.

"Thanks for letting me stop by." Lucy looked tired but composed. Her flowered knit dress accentuated her baby bump, and her coral-pink sweater matched her lipstick. "I know this is a rough day for your family."

"Oh, Lu, I'm so sorry." Rayna drew Lucy into a long hug. "How are you holding up?"

"Taking things one minute at a time, like you said." They stepped apart. "Or fifteen seconds at a time. Sometimes the next fifteen seconds is all I can handle. How are you and Annemarie? I couldn't believe it when I heard about Seth. How is he doing?"

"Much better. Still very sick, but he's awake, and he's stable."

"That's hopeful news."

Rayna couldn't imagine how much Lucy must be hurting. Ben and Seth had both been poisoned, but there had been no hopeful news for Ben. "Would you like to sit down? No pressure if you'd rather not."

"No, I'd love to. Are these the candleholders?" Lucy indicated the open box on the kitchen table.

"Yes." Rayna picked up the box. "Come into the living room, and I'll show them to you."

They sat together on the sectional. Rayna took the pieces out one by one. They both cried as Lucy examined and praised each design and guessed what Ben would have said about it.

"I think this would have been his top choice." She rotated the most playful of the pieces and traced her finger around the outline of the bug-eyed sanddab. "It would have made him laugh. But it would have been a close race. They're all fantastic." She tucked the candleholder back into the shredded paper that cushioned it. "I'm paying you. You're a professional, and this was a business deal, and you must have spent hours on these."

Rayna took a Kleenex from the box she'd brought in after they'd used up the supply of tissues from Lucy's purse. "I cannot even begin to explain how much I don't want money for these. *Please*, let me give you this gift. It would mean a lot to me."

"You're very kind. Too kind." Lucy set the box on the ground. "May I ask you something awkward?"

"Of course."

"I told you Detective Stafford asked me about you, and I keep hearing rumors that you . . . well . . . are a suspect in what happened to Ben."

"The police have talked to me twice," Rayna said. "But I swear to you, I didn't—"

"I know. Do you think I'd be sitting here with you if I thought you were a murderer? But . . . because of your situation, and now with Seth . . . I figure you've been giving this a lot of thought. Do you have *any* idea who might have wanted to kill Ben or Seth or both of them?"

"I wish I did. Do you know about the ice cream?"

"Yes." Lucy's bloodshot eyes welled up again. She took a Kleenex. "I think Detective Stafford suspects me."

"Oh, Lucy. I'm sorry. I guess they always look at the spouse, even when the marriage is strong."

"They're looking at me, all right. 'You were supposed to be there that night, Mrs. Orozco. Why were you late? You grew up here, Mrs. Orozco. Was the traffic a surprise to you? Are there any witnesses to your activities in Sunnyvale? Tell me about your marriage, Mrs. Orozco.' Then there's the coconut in the ice cream—how convenient that it was a flavor it wouldn't be suspicious for me not to try."

"Maybe I'm not her favorite suspect after all," Rayna said. "She has a collection of us."

"Part of me is in denial." Tears ran down Lucy's face. "Like this can't be happening. Rayna . . . I didn't get stuck in traffic. I wasn't there that night because I didn't want to be."

"Did you decide you didn't want to work with me after all? I get it. You were trying to be nice, but it was awkward."

"No, it wasn't you. I had a meltdown that afternoon and told Ben he needed to get his act together and stop putting all his attention into what he considered the 'fun' aspects of the planning while leaving everything else to me. He told me I was being ridiculous and blamed pregnancy hormones, which made me livid. I said I was taking a break and he could deal with the rest of our responsibilities for the day. I walked out. I did go to Sunnyvale but not for restaurant supplies. I went to a movie. I went clothes shopping. I took myself out to dinner."

"Did you tell that to Detective Stafford?"

"No. I felt horrible that I hadn't been there with him. Out of pride, I claimed I'd been taking care of business matters and got stuck in traffic. Then when she told me it appeared his death hadn't been due to natural causes, I got scared. What if she learned we'd been fighting and she suspected me of killing him?"

"But you didn't have any reason to attack Seth, and his poisoner must be the same person. Stafford's probably eliminated you as a suspect."

Lucy pulled on the hem of her skirt, smoothing the fabric over her lap. "Seth and Ben were friends. They hit it off when we were buying the restaurant."

"I didn't realize that."

"Because Seth was always saying, 'Better not let my wife know. She'll have my head for hanging out with the guy who dumped her little sister.'"

"I wouldn't have cared if he and Ben liked to hang out," Rayna said.

"Ben said your sister flipped out on Seth about the restaurant sale when she learned who the new owners would be."

"That is totally unreasonable." How fragile did Annemarie think she was? "She takes big-sister duties to an extreme. But Ben and Seth being friends doesn't give you a motive for trying to kill Seth. Does it?"

"Ben and I . . ." Lucy's voice trembled. "We'd been fighting a lot. I didn't really want to own and run a restaurant, but it was so important to Ben, and I was willing to support him in it. But the more he kept leaving the serious work to me, the more frustrated I got. I even started to suspect that . . ." With her thumbnail, she scraped at the row of diamonds on her wedding band as though trying to clean something off them. "He moved here about six weeks before I did. I didn't want to leave my job earlier than that. While we were apart . . . I'm afraid he had an affair."

Rayna touched her shoulder. "I'm so sorry."

"If you want to say it serves me right, you can."

"I would never want to say that."

"He never admitted to anything, and whatever was going on, I don't think it continued after I moved here."

"What made you suspect him?"

"One of our neighbors said to me what a relief it must be to finally be living here, the trips to visit Ben must have been exhausting, that she was always tired when she was pregnant. I said Ben had been doing the traveling; he'd come to visit me. I'd only flown out here once, and that was with Ben, when we were finalizing the sale on The Sanddab property and signing the lease on our apartment—that's when I'd met this neighbor. She got flustered and said she must have been thinking of someone else in the apartment complex. She looked so embarrassed that it bothered me, so I said, 'Why did you think I'd been here?' and she cracked a joke about the state of her brain since her son is teething and keeps waking her up at night and she has no idea what she's talking about and she'd better go put the laundry in the dryer. The laundry? She'd been leaving her apartment with both her kids in the stroller, and now she suddenly needs to go back inside and do the laundry?"

"Did you ask Ben about it?"

"I mentioned it to him in a casual way and said when our baby is teething, that'll be us imagining things. He laughed and said, 'Forget exhaustion; she must need glasses.' I know he had friends over—he was gathering up any old high school friends he could find, plus making new friends, like Seth. But why would friends coming and going get my neighbor flustered? She must have seen something else that made her think a visitor was . . . Ben's wife."

"Did you try to talk to her about it again?"

"Yes. Yesterday morning. I couldn't stand not knowing." Lucy kept picking at her ring. "I knocked on her door and asked her directly what she'd seen. She admitted that when she'd been pacing her living room with her fussy baby, she'd seen a woman arriving at our apartment late one night. The woman was wearing a floppy hat covering her hair and part of her face. She had a build similar to mine, it was dark, and my neighbor had no reason to take a close look. She assumed it was me, arriving from the airport."

"Lucy . . . you need to tell all this to Detective Stafford."

"I know, but I'm afraid she'll take the information about this woman as a motive for the attack on Seth."

"On *Seth*?"

"Because of the timing." Lucy switched to picking at a tiny chip in her coral-pink nail polish. Rayna didn't remember her being prone to fidgeting, but it was no wonder that this conversation had disrupted her usual composure. "Yesterday morning, after I'd learned about this woman, I had an appointment to speak with Seth about selling The Sanddab, but that wasn't the main thing I wanted to speak with him about. I wanted to ask him if he knew what Ben had been up to."

"Did he?" Rayna hoped Seth wouldn't have shielded a friend's infidelity.

"He said he'd never thought Ben was having an affair and if there was a late-night mystery woman, it was probably Kaitlyn Wyeth, there to talk business."

Kaitlyn at a late-night business meeting? A late meeting would have been fine for night-owl Ben, but Rayna had difficulty believing Kaitlyn would have agreed to that appointment.

"I know what you're thinking," Lucy said. "I remember Kaitlyn saying she was a morning person. It didn't seem believable that she'd meet with Ben at that time, and if they did meet, why go to our apartment? Why didn't he meet her at the Grill? I said that to Seth, and he said, 'Who knows—Kaitlyn was really accommodating to Ben,' so much so that it surprised Seth."

"I doubt she'd be *that* accommodating." Granted Ben had been charming and skilled at getting what he wanted, but charming enough to get Kaitlyn to stop by his place to give him restaurant advice after she'd spent a tiring day at the Grill? "It wasn't Kaitlyn," Rayna said. "That doesn't sound like her at all."

Lucy bit her chipped fingernail. "Might she have stopped by late at night if it . . . wasn't for business reasons?"

"I doubt it," Rayna said gently. "Ben annoyed her, to be honest. And messing around with a married man for a month before his wife arrived in town doesn't seem like her style."

"That's what I thought. I suspect Seth was scrambling to come up with the most innocent explanation he could for what my neighbor saw. As to whether he actually knew who the woman was, I don't know. But then . . . yesterday evening, I heard Seth had been taken to the hospital. I rushed over there to see if I could learn anything, which upset my mother."

"It upset her that you went to check on him?"

"She knows the police have their eye on me. She marched me over to her office and ordered me to stay there, telling me I'd be a fool to be seen lurking in the ER like I had something to do with Seth's illness."

That explained why Rayna had sensed Lucy at the hospital last night. "But why would Detective Stafford think you'd go after Seth?"

"Out of rage? Bitterness? She might assume I thought Seth was hiding Ben's infidelity or had been enabling it."

Rayna laid her hand on Lucy's arm. "Lu, you need to talk to Detective Stafford right away. If your neighbor gets suspicious, she might contact the police and tell them about your conversation. It would be better for Stafford to hear the whole story from you. No matter what, this is important information. If Ben *was* cheating, maybe the other woman is the one who killed him—for instance, because he broke off the affair after you got here."

"I thought of that. I just want more information before I speak with her. Do you have *any* idea who this woman might be? Any guess at all?"

"I'm sorry, but I don't. All this happened before I moved back to town."

"You're sure Seth never hinted at it or joked about it or . . . mentioned a woman accompanying him and Ben on a surfing trip, for instance?"

"Not to me. But I can ask Seth about it as soon as I get the chance."

"Thank you. Yes, please talk with him. I'm sure he'll tell you things he wouldn't tell me." Lucy rested her hand on her belly, where Rayna could sense the baby moving. "What if I get arrested? What happens then? My baby ends up with no father and a mother in prison?"

"They can't arrest you simply because you suspect Ben was cheating. It would take a lot more evidence than that."

"You're right." The spilling of Lucy's tears resumed. "I really did love him. I'd never have . . ."

"I know."

"We could have worked it out. I'd been researching marriage counselors. When I was driving back from Sunnyvale that night, I was planning how I would talk to him about counseling, that we needed it. I think he would have gone with me. He *did* love me. He was truly excited to be a dad, for us to have kids. He just . . . didn't think things through very well sometimes. He could be . . . impulsive. Self-centered. But he didn't intend any harm."

Hoping your flagrantly harmful acts wouldn't cause harm sounded to Rayna like a worthless hope, but she refrained from saying so. She drew her hand away from Lucy's arm. "I'll tell you what else I can do. I'm friends with Damon Hale, the writer doing the book about Willet Beach. Jody Wyeth is his assistant, and she's always gathering news for him. I'll ask him if she's said anything about Ben having an affair. She might have told him something she wouldn't say in front of me since she knows I have a past with Ben. I don't dare ask Jody directly. Right now, she's certain *I* murdered Ben, so I don't think she'd confide in me."

Lucy's response began as a groan and ended as a chuckle. "Jody Wyeth. That woman is a character. Thanks for doing that for me."

"I want answers too."

"How did we end up here?" Lucy picked up the box of candleholders. "I thought we were such normal, boring people."

"I wish we were," Rayna said ruefully. "Talk to Detective Stafford *today*, and tell her your story. Don't wait for us to learn anything else. Maybe she can figure out who the other woman was."

"I hope so. I want to talk to a lawyer before I talk to Detective Stafford though. I don't want to risk bungling my way into a murder charge."

Rayna walked Lucy to the door. "Call me if you think of anything else I can do to help you."

"Thank you." Lucy wrapped an arm around Rayna and pulled her into a hug. "I don't know why you're still my friend, but thank you."

CHAPTER 28

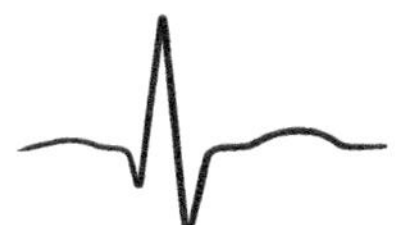

Rayna didn't want to disturb Damon's much-needed sleep by contacting him with her question about Ben's possible affair. She'd wait until he contacted her. Annemarie, however, was awake; Rayna could sense her sister moving around the house. If Seth was up to it, maybe she and Annemarie could go to the hospital and Rayna could ask him Lucy's questions . . . though that wasn't a conversation she wanted to have in Annemarie's presence. Seth hadn't told Annemarie that he'd hung around with Ben socially; Rayna didn't want to be the one to start that discussion, especially when the context would imply that Seth might have been poisoned because he'd known Ben was cheating and concealed it.

Rayna stretched out on the sectional and crossed her arms over her eyes, pressing against an escalating headache. *Ben is dead, and someone tried to kill Seth. You can't tiptoe around this because he didn't dare tell your overprotective sister that he was friends with the guy who once broke your heart. How about everybody, including you, grows up and faces this?*

What if Annemarie *had* faced it—and dealt with it—along with other problems she'd been facing? Stafford's Southern drawl spoke in Rayna's head. *"Were you aware that earlier this year, Mrs. Bristol's store was on the verge of bankruptcy? What perfect timing, receiving an inheritance from your father."*

No. Annemarie would never have killed their father. Or Ben, though she'd despised him. Despised him more than Rayna had. Been upset that he was back in town. Or Seth. Never mind her frustration with him, the friction between them. Never mind her dark joke on the beach the night Ben had died about making a profit if Rayna killed Seth since he'd taken out a life insurance policy.

Life insurance policy? Are you kidding me? This is not a movie. She's not going to murder her husband for his life insurance.

Annemarie had hated reporter Collin Burgess too. Been even more furious than Rayna. She'd been upset when Rayna had let the matter go, upset that Burgess had received no consequences for what he'd done to Rayna.

Annemarie is not a murderer. Your brain is a snarled-up, paranoid disaster if you can even think this way.

Rayna would go over to the house, see how Annemarie was doing, and learn when they could visit Seth. First, though, she needed to figure out lunch. And knock back some ibuprofen.

She sat up. She wouldn't have to go to the house to check on Annemarie. She could sense Annemarie approaching.

Annemarie knocked, then opened the door without waiting for Rayna to answer it. "Excellent, you're awake." She was carrying a plate with a grilled sandwich on it and a large pottery soup mug Rayna had given her when Annemarie was in college. "Did you sleep?"

"Yes. Did you?"

"Yes." Annemarie set the food on the table. "I threw a batch of tomato soup together and brought you some. Figured you could use lunch."

"Thank you." The aroma of the food brought Rayna's promise to Damon into conflict with her empty stomach. Annemarie wasn't going to poison her. But she'd given Damon her word not to eat anything Annemarie offered. How could she manage this without offending her sister? "I should be cooking for you, not the other way around. You must want to get back to the hospital as quickly as you can."

"Seth's asleep. I just talked to the nurse. I needed something to do, and I couldn't endure the idea of going to the Umbrella. Mike called in extra help. They've got it covered for now. Don't worry—I was excessively cautious in cooking. Everything I put in the soup, including the spices, is something I bought at the grocery store today."

"It looks amazing," Rayna said. "But I think my stomach has no idea what time it is. I'm not ready for lunch. I'll stick this in the fridge to eat later."

"To eat later?" Annemarie stared into Rayna's eyes. "Or to toss later because you're afraid it's poisoned?"

"Of course I don't think it's poisoned."

"Did Damon convince you I killed Ben and tried to kill Seth?"

"No. You were the one throwing accusations at him."

"Is he hoping to make a book out of this?"

"No."

"His sponsor is interested in curious things, Kaitlyn told me. Like local ghost stories or supernatural abilities."

Without intending to, Rayna broke eye contact. Hastily, she looked back at Annemarie. "I know. You told me that."

"Did you tell him?"

"Do you think I'd want to end up publicized as a Willet Beach curiosity?"

"I know you wouldn't want that. But I know something's going on with you and Damon. I know you're hiding things."

"We already had this conversation." Desperate to change the subject, Rayna broached the topic that, before Annemarie's arrival, she'd dreaded bringing up in front of her. "Lucy stopped by to pick up the candleholders. She told me that before she moved here, a neighbor saw a woman entering Ben's apartment late at night. Lucy's afraid Ben was having an affair. She asked Seth if he knew anything about—"

"Why would Seth know anything about it?"

"Lucy said Ben and Seth were friends."

Annemarie's jaw tightened. "Yeah, I know. Seth and I already screamed at each other about that."

"You didn't need to come down on him for my sake. I don't care if he was friends with Ben."

"You don't have much sense."

"Wow. Thanks. Seth said he didn't think there was any affair going on, but Lucy wondered if he might not have wanted to admit to her—"

"Lucy's paranoid. Sit down and eat the soup."

"I'm going to save it. I told you I'm not hungry yet. My stomach is a little off."

"You'll feel better if you eat. You need energy. I cut back on the red-pepper flakes. The soup is mild. And I added more cream than usual. Soothing, feel-good food." Annemarie smiled, but there wasn't a smidgen of good humor in her expression. "Our stomachs are in the same mood."

"I wonder why we're feeling off." Rayna smiled back but knew her expression must appear as fake as Annemarie's. "I'd rather save it for when I can enjoy it."

Annemarie slid a chair back from the table. "At least have a few mouthfuls. Seth's parents will be here later this afternoon to take the kids home with them for the weekend, and his mother likes things to be flavorful. I need to know if I made the soup *too* bland so I can zest it up before they arrive."

"Your judgment on what she likes would be better than mine."

"I'd like a second opinion." Annemarie tapped one fingertip against the back of the chair. "Have a seat."

"Good grief, give me a break. I told you I'm not in the mood for—"

"Sit down and try my soup, Rayna." Annemarie's smile grew wider and colder. "Eat. The. Soup."

This had gone beyond the point where Rayna could feign normalcy. "What's wrong with you? Back off."

"You're right." Annemarie's clownish smile went flat. "I'm being too pushy." She picked up the mug, carried it to the sink, and dumped steaming soup with such force that it splashed over the counters, onto the floor, and all over Annemarie's clothes. Annemarie winced, grabbing her shirt and pulling it away from her skin.

Rayna sprang forward and grabbed the sprayer attachment from the sink, ready to douse any burns in cold water, but Annemarie shook her head.

"I'm not hurt," she said and started crying. "You honestly think I'm trying to poison you."

"No . . . Annie . . ." Rayna stuck the sprayer in its holder and grabbed a dishcloth instead. She wet it under the faucet and passed it to Annemarie. "You have soup on your face."

"Are you acting suspicious of *me* to try to hide something *you* did?"

"I did not kill Ben or Dad or anyone else. Didn't you tell me last night that you knew I wouldn't have hurt Ben?"

"I don't even remember what I said to you last night. All I know is the night Ben died, you were making up creepy stories about killing with your mind. Either you're having a breakdown, or there's guilt you're not dealing with."

Since Annemarie wasn't using the rag, Rayna snatched it and started wiping tomato soup off the counter, giving herself an excuse not to look at Annemarie while reciting the lines she was supposed to speak. "Please forget everything I said to you that night. After having Ben die in front of me, after getting questioned by the cops . . . my brain short-circuited."

"You were lying?"

"Yes. I don't know why I made up such morbid stories. I'm sorry."

"You made all that up?"

"Yes. I'm sorry. I didn't mean to take it that far. I don't know what I was thinking." Rayna rinsed the rag under the faucet. "Please forget about it. Don't tell Seth or anyone else. Wipe it out of your head."

"'Don't tell Seth,'" Annemarie quoted her. "Here we go again."

Rayna wiped soup off the faucet. "Promise me you won't. You've been so good about keeping my secrets. Please keep this one."

"I'm not sure I should make that promise this time."

"*Please*, Annie. It was just a . . . glitchy moment."

"*Glitchy*? Quoting Dad now, are we? I'm not sure it *was* just a glitchy moment."

"I didn't kill anyone. Do you think I'd poison Seth?"

Annemarie yanked the dishrag away from her and threw it in the sink. "Do you think *I* would?"

"No." She forced herself to face Annemarie. "But you've been hiding things too. Why didn't you tell me you were having such serious financial problems that The Beach Umbrella almost went bankrupt?"

Annemarie's eyes widened. "Who told you that?"

"Detective Stafford. Last night, she saw me coming out of the hospital and pulled me in for an interview. She made the point of how Dad's death had kept you financially afloat. And no, she didn't ask about the fact that Seth recently got a life insurance policy, so maybe she doesn't know that yet."

"*I did not kill Dad or anyone else*," Annemarie shrieked.

Rayna stared at Annemarie. Annemarie stared back. Silence whirled around them and between them, spinning Rayna's thoughts into a disorienting storm.

"What is *wrong* with us?" Annemarie whispered. "We're accusing each other of *murder*? Is that how little we know about each other, that we don't even know if the other is a killer?" She seized Rayna in a hug so tight that Rayna gasped for air. When Annemarie stepped back, she skidded on a patch of tomato soup and landed on one knee, dragging Rayna with her. They both ended up sitting on the floor, crying and laughing amid splatters of soup.

"I'm sorry," Annemarie said. "I scream at you and dump tomato soup all over your kitchen while accusing *you* of losing it?"

"We can both lose it," Rayna said. "There's not a limit."

They both plunged back into laughter mixed with tears. Rayna lifted her hands to wipe her eyes but lowered them at the sight of tomato soup on her fingers.

"Yeah, don't get that in your eyes," Annemarie said. "When I told you I cut back on the pepper flakes, I was lying."

More laughter. Rayna rested her elbows on her crossed legs and tried to collect herself. Flecks of parsley in the splotch of soup she was staring at were arranged like two eyes above a scrap of onion mouth, an image that didn't help end Rayna's giggle attack.

Laughter gradually settled into silence and sniffling, but neither she nor Annemarie stood. Stepping out of giddy nonsense into reality was something Rayna couldn't bring herself to do, and apparently, neither could Annemarie.

"I've been an idiot," Annemarie said at last. "A spectacular idiot."

"How so?"

"Forgetting what I *do* know about you. Panicking instead of thinking. You lied to me just now, didn't you? About your ability to kill with your mind not being real?"

This reversal spun Rayna back into confusion. "Why would you . . . ? You're the one who accused me of lying about those alleged abilities in the first place, and now . . . Never mind. How about we talk about this another time when we're not sitting on the floor in a puddle of soup?"

Annemarie reached toward Rayna and cupped Rayna's face with both hands, tilting her chin upward. "Stop staring at the floor. Look at me."

Rayna didn't want to meet Annemarie's gaze, but flagrantly avoiding it would be even more suspicious. She looked into her sister's dark-blue eyes.

"You told me I'm good at keeping your secrets," Annemarie said. "I'll tell you what *you're* good at. Evading. Avoiding. Dodging. Hiding."

"Annie—"

"I'll tell you what you're *not* good at. Making up full-on lies from scratch. That's never been your pattern. You get uptight and terse when you lie—like when you pretended you were missing my calls instead of ignoring them or when you claim there's nothing going on with you and Damon. You don't create elaborate stories."

"I'd never had someone die in front of me. That's why I reacted so . . . erratically." Rayna tried to turn her head, shaking off Annemarie's hands, but Annemarie held on.

"'Keep my secrets, Annie,'" Annemarie mimicked. "'Don't tell anyone what I said. Don't tell Seth.' I'm accusing you of murder, and *that's* your biggest concern? That my husband might find out you were babbling nonsense?"

"Can we talk about this later?"

"*There's* classic Rayna." Annemarie released her. "Avoid and evade. No, we can't talk about it later. Suggest that one more time and I'll run outside yelling your secrets to the entire neighborhood. No, I'll text your secrets to Jody Wyeth."

Rayna closed her eyes. "Could you please—"

"Open your eyes. You hate eye contact when you're being evasive, don't you? You couldn't look at me the whole time you were claiming you lied about your powers. Open your eyes."

Rayna opened them. "I'm not up for this."

"Tough. We're talking about it. What you told me on the beach was bonkers, but I already knew you could do incomprehensible things, so I was ready to believe you. Then when you ran off, it was plain you weren't in your right mind, and I thought maybe you'd been in shock when you'd talked to me and you *couldn't* kill with your thoughts; who could even do that? Then I *really* got scared, afraid you'd been rambling about that because you'd actually killed Ben and you were falling apart. I was so rattled that I was jumping to all the wrong conclusions. But now, watching you try to backtrack on what you told me . . . that brings things into perspective."

"What do you mean?"

"You *were* telling the truth about what you can do. I should have known you'd never fabricate an outrageous story like that, even if guilt was ripping you to pieces."

What on earth was she supposed to say now? She didn't want to reveal anything that might increase the danger for Annemarie and her family, but would clinging to her flimsy lies keep them safer? She hated lying to Annemarie, and this strategy wasn't helping. It would only feed Annemarie's frustration and drive her to ask more questions.

"It's all right, Ray." Annemarie touched her cheek. "I don't think you're a monster. I'm sorry for doubting you. You trusted me, and I freaked out on you. That was an awful way to treat you."

Damon had said they could reevaluate their strategy if an attempt at retracting the story was creating problems instead of solving them. While he probably hadn't intended for her to make that decision without consulting him, delaying it served no purpose that Rayna could discern.

"My timing was appalling." Rayna abandoned the lies and willingly met Annemarie's gaze. "I'm sorry for throwing that news at you when I did. I just . . . needed you to understand me. But telling you right after Ben died, and not long after Dad died . . . that was a terrible decision."

"The terrible decision was running off without telling me where you went." Annemarie rose to her feet and extended her hand to Rayna. "And dodging my messages and acting strange when you did respond."

"I'm sorry." Rayna gripped her hand and let Annemarie help her to her feet. "I know that was maddening. But I really need your promise that you won't tell anyone, Seth included, about my new ability, no matter what the circumstances."

"I won't," Annemarie said. "I understand why you wouldn't want word of that to get out." She went to the sink to wash her hands and face. "But we still need to deal with whatever you're hiding. If we're going to understand each—" Annemarie's phone pinged. She hastily dried her hands on a dish towel and yanked the phone out of her pocket. "Seth's awake. I need to change and head to the hospital."

"May I come with you?" Rayna asked, grateful both that Seth was well enough to text Annemarie and that he had derailed the oncoming interrogation about more things Rayna couldn't discuss.

"I don't think they're allowing visitors other than me right now, but I'll let you know."

"You'd better soak that shirt."

Annemarie peered at her soup-splotched white shirt. "I can't believe I did this. And the mess—your kitchen—I'll clean up—"

"No. I'll mop the floor. Go."

"Thanks, Ray. I'll . . . ask him Lucy's question, see if he knows anything about Ben having an affair."

"Thank you. Lucy would be grateful."

"And I *won't* criticize him again for hanging out with Ben. What is he, my child?" Annemarie groaned. "I'm rotten to Seth sometimes. I kept thinking about that last night when I was terrified he was going to die. The way I say things to him, then realize I sound like Dad."

"Go be with him. Go start over."

"If you need a car before you get yours back, borrow Seth's. His keys are on the entryway table."

"Thanks. I'll take the surf-mobile truck, but I'm not touching his new car."

Annemarie hugged her. "I love you."

"I love you too," Rayna said.

* * *

"That was a solid judgment call." Damon picked up the half-full takeout container off his desk. He'd tried to project a nonintimidating demeanor while Rayna had reported on her conversation with Annemarie, but Rayna, sitting across from him, had delivered her report in anxious surges of words while clutching the arms of her chair. She was afraid—reasonably so—of how he'd react, but she'd voluntarily told him what had happened. She could have tried to hide it. For that matter, she could have run away altogether, fleeing town the instant he'd left her on her own. But when he'd awakened from his nap and sent her a message, checking in with her, she'd immediately asked to meet with him. This was encouraging progress that—along with a nap, a shower, and the food he was eating—was rejuvenating.

"I hope it was the right call." Rayna's fingers wiggled slightly as though she were trying to release her death grip on the chair but couldn't get her hands to relax. "If I'd kept denying it, I think it would have made things worse."

"Agreed."

"Annemarie's been reliable about keeping my secrets." Rayna shook her hands out. "Even if . . . I don't think she's . . . done anything she doesn't want me to know about. But no matter what, there's no reason she'd reveal what I told her. I hope."

"We do the best we can," Damon said, accidentally quoting Logan. If Logan found out, his smugness would level up. "Eat before your food gets cold." Rayna hadn't yet opened her lunch.

"I have more to tell you," she said. "Lucy Orozco stopped by."

"Eat first, then tell me. Or eat and talk." Damon wanted to learn what had happened with Lucy, but he could wait until Rayna had eaten. She must be hungry, and it was by his request that she hadn't eaten the food Annemarie had offered.

"Thank you for lunch." Rayna fumbled to open the container. "I'm starving, and this smells amazing. I can eat and talk." With pauses for bites of chicken, grilled vegetables, and rice, she told him about the visit and Lucy's hope of identifying the woman her neighbor had seen at Ben's apartment.

"Jody hasn't said anything to me about rumors of Ben Orozco having an affair," Damon said. "She hasn't speculated about that angle at all. I heard Seth mention it, however, when I was talking with him and Kaitlyn at Wyeth's Grill."

The handle of Rayna's plastic fork snapped off, leaving the tines stuck in a chunk of chicken. "What did he say?"

"He was complaining that people were gossiping about Ben's death and mentioned a possible affair as one of the topics of gossip. Kaitlyn asked if he was referring to an affair with you, and he said that was one of the rumors."

"I would *never* have considered getting involved with Ben again. I hope you know that."

"He also expressed the opinion that when someone dies, if you have dirt on them, you keep it to yourself."

Rayna tugged the broken fork piece loose. Damon opened the center drawer of his desk, found a cellophane-wrapped fork and knife left from an earlier takeout order, and handed the utensils to Rayna.

"Thank you," she said. "You're well prepared. Did you get the impression Seth has dirt on Ben?"

"I wondered about that, but I don't know. If Ben and Lucy's marriage was troubled, chances are Stafford's already figured that out and she's been investigating the possibility of an affair as a motive."

"I hope Ben *wasn't* having an affair. It must be excruciating for Lucy to have the fear that he betrayed her all jumbled up with her grief."

Damon could see no satisfaction, no spite on Rayna's face. Only sorrow. "If there was an affair, it shouldn't be too hard to figure out who the woman is."

"Not Kaitlyn. She'd never get involved with Ben."

"What about Annemarie?"

"Annemarie!" With her new fork, Rayna stabbed a piece of bell pepper. "Are you kidding? She's been angry all along that he and Lucy moved back here. I kept telling her she was overreacting." She stabbed a second piece of pepper without having eaten the first.

"You were speaking of red herrings earlier," he said. "What about exaggerated annoyance and relentless distaste as red herrings?"

"If she killed him," Rayna said tartly, "then the distaste must not have *all* been fake."

"Fair point." Damon sensed Jody approaching the office. "Are you up for company?"

"Sure," Rayna said. "Bring Jody on. I'll ask straight out if she's killed anyone."

"Is that a battle you want to start?"

Rayna shrugged and shoved the forkful of peppers into her mouth.

The door to the reception area opened. Footsteps. A rap on Damon's closed office door.

"Come in," Damon called.

The door opened. "Oh stars!" Jody squinted at Rayna. "Hello, dear. I saw Seth's truck in the lot and got hopeful that he was out of the hospital."

"I'm borrowing his truck," Rayna said.

"What happened to your car?"

A scrappy gleam flared in Rayna's brown eyes. "I left it at the scene of the last murder I committed."

Jody gasped.

Rayna scooped up a piece of grilled onion. "Homicide doesn't always go smoothly, Jody. It's an art, and I'm fallible. Sometimes I have to escape on foot and return for the car later."

Damon sympathized with the urge to tweak Jody, but such punch-drunk behavior from Rayna put him on alert. "I think Jody is taking you seriously."

"Sorry." Rayna set her fork down. "Jody, I was joking. I promise you, I haven't killed anyone. If you could please stop assuming I have, I'd be grateful."

"You know the old adage, dear." Jody's rattled expression steadied. "Many a truth is spoken in jest. Mr. Hale was reckless to tell you my suspicions, but he's a pushover when it comes to you, isn't he? You've bewitched him."

Rayna aimed a wry smile at Damon. "I have definitely not bewitched him. But you've known me since I was a baby, and you're ready to jump to the conclusion that I've committed multiple murders?"

"You're generally a good girl." Jody edged farther into the room, keeping a wide swath of floor between Rayna and her.

"Generally a good girl," Rayna echoed. "Except for . . . killing people?"

"Well, I'm not saying you don't have issues, but I'm sure what you've done is bothering you. Don't you think it would be a relief to go to the police and get the waiting over with? You need help, dear."

"Don't you think it would be a relief," Rayna said, "to be candid about why you're so eager to blame Ben's death on me—and even to blame me for what were ruled natural deaths or accidents?"

"I don't know what you mean." Jody took hastier steps, placing herself on Damon's side of the desk. "I was coming to tell Mr. Hale about another incident I discovered, but since you're so intent on bickering with me, I'll say it in front of you. Mr. Hale, there was a newspaper reporter who wrote a vicious review of—"

"He knows about Collin Burgess. I didn't kill Collin either."

Jody gawked at her, then turned to Damon. "I hope *you* provided that food, not her, and that you had your eye on it the entire time."

Rayna patted the chair next to her. "Sit down and we can watch together to see if the poison I fed him works."

Hands on hips, Jody faced Rayna. "I always thought your father was a bit harsh in saying you were odd, but I see he was understating things."

"You told Damon you suspect me of killing your husband."

"You'll feel better if you admit to it, dear." Jody cushioned her angry voice with a layer of coaxing.

"I wasn't even in Willet Beach when Elliott died," Rayna said.

"Yes, you were. I remember you were here."

"At the funeral, yes, but not at the time of his death. If you don't believe me, have the police call Evan and check with him."

Jody's face went pink. She was twisting her ruby pendant so vigorously that Damon expected the fragile gold chain to break. "You might have sneaked into town, then sneaked back home before your husband knew you were gone."

"Sneaked into town all the way from Denver just to push Elliott off his boat? How could I have timed it *that* perfectly?"

"You're a clever girl. And Elliott was out on his boat every day once he retired. Your hairstyle is off-center, dear. Did you not check a mirror when you were getting ready?"

"My hair . . . what?" Rayna groped at the knot of hair on her head. "What does my hair matter? We're talking about Elliott. Why are you making accusations you *know* are untrue?"

"I know Elliott was unkind to you. I understand why you felt he deserved to die."

"Did *you* kill Elliott? Is that why you're so fixated on blaming me?"

Jody lurched backward. Damon jumped to his feet, ready to grab her if she needed support.

"How can you . . . ? What a vicious . . ." Jody pressed both hands over her heart, tears filling her eyes.

"I'm sorry," Rayna whispered. "I'm sorry, Jody."

Jody clutched Damon's arm. "Do you see why I've been warning you about her? Do you see what she is? I was *heartbroken* when Elliott died and heartbroken when Glenn died, and, Rayna, don't you *dare* try to deny you killed Glenn. I *saw* the loathing in your eyes that night when he was teasing you. And you looked *so* strange during dinner, all zoned out, and Glenn whispered to me, 'That girl is warped. She ought to be locked up,' and I said, 'Do you mean she needs psychiatric treatment?' and he said, 'She belongs in a cage at the zoo,' and I was so naive, I thought he was joking. It wasn't until the police started asking questions that I realized he was telling me he was afraid of you. That beneath the innocent surface, you were a deadly predator."

"Jody, have a seat and take time to calm down," Damon said. "Rayna, please come with me." He guided Jody into his chair and headed for the door. Rayna accompanied him, her gait slightly wobbly.

He closed the office door, crossed the reception room to stand near the exit—too far away for Jody to eavesdrop—and faced Rayna.

"I don't know why I said all that." Feistiness and blood had both ebbed from her face. "I'm totally unraveling."

"The most unraveled thing you did was to apologize to Jody, but the rest of the conversation was . . ."

"On the same continuum?"

"It's probably better if you and Jody steer clear of each other for now."

She curled her trembling fingers into fists. "She's not going to trust you anymore since she knows you pass things on to me."

"She already thought I was too enthralled by you to make sensible decisions."

"Does what she told you change your assessment of whether I killed my father?" Rayna's eyes went hazy; she didn't seem to be seeing Damon. "I wonder if it was the last thing he ever said about me."

"I don't think he said it at all."

"It's the sort of thing he would have said."

"Jody knows your father's style; she could put words in his mouth. She was lashing out at you. I doubt it's any comfort after everything he *did* say to you or about you, but he didn't whisper that zoo statement in her ear. It's far too juicy for her to have forgotten about until now. She'd have already thrown it in my face as evidence against you. Rayna, let's do this. I'll deal with Jody. You check in with Annemarie and get a sense of how things are likely to go for the rest of the day. Since the kids are with Seth's parents, if she's planning to stay at the hospital for a while and she doesn't need you at The Beach Umbrella, we could go pick up your car. We'll drive Maggie's rental out there, leave it for her, and take your car home."

"Just be honest," Rayna said flatly. "Are you wanting to get me to the cabin so you can keep me there until I'm less . . . unpredictable? I have no idea what discussion about me is happening between you and your team. I have no idea what my status is or what happens next or anything else."

"I won't keep you there against your will," Damon said.

"Not today, or not ever again?"

"I can't promise you never again, not while things are this unsettled. There are too many factors at play. I shouldn't even promise you today, frankly, since things change minute to minute, so I'll amend my first answer: I won't keep you there unless it's necessary. Right now, it isn't."

"And if it is necessary," Rayna said, "it doesn't matter if I agree to go to the cabin or not; you'll take me there." She looked at her still-trembling fists and tucked them under her arms, apparently deciding that if she couldn't steady them, she'd hide them. "If you don't think I'm dangerous, what are your responsibilities toward me?"

"Right now, to assist you in keeping classified matters classified and to keep you cooperating with us. And to keep you safe, which seems increasingly vital considering the people around you."

"I don't think Jody—" Her phone pinged. She pulled it out of her pocket to read the message. "Annemarie says I can visit Seth now. Only me though. They're allowing one visitor along with her. I'd like to go now."

"That's fine. Be careful."

"I will." Rayna's drawn expression relaxed a little. "Should I come back here after I visit him, or should I go home?"

"Come back here."

"All right." She inhaled and exhaled a slow, full breath. "I'll do my best not to worry you. I'm amazed that you're willing to . . . I can't imagine how difficult it must be for you to trust me after what . . . happened before."

"What happened before isn't a burden that should be on your shoulders," he said, pretty much quoting Maggie this time. He ought to notify both Logan and her that they'd earned an "I told you so." "Give Seth my best wishes."

"I will. Um, I need my purse. It's in your office."

"I'll get it for you."

When Damon opened his office door, Jody said loudly, "I hope Rayna knows that if she tries to hurt you, she'll be dealing with me. I'm a mother bear, you know, and I consider you one of my cubs."

"I'm sure she'll heed the warning," Damon said, retrieving Rayna's purse.

In the reception area, Rayna thanked him for the purse and said under her breath, "I wouldn't put too much stock in your bear-cub status. She used to say that about me too."

CHAPTER 29

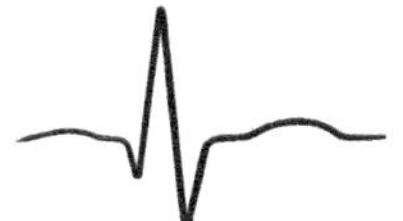

As Rayna was driving Seth's truck into the hospital parking lot, her phone rang. She pulled into the nearest space so she could check who was calling.

Kaitlyn. With no idea what Kaitlyn had heard, Rayna steeled herself and answered. "Hello?"

"*What* is going on?" Kaitlyn leaped to the point. "I just got the weirdest text from my mother."

Rayna leaned against the headrest and shut her eyes. Her headache was mounting again. "What did it say?"

"I'll read it to you. '*I'm at work. I had a terrible confrontation with Rayna. She screamed accusations that I'd murdered your father, reducing me to tears. It was so appalling that Mr. Hale threw her out, even though he's so infatuated with her. She's insane, and I'm certain she's dangerous. Keep away from her.*' I assume she's exaggerating, so could you tell me what really happened?"

"Yes," Rayna said. "Are you aware that she's convinced I murdered Ben, my father, and yours?"

"I know she's been nosing around and coming up with theories about Ben's death, bragging to me that Damon trusts her with the most confidential things. I know you're on her list of suspects."

"She's narrowed the list to me. She's been warning Damon that I'm a murderer. I was at his office for lunch today, and when she arrived, we did have a confrontation. But I didn't scream at her. I did ask her if she'd murdered your father and if that was why she was so intent on blaming me. It was a cruel thing to say, and I apologized for it."

"Why would you ask her that?"

"I'm sorry. It was after she accused me of killing him. I told her I wasn't even in Willet Beach at the time he died, and she suggested I flew here, murdered him, then left with no one knowing I'd been here."

"She said *what*?" Kaitlyn started laughing. "You've got to be kidding. And you felt the need to apologize for clapping back at her? Oh, Rayna. She deserved a lot harsher of a response than that."

"How did you respond to her message?"

"I told her to call me, but she said she couldn't yet. She was having an important discussion with her boss and she'd call me when they were done. Did Damon actually throw you out?"

"Sort of. He asked me to step out of the office with him while your mother calmed down. Then Annemarie texted to say I could come visit Seth, so I left. I arrived at the hospital just now."

"No offense to your boyfriend," Kaitlyn said, "but he's part of the problem here. He encourages her to share information about people, and he's got her viewing her own gossip as valid book research. Then having *murder* committed in our town . . . and having the victim be someone she knew . . . This is so thrilling that her brain has overloaded. It's no wonder she's throwing wacky accusations around. I'm sorry you're her favorite target. I'll talk to her about it."

"Thank you." Why *had* she taken Jody's accusations so seriously, suspecting they reflected on Jody's guilt? Jody loved drama. Jody thrived on presenting Damon with what she felt was vital information. No doubt Damon had particularly encouraged her to share information about Rayna.

Yet, if Damon was correct, she'd fabricated that comment from Rayna's father to shore up her claim that Rayna was dangerous. Jody was fond of exaggeration, but an outright lie?

"Are you doing okay?" Kaitlyn asked.

"I didn't handle the conversation well today, and I'm sorry. I'm not . . . managing my life very well at the moment."

"Will you quit apologizing? She's the one at fault. I'll tell her to knock it off. And of course you're not managing your life well at the moment. Look at everything you've been through. That takes a toll, Rayna. I know you hurt a lot more than you let on. You really scared Annemarie when you left town without telling her where you were."

"I know. That was dumb."

"I'm glad you're back. She said Damon drove you home?"

"Yes. He was visiting, and I was so distraught when I heard about Seth that I didn't dare drive. We'll pick up my car later."

"You two are—"

"Friends," Rayna said.

Kaitlyn snickered. "If you say so. You told *him* where you were hiding, but you wouldn't tell your sister. But you're just friends. What are you doing for wheels now?"

"Borrowing Seth's truck." Rayna opened the truck door. "I'd better go see him now. Annemarie will wonder why it's taking me forever to arrive."

"I have a gift I need to drop off for him. How's he doing?"

"Much better," Rayna said, grateful to be sensing the regular beating of Seth's heart.

"He's incredibly fortunate."

"Yes, he is."

"One more thing—Annemarie told me the story about the neighbor who thought Ben was having an affair. That woman she saw was *me*, and I feel horrid that Lucy was worried."

"That was *you*?" In her relief, Rayna all but bellowed the words and was glad no one was near enough to wonder what she was shouting about. "I told Lucy it couldn't be you. I thought you hate staying up late."

"I do, but for a while, I was having trouble with insomnia and found it helped if I stayed up until I was about to fall over. When Ben kept bugging me, I dropped by a few times after the Grill closed because why not get it out of the way rather than have him pester me during the day. In retrospect, it was dumb going over there at that hour. I should have known it would start rumors."

"Have you told Lucy this?"

"Yes, I called her right away and explained. I reassured her I didn't have an affair with Ben, that it was enough of a trial putting up with him when we were talking business."

"You said that to her?"

"Okay, I could have been more respectful of his memory, but I'd rather be real. It made her laugh. She'd seen us interact; she knew what I meant."

"Thank you for clearing up the question of the mystery visitor." At least this was one portion of grief removed from Lucy's plate.

"Happy I could do that for her. I'll talk to you soon." Kaitlyn hung up, and Rayna headed into the hospital.

Seth had the stamina to speak with her for only about fifteen minutes, but he was cheerfully himself, joking that he'd probably been poisoned by too much microwave popcorn, teasing her about her alleged relationship with Damon, and instructing her not to clean his truck—he liked the colossal amount of sand ground into the floor mats and the mud spray in the wheel wells. Rayna matched the lightness of his conversation, not mentioning her clash with Jody or anything else serious. When he started dozing off, she stepped out into the hall for a talk with Annemarie. They wandered away from the police officer who'd been standing in the doorway throughout the visit.

"Would you like me to work at the Umbrella this afternoon?" Rayna asked.

"No, the store's fine. Mike's running things, my part-timers are stepping up, and Mike's girlfriend has offered to pitch in if we need her—she works off and on for us. We're more than covered. Seth will probably sleep a lot this afternoon, so I'll drop by there myself at some point."

"I can take care of things at your house, then. Get everything cleaned up, do your laundry—"

"I just did the laundry. And I doubt the police will want another look at the house, but just in case, I don't want to start scouring the place. You should go get your car before the owner of your hideaway has it towed. I assume Damon would be happy to give you a ride to pick it up."

"He would be," Rayna said, wishing Annemarie had given her an excuse not to return to the cabin today. She didn't think Damon was trying to trick her, but she couldn't help feeling apprehensive about walking through that door. Still, better to get it over with than to make up weak excuses to stall, possibly feeding Damon's concerns about her.

They reached the elevator.

"Take it easy, all right?" Annemarie said. "You look worn out. Maybe forget the car today and go take another nap. Also, your topknot is crooked. Let me fix it." She grasped Rayna's shoulder and spun her around.

"Okay, my hairdo doesn't matter right now." First Jody, now Annemarie.

Rayna started to step away, but Annemarie pulled her back. "I can do it fast." She removed bobby pins and unrolled Rayna's hair. "I have a brush in my purse. That would make this even better."

"*Don't* go get your brush. I don't care how my hair looks today. Why are we playing beauty shop in a hospital hallway?"

Annemarie slid the elastic off Rayna's high ponytail.

"Annie, this is ridiculous. Let's at least not block the elevator." Rayna sidestepped. Annmarie moved with her, energetically finger-combing Rayna's hair.

Derailing Annemarie from stress-fueled fussing was a lost cause. While Annemarie messed with her hair, Rayna said quietly, "Kaitlyn called to tell me she was the mystery woman visiting Ben."

"Oh, good *grief.* Yes. Seth thought it must have been Kaitlyn since she and Ben met a bunch of times to talk about his restaurant, so I called Kaitlyn to ask. She was mortified and was going to call Lucy right away to clear that up. I said, 'What were you thinking, creeping over to his place at night? No wonder the neighbor thought Ben was up to something.' She said she hadn't thought about it in those terms because Ben is so not a temptation; he's an obnoxious kid." Annemarie smoothed Rayna's hair, drawing it up into a ponytail. "I said, 'Next time you decide to help an obnoxious kid start a restaurant, don't make it look so sketchy.'"

"Thanks for taking care of all that."

"No problem."

"Kaitlyn also wanted the scoop on an . . . argument . . . I had with her mother right before I came over here."

Annemarie divided Rayna's ponytail in half. "You argued with Jody?"

Rayna recounted the conversation.

"Damon's right," Annemarie said grimly. "If Dad had said that about you, she wouldn't have held it back for this long. She's making stuff up for Damon. I wonder if she's making stuff up for Detective Stafford too."

"I don't know."

"Tell Stafford about this. Maybe it'll distract her and slow her down on arresting me for attempting to murder my husband."

"Do you think it will come to that?"

"I don't know. Detective Stafford makes everything I do or say seem suspicious."

"She's the same with me. And with Lucy."

"I think I know how Seth was poisoned though."

Rayna tried to look at Annemarie, but Annemarie said sharply, "Face forward. You'll wreck my work. I haven't heard anything official yet, but he told me everything he ate yesterday, same list he gave Stafford. One thing was a big extra-dark-chocolate mint cookie. The receptionist at his office gave it to him, saying it had been left by the door. It was in a Dorotea's Bakery box with Seth's name on it and a 'Thank you for all your help,' signed with the names of a married couple he sold a house to recently. I don't dare try to contact them to ask if they really left him the cookie—I don't want to get in trouble with Stafford for interfering with her investigation—but I did dispatch Mike to scope out the bakery on his lunch break. Not to talk to anyone about the cookie—just to look."

"And there were no extra-dark-chocolate mint cookies for sale," Rayna guessed.

"Nope. I don't remember Dorotea's ever selling that flavor. Seth loves chocolate and mint, and he would have talked about them, or I would have bought him one at some point."

"The killer chose a flavor combination Seth loves? Like the killer chose an ice-cream combination including an ingredient Lucy couldn't eat?"

"Right? Is it coincidence or knowledge of their victims . . . or of the victim's spouse, in Lucy's case, if the killer was only targeting Ben?" Annemarie slid a bobby pin into place. "I'm freaked out at the thought that I probably know the poisoner."

Suspicions of Jody flickered again in Rayna's head. Jody was an accomplished baker and Seth's neighbor. She might well know he was a fan of chocolate and mint. And she'd known Lucy since Lucy's childhood. *Why would Jody try to kill Seth or Ben? She has no motive.*

"Does Seth have any idea why someone would try to kill him?" Rayna asked.

"No. I said—in a nice way, I promise—that it must be connected to the reason Ben was poisoned and was Ben up to anything? He said Ben was up to opening a restaurant and showing off on a surfboard, and the only person Seth was afraid would murder him due to his connection with Ben was me."

"He doesn't—"

"No, he doesn't think I poisoned him. He was teasing." Annemarie patted the redone topknot. "There you go. It's a little ragged, but it's better than it was. I'm going to go sit with Seth for a while, or maybe grab a bite at the cafeteria. I didn't have an appetite for that tomato soup either after the scene we made."

"Keep me posted on how I can help you."

"I will. And Ray . . . don't eat anything, tomato soup or otherwise, unless you buy or prepare it yourself."

Rayna chose not to mention that Damon had provided her lunch, lest Annemarie drag her to the ER to get her stomach pumped. She pulled Annemarie into a hug and kissed her cheek. "You be careful too."

"I will."

On the elevator ride to the main floor, Rayna drew her attention away from Seth and Annemarie and wandered mentally through her range, checking to see if Detective Stafford or anyone else familiar was nearby. Kaitlyn's presence caught her attention, out in the direction of the parking lot. She must have decided to come drop off the gift she'd mentioned. If Rayna could do so in a natural way, she'd intercept her, let her know Seth was asleep, and offer to take the gift to Seth and Annemarie's house.

The wind was brisker and the clouds darker than they'd been when Rayna had entered the hospital. Was it supposed to rain today? She walked slowly toward Seth's truck, but Kaitlyn didn't come into view. Rayna could sense her standing several rows over, not advancing toward the hospital. She must have stepped out of her car, then gotten distracted by something—possibly a call from her mother reporting on her "important discussion" with Damon. How *had* Damon handled that conversation?

Kaitlyn still wasn't moving, and Rayna couldn't see her. She and her car must be hidden behind a van or truck. Rayna couldn't think of an unweird way to pretend to notice her, so she gave up the idea of intercepting her and climbed into Seth's truck.

She was backing out of her parking space when she sensed Kaitlyn walking in the direction of the hospital, moving at an angle. Rayna braked and glanced in Kaitlyn's direction just as Kaitlyn adjusted her trajectory so she was heading toward Rayna. She must have spotted Seth's truck.

Kaitlyn cut between cars, waving. Rayna waved back and rolled down her window. If it hadn't been for her ability to sense Kaitlyn, she'd have done a double-take, wondering who was waving at her. Kaitlyn was wearing a straw sun hat, an oversized navy-blue windbreaker, and large, round sunglasses that weren't her style. Had she taken them from the Grill's lost and found? She wouldn't need the sunglasses for long, considering what the weather was up to.

"Good timing." Kaitlyn reached Rayna's open window. She was carrying a brown paper sack. "You saw Seth? How is he?"

"He's in good spirits but very tired," Rayna said. "We didn't talk long, and he was falling asleep by the end of the conversation."

Kaitlyn held up her paper sack. "I shouldn't go give him this right now, then."

"Would you like me to take it home with me? Annemarie can deliver it to him later, or he can get it when he comes home."

"Thanks, yes. She can keep it at home for him. Not like he'll need it in the hospital. I was trying to think of something he'd like better than flowers. Want a look?"

"Sure."

"Hang on; I'll get in the truck so you can stop blocking the lane." Kaitlyn circled to the passenger side, hopped into the seat, and shut the door. Rayna rolled up her window and pulled forward into her parking space.

From the bag, Kaitlyn took a small basket wrapped in blue cellophane tied with a burlap ribbon. She untied the ribbon. "This is all top-quality stuff—especially the gift card—so I hope Seth likes it." She showed Rayna a bottle of natural sunscreen, a tin of surf wax, a tube of pure aloe vera gel, and a gift card to Wyeth's Grill.

"He'll love it," Rayna said. "This is very kind of you."

"Well, he was almost my stepbrother-in-law." Kaitlyn retied the bow and stuck the gift basket back in the paper sack. "Hey, would you mind giving me a ride to my car? I'm parked at the bookstore down the street. That's where they sell this sunscreen—the new owner makes it. I wanted to stretch my muscles, so I walked from there to the hospital." She set the bag on the sandy floor mat next to Rayna's purse and fastened her seat belt. "While you play chauffeur, I'll give you a report on my mom's conversation with Damon . . . if you want to hear it."

"I want to hear it." For the second time, Rayna reversed out of her parking place. Kaitlyn's heart was beating so fast it triggered Rayna's apprehension. That pulse rate wasn't all due to exertion; Kaitlyn hadn't walked *that* quickly toward the truck. If Jody's report had been enough to upset unflappable Kaitlyn, it must have been a doozy. "Did she tell him I've killed someone else?"

"No. She lectured him about how dim men are when they're dealing with a woman who knows how to bat her eyelashes. That it takes another woman to see the danger behind a pretty smile, and you've been evil since birth."

"Evil since birth?" Rayna reached the parking lot exit and turned in the direction of the bookstore. "She's always liked me, claimed she was excited to have me as a stepdaughter, and now I'm evil since birth? She's escalating her accusations by the minute. How did Damon respond?"

"She claims he listened closely and asked sincere questions, so she's hopeful she got through to him. She gave him a list of warnings: don't be alone with you, don't eat anything in your presence because it would only take a moment of distraction for you to poison it, watch out for you trying to steal his phone because that means you're about to strike and don't want him to be able to call for help . . . I don't remember what else. Oh, she's planning to track down your ex-husband to warn him because he must be on your hit list."

"Oh my word." Rayna shriveled at the thought of Evan getting a call from Jody ranting about how evil Rayna was. "Something is wrong with your mother. It made sense to be suspicious of me after Ben died, but she's getting less and less rational. When's the last time she saw a doctor?"

"She's definitely behaving irrationally," Kaitlyn said. As Rayna signaled to turn into the bookstore parking lot, Kaitlyn said, "No, not here. Keep going. I'm parked farther down, on the side of the street."

Rayna drove past the bookstore. "Will you talk to her about seeing a doctor?"

"Yep, I'll try."

Thinking about chocolate mint cookies and motives, Rayna decided to risk an offensive question. "This is going to sound incredibly rude, but . . . is there any possibility that your mom had a reason to . . . that she might have . . . ? She reacted so strongly when I asked—"

"If she'd committed murder?" Kaitlyn finished the question matter-of-factly. "Before any of this happened, I'd have said there's no way she'd take a decisive action like that on her own. Mom is usually sea-foam. She lets life toss her around. But when she gets scared enough . . . At this next intersection, turn right."

Rayna did so. "When she gets scared enough . . . what?" she prompted.

"It turns out she does crazy things."

"What kind of cra—"

"Rayna, I need you to take me to the fishing hut. Could you do that?"

"The fishing hut!" Baffled, Rayna glanced at Kaitlyn. The Wyeths' fishing hut was twenty minutes away. "I thought I was taking you to your car."

"I don't feel like driving. You can relate, right?"

"What is going on with you? First your car's at the bookstore, then it's farther down the street, then it's on a different street . . . and now you don't want it at all?"

"I'm under a lot of pressure, all right? That's why I want to go to the fishing hut. To unwind."

It wasn't like Kaitlyn to be this capricious. "I'm sorry, but I don't have time to take you to the fishing hut. I'd be happy to take you to Damon's office though. That's where I'm headed. I'm sure your mother can give you a lift to the fishing hut."

"Mom will be busy with whatever nonsense project Damon has assigned her." Kaitlyn bent forward, both hands rooting around inside the paper bag holding Seth's gift. "You can spare the time. After what you've been through, no one expects you to be productive today. You remember how to get to the hut, don't you?"

It also wasn't like Kaitlyn to demand that people cater to her. Rayna pictured the location of the fishing hut—a lone house on the water, accessed via a narrow, winding road, and surrounded by trees. No neighbors.

"Damon's expecting me." Rayna tried to sound casual. Kaitlyn's rapid heartbeat had accelerated further; beneath her composure, she was agitated. "We're going to get my car. Don't you need to get back to the Grill anyway?"

"I need a break. They can survive without me for an afternoon."

Tiny shards of glass seemed to form along Rayna's spine, then snap loose, stinging her from head to feet. Kaitlyn was as likely as Jody to know about Lucy's allergy and Seth's taste in baked goods; as a restaurateur, she paid attention to what friends ate. Kaitlyn had been exceptionally helpful to Ben in establishing his restaurant, even as she claimed he irritated her. Could her disdain for Ben have been a cover—as Damon had suggested it might be for Annemarie? Maybe there had been no insomnia-inspired business meeting. Maybe there had been an affair that had ended badly, wounding and infuriating Kaitlyn.

But that doesn't sound like her at all.

No matter what, Rayna wasn't going off to an isolated location with her. "I can drop you right here, or I can take you to Damon's office. Those are your choices."

"Let's go to the cabin."

"Kaitlyn—" Rayna glanced at her and saw the gun in her hand.

"The cabin," Kaitlyn said. "Turn right at the next intersection."

CHAPTER 30

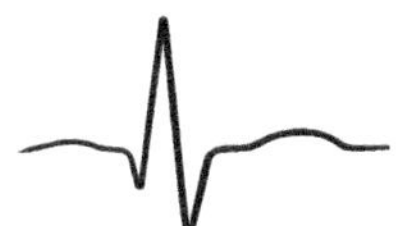

Fear made it impossible for Rayna to organize thoughts that had jumbled and frozen in the wrong order. She couldn't focus on the important question of what to do now. All she could think of was Kaitlyn in the hospital parking lot. Kaitlyn hadn't been coincidentally concealed by a tall vehicle as she'd talked on the phone or answered a message while Rayna exited the hospital. She'd been hiding, waiting for the chance to approach Rayna away from the hospital building, where she was less likely to be seen. But surely there were security cameras—

The big sun hat covering her hair and shading her face. The sunglasses. The too-large windbreaker. Even her jeans were baggy, with the hems dragging on the ground, a style Rayna had never seen her wear. If a camera had caught an image of Kaitlyn, Rayna would bet it wasn't identifiable.

"*Turn.*" Kaitlyn jabbed the muzzle of the gun into Rayna's rib cage.

Rayna twisted the steering wheel too sharply. The tires screeched.

"If you get yourself pulled over, you're dead," Kaitlyn said.

Rayna corrected the truck's position on the road. "Where are we going?"

"To the cabin, like I said. Do you remember the way?"

"Yes." Rayna drew a halting breath. "But I told Damon I was coming back to his office right after I visited Seth. If I'm gone too long, he'll get worried."

"Controlling guy, huh? Bad choice of men."

"He's not controlling. He's nervous because a murderer is running around Willet Beach." Rayna shrank away from the metal poking her side. "Did you kill Ben?"

"Where's your phone?"

"In my purse."

With one hand keeping the gun aimed at Rayna, Kaitlyn reached with her other hand to unzip Rayna's purse and pull out her phone. "Passcode?"

"Why do you need it?"

"Once we're out of town, you're going to send Damon a message. Passcode?"

Rayna recited the passcode. Kaitlyn fiddled one-handed with the phone. She was wearing surgical gloves. She must have put them on while digging around in the paper bag.

When Rayna was speeding down the highway, Kaitlyn said, "Keep quiet while I do voice-to-text." She tapped the screen and lifted the phone to her mouth. "Visiting Seth was awful," she dictated. "I faked it for Annemarie, but I thought I'd melt or blow up or shatter . . . end up in pieces, tiny pieces, horrible pieces . . . I am in pieces. I can't deal. I can't sort any of it out. I can't keep feeling this. I don't know anything. Why do I hurt people I love? But they deserve it. But they don't . . . I didn't understand that until I saw Seth. I don't understand why I hurt Seth, but he brought Ben to town, but it was his job. He didn't mean to hurt me. Not like Ben. Ben hurt me. Not like Dad. I need to be gone. I can't tell Annemarie what I did. She'll never forgive me. I need to be gone. I'm sorry. I'm sorry. I really do care about you, and you've been so nice to me. You won't understand. You'll never believe I could be this terrible, but I'm a mess . . . a junk pile I can't sort out. I'm sorry for everything. I need to be gone." Kaitlyn tapped the screen a couple of times and lowered the phone.

"'I'm a junk pile I can't sort out'?" Rayna quoted. "So, confessing to murder turns me into a lousy poet? What was *that* about?" She already knew the answer: it was about giving Damon the impression that guilt over what she'd done to Seth and others had overwhelmed her and she was emotionally disintegrating.

"Get into the left lane," Kaitlyn said.

Rayna signaled and changed lanes. Kaitlyn rolled her window partway down and dropped Rayna's phone into the center of speeding traffic. She rolled the window up. "Get back in the right lane. Exit's coming up."

Rayna returned to the right lane. "Damon knows I didn't poison Seth. I was with him, out of town, when Seth got sick."

"You could have arranged to leave something behind, knowing he'd eat it while you were gone."

Something like a dark-chocolate mint cookie? Dread enveloped Rayna like frigid water. What if Damon *did* believe she'd written that text?

He won't. He knows if you wanted to kill someone, you wouldn't bother with poison.

But that didn't mean he wouldn't believe she was unstable and dangerous, spewing dark nonsense.

How could she escape this situation without taking Kaitlyn's life? She did *not* want to kill her, no matter what Kaitlyn had done.

But there might not be another way to survive this.

* * *

Had he misjudged both Rayna's innocence and her mental stability? Damon couldn't rid his mind of that piercing self-condemnation, but he forced himself to think around it while he reread Rayna's text several times. Yes, she'd been on edge during their lunchtime conversation and the clash with Jody—how could she not be struggling after so many threads of her life had been knotted or broken?—but she'd been rational and calm. She'd willingly gone to visit Seth as soon as she'd had the opportunity, and now, just over an hour later, she was sending Damon an incoherent message filled with anguished, rambling confessions?

She'd poisoned Seth? That was extremely unlikely. Even setting aside the fact that if murder was her goal, she had an easy and untraceable means of committing it, she'd been imprisoned in the cabin from the day after Ben's death until Seth was already sick. She'd have had no opportunity to plant poison or to enlist someone to do it for her—unless she'd plotted it all out before Damon had kidnapped her. Poisoning Ben . . . arranging things so Seth, too, would be poisoned . . . waiting for Seth to die. A cold-blooded, long-premeditated attack on her sister's husband followed by a credible display of shock when she'd gotten the news that he was in the hospital. Damon had witnessed the loss of color in her face, the speeding of her heartbeat, the agony in her eyes.

"You've been so nice to me." Nice to her? Like drugging and kidnapping her? "*You'll never believe I could be this terrible."* He'd held her prisoner precisely because he thought she might have committed multiple murders. *"I really do care about you"*? All of these comments sounded like ones an outsider would create when they had no idea what Rayna's interaction with him had truly been.

He knew better than anyone that not all messages sent via Rayna's phone came from Rayna.

If she hadn't sent the text, who had? He tried to call her. She didn't answer. He texted her, certain he wouldn't get a response. *"I need to be gone."* She was going to disappear, either without a trace or leaving evidence behind that she'd committed suicide.

She was in danger, and he was an absolute idiot. He should have insisted on staying within range of her at all times, not sent her off on her own. She'd have been cautious enough not to eat any food offered to her, and she could defend herself against a direct threat. But what if the threatener was her sister?

He called Annemarie.

She answered promptly. "Hi. What's going on?"

It took all his effort to keep his tone civil. If he stayed calm, he'd have a better chance of gauging whether or not she was hiding anything. "How long ago did Rayna leave?"

"Why?"

"Because I'm worried about her. I got a strange text that I'll forward to you for your opinion, but first, tell me when she left."

"Uh . . . let me think. Not long ago. I stayed in Seth's room for a few minutes after she left, then came down to the cafeteria . . . so, maybe . . . twenty minutes ago? What is this strange text?"

"I'm sending it to you." Damon forwarded it. This would have been better in person, when he could have monitored Annemarie's physiological reactions, but he didn't want to wait.

"Okay, got it . . . Hang on . . ." Silence from Annemarie and faint background noises of conversations. She'd lowered the phone to read the text.

"Oh *no. Oh no.*" Her cry was soft at first, then strident, punctuated by the thud of footsteps. "*No.* This is *wrong.* This is so wrong. I *know* she wouldn't have hurt Seth. I got scared about Ben when she ran away; fine, I admit that, but *not* Seth. I'm positive about that. *Where is she?* We need to find her *now.* When did you get this text?"

"Right before I called you." Would Annemarie undercut the message of the text if she'd sent it herself? "How did she seem when she was with you?"

"She seemed . . . tired and worried but calm, offering to help me with everything under the sun. I told her to go pick up her car with you or go take another nap. If she'd been on the verge of . . . *this* . . . I promise you, she couldn't have hidden it from me *that* well." Annemarie was panting. Wherever she was going, she was running. "She *never* sounds like she sounds in that text. She's 'tiny pieces, horrible pieces'? She's a 'junk pile'? No. I don't think she wrote that text at all."

"You think someone else did?"

"Yes, someone who wants her to get blamed. You have no idea where she is? I assume you tried to call her."

"I tried. No answer. I have no idea where she is. Did she say anything about where she planned to go after leaving the hospital? Any errands?"

"The only errand we talked about was her going to pick up her car with you. I'm calling Detective Stafford."

Damon planned to call Stafford as well. "Did she mention speaking to anyone or even . . . noticing anyone near the hospital?"

"No."

"Did she mention telling anyone she was going to visit Seth? Or even mention speaking to anyone at all today besides me?"

Annemarie spoke faster, with ragged breaths between phrases. "Sorry . . . out of breath . . . checking the parking lot to see if Seth's truck is still here . . . I know she spoke to Kaitlyn Wyeth."

"Did they speak after Rayna knew when she was coming to visit Seth?"

"Let me think . . . It was after I'd talked to Kaitlyn, and that was only . . . maybe . . two hours ago? Oh, and Kaitlyn talked to her about the argument that happened between her mother and Rayna right before Rayna left for the hospital. So yes, she probably told Kaitlyn she was coming to visit. I'll check to see if Kaitlyn mentioned that to anyone else or if anyone could have overheard their conversation. Not that it would have been hard for the killer to guess Rayna would be here visiting Seth at some point. But unless they knew when, they'd have had to spend a long time waiting."

"Let me know if the truck is there. Or if you learn anything else. I'm going to talk to Jody."

"Good idea. If anyone is set on blaming Rayna, it's her. Maybe she's nutty enough to create fake evidence. I'll call Stafford immediately to get her searching for Rayna, and I'll head home to check for Rayna there. Tell me if you learn anything from Jody."

"I will."

Annemarie hung up.

Damon trusted that she'd make that call to Stafford. Claiming she would and not following through would be too suspicious of behavior. He'd follow up with Stafford himself after speaking with Jody. Through his office door, he could hear Jody on the phone, happily explaining to a caller that this wasn't a travel agency but she could suggest an excellent one.

Jody, obsessed with Rayna's guilt.

Jody, whose daughter had been so helpful in advising Ben Orozco, to the point of meeting him at night at his apartment—an uncharacteristic thing for Kaitlyn to do. And Kaitlyn had likely known Rayna would be at the hospital this afternoon.

Jody, proclaiming herself a mother bear who defended her cubs.

Damon called Kaitlyn's cell phone. No answer. He looked up the number for Wyeth's Grill and called it.

"Wyeth's Grill, good afternoon, this is Shelly."

"Hello, Shelly. This is Damon Hale. I need to speak with Kaitlyn. I apologize for interrupting her, but it's an urgent matter."

"Wow, sorry, Mr. Hale, she's not here. She took the afternoon off. Could I help you with something?"

"Thank you, Shelly. No. Just let her know I called." Damon hung up and walked into the reception area. Jody gave him a perky smile. After the interest he'd feigned in her lecture about Rayna, her mood had transformed into a chipper one.

"What can I do for you?" she asked. "Stars, you have such a stern expression on your face. Is something wrong?"

He stood in front of her desk. "I need to speak with Kaitlyn immediately. Please call her for me."

"Well, of course I can do that, but I thought you had her number."

"I do. She didn't answer. Maybe she'll pick up for you."

"Why do you need to speak with her now? She'll be busy at work."

"She's not at the Grill. I already tried there as well. Call her."

"I'm happy to help." Jody took her cell phone, tapped the screen, and lifted it to her ear. "Oh . . . she must be busy . . . Dear, hello, Mr. Hale has an urgent need to speak with you. Call him back as soon as you can. Thank you, darling." She lowered the phone. "She'll return your call as soon as she has a chance. She's very responsible."

"Answer a question for me," Damon said. "Did Kaitlyn have an affair with Ben Orozco?"

"Mr. *Hale*! Of course she didn't. Get your mind out of the gutter. Why would you think that?"

"Are you determined to convince people that Rayna is a murderer to keep them from suspecting your daughter?"

Jody gasped. "What a spiteful thing to say! I thought you listened to my warnings about Rayna, and now *this*?"

"Answer my question."

"Men are so gullible. Rayna manipulates your brain like a blob of clay. You tell her she's *not* pinning this on my Kaitlyn."

"You haven't answered my question. Did Kaitlyn kill Ben?"

"Of course she didn't!" Jody's pulse was galloping. "I thought you were a nice man. Men are so skilled at faking that. Elliott was charming, too, when we were dating. You need to apologize, or I'm quitting. I won't put up with you making up lies about my child."

"Jody," Damon said, "do you know anything about a text sent from Rayna's phone making it sound like she was in a deteriorating emotional state, suffering crushing guilt over being a terrible person who hurts people she loves?"

"She *said* that?" Naked astonishment and confusion showed in Jody's face. "She told you those things? That . . . that poor girl. Of course she regrets what she's done. Of course she does. Of course she couldn't keep her crimes hidden." Jody smiled radiantly for an instant before she damped her expression down. "We should help her find a brilliant lawyer." She started typing. "I have lawyer friends. I'll start with them."

"Rayna didn't send that text," Damon said. "There are elements of the message that indicate it was written by someone other than Rayna. Kaitlyn knew Rayna would be at the hospital this afternoon. Now Rayna and Kaitlyn have both disappeared."

"Oh stars, you have the worst case of denial I've ever seen."

"You reacted dramatically when Rayna asked if you killed Elliott. You've accused her of multiple murders, but the moment she threw an accusation back at you, you burst into tears."

"It was a very painful insult." Jody kept typing. "I couldn't help crying."

"I think you could. I think you knew tears were the best way to shut Rayna down. Tears followed by a vicious insult you falsely attributed to her father."

Shoving her keyboard away, Jody glared at Damon. "*Falsely* attributed to? He said it!"

"He said it? Yet in all your trying to convince me she's dangerous, you forgot to mention it—until you needed a verbal weapon against her?"

"A verbal weapon! I was simply stating what—"

"You needed a way to distract her before she started presenting far more credible scenarios than her slipping into town to murder your husband. You told me you were going to call Rayna's mother to see if anything happened around that time that might have set Rayna off. Did you learn anything?"

"I haven't had a chance to speak with her," Jody snapped. "I've been busy keeping your photos and interviews organized."

"Or have you been delaying because you're afraid Jeanette will recognize what you're trying to do to her daughter?"

"Do you want me to quit this instant?" Jody pushed back from her desk. "I don't need this job, you know."

"Once you found out Rayna wasn't in town when Elliott died, why would you cling to an accusation that no longer made sense?"

"I'm finished here." Jody started to stand, hesitated, and settled back into her chair with a twittery laugh. "Oh, listen to us growling at each other. These murders have us both out of our minds. You're right. It doesn't make sense to think Rayna would come all the way back here to kill him. I got carried away.

It's hard *not* to get carried away, considering everything else she's done. Why don't you go for a walk and take a break, and I'll put together a list of lawyers."

"Why did you feel a compulsion to add Elliott to her tally in the first place? Guilt? Preemptive action in case the authorities ever questioned his death?"

Jody shrank down in her chair, but she wasn't cringing. Her body was taut, muscles ready, eyes fixed on Damon, heart pounding frenetically. She didn't look like a mother bear. She looked like a cat poised to launch herself at her prey. He shifted his right foot behind him to stabilize his stance in case she did lunge at him.

"*Did* you kill him?" Damon asked. "Or did Kaitlyn?"

"You have crossed the line. I *quit*." Jody yanked open a desk drawer and grabbed her purse.

"I'm calling the police," Damon said. "I'll tell Detective Stafford everything I just discussed with you."

Jody stalked toward the door. "She'll tell you you're a dim-witted plaything of Rayna Kirkpatrick's. That evil girl will get locked up for life. I hope you get locked up too." Jody exited.

Damon waited until he sensed her driving out of the parking area, then sprinted to his car and followed, tracking her with his mind. How had this assignment become so improbably tangled? He'd come to Willet Beach to investigate and possibly apprehend one potential murderer, and now he was scrambling to protect that potential murderer from another potential murderer?

He tapped the Call button on his steering wheel. "Call Claire Stafford," he said.

CHAPTER 31

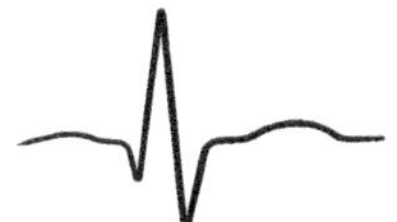

"You poisoned Ben and Seth?" Rayna kept subtly lifting her foot off the accelerator, letting the truck drop as far below the speed limit as she dared. She had to gather information, stall as long as she could before she took action against Kaitlyn. Kaitlyn was unlikely to pull the trigger while Rayna was driving. It would cause an accident that would risk Kaitlyn's life, and it would be difficult for Kaitlyn to make it appear that Rayna had shot herself. "*Did* you have an affair with Ben?"

Kaitlyn snorted. "No. I'm sorry, Rayna. Honestly sorry. This isn't how I ever wanted things to end up."

"Then . . . please don't let them end up here."

"Stop driving at forty-five miles an hour like you think I won't notice. Keep up with traffic."

Rayna pressed the accelerator. "You won't really kill me, will you? There's got to be a better way to work out . . . whatever you need to work out."

"What I need to work out is stopping the police investigation. I need them to stop asking questions. I need them to have their perpetrator. I need them to close the case."

"Then why didn't you just frame me? You could have planted poison and ice-cream ingredients in my house. That would have done it. Detective Stafford is certainly suspicious of me. And of Annemarie."

"I *will* plant evidence, but I'll have to be more creative about it now. I didn't do it before because I wasn't planning to frame you or anyone. But things have gone sideways."

"Why did you try to kill Seth?"

"I didn't. That's what went sideways. What a mess."

"The least you can do," Rayna said coldly, "is explain what you mean."

Kaitlyn gave a curt laugh. "Yeah, I at least owe you that. Mom poisoned Seth, which I never wanted. And when you told me the crazy things she said to you today, about you sneaking into town to murder Dad, that was the last straw. She's losing it. I can't let this go on."

Rayna slowed behind a minivan traveling at a sluggish speed. "Why would your mother want to poison Seth?"

"Because she was afraid Seth knew too much about Ben, and he's such a talker, he'll eventually crack and blab it."

"Why—"

"When Seth, Damon, and I were chatting at the Grill, Seth made a comment about how if you have dirt on someone who's died, you keep it to yourself. *I* didn't tell Mom he said that, but someone did—Damon, maybe, or one of our servers. She started hounding me about it—did I have any idea what it meant? Did Ben have secrets? Did Seth know about them? She guessed something was going on between Ben and me. There was, but *not* what you think. He was blackmailing me."

Rayna veered too far to the right, tires nearly reaching the edge of the pavement. Fingers tight around the steering wheel, she eased back into her lane. "He was *blackmailing* you? Over what?"

"He claimed it wasn't blackmail, but it was. He saw me, Rayna. The day Dad died. He and Lucy were visiting her parents, and he was out hiking. He spotted me paddling to shore in an inflatable raft. I didn't know he'd seen me, and he didn't know there was anything significant about it until at Dad's funeral, Mom was bemoaning how I'd been off at a restaurant trade show on the day he'd drowned and she'd had to deal with that alone."

"Wait—you were . . ." Rayna's thoughts jostled into place. "*You* killed your father. You were supposed to be out of town, and you sneaked back home. That's what put that idea into your mom's head in the first place."

"She never confronted me, but she must have suspected me. Maybe she was talking to friends in the business and found out I hadn't been at the trade show I was supposedly attending, or maybe someone besides Ben saw me and told her."

"Maybe she suspected all along without any tip-offs," Rayna said. "I also remember her complaining at the funeral about how you were gone when he died. She made a production out of that. Maybe she wasn't seeking pity. Maybe she was afraid you'd killed him and she wanted to bolster your alibi."

"You might be right," Kaitlyn said. "She knew how sick of Dad I was, sick of the way he treated her, treated me, wouldn't stop interfering at the Grill even though he'd retired and I'm much better at running a restaurant than he ever was."

"Ben threatened to tell the police he saw you?"

"He didn't say anything at the time. Not until he bought that restaurant property and came flashing his charisma and wanting me to advise him. I pointed him to some resources, but that wasn't enough. He kept pestering me. His entitlement drove me up the wall, that he'd assume I had the time or interest in being his mentor. I finally got angry and told him, 'Ben, you get on my nerves. Mentoring you would be torture *and* a waste of time because you don't have the grit to succeed and you'll go under within two years.'"

"Oof," Rayna said. "Ben's not used to getting told off like that."

"Oh, I know it, and it *really* stung him. He told me he had something private he needed to discuss with me and to come by his apartment that night after the Grill closed. I told him to get out of my restaurant or I'd call the cops. He whispered that if I did that, he could tell the cops some interesting things about where I was the day my father died. Then he walked out. That night, I went to meet with him." She gestured at the car in front of them. "Will you pass this minivan already?"

Rayna signaled and pulled into the left lane. Kaitlyn was keeping the gun aimed at her, but she was holding it lower, bracing it on her thigh. Her heartbeat had slowed. If Rayna could keep giving Kaitlyn an empathetic ear, keep letting her unwind, maybe she could coax her into putting the gun down altogether. "What did he say when you went to meet him?"

"He told me what he'd seen, and he knew details—like the color of the raft, the time of day, and where in the cove I was when I reached shore—so I knew he wasn't making it up. He said he'd figured out what I'd done, but he'd never planned to say anything to anyone. He knew what a lowlife my father was, and he wasn't going to get involved. But if I was going to treat him like scum after he'd been kind enough to keep his mouth shut, he wasn't okay with that. This was my chance to return the favor and help him out. He didn't want money—he kept claiming he wasn't blackmailing me. He only wanted my knowledge, my guidance. My encouragement and public support. I was a respected and successful restaurateur. My assistance would get his feet on the ground, and my endorsement of his business would give him credibility and help him make professional connections."

"I doubt the police could have made a case against you at that point, even if Ben did tell them what he'd seen."

"Probably not, but he sure could have stirred up gossip, and the timing was dicey. This was right after *your* father died."

The sensation of slivers of glass fanning out across her nerves hit Rayna again. "Did you—"

"Yes, I poisoned your father. Slipped him an overdose of his heart medication."

An overdose. "If the medical examiner had required an autopsy . . . or if Annemarie and I had requested one . . . would that have shown up?"

"I hoped not, or if they did notice levels were high, I hoped they'd assume he'd taken too much by accident. I did take the pills from his own bottle. But no matter what, it would have gotten the cops interested in me if my almost-stepfather had dropped dead while I was nearby and Ben promptly started telling everyone what he'd seen the day my father died. I figured I'd better cooperate with Ben."

"Why . . . my father . . . ?"

"I hope you don't expect me to apologize. Do you think I got rid of my dad so my mother could bring a nightmare like Glenn Kirkpatrick into our lives?" Kaitlyn shuddered. "You're welcome. I know you don't miss him."

* * *

"We'll find her," Detective Stafford said. Damon drummed his fingers on his steering wheel, listening to Stafford's voice through his car speaker and monitoring Jody as she moved through her house. "After I spoke with Mrs. Bristol, I put out an alert on Seth Bristol's truck. When we spot it, we'll have a conversation with Miss Rayna."

"You need to find Kaitlyn Wyeth as well." What was Jody doing? She'd gone into one room, then another, moving fast. Gathering evidence to destroy it?

"We're also watching for her car. We're doing everything we can to figure out what's going on and keep everyone safe. Here's how you can help: give me the address of the cabin where Rayna was staying in Big Sur."

"Whether she was taken against her will this afternoon or she disappeared voluntarily, she won't be headed there."

"You don't think so? If she's planning to run, she might want to retrieve her own car first."

"I don't think she's planning to run. I think someone is planning to kill her."

"What is the address, please?"

"I don't know it. She gave me verbal directions that I jotted down and threw away after I got there."

"In the era of GPS, you wrote your directions down by hand. How lovely and retro. I'm sure you can reconstruct most of them from memory. I have my pen ready; go ahead."

"I'm certain Rayna isn't there. Can we focus on finding her?"

"My colleagues are searching for her now. Our conversation won't delay that."

Damon hastily inventoried his options. None of them were solid. If he refused to answer the question, that lack of cooperation would be a significant red flag. If he gave Stafford the address, she would contact law enforcement closer to the cabin and have them check it out, which wouldn't give Maggie time to pack up and clear out. Even if Maggie did have time to remove the evidence of what they'd been doing there, she'd have to flee in Rayna's car, the only vehicle at the cabin. And if Stafford spoke to the owner of the cabin, she'd learn that Damon, not Rayna, was the one who'd rented it, that he'd done so weeks ago around the time he'd moved to Willet Beach, and he was still renting it.

"Mr. Hale? Are you there?"

"Yes." Jody had emerged from her house. From where he was parked down the block, he could see her rushing toward her car, wearing her white raincoat.

"Since this seems to be a difficult question for you, let's try a different one," Stafford said. "Did you know where Rayna was all along when you were claiming to Mrs. Bristol and me that you didn't?"

Damon shifted into drive and followed Jody's car through her neighborhood. "I'd be happy to answer your questions later, but this is not relevant to—"

"It's relevant." Stafford's mellow drawl became clipped. "Under normal circumstances, I wouldn't consider it my business what you've been up to with Rayna Kirkpatrick, but I have a murder victim and an almost-murdered victim, and in the middle of things, I have Rayna, her sister, and a stranger with an unverified story who recently strolled into town. A stranger who is fond of lying to me."

"Did you speak to Logan Tilburg?"

"Yes. He's delightful, one joke after another, but he's no better than you are at offering definitive evidence, saying only that he'll try to persuade your reclusive sponsor to allow herself to be identified. And now we have Rayna seemingly experiencing a guilt-induced breakdown with you wanting my help in locating her even as you refuse to provide basic information to assist me. Mrs. Bristol is concerned that Rayna's behavior regarding you has been abnormal for her and that you've been manipulating her. Tell me: Does Rayna want you to find her, or is she running from you?"

This was beyond what Damon could fix, and he was tired of this whole ill-considered effort to keep Stafford in the dark. After Ben Orozco's death, Logan had been too optimistic, thinking they could continue without giving her at least minimal information. "I haven't been straightforward with you," Damon admitted. "We have things we need to discuss, but I can't do that over the phone. Once we've found Rayna, I'll sit down with you and explain what I can."

"Why can't you discuss it over the phone?"

"There are sensitive matters involved."

"Sensitive matters your shy sponsor wants kept private?"

"Yes."

"Interestingly enough, Rayna has also asked that a sensitive matter concerning her be kept private. Is that a coincidence, or are the two of you talking about the same sensitive matter?"

That was a perceptive question. "As I said, I can't discuss this over the phone. If you'll save your questions, I'll answer them when we can meet in person."

"Where are you now?"

"In my car," Damon said. "Tailing Jody Wyeth."

"Would you like to get arrested for harassment?"

"I'd like to find Rayna before someone else dies. I'm not harassing Jody. She doesn't know I'm following her. I'll keep you posted on where she's headed. She might be armed. She's mentioned to me that her husband owned several guns."

"Mr. Hale," Stafford said, "I'm out of patience with you. Do you understand that giving me false information and interfering in my investigation has consequences?"

"I understand that, and I apologize for the trouble I've given you." Damon decelerated to allow yet another car to pull between his car and Jody's, additional assurance that she wouldn't notice his pursuit. "I'm going to give you a different phone number to call. This one will also connect you with Logan Tilburg, but the fact that I gave it to you will signal him to give you better answers. Tell him what's going on, that you're at the point of arresting me, and I'd appreciate it if he could persuade you not to do that."

"I'm not interested in wasting time on another chat with your friend."

"You'll waste a lot more time if you arrest me," Damon said. "And whether or not he considers himself a friend after this debacle remains to be seen. Just talk to him, please. Give him my apologies, and tell him I did my best to keep things under wraps but that he needs to provide you with additional information immediately because I need your full support in protecting Rayna Kirkpatrick."

"I see," Stafford said.

"And if you could please not—"

"Mention this conversation to anyone?" Stafford cut in.

"Yes," Damon said. "We'd appreciate that."

CHAPTER 32

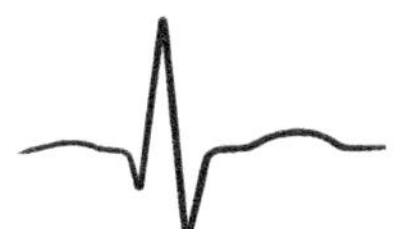

Rayna's throat was so parched that her comment started out as a squawk. "I can—" She swallowed. "I can see why you targeted our dads. But you and Ben had reached an understanding. An agreement. Why did you decide to kill him? That was a lot riskier than a murder that appeared to be an accident and a murder that appeared to be death from natural causes."

"I know it was risky, but he kept getting more arrogant." Kaitlyn switched the gun to her left hand, shook out her right hand, and switched it back. "You heard him talking about being our fiercest competition, about unseating us as Willet Beach's most popular restaurant. He was determined to use *my* expertise as a tool to outshine *my* restaurant. Do you remember that night you met him and Lucy at the Grill and he was joking about outdoing the Grill's success?"

"Yes."

"And Lucy tried to rein him in and he said it was cool, that he and I were old hiking and fishing buddies?"

"Yes."

"Cute, huh? Hiking and fishing buddies. He was literally cracking jokes about his blackmail. *So* cocky. He was going to keep demanding things, reveling in his control over me, and I'd have to keep smiling and building him up, undermining my own hard work. I could have lived with the arrangement if he'd been reasonable, but no, this was Ben Orozco, so it's all about Ben, and we'll all adore him no matter what. I was scared to go after him, knew there'd be a big investigation, but I was less scared than I was angry. He pushed me too far."

Rayna glanced again at Kaitlyn, wishing she could see her expression behind those huge sunglasses. "Do you think Seth *does* know about the blackmail?"

"No. Ben liked to flex with those wink-wink jokes, but he didn't want word of our arrangement to leak out any more than I did. I think Mom put all the puzzle pieces together, and she panicked. Scared for me."

"Not . . . angry that you killed . . ."

"I guarantee she was relieved to be rid of Dad. Your father . . . I don't think she was in love with him. She was lonely, and she liked the attention he gave her. But I'm the priority."

"And she's the mother bear."

Kaitlyn coughed out either a laugh or a hiccupy sigh. "Yep, the fierce mother bear. Swoops between Dad and me so he hits her instead. Did she think I was okay watching him hit her? Did she think I was okay with being screamed at even if he didn't hit me until she wasn't around? How about taking us both *away* from him? Sorry. I'm dragging you way too deep into my family drama."

"I care about your family."

"I know you do. I'm grateful. I'm sure Mom meant well, going after Seth. She was trying to fix things for her little girl, but she's so terrified for me, so overwhelmed that I think her brain is fraying. Like trying to attach my Dad's death to you when it would have been better if she'd never called his accident into question at all. And she was upset with Seth anyway. You know how he was trying to get Owl Cheney to relocate to bigger premises? She'd fume about how Seth was attacking our business, trying to deprive us of the benefits of being next to Cheney's."

"Oh my goodness. She took that personally?" They were approaching the turnoff to the Wyeths' property—a turnoff Rayna planned to miss. "You won't let her go after Seth again, will you?"

"No. He'll be safe. I promise you that. It would be too devastating for Annemarie to lose both of you. Keep an eye out. The road's coming up on your right."

Rayna pretended to watch for it. "You said your mom was panicking and making things worse, but so are you. Why didn't you sit down with her and tell her to knock it off instead of involving me?"

"I told you I need to *end* the investigation, not just quiet Mom—Slow *down*; that's the road—"

"Where—Oh . . . sorry." Rayna had sped past it. "I haven't been here in ages."

Kaitlyn jabbed the gun into her side. "Nice try. In a couple of miles, there's a place where you can turn around."

Kaitlyn's heart was racing again, and a weighted sensation in Rayna's chest made her question how well her own heart was functioning. "Kaitlyn . . . this isn't going to help you or your mother. The investigation won't end with my death. For one, Damon won't believe I suddenly confessed to the killings and ran away or committed suicide. He'll dig deep to find out what happened."

"Considering that you ran away after Ben's death, I don't think people will have trouble believing you freaked out and ran away after you poisoned your own brother-in-law."

"Damon knew where I was the whole time. I didn't run away from him."

"Yeah, I figured he was with you, but he lied to Annemarie about knowing where you were, so his credibility is worthless. Here's the problem with counting on Damon: there's something off about him, and Detective Stafford knows it. She's asked my mother all kinds of questions about him. Mom's clueless enough to worship the ground he walks on, but the guy's a con man."

"A con man?"

"Roaming all over town, learning about people, tricking them into letting their guard down, flattering them that they might see their names in print. Even hiring my mother and using her as a source of information on the locals. He's not gathering material for a book that no one will buy. He's gathering information he can use to exploit people. Blackmail? Extortion? Theft? Whatever he's up to, it's shady, and he's the last person who'll nag the police about your disappearance. He doesn't want their attention. He wants to use us, gather his spoils, and run."

"That's not true."

"Oh, Rayna. You naive kid. Mom thinks you've been manipulating him, but it's the opposite, isn't it? He's been manipulating you. He finds out enough about you to realize how vulnerable you are, and he pounces. Okay, you're going to reach an old barn soon. Pull into the dirt lot in front of it, turn around, and get back on the highway heading toward the fishing hut. If you pass the barn without stopping, I *will* shoot you." She touched the muzzle of the gun to Rayna's temple. "I'll have a scary moment while you die and I grab the steering wheel, but I think I can regain control in time. I'll put your fingerprints on the gun and park Seth's truck in a spot where it will be a *long* time before anyone finds your body."

Rayna couldn't fathom how Kaitlyn could stage that scenario so it didn't appear to be a homicide, but she didn't want to push her to the point of trying. She couldn't let this escalate to where she had only an instant to defend herself. It would take her multiple seconds to stop Kaitlyn's heart whereas it would take Kaitlyn only a fraction of a second to pull the trigger.

Do it now. End this. There's no reasoning with her. Do you think she'll let you go after what she's told you? Do it.

Nausea seared her stomach. *Not yet.* When they stopped, maybe she'd have a chance to escape.

When she reached the barn, Rayna braked and veered into the dirt-and-weed patch in front of it. She looped around and pulled back onto the highway, heading for the Wyeth property. No other cars were in sight or even within Rayna's range.

Kaitlyn lowered the gun, again pressing it against Rayna's side. "I'm sorry about all this."

"Instead of worthless apologies, how about you figure out another way to handle this? There has to be another answer for you. You must have thought about what you'd do if you had to run."

"Not really. I preferred to focus on how I could stay. Honestly, Rayna, if you're dumb enough to fall for a scammer like Damon Hale, you were in for a miserable life anyway. I'll spare you that suffering."

"Is that how you'll justify this to yourself when you're comforting Annemarie over losing me?"

"I'm not pretending I won't feel horrible for a while, but I can deal with tough decisions. And Annemarie has Seth and the kids. She'll miss you, but she'll get over it."

The gun poking Rayna in the ribs was jiggling; Kaitlyn's hands were shaking. She wasn't as callous as she was pretending to be.

"Taking me to your fishing hut is a reckless plan," Rayna said. "As soon as Damon got that text, I'm sure he started searching for me. He'll check there."

"Why would he check our hut? As far as he knows, I have no motive for harming you. Besides, we're not actually going to the hut itself. It's just the same turnoff. Don't miss it this time. Watch for it . . . coming up . . . Right there."

Rayna made the turn, her clammy hands sticking to the steering wheel.

She followed the narrow road filled with switchbacks and surrounded by cypress and pine trees, but before they reached the steep driveway leading to the fishing hut, Kaitlyn said, "In about a hundred feet, you're going to turn left."

Rayna squinted at the trees and brush. "Turn left *where*?"

"There's a path. You'll see it."

With the lightest of touches on the accelerator, Rayna kept the truck crawling forward.

"There." Kaitlyn pointed.

"That's not a road."

"The truck can handle it. Go."

Rayna turned onto a dirt path. Brush scraped both sides of Seth's truck. "Is this a hiking trail? We're going to get stuck."

"Go as far as you can."

Rayna inched along. They were traveling parallel to the shoreline. Between the trees, far down the slope, she caught brief views of water rendered silver-gray by the overcast sky. "What happens when we come face-to-face with a hiker and we're blocking the entire trail and then some?"

"We won't see anyone. There's hardly ever anybody out here, even when the weather's good. Why do you think my dad liked having our fishing hut here? No one to hear him screaming at us or breaking things."

Kaitlyn was correct that no one was nearby. Rayna still couldn't sense anyone within her range. "Is this where Ben was hiking when he saw you?"

"Yes. Most people have no idea there's anywhere to hike here. The trail isn't in any guidebooks and it's not maintained."

"Where are we going?"

"To the little cove where I buried the raft I used to row back to shore. I discovered this place when I was a kid. It's where I'd hang out when we stayed at the hut and I wanted to get away. My private spot. There's a small cave there that's partly underwater. Almost completely underwater at high tide."

But accessible enough for hiding a body? The truck bounced hard over a rut, then crunched over low bushes. "We're leaving an obvious trail," Rayna said. "But you think no one will find me?"

"No one will know to look here. And I won't leave the truck. They'll find it parked miles away at the edge of an ocean cliff."

"So it will appear I jumped off a cliff?"

"At least Annemarie can have the closure of thinking she knows what happened to you instead of wondering if you're hiding somewhere."

"Will they find my body?"

"No. Sorry."

Because Kaitlyn couldn't think how to kill her without leaving physical evidence of murder. She couldn't drive Rayna to the cliff and push her off. Rayna would put up a fight. The only way she'd get her over the cliff was by shooting her or in a hand-to-hand battle that would leave Kaitlyn injured and Rayna with marks that a coroner would know hadn't come from the rocks.

The truck jolted over roots, and branches slapped the doors. "There are going to be scratches all over Seth's truck," Rayna said.

"There are already scratches all over Seth's truck. It's a piece of junk. Nobody will notice anything different."

Ahead, a fallen tree, weathered and splintered, blocked the path. Rayna braked. "We're not going to make it over that."

"Yeah, we'll stop here. Turn off the engine, and give me the keys."

Rayna handed her the keys. Kaitlyn stuck them into the pocket of her windbreaker. From the paper bag at her feet, she drew out a handful of heavy-duty zip ties, some already fastened into loops, and set them on the dashboard. From the pile, she took five ties and dropped them on Rayna's lap—two loose ties and three looped together.

"Thread the loose ties through the end loops," Kaitlyn said. "Then fasten the loose ones around your ankles."

Thus creating a short chain between her ankles, allowing her to walk but slowly. "Are we hiking down to the cove?"

Kaitlyn shoved the muzzle of the gun into Rayna's side. "Hurry."

Rayna picked up the zip ties. Being tied up wouldn't impair her ability to stop Kaitlyn, and cooperating would give her a bit more time to think up another way to deal with this.

You're stalling. Fooling yourself. You don't have any other options. Rayna couldn't run; she'd get shot before she even got the car door open. She had no chance of disarming Kaitlyn. Kaitlyn was too alert, too careful with the gun. No one knew Rayna was here. No one was close enough to help her.

Rayna bent and began fastening the zip ties as instructed.

"Open your door, but don't get out," Kaitlyn said when Rayna had finished. "Any sudden moves at all and I'll shoot."

Rayna opened the driver's door, crunching branches that were in the way. Cool wind whipped into the truck.

"Put your feet outside the truck so your back is to me but don't get out," Kaitlyn said. "Cross your wrists behind you."

Rayna obeyed.

With one hand pressing the gun against Rayna's spine, Kaitlyn used her other hand to guide a plastic loop over Rayna's hands and cinch it tight around her wrists.

"Did you kill Collin Burgess?" Rayna asked.

"Collin Burgess! That buffoon of a reporter? No, but good riddance. Taking a drunken header down the stairs was poetic justice for him." Kaitlyn opened her door, shoving hard against the bushes to give herself room to squeeze out. "Stay in the truck until I tell you to stand up."

Rayna waited as Kaitlyn tromped through brush, came around the front of the truck, and tromped through more brush to reach Rayna's open door. She reached in and pulled Rayna to her feet.

Even with Kaitlyn's help, Rayna's shaky legs, limited stride, and bound hands made it difficult for her to manage the uneven ground, let alone climb over the tree blocking the path. By the time they were clear of the tree, Kaitlyn's eyes were stormy and her fingers gouged into Rayna's arm as she hauled her forward. The only words she spoke were threats whenever Rayna stumbled. It was plain that the slowness of the trek toward the cove was unnerving Kaitlyn. She wanted to finish this and get out of here. Rayna had intended to ask her for more specifics about the murders to gather information for Detective Stafford, but now she didn't dare.

Overgrown plants finally clogged the trail completely, and Kaitlyn propelled Rayna forward into the bushes, saying it would clear out soon. The zip-tie loops linking her ankles together kept catching on branches, and she fell, causing Kaitlyn to fall as well. Kaitlyn yanked her up, and they continued, but the second time they went down, Kaitlyn yelped in pain. A branch had clawed the side of her neck, marking it with a bright crimson scratch.

Panting, Kaitlyn sprang to her feet, not bringing Rayna with her. Rayna looked up and saw Kaitlyn pull the gun halfway out of her pocket, then stuff it back in.

Resignation filled Rayna, icy clear. Kaitlyn was losing control of herself, and Rayna couldn't wait any longer to end this.

I'm sorry. She linked with Kaitlyn, zeroing in on the electrical impulses controlling the beat of her heart. Kaitlyn moved past Rayna, stomping out a path for them.

The sense of another person entering her range diverted Rayna's concentration. Jody. Jody running. Confused, Rayna held back, not completing the block but not dropping the link. Had Kaitlyn told Jody where she was going? Why was Jody rushing toward her now? To warn her that something in her plan had gone wrong?

To beg her not to kill Rayna? Might Jody intervene for her?

Or should she kill Kaitlyn now and stagger off the trail in an effort to hide from Jody—leaving her daughter's body for her to find?

Her daughter murdered three people and is planning to kill you.

"Let's go." Kaitlyn helped Rayna up.

Rayna released the link. She'd wait for an indication of how Jody's presence would affect Kaitlyn. "This would go a lot faster if you'd cut these zip ties off my feet. I still wouldn't be able to get away from you."

Kaitlyn didn't respond. Rayna shuffled along, monitoring Jody. Able to move much faster than Kaitlyn and Rayna, Jody was drawing closer. Soon Kaitlyn would hear her footsteps. Would she be able to see who was approaching? Or would she panic and shoot Rayna?

It was foolhardy to wait to see how this unfolded. Rayna reformed the link with Kaitlyn.

"Kaitlyn!" A distant shout caused Kaitlyn to spin both herself and Rayna around, jolting Rayna into losing her focus. Kaitlyn dropped Rayna's arm and reached for her gun.

"Darling, wait for me!" Jody was jogging toward them, waving both arms above her head.

Kaitlyn groaned and drew her hand out of her pocket, leaving the gun out of sight. "Why . . . ? How did she . . . ? Rayna, keep your mouth shut."

"Stars." Jody was panting as she neared them. "It's a good thing my pickleball keeps me in shape."

"Mom, what are you doing here?"

"Finding *you*." Jody pulled a tissue from her pocket and blotted her forehead. She was carrying a canvas tote bag over her shoulder.

"How did you know I was here?"

"Darling, it's not hard to guess where you'd go if you needed privacy. The cove was always your little hideout, wasn't it?"

"You knew about it?"

"Of course I did. I never told your father though. I knew you needed a place where you could hide from him. Do you have one of his guns? There's one missing. Goodness, you and Rayna are both a mess, aren't you? And those sunglasses look silly on you. They're the wrong shape for your face."

"Mom . . . we'll talk later. Right now, I need you to go away and let me take care of things."

"Take care of *things*? What are you doing to this poor girl? Did you have to tie her up? How can she hike like that?"

"*Mom. Go away.* I know what you did to Seth. You know what I've done. We have to give the police a culprit and end this. As *you* kept pointing out, the obvious culprit is Rayna."

"I didn't want you to torment her, for goodness' sake." Jody marched forward and elbowed Kaitlyn aside so she could put her arm around Rayna. "Are you all right, dear?"

"I'm fine." Rayna reformed the link with Kaitlyn. She didn't think Kaitlyn would shoot her with Jody at her side, but she needed to be ready to act if Kaitlyn's aggression spiked. "Kaitlyn does have a gun. She's planning to kill me and hide my body in the cove."

"Oh stars! Kaitlyn, you are *not* going to shoot Rayna. What a nasty, painful thing to do to her. I'm ashamed of you. Rayna, dear, don't you worry. We'll figure this out together."

Kaitlyn faced them. "There's no backtracking on this," she said. "Leave, Mom. I'll take care of it. You need to keep quiet and stop trying to help because when you do, you create catastrophes."

"What a rude thing to say! You *do* need help, you bossy child. This isn't the way to handle things." Jody released Rayna and stepped between her and Kaitlyn, her back to Rayna.

Head aching, Rayna loosened the link slightly and held it there. Maybe Jody *could* get Kaitlyn to stand down.

"I need you to leave." To Rayna's surprise, Kaitlyn's voice was choked. "Let me deal with this. I'll keep your life running smoothly. Everything will be fine."

"Bullets flying around do not make things fine." Jody turned toward Rayna and patted her shoulder. "I'm sorry for what you've been through. Kaitlyn means well."

"Is there somewhere you could take her?" Rayna asked. "She needs to get away from here. To escape."

"Don't worry, dear. I always take care of my daughter." Jody reached into her tote bag and took out what appeared to be a double rolling pin made of marble. "Look what I bought for her! This is a pastry roller. She makes delicious pastries."

"I've tasted them," Rayna said. Was Jody losing her sanity? "They're almost as marvelous as yours."

"Don't worry, dear," Jody repeated. "This won't hurt." As Jody lifted her arm high, comprehension flooded Rayna. Dropping the link with Kaitlyn, she lurched away from Jody, lost her balance and went down hard on her stomach. Gasping, she fumbled to link with Jody, a process interrupted by the marble pastry roller crashing down on her skull.

CHAPTER 33

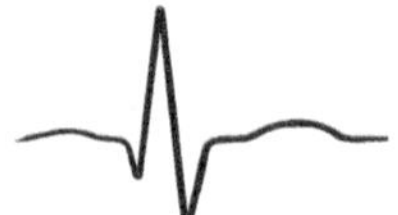

It had quickly become obvious to Damon that Jody's destination was the Wyeths' fishing hut. That small vacation home was in an isolated location where anything that occurred would likely have no witnesses. But as he'd followed her car along the switchbacks leading down the slope, keeping far enough back so she wouldn't notice him, she'd made a turn that had surprised him. Instead of following the road toward the hut, she had turned south, driving where Damon's GPS showed no road at all.

Afraid he'd lose cell service any second now, he called Stafford and updated her.

"We'll check it out," Stafford said. "We're a few minutes behind you."

"I'll stay in touch as long as I can." In the direction where he could sense Jody, Damon spotted the entrance to a path. "You'll see the path on your left . . . I'm sending you a GPS pin. Looks like a hiking trail. Broken branches on either side of it."

Stafford responded, but Damon couldn't discern what she'd said; the call was breaking up. "Detective, I can't hear you. Say again."

The call dropped.

Damon kept driving, vegetation thrashing the sides of his car. Jody's car came into view, parked on the trail behind Seth's truck. His sense of Jody was fading; she was at the boundaries of his range. She must have run at an impressive pace to be that far away from him already.

From his jacket pocket, he dug out the syringes he'd been carrying and threw them into the glove compartment. In a situation involving guns, their effect would be too slow to help him, and they'd make things more complicated to explain to Stafford. He climbed out of his car, scrambled over the tree blocking the road, and ran along the trail. As three familiar life senses became clear in his mind, his fear for Rayna grew: Jody and Kaitlyn were walking slowly, Rayna between them. Rayna was nearly horizontal, close to the ground. They were dragging her, and she wasn't putting up a fight. She was injured or drugged.

Before he got close enough for the Wyeths to notice him, he veered off the trail and headed uphill. Keeping out of sight as much as possible, he resumed the chase, scuttling along the side of the hill, grateful that the rustling and rattling the wind created concealed the racket he was making. When he was well past the slow-moving trio of Rayna and her captors, he worked his way down the hill and hid behind a cypress tree near the trail, waiting.

Voices joined his impression of three people approaching.

". . . exhausting. Goodness, I'm all sweaty in this coat."

"If you hadn't interfered, I could have walked her down here."

"Oh, hogwash. She wouldn't have cooperated. You'd have had to shoot her. Gunshots can be heard for miles, and bullets can be matched with guns. If her body is ever found, you don't want a coroner finding Elliott's bullets in her."

"I'll get rid of the gun too, Mom. They'll never find her anyway."

A moan. Rayna?

"She's waking up," Jody said breathlessly.

"Knock her over the head with your pastry roller again, if you want to."

"I didn't like doing that the first time, but you were being so cruel, kidnapping her and making her hike to her own doom. She doesn't deserve to suffer like that. This is a dreadful situation as it is; you don't have to make it harder. Stars, I need to rest. I feel sick."

"We don't have time to rest. If you'd gone home like I told you to, you wouldn't have had to deal with any of this."

It was time. Damon drew his gun and sprang into the center of the trail.

Jody screamed.

"Very slowly, keeping both your hands visible, lay Rayna on the ground," Damon said. "Then put your hands in the air."

Jody released Rayna with an abrupt motion, causing one of Rayna's shoulders to crash into the trail. "How on *earth* did you find us?"

Kaitlyn lowered the rest of Rayna to the ground more carefully and straightened up, lifting her hands. Between the sunglasses and the sun hat, Damon couldn't see enough of her face to read her expression.

"What did you tell him, Mom?" she asked quietly.

"Absolutely nothing!"

To Damon's relief, Rayna was wriggling now, fighting the zip tie around her wrists. If she had the energy to struggle, that seemed like a good sign. Wanting distance between her and the Wyeths, he said, "Jody and Kaitlyn, walk toward me."

The women moved forward, Kaitlyn with stiff motions and Jody with small, jittery steps.

"Stop there. Kaitlyn, moving one hand *very* slowly, take your gun, drop it, and kick it toward me."

"I don't have a gun."

"Yes, you do. Drop it, or I'll interpret your lack of cooperation as a threat on my life."

"You're not a travel writer." Kaitlyn inched her hand toward her jacket pocket, removed the gun, holding it by the barrel, and let it thump to the ground. With her foot, she shoved it toward Damon. It didn't make it far over the rough ground. Keeping his eyes on the Wyeth women, Damon stepped forward and picked it up.

"The police will have a lot of questions for you," Kaitlyn said. "You're not getting away clean."

Damon stuck Kaitlyn's gun in his jacket pocket. "I'll be happy to answer their questions."

"I doubt that." Venom infused Kaitlyn's voice, but she remained in place, hands in the air. She didn't seem inclined to make a reckless move that would get her shot.

"Jody, toss your tote to me," Damon said.

"I will not! You have no right to rifle through my belongings."

"The police are nearly here." They weren't yet as close as Damon would have liked; he couldn't sense Stafford or anyone else.

"I don't believe you." Jody retreated two steps, bringing herself closer to Rayna. "The police aren't coming. They'd never believe your lies about Kaitlyn."

He formed a precautionary link with Jody. "I don't want to kill you. Move away from Rayna, and throw me your tote."

Rayna lifted her head, looked blearily at Damon, and lowered her head again.

"Mom, do what he says," Kaitlyn barked. "Are you going to bat away bullets with your pastry roller?"

Jody wrapped her arms around her bag. The flush created by strenuous exercise was dwindling rapidly; her cheeks were a chalky pink. "Kaitlyn hasn't done anything she should be punished for."

"That's up to the police and the courts to figure out," Damon said.

"*You're* the one holding us at gunpoint. We'll testify that you kidnapped all three of us and made us carry Rayna to the cove."

"I don't think Rayna will endorse that story," Damon said as Rayna squirmed, attempting to roll onto her back. Raindrops spattered the trail.

"Oh, she'll have no idea what happened," Jody said. "She won't remember a thing."

"Jody, this is your last warning. Step away from Rayna and toss me your bag."

"Mom." Kaitlyn removed the sunglasses and hat she was wearing and flung them at her feet. "*Mom.* Look at me. You're being ridiculous, and you're going to get yourself killed. Just do what he says, and I'll sort things out later."

"You can't *sort this out,*" Jody screeched at her. "You think I'm useless, don't you? Someone *you* have to protect? The only one who can keep you safe here is *me.*"

Jody fell to her knees, lowering her tote to the ground. For an instant, it seemed a promising indication of surrender until she pivoted and flung herself on top of Rayna, her body flat against Rayna's, her cheek knocking into Rayna's cheek, pinning Rayna's head to the ground. Rayna groaned.

"You can't risk shooting me now, can you? You might hit your sweetheart. If you want her to live, you'll let my Kaitlyn go." Jody jammed her hand into her bag. "Kaitlyn, *run. Now.*"

"Are you *crazy*?" Kaitlyn shrieked.

Damon stopped Jody's heart.

The gun Jody was pulling out of her bag fell from her grasp. "Something's wrong, Katie," she whimpered. "I . . . I think I . . . ran too fast."

"Mom!"

Jody went limp. Damon leaped forward and snatched her gun and bag.

"She's having a heart attack!" Kaitlyn screamed. "Let me help her. *Let me help her!*"

Keeping his own gun aimed at Kaitlyn, Damon stowed Jody's gun in his back waistband and dumped the tote in search of other weapons. A tool clonked to the ground, a double-sided marble roller. The pastry roller Kaitlyn had referred to. He tossed it into the bushes to keep it out of Kaitlyn's reach, dragged Jody off of Rayna, then beckoned Kaitlyn toward her mother.

Kaitlyn dropped to her knees next to Jody and rolled her onto her back. The police were approaching now. Damon could sense Stafford and three other people on the trail.

Kaitlyn started CPR. Damon leaned over Rayna. Rayna's eyes were open but foggy.

"Rayna, it's Damon," he said. "Can you hear me?"

"Yes," she mumbled. "Kaitlyn . . . she . . . Jody . . ."

"Don't worry about explaining anything now. I'm going to cut the zip ties off your wrists and ankles. Lie still." He pulled out his pocketknife, opened it one-handed, then switched the gun to his left hand so his right hand could maneuver the blade. By the time he'd freed her, Stafford was in sight with another officer behind her and the other two officers on either side of the trail. The three officers he could see all had their guns drawn.

"We . . . need . . . help!" Kaitlyn rasped out her plea as she continued her compressions of Jody's chest. "Damon's threatening to . . . kill us, and my . . . mother collapsed. I think it's a heart attack—"

"Drop your weapons!" Stafford yelled.

Instantly, Damon dropped his gun and pocketknife and lifted his hands into the air. "I have two more guns: one in my left jacket pocket and one in the back of my waistband."

An officer confiscated the guns Damon had taken from Kaitlyn and Jody and searched him for any additional weapons. "Lie on the ground, sir. Hands behind your head."

Damon stretched out on the trail as ordered. The officer handcuffed him and walked over to assist the officer who was now performing CPR on Jody. Kaitlyn, too, was lying on her stomach, hands shackled behind her, tears spilling as she watched the attempt to revive her mother.

Stafford was leaning over Rayna. With Stafford's back to him, Damon couldn't catch her quiet words, but he could hear Rayna's semicoherent struggle to defend him. "No . . . let him go; it wasn't him . . . I can't remember what . . . He didn't do this; he's the one who stopped them . . . They were . . . Jody, I think . . . No . . . Kaitlyn . . ."

Wind gusted, and another round of raindrops pelted Damon. He wanted to tell Rayna not to strain herself, not to worry about him, but he couldn't interfere. He closed his eyes. This was in Stafford's hands right now, and all he could do was lie here with his face in the soon-to-be mud, feeling the comforting beat of Rayna's heart and the hollow silence of Jody's.

Sensing Stafford approaching him, he looked up. She leaned over and spoke in his ear. "Sorry, hon. I know you're uncomfortable, but this is how your friend wanted me to manage the situation. We'll have a candid chat later on. For now . . . relax and hope the rain doesn't get heavier."

"Thanks," Damon muttered.

CHAPTER 34

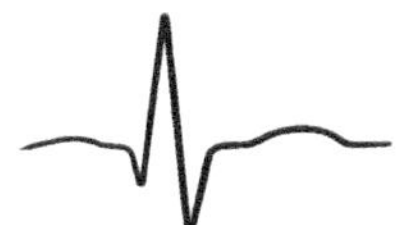

"YOUR DOCTOR SAID I COULD have fifteen minutes with you." Detective Stafford sat in the chair she'd pulled up to Rayna's hospital bed. "But if that's too much for you, we can do this later."

"No, it's fine. Please. I'm ready." Aching head notwithstanding, Rayna was eager to speak with Stafford. From the darkness outside her window, she knew hours had passed since she'd been brought to the hospital. She'd had no visitors—she'd been told Stafford had requested that no one besides medical personnel and law enforcement have contact with her until Stafford had had the chance to interview her. Rayna didn't know if Stafford could make that isolation mandatory, but she hadn't asked. She didn't want to give Stafford reason to think she'd coordinated her statement with anyone.

Annemarie had tried to visit her; Rayna had sensed her in the ER waiting room earlier and could now sense her with Seth in his hospital room. Damon had arrived at the hospital not long ago. He'd sat for a while in the area Rayna judged to be the main lobby, then he'd begun pacing. Now his pacing was covering far more ground; he must be prowling around outside the hospital. He was plainly waiting to speak with her. What did he know about whatever had occurred on the hillside near the Wyeths' fishing hut? Rayna had no idea what had happened or how the confrontation had ended or how she'd ended up at the hospital.

Or whom she'd killed.

"We spoke at the scene," Stafford said, "so some of my questions might be repetitive."

"We spoke at the scene?" Rayna blinked at Stafford's pleasant face, at the hearts in the corners of her pink-rimmed glasses. "I'm sorry. I don't remember that. The doctor said that . . . amnesia around the time of a . . . traumatic brain injury is common."

"In that case, my questions won't be repetitive." Stafford smiled at her. "Don't worry. We'll focus on what you do remember. I'm going to record you, if you don't mind."

"That's fine."

"Why don't we start at the beginning. You were at Mr. Hale's office this afternoon. You also came to visit your brother-in-law here at the hospital. Do you remember that?"

"Yes. When I got here, I got a call from Kaitlyn Wyeth . . . I'm going to close my eyes. I'm not nodding off on you. It just makes my head hurt a little less."

"Whatever makes you the most comfortable."

Rayna closed her eyes. As methodically as she could, she told Stafford everything she could recall, omitting only her certainty that she'd have to link-kill Kaitlyn. "The last thing I remember is Jody arriving . . . calling to us on the trail. That's all, until I found myself in the ER, throwing up, dizzy, and completely confused, with the doctor telling me I have a concussion."

"Do you know how you got that concussion?"

"No."

"Thank you, hon. This is all very helpful."

Carefully, Rayna turned her head toward Stafford and opened her eyes. Apprehension was reigniting nausea; she had to either get this question over with or ask for a basin. "Could you tell me what happened after my memory fails? Where are Jody and Kaitlyn now?"

"We've arrested Kaitlyn. I'm afraid Jody is dead."

Shards of pain crowded against Rayna's skull. "How did she die?"

"They're not sure yet. Kaitlyn suspects a heart attack." Stafford rose quickly. "Oh, honey, let me get your nurse. I've had you talking too long; you look ready to pass out."

"No, no, wait." Without thinking, Rayna clutched the hand Stafford had rested on the bedrail. "I'm okay. Just tell me quickly. How did you find me?"

"Your friend Mr. Hale," Stafford said. "He's an interesting man."

* * *

"No, you stay *right there*." Annemarie planted herself in front of Rayna, who had attempted to rise from the recliner, where she'd been lounging, watching pottery videos on her laptop. "*I* will answer the bell."

"I'm not on bed rest, Annie. That's Damon at the door. He's coming to take me for a drive."

"No, he is not," Annemarie said.

Seth laughed. He was on the couch, helping Nancy with her math homework. "Hey, Nan, go pop some popcorn. I'll eat it while I watch the battle that's about to happen."

"There will not be a battle. The battle is over." Annemarie marched to the door and opened it. "Hi, Damon."

"Good . . . evening." At the hesitation in Damon's greeting, Rayna pushed herself to her feet. Annemarie was standing in the entryway with her fists on her hips, body language radiating *go away* messages. Rayna didn't want her getting rid of Damon. She desperately needed to speak with him in person, in private.

"It's nice of you to stop by," Annemarie said. "Thank you for the flower arrangement you sent us. Loved the magenta roses."

"Let him in," Rayna called.

"You can come inside," Annemarie told him, "but only on the condition that you drop the field-trip idea."

"We aren't dropping the field-trip idea," Rayna said from behind Annemarie. "Let me get my shoes."

"Rayna is supposed to be resting," Annemarie said.

"I've spent the past four days doing nothing but resting," Rayna said. "I'm not dizzy. I don't have a headache. I'm perfectly capable of riding in a car for five minutes and walking one hundred feet onto a beach to watch the sunset, which is what we're going to do. I won't go farther than that."

Annemarie wheeled around and subjected Rayna to a long, assessing look. "You're pale."

"That's because you won't let me into the sunlight." Rayna sat on the bench in the entryway and reached for the tennis shoes she'd left underneath it. "Come in, Damon."

Damon stepped over the threshold. Grudgingly, Annemarie shut the door behind him.

"How about we all relax in the living room and chat . . . restfully?" she said.

"Babe, your sister's a big girl." Seth joined them. "Let her get out of the house if she wants." He offered his hand to Damon. "Hey, haven't had the chance to thank you in person yet. Ignore the way Annie's scowling now—she's spent hours crying about how grateful she is to you."

Annemarie sighed. "He knows that," she said. "I cried plenty of those tears on his shoulder at the hospital after Rayna's nurse would only let us into her room for about thirty seconds because Detective Stafford had already worn her out. I'm just worried about her overexerting herself."

"I won't overexert myself." Rayna stood. "I promise."

From the kitchen came the hum of the microwave. Nancy had taken Seth's popcorn request seriously.

"How are *you* feeling, Seth?" Damon asked.

"Good, mostly. Just tired." Seth wrapped his arm around Annemarie's waist and grinned. "She won't let me out in the sunlight either."

Rayna grabbed her jacket off the coatrack.

"What time will you be back?" Annemarie asked.

"She's thirty-something years old," Seth said. "She doesn't have a curfew. Bye, guys. Have fun." He kissed Annemarie's neck. "My wife and I are going to make out on the couch until one of our kids comes into the room."

"Seth!" Annemarie was laughing as Seth drew her toward the couch.

Rayna exited the house with Damon. "I cannot begin to tell you how marvelous this fresh air feels," she said. "Thank you for doing this."

"Glad to help. You're feeling all right?"

"It depends on the moment, but things are trending in the right direction." Rayna touched the tender area on the side of her head. "The doctor said the recovery process for concussions can be hard to predict, but so far, so good."

They settled into Damon's car. "Any particular beach location in mind?" he asked.

"Remember where you ran into me the night I got myself soaked? Go there. One flight of stairs and a thirty-second walk to the best sitting rock in Willet Beach."

He started the engine. "I remember it."

"I assume you finding me there wasn't coincidence. Were you keeping an eye on me? You'd figured out I was meeting Ben and Lucy that night and wanted to know how it had affected me?"

"Yes. And I should admit that I had your lost keys all along. Before I even spoke with you, I spotted them on the sand near the rock where you'd been sitting."

Rayna swiveled her head too sharply toward him, causing pain to flare. "Why did you . . . ? Oh, I see." Gingerly, she faced forward and leaned against the headrest. "You used my missing keys as an excuse to prolong our time together so you could get a better read on me."

"Yes. The more time I had to evaluate you, the better. But I apologize for the added stress."

"Thanks for telling me. Any other confessions?"

"I copied the keys to your house, Annemarie's house, and your shed before returning them. Never used them though. Here." Steering with one hand, he reached into his pocket, took out a metal key ring, and passed it to her. "In case you'd like the extra copies."

"What I *won't* do is give these to Annemarie. Talk about an awkward thing to explain."

"How is she doing?"

"She's . . . stunned. Nearly losing Seth, nearly losing me . . . finding out our lifelong friends were responsible . . ."

"It must be excruciating for all of you."

"Seth feels guilty that he didn't tell her he was hanging out with Ben. Annemarie feels guilty that he was scared to confide in her because he knew she'd flip. Lucy sent them a list of the marriage counselors she'd researched when she was hunting for someone to help Ben and her. She said this was probably an intrusive thing to do, but she didn't care much about tact anymore, and she figured Annemarie and Seth might be able to make use of her research."

"Do you think they will?"

"Yes. And Seth *didn't* know anything about the blackmail. Lucy . . . She had no idea either. She called yesterday. Neither of us knew what to say—'I'm glad your husband wasn't cheating on you; sorry to hear he was a blackmailer'? So I kept saying, 'I'm so sorry. What can I do to help you,' and she kept saying, 'What do you mean help *me*; you're the one who ended up with a TBI because of his stupidity,' and then she said, 'At least I made sure you didn't get stuck marrying him,' and I said, 'I owe you big for that; thanks for taking one for the team,' and we were both bawling so hard by that point that Annemarie was ready to pry my phone out of my hand and call my doctor. But Lucy and I both felt better afterward."

"I'm glad you were able to comfort each other."

"Everything feels so strange that my brain . . . especially in its shaken-up state . . . has no idea how to process it. Thanks for asking if we could go for a drive. I've been wanting to talk with you. Face-to-face, I mean. Privately."

"I've been wanting to speak with you as well," he said. "Start us off. I'm listening."

Rayna fidgeted with the keys Damon had given her. Except for the brief hospital visit Annemarie had mentioned, she hadn't seen him since her injury. They'd spoken on the phone, sharing some of the nonconfidential facts of what had occurred, but she hadn't had the chance to go deeper. Now that she had that opportunity, strong emotions were stirring, something she hadn't anticipated this early in the conversation. "I don't know where to start."

"How about with whatever is troubling you the most?"

The gentleness in Damon's voice coaxed Rayna's emotions farther into the open. She breathed steadily, trying to keep her throat from knotting. "I don't want to cry in front of you again. Why do I always end up crying in front of you?"

"Ah . . . Rayna . . . I'm guessing that has a lot to do with what I've put you through. I'm deeply sorry."

"That accounts for maybe half the tears." Rayna blinked, adding two more tears to her total. "You don't have to apologize. The evidence pointed to me, lives were at stake, and you have severely limited options for dealing with a potentially murderous Trespasser. I have no idea how you could have handled the situation better."

Damon parked near the stairs that led to the sand. In silence, he studied Rayna, his expression pensive. "Thank you for your patience and your lack of enthusiasm for holding a grudge," he said. "And for understanding the complexity of the situation." He reached into his jacket pocket and took out a packet of tissues. "Here. In case you need them."

With a raspy giggle, Rayna took the tissues. "You came prepared for the waterfall."

"Stay there. I'll open your door."

As they approached the stairs, Damon offered her his arm, and Rayna grasped it. Her legs were wobblier than she'd expected as they walked down to the beach. The evening sky was cloudy, and the wind was turning cold. No one else was around.

They settled on the flat rock. "It won't be much of a sunset tonight," Rayna said.

"That's all right. I'm here to talk with you, not watch the sunset. Tell me what's on your mind."

Rayna pulled off her shoes and socks and stuck her toes into the sand. "When . . . Kaitlyn and I were in Seth's truck, it was so . . . surreal . . . listening to her explain what she'd done and how she didn't *want* to kill me but that was the solution to her problem. And I'm trying to gather as much information as I can, knowing I can kill her if I have to . . . knowing I'll probably have to . . . but holding off . . . hoping somehow, miraculously, it won't come to that . . . Then we were on that trail, and she's herding me along . . ."

Wind tugged wisps of hair free from the loose braid Annemarie had woven for her to keep her hair from getting snarled while she was spending most of her time lying down. Rayna gazed out at the breaking waves. "Sorry. I lost my train of thought. That keeps happening . . . The doctor said it will get better . . ."

"Take your time. You were on the trail with Kaitlyn . . ."

"Thanks. Yes. I kept falling, and Kaitlyn was getting agitated, and I knew this was it. I had to end it. I remember linking with her . . . then sensing Jody approaching . . . deciding to wait before . . ." She paused, burrowing her toes deeper into the sand and tugging her jacket zipper to the top.

"Did you think Jody might help you?" Damon asked.

"I . . . don't know. I wanted to see how Kaitlyn would react to her. I've . . . regained a few scraps of memory from after Jody reached us." Why was she shivering? It wasn't that cold.

Damon removed his jacket and draped it around her.

"You don't have to do that," Rayna said. "You need it."

"I'm not cold. Please use it."

"Thank you." Rayna slid her arms into the sleeves. "Every time we're on this beach, you lose a jacket to me."

"I don't mind. What else do you remember?"

"Only fragments. Jody's white raincoat . . . her heart beating very fast . . . Kaitlyn asking how she found us. And Jody saying something about pickleball. Pickleball. Of all the things to remember when so many other things are a blank." Rayna tucked blowing strands of hair into the braid. Her fingers were getting clumsier, and her eyes stung. "I . . . assume Jody's death wasn't . . . natural causes."

"No," Damon said.

"Detective Stafford said I was conscious and talking to her at the scene, but I don't remember any of that. I have no idea what else I might have done that I . . . don't remember."

"You didn't kill Jody," Damon said. "I did. At that point, you weren't nearly coherent enough to form and sustain a link. Jody had thrown herself on top of you and was drawing a gun with the intent of using you as a hostage to hold me and the police off while Kaitlyn escaped."

"*Jody* had a gun? Oh . . . it must have been her husband's. He owned a few of them."

"Yes. Kaitlyn took one. Jody took another. Rest assured that I gave Jody more than ample opportunity to surrender. She'd already tried to kill you once via blunt-force trauma, and I wasn't going to let her put a gun to your head and launch a standoff with the police that could cost your life and more. She had the chance to stay alive. She chose otherwise. I assume her death will be ruled natural causes."

Relief that she hadn't been the one to kill Jody filled Rayna, but guilt promptly tainted it. "I'm sorry I left that job to you. You didn't want it."

"I'm glad you didn't have to do it."

"I should have acted sooner. I was *not* planning to let myself get killed. I *was* ready to defend myself, but, Damon . . . how do you make these decisions? For me, it was one thing to act in a moment of panic, like I did when you were kidnapping me, when I thought it was now or die. But to rationally weigh a situation . . . decide at what point taking a life is justified . . . but not wait so long you lose control of the situation, which is where *I* failed . . ."

"It's never easy," Damon said.

"It's *brutal.* I do not envy you your job. Thank you for coming after me. For saving my life."

"I'm sorry I wasn't in time to prevent you from getting injured."

"That's my fault. I'm grateful I got off with a concussion. Do you know what she hit me with? You never told me that."

"A pastry roller," Damon said. "A marble pastry roller."

"A *pastry* roller? Are you serious? That's the perfect weapon for Jody Wyeth. She made amazing fruit-filled danishes. Cherry and lemon and apple. She'd bring them to us every year for our Christmas breakfast." Rayna pictured Jody on the front porch, wearing one of her many Christmas sweaters and holding out a tray of pastries. *"Merry Christmas, dears!"*

"Oh, Jody." Tears spilled down Rayna's face, and her muscles constricted as she fought to keep her breathing smooth. A cluster of shorebirds were skittering back and forth at the edge of the water. Rayna focused on them and tried not to wonder what had passed between Jody and her in the moments before Jody had struck her . . . tried not to remember Kaitlyn's cool voice as they'd sat in the cab of Seth's truck . . . *"I need them to stop asking questions. I need them to close the case. Sorry, Rayna."*

Rayna pressed her hands against the rock she sat on. Her fingernails scraped back and forth over the stone. *Stay calm. Watch the birds.* "I might . . . need a minute to get myself under control."

"Please don't waste energy trying." He touched her shoulder. "Let yourself grieve."

His kindness tore through the rest of her composure. Pain crashed free in sobs she couldn't mute even with both hands over her face.

She felt his arm curving around her, a gentle and comforting touch she hadn't expected. Why was she fighting to hide her pain from him? It made no sense, not at this point. She lowered her hands, leaned against him, and let herself weep, Damon's heartbeat a soothing rhythm beneath her roiling grief and fury.

Orange hues were tinting the clouds at the horizon when Rayna finally managed to sit up straight, her head aching and a ball of damp tissues in her fist. "What happens now?"

Damon withdrew his arm. "You take it easy. Maggie's back in D.C. She won't resume interviewing you until you've healed, and we'll go forward from there."

"Okay."

"She wasn't happy about leaving—she's already possessive of you as a patient and didn't like walking away while you're dealing with a traumatic brain injury. I swore I'd make sure you're taking care of yourself and getting enough rest."

"Oh, please no," Rayna said. "Not you and Annemarie both."

He laughed.

"Does Detective Stafford know any of the truth about what you're up to?" Rayna asked.

"It was necessary to give her some information. She knows I'm a government agent. She knows I'm interested in your extrasensory abilities, and she knows the importance of keeping both your abilities and my real work confidential. She knows nothing about link-killing."

"Did you tell her you have the same abilities I do?"

"No. She doesn't need to know that. If she suspects that's how I was able to track Jody, she hasn't asked me about it. She's been helpful in publicly minimizing my role in what happened."

"I saw how the press reported it. You're a 'friend of the Wyeth family' who was able to tip the police off to my possible location once Annemarie reported I was missing."

"Yes. It's not complete anonymity—multiple people know I was there—but it's better than a big stir and reporters hammering on my door. Thank you for your discretion as well."

"It's not hard to be discreet with Annemarie scaring away anyone who tries to talk to me about it." Rayna massaged the back of her neck. "Has Detective Stafford told you anything about the investigation? With only my word for what Kaitlyn confessed to, I've wondered if I—or Annemarie—are still somewhere on her list of suspects in Ben's death. And my father's death."

"I've spoken with Stafford about that," Damon said. "She has more evidence against Kaitlyn than your testimony. At the cove where Kaitlyn was taking you, there's a cave that's largely underwater."

"Yes," Rayna said. "I told Stafford that's where she hid the raft she used to row back to shore after she killed her father. And where she was planning to hide my body."

"The raft wasn't the only thing she hid there. The police also found a watertight box buried in the sand. This is confidential information, so don't share it, but one of the things it contained was a collection of dried plants and pharmaceutical substances. Stafford indicated one or more of the substances is a likely match for what killed Ben. There were also several books on pharmaceuticals and poisonous plants."

"Because, unlike me, Kaitlyn was smart enough not to ask Google sensitive questions. I wonder if she kept those supplies in case she wanted to use them again."

"I imagine so. I'd also guess she was planning to retrieve them after she killed you, wipe them down, get your fingerprints all over them, and stash them somewhere to implicate you."

Rayna swallowed. If Damon hadn't showed up, Kaitlyn would have succeeded with that.

"I don't know what other evidence Stafford has found or will find," Damon said, "but I know she's confident they have a strong case against Kaitlyn in Ben's murder. As far as your father's and her father's deaths, and as far as your kidnapping, let me tell you what might happen."

Rayna folded her arms, grateful for the warmth of Damon's jacket.

"As you know, we want as little attention on you as possible," Damon said. "But Kaitlyn's lawyer will do whatever she can to undermine your credibility. She'll dig into your role in what happened the night Ben died. For instance, she might uncover the fact that you called 911 for Ben before you arrived at his restaurant."

Dread kicked a surge of adrenaline loose. "Will you have to take me—"

"I'm not saying we'll have to remove you from Willet Beach. I'm saying there might be talk between my team and the local prosecutor. One way to keep control of things would be through persuading Kaitlyn to plea-bargain. For example, offering to drop the kidnapping charge and the other murder charges if Kaitlyn will plead guilty to the murder of Ben Orozco and offering her something short of a life sentence. It would still mean a long prison term but less than she'd otherwise be facing. But that's nothing you need to worry about. I'll keep you updated. I just want to reassure you we're doing our best to maintain security while not disrupting your life more than we have to."

"Thank you," Rayna said. "And tell your people, whoever they are, that I'm very grateful."

"I will. We're very grateful for your cooperation."

Rayna lifted her feet, brushed sand off them, then rested them back on the sand, with no clue why she'd gone through that process. "While I rest and recover, what do *you* do—besides join forces with Annemarie in nagging me?"

"I work on my alleged book with the additional cover story that my sponsor is more determined than ever to tell the deep, rich story of Willet Beach instead of letting murder be what the town is known for."

"That's a nice spin. Are you staying to keep tabs on me?"

"Yes, though not in the same way as before. But I have more research to conduct in this area, and we do need to stay in contact. I'll be coordinating things with you, such as the schedule for Maggie's endless testing."

"Okay."

"There's a question I need you to consider," Damon said. In the corner of her vision, Rayna saw him turn to look directly at her. "I don't want you to answer it now, but keep it in the back of your mind while you learn more about the Trespasser team and what we do."

She met his gaze. The cloudy evening sky wasn't doing much for the sunset, but it somehow brightened the color of his eyes. "You're wearing an eye shirt," she said.

He aimed a puzzled glance at his green T-shirt.

"Sorry." Rayna felt herself blush. "I used to say that to Annemarie when she'd wear a dark-blue shirt. Your shirt is the same color as your eyes; that's what I meant, and it's completely irrelevant. Did I mention my brain's a bit rattled up? You have a question. What is it?"

"When I came here to investigate you, one of my purposes was to determine if you would be an asset to our team," Damon said. "It's clear you would be. We'd like you to consider joining us."

Rayna stared at him. "Joining . . . ? Like . . . doing what you do?"

"Not necessarily what I do." He smiled slightly. "After what you've witnessed of my job, that would be a tough sell right now. There are other aspects of our work you could assist with."

Rayna brushed sand off her knees, then picked up one of her shoes and brushed sand off it. Why couldn't she keep her hands still or at least do something with them that wasn't pointless? Next she'd be trying to brush the entire beach into the ocean.

"This isn't a decision you need to make anytime soon," Damon said. "You hardly know anything about us. Just keep the offer in mind while you learn more."

"Damon . . . I'm a potter living in a little beach town. I can't imagine I have any skills that would be of use. I'm not a . . . secret agent . . . or a doctor . . . or a researcher or . . ." She sighed. "None of this is getting me off the hook, is it? It's my Trespasser abilities you're interested in."

"You'd be a tremendous help," Damon said. "We need you. But this is an offer, not a conscription. Will you keep it in mind?"

"Would I have to leave Willet Beach?"

"Not necessarily."

"Okay, I'll keep it in mind."

"Please don't let it be a source of worry. Just let it be a possibility."

Rayna nodded. She'd let it float in her thoughts, but for now, she couldn't spare it more attention than that. The present was all she could carry.

"One more question for you to consider," he said. "And I do need an answer to this one soon. As you're aware, most people who know both of us assume our relationship is . . . personal. In order to keep the nature of our interaction confidential, I haven't done much to correct that assumption. At times, I've even leaned into it."

"Same," Rayna admitted.

"Going forward, however, it's up to you what cover story you'd like to use. If you're uncomfortable having people assume we're . . . romantically involved . . . we can cut those rumors off and come up with another way to explain the time we spend together—or take precautions to conceal our interaction entirely."

Damon's words sounded formal, preplanned, and his pulse rate had noticeably accelerated.

"What would *you* prefer?" she asked, squirming inside at the way her own heart was thumping. He'd notice that.

"It's up to you," he said. "I'll respect whatever your wishes are."

They sat in silence, both staring toward the ocean.

"It's easier to let people keep thinking what they're thinking," Rayna said. "We can go with that. If you're sure you're okay with it."

"I'm fine with it," he said.

A wave collided with a jagged rock, sending up spray. A seagull crossed the darkening sky, letting out a screechy call.

"We can try for a better sunset tomorrow if you'd like another chance to get out of the house," Damon said. "Right now, I'd better get you home. You must be tired."

"And you answer to Maggie."

"How's your head feeling?"

"It's . . . hurting. But just give me five more minutes. May I make use of your shoulder again?"

"Feel free." He wrapped his arm around her. She rested her head on his shoulder.

"This will be a good look if anyone wanders by," she murmured. "Strengthening our cover."

He laughed softly. With a light touch, he lifted a stray strand of hair off her cheek and tucked it into her braid.

ABOUT THE AUTHOR

Stephanie Black has loved books since she was old enough to grab the pages, and has enjoyed creating make-believe adventures since she and her sisters were inventing long Barbie games filled with intrigue and danger or running around pretending to be detectives. She is a four-time Whitney Award winner for Best Mystery/Suspense and a finalist for Best Speculative Fiction.

Stephanie lives in Northern California. She enjoys taking pictures of birds, playing the violin in a community symphony, and eating cookies for breakfast. She loves spending time with her husband, Brian, and their kids and kids-in-law.

Stephanie enjoys hearing from her readers. You can contact her via email at info@covcorp.com or by mail, care of Covenant Communications, PO Box 416, American Fork, UT 84003-0416.

Website: stephanieblack.net
Facebook Group: Stephanie Black's Mystery Chat
Instagram: @stephanieblackauthor

"An inspirational pag
Gigi Salmon, Sports Comr

WHAT'S

Redefining

WRONG

What's Possible.

WITH

Unapologetically

YOU?

Unstoppable.

LOUISE HUNT SKELLEY

Designed and edited by Turquoise Tiger Press, Lincolnshire, UK

Published by Louise Hunt Skelley

Manufactured in the United Kingdom.

ISBN: 978-1-7398221-7-0

Back cover image by João da Conceição Nunes

For Chris and Milo,

For filling my heart with love, for making me feel adored and happiness like I've never known, for giving me a safe place to call home, and for being my calm through every storm – this is for you.

Dear Trudy,
All my love
Louise x
02/06/2025.

Table of Contents

Foreword 1 ix

Foreword 2 xi

Prologue xiii

Chapter 1: Breaking Rules and Speaking Up 1

Chapter 2: Hello World: I'm Here to Prove You Wrong 15

Chapter 3: Floating Hips and Funky Cushions 19

Chapter 4: Being Me: Competitive and Reckless 25

Chapter 5: From Child's Play to Tennis Camps 31

Chapter 6: Bully to Bodyguard 37

Chapter 7: Listening Without Judgement 43

Chapter 8: Treetop Quarrels 47

Chapter 9: All Hail the All-Conquering Leg Bag! 51

Chapter 10: My First Wimbledon 53

Chapter 11: Striking a Balance: Tennis and Education 59

Chapter 12: The Long Goodbye 63

Chapter 13: A Quick Guide to Wheelchair Tennis 73

Chapter 14: Too Nice and Never Going to Make It 77

Chapter 15: Stubborn Streak Versus Self-Care 85

Chapter 16: Feeling Hot, Hot, Hot! 89

Chapter 17: Gratitude for Ghana 95

Chapter 18: Going Undercover 105
Chapter 19: Pressure Sores Can't Stop Me 109
Chapter 20: My Tennis Mind-ers: Calm Amongst The Storm 115
Chapter 21: Money, Health and Getting Out of My Head 121
Chapter 22: Let's Hear It for the 'Humble' Wheelchair! 129
Chapter 23: London 2012: Missing Face in the Crowd 137
Chapter 24: Everything Only Lasts For a Moment 147
Chapter 25: Living Our Dream Together 159
Chapter 26: Meeting My Soul Mate 161
Chapter 27: Sponsorship and Shifting Mindset 167
Chapter 28: From Top To Bottom and Back Again 173
Chapter 29: Tennis Takes a Back Seat 179
Chapter 30: Double, No Trouble 209
Chapter 31: Popping The Question 215
Chapter 32: Hooray For the Happy Van and Magical Milo 221
Chapter 33: Taking My Career in a New Direction 225
Chapter 34: True Colours 229
Chapter 35: Travel Nightmares: Time For Change 231
Chapter 36: I'm A Fire Hazard 251
Chapter 37: Independence Is Asking for Help 257
Chapter 38: Ableism: Why It Needs to Stop 265
Chapter 39: A Life of Contrasts...Still 267
Chapter 40: PEEP Show 273
Chapter 41: Choose Your Words with Kindness 275
Chapter 42: Language Lessons for Us All 277
Chapter 43: Boobgate, Blunders and Sporting Heroes 279

Chapter 44: Loving Lockdown, And Then Not So Much 283
Chapter 45: Travelling Trickstar 295
Chapter 46: Gold! Living The Pie Life 299
Chapter 47: Rollercoaster 303
Chapter 48: Introducing The Bride Squad 335
Chapter 49: Positive Progress: A Family Affair 343
Chapter 50: Find Curiosity and Joy in Others' Success 351
Chapter 51: The Smallest Room, But the Biggest Comfort 353
Chapter 52: Limitless Future 355
Chapter 53: Welcome to the World of Celebrity 365
Chapter 54: Ever Evolving Relationships 369
Chapter 55: Time For Equal Play, Equal Opportunity 373
Chapter 56: What's A Winning Mentality for You? 377
Chapter 57: Some Louise-isms For You to Ponder 381
Chapter 58: 76 Reasons to Believe in Myself 383
Chapter 59: C'est La Vie: Paris and Beyond 385

Foreword 1

By Christopher Hunt Skelley MBE PLY

My darling wife,

You have shown me how to live, how to love and how to be the best human I can be, and I'm incredibly grateful for you coming into my life and changing it for the better.

You are a best friend, my wife, a daughter, a mum to our fur baby Milo, you mean so much to many people, and we are all so proud of what you've achieved.

You are a role model to so many and I am so proud to call you my wife. You have taught and shown me how to grab life with both hands and roll with it. I love your sense of adventure and your abnormally ambitious character.

I am so proud that you are finally sharing your amazing story of thriving and showing the world that anything is possible with a disability.

For the people who are going to read this, you should know that this has been a lifetime ambition of Louise's to create this book and share her story. She is a true example of how to strive and overcome in the face of adversity, and do it with a smile on your face and maintain a good sense of humour.

Her determination to be the best version of herself makes me love her more than anyone can ever know.

Louise's transition out of professional sport has been amazing; to the extent where I am aspiring to follow in her footsteps and I hope many transitioning athletes can take comfort in that they can smash this step too. It might be scary, but Louise has shown how successfully it can be done.

Her career post-tennis has been impressive to witness; the amount of doors which have opened for Louise is testament to her professionalism and spirit. From commentating, supporting people with disabilities, athlete mentoring, tournament directing, public speaking, the list is endless and carries on. What she has been able to do post her tennis career is truly remarkable.

You will not believe what Louise had had to deal with and overcome to reach success and feel content with who she is as a person.

I am honoured to have played a small part in her life and can't wait to see where our lives are going to take us next. There's plenty more chapters to come and I can't wait to be a part of each and every one!

So when you read this book, be ready to go on Louise's journey of triumph, overcoming challenges, and love, and remember that if you surround yourself with the right people and are willing to work hard, the unimaginable can become possible.

With love, from your husband,

Christoph xx

Christopher Hunt Skelley MBE PLY

Foreword 2

By Gigi Salmon

Hello World: I'm Here To Prove You Wrong; the title of Chapter 2 and something I saw in Louise from the moment I commentated on her for the first time - fierce, feisty, fair. I was looking at an athlete who was at the top of their game and at a person who had fought a number of battles to get where she was. Little did I know how many battles she had fought until reading *What's Wrong With You?*

From watching from the outside and, at times, coming to conclusions from just what I saw on the tennis court, I had the opportunity to get to know Louise during the Tokyo Paralympics, when we spent a thoroughly enjoyable week in the basement of a building in London commentating on the wheelchair tennis event in the early hours of the morning. It was a week in which I learned a lot; we laughed a lot and even cried together when her now husband Chris Skelley won Paralympic Gold, which we were watching on a tiny screen while also commentating on the wheelchair tennis!

I have worked in sports commentary for a number of years now across a variety of sports in radio and television and with each person and team you work with, you learn, but there was something different and special about this time we spent working together, even before Chris won his gold medal when we were live on air. Louise has a way of drawing you in, which you will discover over the pages of the book, and motivating you when you don't even realise that you need motivating; greeting me with a smile and a cup of tea at 3am, night after night, and helping me shape the narrative of the players as we told their stories to viewers.

What will come across when you read this book, and what I have been lucky enough to experience in real life, is how inspirational Louise is in everything she does. Imagine, as a teenager full of hope, being told by your careers advisor that your dream of being a Paralympian is unrealistic - that would crush most people; not Louise who went on to become a two time Paralympian.

Her list of achievements is lengthy, a smile is never far from her lips and I'm happy that what I know about Louise will now be shared with others through this unique and personal insight into her life and experiences. Thank you, Louise, and I look forward to sharing a commentary box together again soon!

Gigi Salmon

Prologue

"Oh, you're a Paralympian, what's wrong with you?" A stranger at a Business Expo where I was the keynote speaker in February 2024.

Me: "Okay, to answer your first question, there's nothing wrong with me.

"I have a disability called Spina Bifida."

On reflection, I'm not sure why I said that or even bothered responding, because I owed this man nothing.

He was a total stranger and, frankly, quite rude. My medical history, my diagnosis of my disability is no-one else's business.

I guess it was my way of trying to educate, something I often feel obligated to do.

A pause, then...

Man: "I've just realised I've asked that wrong, haven't I?"

Me: "Yes, you have."

Paralympian. Speaker and mentor. International sports commentator.

Tennis Player. World Traveller. Conversationalist.

Businesswoman. Partner to Chris. (The ultimate team). Mum to Milo (my canine companion).

Cripple. Fire Hazard. Space Stealer (The phrase thrown at me was 'taking up space', actually).

First three sets of descriptors are fact.

The rest, insulting, but all too common.

This is me in 2024. Achieving, motivating, mentoring, inspiring, exploring, celebrating, loving, laughing, living.

London 2012. For two weeks of my life, I was treated how I think we (people with disabilities) should be treated. I felt respected.

The title used in all the promotion/marketing was Superhuman. That was pivotal because I learned what it felt like to be respected with a disability, and people almost started to view that as a cool thing. It felt incredible and it showed me that it can happen again and again.

Twelve years later and it's time to go beyond the Superhuman label and figure out how we can all work together to continue to change attitudes.

I hope this book, charting my life from a risk-taking teenage rebel to world class tennis player, proud Paralympian, public speaker, athlete mentor, sports commentator and businesswoman, via the catwalks of London Fashion Week, will open minds and hearts to that change, including yours.

Chapter 1:

Breaking Rules and Speaking Up

I didn't realise I was disabled. With family and village life, it was barely spoken about. No-one ever questioned my abilities. I was just Louise.

It was secondary school where I first experienced rules being imposed on me for the very first time just because of my disability. Anti-tip bars on wheelchairs, and seatbelts were compulsory, but with the support of my parents, I said no. I'd been taught how to fall out of my chair safely and all I could think was, if I had a seatbelt, I would be trapped.

The contrast was a real shock to the system because it showed me (really for the first time) that I was different.

It was at secondary school that, without choice, I had a teaching assistant in all my lessons which, rather than helping me, stopped me from making friends. Who wants an 'elderly' grown up cramping your style, right? We pushed for this to stop too. Now to be clear, I know that none of this was imposed upon me with any other intent than to help me, however, when I started secondary school, that was just how it had always been done with previous students, and it became very clear I was the first student who'd really spoken up against this one-dimensional approach. More on this later, as my secondary school truly did play a lifechanging role in where I am today; the start was just a little shaky.

It was especially hard to deal with because it was such a contrast to the help and support I had received at Wanborough Primary School from one wonderful woman, Mrs Petersen.

Mrs Petersen was a tall, slender, short haired blonde woman, who I always felt had a real sense of calm about her. She'd take no messing and would always have your back. I really respected her from day one.

She was fun, completely professional and always made me laugh. She was just cool. Cool in the classroom, cool with the kids. She never changed. Consistent. Wherever she was, whatever she was doing. And she made me feel safe, capable, and not like a burden, which is massive when you're a disabled child.

She was by my side throughout the school day, all day, every day, but she'd give me space which she knew was so important. She was there if I needed her, and she instilled in me that element of independence from early on.

The time spent with Mrs Petersen was amazing. Now I've grown up and witnessed others that support young people with disabilities, I truly understand she was one in a million, and that somehow I struck gold.

She was so cool. And when you're a kid, you want someone that's cool and lovely. She was there because I couldn't catheterise myself 'til I learned how to do it, so she would take me to the loo, basically.

At secondary school they had consistently been a bit too clingy in trying to support me, which made me want them to back off. I hadn't had that at primary with Mrs Petersen. She allowed me to thrive and enabled me. She didn't suppress me, she was just there to do the practical things to help.

To this day, I firmly believe that, whether it's care or support, it should be about helping someone thrive, not survive, and this is what Mrs Petersen did. I'm going to get this on a t-shirt one day.

What was amazing about her? She was always there when I needed her. She never imposed herself. She never made me feel like I needed her, which now is a massive deal, because, actually, I did for a few years, and that's clever.

I realise now she clearly wanted me to be independent and just be me; to make friends just like all the other students in my class. To my knowledge I was the only one who had a disability, but I never even really noticed.

At school I was given a 'special' table that was too high. Giving people in wheelchairs high tables is a thing – a weird assumption that's what we need. I don't know why, but it just is, it literally happened to me recently in a restaurant and the waiter said as I came in: "Don't worry we've saved you the highest table we have." I didn't want to sit at the high table then, nor do I now. At school, I remember saying: "I just want to sit here with my friends. It's normal. I'm sat down, I'm chair height."

Mrs Petersen told the school: "Louise isn't going to use that. She is going to sit with her friends and I'm going to have this table as a desk. I need the space."

It's only now that I realise she did that so I was sat with my friends. I very easily could have ended up the only kid in the wheelchair, sat on a table on my own. And, yeah, the table was inappropriate, not just practically as I could barely see the top of it, but also socially. It would have been completely isolating as it really was only big enough for one person. I would have been completely alone in the corner of the classroom away from everybody else. It just wasn't suitable for me and my needs.

She just put her things on it and made it hers, which was so clever.

She was always there, but I felt like I never spent time with her. She would be with me for a bit, but she'd then help and play with all the other kids as well. It was never a case of here's Louise's adult that follows her around because she's different, because that stops you making friends.

I saw that happen to so many kids in secondary school and initially, it started to happen to me until I stood up for myself.

When we were in a lesson, I never needed help intellectually, I never struggled with any subject. I'm like that middle of the road student, always going to be an A to C girl. I was always going to pass everything with a decent grade, but never going to be a genius either. I got one A star in Art, and I'll remember that forever. But I got B in PE, which is quite funny. I was always going to pass exams because I picked things up well. I'd revise a bit and I didn't need any additional help, *except* for a bit of extra time given to me in exams, which I was so grateful for. That was in case I needed to toilet, as medically I couldn't wait, nor was it a quick job as it is for most people.

I was more than capable of sitting in a lesson, producing all my work. There was nothing that separated me from the other students, and I think Mrs Peterson noticed that. So, I just never felt patronised.

I didn't need full time help, I just needed someone to help me go for a wee. She was always so discreet. Always there, I never had to look for her. We'd exchange a look and then we'd go to the loo. She never made me feel uncomfortable, difficult or awkward. After helping me get sorted, I'd be back in my chair and then I'd be off. I wouldn't see her again until I needed another trip to the bathroom.

And while we're on the subject, let's tackle the first elephant in the room, shall we? Let's talk about wee! Well, actually catheterisation and what that means for me day to day.

I'm not embarrassed or ashamed of it in any way, and actually, it's a really big part of me gaining my independence.

Going to the loo is one of the many challenges you may have to deal with when you have a disability, especially as a child. I couldn't go to a sleepover until I learned how to go to the toilet myself/self-catheterise, whereas my non-disabled friends didn't have to give it a second thought.

So, catheterization, a big part of my life, a pain in the ass of my life, but necessary. For many of you reading this, your experience of it may be when you've gone into hospital and had an operation. Just in case you're not too sure what it means, it's a tube that goes straight into your bladder which allows you to go to the toilet. That's probably the easiest way to describe it. So, I can hold my wee, but I can't release it. The catheter helps me to do that.

For the early years of my life, I had four people I couldn't exist without – Mum, Dad and Nan learned how to catheterise me, and then there was Mrs Peterson, who was like my family in that she just got on with it. It's what I like, and I think what you need as a youngster.

We talked about it enough that I was comfortable, but we didn't over talk it, so that it became awkward.

Being supported going to the toilet is a very personal thing, of course. Very personal. It's not a very nice thing, but I just remember chatting with her. Chat, chat, chat, chat, chat, and I'd almost not realise that she had catheterised me. I think that's why she did such a good job.

So, going to the loo in this way. Why mention it at all? Do we need to include this in a book about a Paralympian? Yes, I think we do.

I don't believe as a disabled person, I have any obligation to share my personal medical stuff just for the sake of educating others, however I do care about this. So, if you're someone with a disability or a parent with a child with a disability, and this gives you a little bit of support and knowledge, then it's what motivates me to talk about it.

If your child has to rely on a catheter it's so important they can learn as much about it as possible, so they can be fully independent and feel empowered as early as possible in their life.

I certainly learned early on that this was my life, and that I wanted to live the very best one I could, so learning how to catheterise myself was an important part of this.

It's also really good to encourage those of you without a disability to stop for a moment. Please never take for granted how lucky you are to be able to walk into a toilet, that you can get into for starters (more on this later) and then go for a wee with no faff or medical device.

At primary school, the loo was the only place where I really needed help. I was always out hanging on and falling off monkey bars. My friends would just push me along the bark track or field in my wheelchair and there I'd be outside, like everyone else, having fun.

I still remember the first time I was able to catheterise myself. It wasn't until I was invited to my first sleepover, aged 10, when things changed.

To stay over, I needed my mum's help, and she didn't want to come with me to a child's sleep over, believe it or not. Unsurprisingly, I didn't want her to come with me either.

I had a week to figure things out. Could I finally catheterise myself so I could join the party with my friends? Then, at a family dinner one night, I needed a wee.

"Come on, you're going to do it yourself," said Dad.

With a little mirror clipped on the loo, I managed it. I remember getting my catheter in, hearing the wee and saying: "I've done it!" From then on I never had someone do it again.

For me, catheterisation is one of those things that once you've done it, the act is not hard, it's more about the anxiety and stress around getting it right.

Once I could self-catheterise, it meant so much more independence. I could go on that sleep over and do so many other things, on my own.

As for the amazing Mrs Petersen, I didn't need her help on a daily basis anymore, but she was still in the background, giving me confidence to be me and live my best life.

During my last couple of years at primary school, though we didn't see each other regularly, I still felt her presence and positive influence. Knowing she was there if something went wrong was a huge comfort.

It meant that when I went to secondary school, I didn't need anything and that when my parents put me on a plane around the world on my own, two years later, I knew I could do incredible things. Mrs Petersen had done her job beautifully, and for that I will be forever grateful.

That sense that anything and everything is possible has always been with me. My whole family deserves credit for this approach to life. Now I'm getting older, I'm realising it never occurred to them that I wouldn't be able to do anything I wanted one day.

I was in a family with the attitude that she will do that one day because she'll want a 'normal' life, she'll want to be independent. She won't want us with her all the time, in the nicest way possible.

Growing up I got treated just like my brother. Disability was never a factor. My parents never wrapped me up in cotton wool. Their mantra was, and still is: "Just try it."

Their mindset was incredible and it gave me the confidence, at a very young age, to think I could do anything.

Village and small primary school life had been so good, but then came the big change. My catchment secondary school wouldn't have me, because they didn't have wheelchair access around the school, nor were they willing to try and accommodate me. So, I was placed outside the area, on my own, away from my friends, Mrs Peterson and familiarity.

The change was massive. My new school just didn't 'get me'. Simple things like they couldn't understand why I didn't have a seat belt on my wheelchair. They wouldn't let me do lots of things I'd done at primary, like take part in PE without help, and everyone was talking about me.

With this came the realisation that I was 'different'. It was a huge blow for my confidence and independence.

Yet again, there was I being forced to be confronted with the contrasts in my life. Outside school, I was already competing in wheelchair tennis at a high junior level, but in the classroom I couldn't do anything. I felt trapped and cried every day for a year.

To top it all, when I told the careers advisor I wanted to be a Paralympian, she told me to "aim for something more realistic!"

The conversation went something like this:

Careers adviser: "So, what do you want to be when you grow up?"

Such a daunting question for anyone of any age to answer.

Me: "I know what I want to do. I want to be a Paralympian."

I'd seen the Paralympics/Olympics on TV and I was doing really well in my sports. This felt like an achievable goal.

Careers adviser: "Maybe, you should look at something more realistic."

My heart sank to my stomach.

Me: "Oh!"

I felt stupid.

Me (thinking): 'Am I an idiot? I thought I could do this, and now I'm not so sure.'

Then, in true Louise fashion, I quickly changed my thoughts to: 'Why can't I do this?'

It was the first and last time I met the careers adviser.

It was a bizarre experience which, for a few moments, left me feeling useless, inadequate, rubbish.

In the end it was that inner belief and drive, nurtured by my family, that turned things around and spurred me on.

Every day they would tell me I was capable and could do anything I set my heart and mind on. They deserve credit for getting me through this experience.

At this point, with so many things mounting up to squash my potential to be independent, I could have gone backwards.

Instead, my strong mind and determination, combined with the love and support of my parents, saw me through.

Eventually my secondary school began to understand just how much I could do for myself, and allowed me time out for various tennis events, showing incredible support.

At this point, my junior tennis career was really starting to develop, and I was being invited to international camps and competitions across the globe. I was competing and playing in countries like, Holland and Brazil, which was mind blowing for someone of my age.

As my confidence and level of independence grew, there were two people who really helped shape me as a young adult – headteacher, Mr Defter and tutor, Miss Butler.

When, aged 15, I was selected for my second World Team Cup, in Brazil, I went to both of them with a problem.

The World Team Cup (Wheelchair Tennis' equivalent to the Davis Cup), which was an incredible opportunity for someone so young, clashed with my GCSE exams. I so wanted to go, so what could I do?

With my parents' support, I was the first person that was not afraid to have a voice and speak up.

Me (to Mr Defter): “I really want to do this. What do I have to do for you to let me go?”

Mr Defter: “Okay, you can go and we support you in this, but you must keep your grades above C across all subjects. Your studies cannot suffer.”

So, that was the deal.

From this moment on, whenever I was away for competition, I was always given work to take with me.

This meant that when I wasn’t on the tennis court training and competing, I was in my hotel room or somewhere quiet doing my homework to ensure I could keep enjoying these amazing opportunities. I knew how lucky I was to be given this chance; others in our team didn’t have such understanding schools so missed out on a lot of opportunities. I was determined to stick to my promises and make everyone proud.

I was always expected to have my work complete when I returned to school, and I always did.

It was hard, at times, but so worth it.

Looking back, I think my secondary school experience was an incredible example of how if you just listen and adapt, you can help somebody fly and flourish.

If the school had just engaged those so-called rules without taking into account my wishes, I wouldn’t have achieved half the things I have. I would have been so suppressed. Instead, they did listen, and they took positive action.

I truly believe that it's because of Mr Defter and Miss Butler working with me in this way, that I could do my college and university studies alongside tennis later on in my life. This set me up so I could work alongside tennis because it was no longer a strange thing to balance the two. It wasn't an alien concept. I just thought, 'This is really going to benefit me to do this. I can do this' and that was so powerful.

They taught me the importance of education and kept me accountable. It was a case of you can have these privileges, but you have to work hard for them. That was such a good lesson to learn when I was so young.

All of this is still with me today. I balance so many different elements of my career, and I know I succeed with this as it's just something I have always been used to. I know I can do it, and actually really enjoy the variety.

I loved watching the school evolve and make changes which impacted on how they treated other kids too.

After I was given permission to go to the World Team Cup, I discovered that other students at the school were also grateful for the changes.

It was so cool watching them and the staff evolve too. Everyone flourished in that environment.

I have so much respect for everyone at Commonweal school because they listened to my concerns and wishes and smashed it out of the park in terms of changing things for the better. Sometimes it just takes someone to encourage you to see things differently, and take the fear of trying something new away.

Towards the end of my time at the school, and since, when I've been in to deliver talks or just visit, I've had staff say to me: "You were the star of a little, bitty revolution." I love that. What a wonderful way to leave a mark.

Chapter 2:

Hello World: I'm Here to Prove You Wrong

Louise Ann Hunt

Born: May 24, 1991

Weight: 7lbs 12oz

Mum doesn't really remember much about my birth. She was really poorly when I was born, so her memory often tricks her a bit.

There are a few things she does recall though.

"Congratulations, you have a little girl!"

I have to be delivered by Caesarean section because I am born with my legs across my chest. I arrive in a folded in half position, because due to a cyst, there is nowhere else for my legs to grow.

Hospital staff tell Mum and Dad I have a cyst on my back.

Mum asks to see me, but I am already being prepared to go by ambulance to John Radcliffe Hospital in Oxford. Here there are more specialists to help me.

Mum is in a bad way and asks a second time: "I need to see her." She's so worried that she'll never get another opportunity.

I'm brought to Mum briefly. Just a few precious moments together.

At this point there is no mention of Spina Bifida.

Dad travels with me in the ambulance to John Radcliffe.

Mum tells hospital staff: "I want to be transferred with Louise."

A few days later, against medical advice, she gets her wish.

Despite being very ill, in considerable pain and still healing from surgery, Mum travels by ambulance on a floating bed to be with me.

I'm now just a few days old and Dad is told I have Spina Bifida. He knows nothing about the condition. This knowledge will come later.

I undergo a six-hour operation to remove a big cyst on my back and a smaller one on my leg at around 10 days old.

At John Radcliffe, my parents are told I'll probably have Hydrocephalus (It's a neurological disorder caused by an abnormal build up of fluid in the ventricles (cavities) deep within the brain. This excess fluid can put harmful pressure on the brain's tissues) which can develop later in life and is common with my disability. They are advised to look out for headaches. Luckily for me, this never happens.

Mum and Dad are bowled over by the hospital's high levels of care.

Mum is shown how to catheterise me. I'm so tiny that she catheterises me into an ashtray.

I remain in hospital for a month.

It's not until I am several months old, a lovely physio shows my parents how to stretch my legs down, to help me get into a seated position, tiny movements at a time.

Both mum and I are in tears during these sessions as it is so painful, but Dad is always the ultimate master of distraction, trying to make me laugh and take my mind off what is happening.

Dad draws me endless pictures of Donald Duck and brings me talking and singing animals as distractions; these will make regular appearances in my hospital visits as a child too.

This is where my parents demonstrate they are the ultimate team. Mum is able to crack on with tending to my medical needs, only made possible by Dad providing constant entertainment and distraction. Together they always ensure I have the care and support I need.

My incredible parents are determined to give me the best possible start in life.

With their love and care, I am able to use a walking and standing frame.

We call the standing part, the clicker frame because it clicks as I move with it, the most annoying sound.

It's a brilliant piece of equipment though, which helps me to stretch and move around, by strapping me in tightly in a standing position. I would then hold onto a walking frame which would allow me to balance and shuffle along.

It's particularly good for my internal organs as bodies just aren't designed to be cramped up all the time.

I hate it and it's a constant battle to get me using it, as it's uncomfortable and I'm really slow in it.

Mum and Dad resort to bribery, reading, drawing (Dad and I's shared passion and talent), treats and trips out, and it works. Playing pool is the perfect distraction for me too, another family favourite activity.

As Mum and Dad continue to encourage and guide me, medics tell them I'll need a huge amount of care throughout my life.

"It's very unlikely Louise will be able to live an independent life,' they say.

My wonderful parents have other ideas.

We are ready to prove them wrong.

Chapter 3:

Floating Hips and Funky Cushions

I can't explain how important it is for parents of disabled children to instil independence in their kids from a young age.

I'm so grateful I have always been surrounded with positive mindsets, encouraging me to try things and adopt that 'can do' attitude.

I'm not saying my family are perfect, but I am saying that at 33, in a house that I've earned the money to buy myself, I can do everything on my own.

I learned about my medical care very young and that made me physically and mentally stronger.

It's not to say that sometimes I don't need help, because everybody does, but my help looks a little bit different.

When I'm super poorly, guess who helps me physically if I'm struggling, like helping me empty my leg bag? (more explanation on this later) It's my husband, Chris (my love and fellow

Paralympian), because I'm hurting and I'm ill, and that just so happens to be the thing that I need help with. But when he's ill, guess who's the one getting his lenses sorted (he's visually impaired), helping him? It's me and it's no big deal. We just do what needs to be done.

I'm so grateful that when I was young, when you're kind of learning everything, I learned that this was my life and from day one, I never believed I couldn't do things. It was always a case of how will we do that? It might look different to someone without a disability, but I'm going to do it.

So, when I meet someone who expresses surprise that I'm in a wheelchair and I can drive, I'm all too eager to explain, it's not that difficult. You do your lessons, take your test, get your car adapted and away you go!

I actually failed my first driving test because I made a major boo, boo, well they classed it as major. I crossed the central line when turning right which is an instant fail apparently, but I passed on the second attempt, because I'm human. It's actually not that amazing.

It's at times like this, when I come out of my own little bubble, that I have to deal with a stranger's ignorance about my capabilities, but more on this later.

First, let me tell you about my disability.

Those of us with Spina Bifida either are born with a cyst or a hole in our spine and this denotes the level that it affects us. I had two cysts, one on my leg and one on my lower back. As you learned earlier, both had to be removed when I was a baby.

At John Radcliffe hospital in Oxford, I was in the baby ICU unit and Mum in the maternity ward. She could see me out of her window if my Dad carried me to his nearest window.

Spina Bifida is a congenital disability, which develops when the baby is inside the mum's tummy, and it affects the growth of the spine.

To remove my lower back cyst, they had to take most of my left bum cheek away with it due to its low positioning, which is why I now have to use a specialist cushion to help me sit straighter.

Both my hips have no joints and I get a lot of discomfort in them. It also means I've got really bad balance. If I'm being completely honest, there's only so much a cushion, chair and propping yourself up can do, so it can be pretty challenging.

I also have one leg longer than the other, because I needed surgery to remove the other cyst on my left leg. In doing this, I had to lose my ankle. Surgeons cut bone and tissue from the back of my calf on my left leg to create an ankle for me. It's why, as a child, I had to have special shoes with a build-up on one side to make sure I grew straight.

I also had to wear splints as both of my feet are completely floppy. I have no resistance in them at all.

I've always had partial feeling and movement from my waist down.

I can feel my thighs and between my legs, but I can't feel anything else, like my bottom or lower legs.

I can move my knees and my hips a little bit, but as I don't have hip sockets, my hips are completely out of joint. My pelvis is twisted. I can't feel or move anything from my knees down and I can't feel or move my feet.

I'm always really conscious that when I talk about my disability, all I can explain is how it affects me. Spina Bifida, like all disabilities, affects everybody in very different ways.

Medically, I'm unable to go to the toilet to empty my bowels or bladder in the conventional way.

Because of where my lower back cyst was removed, they effectively removed 90% of my left bum cheek.

The doctor used to describe me as having floating hips, i.e. they're not in their sockets.

My funky cushion that accompanies me everywhere, allows me to sit more comfortably, although I use the word comfortable loosely. I don't think I ever truly sit comfortably. I don't know it's a feeling I've ever had.

For anything active, like playing tennis, I need to wear splints on my lower legs and onto my feet to hold my ankles in place. Without the splints, they're just like jelly. There's no support there, no rigidness to keep shoes on. So, even though I don't wear them all the time, I pop my shoes on and wear them, and my wheelchair foot plate helps me keep them on due to its side guards. If I move, they'll just fall off, because I've got no tension in my feet to hold them on.

I was a little bit lopsided when I was younger, to be expected with all the things I've got going on, but I wanted to have straight shoulders as I was really conscious about it. I can remember forcing myself to hold myself straight. I was so adamant that I wanted my posture to be good, I used to put a sticker on my phone to remind me to sit up straight.

I suppose it could be said that I didn't luck out on the Spina Bifida front, but my parents were great. I was educated by them and my doctors. Because I grew up around a lot of disabled people, I think I learned and got my knowledge from them plus a lot of physios when I was on the tennis tour.

I don't think I've ever felt the need to Google about my condition because of all the help and support I got and still receive from people around me. I never felt hung up by the term, Spina Bifida. For me, it was simply a case of, this is the way my disability affects my body, so this is what doesn't work for me and this is what does. I just got to know my body, and it's the way I've always approached things.

Chapter 4:

Being Me: Competitive and Reckless

I can remember everything. The first time I went there, I was five years old. That massive sports hall. Cold, with that musty sports smell that I like to this day. It's still there, even though the hall must have been renovated 100 times since.

Through the doors and the hall was split into two sections. In those two halves there were all sports. In front of me zone hockey, the one I ended up loving the most. Table tennis, basketball and too many others to remember.

The space was rammed with disabled kids. A lot of wheelchairs, a lot of fake arms and legs lying around, and I was overwhelmed, but in a nice way, in a 'My God, they're all like me' kind of way.

There were so many disabled people there that I didn't even know existed. I remember thinking, they have no arm, no leg, what? I thought I was the only one that was different in the world because up until that point, I didn't have any friends who used wheelchairs or who had disabilities.

It was another moment where I realised I could belong somewhere, and these people were like me.

Zone hockey was so fun. I used to love playing that game and I was really good at it. I'm fast and I was fast then too.

For the uninitiated, Zone Hockey is a 4-a-side game in which girls and boys can participate in a high scoring, fast moving game of hockey. It enables electric wheelchair users, manual wheelchair users, ambulant and semi-ambulant competitors to play together. Basically, everyone can play competitively together.

One lane is for those with manual chairs, one for electric chair users. Middle section is ambulant (Two people on their feet) and then the goalie which could be anybody. It was brilliant. Everyone could play.

So you were in a team, but you were against your counterpart. I was fast and I had good long arms, so I could smack the ball anywhere.

By the time I went to Stoke Mandeville (birthplace of the Paralympic Games) for the first time, I'd been to a couple of junior tennis camps. I think Mum got contacts that way, and then, just like that, booked me a space because it was interesting. I went for years.

I visited on my own to start with and then the next year, a few of us from the wheelchair tennis camps, went there as a team and played the sports together.

But then, when I went to secondary school, I used to go with my school and we'd sign up for Zone Hockey as a team. That was really fun, too.

So it was that and fencing for me. I always got told off for being too powerful. I wanted to win and I could win at that. These were my early memories of winning, and I loved it.

Maybe from then I had a passion for inclusion without realising it, because I loved that I could do something with my friends that were all different, but somehow sport put us on a level playing field.

A lot of the time, in other situations, it had often been a case of: "Oh, Louise, you can do the scoring because you're in a wheelchair, right? Yeah, do that." Whereas with Zone Hockey, everyone could play, which was brilliant and really fun.

It was the first team thing I did. So, although I prefer individual sport, I think there is definitely a bit of a team player somewhere within me because I really enjoyed playing.

What I also love about the zone system is that it can be used for so many sports. You could zone a basketball game, for example. Basically, if it's pressure sport, sign me up. Really. I'll come out of retirement for Zone Hockey.

Stoke Mandeville became a big part of my childhood. I went every year from the age of five 'til I left school at 16, and had the time of my life.

We used to do some really crazy stuff which smashes down every perception of disability.

The dormitories were so basic and old fashioned. Although the girls and boys would be in different dorms, the wall between them was several feet off the ceiling so you could hear everything.

We used to climb up the bed, the tables, wardrobes and go over the wall. As none of us could walk at all, or well, we would just drag our bodies up there, jump and land on a bed the other side of the wall. It never hurt, and if it did, I couldn't feel it anyway. We were kids and it was just madness. We used to get in so much trouble.

There was a very long ramp that went from the sports centre down to the dormitories. We used to get in our sports chairs, take the big wheels off and then shove people down the slope so you had no control. It was lethal. How we didn't break arms and stuff, I don't know, but we'd put mattresses from the dormitories at the end of the slope, so people would have a soft, and hopefully, safe landing. We were just a group of disabled kids having fun because we didn't feel fear.

When it came to the sports available to us, I just loved that you could choose what to compete in. I did everything because I wanted to win. You could try out a sport for a few days, and in the last couple of days then compete in it.

I won in quite a few things, winning many medals. It's funny in that I don't really think I was that naturally gifted, but I would try things and be successful in quite a lot of sports like swimming. I think it all boiled down to the simple fact that I just really tried.

When I was little, though I wasn't winning as much as I would do as an adult, I always wanted to win. Those medals meant the world to me, and we hung them up every time. I've still got them.

My parents should take some credit because they taught me that it's okay to be proud of yourself, that achieving is a good thing. Sometimes that's suppressed by people, by our parents and often our peers.

The impact of this, long term, can be very damaging. I see so many young people who don't know how to celebrate their successes, because it's not 'cool' or something they've been taught. The tragic result of this is a huge lack of confidence and motivation to work hard towards any goal, because they simply don't see the point or understand the value in how good that can make them feel.

Mum and Dad believed, and still do, if you want to do it, work hard and do it, and we'll celebrate whatever the outcome. So those medals would always be hung up in my room so I could see them, and that made me feel good. I loved it and loved that feeling of winning.

In this environment, I felt the safest I ever did as a child. Being there I could be 100,000% authentically myself, which was competitive, disabled, and reckless. This instilled mindset helped me power through some pretty dark times in my life, and lifted me through those many moments when others didn't believe in me or treat me fairly.

How I've managed to hold onto that winning mentality and taken it out into the world, is something I'd not really put much thought into until I was asked that question fairly recently during a motivational speaking/mentoring gig.

I think I'm competitive in a different way now. So, when I was an athlete, the biggest opponent was me. The pressure from other opponents is nothing compared to the pressure you put on yourself.

Chapter 5:

From Child's Play to Tennis Camps

I was five years old when I started playing tennis.

The first time I played I was in my old NHS chair that weighed a tonne.

It was on a family friend's court, at the back of our house, and I was there with my brother and Dad just messing around. Playing for fun.

It was something I could do with everybody else. Whether you were standing, sitting, it didn't matter.

My family played tennis, so I played too.

I didn't feel disabled. I remember playing in a tennis chair for the first time and suddenly I was so able. It felt so cool.

Any wheelchair can change your life, but sports chairs can in a special way. It certainly did mine. That first time, I felt free and unstoppable. I knew it was a feeling I never wanted to lose.

The ease of manoeuvring it, the speed I could reach, indescribable freedom.

Suddenly, I was as fast or even faster than anyone else on the court, and I was actually better. Wow, I was on a level. I could really play. No just sitting there, hoping as someone tried to hit the ball to me. I could move to the ball and hit the ball to them, and I was quick, so quick!

I could play and play well. I could play socially, for fun, just like everyone else, without needing special allowances to make it work for me.

At the same time, I discovered wheelchair racing and that led me to compete in the London Mini Marathon 10 times. These are such special memories, especially my first marathon which I did in my tennis chair, as I didn't even have a racing chair then. I was so nervous, Dad ran alongside me which was so magical. A couple of years later, he ran the actual race (as he had done many years prior) so that was a special year for us both too. I love a photo I have of us with our medals.

It was a great experience, pushing through the closed off streets of London. An electrifying atmosphere with fans cheering you on your way.

I then did a couple of track events, but racing wasn't really for me. On one hand, I loved competition day, but on the other, hated the training.

In contrast, I loved training for wheelchair tennis. I'd happily get up early in the morning for it, which says a lot, especially as mornings, when I was younger, weren't my thing. I just never found it boring, there was always so much to learn.

The thing is, when you're an athlete, 70% is spent training or on a practice court, so most of your life isn't about competition. Many people don't realise that as they only see competition days.

The racing training was too easy, basically. Don't get me wrong, I had to train hard. I didn't win those mini marathons that easily, but it was a case of go from there to there as fast as you can. My good pushing technique meant I never had a coach. It was just a bit too straightforward.

In contrast, tennis felt much more of a challenge, so interesting. Even now, when I go and hit for fun, I'm learning all the time on a tennis court. I'll notice my forehand technique could be better with an adjustment, I'll notice changes in my game on different surfaces or I'll work on improving my pushing technique.

In tennis there's always something to get better at or to challenge you, and that was a massive pull from the beginning.

I did both sports for 10 years, but in the end it was going to the Beijing Paralympic games in 2008, that made me put all my focus on tennis. I was invited to Beijing as a part of an inspiration programme, which aims to give athletes who have the potential to reach a Paralympics in the future, the experience of what a games, is truly like, the ultimate motivation.

I didn't want to be a racer, I wanted to be in the next games as a tennis player. It just felt right. I knew it was the sport for me, but some people around me weren't so sure about my choice. They thought I was crazy to opt for tennis because I was more naturally gifted at racing. My first challenge was to overcome other people's opinions. Story of my life.

So, I followed my dream and got to work.

My early focus was on adapting my pushing technique.

I naturally pushed with these big, long sweeping pushes, perfect for distance, whereas for tennis I needed to use short, sharp pushes.

My natural abilities meant that I could always push longer than many other players on court, but initially I was a bit slower off the mark.

It just took a lot of practise and training drills such as the dreaded fan drill, which I and many players always hated. Basically, this is a drill where you have to recover back to the centre point at the back of the court every time after pushing around four or five other points on the court. It was repetitive and dull, but it was a great drill for me to work on those short, sharp movements to ensure I nailed the technique as best I could.

It was a life changing moment. I felt so happy and heard my Grampy's words (Mum's Dad, my hero) in my ear: "Success is waking up every day doing something you love," and I loved tennis.

My eyes were opening to a world that would bring equality and opportunity. Tennis had captured my heart and my imagination.

Part of this new found love was that tennis offered me a huge learning curve in so many ways.

I have always loved to learn. It's part of my personality. I'm always striving to learn something new, whether I'm following someone on Instagram, chatting with someone I meet on the tennis circuit or reading a good book.

As I got older and better at my sport, it literally opened up my world, and I strongly believe the best education you can ever have is through travelling and meeting people. Tennis has given me all this. It's taken me around the world, to countries that I probably never would have been to. If you work hard, the rewards are amazing.

That reward came early on when, aged 11, I was on a plane to Holland without my parents for the first time. I was going to a junior tennis camp with all these other juniors from across the world.

As I got good at the sport relatively quickly, through my teens, I was missing school and college, and flying the globe and being funded to do it. If I was playing in the main tournament, I was also earning prize money too. What more could I want? It was certainly more fun than school, and I felt I learnt so much on these trips.

It was this that got me up in the morning. Easy to see why the world of tennis had made such an amazing impression on me. It was the perfect opportunity for me to shine.

Chapter 6:

Bully to Bodyguard

Bullying is always unacceptable. However, people don't act out and treat people awfully for no reason at all, and that reason is nothing to do with the person that's being hurt.

I had a really hard time in my first year at secondary school. I think it had something to do with it being the perfect storm. As my catchment secondary school wasn't accessible, I had no choice about where to go to continue my education. I had to go to Commonweal secondary school.

I was really easy to prey on because I stood out. I had no friends initially, and I was different because I was visibly disabled. So, I was a perfect go-to for a bully.

There were a couple of bullies in the year above me who were pretty awful. They would frequently shove their feet in my wheel so I'd fly into the wall.

This was so humiliating and embarrassing, and made me feel so self-conscious. I remember these experiences were one of the first times in my life where I just hated myself for being different.

It was something I'd never really felt before as I was always supported to embrace my uniqueness, but suddenly, this was the thing that was making my life hell.

This went on for months, and months, and months. I felt there was no end in sight and that this was going to be my school life for the next 5 years. I saw no way out.

Then one day, I'd had enough. As one of them put their foot in my wheel once more, I shouted: "Stop doing that!", put my hands on the rim of the wheel and turned sharply, trapping them.

From that day onwards, it never happened again.

I remember seeing the bully the next day and he was limping a bit. I think he had probably twisted his ankle.

Though it had been a minor victory, that wasn't the end to me being bullied though. There was a bully in my year group too. He stole my bag and emptied it, spilling my catheters across the floor. I was mortified.

When you're young, trying to make friends and find your way and your place within that weird secondary school dynamic, it can feel even more crushingly embarrassing.

I was bullied for ages. Being picked on all the time, name calling, drawing attention to me for no reason, it became intolerable. In desperation, I reported it to my tutor, Miss Butler.

It was her idea to bring my bully and I together. So, she put us in a room together and we had *the* conversation. It wasn't easy, but we both committed to it.

When we met, I remember being struck by how sad, ashamed and guilty he looked.

"I'm really sorry. I've never met someone in a wheelchair before and I didn't know how to talk to you or how to treat you," he confessed.

After taking a minute to mull over his comments, I replied:

"It's no excuse what you just said. You should treat me the same as everybody else."

I told him how his bullying was unfair and how it had made me feel, then said: "Let's just move on from it."

Despite his actions, I appreciated his honesty and bravery in speaking as he did. He was clearly clueless, and it took a lot for him to say what he said.

I've never been one to hold a grudge. If you can admit you're wrong, I think that's one of the bravest things you can do. And that's what my bully did.

I made it very clear to him that just because you don't know someone or why they're different, or haven't met someone like that before, it's never an excuse to treat them poorly.

Amazingly, from that day on, we became friends, of sorts. He became my very own protection officer.

A few days later he asked if a couple of lads were bothering me, when they were just chatting to me. Anytime he saw anyone talking to me he'd come over and see if I was okay; he took it to the opposite extreme really.

My former bully would continue doing this until he changed schools, around a year or so later.

His actions showed me that he was clearly very uneducated before our chat and just how sorry he was for his past behaviour; he wanted to do all he could to make up for them.

It was a huge lesson for the 11-year-old me. It taught me there is absolutely no excuse for bullying, but when people get bullied, it's always on the bully. It's a reflection of that individual and what's going on for them. Often, it's because they've got internalised insecurities. They're trying to take attention away from themselves because they struggle with who they are.

I think my bully was just so embarrassed at getting things wrong that he would take things a little too far the other way.

If he saw anyone speaking to me, he would panic and intervene, to which I would reply: "I've got this."

We would chat and in the end, got on really well.

Bullying taught me to stand up for myself.

Thanks to Miss Butler, that 15-minute conversation with my bully gave us both new perspectives on the situation and a way to move forward together. Just imagine what sort of world we'd live in if we could all try this approach.

To this day, I try really hard to take a step back if I hear or see behaviour I am uncomfortable with, as this taught me that there's often more to what you first witness. Of course, it's super hard to do this sometimes as we're human and are programmed to react on instinct and first impression, but so often there's more to someone or a scenario than first meets the eye.

Now, all these years later, my experiences have shown me that not everyone is exposed to everyone. So many people live in a tiny little box and may not meet a diverse range of people.

There is always a reason why bullies behave as they do and my bullies taught me that and why it's important to look beyond the nastiness. Their behaviour actually had nothing to do with me - I just ended up being in the firing line.

When this was happening, I was adjusting from being this little sheltered girl in a village bubble, where I felt ordinary, to a world that was so different to mine. It was a massive shock to the system.

This perspective is something I'll often share when I'm talking to young people in the hope that it may help them in their journey too.

Chapter 7:

Listening Without Judgement

I have a beautiful photo of Mum taken when I was playing in Turkey. I was in my late teens.

She's wearing shorts and a t-shirt because it's bloody hot. She's sat between two women dressed all in black with hijabs. They're all smiling.

The photo is wonderful because the visual difference in culture is so apparent and there they are together, laughing, joking and bonding. Even more special, they were watching my match where I was playing one of the other women's daughters, yet the atmosphere was lovely and supportive.

This is what I love about sport, it brings so many different people together who probably wouldn't have met otherwise.

At the time, world events led to the ITF (International Tennis Federation) approving separate draws for competitors from nations in conflict with one another.

This was the first time I'd spoken to people from another country where the news was so prominent.

About eight or nine of the athletes I chatted with on this trip, had been injured by bombs. Each one had at least one limb missing.

This experience set a groundwork for me on tour, where I began really talking to people and asking those difficult questions.

"How do you feel about this situation?", "What's your country's view on this?" and "What's your view?"

The replies received were interesting and enlightening. I was given so many different perspectives and told things that I would never have known just by listening to what was being fed to us through the media.

It made me realise really early on in my life just how we can be given just one narrative, and how important it is for us to take on board many.

Once, I confessed to my fellow athletes that I had worried that they wouldn't want to speak to me because I was British, and yet how wrong could I be?

It was such a big teaching for me and it's why I'm so much about talking with people and listening to their views.

I'm in a very privileged position where I know people all over the world and those connections, those conversations, have provided me with a more balanced and educated view on things. This is why I avoid the news. What we're told is such a biased narrative, I just don't trust it.

It makes it even more frustrating and disappointing when I meet people that have only ever spoken to people of the same class and culture, who, in some cases, have never left their home country or even town, and hold very narrow-minded views. I do, of course, appreciate that having the ability to travel is a privilege and not something everyone gets to do, but I can't encourage you enough that if you get the opportunity to see somewhere new, do it! You won't regret it!

I love how on tour, sport connected us and then allowed us to go deeper with our conversations. Listening to one another, we were able to talk through our challenges, our differences and find common ground to help us build on our understanding and our humanity.

A few days after the pic of Mum and the two women was taken, a boat was hired for us. In the middle of the sea, we jumped off the boat and swam.

It was quite a sight. People with various injuries and disabilities, throwing themselves off the top of the boat, relaxing together. This was still early in my career so, at the time, this felt very different, but so exciting, and created such a positive atmosphere of total acceptance of each other.

There had been all this talk about keeping people from different nations in conflict separate from one another, and here was this incredible group of athletes bonding and partying.

It was amazing and, if I'm honest, quite confusing. Still very young, I just didn't get why we had received warnings not to mix. I didn't understand what all this division was about.

When I look back at this time I'm reminded of all the good things that came out of these moments. The photos of me with one guy from Israel on one side and another from Iraq on the other. All of us laughing together.

During the tour I made some really good friends within the Iraqi team, at a time when the Iraq war was going on. My family had actually lost a friend in the war. He was an inflight engineer who was shot down in a Hercules aircraft sent to Iraq.

This experience added to my preconceived perceptions that all Iraqis hated us so, as I got to know members of the Iraq team, I asked those challenging questions and listened intently.

That listening without judgement opened up many more conversations and provided me with a much more balanced perspective. I enjoyed my time with them more than words can say. I'm so thankful for every person who spoke to me, judgement free, and helped me see the reality of something I never would have known about if it wasn't for their good nature and welcoming spirit.

Chapter 8:
Treetop Quarrels

I've always had a sense of adventure; it runs in the family. We all have it.

The other day, as I was thinking about preparing this book for publication, a childhood memory popped up that perfectly illustrates the adventurous spirit I've been blessed with.

A 'home-made' treehouse complete with zip wire. It's what childhood dreams are made of, and I had one in my back garden.

Gramp and Dad built one for my brother and I, and it was the coolest treehouse ever.

Constructed with part of it in the trunk of the tree, it had a little castle bit on the side.

Gramp and Dad ensured it was built with different levels, the idea being that I'd probably only be able to use the lower level. It made it even more magical, but there was no way I was just using part of it.

My brother would climb up to the top and, very quickly, I found a way to do the same.

Mainly using my arms and dragging my legs behind me, I'd climb up the treehouse. Then my brother and I would hoist each other up and down, using some rather dodgy abseiling gear.

I loved that tree house so much and the zip wire which went over the pond.

Rob and I would spend hours and hours playing up there and would abseil into the field next to our house. We had so much fun.

I can still remember the first time my parents and grandparents caught me right at the top. Their faces were a picture.

When my Gramp asked how I got there, Rob and I smiled. "That's for us to know and for you to never find out," we quipped.

As with most sibling relationships, we didn't always get along.

One day we had a bit of a fall out. I think Rob might have been in his teens. Anyway, we were really young and, for whatever reason, had a bit of a spat about goodness knows what.

Rob's reaction was to leave me hanging over the field for ages.

Now, some people may cringe at this scenario, and that's okay. A child with Spina Bifida being left alone, dangling from a tree? How awful!

But this memory makes me smile for several reasons. It shows that Rob didn't allow my disability to dictate how he treated me. To Rob I was just Louise, his annoying little sister who he'd fallen out with.

My disability was irrelevant. It was never a case of 'my sister's disabled, I can't treat her like this'. He would have left his mate dangling from the treehouse, so why wouldn't he do the same to me?

We did so much climbing, abseiling and zip wiring from our beautiful treehouse over the years. It taught us so much about getting out of our comfort zones, pushing ourselves and letting our adventurous spirits out to play.

In these moments, we were just your average brother and sister - high on life and high on adventure. We couldn't wait to see what life had in store for us.

Chapter 9:

All Hail the All-Conquering Leg Bag!

It had been in my teens I discovered that my one and only kidney had deteriorated due to my bladder refluxing. This had happened because when I was playing tennis or travelling, I wasn't emptying my bladder as much as I should.

A leg bag was suggested by my consultant for long flights and tennis matches. Very reluctant to use one initially, but when I did, it changed my life and made things so much easier.

I'll never forget when I first used one at school. My dear friends who waited for me outside the loo, noticed the difference immediately. They had got used to waiting ages when I catheterised, basically missing most of their break times, but in came the leg bag and I was in and out of the toilet in seconds. A game changer for all! They loved it as much as I did.

Then there was the flights game changer. No more panicking about negotiating a tiny, awkward loo. Worst case (of course, not ideal), I could empty into a bottle. Life changing and so much peace of mind.

Chapter 10:

My First Wimbledon

My first time at Wimbledon and it felt like I had just jumped into the TV screen. I was five.

Growing up in a family that loved tennis, we always had the television on during the tournament, so for me to see it in the flesh was incredible.

An unbelievable atmosphere, tennis at this level was, and still is, unparalleled to any other sport I know.

On this very special day I had the most magical experience. Not only because I saw my first match in person, but I was given my first tennis wheelchair by the incredible charity, Get Kids Going!

This national organisation gives disabled children and young people, the wonderful opportunity of participating in sport and provides specialist wheelchairs and funding to help them from start to Paralympic level.

The Get Kids Going gift was to be the first of many as the charity supplied all my tennis and racing wheelchairs until I retired. They also provided valuable funding to help pay for my training and competition costs.

As a young kid starting out, who needed an incredibly expensive sports chair to compete, they gave me the perfect start.

To make things extra special on the day, Sir Cliff Richard presented me with my chair. It would be the first of many meetings with him over the years as our careers overlapped.

My presentation took place in the stunning members area. So many beautiful flowers, an eye catching water fountain, and such a sense of occasion. Then tea and cake to follow.

I have so many gorgeous photos to remind me of this moment.

The whole experience was a credit to Get Kids Going for their generous donation and my parents for getting me there, not just in a physical sense, but in an emotional way to help me believe I could play wheelchair tennis at all.

There I was, in the home of tennis. Can you imagine how that felt? There aren't enough words.

Around 9 years later in 2005, I was at Wimbledon to watch the first ever wheelchair tennis match being played. This was just one match, effectively a demonstration of the sport, between two doubles teams. I'll never forget seeing the players on court and thinking, this could actually be me one day.

Just one match, but such an important one. To see this match on grass, at Wimbledon, was something else. It brought everything to life for me.

To play at the place I held in such high regard and which, for me, was the peak of any person's tennis career, was phenomenal.

It brought everything to life and with it one big realisation: I could do this. This was my future.

Ten years on and my dream came true. It was my time to play at this incredible venue.

Surprisingly, the memory that stays with me all these years later is not the first match I played here, but the first time I went out on court to practise with my coach, Ali.

At our first practice session on Court 14, I think, a few days before the tournament, we just looked at each other in amazement. "Are we actually here?" we murmured. Bearing in mind that we first started our tennis journey together when I was just 5 years old.

This practice court is right in the middle of Wimbledon and my favourite spot. It's amongst the run of courts that are situated between court one and centre court, so it's a really bustling, exciting part of the grounds where lots of good matches happen. Loads of energy, loads of noise.

I was hooked from the start. It was most definitely my 'Oh my goodness, I'm playing at Wimbledon' moment, but with a successful session those newbie nerves settled down.

Prep was done, practice was done, and I was ready to make my Wimbledon debut.

My Doubles partner was Katharina Krüger, from Germany who I had known since my junior days on the international tour. We had teamed up for a year or so before the championships and had got some impressive results together, such as reaching the doubles Master's final. We'd received the wildcard to be the fourth doubles pairing for Wimbledon, but we were actually the fourth best ranked pair in the world at that time too.

After all the build up, all the preparation, it was time to play. A childhood dream coming true.

Of course there were nerves. There was the grandeur of where we were playing, but once we were out on the court, I was just playing tennis.

I had done lots of practise on grass, so I was ready.

'I know this. I know it's something I can do. I do it day in, day out,' I told myself.

I can't remember the score, but sadly we didn't win.

Though Wimbledon is my favourite tournament and grass is a wonderful surface, it's also my worst nightmare.

My game's biggest strength is heavy top spin. My strongest shot being my reverse backhand. I really relied on those high, kicky balls to put my opponent under pressure, and on grass, that just isn't effective. The ball just dies.

A heavy slice is so effective on grass and that was just not my game. For me, the surface was really de-weaponising and I found it really, really hard.

Also, for me, playing on grass meant making adjustments. The main one was raising the back wheel on my chair to reduce the drag. A tennis chair has two big wheels and three little ones, two at the front, one at the back.

I also went for a slightly smoother edge on my back tyres. By opting for tyres that I'd used for a couple of weeks beforehand, it stopped them cutting into the grass too much, making it quicker and easier to manoeuvre.

During the match, I tried to incorporate my slice a bit more. I had a good slice, but it wasn't as effective as my top spin.

It's hard to push on grass in a chair, so anything you can do to make your opponent move more gives you a better chance of creating space and hitting to that space.

Of course, the loss at Wimbledon was devastating initially, but it didn't take long to pick myself up and go again.

After all, I had just achieved my childhood dream, played on the sacred grass courts of Wimbledon and picked up a handsome pay packet. Life was good!

A year later and I was back at Wimbledon making history. Wheelchair Singles was introduced for the first time, so I played in both Singles and Doubles this time.

My second visit to the home of lawn tennis was equally magical, but a little easier to manage.

I wasn't quite so rabbit in the headlights. I knew what I was doing, and I was in a different headspace.

When you go to any big event as a player, it's always a challenge. Not just when you're on court, but also when you're behind the scenes.

Even just navigating those spaces, understanding where the locker rooms are, where the restaurant is, where you can and can't go, means you're on a constant learning curve.

Another thing that impacted me later on at Wimbledon was the 'all-white' dress code for players.

At a time when I was struggling with body image issues, I was really conscious of my lumps and bumps, plus my leg bag under my clothes. White is very unforgiving and my self-esteem felt that. Due to my splints and leg bag, I didn't wear shorts or skirts, so finding completely plain white sports trousers was harder than you'd think, plus surprisingly uncomfortable.

It all added a layer of stress I could do without in competition.

Imagine what it was like, about to play a crucial point or serving for a set, when in the back of my mind was worry about how I looked.

I was always worried about my leg bag, becoming too obvious as it filled up. That's why when Wimbledon relaxed its white dress code ruling in 2022, I was so excited. It was such a big deal for wheelchair users and women players in general.

After those first couple of Wimbledon experiences as a player I still felt very privileged to be there, but I'd lost that newbie buzz and was starting to feel more at home.

Little did I know at this early point in my career that I'd be returning again and again and eventually broadcasting live as a commentator for the BBC.

All part of the build of my post retirement career which would also see me mentoring, supporting, and advising young athletes in a variety of sports.

Chapter 11:

Striking a Balance: Tennis and Education

I'd never planned to go to university. I wasn't bothered about going at all. In fact, it wasn't even an option in my mind.

I was pushing to qualify for my first Paralympics in London and never felt, in a million years, that any university would accept my inevitable lack of attendance as training and competing ramped up.

I always wanted to further my education and qualifications, but the chance of uni life just wasn't on my radar.

Then I had an interesting chat with a mentor I was working with through some funding I received.

I explained that I wanted to continue my qualifications, but qualifying for London 2012 was my priority. I wanted tennis in my life, but not only tennis. I knew balance was crucial, but I couldn't see how I could achieve that. I didn't know what to do.

He provided a simple solution.

An athlete's degree course, which was designed specifically for elite athletes to gain their degree alongside their sporting commitments. As long as I fulfilled the work, I would have an extra year to complete it and attendance percentages wasn't a deal breaker. Perfect for fitting in with my busy training/competition schedule. It was an incredible opportunity; I could get a degree which would be a great thing to have ready for work opportunities post sporting career.

Just five weeks later I went to Bath University, where I studied three years for a Sports Science and Performance degree.

Truthfully, I was barely there. Access was great and I never felt anything other than an elite athlete on the course because it was only open to those who were the best in their sports. Everyone's schedules were equally as hectic and they just understood what we were juggling day-to-day.

Although it felt like I was on a level playing field with other students, I never got to know anybody. Unsurprising, as I was always in and out of campus, but it didn't bother me in the slightest as I was solely there for the degree, no other reason. I never had the desire to experience 'uni life' as I was basically getting an even better version of that independence, by travelling around the world doing the sport I loved.

Having said that, there were times when I lacked confidence and felt quite insecure though. I don't think this was created by anyone other than me. I never lacked friends in my life, but as my tennis was taking up so much of my energy, I didn't really work on building those social connections at the university as it wasn't a priority then. I couldn't tell you the name of one person on my course. I suppose that's a bit sad really, but I was so focused on getting the work done so I could qualify for London, plus I didn't lack friendships and my childhood and college friends were so supportive and ever present in my life.

I graduated in the winter of 2012. I actually missed my official graduation ceremony as it clashed with the Paralympics, so the uni gave me a place at a ceremony later in the year. This was such a magic moment for me. It was tough to gain my degree with my hectic schedule, but also, so many people had encouraged me not to pursue my education as it was deemed too much of a 'distraction' from my tennis. I knew in my gut that it was the right thing to do for my future self, and I am so proud I followed my instincts.

Chapter 12:

The Long Goodbye

Sam was sweet. One of those people who didn't have a bad bone in his body. I never heard him make a bitchy comment about anyone. He was good to the very core. Really kind, patient, generous with his time.

I always felt happy with him. Our friendship developed out of a larger group of friends and was beautifully low maintenance.

I met Sam at Commonweal secondary school, in Year 8. I knew no-one in my first year, as mentioned earlier, I had been studying at a different primary school to everyone else and I couldn't go to my catchment school as it was not accessible.

At my new school, my amazing tutor, Miss Butler, brought me together with Becky. As we got to know one another, we became close friends. I can still recall us having fun playing the Malteser game at lunchtime. For those that don't remember it, I invite you to lay flat, grab a Malteser and place it on your lips. Then try and blow it into the air and catch it on the way down. Enjoy, you're welcome!

Via Becky, I then met others and that's how our lovely group of friends was created. Becky is still one of my best friends in the world and was my first real friend at Commonweal; I think that makes our friendship so special.

At the time, Sam was in a relationship with one of my closest friends, Jack. I never used to get told off at school, but I always managed to get Jack into trouble in class and he'd get kicked out of lessons....a lot.

In our maths class we'd all copy work off each other. I'm not kidding when I say it was so obvious what was happening, as, as you'd go down the line, the grades gradually declined, with mine and Jack's being at the lower end. I just really hated maths so didn't want to put time into it and struggled to concentrate.

We would talk, talk, talk in class and when challenged, I'd say: "It was him!" Jack would be told to get out of the class, which was a cabin style classroom separate to the main building. My response was always the same: "I can't stay outside, I've got circulation issues. I'll get too cold."

The teacher would separate the two of us, with Jack sent outside while I stayed in the warm. I did feel bad, to be honest, when he'd stare at me through the window.

The only time in my life, when I have played on my health issues as a youngster, was to avoid getting into trouble or doing things I didn't want to do. I know how this sounds, and I'm certainly not suggesting it, but I was young and learning my own and others' limitations.

Despite moments like these, Jack and I became such good friends and through that friendship, I got to know Sam too.

Sam and I developed a really sweet, lovely bond, but then he started to become unwell.

As his health deteriorated, he spent a lot of time in hospital, and I would go and visit him regularly.

We'd sit on the benches outside and always get told off by nursing staff because Sam was out too late.

When he ended up with a colostomy bag, it may sound weird, but it kind of bonded us together even more. I think it was a case of me 'getting it'. I understood what it was to live with something attached to your body to help with bowel/bladder function. I was able to say: "Yeah, me too." We talked about all of that stuff. All of our friends were good with those conversations too. No-one had an issue.

Every hospital visit I'd always smuggle in treats Sam wasn't supposed to eat - anything unhealthy that he wasn't allowed, basically.

We knew Sam was really ill, but when the end came, his death was the first thing that sent me into therapy because I just could not deal with how it happened.

Sam had been very poorly and was in hospital again, so we hadn't heard from him very much, until one day I received a text message:

"I need you to come here now. Please will you come and see me?"

I got in my car straight away and drove to the hospital. Sam was in ICU.

I asked to see him, but the nurse said no. Family only.

At this point I was beyond despair or anger. I think somewhere in my head I knew this was really bad.

I showed the nurses Sam's message, but they still refused entry, even when I pleaded with them to let me in because he'd asked me to be there.

Sat on the other side of the door, I was so close to him, yet felt so helpless.

It was a horrible situation and, for a long time, I hated that nurse.

I never saw Sam again; he died the next day.

On the night of Sam's death, Jack cried in my arms. I made him a bed next to mine on the floor, and we just cuddled there all night.

At first, I wasn't sure I was strong enough to get through the funeral, but I knew I needed to be there for Jack, our friends and for Sam.

It was a really hard day. Sat in a pew as everybody left the service, I waited for my wheelchair to be returned.

At that moment Jack fell into the seat next to me and fell apart. I held him again. This experience was to bond us for life. Jack remains a dear friend. There is something so special about our love for each other, and when I spend time with him I just feel so safe and content as I always have done. He's just an all-round, lovely human that I am so grateful for.

Sam's wake took place at the local Steam Museum where he'd worked. At this point, none of us knew how he had died.

Being as sensitive as I could, I asked his step mum what had happened; she told me he had died of sepsis. His bowel had split which then poisoned him. He was 20 years old.

As strange as this may sound, knowing how Sam had died felt like a weight off. We had all needed clarity but hadn't had a chance or way to get that information until then.

After the funeral, for many years, I found random items on my travels around the world that I thought Sam would have appreciated and I would place them on his grave. These included a blue train and a pretty rock I found in France. Random, I know, but somehow it helped. Another dear friend, Elise, would often come with me to Sam's grave. I remember the first time we went there - it took us forever to find it, and the most surreal thing happened. At the very moment we felt like giving up, a gorgeous little cat approached us. We decided to stroke it and follow it and it led us right to where he was. So surreal but also, completely meant to be.

I sometimes think my anger towards the nurse who had not let me see Sam, overrode my sadness for a long time. Maybe I was meant to grieve in that order, at that time, so I could step up and take action to gain clarity for all of us that loved and missed our friend.

Whatever it was about, my real grief came about four or five months later.

It was Spring 2012 and I had arrived at London's Olympic Park in Lee Valley for the first time.

This very special place represented so much for me; a culmination of all that hard work, the training, the traveling, the competing, the sweat and tears, and here I was, trying to take it all in.

I was on a tour of the venue to see what was lined up for us a few months later for the Paralympics.

My first ever Games. The nerves, the pressure, the excitement, were really mounting.

I was in the player area with my lifestyle adviser. This area was converted into indoor courts.

A lot of elite athletes have a lifestyle adviser to help them with everything from managing things alongside sport, such as education and signposting to other professionals who can help them on their journey.

As we looked at this incredible venue, as I was about to prepare for one of the biggest moments of my sporting life, the adviser pulled me aside:

"I can see that you're not getting over the loss of your friend, and you need help. I want to help you," she said, or at least that's how I remember it.

"I think it's time to deal with this. How do you feel about me trying to arrange a counsellor for you?"

I said 'yes' immediately and sobbed my heart out there and then in the middle of the tennis centre. I knew she was right and the sense of relief was palpable. I felt seen, heard, cared for and comforted by the fact that someone had nudged me towards something deep down I needed to resolve.

The tennis centre at Lee Valley was state of the art and brand new. I can still remember exactly where we sat – right at the corner where the entrance for the player area was going to be. It was really beige and a bit clinical at the time as they hadn't done anything with it. It was just a shell for what was to become an iconic building in 2012.

And in this moment, here was that contrast again. On one hand, I was this elite athlete, about to compete at the greatest show on earth, and touring around this sporting theatre of dreams; on the other hand, I was being crushed by the weight of complicated grief while still trying to get my body and mind into the zone for playing for Paralympics GB.

Luckily for me, my lifestyle adviser spotted I was in trouble. She set up counselling, which was all funded through our private healthcare - something you get when you're on the elite programme as a funded athlete.

That was when I met Sheila for the first time.

Sheila was my counsellor and would prove to be an invaluable support for me, both pre and post London 2012.

She was absolutely not what I expected. To begin with, I thought she'd give me all the answers and talk a lot. Instead, she was calm, quiet and only spoke quality, giving me space to cry, talk, but inevitably work out my own solutions. She was brilliant at her job.

A really interesting time in my life because it gave me a space to talk about Sam and all the other things that I'd been holding in.

It was to be something I went back to when I got kicked off the national wheelchair tennis performance programme in 2016.

In a strange way, I think Sam's death, though shattering, set me up for change in a positive way. His death made me go to therapy which taught me so much about how I grieve and how to communicate with people around me in those times of grief.

It helped me to understand that we all process things differently; there's no right way and it's crucial you choose the appropriate people to support you and talk you through tough times. It doesn't mean that the ones you don't lean on don't care or love you, it's just that they cannot support you in the way you need them to in that moment. It also taught me that things can bloody hurt, but there is always sunlight somewhere. You just have to push through that pain to find it.

I also think that losing Sam meant that when my dear grandfather, Gramp, died not long after, I handled it in the best way I could have done.

I do believe the stuff I worked through and learned with Sheila has helped me cope with so many things since.

I really liked what she did at the start of our time together. She got me to write down things about the key people in my life, to help her, and me actually, understand how these relationships work in my life.

She taught me that we probably all hurt in the same way, it's just that we all deal with that hurt differently, and that's okay.

When I was younger, I'd think, if you're not crying then you're not showing me that you're sad and so I struggled with responses different to mine.

I held a lot of guilt about not being able to see Sam the day before he died. I replayed things in my head, over and over, and re-read that final text from him so many times. He wanted to see me... he asked me to be there, and I wasn't.

Then the guilt turned into anger, and I behaved irrationally for a while.

Now I know that the nurse who denied me access to Sam was just doing her job. There have still been moments when I have thought, did Sam know I was there? At times like this I've been able to tap into the supportive words of Sheila. Sam would have known because I was someone that always showed up for him. That's a powerful realisation that has helped me enormously.

It's only in recent years I've realised that holding onto all the negative thoughts and feelings around Sam's death weren't serving me and that I needed to move on.

I have so many happy memories of Sam. He was such a nerd and I loved him for it. He'd volunteer in the school library during lunch and break time, and he seemed to be living his best life at the local miniature steam railway before his death.

His interests made him who he was and there was nothing more wonderful than seeing him in his favourite places embracing his hobbies and interests.

I used to go and see him at the mini railway because it was a few miles from my house. I would cycle as part of my training, so we'd meet up and then we'd sit eating chips by the trains. Nice healthy training snack during a training session, I know.

One day, my friend Becky and I decided to bike over together to see him. I had two hand bikes. These are cycle bikes you propel with your hands while sitting like you're in a standard wheelchair. The pedals that you propel with are shoulder height.

Becky didn't have any sports gear with her, so she said: "Can I put one of your GB kits on?" Minutes later and we were both on our way, dressed in GB kit cycling to meet Sam. How cool were we?

Sam's reaction when we arrived? (while giggling away): "You two look ridiculous." A typical Sam response which still makes me smile.

We all went to get chips. I love the photo I have of all three of us. Becky and I in our GB tops, Sam in the middle. Weird but wonderful.

These are some of my favourite memories of our time together.

Chapter 13:

A Quick Guide to Wheelchair Tennis

So, let's get a few things straight when it comes to wheelchair tennis.

Firstly, here's a quick history lesson, with thanks to Paralympic.org for the info.

Wheelchair tennis was founded in 1976 following work by former US freestyle skier, Brad Parks.

It grew in the 1980s as France became the first European country to put together a specific wheelchair tennis programme.

The sport debuted at the Barcelona 1992 Paralympics and has become one of the fastest growing wheelchair sports in the world.

There are three categories: men's, women's and quads, with each division having singles and doubles divisions.

Athletes compete in a series of tournaments around the world (there are literally hundreds), including well known events like

Grand Slams: Australian Open, Roland Garros, Wimbledon and US Open, plus the singles and doubles Masters.

We use the same nets, rackets, balls, scoring system, everything, but let's talk about the double bounce.

The double bounce is an important rule, but I want to be really clear here; you don't have to use two bounces if you don't want or need to.

In the higher ranked player matches, the less this is used. Tactically, it's not an advantage to use two bounces because it gives your opponent more time, and can often put you in a defensive court position.

Only the first bounce needs to land inside the court, the second can land anywhere, but you really don't see two bounces very often in the elite level of the game.

Aside from this, the main technical difference for a wheelchair player is my favourite shot - the reverse top spin backhand.

It was my strongest shot when I was competing, and I still love it.

Tactically, there are a few game plans which are super effective. One is returning a serve into the body of the chair user because of that inability to sidestep out of the way.

Actually, if you can jam a player up (hit the ball into the body) and catch them when they're not moving too much, it's really difficult for them to move into a position to create a good contact point and produce an aggressive or neutralising shot.

Hitting back behind the player is also a really effective tactic, because again, that lack of ability to move side to side, all our movement is incredibly fluid.

It's a great tactic because the momentum of the chair is going one way and the direction of the ball is going the other, therefore taking a lot of time away from your opponent.

If you haven't seen wheelchair tennis before, I really encourage you to come and enjoy our sport, in person or on a screen; it will really open your eyes to the speed and pace of our sport.

MY TRAINING SCHEDULE AS A PARALYMPIAN

- ✓ 5 days a week, sometimes 6
- ✓ 2 tennis sessions a day (usually 1 ½ - 2 hours)
- ✓ 4 gym sessions a week
- ✓ 1 sports psychology session
- ✓ 1 sports massage session
- ✓ 1 physio session
- ✓ Occasional nutritionist session

Chapter 14:

Too Nice and Never Going to Make It

I've *always* been curvy. I'm bigger than I was, less fit than I was, because I don't train all day, every day. I now feel more confident and happy with myself than I ever did when I was at my peak fitness, when I was strong, super fit, an athlete with less weight.

Some people won't grow fat and muscle on their lower part of the body because of the way that disability affects them, but mine doesn't work like this. So, I always felt that I just looked different to other girls on the tennis tour. There was nobody else that looked like me, that was curvy like me and so I always felt so insecure because they all looked so drop dead gorgeous and I felt I never did. So often, I just felt like a fat blob in a wheelchair on the tennis tour.

In comparison to everyone else, I thought I'm never going to look right. What made it really tricky was that my national performance team, who funded me, used to put quite a bit of pressure on me to lose weight, which now, looking at pictures from back then, really wasn't necessary. Body dysmorphia is a real thing, and I had it severely back then. It's just that neither I or anyone around me noticed, which meant that pressure was by far the wrong approach. When I look at old photos, I feel proud of how I looked - fit, athletic, and strong - maybe not like everyone else but I was fine the way I was. Sadly, the sports world attracts people who obsessively make comparisons and I ended up on the receiving end.

At a time when that weight conversation was really common, I look at myself in those photos and think I'd love to be that size now. I think 'wow', I really was okay. I wasn't skinny, but I wasn't unhealthy. I was actually really healthy, but not identical to their idea of the perfect athlete.

In top level sport, they keep an eye on you medically and out of sport; my GP was amazing, checking everything – heart rate, blood pressure, all fine.

Away from the court, this became such a distraction that they were so focused on my size and body that no-one really paid attention to my technical and tactical game. Actually, if we'd put in time there, what would that have led to? The irony was that when I was doing fitness drills, I was so often faster than others on our team, and international players.

My best friend Dana, who came over to train with me several times from the USA, and who's always been beautiful, tall, slim, athletic, would be gutted as I would kick her ass in every fitness session - in the gym or on court - and it's still an ongoing joke now.

She was always so kind to me then, reminding me that my potential and ability was not defined by a number on a scale, but by my performance, in the gym and on court. I love her for that still today.

I'd have a 20 kilo ball, she'd have a 10. My fitness, my speed, I was so quick. One of the quickest girls around. I was so fit, so strong, I'd never get injured. Just one horrendous injury for me where I tore a ligament in my wrist. I was a junior and had to play through it. A team member broke his arm at the same tournament, and there was no-one else to play. Apart from that, I stayed injury free. I was robust and simply followed the advice I was given about warming up and cooling down.

I took care of my body. I'd listen to everything, in terms of prehab and rehab and I think having that little bit of extra meat kept me well, because my body had more to take from.

I'm not saying I had a perfect body by any means, and yeah, in their eyes, I could have lost a bit of weight, but it became a focus over so many other things, until it took over everything.

One summer all my tournaments were taken out of the schedule, and I was told you've got two months. No focus on tennis, just fitness, fitness, fitness to get me really slim. I was utterly miserable and then guess what I did? I went to food for comfort so then it became a vicious cycle. I was miserable. When I should have been focusing on my technique and the game itself, the mental stress was horrendous. It's hard to look back on this time now as I really didn't feel I had the choice to challenge this; after all they held the purse strings to my job, my life, my everything (or so it felt at the time). I went along with it and didn't speak up, through fear of losing their support.

Why did this happen? At the time, when I was at the highest point in my career, I felt like very few people in and around our sport cared about me as a person. It's really sad to think like this, but it was just always a focus on results, and for me, how I looked.

There was also the added complication that because I was from a country where we were really good at the sport, there were other players doing better than me, so I looked a little worse as I was 'only' ranked 10 in the world. There were two women from GB ranked above me for the majority of my playing career.

In other countries I would have been number 1 by far, so because we had all the success, it was a blessing and a curse. I suppose I was lucky and unlucky in a way.

I got through it largely thanks to my individual team who deserve so much credit, Ali, Shaun, Chris, James, Danny, Karl, I'm forever grateful to you all. They remained professional at all times and supported everything I did. They struggled with things as I did, and we had open conversations. They never sugar coated it. They were so good because I knew they were as frustrated as I was, but also knew what I wanted to achieve, so always brought us back to why we were doing what we were doing in the first place.

"You still have tennis. You still want to do this. You want to achieve that, so that's what we're going to do."

It was a stark contrast to my experience with our national organisation. I felt I rarely gained anything of quality or substance from them in terms of how to be a better tennis player. They were often too busy with other players who were, in their eyes, a priority, and the fact that I am, and was, so self-sufficient and just 'got on' with things, meant they thought I was fine. In reality, I was too afraid to ask for help, through risk of being seen as a nuisance.

It made me recall one training session on court when a national coach stopped me half-way through to pronounce: "Louise, you're never going to make it because you're too nice."

I wanted to cry. Recalling this again makes me want to cry.

I remember coming off court and thinking, 'shit, is that true?'. That comment really messed with my head. I'd been brought up to be kind and I didn't want to be a dick. I don't feel the need to trample over people to get to where I want to go because I'll just get there, my own way.

Telling me I'm not going to make it, even though you're funding me and I'm on your tennis court. Great!

Those words stayed and messed with me for a long time. I kept quiet about it.

In the meantime, my head was full of questions and confusion.

Okay, so I could either choose to be a good person or a good athlete - I couldn't be both. Why couldn't I be both?

It was a chat I brought to my individual coach, Ali, that changed things for me:

Ali: "Louise, that is so ridiculous."

My answer? "Yeah, but is he right? Is that true?"

Ali's next move to help shift me out of the confusion was perfect.

"Roger Federer. Is he nice?"

"Yes, he's lovely," I replied.

"What about Shingo Kunieda?" (retired Japanese gold medal winning Paralympian tennis star who is one of the nicest guys you'll ever meet.)

"He's number 1," he continued, "and he's smashed records. He's nice, right?"

I nodded.

He'd made his point powerfully in a way that helped me break things down.

The language I heard on the professional tennis circuit and the way people would be talked about sometimes, was horrible.

I can still remember one bus journey at the Israel Open. I sat next to a player from another country who I was competing against later that day. She was lovely and a similar size to me. The same national coach, who had made the 'nice' comment, told me, on a bus full of athletes: "You'll be fine" then looked at the other athlete and made a derogatory comment about her weight.

He didn't know she spoke English. I just wanted to cry, I was mortified for her and me. 'If you're saying that here like this, what the hell are you saying about me?', I thought.

Experiences like this with the national team hit hard and showed why I never fitted in properly.

I'm a positive person and my natural reset is to see the good in life and people. I love people and I'm grateful for everything I'm given.

At various points in my career, I was dumped into a world where everybody seemed entitled and were happy spending a lot of their time bitching about someone else, about not getting what they thought they deserved.

Conversations were so narrow that I'd be there saying: "Shall we talk about this film, what about the news, shall we play a game?" Anything to stop the negative cycle. Bitching became some people's default, and it was horrid. It also showed me there were very few people I could trust. My natural default was to just retreat into my own little safe bubble.

The negative effect this had on my performance was huge.

Before I learned how to manage things, I would be playing matches, everything going well and then someone from the national team would rock up. I'd absolutely bottle it and I'd lose. I might be kicking ass and then they'd sit down. Going through my head would be: 'What are they thinking about me? Are they going to cut my funding?' I felt bottom of the pile.

It's amazing what words can do, even when you don't respect the person who has thrown them at you.

I'm still not exactly sure how I made it through all this, but I did. Even though I was on my own in these moments, regardless of how crappy things were, I think it was that innate feeling within me of don't let the haters win. Just because he says you're fat, or you're too nice, that doesn't mean you can't go on and achieve great success.

I don't feel the need to be mean and horrible to get where I need to go. I'm just going to go there. Others can do their thing and they might get there, too, but it's not my way.

In challenging moments like this I had to keep on reminding myself I was doing all of it for me and the people I love, not for someone I didn't love and didn't respect.

Something that has always helped me is the belief that if the good is outweighing the bad, then you're doing alright.

It's this that kept me going, that still does.

So, back then, for every negative comment, there was a match, another country to explore, new people to meet, more opportunities and more prize money.

A deep breath then... 'I'm not here for you. You don't define who I am. You won't define my success.'

My resilience had well and truly kicked in.

Chapter 15:

Stubborn Streak Versus Self-Care

My determination has got me through so many tough matches over the years and I have never pulled out of a match.

But confession time now. I have also played through too many when I shouldn't have done. I didn't tell anyone how ill I was.

When I look back, I'm horrified at myself, but that's just the space I was in.

On one occasion, I was playing in Nottingham with a stomach problem. I was in so much pain I was taking painkillers on court and went straight to A and E after the match.

I lost to somebody who I would often beat. When I came off court, one of the national coaches asked me: "What happened there? That performance wasn't your best, was it?"

They were right, it wasn't good enough, but I didn't tell them I was ill. I can still be a bit like this now. I don't like to moan if I'm poorly and I don't like to put that on other people.

I have this obsession of powering through because I like to prove what I can do. I also get FOMO and can't bare it when people say things like: "You're always ill." It's not helpful and makes me feel so useless and self-conscious.

I should have told the national coach when I was ill, but I didn't.

The thing is I love playing tennis. I wanted to play.

As for the A & E visit, Becky drove me. She was there watching the match and gave me a good, tough love friend talk about being honest about how I was feeling and reassuring me that it's okay to sometimes not be okay.

Some may describe this as a stubborn streak, and that's okay. Looking back at things now, I realise this was going on before I learned the importance of self-awareness and self-care.

There are still moments today when I have to have a strong word with myself to slow down and take care of me. If I don't, I know it will take twice as long to come back to full strength.

Even small adjustments can make a big difference. Today I avoid caffeine. Experience has taught me it can increase the likelihood of a UTI and isn't the best thing for my solo kidney (I was only born with one). I'm more a herbal tea girl these days. As a non-alcohol drinker, I'll have a soft drink as my go-to, but fizzy drinks are not great either.

Now, I add to the mix cranberry, fish oil and vitamin D supplements every day. I take a gut health supplement in the morning which has definitely helped reduce the amount of UTIs, and I do everything I can to stay well. Whether or not it's making a massive difference, I don't know, but I'm trying my best to follow the best diet to support my overall health.

Over the years I've also learned to seek out the people and safe spaces I need for good mental health. Those that can help me understand myself better and where I can look at all sides of a situation.

Sometimes a particular person who I'm close to is not necessarily the person I need to go to and so I need to lean on someone else.

Taking this approach has helped me love people around me even more, because I feel like I can understand *them* more.

This knowledge has helped me in the tennis world and outside it. It's taught me where to put my heart and my emotions at the right time.

Chapter 16:

Feeling Hot, Hot, Hot!

I've never quite understood the heat rule in tennis. It's not just about the temperature, it also depends on wind and humidity, so it's not black and white. As competitors we just let the referee tell us whether we can play on or not.

I personally love playing in the heat, so it never bothered me. When the temperature rises, my body just feels so good. I have no pain, no stiffness, I just feel great.

Of course I feel hot and clammy when I'm playing, but it doesn't adversely affect my performance.

One of my key strengths when competing is that I've always had good stamina and have played loads of long matches. The longest one was played in a doubles match in Belgium.

It lasted for just over 5 hours, finishing at 2am. Just a teenager, but we won! I remember it so well because I was playing with Karen Korb from the USA, who at the time was one of my idols. She was always so cheerful and vibrant inside and out and had this infectious energy which I gravitated towards.

I felt exhilarated as I did with every long match, many that were over four hours.

I think my stamina comes from my racing days; I was certainly built for endurance.

When you're in the match you just don't notice how long you've been on court for. I would always be buzzing after a long match, but give it half an hour and I would hurt. Going to bed, my body would be killing me. Not my arms, my shoulders, my head, it was my lower body where I'd been strapped into my tennis chair, super tight, for hours.

Oh my God, that feeling. It was horrendous. I would struggle to get my body out of that seated position. It would take a while and a lot of stretching, a hot bath, because I'd be so stiff, frozen almost, in that seated position.

Playing singles and doubles at competitive level, I'd often have another match later on that day, so I'd have to get on with it.

Coming down mentally from competition was equally important.

Working with my sports psychologist, Karl, helped with this a lot. Recording voice notes was really useful because I would vocalise things straight away and get things out. Karl would listen to my notes and then we'd talk things through a couple of days later.

It was an easy way to get those initial thoughts out of my head and helped me to process them in a positive and effective way.

As for adjusting back to 'civvy street' after a competition, ie the non-tennis world, that never seemed to be an issue for me.

It didn't take much time at all, probably because I'd always had such a good work/life balance. I love my life outside of competition, and I always did. I managed to strike a good balance in terms of maintaining college and uni alongside tennis.

I was used to juggling, so later on in my career I then did things like athlete mentoring, which is still one of my favourite roles to play today. It's such an honour and privilege to share my stories with young people. They're at such an important age; I love helping them to explore their passions and goals, and to support them in building their self-belief and confidence.

Karl's support before, during and after matches was crucial to my health.

One of the things I struggled with most on court, especially during those crunch points, was staying in the present. I'd always be thinking ahead, like 'If I don't win this match, I'll lose these points' or 'If I miss this forehand, it'll be this' or 'Or if I do this, the score will be...' I'd be worrying about the future all the time.

Thanks to Karl, I discovered ways to help me remain focused in these moments. We had a couple of methods which worked well.

I had a little dent in my wheel (caused by an airline) that I would have to find and feel, and that would instantly bring me back to the present. I'd be so focused on trying to find it that it would stop other thoughts from taking over and distracting me.

I would also readjust the straps on my chair and this would help me focus on the present moment.

Both of these simple actions would help me on those big, match winning points.

Then I'd have routines like bouncing the ball in rounds of three, which is ironic because for some strange reason I can't stand odd numbers. Everything has to be even in everyday life, like the TV sound level, for example.

These routines in my tennis would help make each match and point feel familiar, because it felt safe, familiar and helped me feel calm.

These were some of the positive lessons I took away from my time on the tennis tour and that have helped me in other areas of my life, especially the staying in the present. I do tend to worry and my thoughts always go to the future as they did when I was competing. I now have other methods in daily life, which help pull me back. Karl's words of wisdom have supported me far beyond the court itself. They have stayed with me and will do forever.

The one thing I did find hard when I came off the tennis tour initially was not being around like-minded people. One of the most amazing things about the tour is that you are totally absorbed in an environment where everybody believes you can.

There are never conversations with questions and phrases like 'Should you? Can't you?'. Instead it's more like: 'Yeah, you played good', 'Yeah, tough match today, you played well'. Just normal chats about performance, but never about disability, what you can't do.

It's an environment where everybody is achieving and overcoming barriers/stereotypes, but not talking about it, it's just happening!

Now and again, I will admit to missing that environment. So, when I dip back in as an event organiser or commentator, it's lush.

Of course it's not just about being around like-minded people who get it and get the struggles, it's about being around people who are kicking ass with a disability. It's just the 'norm' there, so refreshing.

In many ways, going solo on the tennis tour, without official backing, was the best time of my life. I had nobody telling me what to do or making me feel inadequate. I wasn't obligated to speak to people I didn't want to speak to, I didn't need to go to training camps that made me feel insecure and like I'd be punished if I didn't turn up.

Obviously, in terms of my professional profile, my ranking did drop slowly over the last two years I played. By then I was balancing work and training, which meant I was no longer dedicating all my time to tennis. I just plateaued, and that was okay; I was doing my best.

Chapter 17:

Gratitude for Ghana

They took me to my room. A step so high I couldn't get up it on my own. Luckily, USA coach, Dan James, was there to help. We managed to get me up the steps and he promised to return to help me again the next morning.

7.30am the next day. I open my door and there's a freshly laid concrete ramp waiting for me. Overnight, the hotel had sourced concrete and set it ready for my use.

I went to the restaurant, which had quite a few steps, and a wooden ramp had been installed for me.

Dan just stared. We couldn't believe it.

I remember thinking, 'can you imagine if the world had this attitude? Imagine a world where people adopted the attitude of here's an issue, I'll fix it, rather than here's an issue. So, let's go through 17 people to do a risk assessment and find out if that's going to kill them.'

This was Ghana in 2012. I was at an interesting turning point where I didn't know which direction I was going in next and yet this country, and its people, changed my life. It was just one of the best weeks of my life.

It was here the world taught me what access and inclusion truly means.

Ghana showed me that it's not about having a perfectly built building or about health and safety guidelines, it's about making people feel included.

How is it that I went to a developing country and felt the most able and accepted that I ever have in my life?

I had the privilege of travelling to this amazing place twice, thanks to the International Tennis Federation's, Johan Cruyff Foundation's development fund.

The fund allowed players like me, and coaches from around the world, to take wheelchair tennis to developing countries like Ghana, introduce the sport and its benefits and help educate and build opportunities for disabled people.

In 2012, while still competing, I travelled there for the first time. I really wanted to introduce people to the joy of wheelchair tennis and help them discover what it could offer - a true passion of mine.

The purpose of these trips was to introduce wheelchair tennis to the Ghanaian people and show them the beauty and power of the sport, specifically in terms of the benefits to health and social aspects sport can have. It was also about changing perceptions on what could be achieved as a disabled person.

During my stay, I met key partners and stakeholders in the country in a bid to provide opportunities for those who normally would not get a chance.

The trip was so cool. We took out wheelchairs, rackets, balls and all sorts of tennis equipment.

I learned so much in Ghana. When I talk about accessibility, I often use it as one of the best examples in the world.

As a developing country, we had a lot of challenges on this trip, but more physical challenges than accessibility and attitude challenges – in many ways, the opposite to the UK and other more 'developed' nations.

On one trip, we planned to visit a set of courts seven hours away from where we were staying in the capital, Accra, but couldn't get to them because the terrain was so difficult to tackle.

As we struggled to gain access, someone from the local village rocked up on a quad bike and drove me up on the back of his bike to the courts. I had my wheelchair in one hand while holding on for dear life with the other.

In that moment we made it accessible.

This was my first eye opener to the forward, switched on thinking of this fabulous country. It was so refreshing. I felt so able and seen, somewhere where it could have been so different.

On another trip out, I met one guy with no legs. He couldn't afford a wheelchair, so he went around on a skateboard. He was quicker than most of us and showed us how easily he could get around. He found a way to make his world accessible.

Then there was the day I went to a market on an afternoon off. Throughout the village were super deep sewers with really high curbs either side. They were impossible to get over in a wheelchair, so I found myself stuck in a place I didn't know, unable to move on.

Feeling a little unsettled and trying to work out what to do, suddenly I was levitating, at least that's how it felt. Several locals saw my predicament, picked me up in my chair and lifted me over the sewer.

I was stunned, but incredibly grateful.

As I chatted with the local friend I had made, he told me: "That's just what we do in Ghana, Louise. If someone needs help, we help them."

The people I met on this trip changed my life. They showed me what it meant to smash down barriers and what you can achieve with the right, open minded attitude.

I went there to help people, but they were also helping me with their attitudes, humanity, their relaxed way of thinking and no fear perceptions, time after time.

I love to meet people who are innovative with accessibility, and there were many people like that in Ghana.

At the start of the trip, I had an overwhelming feeling of guilt, for having so much when those around me did not, as I perceived it. There I was, sitting in a five grand chair that someone else had bought for me, with a bag full of rackets that were gifted through a sponsor. I was going home to a fully adapted house with free medical supplies, and I was here.

I'd seen people with complex disabilities, like the man getting around on a skateboard, who I knew didn't have the medical stuff they needed to stay well, healthy and thrive.

I knew that their prospects of work weren't high and that their life expectancy was lower because they didn't have access to the same levels of care as I had, and that just killed me.

Dan helped me work through my feelings of guilt by telling me I needed to change this narrative.

"That's enough," he said. "Just appreciate what you have. Be respectful and appreciative of that, and then while you're here, have an impact."

He added: "You've got to remember that if you didn't have that medical equipment, that amazing chair, how would you be here helping others?"

His wise words really helped me make sense of things and encouraged me to drop the guilt.

The next day I visited an orphanage. I'm lucky that I'd had the chat with Dan the night before as I know it helped me digest the experience better. He was always so wise with his words. We'd met at my first junior camp when I was 11, so we'd known each other a really long time. Dan's still one of my favourite coaches I've ever been privileged to spend time with, I've always looked up to him. He was always kind and professional, a combination I really value and respect.

There were so many kids at the orphanage, and they were all so excited to meet me. We were all chatting and none of them cared less about my status as a tennis player, a Paralympian. Once again, I was just Louise, and that felt so good.

They just wanted to chat and show me around their homes.

I will always remember two little girls - they were so cute. They took me by the hand, one pushing me in my chair.

Their home was an empty shell of a concrete block. No windows, nothing painted. A bedroom with around 10 beds, and when I say beds, I use the term loosely. They were makeshift mattresses on the floor with fly nets over them.

Each bed had something like an old teddy on it. They each had one thing and they were so proud of it.

They loved showing their home to me.

I thought, 'they're grateful, I need to be grateful. Dan's right. We need to be grateful for what we have.'

It was really beautiful because I could see this was making them happy, and so I loved this too.

All these kids had been saved after being abandoned by parents who had given birth to disabled children. Sadly, in some parts of Ghana, being born with a disability has quite the stigma attached to it. Some parents feel they have no choice but to give their children away due to the negative reputation it could bring on their family. It's incredibly sad.

A couple of years after my trip, I watched a horrific documentary about Ghana and the many children with disabilities who go missing. It showed how people get paid to kill and dispose of them.

Watching that broke my heart.

In contrast, I went somewhere that saved and loved those children, that taught them skills. Children were shown how to make leather shoes and were taught carpentry.

It was so cool because not only had the children been saved physically, but they were learning new skills so they could contribute to society and move forward in the world positively. They were so happy; that place's energy was pure magic. I could've stayed forever.

These trips captivated my heart. I left the country feeling totally fulfilled. I learned more than I ever could have imagined. It really changed my view and perspective on so many things.

After my first trip, I came home with no rackets or kit because I gave everything away.

My second trip to Ghana with Dan again, four years later, was really interesting.

It was wonderful being back there with him and seeing all the positive action that had been taken since our first visit.

Every bit of advice we'd given, they'd taken; they'd worked so hard. All the places we went back to had developed. Players had managed to acquire some sports chairs and they would rotate their use on their Saturday sessions.

Players would play for 15 minutes, then jump out and sit on the floor and give someone else the chair. Suddenly there were 30 people there, all coming to play tennis with eight wheelchairs, but it was so much fun. The atmosphere was electric.

A successful businessman we'd met on our first visit had invested in the project and now there is an international tournament at that same venue where they're rotating chairs.

We just gave some advice, they listened and they acted. It just shows what can be achieved.

During my visits I went to some incredible places, but they did take a toll on my health.

Nine hour car journeys on rough roads and I came back a bit of a mess.

Intense heat, the rigorous movement of the car, I got so many pressure sores all over my feet. Because of the hygiene risk, I was unable to use the running water so it was really hard to keep my sores clean, though this was nothing to what I was witnessing on a daily basis.

I had to use bottled water and emergency dressings, which I always had with me, to take care of them.

Trips like this went beyond let's get people good at wheelchair tennis; it was about transforming lives, perceptions and giving opportunity.

It makes me so happy to see how far they have come since we started working together. The development across the country in the sport has been extensive and they are now creating some great players who compete internationally.

Ghana and its people, once again, showed me it should never be about what you can't do, but about how you CAN do - just as my parents, Gramp, Chris, Mrs Petersen and many others mentioned in this book, have shown me.

I'm still amazed at just how quickly I fell in love with Ghana and its people.

Although I was exhausted throughout my visit, I didn't care. I felt totally loved and appreciated, and I can't wait to return.

Chris (more on my ripped Romeo later!) is really dying for us to go because I talk about Ghana all the time. It's on our 'to do' list and it's staying in my heart forever.

What we'll probably do is stay at a rehabilitation centre there, which is very cool.

The centre repurposes used prosthetics and mobility equipment, adjusting them for people.

We want to spend time in their workshop, so we can understand how they work and perhaps run some activities there.

What's really wonderful is that parents can come and stay with youngsters while they go through rehab, adjust and come out strong, so they can go and smash it in life.

I'd like to spend some time with the parents to help reassure them that their children are going to be fine.

I also want to revisit the places I've been to before, plus deliver tennis programmes. I can't wait to go play tennis with the children and see how I can have a positive impact again.

Ghana gave me perspective, especially during my second visit in 2016, as I was there just after losing my funding and was really emotionally struggling. That trip acted as a reminder that there are so many paths you can take to achieve a desired outcome; it doesn't always have to be the traditional path. I'll never forget the kindness I received on those trips and how welcome I was made to feel. My gratitude to every person I came into contact with, is indescribable.

My drive was always, and still is, to help the Ghanaian people, but I had no idea that I'd be the one being helped.

Chapter 18:

Going Undercover

Sometimes I like to go undercover. I've been like it since I was a kid.

It all started when I'd go out with friends, out of school time.

Out of my wheelchair, I'd sit on a bench with everyone else.

The chair would be carefully positioned, away from us, but near enough for me to keep an eye.

Then I'd sit and wait. This was the really interesting part.

As people walked by, I'd be watching their reaction. I could see them trying to work out who the wheelchair belonged to.

Sat on a bench with everyone, no-one knew. There was none of this, 'what's wrong with you?'

Sometimes it's kind of fun to not be disabled and for people not to know.

I know it sounds odd, but especially when I was young, this was my only opportunity to feel 'normal' or like everyone else.

Years later, I was at a business event in Swindon when I was sat behind a table with a colleague and they asked me for advice. It was a good conversation and they were really appreciative. We said our goodbyes, but then, as I wheeled myself out from behind the table, they left me with this parting shot.

Visitor (looking down at me): "Oh, I didn't realise you were one of them."

Takes a lot to make me speechless, but what do I say to that?

Behind that table, this man had treated me like a 'normal' person, but once I wheeled away, it was a different story.

It was a stark reminder that this narrative still exists, and that people view me as different based on the fact that I simply can't walk.

The 'What's Wrong With You?' type comments happen all too often in my world, even though I'm an independent woman, living my own life, my way. I cannot help but reflect on the contrast.

The irony is that, in many respects, people don't know that I'm disabled unless I say anything, and that is the most powerful thing, because, in these moments, it feels like I am undercover again, just as I was as a child. I have the choice whether I want to say anything. I choose to only say something if it's relevant.

If I am offering online support to a group, such as I do for young people, or leading a call when organising an event, I may tell my audience I was a Paralympian (if relevant), but I can pick and choose when to disclose this. There's something quite empowering about that, that I'm just being judged on my personality, and not what I have achieved or the fact I have a disability.

At times, working as an athlete mentor, with young female footballers online through the Youth Sport Trust, I've had to work through my own imposter syndrome. I've overcome my worries around being a wheelchair user and delivering a football themed session when my sport is tennis.

Ironically, I can't play football, but I am big on girls in sport doing what they want to do, and I can talk about how they can achieve their passion. I am very passionate about equality.

For this work, the Youth Sport Trust has not thought twice about any of this. They've just taken the approach that Louise is a good athlete mentor, we want her to deliver these sessions, and this is how the world should be. I love them for that! They make me feel equal, capable and empowered to do my role.

Since the initial 'what's wrong with you?' comment, a business friend of mine and I decided to use this as a little test of the attitudes around us.

Often, when we meet, he'll publicly and audibly ask me: "What's wrong with you?" It's so interesting to sit back and observe people's reactions.

The results so far have been fascinating and offered real insight into how people really feel around people with disabilities. Some challenge, some ask questions and some laugh, but it can be a great ice breaker.

It's an ongoing thing now, and it may seem silly, but I guess it's a coping mechanism to make light on how ridiculous this question is, as well as a mini social experiment. At its heart, I hope it ignites interesting conversations which gives me the opportunity to change perceptions and attitudes towards disability.

Chapter 19:

Pressure Sores Can't Stop Me

Without sounding dramatic, I'm dragging blood through the house right now.

Pressure sores: my nemesis and my constant. I've got one as I'm writing this. Hit my foot in the swimming pool and then again at home. They are always on my feet. It's the first one I've had in a while actually. It usually happens because of the splints needed on my feet for training and competing, but they can also appear with general rubbing in my shoes, especially on warm days (and due to having no feeling, I have no idea it's happening).

Sores have been a massive part of my life, especially during many years of competition.

On tour. Sweaty feet, which I can't feel, in sweaty splints. Never a good combination. That constant rub, no air. The sores were horrific.

Today it was a classic case of blood everywhere, 'Where's it coming from?' I can't feel cuts or sores, and without being too gross, the really bad ones can smell - A death like smell. Okay, I know that sounds dramatic, but that's what it smells like to me. You wouldn't believe the state my feet have been in over the years.

I remember seeing my bone with one of them. After winning a tournament, I went to the changing room to quickly get showered and changed before my flight home and, as I took my right shoe and splint off, I could smell my wound before I saw it. It had worn down so far that, yep, there was my bone. It didn't matter how many precautions I took, I was in this situation regularly. Luckily, I always carried many types of dressings with me so I was well equipped to dress them and take care as best I could.

There have been times when I probably should have been hospitalised or on bed rest, but I wanted to keep playing, I wanted to compete, so I kept going. I couldn't stop because I wanted to achieve my goals.

Thankfully, my amazing nurse and doctor at my local GP surgery, have enabled me to care for myself. These days I'm like a wheeling pharmacy with all the dressings and medications in my kit bag. I need to keep me well, so I always carry back up dressings etc so I'm prepared for every eventuality. I have followed their advice to the book and now I can call them if I get a pressure sore and say what kind of dressing I need. There isn't the need to see me as they have trained me to assess, clean my wounds and re-dress them; more amazing people in my life who have empowered me with the tools to be independent.

I could tell you exactly what dressing you need for what wound, based on the colour, smell and depth of the sore.

Luckily, I've had the right doctors and nurses who respected and trusted me to do this - they got me. It was also helpful that I was very willing and open to learn. I was like a sponge, listening and soaking up their advice.

I didn't want to have to go to the surgery three times a week when I was so busy, so I told them to tell me everything - I wanted that. I think sometimes it's easy to be scared or to not bother learning how to do things for yourself, because it's easy, or lazy - I'll let you decide on that one. I just always had the attitude that if I can do anything for myself, I will.

Treating a pressure sore is quite hard work and would take up so much of my time. If I had a gaping wound on my foot, I'd have to try and have a bath with my foot out of the bath. Moving my body is hard enough as it is.

Then I have to wash the pressure sore with salt water/saline and dry it with a hair dryer on the cool setting. I can't feel it, of course, but the foot needs to be completely dry so I can dress it.

I love that, these days, my nurse doesn't feel she has to see me because she's taught me what to do so well, and there's that trust.

Of course, there have been times when having pressure sores has really affected my mental, as well as my physical, health.

The fact that I can't feel my feet and seeing them in such a bad way has been really upsetting. There have been moments when I've broken down in tears because it's been horrible to look at my body and despair at how bad it is. Wearing splints for more than 12 hours a day sometimes, in hot weather, it can get to the point where the sore is infected, but I have no idea. That's pretty awful and hard to get your head around when it's your body, but you just have had no idea what's happening.

There are a couple of moments that come to mind when thinking about how my pressure sores have really affected me.

I had won in the German Open final, and it was really hot. It had been full on and I had a flight that night. I went to the changing rooms to get showered and a pressure sore had appeared that day. It wasn't there in the morning.

I remember taking my shoe and sock off, and I smelt it before I saw it. I had a hole in my foot the size of a one pence piece, and it was black. It was pretty deep.

I had basic dressings with me so I started dressing it, but I knew I needed more help.

My mum was picking me up from the airport, so I rang her and explained it was bad. When I landed we had to go straight to A and E where I spent the next few hours having the wound cleaned and re-dressed. I was given antibiotics to fight the infection, but it took a good few months for my body to fully recover. It actually wasn't the hardest one to heal. Once it took 18 months for a wound to fully bugger off.

Pressure sores have been a constant throughout my playing career. It must have been six or seven years where I wasn't without one.

The sheer volume of my training and travelling meant they never had a chance to heal. The better I got at the game, the higher my world ranking and the higher my workload. The only thing that would heal them would be to stop. I needed to be out of my shoes, out of my chair and out of training, and that just wasn't going to happen.

Only when I retired did I discover what life could be like without pressure sores. Within a couple of months they'd all gone.

It had been the best part of a year before I got another. To say the timing was lousy is an understatement.

Two weeks before my wedding in 2022 and I was on the phone to my nurse, Tracey, in a complete panic.

I had no dressings because I'd not needed them in so long, and it hadn't occurred to me to restock as I was no longer competing.

Anxious Me: "We have to heal this. I'm getting married and I'm going on honeymoon to the Maldives, where I'm going to be swimming in the sea, having adventures etc."

(Sand and sea not conducive for healing a pressure sore.)

Anxious Me: "Please help. I don't want to miss out on anything."

Tracey: "Louise, you don't play tennis anymore. We'll heal it."

And heal it we did. I can't tell you just how good that felt.

My lifestyle allowed me to heal. My feet weren't being squashed into tennis shoes. I could wear shoes without splints in my day chair or take them off completely under the desk at work. My foot could have air.

Two weeks later I rang Tracey.

Me: "It's gone!"

Tracey: "You're joking! I told you we could do it." I could sense her smile.

Gone in two weeks! Result!

I have a scar from my first sore. It happened when I was little, about 3 years old. This is a tough one for Mum and Dad to manage as it came from crawling around the house a lot. I had a carpet burn right across the front of my foot. As I crawled, my socks would always fall off and I wouldn't know. The carpet burn would create the wound. Of course it wasn't my parents' fault; I was just being a typical toddler, exploring and navigating my way around places. I never learnt to walk, so crawling for a few years was my means of getting about.

I'm so grateful for the care I received from my family and also from Tracey – another super woman like Mrs Peterson. Once again, she empowered me, never made me feel anything but capable.

I valued, and still value, independence and my career over being dependent, and this includes practising self-care in a practical way when needed. Learning how to treat and dress my own wounds has been a small, but invaluable part of the journey.

Chapter 20:

My Tennis Mind-ers: Calm Amongst The Storm

There aren't too many people outside of my closest friends and family I have allowed to take up residence in my head and heart, but Ali and Karl are two of them.

Outside of family and close friends, these men have seen me at my strongest and my most vulnerable, on court and off.

When I got kicked off the national performance wheelchair tennis programme and lost my funding, it was Karl that helped me put myself back together.

When favouritism reared its ugly head on the tennis circuit and frustrations bubbled over, it was Ali who kept me on track.

Both of these incredible men have been with me for the highest highs and the lowest of lows.

They have supported me throughout because they cared and believed in me. There was no ulterior motive other than trying to make me the best player and person I could be, and that's why I love them.

Ali has been with me from day one, from that first hit of a tennis ball. We learned wheelchair tennis together.

We first met when I was five years old. He was working in our local tennis club, across from our house.

I'd been playing tennis with my parents for fun, but they'd recognised I wanted to take it further.

So, in true Mum and Dad style, they headed over to the courts and asked Ali if he was up for doing some coaching with me.

At the time, he didn't have any experience in wheelchair tennis, but he was keen to learn.

I think what's really cool about our relationship is that we learned about wheelchair tennis together.

He wasn't an expert, he wasn't highly qualified then but, like me, he wanted to learn.

I was so lucky that I joined him right at the beginning of his journey to become a tennis coach.

We learned the sport together and now he's 100% an expert. He would never say that about himself, but he is, so I'm saying it for you, Ali.

I'll always remember how I felt when I saw Ali step on court at Wimbledon for the first time. His face - I've never seen him light up quite so much.

He gave me a look that said, 'we're about to hit, you're about to play, and this is massive.'

That 'we did it!' moment will stay with me forever.

Up until this moment it had all been about getting me there, but now it was about us, and just seeing his reaction, I could relive that tomorrow. It was his dream too.

Throughout our time together, Ali was so calm and collected. I knew he felt my frustrations and struggles in terms of the way I was treated and how I felt, but he always managed to remain professional; he never went down the route of bitching or moaning about things.

He would listen to me and validate my feelings, which really helped. In those challenging moments, it made me realise I wasn't going crazy or just imagining things.

He had a brilliant way of bringing me back to centre.

He would say: "Okay, but that is how it is. Let's now focus on the things we can control, we can change, and that's your tennis.

"We can't change how you're being treated. We can't change that system, but we can change the here and now on court."

That approach is what helped ground and calm me. He was just brilliant at doing this - a constant support throughout my entire tennis career.

It's no exaggeration to say a big part of Karl's job was keeping me sane. When I got kicked off the programme, I've talked about the positive impact he had on my tennis career, but he also positively influenced my personal life too.

His advice was never just about what was happening on court. Sometimes, unfortunately, the on-court stuff had to come second because I couldn't get on court if I wasn't in the right headspace.

Karl is very calm and totally got me and the way I tick. He was always very good at getting to the point, being serious and doing the work, but he had a great balance of bringing in a sense of humour with it, which was what I needed.

He was kind beyond belief, incredibly honest, which I found so helpful, and it kept me on track. I loved how we would manage to have a little joke and he would bring us back on track; he was really good at that.

Karl came into my life, via the national programme as the 'national team psychologist', between the London and Rio Paralympic Games.

He would come up with so many great tips and was so creative. If we'd tried 10 things, we'd keep exploring until we found something that would work.

Incredibly professional, but still managed to feel like your friend, and that's a hard balance to strike.

He never made me feel like any emotion was invalid.

One of his greatest pearls of wisdom was helping me see how I would try and run away from my negative emotions.

He said: "That's never going to work because you're human, and you're going to feel those things, so feel them."

What we worked on together then was moving away from those feelings or changing the narrative.

He encouraged me to feel the emotions and then redirect that energy in a positive way.

"You can't change how you feel about something, but you can, over time, redirect the energy." This advice has genuinely got me through life.

His advice was always practical, so when I struggled to move on from a previous point on court, he helped me come to a powerful realisation.

The reason why I would try and rush to the next point, if I'd lost the previous one, would be to get away from the emotion.

Also, if I won a good point, that wouldn't exist anymore in my rush to move on. In both cases it would mean I wasn't ready for the next point, and so therefore I may not have played it as well as I could have done.

Karl helped me recognise that I was always running away from what I felt, both on and off court, and that was a huge moment for me.

That realisation that everything on court translated to off court was a real light bulb.

Even when my funding was lost, we found a way to work together, and that says so much.

It showed me I wasn't just a number to call. He genuinely cared and believed in me.

Karl also struggled with the dynamics and politics behind the scenes so developed a career outside of this. We would see each other at the National Tennis Centre and our training bases in Swindon.

We'd be on court together and have online calls and group chats where we'd all link up.

Both Ali and Karl are amazing people that were there at exactly the right time for me and provided exactly what I needed without wanting anything in return.

They worked super closely together and got on incredibly well, which was a huge benefit.

For me, these two incredible men provide us with a big reminder that we all need to surround ourselves with the right people that only have our best interests at heart. No game playing, no agendas, just genuine support, and kindness on tap.

Chapter 21:

Money, Health and Getting Out of My Head

The adrenaline. The endorphins. The reason you're an athlete. Suddenly winning was about far more than this.

I'd always found going on tour tough - mentally and physically - but going it alone, without funding and the support from your national governing body, was something else.

With everything covered when I competed, I was focused on the competitions only but, in the last few years when funding myself, cost came into a lot of the tournaments I chose.

For financial reasons, I didn't do the Australian tour, where a lot of players competed, so I had to do other tournaments in Europe, and that took away a lot of my social connections, and safety nets, like Dana for example. I lost the connections I'd built up with people that I loved, and that was really difficult.

This was hard on performance because I'd shift from being focused on the match to feeling, 'I really need to win this tournament to cover my costs here and pay for my flights home.'

It was massive pressure and the effect was huge over those five years going solo, but I'd still take that over how I'd been feeling during the days when I was funded and on the team.

No more 'Louise, you need to lose weight,' 'Louise, you can't go to that because of this' or 'Louise, you need to do this', and that felt good.

The thing I never fell out of love with throughout my tennis career was training. I really loved it.

But keeping myself fit and well was actually really, really hard. My individual team knew this and were sweet and understanding, but my national team were totally unaware. They didn't know how my disability and health were really affected by the rigorous schedule of training and competing.

Now, I have to take part ownership here because I didn't talk about this much. I never wanted to look like I was weak because I was always conscious of coming across as incapable, but I was ill a lot of the time, especially with UTIs.

I hid this from the national team, but I think there was a general lack of awareness too.

I tried to keep a really well balanced diet and took supplements, especially when I went to countries where there may have been a higher risk of infection.

As athletes we had to be really careful of contamination. A lot of people don't realise it isn't just medication that can be affected on the drugs list. It's things like drinks and foods too. It took a lot of time planning. When I was travelling, alongside the supplements, I'd take backup stuff like energy gels, hydration tablets and snacks.

In some countries, when I was competing, it was impossible to check the supplements were safe for me to have, so I always took care with this.

As for my diet on match day, it didn't really change. I would have more things like energy gels because sometimes matches would be longer, but what I ate stayed pretty much the same.

Protein - ideally fish, as that's my favourite go to – carbs, such as pasta, and lots of fruit, were the regulars.

One of the toughest competitions for me at this time was the Israel Open which qualified me for London 2012.

Winning that final, although it wasn't the longest, was so tough mentally because of what it meant.

I'd already done 24 tournaments so far that year, but it was this match that was going to qualify me for the home games.

The tournament was terrifying. A week before, I had dropped to 23 in the world (one place outside the automatic qualifying bracket) and I had worked out that the only way to get back inside the top 22 and to qualify, was to win the whole thing.

As had been the case in so many key moments, Mum was there by my side to step up and support me. She wasn't originally coming, but when I told her I needed her, she was there.

Although it was a highly pressurised environment, when I think back to that time, Mum's behaviour still makes me laugh.

In these high performance moments you want a hyped person in the crowd that you can look to with that 'Come On!' attitude. Mum was normally pretty good at that, but this time things were a little different.

The grandeur of the occasion, the fact that she was my mum and feeling everything I was feeling 10 times over, I just have these memories of looking to her during the match and she's sweating, getting up and pacing, not making eye contact with me.

I remember thinking, 'this really isn't why I brought you, but you want this as much as me. I've got to do it for both of us.'

Sweating and stressed too, I was also thinking, 'Shit! I need to hurry up and see if she's okay.'

I was on court for about two-and-a-half hours and we were just one degree off the heat rule which would have automatically halted the match.

Those last few points felt like they went on forever; the closer we got to the finish line, the more time dragged on.

I had never won a tournament at this level, at this point (The Israel open was an ITF2 – which is middle tier international level event) and I had never beaten two of the girls there either.

Somehow, I seemed to thrive on the pressure. I won the final in straight sets.

This put me back to number 18 in the world and qualified me for my first Paralympic Games. I had done it!

Chatting to Mum afterwards, she admitted she couldn't look at me because she was just too nervous, to which I replied: "How do you think I felt? This is my dream."

The main thing was that she was there, and sometimes just being there is enough.

On the flight home I was utterly unbearable. About 10 times an hour, probably more than that, I would say to Mum: "I've qualified for the Paralympics! I won the Israel Open."

Her response, with a huge smile on her face? "I know, and I'm really happy for you, but you've told me a thousand times in the last five minutes. I haven't slept for a week because I've been so stressed. I'm so proud of you, but can I actually rest now?"

She'd most definitely earned it.

Re-living this conversation in my head now still makes me laugh so much. I really do have the best mum in the world.

Mum came to quite a few tournaments each year. I loved it because she would pick ones that were in a really beautiful place so she could enjoy a bit of a holiday or, if I was going somewhere not quite so nice, where I'd be really lonely, she would just come and keep me company. We'd play games in the room, watch soaps and reality TV shows via VPN, in bed, and we loved that it was such quality time for the two of us. She was just brilliant.

Dad was still working hard as he always had done and, of course, taking care of my brother, so it was hard for him to join us in the same way, but he came to every tournament he could, especially the British ones.

Being an athlete, especially when I was younger and travelling, meant Mum and I spent a lot of time together, as did Dad and my brother, Rob.

Rob is three years older than me and, in my early years, I needed more attention and time due to my complex health needs.

There were plenty of moments when Rob could have felt like he was handed off, but never has he made me feel anything but equal. I often felt incredible guilt about the time and attention I took up, but he was always so understanding and cool about everything - whether it was because of tennis or health, he just got it.

He's always understood, our whole family has always understood.

From when I was born, Rob had to stay with my grandparents while Dad stayed with me and Mum. At this point we didn't know if either Mum or I would even survive.

I never felt like Rob was annoyed that I needed more help and attention and, when we were young, he never treated me any differently.

I think this attitude is something my parents deserve so much respect for because they managed to get it right. I can't imagine how hard things were to juggle for them at times.

Rob is so different to me in so many ways, but so similar at the same time. We have a similar sense of humour - just a bit silly and immature.

We bond over our childhood memories, especially when it comes to musicals that we loved, like Mary Poppins and Chitty Chitty Bang Bang.

His favourite film in the world is The Sound Of Music and, if you put Edelweiss on, he'll cry because he thinks it's so beautiful.

He'll hate me for writing this, but it's true and it's one of my favourite things about him. He puts on a tough act, but he's such a softie inside.

The most supportive big brother I could ever ask for, but he does it in such an understated way. When I was competing, he'd always like to celebrate the wins with me and would check in when I was away. He kept me grounded.

He was my biggest protector and defender too. He even hung a kid on a coat hook when they bullied me at primary school. This story still makes me laugh so much. He's always been tall and strong, so he went up to this boy, said: "You just don't talk to my sister like that," hung them on the hook and then walked away. No harm, no fuss, and that's him. I think that kid got the message loud and clear as it never happened again!

I thank my lucky stars for him every day because without him, my life could have been so different.

Chapter 22:

Let's Hear It for the 'Humble' Wheelchair!

I have lost count of the number of chairs I've had through my life. Tennis chairs and day chairs are like chalk and cheese – completely different experiences.

Being strapped into a tennis chair still, to this day, makes me feel good. I love being all snug in it and feeling so free, like I can do anything. My ability is vastly increased, I'm so able in it. It's the best feeling ever.

I remember the first time I got into a tennis chair. It belonged to the British Number 1 guy of the time and, oh my God, it was so fast. It made me feel totally able and level with everybody else. Amazing, and that's what the right equipment does for you; that's how you should feel.

Getting my own tennis chair was out of this world. I can remember playing tennis with my family. I was faster than them. Up until this point, though I'd had the tennis abilities quite young, I was still pretty slow as I was using an everyday chair. Getting the tennis chair meant I was just as quick, as able as my relatives, and that was a real game changer.

Being strapped into a tennis chair is like being given a set of wings. What's possible changes in an instant and that's what helps your performance. Your chair becomes part of your body.

Transferring across to my match chair means transferring my upper body first and then my legs. Everyone's chair is set up differently, so for me it includes an adapted foot plate with side and front guards (All created by my Dad. I can't tell you how handy it is having a mechanic in the family. Dad can literally create anything). This means my feet are wedged in, which is brilliant as I have no control or movement over my lower body. If they're not in securely, this would severely knock me off balance and affect my ability to perform to my best.

Most tennis chairs have a knee brace now, which goes in front of your knees and helps to keep you secure. So, you're boxed in, basically. On my chair there's also a lap strap, which is a ratchet one - so secure, it's near impossible to undo.

My tennis chair really does feel amazing. I love the tennis chair because it's holding me, doing the work for me so I don't have to put effort into my core/supporting my body in the same way. When you've got a physical disability, your body is always making up for what you lack. So, for me my left side has a terrible time fighting hard to keep up with my right side because I'm missing so many things, such as my bum cheek, fully formed left foot, the list is long.

I often liken being in my tennis chair for the similar reason I love swimming in terms of freedom. I love being in water because I love that weightless feeling. Again, it's really nice not needing to have anything else holding me up. When I'm in the water, even with the bits I can't feel, I can tell my body's going 'thank you'. Not having splints, straps, sideguards, it's the best feeling ever.

That's not to say I've not been desperate to get out of my tennis chair. During a match you don't think about that at all, but on the odd occasion when I've been on court in a five hour epic, for example, it's so liberating and such a relief. I liken it to when you've had a belt on all day but not noticed it's dug in until you take it off later. That's what it feels like, but en- masse.

That's why you always see loads of people on tour laying on the floor, stretching - the ultimate feeling of release. It's hard to explain, but it's like everything separates in your body as it's all been strapped so tightly together whilst you're competing; everything re-aligns.

When I stop playing, get out of the tennis chair and into a day chair, there's often an awareness that I want to get out of any chair, I just need to not be in this L-shape anymore.

The stigma around wheelchairs is one I'm keen to smash and one I talk about all the time.

Whilst my wheelchair is seamlessly just a part of my daily life, taking a moment to recognise its true purpose, just shows how integral it is to my everyday existence.

I find it very disheartening that some people still view mobility aids, particularly wheelchairs, negatively. Comments, often from strangers, expressing sentiments like "being in a wheelchair is the worst thing I can imagine happening to me" are not only rude but stem from an uninformed perception of my life. My response? "Really? I can think of a lot more things which are way worse." I find this perspective pretty horrendous and something I'm pushing back against in the work I do today. Is it really the worst thing? Because that chair I'm sat in, is the very thing that gives me total independence and freedom, so I think it's freaking awesome. I find it absolutely amazing that anybody would struggle with this.

My wheelchair, an incredible piece of technology, has evolved over the years, granting me limitless possibilities. It provides me with absolute independence, enabling a life that, as a child, I could only dream of. Why would needing it to get around be considered a drawback or negative?

Today, I cannot express enough gratitude for my wheelchair and the daily freedom it gives me. My appreciation extends to those continuously enhancing equipment accessibility and the supportive people who refrain from judgement or pity based on my seated lifestyle.

Of course, I appreciate that everyone's situation is different. I can't walk at all, but I have plenty of friends who use a wheelchair when it's appropriate and will walk when they're able to. It's all about finding a balance and what works for you.

There does seem to be a bizarre obsession with walking for walking's sake though. 'Walking is the best thing.'

Well, it's not if you then can't carry anything, can't be independent, can't open a car door, can't carry your shopping, struggle to get something out of your pocket, need to lean or stop every five minutes to sit down. In these situations, walking sounds pretty shit to me.

Before anyone gets on my case, I'm not saying give up every chance of moving your body. If you're able to keep your body upright and move around, then do it.

But, if this is causing you pain and making your life significantly more challenging than it needs to be, why would you struggle? I find it incredible that someone would rather struggle around with walking sticks, for instance, and perhaps need someone to help them, when you could get in a chair and live a completely independent life.

Bizarre, and yet I see it happen a lot, even on tour in the tennis world when some have been, in my opinion, brainwashed into using crutches because 'walking is always the most ideal solution', even if it makes them dependant on others, and it's a real struggle. Sometimes this comes from cultural beliefs and pressures, I believe.

We'll go out together and they can't carry their tennis bag, they can't push their sports chair around the airport, for example, they can't carry their food when they order it from the counter; they can't keep up with the rest of us.

But then we go get a chair for them and their whole life changes. In the hotel room or the lobby they might walk around a bit because it's good for them, but they don't struggle and they discover that wheelchairs can be amazing.

There can be so much shame associated with wheelchairs, so much stigma attached. There are those who will struggle to the end of their life because they will be stuck with this old-fashioned mindset, when a wheelchair could transform their world.

This really emphasises to me the importance of the language we use and how we communicate with each other.

I've watched my Nan and my Nana go down really different routes regarding wheelchairs. With one grandparent, she refuses to use a wheelchair and hasn't really left the house in several years, whereas my other grandparent does use one, but only when she needs to, so she doesn't miss out on trips out with the family.

When she first needed a chair, it led to some interesting discussions that went something like this:

Nan: "Oh, I don't use a wheelchair."

Me: "Nan, hello, I'm 33. I've used a wheelchair my whole life."

Nan: "It's different."

Me: "How is it different in any way?"

Pause

Me: "I can't do something so I've got an aid to help me. You can't walk long distances anymore, but want to come out with your family. Sit in a wheelchair. It's no different."

Guess what? She did, and it's been great for her. Now, if we do anything long distance, it goes something like this:

Nan: "I will take the chair."

Me: "Yeah, let's take the chair."

It's beautiful, and most importantly, she has quality of life and never misses out on those precious outings.

We need more open, honest conversations like this.

Chapter 23:

London 2012: Missing Face in the Crowd

I'll never forget the sound. A sound so breath taking, I felt its vibration come up through the floor, its sheer power vibrating my chair.

I say it was a sound, but it was so much more than that; it was an indescribable feeling. Magical.

I was so consumed by how amazing it was, I almost forgot there were 80,000 people sharing it with me.

I've never heard a sound change like that, before or since.

The crowd in the stadium erupted.

They had been waiting for us.

When we rolled into the Paralympic stadium, the noise took my breath away. Those cheers will stay with me forever.

The lap we did around the stadium was unbelievably special.

Union Jack spoilers clipped on our wheels, all dressed in Team GB white tracksuits with gold trim.

I was so excited when we found out that Peter Norfolk from the Wheelchair tennis team was going to be our flag bearer for London 2012.

It meant that all Paralympics GB tennis players would be at the front of the parade. What an honour!

Being part of the home nation's team meant we would be the last team welcomed into the Paralympic stadium.

We couldn't wait. As the opening ceremony grew closer, excitement built.

People often moan about Olympic and Paralympic ceremonies being ridiculously long, but it's even longer for athletes.

We had started queuing mid-afternoon on the big day, even though we wouldn't get into the stadium until towards the end of the ceremony - usually mid-evening.

They say the Brits are good at queuing and, on this special day, we had every reason to enjoy the experience.

Music, snacks, enjoying each other's company - time seemed to fly by.

This was something new and so special for every person in our team. We had never experienced anything like it. We wanted to soak up every tiny detail.

Every one of us united, all in the same boat.

After around five hours of waiting, it was time for the opening ceremony to begin.

We could hear the cheers from afar as nation after nation was announced.

As we edged closer to the stadium, the crowd grew louder.

Then, finally, it was our turn. Paralympics GB was in the house!

As soon as we reached the entrance, the stadium erupted.

The change in volume was insane.

I'll never forget that sound. It was magic.

Then a funny thing happened.

As all our tennis players had to be at the front, we were all lined up, ready to go, when we reached a bit of a bottleneck.

We all got squished together and I ended up being pushed really far back. I'd lost the tennis team!

So, in an effort to catch up, I pushed myself around the outside of the TV cameras so I could cut back into the procession.

If you ever look at the parade online, look out for the little white blob. That's me going around the outside in an effort to get back to my tennis teammates.

Consumed by the experience, I rolled so quickly that I overtook our flag bearer, Peter, and had to reel myself back in.

The upside of my faux paus was that I ended up with an amazing photo you can see in this book. It's one of my favourites.

I also ended up on a Royal Mail stamp which was so cool.

Being right next to the flag felt unbelievably special. It was iconic to be part of the parade; the best experience of my life.

I feel incredibly lucky to have competed at a home games. A once in a lifetime moment.

Three days later and I was ready to compete in tennis singles for Paralympics GB.

First round in the women's singles and I was drawn against Japanese top seeding, Yui Kamiji. An amazing player, who has gone on to become a multiple Grand Slam champion.

Some may say I got pretty unlucky drawing Yui at London 2012, but it was an incredible opportunity on home soil.

I was terribly nervous before the match, to the point where I felt unwell, but then Ali, my coach, worked his magic, as usual.

"Just remember, as soon as you get out there, it's just a tennis ball," he said. "It's a yellow fluffy thing that you hit every single day of your life and you're going to be fine. It's a place where you love to be."

Ali's words worked wonders. Terrified and sick with nerves beforehand, once I wheeled out on court, I knew I was in my safe space. I felt good.

Everything about this home games was different from any other matches I'd played before. From the way the crowd was so heavily weighted in my favour to the fact that suddenly all these people I knew were watching me. That was a really wild thing.

It had taken me 25 tournaments around the world that year alone, plus the countless years of hard graft, to get me to this one special moment.

Sometimes my parents or grandparents would turn up at the odd match. Mum would come to a couple abroad tournaments with me, and the odd friend too, but most of the people I knew there at the Paralympics, had not seen any of the matches I played to qualify.

It meant I wasn't used to playing in front of people I knew. It was really bizarre to hear familiar voices in the crowd and have that realisation, 'oh you're here to watch me'.

Just squeezed in for qualification at the Games and playing against someone like Yui, the pressure felt unreal at times.

What made everything worth it was having so many people rooting for me. It was an amazing feeling that you can only really get at a home Games.

The match was on quite a big court, which added to the atmosphere perfectly. All those cries of support from people I knew and loved, alongside complete strangers; it was a heady mix.

In amongst the voices, I definitely heard Mum's cheers of encouragement, but where was Dad? It was so unlike him to keep quiet. Dad would always make his presence known when I was on court. He would often cheer in all the wrong places, which was slightly embarrassing, but that's part of his charm. Him being there always meant the world to me.

When I looked into the crowd occasionally between games, I just couldn't see him. I wouldn't let it impact my performance. I'd worked so hard to be there, I was determined to give it my all.

After a hard fought match, I lost to Yui. Coming off court, all my friends and family surrounded and congratulated me.

Hearing the words: "We're really proud of you" softened the blow of my loss.

I looked again for Dad. He was nowhere to be seen.

"Where's Dad?" I asked, looking at mum.

"He's hurt his collarbone. He couldn't come on the train, it was too painful," she explained.

Something didn't feel right. This was my dad, the most hard-core man in my life, and my biggest supporter. I knew he would do anything to share this special moment with me.

"What's really happened?" I asked.

That's when I found out about the accident.

The night before the opening ceremony, before one of the biggest matches of my sporting career, Dad had come off his push bike and was in intensive care.

Knowing just how important this match was for me, my family had decided to keep the news to themselves.

22 bones, broken and fractured, including his back, shoulder blade smashed into 10 pieces, ribs, vertebrate, dislocated shoulder and lots more injuries that even now Dad doesn't like to remember.

The news was shocking and took a while to sink in.

Mum had tried to lie in the gentlest way to protect me. My family were adamant they wanted me to enjoy the Games.

I still don't know how they managed to keep things quiet, but as I chatted to Mum, it became evident just how much had been going on behind the scenes.

Despite her huge concerns for Dad, she'd also been talking to the top people within Paralympics GB.

Mum had contacted our team manager to warn them I might have to suddenly leave the Paralympic village and the competition.

Aware of the situation, they were on standby in case Dad took a turn for the worst.

Despite many difficult conversations, my family bravely carried on, choosing not to tell me until they knew Dad would be okay.

Luckily Plan B was never put into action. I was able to stay for the whole games.

It was an amazing experience, but still really hard not having Dad there with me.

Dad has always believed in me and played a big part in supporting my bid for London. Always rooting for me, always so proud.

I was really sad that he never made the home Games. I missed my Nan and Gramp being there too.

Mum, brother, Rob, family and friends were just utterly unbelievable in this moment.

Ether Mum or Rob came to the Games most days. It was incredible to see them there, for us to hang out and go see other sports together.

I still wonder how on earth they managed to keep things together and support me when Dad was so badly injured. Rob was poorly with stomach issues too and then there was a very poorly Gramp. Everything was hitting at once.

What an incredible family I have. Adamant that I needed to stay at the Games, that this was my dream. They knew it was the right thing, that there wasn't anything I could do for Dad if I came home. They, like me, have the most amazing friends who stepped in to help, just as they have done on many occasions in their lives.

Me missing out on this once in a lifetime experience would have upset them all so much, including Dad.

My family is so selfless in this way - it's just how we are. I love this about us.

Family comes first, but with a view that if you're doing something amazing and it's something you've worked hard for - an incredible experience - there's no need to miss out unless you really have to.

In taking this approach, they were right. The Games were amazing. Going to see other sports, being a British athlete, there was always so much going on. For two weeks, I had the time of my life.

Rihanna, Coldplay, the closing ceremony was incredible and the atmosphere unreal; memories I'll hold onto always.

The next day I came home to find Dad back from hospital. I think he was home a little too soon, but in that classic, British 'keep calm and carry on' way; typical Dad, really.

While he laid in bed, I sat with him to show off all my Games goodies and the gifts I had bought him. Extra Paralympics GB kit, an iPod, a kilo of personalised Cadbury's chocolate and lots and lots of photos - we were so spoilt!

Dad loved seeing my mementos, but I could feel his sadness at missing my big moment. I knew in my heart just how much seeing me at London 2012 had meant to him.

'Rio, we're going to Rio'. The thoughts came loud and clear. 'I've got to do this again. Dad's got to be there.'

Here was my biggest motivation for competing at the next Paralympics in South America.

As time went on, my motivation developed even further. I wanted to be one of the best in the world. I wanted to be top 10. My goals and ambitions were getting bigger.

And holding it all together? My dream of sharing Rio with Dad. I was going to make it happen.

Chapter 24:

Everything Only Lasts For a Moment

I'm so lucky to have my family and friends around me.

My Gramp was the most amazing man on earth. He was the Grampy that everyone wanted as their own, and the coolest thing about him? He actually was that to so many, and opened his arms to everyone.

I loved how he embraced and supported my friends like they were his actual grandkids.

He never failed to offer them a judgement free, kind, safe space, like he did me and my brother. So much so that even when we were teenagers, Becky and I would go for sleepovers at Nan and Gramp's house because we loved their company so much!

Of course he had his flaws, but he was my absolute super-hero. He helped shape my positive and determined attitude.

Thanks to him and other close family members, such as my parents, Nan and brother, it was the only attitude I knew until

I stepped out into the world and realised not everyone is as positive or as accepting of me being different.

Gramp taught me there's always an alternative way. It was never a case of 'Louise can't'.

My family comes from a motorbike/car background, so we were always surrounded by motorbikes and other stuff like that. We are so adventurous and have a need to speed, let's say. Dad was a successful speedway rider (he even had a fan club) and my Grampy owned garages and sponsored the local speedway team too, so this just always surrounded me.

Growing up, Gramp always had old motorbikes for my brother and cousins to mess around with and learn to drive. He was also convinced this was what would help us all pass our car driving tests.

When I was old enough, I wanted to play, so he got me a quad bike with hand controls so I could join in too. It was never a case of you can't do this because... It meant I could have the same experience as Rob and my cousins.

Little did I realise at the time, but he was definitely showing me what inclusion really means and how there's always a way to get to the same end result; we just sometimes need to find a different route.

One of my favourite memories with Nan and Gramp was on a beautiful snowy day, where the small field they owned was completely covered in fluffy, fresh snow. Gramp rang me and said: "Want to come play on the quad bike?" The answer was so obviously, 'yes', and within half an hour I was making perfect donuts in the field, snow spraying up from the back tyres. Gramp was beaming with pride and Nan was smiling through gritted teeth, hoping I didn't hurt myself, although I could see she loved every minute too. It was magical. These memories will stay in my heart forever. It was quality time with them both that I was so lucky to have, so often. I'll be forever grateful for this. My love for them is indescribable.

When I wanted to learn to dive in the pool, Gramps made me a little diving board from some dodgy wooden pallets he found in the garden. It meant I could jump into the water, as from the side of the pool, in a seated position, just didn't feel exciting enough. Basically, diving this way resulted in a belly flop every time. It makes me cringe a little now because I probably got splinters from those blooming pallets - not that I could feel them, and they were totally unsafe in hindsight, but Gramps would always find a way. He taught me to be the same, to be adventurous and fearless.

Gramps embedded in me, to the depths of my core, how able and how capable I am. It was never 'you're not going to be able to do that.'

He gave me some of the best advice I've ever been given:

"Everything only lasts for a moment."

I have these precious words on a bracelet on my wrist.

I was young, distraught and crying when he shared them with me for the first time.

I had just ballsed up. The long story short was that I'd made a genuine mistake in terms of committing to another player in doubles and misinterpreted another commitment. Instead of owning my error, I tried to pass the buck which resulted in things escalating ridiculously and then me getting in trouble. I'm still embarrassed by it, but I realise now that it was a spur of the moment panic which came back and bit me, and that I will never make the same mistake again.

A big lesson to learn as a young teenager, but it really taught me to own my mistakes, and to be honest with those around me.

So, with this going on, and as I struggled to deal with my emotions, Gramps said:

"At some point in your life this is not going to matter. It might be a week, a month, a year, 10 years from now, but at some point you're going to forget this even happened.

"Everything in life - good or bad - is momentary; so if it's a good thing, just love it when it's happening, absorb it, because it will go eventually. Be present. If it's awful, just know that you're not going to feel like this forever."

His advice helped so much then and to this day. I live by these words.

When I was playing tennis, if I'd had a shocker of a match, it was such a good reminder to stay positive.

His words helped me change my thoughts, to put me in a more empowering place. The result?

'Today wasn't my day. I'm better than that. This isn't going to hurt as much tomorrow and the next day, and the day after that.'

In challenging moments, I always try to live by Gramp's words.

Another 'Gramp-ism' to make me smile:

"If you find something you like, buy two or buy it in every colour, in case you can never find it again." Now, that is great advice, right? My best friend, Claire, still lives by this advice to-day, just ask to see her sunglasses collection. His impact lives on!

One of my favourite memories of him revolves around shoes. My special shoes, built up on one side, were the most ugly foot-wear you could ever imagine. Trust me, they weren't helping me to make friends for sure, but they were crucial in ensuring I de-veloped as best as I could physically to give me a good, comfort-able life.

I have one leg longer than the other, so when I was growing, it was really important that my spine, hips and legs grew as straight and in sync as possible, to ensure I didn't become any 'wonkier' than I already was. The shoes were actually life chang-ing, but at the time they were just a call for the fashion police.

As I grew, to ensure my legs and hips aligned, they had to be adjusted and so 'normal' shoes were out of the question. These were really grim, not cool for street cred. I hated them.

So, when the doctor told me I'd grown sufficiently to wear 'normal' shoes, I was so excited.

Suddenly, I could wear whatever footwear I wanted. (Side note: within reason, as splints and floppy ankles don't fit into all styles, such as high boots, heels or sandals, for example, however a whole new world had opened up to me and the excitement was so real).

Gramp had always said that when this moment came, we would go shopping, so that's what we did.

He took me to a huge warehouse full of shoes. Some of them were naff and tacky, but there were so many cool pairs too. Gramp used to love a bit of retail therapy. "You need boots, you need trainers, you need smart shoes, and you should probably have a pair for every year you missed out on wearing them, at least," he said. He really understood what this moment meant to me, it was about so much more than just the physical shoes, it was a moment of freedom and another chain unlocked!

I came home with 11 pairs of shoes.

I wore all those shoes into the ground. They lasted me ages because my shoes take forever to wear out. Basically, he bought me a lifetime's worth. I think that's why I love shoes so much now.

Today I only buy really nice, fancy ones that are bright and branded because I love them and feel privileged to wear them.

Gramp's love of shopping was in total contrast to my nan who really wasn't that bothered. I remember he took me to this amazing place to buy my prom dress. It was in Cirencester, about 30 minutes away. A lovely town, I couldn't believe he took me there as this was where Nan got all her stunning holiday/cruise outfits from. I felt like a princess.

Those outfits were just beautiful and, with every outfit Nan owned, Gramp would always insist she had a matching pair of shoes, bag and accessories. She looked like royalty.

He used to spoil her just like she deserved and he relished in buying her lovely things to make her feel special. It's just so cute to me that he actually enjoyed this more than her. Nan, day-to-day, is super down to earth and very happy in joggers and a t-shirt but, my goodness, did she shine when she dressed up. His taking me to this Cirencester shop made me feel like the most special girl in the world.

Gramp spoiled me rotten, he really did, and I'm so grateful for everything he ever did for me or said to me. I miss him so much.

He was an amazing man who came from nothing and achieved massive things. A successful businessman, who eventually owned multiple businesses - from farms to garages.

It all started with him getting things off the scrapheap, such as old steering wheels, bikes and car parts, doing them up and reselling them.

When he married my nan, they had very little money, so Nan borrowed a wedding dress from a lady she worked with. Nan and Gramp married on 8th October, 1955 in Farringdon, with a very small reception afterwards.

Gramp's actions and wise words helped me to believe in myself and to recognise that if you work hard, anything and everything is possible.

Just like my parents, he was just one step ahead when it came to my development. He never made me feel different. Gramp helped me realise that though people without a disability may go from A to B, I may sometimes have to go via C, but I could always get there. I could get to the same ending, the same goal, the same finish line, but I might need to go a slightly different way, and that was okay.

I don't have a memory of hearing he had cancer. I find I have two responses when dealing with hurt, grief or trauma – I either completely blank and have no memory of it or I can relive every detail. So, I don't remember how or when I was told, but I do remember when he passed away like it was yesterday.

For the last two weeks of his life I saw him every day. He wasn't really able to speak. Confined to bed, I watched him slowly fading away.

His illness began with bowel cancer and, as the cancer spread, I was preparing for London 2012. He was so proud and kept telling everyone that his granddaughter was competing in the home games.

A couple of days after surgery he had to have a colostomy bag fitted; he kept telling the nurses that all he wanted was to see me at the Paralympics.

It was pressure, but welcome pressure given the circumstances.

The nurses knew everything about me. I was Gramp's little girl.

Not long before he died, we were in the local bank together where everyone knew him. He used to love it when people would ask me: "Are you Tony Wooster's granddaughter?" On this occasion the tables were turned when the lady behind the till commented that she didn't realise he was Louise Hunt's grandfather. It was so funny because someone associated him with me, rather than vice versa. I'll never forget the look on his face. It still makes me chuckle now. A combination of horror and pride. Secretly, I could tell he was proud that someone had recognised 'his granddaughter' for what she'd achieved.

It breaks my heart that he couldn't come to London in person. However, he knew I went, saw me on TV in the ceremonies and got to hear all the stories on my return. He just wasn't well enough to travel, but he did see me go.

I gave him some bits from my kit too which he wore with pride, including a bright red bucket hat which turned out to be ideal for gardening. I still have that hat and keep it in the safest place.

Another beautiful thing was the bond Gramp had with my dad – his son-in-law. They had similar mindsets and I love what kernels of wisdom Gramp passed on to him. Similar to what he shared with me, Gramps had that belief in my dad that he could achieve great things with hard work and persistence.

He also passed on endless practical skills to him too, giving Dad the confidence to create some incredible things. I don't think there's anything my dad can't make – from buildings to sculptures – he's so incredibly clever, and I know some of that skill and confidence was passed on from Gramp.

I love watching my dad pass that same wisdom on, how he teaches Chris things. Gramp and Dad were like my dad and Chris are now. I feel they were meant to find each other.

When Gramps passed away it was super hard.

At his funeral, I played on the piano the theme tune from Last Of The Summer Wine - one of his favourite TV shows, which he loved me playing.

Piano playing is one of my only natural talents. I've been playing since I was five years old, and I've just always picked up music and rhythms so naturally. Music has always touched me in a way nothing else does. I love the escapism it gives me. I get lost in it and forget about everything else. I love creating new sounds on the piano and tweaking songs, into my own versions, such as turning classic Christmas carols into jazzy, jolly versions.

After I had showed commitment to playing for a couple of years, Gramp bought me an upright grand piano. It's my most prized possession today and I will never have a different piano.

When he took me to the piano shop, he insisted I have an actual grand piano. Classic Gramp! The look on my parents' face was hilarious. Where was it going to fit into our house? It simply wasn't. So, we managed to persuade him to stick to the upright version. It meant we could create the same sound, but we would have room for it.

I have a picture on the piano of him next to it, so whenever I play I feel like I'm with him.

Playing for his funeral was one of the hardest things I've ever had to do, but saying goodbye by playing his gift to me felt so right.

Nan was so proud of me that day and thanked me endlessly for contributing to the service. I feel so incredibly grateful to still have her in my life. There is nothing more magical than seeing Nan at the heart of our family, especially the bond she shares with her great-grandchildren. My nephews light up her world, and despite everything, she continues to fill ours with her warmth.

Our bond is so strong and I'm so grateful for the fact we're still making memories together, making each other laugh and sharing precious moments. Thanks to my parents' tireless efforts,

Nan's life is full of love, laughter, and precious moments all these years after losing Gramp. Her life is fulfilled in the truest sense, as she is always surrounded by those who cherish her most. The way my family has rallied around her shows that love endures—and that is the greatest gift of all.

Chapter 25:

Living Our Dream Together

Rio 2016. I'm at the opening ceremony of the Paralympics. My dream has come true.

Somehow, among thousands in the stadium, a friend manages to pick him out in the stands. There he is – Dad, living his best life alongside my mum.

Seeing him cheer me on is up there with one of the best memories of my career. It was pretty special.

How my friend spotted him in a huge stadium is beyond me, but once seen, I just couldn't take my eyes off him.

Dad saw me in the ceremonies, saw me compete, and I even got him and Mum into the Paralympic village for the day for a tour. It was just such a brilliant two weeks where the three of us created some magic memories.

He was with me for the closing ceremony too.

In true Dad fashion, he made it through security to the athletes' area on ground level of the stadium where he found me.

There we were, in a sea of people from across the globe, having a great big hug. It felt so lovely. Just thinking about it still makes me smile today.

All these years later, Dad is okay, although his body still hurts from the bike accident trauma.

He has yet to fully recover, but continues to be the incredible driving force in my life that he's always been. I'm so thankful for the inspirational, indomitable spirit that runs through his veins. I have no doubt it helped us both get to Rio. I like to think a little of that spirit has rubbed off on me.

Chapter 26:

Meeting My Soul Mate

Christopher Peter Hunt Skelley MBE: a British Paralympic Judoka Champion who won Gold for Paralympics GB in the under 100kg category at the Tokyo 2020 Paralympic Games.

When we're together we can achieve anything and everything.

We always say this: "We are like an 'able bodied' person combined because Chris becomes my legs and I become his eyes."

I love our marriage.

Chris was diagnosed with oculocutaneous albinism at 19. This is considered the rarest form of albinism and means he has significant sight loss, only sees in black and white and that his vision is vastly affected by light. He also relies on hearing aids as he has profound hearing loss too. We are still not completely sure if this is linked to his eye condition or not... we seem to get mixed messages on that one.

The first time we met was July 2016 at the launch dinner in London before the Rio Games.

The dinner is a place where all competitors are announced and is a chance for athletes to spend a weekend together, get all their GB kit and do some pre-publicity with media.

It was a big weekend in London for the team and for us as individuals.

Chris and I ended up on the same table. The tennis team was too big to fit onto two tables so GB number 2 female player at the time, Lucy Shuker and I, were... let's say 'promoted' onto the British judo table.

I'd never even heard of Paralympic Judo back then and had no idea what it was about.

Chris was sat a person away from me and I was sat next to his best friend, Jack. The same Jack who was to become a groomsman at our wedding.

I didn't really speak to Chris much that night, to be honest. I had a bit of a laugh with him and the rest of the judo team, but it wasn't until Rio that we really spoke.

We didn't even cross paths much in the athletes' village, but said hello from a distance.

Chris always makes me laugh when he talks about it. He says he never really knew if he was saying 'hello' to me as there were so many people in wheelchairs there and he couldn't tell who was who. Charming! ;-)

It was actually on the flight home in September 2016 when Chris made his move. He literally kept coming back to speak to me, bringing up all sorts of weird and wonderful topics to talk about.

On the last trip down the aisle, he popped the question. No, not that one. You'll have to read on for more on that.

"Can I have your number? Can we go on a date?" he asked.

"Okay," I replied, playing it cool, because I was genuinely unaware that he was hitting on me.

Two weeks later and we went on our first date, to a Japanese restaurant in Birmingham, close to where he trained and lived at the national centre in Walsall.

One hilarious story from that date Chris and I laugh about today is when he was telling me about an operation he had and how he had to have a catheter. He proceeded to tell me, in full detail, how it was the worst experience of his life and that I should avoid it at all costs. You should have seen his face when I told him about my reality. He was so embarrassed, but you know what was great? It meant he knew about my medical set up from super early on, taking that pressure away from me that I'd had in other relationships. No more awful moments when I'd struggle with whether I should tell them about my situation or hide it. No secrets needed, it was the perfect start.

After this, we saw each other a handful of times, but we very much fell in love through our phones. Our busy schedules meant we weren't able to be together much in person, so phone chats had to be the way forward.

We think this is why our communication is so strong today. From day one, we had to make time for each other and speak honestly and openly.

We talked about everything and anything in those moments – from our families, our careers to future plans and ambitions. Nothing was off limits.

Phone calls and text messages from opposite ends of the country, sometimes from different countries and time zones. Once Chris got hit with a £1,000 phone bill when he was in Mongolia. He got the money refunded in the end as they gave him the wrong information about what was included in his phone contract, before he left. We got lucky there!

In between training, travelling and competing, we would find pockets of time to be together, thanks to the wonders of technology.

Our love for one another grew during the next couple of months, but then came the big 'kick in the teeth'. I was off the national performance programme and felt utterly broken.

The next day I went to pick Chris up from the airport. He'd been away training abroad.

I was a mess and at the lowest I'd ever been. I just cried and cried. Chris really supported me through it. I can still remember ringing him late at night the week after I had been told the news, when I was having a full-blown panic attack. Distraught at what had happened, I couldn't cope, with my confidence and self-worth just shot away.

Chris jumped on a train, got to me at 1am and then had to go back to Walsall for training five hours later.

It was early on in our relationship, but he travelled all that way just to be with me. He loved and cared for me from the start.

Chris was there for me and understood the magnitude of how it must have felt to be kicked off the programme.

It's weird how people come into your life at exactly the right time. Chris came into mine at the lowest time and, thank goodness - lucky me - he stayed.

I think it's incredible that he was so there for me at the very start of our relationship. At a time when the lack of communication and support from the national performance programme broke my heart.

In truth, being on the programme was the loneliest, most isolating time of my life. It was the place where I felt the most insecure – in stark contrast to how I felt with Chris and in my bubble at home, where everyone loved and embraced me for my differences.

Being around the national team, I felt these things were frowned upon and people just didn't get me. I felt pushed out and often completely ignored.

Chris was the perfect antidote. Since those very first days of snatched phone conversations, we've always been able to communicate openly, honestly and lovingly.

However busy our schedules, wherever we are in the world, our quality time together is sacred.

Time for me, Chris and Milo (I'll introduce you to our pooch properly later!). My favourite days are long lie ins together, a good old roast with Chris' world class Yorkshire puddings and a walk around our village, just the three of us.

Being dropped from the tennis programme was brutal, but it led to a massive transition for me and, then for Chris.

I was able to get a job which meant I could buy a house - my dream house. I had a lovely time living with my parents; gosh, they went above and beyond, even building me an apartment in their home so I could have space and feel independent... but I wanted my own home. Suddenly, I had my own place to come back to, my base. My friend, Claire, calls it my castle. I like to refer to it as my big security blanket.

My home, my amazing family, my stability. Chris, Milo.

When I stopped playing competitively, it wasn't a case of 'I'm an athlete and now it's gone.' Being an athlete was part of my identity, but I had all these other identities of friend, daughter, partner, mentor, so I just grew and pushed on with those. Chris and I grew and pushed together.

Chapter 27:

Sponsorship and Shifting Mindset

Wheelchair tennis is a massive disability sport and one of the most expensive Paralympic sports.

Why? Tennis tournaments are all over the world and the only way to build your ranking is to compete in them.

Although you can start off in one country, no country has enough tournaments to help you place high in those world rankings.

So, to become a top player you have no choice but to fly around the world to compete.

Currently, there are around 180 international tournaments on the wheelchair tour, at different playing levels.

When I stopped being funded, how well I did in tournaments really mattered more in terms of financial gain.

It majorly affected my thought processes. Suddenly I was thinking so much more about cost. 'I really need to win this because I'll win x amount of money and that will cover the cost of my flight,' I'd frequently think to myself.

Not an ideal mindset to have when all your focus needs to remain in the game.

Being a self-funded athlete put a lot more pressure on me mentally as well as financially. That's why my sponsors were such a vital lifeline.

Things are getting better for wheelchair tennis athletes, and that's something to celebrate.

Today, there are a lot more free entry tournaments, but these tend to be at the very top end of competition. In other words, they are only played by those established players who already have a high ranking.

In contrast, those wheelchair tennis players still working their way up the rankings must pay entry fees of around £500 - possibly a little more or a little less - and that's without the cost of flights and food.

Playing tournaments in Europe can average between £500 and £1,000 every time, and that's if a player is securing good rates on air travel, of course.

Then there's training and equipment costs. Coaches charge an hourly rate and bespoke tennis wheelchairs start at £5,000. The more bespoke things on it, the more that cost goes up. I know of someone's tennis chair that cost £10,000.

All these costs come with an enormous amount of pressure and can have a massive impact on a player's mindset and performance.

I discovered this for myself, particularly when I was taken off the national squad.

When I had to self-fund my tennis career, I learned an awful lot about myself and the incredible people who continued to support me.

My sponsors were, and are, my support team. In many ways, they are the unsung heroes who can bolster an athlete's belief in themselves. I know mine have certainly fulfilled that role throughout my career and post retirement from competitive sport.

Get Kids Going, my first ever sponsor, stuck with me right to the end of my career. I know I couldn't have done what I've done without them.

From buying my first ever tennis chair, they kept the faith in me. That's what they do so well. A lot of the athletes they supported, like me, made it to the Paralympics, won medals and other international titles. They grew with us and stuck with us.

When I lost my place on the national performance programme, it was Jane from Get Kids Going who I rang. A magical woman who never stopped believing in me.

"I believe in you Loui (her nickname for me which I love). We've got this, we've got you. We're going to do this together," she said. Her words meant so much. The organisation helped fund my tournaments, training and equipment.

I've had several different sponsors throughout my life and all of them have been so supportive.

One of them was a local hairdresser which meant I got my hair done for free. Another was Mondelez International, which owns Cadbury. I was in sweet heaven! A kilo of chocolate with my face on it, personalised goody bags, loads of chocolate treats. It was pretty cool as part of the pre London promotion.

Then, on a local recommendation, I contacted James Phipps of Excalibur – a communications and IT provider.

I was hoping James' company might want to sponsor me, but unfortunately, he'd already reached his sponsorship limit for the year.

Apologising, he said: "I really love what you do, so I want to help you gain another sponsor."

He helped me to reach out to Imagine Cruising, based in Swindon, and even offered to come to the meeting with me. A very kind and special guy.

A friend from Chile, who'd picked up a massive sponsor, recommended I create a leaflet showcasing my achievements as she had done.

At the time, letter writing was the standard sponsor approach, but this was a little different.

It worked. Imagine Cruising wanted to be my sponsor and, just like Get Kids Going, became my biggest cheerleaders.

Once again, they helped me believe in myself and supported me to the end of my career. This belief helped me to keep going.

What's even more special is that they now sponsor Chris. It's been an amazing link up for which I'm truly grateful.

Incidentally, James Phipps has continued to pop up in my life at exactly the right time. He was there to offer advice when I went self-employed and, as a trustee for Wiltshire Air Ambulance, it was him who put me forward as an ambassador for the charity. This all evolved on the very night I won an award, which I later found out he nominated me for.

He's also put me in touch with the amazing Fiona Scott, who helps both Chris and I with our PR; we'd be lost without her now. So many opportunities have come my way because of him, so thanks James.

A great reminder of the positive power of networking in your local community.

Chapter 28:

From Top To Bottom and Back Again

2016. The year of the Rio Paralympics and this was a huge turning point in my life. Everything changed dramatically.

For London, I had given 100% and had scraped qualification. At Rio I wanted to do better. I had to give 110%.

The difference between these two Paralympic cycles was recognising the need for that extra 10%. It was the first time in my life I understood I had that bit more gas in the tank to work with.

I was in top form, having my best ever year of tennis. I was beating players I'd never beaten before. I was at my highest ever ranking - Number 10 in the world.

Having only played ten tournaments that year, it was a time of self-reflection and realisation. I was doing really well, and I was performing well at the right times.

It was a major contrast when I looked back to the four years prior to London 2012. To qualify for the home games, I was ranked 18 in the world but had been scraping around for points on the tennis tour and played 25 tournaments to get there.

It made the 2016 ranking even more of a big deal. For the first time ever, I felt like I had that really deep inner self belief in terms of my capabilities.

I felt strong on court. I felt like I knew what I was doing, and I was so excited to build on that.

At Rio I drew Dana first round. Could you believe it? Out of 32 women in that draw, I drew one of my best friends. Up until that point, we had both beaten each other in competition, but in Rio it was her day, not mine. She played super well and outperformed me.

It was such an odd feeling because I was devastated, but if I had to lose to anyone, I was glad it was her. I genuinely wanted her to do well but, of course, in that moment, it didn't matter who it was. I had lost and I was so disappointed.

The irony is that Dana was the one who comforted me that evening and talked me through our match. The same, beautiful friend who'd been there for me on tour, sharing bedroom picnics which became our escape and safe space. Making me smile at a time when I felt so low and alone.

No-one from the national team offered me any support or words of feedback on my performance. It was my opponent who supported me afterwards. Such a bizarre scenario, but how lucky was I to have a friend like Dana?

When I returned from Rio, I was feeling pretty good going into my annual performance review.

A review like this is a chance to assess an athlete's performance over the past 12 months, evaluating whether goals have been met and plan for the coming year. All this is linked to athlete funding.

Traditionally this would be a time when I would lose sleep the night before worrying. I would often go into the meeting in tears. I'd be so worried about being kicked off the programme, losing all my funding and having my dream, my life, my job taken away.

But in 2016 things were different. I'd had such a good year, my results were so good, my highest ever world ranking, that I went to the review with my coach, Ali, who'd been working with me since I was five years old, and everything felt great.

I can still remember the conversation in the car with him, it went something like this:

Ali: "You're a bit quiet." (Always a worry, as I'd usually be in a bit of a state at this stage).

Me: "Well, I feel really good about this, like I've done everything I could possibly do. I've met my goals, I've done really well."

Ali: "Exactly."

When we got to the review, however, there was an odd atmosphere in the air. Within the first few sentences, I heard:

"You're off the programme."

Then this...

"We're not going to fund you anymore."

In that moment I felt like every ounce of self-belief I'd managed to find had been ripped from my soul.

During that horrendous meeting, I basically begged for them to give me a chance to get back on the programme. I kept asking what I could do to change their mind.

We drove home and Ali asked me what I was thinking.

"I'm just not done yet", I replied. "I don't want to be done. I'm the best I've ever been."

Ali's response was perfect: "Don't be done then."

Me: "Well, how am I going to do this? My tennis programme is extortionate. It's so expensive to be a wheelchair tennis player (at the time I was looking at a minimum of 40k to cover my costs alone).

Ali: "Okay, so if you don't want to be done, we're going to find a way. Go home. Think about it."

The next day I picked Chris up from Birmingham airport. He'd been abroad training, so we had a big chat on the way home. This was a huge thing for us to deal with at such an early stage in our relationship. At this point, we'd only been together for a couple of months.

Chris was horrified by the outcome of my meeting and as he was an athlete, really understood how much this situation hurt me.

He spoke so similarly to Ali and promised to support me in whatever choice I made, but encouraged me to carry on. He told me that he would help me find a way to do this if that was what I really wanted.

The following morning, I woke up with Chris and together we made a plan.

I rang Ali and we made more plans. Three crucial elements to success. First up was funding.

I spoke to my sponsors: Imagine cruising had been so incredibly supportive for the past couple of years of my career, and Get Kids Going, the charity who supported me from day one with my sports chairs and other funding. Alongside this, the wonderful Danny Clayton had also sponsored me with all my physio and massage needs.

I explained my need for more funding and what had happened, and they all stepped up for me. I couldn't believe it. Their emotional support and belief in me made all the difference. I had just been told I wasn't good enough, but they thought differently. They believed in me and felt I was still worth investing in and supporting. That meant the world.

In contrast, after a few weeks of conversation, the national performance programme, agreed to give me 3k a year for a couple of years – I think to keep me quiet. Access to some training camps was offered, but it felt like a token gesture which didn't help much.

Step 2 was about helping my mental health. Cue some honest conversation with Ali. He recognised I was not in a good space. His words of wisdom? "You're unhappy and you know a happy athlete is a good athlete, right? You need to get some support."

It was time to acknowledge that when I was in a terrible headspace, I was never going to perform like I wanted to, so something had to change.

Counselling had worked for me before and I knew it would work for me again, so I got back in touch with counsellor, Sheila, explained what had happened and booked myself in with her for more sessions, this time funded by me.

Chapter 29:

Tennis Takes a Back Seat

Off the tennis programme and I needed an income.

Who was going to employ me when I would have to regularly be away training and competing?

Luckily for me, the DWP (Department for Work and Pensions), gave me a job.

I'd always done work alongside my playing career, giving talks and working as an athlete mentor, but the DWP role was a big deal. When I was on APA funding (which is lottery funding), mortgage advisers would not recognise it as an income. So, this would change everything.

I'd be working across our district of job centres, which was massive.

Working two days a week, my role was to upskill job centre staff in how to work with young people with disabilities. I would help them move off benefits and find employment.

It was a really cool job and I loved having the chance to work with some customers face to face.

My whole aim was to change attitudes and perceptions, build better relationships with local providers and help people find independence.

I covered the whole of Dorset, Wiltshire, Hampshire, Isle of White and learned so much in the role. One of the biggest things it did for me was to break down a bit of the pre-perception and stigma I sub-consciously carried around job centres.

I learned that everyone working there really wanted to help people, but had to work within very strict rules and regulations.

I had a fixed term contract, but after they extended a second time, I couldn't stay in the role. I left because I couldn't bear how tight the rules and regs were. There was no wriggle room which meant I couldn't help people in the way I wanted.

I became increasingly frustrated in the role. I'd come up with lots of great ideas, but because it went against 'normal' procedure or wasn't involving one of their products or contacts, it would be shelved. On the rare occasions when something was given the green light, it would take months and months to action, and by then we would lose the person we were trying to help. It was so frustrating.

Then there was the other thing that drove me nuts. My main base was at Swindon Job Centre. I had a nice, separate office. That was great, but the only accessible toilet was on the 4th floor and I wasn't allowed to use the lift due to health and safety concerns.

So, I worked there for 18 months and couldn't use a toilet in my building for the vast majority of that time. Ironically, they managed to get things sorted in the month I left the role. For the time I was there, I used to push across the road and use the toilet in a retail store.

The set up in my office meant there was a men's toilet downstairs and a women's toilet upstairs.

"Why don't you just convert the men's toilet into either a disabled, unisex or multi-purpose toilet?" I suggested. "You could do that by just shoving an appropriate sign on it to start with, and then eventually you could make a bigger cubicle for wheelchair users in there. That would solve the problem in the short and long term," I added.

But no go. In typical government fashion, DWP wouldn't budge.

So, for 17 months things stayed the same. It was one of the main reasons why I decided to move on.

Having aired these frustrations, the DWP role paid well and allowed me to fund my programme and buy a house.

It was the first job which paid a salary, that I had alongside my training and competing, and it was a real silver lining moment.

I loved the experience as it introduced me to a variety of people and enabled me to get my first step on the mortgage ladder.

After 18 months, I moved to a mental health and learning disability charity, Phoenix Enterprises in Swindon.

I'd been working with a young person and took her to meet the team at Phoenix which is when I was asked to get involved.

I spent time at their offices and loved their holistic approach. One thing that's really important to me is being really open and flexible when helping people with disabilities and mental health issues; everybody's different and require different things.

Phoenix allowed me to work in this way. The staff said they didn't mind what I did as long as it was the right thing for the person I was working with, to get them where they needed to go. I fell in love with that concept. Even today we still have this lovely, flexible working method. We've all got our roles, but if we want to do something outside the box that's going to help a person, then that's what we do. I find that really empowering and I can see the massive difference from it.

Both DWP and Phoenix always appreciated my honesty that tennis was still a big part of my life, and my roles would need to fit in alongside my sport.

The great thing is that both organisations were really understanding and flexible.

With so much changing for me, from the beginning of 2017 until the start of lockdown, I was pretty exhausted. I had also been working for an amazing organisation called Wilts CIL at this time too, and was starting to investigate the world of self-employment.

Being constantly busy meant I was ill quite often. A big part of my disability means if I get run down, don't get enough rest or sleep, I can be affected quite badly; guaranteed UTIs, and I had lots.

During this time, I can still remember one heart sinking moment at a tennis training camp.

I'd got really bad blisters on my hands after training for a couple of hours, which was a real first since I'd seen the work/tennis balance shift for me.

"Oh, not been training, have we? Look at those hands," commented one of the players. That comment ripped through me. I wanted to burst into tears.

With less time to train, I wasn't as robust which meant my beloved tennis had to take a backseat sometimes. It was a tough adjustment.

I have no idea how I found the energy to keep going with work and training, but I did.

I was certainly running on empty, but although relentless and exhausting at times, it was also one of the most empowering chapters of my life.

Yes, I was tired and juggling things, but I was in control - the master of my own destiny. It felt incredible.

Emotionally and physically drained, I was still able to get my head in the game and my self-confidence and belief back. It made me realise I could do anything if I put my mind to it.

To those who had said: "You're not good enough, we're not going to support you, we don't believe in you," it was most definitely a two finger gesture moment.

It was up to me to decide what I wanted to believe and what I wanted to achieve.

In my employment specialist role at Phoenix, which I still do part-time today on a self-employed basis, I help adults with learning disabilities and mental health issues find employment.

I love working with people there. I have always been determined that my disability will not hold me back, so now I help others feel the same and reach their full potential.

I strongly believe that having a disability, mental health issue or learning disability can actually become your superpower.

Facing adversities and struggles every day can teach us many things, such as becoming super resilient. It's a huge advantage, especially in the workplace.

I've learned through my own life experiences how having independence and earning your own income can change your life. It's a game changer in terms of growing your confidence and creating opportunities, so I love sharing my knowledge with others.

Bitten by the tennis bug: All smiles at Delta Tennis Centre, Swindon in 1996.
Swindon Advertiser

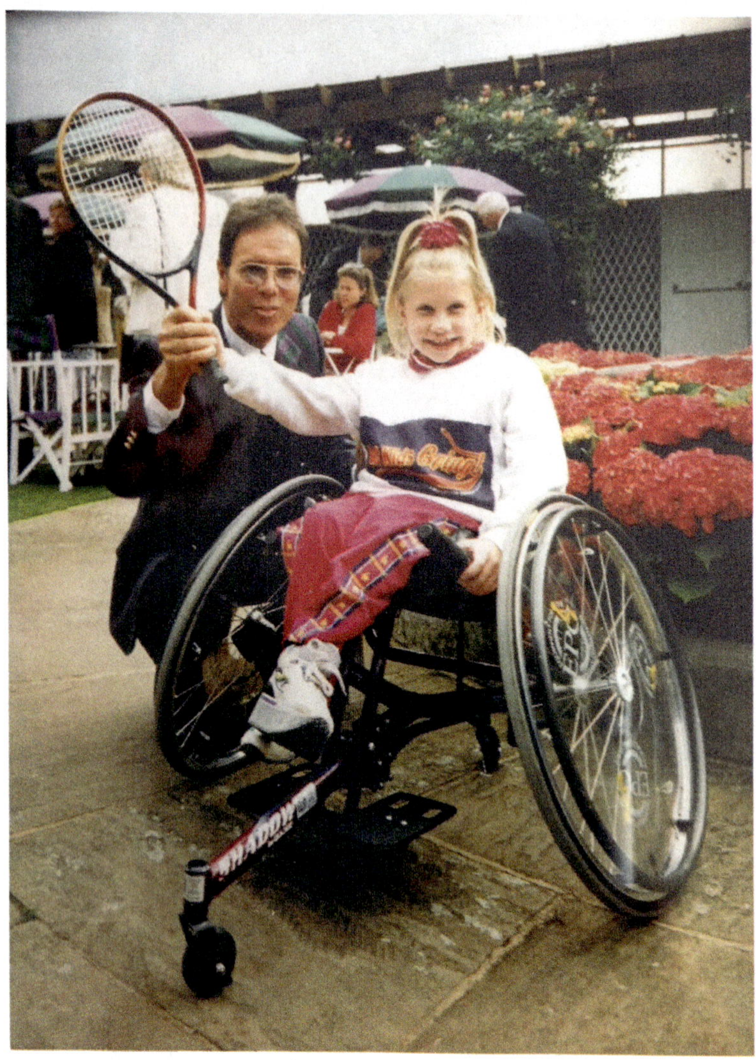

Receiving my first tennis chair, funded by Get Kids Going, from Sir Cliff Richard, Members Enclosure, Wimbledon, 1997.

Celebrating a London mini marathon win.
Swindon Advertiser

Flying the flag in Holland for my first trip abroad for a junior tennis training camp.

School life rebellion: Our classic go to pose with Sam (left) and Jack (right).

My beloved Gramp taught me so much. Here we are in his sacred field where we quad biked.

I'm so blessed to have the most amazing family who have supported me every step of the way.
Swindon Advertiser

My first trip to Ghana in 2012 changed my life in so many ways. I can't wait to go back.

Having fun with Rob, Nana and Grandad at a family celebration in Worlingworth, Ipswich.

Hannah, me, Lorna and Mum in our beloved bluebell woods, recreating a photo taken when Hannah and I were children.

A dream comes true: This image with my fellow Wheelchair Tennis teammates at the opening ceremony in London is my favourite pic of my whole career. It even made it onto a Royal Mail stamp!
David Davies/PA Images via Getty Images

We made it! Ali and I at our first Wimbledon, circa 2015.

In action at Wimbledon in 2016.
Shaun Botterill/Getty Images Sport via Getty Images

Chris and I celebrate our engagement with my 'beautiful rock' clearly on display.
Claire March

Run away bridegroom (and bride): The look on my face says it all. What a beautiful day!
Neil Bryars, Holbrook Manor

Sharing our big day with the family was so special. Left to right:
Dad, Nan, Chris, Me, William, Abby (Benji in belly), Rob and Mum.
Neil Bryars, Holbrook Manor

My Bride Squad with Chris and I on our special day. Left to right
(me, Josh, Bethan, Abby, Hannah, Becky, Claire, Jordy and Chris).
Neil Bryars, Holbrook Manor

Our Honeymoon in The Maldives: Jet skis, parasailing, swimming with sharks.
We did it all and I loved it. I felt amazing.

However busy our schedules, wherever we are in the world, our quality time together is sacred.
Barbara Leatham

Bravo for Beach Chairs (but we need more available):
Dad and I relaxing in the Bahamas on a private island - Ocean Cay.

Precious poolside family time: Chris takes a selfie with me, William, Mum, Dad, Benjamin, Rob and Abby.

Such a proud moment at Windsor Castle in 2022 as Chris and I celebrate his MBE.

Dana and I in Bolton in 2023, where I was tournament director and she won the title. The best doubles partner and friend I could ask for.

The two main men in my life: Chris and rescue pup, Milo.
Claire March

Tennis runs through my veins and will always be part of me, but now there are new dreams on the horizon. I can't wait to see them develop and flourish.
Barbara Leatham

Our fairytale finale in Paris. So much love, joy and pride to take us 'to infinity and beyond!'

Chapter 30:

Double, No Trouble

From day one of my playing career, I always played doubles. At national junior camps, aged five or six, I was playing both singles and doubles.

However, I got better a lot quicker at doubles and my ranking was higher for a long time. It was definitely the area where I really excelled.

It took me quite a while to get my singles ranking to match my doubles ranking.

I'm not entirely sure why this was the case.

I certainly loved the different dynamics that doubles brought and I felt safe having someone with me on the court.

It felt easier to be braver and more adventurous with my playing style with a doubles partner.

In my singles game I was defensive for so long, whereas in doubles I felt free to try a variety of approaches to my game.

It clearly paid off because I was getting much better results.

Throughout my career, I only played women's doubles, although I did play at the British Open in a mixed doubles event once. My partner was Dave Phillipson who I'd known since I was five years old. We entered a trial doubles competition in Nottingham (where we both first started playing) just for a bit of fun, but made it to the final where we eventually lost to my friend, Jordy and her partner - another British player.

It was so much fun and I absolutely loved the experience. If mixed doubles had been brought in when I was playing, I probably would have pursued it as it made things really interesting. I loved the dynamic of having men on the court as well.

Playing singles and doubles obviously requires the same basic tennis skills, but for doubles, where you're playing matches with different partners, you can assign yourself a different role and be more explorative with tactics, which I loved.

Ninety per cent of the time I would play on the backhand side with any partner because my backhand was so much stronger than my forehand.

On court, my biggest strength as mentioned earlier, was my reverse backhand. It's a topspin backhand played with the same grip as your forehand, using the same side of the strings. This is common in the wheelchair game as it is beneficial due to one less grip change and the fact that with this technique you can generate more height and spin - ideal when you're playing from a chair as you're closer to the height of the net than a standing player. You don't see this version in standing tennis very often as it's not as much of an advantage.

So often, because I was consistent and fast, I'd end up playing the baseline role. I would cover my partner all the time because I could do it pretty easily and I liked doing it.

Dana, who became such a great friend both on and off court, and still is today, was my favourite person in the world to share that doubles court with.

What I really loved about playing with her in particular, was that she could deliver those really hard, fast balls from the back of the court. They were so effective and could really set me up as her doubles partner.

This fabulous partnership meant that my role changed. Though I did some running around at the back of the court, I discovered I was really good at the net. With Dana I could spend so much time there because she had a more powerful baseline shot than me and could set me up for those short balls at the net.

I'd happily just sit at the net waiting for the ball. I loved playing with her as she instilled so much confidence in me that I could play this way. She believed in my ability, as I did hers. As a partner, it was a powerful game changer. It made me feel so safe and trusted. I was always in awe of her tennis ability and together we made an epic team.

We made such a great doubles partnership that we got to the final of the Masters in Holland in 2018 and this is where those tactics shone through.

When we look back on that time, we still can't quite believe how well we played. I just didn't miss a ball that week. I have never played so well in my life, and it was magic.

I think a big part of that was because we were friends and Dana made me feel safe and so capable. I love her for that. What we also did so well, was when one of us was having a blip, we knew exactly how to support the other to ride that wave. It happens in every match; the joy of momentum swings, but we always knew how to keep the other one going if we were struggling.

After I was kicked off the programme, it took me a year to get myself back on track. Dana rode that wave with me.

I was with a partner who believed in my ability, who believed in me. It was a case of 'you go there and do your thing, I've got your back and I'm going to set you up for the winner.' Everything about our partnership just worked.

At The Masters we were unseeded, but Dana said: "We're just going to play, we're going to have fun. We deserve to be here." It was just what was needed.

I would have loved to have felt as successful in terms of my Paralympic doubles opportunities, but unfortunately this never happened.

It really was a case of always the bridesmaid, never the bride when it came to the British doubles team. Even when I was ranked 10 in the world for a couple of years, there were always two other British women ranked above me, so they became the favoured doubles pairing.

The performance team wasn't brave enough to take a punt on me, even though my results spoke for themselves, and that was so hard.

At London 2012 I wasn't experienced enough to be in a doubles pairing. The two women above me in the rankings were absolutely the right choice. However, in Rio, I proved my worth that year. I got my ranking into a place where I'd have matched the seeding of my fellow competitors.

It really hurt that being number 10 in the world wasn't good enough in our country at that time. I think, bar four others, every other country I would have been number one in.

There was such a high level of skill within our national team then, so my timing was so unfortunate.

Today, I'm so grateful for the experience in many ways, but I still remember how brutal it was, that being number 10 wasn't good enough, being a Master's finalist wasn't good enough and the two women above me were always chosen for everything.

Equally, I think this situation is what pushed me to get better. Having that competition, I was so hungry to try and go above them and fight for that place on the doubles team.

Today I can see the benefits of situations like this. It's good when you've got somebody above you that you're trying to beat in competition and get better at. It pushes you in a positive way.

It's also good when someone's coming up behind you. I had that in my career too, and it certainly helped me to improve my game.

Chapter 31:

Popping The Question

Christmas Day 2019 and Chris and I bought each other the same present - Afternoon Tea at The Ritz - a bucket list gift.

That's what you do in a long term relationship, right? You buy gifts that are experiences that you can both enjoy.

I'd long dreamed of taking afternoon tea in one of the country's most luxurious hotels, so discovering that Chris had bought us the same present meant double the excitement.

We were all ready to book in for our afternoon treat in the capital in 2020, but then lockdown hit in March.

As we all kept to our bubbles, Chris was on a secret mission.

An engagement ring, which I now lovingly refer to as my beautiful rock, was finding its way to Chris' mum in Hull for safekeeping, and I had no clue.

Months earlier, Chris and I had been on a cruise around Norway. Chris had been asking me to let him know what types of rings I liked for ages, and I had tried loads, but nothing ever felt quite right.

I was starting to feel really deflated about it actually, and then I saw it. Sparkling away in a very expensive jewellery shop - there it was, pulling me in. I think Chris was meant to encourage me into that shop that day because it was crazy how I just saw it.

It's a stunning white gold ring with multiple diamonds. Nothing like anything else I had tried on before.

I tried the ring on and OMG! It was love at first sight.

Chris looked at me and I could read his mind. 'Shit, why did I bring her in here?' I could hear his thoughts screaming as the ring came with a hefty price tag, but he was always grinning from ear to ear as we'd finally found it.

"That's your ring, isn't it?" the shop assistant asked. Smiling, as I handed the ring back, we left the store. It was just exquisite.

It really was a gorgeous ring, but considerably over budget.

I tried not to give it another thought as we headed back to the ship.

Chris did though. That beautiful rock was coming home... eventually. I just didn't know it yet.

Chris had another big surprise too.

In September, between lockdowns, hotels began to open up. We decided to book in for one of our afternoon teas at The Ritz.

As a special treat, and because we hadn't been able to have a holiday, Chris booked us a room for the night.

He was so organised and took care of everything. He wouldn't even let me sort out the parking.

Being organised is not his role in our relationship. I should have sussed something was going on then.

Arriving at The Ritz the day before our afternoon tea, Chris could not wait to get out of the car. He legged it before I had a chance to say a thing.

I thought it was a bit strange, but I had no idea why he'd gone running inside. It turns out that Chris had arranged for The Ritz to put loads of decorations up, but two days before, those plans were out the window due to Covid rules.

Instead, Chris asked for rose petals in our room, but they could only do it if we supplied them. The only place he could order them from, last minute, was Ann Summers. Hilariously, he had them delivered to my parents' house so I didn't see them. That took some explaining!

The reason for his quick car exit was to hand the petals to Ritz staff before we went to the room. It was a small, but important part of his surprise.

I can just picture him fretting beyond belief as he tried to sort stuff out.

Our room was amazing. So beautiful, and even had two bathrooms. It was perfect.

After sitting down for our evening meal, Chris said he needed to pop back to the room to replace his hearing aid batteries. This is pretty normal for Chris, although he was gone for quite a while.

He came back to the table, we finished dinner and then took some lovely photos around the hotel.

When we got back to the room, I opened the door. The room was full of flowers, non-alcoholic champagne (I don't drink) and balloons spelling out a very special question: *will you marry me?*

Scattered on the bed were the rose petals Chris had done so well to hide from me.

Letting those four important words soak in, I turned around to find Chris, down on one knee, waiting with that beautiful ring, for my answer.

There was no hesitation. Just a heart full of love and a big *'Yes!'* from me.

I was crying, Chris was crying - it was the perfect proposal.

I don't think many words came out for ages. We were both just too caught in the emotion.

When we'd discussed marriage in the past, Chris had always been careful to ask if there was anything I wouldn't want in a proposal. I had told him that all I didn't want, was to include other people in our special moment.

For me, your proposal is the part of your wedding that is yours and yours alone. Chris understood this and completely nailed it.

Half an hour after he proposed, Chris was shattered. He'd had my ring in his responsibility, had planned every last detail and hadn't stopped.

I spent all evening planning the announcement of our proposal and making a priority list of people we were going to tell. Meanwhile, Chris slept on.

Apart from telling our parents, we agreed that we would have the next day just for us before sharing news of our engagement.

I found out later that Chris had asked Dad's permission for my hand in marriage when they were kayaking together. He felt it was right to ask when they were doing something they love -

being active. Apparently, Chris chose a moment when things got pretty rocky and dangerous and he nearly stacked it out of the kayak.

In his wedding speech he joked that Dad had nearly killed him during their watery adventure. Dad was over the moon when Chris said he wanted to marry me because he loves him like his own son and says he couldn't think of anyone better for his daughter.

He talked about that so beautifully in his wedding speech, saying that he loves the two of us together and totally understands how we're the perfect team.

The day after Chris' proposal we enjoyed our wonderful afternoon tea. I look exhausted in many of the pics because I was. I didn't sleep that whole weekend, not one wink, but it was so worth it.

It was an amazing couple of days. A fairytale proposal, a fairytale romance with a fairytale ring and a fairytale prince. Bliss.

I felt, and still feel, so very, very lucky. I just love remembering that weekend. Chris knows me so blooming well. He got everything perfect. I couldn't have imagined anything better.

Chapter 32:

Hooray For the Happy Van and Magical Milo

There has never been a better vehicle than The Happy Van. Why? Because it brought us Milo, our beautiful canine companion.

Our dear rescue pup arrived in England from Spain in what is commonly referred to as the Happy Van which transports dogs looking for forever homes.

He was five months old and the last one in his litter to be rehomed. We fell in love as soon as we clapped eyes on him, via Facebook.

Milo is one of my favourite topics. As I write, he's laid out in the sunshine, basking like the little Spanish sun loving pooch that he is.

He's frequently joining me on Zoom calls and I love nothing more than exploring the Great Outdoors with him.

Milo came into our lives just before the pandemic hit and we named him before we adopted him.

At the time, the CEO of Phoenix had rescued dogs from a shelter in Spain and would frequently share details of animals up for adoption.

Initially, there was talk of Milo becoming the charity's therapy dog, but he had an instant bond with us and we knew we just had to adopt him.

I was still competing at the time, so there was lots of discussion to ensure we could provide the right home and support for his needs.

When Chris and I picked him up for the first time, I cannot tell you how we fell in love at first sight. As we drove home, he fell asleep in Chris' arms. I'd never seen anything so beautiful in my life. I remember thinking, 'Oh my gosh, he is ours.'

His first night at home and he had us wrapped around his little paw. We'd got everything ready for him – toys, bed, cage, blankets for the kitchen – so he could pick what was comfortable for him. We'd never had our own dog before (Chris had family dogs), so we really spoilt him. Was he happy with the cage/bed we got him? He hated what was on offer, basically.

What did we do? We made the classic rookie dog owner mistake. We gave in (as all good dog owners do, right? ;-)) and let him sleep on our bed. There's never been any going back since, and I wouldn't change it for the world.

On that first night, Milo in the middle of the bed, laid on his back, snoring, fast asleep and beautifully content. Chris and I laid either side of him, whispering: "Do you think he's happy?" Of course he was. Chris and I hardly got a wink of sleep because we just kept looking at him. We loved him instantly and wanted him to be able to live his best life.

Lockdown hit just over two weeks later, and it gave us the perfect opportunity to work on Milo's training.

We put so much quality time into instilling good behaviours. Within a few days we realised Milo would need to quickly learn that, post lockdown, we would not be able to spend every waking hour with him. The last thing we wanted was for Milo to develop separation anxiety.

So, we made a massive effort to get him used to being home alone. We'd take him for his daily walk, settle him back home and then pop out around the block. First for 10 minutes, then 20, then gradually build up the time he was left.

When we were allowed to create a lockdown bubble, our neighbours and Mum and Dad helped with Milo's training too.

Milo's behaviour has improved so much since we had him. When he first joined us, he was really scared of all vehicles, so we would sit with him in the car on the drive. He's gone from trembling, when he got in the car, to happily trotting up to it and jumping in.

When he gets in the car with me now, he's so happy. He lays there, puts his little head on the armrest and just stares up at me as I drive.

No matter how long the journey is, he's happy and content. I'm so grateful for our lockdown time together because it totally transformed our relationship with him.

When Chris has been away for training and competition, Milo has been my constant companion.

He's been beside me for some of the highest and lowest points in my life.

In April 2024, Milo and I were featured for #National-PetMonth as a great example of the power of the human-animal bond.

I told the national organisation, which promotes responsible pet ownership, Milo reminds me every day of what truly matters in life; that he needs me and I need him.

I described Milo as my adventure buddy, best friend and ultimate companion through and through.

I'm never truly happier than when he's by my side.

Chapter 33:

Taking My Career in a New Direction

I've seen a lot of friends go through a horrific time transitioning from a sporting life into one outside of that, and it's really hard to see. It was always on my mind. There were moments when doubt crept in and I questioned whether I was making a mistake, but I was determined to take my career in a new direction. I saw how things didn't work for others, so I was determined to carve out a new path for myself.

Ultimately, by taking me off the performance programme, the federation did me the biggest favour around self-reflection and where I wanted to be long term. I got to have five years where I was my own boss. I could play tennis where I wanted, with whom I wanted, and that was brilliant. I may have never been more ill or felt more tired in my life, but there was no-one to make me feel small anymore or judge my worth against others. I was in charge, and that was pretty cool.

Though I never doubted my decision to stop playing on the tour, I was worried about telling my team, sponsors, friends and family, through fear of letting them down.

Of course, nothing was as bad as I'd imagined.

I was at training, on court, in Royal Wootton Bassett, my regular club, when I took this massive decision to retire.

It followed a difficult, but ultimately, positive, life changing conversation with my team.

Ali: "Why are you here?"

Me: "I'm here to train."

Ali: "Why do you train?"

Me: "Because that's what I do."

Ali: "That's not a good enough answer."

The questions continued as Shaun and Chris, my hitting partners, joined the conversation, (these guys have been by my side for years too and contributed so much to my career)

Then....

Ali: "What are you striving to achieve anymore? You've achieved everything you wanted and more. Paralympics twice. Wimbledon twice. Top 10 in the world."

Then Shaun, added: "And you met Chris. What else could you possibly want from this chapter of your life?"

Boom! And there it was.

Eye opening. Life changing. I was done.

The sense of relief afterwards was huge. I felt on top of the world.

I was done, so done. I was not going to train tomorrow. It felt incredible.

The experience of taking ownership, making a decision and sticking to it, built my confidence no end.

For the first time ever, I was able to say: "I am worth more than the label put on me by others."

I am the only person who should be making decisions about what happens to me and what I should be doing.

I am the one who deserves to be happy with my success and where I'm heading.

It was time to put the energy into my own self-care and the people I cared about. Those who would reciprocate.

Leaving all this baggage behind was life changing.

I've always been someone who loves to support others to live their best life, but I think I'm a better person now. I've become more level headed, have a better perspective and a really balanced life. I was never this happy when I was an athlete.

That day was pivotal and I will forever be so grateful to Ali, Chris and Shaun for that... let's call it an 'intervention' chat, because that's just what I needed, just at the right time, and truly shows how well they knew me and how much they cared.

Chapter 34:

True Colours

While footballers and rugby players get caps for representing their country, tennis players get colours.

My colour holder number is 273 and I'm proud to be in a long list of fellow players who have competed for our country in the sport we love most.

I am incredibly proud to have represented Great Britain at 2 Paralympic Games and 13 World Team Cups around the globe.

I was invited to the National Tennis Centre in London, to celebrate the re-introduction of British Colour Holders.

A colour holder status (that's me!) is achieved when a wheelchair tennis player rolls out onto a court to play for Great Britain.

The re-introduction of Colour Holders marked 125 years since the first players went out on court to represent Great Britain at the 1896 Olympics.

It was developed to acknowledge, recognise and celebrate players, past and present, who have represented the country in the Davis Cup, Billie Jean King Cup and Wheelchair Tennis World Team Cup, plus the Olympic Games and Paralympic Games.

As I'm so passionate about equality for all, it's incredibly refreshing to see wheelchair players and able-bodied players being recognised at the same level.

Competing at the top level of any sport and representing your country is every athlete's ambition and I still have to pinch myself to realise that I've done it 15 times.

Chapter 35:

Travel Nightmares: Time For Change

Tickets, passport, money. A familiar mantra before we embark on an overseas trip.

Here's what else I have to add to the mix. Say, I'm travelling to a tournament. I'm in my everyday chair and pushing my tennis chair. Wheels are in a wheel bag. Tennis bag, racket bag, clothes bag. Day chair, tennis chair. I've got five pieces of luggage that I have to get around the world on my own.

It's amazing how you master this but, at times, travelling by plane as a disabled person has been not far from the definition of hell, and one of the reasons why I got so sick of how I was treated when travelling during my career.

Seven tennis chairs broken, two of which had the frames snapped in half. I saw one of them break. I was getting onto the plane and there it was. Up on its front wheels almost with the back wheel sticking out of the plane. I told the grounds people what was happening: "You shut the door and you're going to break it." They didn't listen. I arrived at my destination and there was my chair on the conveyor belt in two pieces.

There is nothing that hurts and terrifies you more than someone taking your wheelchair away and you don't know where it is. You can spend time explaining why you find this difficult and why they can't store your chair in a certain way or fold it up. You can ask them to be careful, but no one seems to listen.

Whether I've been travelling for an hour to Europe or I'm on a 24-hour flight to Australia, I'm always thinking, 'holy shit, am I going to be able to get off this plane? Have they put my chair on the aircraft at all, and if they have, is it broken? Can I use it?' and that is stressful.

Ever needed the loo on a flight? Of course you have. Me too. Well imagine, if you can't get to the loo, or if you can, you can't shut the door.

For me to use a toilet on board I require an aisle chair – a chair small enough to fit between the seats of the aisle which someone else has to push. I've been on flights where this vital piece of equipment has not been on board. No aisle chair, I can't go to the loo, although in desperation I have been known to crawl down the aisle of the plane to get to the toilet.

Other times when I've been taken to the loo in the aisle chair, I've had to transfer onto the toilet with the door open because the space is too small. No privacy.

There are so many stories like this impacting many people with a disability and it's all pretty shocking that it still happens today. I've lost count of how many times I've landed somewhere and they've forgotten to book assistance for me.

Then there's the moment of arrival at your destination. Seat belt signs are switched off and you're raring to grab your baggage from the overhead locker and depart the aircraft. Not me. The longest I've sat on an aircraft after landing is two hours - either because assistance hasn't been booked/turned up or they can't find my chair.

Why can that happen? Often because my chair has been sent off with the luggage, even though I've told them you can't put a wheelchair on a conveyor belt. I need it when I get off the plane.

But instead, I end up sitting in a chair that I can't balance in (remember I need a special cushion to sit upright 'comfortably'), waiting for my chair to be found. That's really uncomfortable.

Travelling by air with a physical disability is hard, but I do it because I love to explore.

It's difficult to explain just how much pain and discomfort I'm in after any flight. Those chairs aren't comfortable for anyone but, for me, having my legs down is really tough. Lack of circulation, swelling, can be awful. Obviously I can't get up and move around and I can't change position. So, I'm stuck and it makes me feel rigid.

On a flight to Australia once I was so desperate to move position that I transferred onto the floor in the aisle and tried to lay down flat for a while. Anything to relieve the discomfort.

Touch down and I've also had chairs not turn up at all. Sometimes they'll end up in the wrong country.

I can still remember coming back from a world team cup to see my friend's chair come off the plane in England with the rest of our stuff. I rang him. "Oh f**K!" was his response. He lives in Australia.

The ground crew had seen the chair, not bothered to look for its destination and thrown it on board because there were other similar chairs on our flight.

All of this can be a bit of a nightmare, but as I love to travel, I have to get on with it and plough through in robotic mode.

I've been flying solo since I was young, but that stress never really leaves me. It's a constant worry. The thing I can't bear is sitting on a flight for a long time knowing that my chair might not even be on the plane with me.

In my competition days I'd be going to countries I'd never been to before, where I didn't speak the language. I'd be thinking, 'if I get here and my chair's not with me, I'm screwed.'

The psychological and physical impact of this could not be underestimated, especially when combined with the demands of preparing for competition.

On arrival, while some would go and train, I would need to go and get out of my chair. I could never even think about going to the courts until I got to my hotel room, sat on my bed and stretched out, moved my body because it hurt so much. A bath, heat, always helps.

I'm always getting out of my chair because it's really uncomfortable being trapped in one position all day.

There's this weird perception that it's alright for anyone in a chair because 'you've always got a seat.' Try sitting in the same position for 16 hours a day and then come back to me on that.

It's why I'm so grateful for the physios and sports masseuses I have worked with over the years. These incredible humans, with the hands of gods and goddesses, are often available at tournaments and are so ready to help.

When you talk to those on the wheelchair tour, they say they often do the same things all day. Shoulder, core. Shoulders, hips are tight because we're pushing a chair all day. They know their stuff and having them available was a massive game changer for me.

Now I'm not competing, I've got my own stretches and exercises, so that helps too.

Sophie Morgan, a disability activist, presenter and all-round legend, is really pushing the movement for better air travel.

In 2024, I saw her documentary Fight to Fly supporting her Rights On Flights campaign, and it made for truly heart breaking viewing.

I genuinely contemplated not watching it because I knew how sad and angry it would make me.

However, I want to support Sophie's work as it really matters to me, so Chris and I watched it together.

It made for horrifying viewing. Did you know that 43% of wheelchair users say they don't feel able to fly and that 1 in 4 wheelchairs get broken during air travel? A third of disabled people that have flown in the past five years have made an accessibility related complaint. Just remember that 1 in 4 of us are disabled, so that's a big part of the population being affected by this awful system.

Shocking stats, aren't they?

This programme reminded me how really shit it is to fly as a wheelchair user, that things are not getting better, and that's not okay.

With the Paris Paralympics just a couple of weeks away as I write this, I'm hearing about some really shitty things some athletes are going through at the moment. I always hoped it was just me having these awful experiences.

I hoped that it was just me that had bad luck with the wrong people, at the wrong time, and it kills me that it's not. It kills me that I am in quite a high statistic that sucks, and that breaks my heart.

I don't want to be part of some big, horrible statistic. The programme reminded me of how utterly traumatic flying as a disabled person can be. Story after story featured in this documentary, happened to me.

I watched as the guy dragged himself along the floor of the plane to just go for a wee because they didn't put an aisle chair on the aircraft. That happened to me.

And actually, you probably shouldn't have put me on the plane in the first place, or at least told me there was no aisle chair.

I saw people crawling down dirty aeroplane steps on their bums because the ground crew didn't plan for an ambi lift (a vehicle lift to take you off the plane if there are steps) or bring a stairlift. That happened to me.

I watched people having to sit on an aisle chair through the airport because airport staff hadn't brought their wheelchair to them. In pain, trying to balance for 30 minutes to an hour. That happened to me.

It reminded me of when a group of us were on route to Beijing airport for the Inspiration Programme.

They wouldn't bring our chairs to the aircraft to meet us as we were connecting, so they put us in aisle chairs which we couldn't push ourselves. We were taken to a room where they left my friend, who is a quadriplegic, facing the corner.

None of us could do anything about it because we couldn't move. We were on these awful chairs you can't control yourself and our friend was just there, looking into a corner.

I remember thinking how fucked up this was. What a way to treat a human being who was achieving far more than any of the rude people treating him this way.

This experience scarred me. Just like the moment when an airline refused to take my chair on the flight.

Flight attendant: "We can take you, but not your wheelchair."

Me: "Okay. Should we just think about that for a second?"

But no, they were absolutely adamant. My chair would not fit on the plane. Ridiculous, as I've seen bags bigger than my chair go on board.

So, it was my problem, not theirs, because I needed a wheelchair, and they wouldn't let me fly. They wouldn't refund my money either.

And then there was this...

Coming home from South Africa. Two of us (both wheelchair users) were told we had to go a different way around the airport to the plane, which sometimes happens. We were taken to an empty gate. We couldn't see or hear anyone else.

Airport staff: "We'll take your passports to check you in."

Me: "I don't separate myself from my passport. I need to come with you."

They kept pushing and pushing for this to happen until another player and I reluctantly allowed them to have our passports.

As we waited, I remember looking at her and thinking, 'We're in trouble. I don't know anyone here that can help us. We don't have our passports. They've taken our stuff. No-one's come back for us.'

It was getting later and later. 'Our plane's going to leave without us.'

We should have been boarding first. I don't say this out of a sense of impatience, but for purely practical reasons. Boarding first means we can get to our seats without having to work around other people. We can transfer onto our seats with dignity before other passengers arrive.

Incidentally, airlines do have an obligation to make this happen, so if you see this happening please bear this in mind and be an ally by speaking up and showing care and understanding.

Half an hour later, airport workers returned. It was 20 minutes to take off. We were stressed and upset because I knew, as a seasoned traveller, we would be unable to meet the departure time.

Boarding a flight, with all other passengers already on the plane, was the most humiliating experience.

As we were boarding and being dragged through the aisles to transfer to our seats, the captain made a public announcement.

Apologising for our late departure, he blamed us, and finding space for our wheelchairs, as the reason for the delay.

Broadcast throughout the plane, he announced: "We are delayed because of the two girls who use wheelchairs and are boarding now." A whole plane of eyes just stared at us!

We were mortified. In that very human way, everyone was looking in our direction. One woman on our aisle went a step further: "Where were you?" she demanded.

Later in the flight, the same woman, who was in the window seat next to us, asked us to get up because she needed to go to the toilet.

In answer to her request, the conversation went something like this:

Me: "I'm sorry, but I can't walk."

Woman: "Oh, you *can.*"

Me: "No, I really can't, although I'd love to actually."

With that the woman huffed and puffed and shoved past me.

Later in the flight, there was the reaction of the cabin crew when I rang the bell for assistance.

Earlier, they had watched me and my colleague be wheeled onto the plane in aisle chairs.

Me: "Could you pass me my bag please?" (In all the hustle and bustle, it had been stored in the top of an overhead locker I was unable to access).

Air steward: "Why can't you get it yourself?"

Me: "You've just boarded me on an aisle chair. Isn't it obvious?"

They handed the bag down then...

Me: "Thank you. Could you get my friend's too please?"

Air steward: "Why can't she get hers?"

Me: "Because we're both paralysed. You've watched us get on the plane. Do you really think I'd go through that rigmarole if I could just walk on and get it myself?"

At this point I just felt completely embarrassed, humiliated and sub-human and simply could not wait to get off that plane.

I can't tell you the ableist privilege that some people have. It makes me sick.

All these years I've just thought I've been really unlucky, yet statistics clearly show just how badly people with disabilities are being treated when they travel.

Watching Sophie's documentary ripped me up inside. Every single thing I was seeing had happened to me.

Ultimately, it all boils down to people and their attitudes to disability.

Sophie has pushed so hard for change, to create a wheelchair space on an aircraft so a person can remain in their wheelchair, move to the toilet and be independent, which is great.

Of course, it's not for everybody. In my case, I couldn't sit on a long flight in my chair. I'd be in agony, but would I take that option if I could? Definitely. It's a fantastic idea and a brilliant invention. I so hope it takes off (no pun intended).

What Sophie is doing is truly wonderful and I love it, but what really pisses me off is that we're having to spend all this money and energy when, very often, all we need is for people to be kind and thoughtful. That's it.

Instead, we've got to spend millions reinventing planes, creating these wheelchair spaces because we can't trust people to be kind, respectful and thoughtful, and that's so sad.

I also think we've got to think what's beyond this? If there's going to be one space for a wheelchair, that's really good. But what if I want to fly with a friend who uses a wheelchair? Who's having that space?

It's utterly tragic that we have to push so much, because for some people with a disability, sitting in an aeroplane seat is not appropriate. It's fantastic for so many people, but for me personally all I (and many others) need is someone to display kindness and thoughtfulness, and take care of our wheelchairs with respect. I don't need a special chair on a plane. Just put my chair in the hold carefully, take it back out and give it to me when we get to our destination. That's all we/I am asking for.

There's a clip in Sophie's documentary where a wheelchair flies down a luggage escalator and it made me feel physically sick. The programme was a hard watch as it brought up a lot for me, as I'm sure it will for many.

It made me so deeply sad because I love travel so much, but I need my chair more.

I'm lucky because I've seen the world, I can travel around the UK and, just like my Gramp showed me, I've found a work around. I've found another way, a method.

This is where taking cruises is brilliant. I'll still fly for things that are absolutely necessary and important to me, like going to see my friend Dana for her wedding. But outside of that, the risk isn't big enough for me anymore. When I was a competing athlete, the risk was great enough because the reward was so great.

Today I have to weigh things up when it comes to air travel. The only way I can do it is by flying first class, only because I know they treat you differently. There's no luggage restriction in the same way, so they'll take my chair on board. I've paid more money and they'll make space. I can't afford to fly first class every time, so there's another limitation there.

Our honeymoon flights to The Maldives would have been 10 grand if it wasn't for all those air miles I collected, along with Chris' British Airways Gold card he got for winning Gold at the Tokyo Paralympics.

Anxiety around air travel came up for me again in 2023 when I was asked to go and commentate on the Para European Games in Holland. I hadn't flown solo for a couple of years, and even though I'd done it a million times, the worries were still there in the back of my mind.

Thinking about this transports me back to some of my last tournaments before London 2012. I was flying back from France when I was stopped at the gate.

It was so bizarre. Here I was doing all these massive things, qualified for the London Paralympics, doing all this amazing stuff, seeing all the Superhuman billboards and then at Charles De Gaulle airport everything stopped.

Airline Staff Member: "Who are you with?"

Me: "Nobody."

Airline Staff Member: "Well, you can't fly on your own."

"Well, I got here on my own. I've been here for a week," I reply. "I live in England."

I remember looking at the woman as she refused to let me get on the plane.

"You can't travel alone," she replied.

I just couldn't understand it. I'm in France, I got here on my own. Now I want to go home to England.

Ironically, I remember looking at her and thinking, 'what's wrong with you?' Sound familiar? ;-)

The conversation continued until she said: "You need to prove to me that you can walk for me to let you on the plane." It was horrible.

I'm qualified for a home Paralympic Games and here I am begging to be allowed to fly back home so I can compete in it.

Next thing I'm making up lies just to get back.

"I can walk," and when she asked for proof, I said I couldn't because it was too painful.

But then something magical happened.

I got rescued by a complete stranger. This amazing man had heard this ridiculous conversation and jumped in to help.

"She's with me," he said.

I remember looking at him and thinking, 'do I go with this or is he a weirdo?'

"Yeah, I'm with him," I replied.

It worked. I checked in. He checked in.

This guy saved me. Even offered to meet me at the gate early so I could board with no hassle, in case they asked crazy questions again.

On the plane, he came over. I said thank you and we travelled onto London separately. What a beautiful stranger, and this is what we can be like, people.

I should never have had to rely on a stranger. It's crazy that this had to happen, but once again, here's the contrast.

I was at the pinnacle of my sport, about to represent Paralympics GB at the Paralympic Games in London and there I was still having problems flying home from a country that I flew to on my own.

Here I was travelling with one of the best bits of equipment on the planet (my sports chair) that we'd paid a fortune for because I'm one of the world's best, with the worry that it's been smashed on the journey. No chair, no competition for me.

Ready to prove that, after all those months of hard training, I was ready to take on the world's best while stressing about how I was going to get to the loo during the flight.

No matter how good I was on a tennis court, my day to day life could be freaking painful.

As you can probably tell, there are many horror stories like this to share. Far too many.

I've spent my whole life travelling solo and flew for the first time alone, when I was 14. The flying doesn't make me nervous at all. It's everything else.

I flew to Australia on my own when I was 20. I've travelled to over 40 countries now. Travel for me is really important because I think the best education anyone can ever have is from this and from meeting people. I've managed to travel, learn and get my education as well. I'm lucky because my secondary school taught me that balance.

I don't think anything of getting on an aeroplane and flying to the other side of the world. I like the independence of it. I like the bubble that you go into when you get to the airport and you can just focus on you and where you need to go.

The thing that can make me nervous and stress is the fear of what are they going to do with my luggage, my chairs, and how I and my things are going to be treated. That never changes. No matter how many times I fly, I can still be dreading what's coming.

Each one of these worries undoubtedly took its toll on my physical and mental health before, during and after competition during my tennis career.

Yet every time, even when a chair was snapped in half, I found a way to play.

One time, after giving staff an earful as I was brought my tennis wheelchair snapped in half, I found a garage near my destination. They were able to weld my chair together so I could get on court and compete. After successfully begging the tournament director and referee to put me on court a day later, I sent my chair off to be mended.

After the work, it was so heavy. I was playing on clay, plus I had the extra weight of the weld. It's probably the worst surface to play on in a welded chair, with all that drag, but at least my game really suited clay.

The show had to go on, and it did.

Moments like this really demonstrated what an excellent problem solver I can be, that I have to be, although things don't always turn out exactly how I'd like them to.

With the chairs with twisted frames, I tried to get them twisted back the other way, but it meant that when I pushed in the chair, I wasn't pushing equally and it would drag one way more than another. An added complication on court I could do without.

It was sometimes hurting my shoulders because I was overcompensating and pushing harder, so it affected me every time this happened.

Ninety nine per cent of the time, tournaments were so understanding when any player asked for a change in the schedule to allow for repairs – just as well as this happens to someone at practically every tournament I've been to. Another depressing statistic that needs to change.

In Bolton, at the start of 2024, at an international tournament which I was the tournament director for, I had two players whose chairs didn't turn up until the third day, and I had another player whose wheels never arrived. I did everything within my power, from working with the referee to tweak the schedule as best we could, and calling the airlines/airports/ anyone who'd listen to resolve these issues. It was a sad realisation that nothing has changed.

One chair was cracked so badly that the player shouldn't really have played. It was unsafe. They bodged it with help from our lovely repair guy, to make it safer, but I don't know how he even played in it.

Moments like this certainly affected the way I played. I couldn't perform at my best level.

I've had to borrow wheels when my own wheels were broken or didn't turn up. Wheels are a little bit less of a problem as, if you can get the right size/axle, they should fit and operate efficiently. Even so, it's an unnecessary complication and they're still not yours, so won't feel the same. People have different push rims, types of grip etc, everything is bespoke.

I must confess that up until my recent trip, I had enjoyed not having the stress of potential air travel problems in my life. However, my flight to and from Holland was a complete success, with lovely staff and efficient assistance. Was it luck? Who knows, but I lapped it up! Let's have more of this, please.

As Sophie's campaign gathers momentum, we're still awaiting more news on the world's first wheelchair accessible plane.

In the meantime, something that really helps resolve a lot of the issues around flying is the use of first and business class travel spaces as you get that little bit more space. The toilets are bigger, but when I was travelling for competition, I could hardly ever afford to upgrade in that way. I'd always ask for it though.

I believe the reason people like Sophie are having to push for this kind of accessibility with air travel is through fear, and that fear is validated by evidence of our chairs being destroyed, left behind and treated like a piece of generic luggage, and not like part of our bodies.

In contrast, travelling by train is such a joy. When Whisper, who employ me to work for Channel 4, asked me to commentate on the Paris 2024 Paralympics, I was clear that it was a deal breaker that I would only travel to the games by EuroStar. They responded, unsurprisingly, with total understanding and reassurance. They, of course, got it!

I would do anything to avoid the world's worst airport - Charles de Gaulle. They just don't care about disability.

Travelling by rail, I will roll onto my carriage on the EuroStar, on my own, in my wheelchair. It's flat. I wheel in, jump into a seat. My chair's right next to me. I need a wee. I get into my chair and go for a wee. I come back to my seat and sit back down again. I want a drink. I get back in my wheelchair and go buy a drink. It's wonderful.

And there's the contrast again, as Sophie points out in her documentary. She was sitting on a train and she pointed out that even though the space was actually smaller than an aeroplane, the carriage had been designed with space for a wheelchair user. So, it's kind of nuts to think that on a bigger form of transport, we haven't managed to do the same yet.

This is such a worthy campaign, but now we have to start thinking about what's beyond this if we are to be afforded the same basic human rights when it comes to quality, safe, comfortable travel. This needs to be led by people that truly deliver customer service with love and kindness for their disabled passengers. And, as I mentioned, in my opinion, this can all change for the better through people, through education, listening to those who know their stuff. There needs to be a willingness to adapt slightly, per individual, to accommodate their needs.

We're all different and that's what makes us wonderfully unique.

Chapter 36:

I'm A Fire Hazard

"Fire hazard." "You're taking up space." "You're taking too long."

Sworn at, patronised, blamed, ignored.

Celebrated, thanked, praised, loved.

This is my life.

Some days simple tasks take on huge significance.

I got fuel by myself for the first time in a year, recently and it was a really nice experience.

So nice that I messaged Becky to tell her about it.

I can't wait for the day when I don't need to message someone to say: "Wow, isn't that amazing." - when this positive experience is normal.

Accessibility has come a long way, but it still has a really long way to go.

My worry about going for fuel on my own revolved around having to park super far away from the pump to get my chair out, meaning I could be blocking space for other drivers.

I'd been avoiding going to the petrol station alone because of the awful experiences I'd had in the past.

Those comments, "you're taking too long, taking up too much space, I can't get my car through to the opposite pump" still stick in my head and my heart.

I get really tired, sometimes, of being treated as a second class citizen. A lot of it revolves around the attitudes and the perceptions that I'm incapable or simply an inconvenience.

Different fuel stations have different set-ups, and that can have an impact too.

Sometimes, those of us with disabilities are asked to beep our horn and hold up our blue badge when we get to a petrol station so someone can come and help us fill up our vehicle.

I did that once and the person in the service window was clearly not happy. They refused to come and help and, unless my lip reading is not as good as I thought it was, clearly told me to F off!

I've also rung up a petrol station or used an app on the forecourt to request help, again with a negative result.

Shopping trips can also be challenging. People won't hand over my things or take money off me. They talk to the person that's with me, instead of *to* me. In restaurants I've had people ask: "What does she want to eat?" rather than speaking to me directly.

Then there was the Peppa Pig World visit with my nephew. It was really fun until he wanted to go on one of the smaller roller coasters with me.

As I went to sit next to him, I was stopped. "You can't sit next to him," said the staff member.

"Why?" I asked.

"Because you need a carer, because you're in a wheelchair." Her response was direct and abrupt.

I'd been on all the other (much bigger and faster) roller coasters in the park, got on and off by myself, no problem, yet for some unknown reason, for this one I needed someone over 14 to sit with me. My nephew was 2 so didn't quite meet the criteria!

I'm a roller coaster junkie. All day this had not been an issue, and as much as I love my mum, brother and sister-in-law who were there with us, I didn't want to ride with them. I wanted to ride with my nephew.

If I'm honest, I had a bit of a moment at this point. I felt really sad. We're in this mad world where I couldn't sit on this coaster with my nephew, but a 14-year-old can be responsible for me. It was really strange. Where is that a rule? All day up until this point it had not been an issue. Why now?

It's interesting where your thoughts go at times like this. So, if I had a child of my own, I couldn't go on a roller coaster with them, which sucks because I'm so adventurous and love stuff like that.

Missing out on that experience made me question how I would handle things if this was with my child?

At times like this it's hard not to feel second class, where there are rules and restrictions on where I can go, where I can sit, without any real explanation or justification.

I've been to places where I've wheeled up to a table only to be told: "You can't sit here because you're a fire hazard." Those words exactly.

Well, no, I'm a person, and people can get past me.

In situations like this, I can't bear the effect this can have on me mentally. I can't bear to be patronised. It makes me feel lonely, isolated and a total inconvenience - the furthest thing from feeling human.

I am exhausted by trying to prove that I am worthy of equal rights, equal opportunity. I shouldn't have to have these conversations. I just want non-disabled people to recognise that just because part of our body may not work like theirs, it doesn't mean we're not capable.

I just want people to be treated like people. As for the pity and people feeling sorry for me, although I'm noticing this a little bit less, at least once a month I'll get a thoughtless comment again.

"I can't think of anything worse than being in a wheelchair..." They don't know me, they don't know my life. It kills me every time.

This misperception has followed me throughout my life.

I was reminded of a conversation with a boy I fancied at secondary school, recently.

After months of growing attraction, I'd finally plucked up the courage to say: "I'm into you." His reply: "I really like everything about you, but I just can't date someone in a wheelchair." "Ouch!" doesn't even cut it.

Then there was the time one of Chris' first girlfriends broke up with him when his sight started to deteriorate, and medics were trying to work out a diagnosis.

Just a few weeks ago, Chris was reminded of people's misperceptions about disability when he was at Heathrow.

He'd pre-booked assistance to help him through the airport and staff arrived with a wheelchair.

Chris has Oculocutaneous Albinism which affects his eyesight. He doesn't require a wheelchair and he didn't request one.

When Chris explained this...

Airport staff: "Well, what's broken then?"

Chris: "Sorry?"

Airport staff: "What's broken with you? You booked assistance."

Chris: "Nothing's broken. I can't see very well, so I need help navigating the airport and reading signs."

Airport staff: "What do you need a wheelchair for then?"

Chris: "I don't need a wheelchair, nor did I ask for one."

Airport staff: "We don't understand what's broken."

Then followed several minutes of Chris trying to explain hidden disabilities and what he required.

This is far too common. Often people hear disabled and think wheelchair! However, us wheelchair users are actually just a small part of the disabled community, the rest is made up of multiple other conditions, many of which you can't see.

I hear many stories like these. It makes me even more determined to share my own life experiences in a bid to open people's eyes to what it's like for people with mobility challenges.

It's also why I'd love you to become a disability ally.

All I mean by that is, please stop and think before you speak. Sometimes, if it's curiosity or a sudden comment that's entered your mind about someone's difference, always consider the impact those words may have on that individual. If you see a scenario like the one mentioned, i.e.: the airport saga, maybe just check in and say: "Can I help at all?" Often, just being seen can feel so powerful. Just remember we're human, so please treat us as you'd like to be treated - with respect, privacy and dignity.

Chapter 37:

Independence Is Asking for Help

It had been a long day. Work had been great, but full on. I was a little tired, and then the heavens opened. A full scale downpour.

I couldn't wait to get indoors, take my shoes off, change into my PJs and relax.

As I opened the car door, I was already dreaming of that cuppa when I relaxed with Milo on the sofa.

Home sweet home was tantalisingly close.

And then...the realisation.

I looked to my left and it wasn't there. No wheelchair in the passenger seat... it was still in the boot.

I had just dropped off a passenger and forgotten to ask them to move the chair from the boot to the seat so I could reassemble it on the drive and go indoors.

Now, I was stuck.

I've done this a few times over the years.

Living where we do, we have the most beautiful neighbours in the world. They are next level kindness. Amazing.

Sometimes, when I have pulled up on the driveway to discover my chair is still in the boot, I'll just ring Trish and Doug next door and say: "I'm stuck. Can you come and help me, please?"

As if by magic, Doug's been known to appear at just the right time as I arrive, just in case I might need anything.

My wonderful neighbours on the other side - Jayne and Graham - will kindly put my bin out every week and help take in parcels and post. With Chris' training base in Walsall, I've been living alone for the majority of the week, as he's been mainly coming home at weekends. It's meant that running of the household chores has been down to me.

Trish and Doug bring us beautiful things from their garden and help with Milo when I travel for work. It's wonderful, and we have struck absolute gold with the people who surround our home. They're much more than neighbours to us; they're friends who we care about and value, and who have made me feel so safe in our home, especially when I'm home alone.

I didn't always find it easy to ask for support.

I can still remember that first time. I didn't want to ask and I was embarrassed. Not only that, I was frustrated with myself.

I was on the drive speaking to Chris on the phone, asking what I should do. When he told me to contact our neighbours for help, I was devastated. "I can't do that. I don't want to make a fuss," I said.

Chris rang our neighbours, explained what had happened, and guess what? They took the chair out of the boot for me. Simple, and made no fuss whatsoever. They made me, and continue to make me, feel human!

From that moment on, I never worried about asking for help again. Chris and our neighbours had shown me it was okay.

Now I realise that asking feels really reassuring. Knowing that my neighbours, my friends, who I really value, are here, feels good.

Only recently, I'd accidentally left the chair in the boot again. I was going to call my neighbours, but when I pulled up on the drive, they appeared. Chris had rung them and there they were. They had been taking care of Milo for me, so it was perfect.

Do you know what? My incredible neighbours have made me feel more empowered asking and accepting help because I'm never stranded.

Independence doesn't have to be hard. It can look like a little bit of help sometimes. You *can* be independent and receive that support.

It's not like it happens every day. These situations happen rarely, but if they do, I know I'm safe, and that means the world.

Some things are hard work and exhausting. Those days when it's pouring with rain and my chair is filling up with water before I can get in it… they're no fun.

So why would I not want to ask someone to help, if they can? The feeling of someone taking my chair out of the car and me not having to struggle, can be the best feeling ever.

Pulling that chair out of the boot may be the smallest thing for someone without a disability, but for me it is massive.

In living on my own, particularly post retirement, I've learned that independence looks like asking for help when you need it, and being okay with that.

I've never understood why people would choose to do something themselves that's incredibly difficult for them, rather than asking for help. If someone could help you do something quickly and easily, without struggle, that makes total sense to me. This approach works for all of us.

For example, why would Chris struggle to read something when he could ask me to read it for him? Him asking me to do that *is* being independent. It's all about recognising someone else is better equipped in a particular area and letting them do that.

Chris is better equipped to put my chair in the car quickly, so he'll do that. That is independence.

I don't get why people struggle on their own. Out of what? Out of principle to say that you can do something?

No-one's questioning that you can't do it, but why struggle?

Mum and Dad encouraged me to live independently from an early age. Dad even built an extension to the family home where I had my own apartment. It was the perfect bridge between adjusting from family life to full independence, in my own house.

Every year I drive thousands of miles for business and pleasure. I have an adapted car with hand controls.

When I'm travelling solo, I transfer out of my chair into the passenger seat. With strong arms, I use the steering wheel to pull myself into the car. Legs first and then my upper body.

My chair collapses down. Side guards fold in, backrest folds down and then I take the back wheels off. They have a quick release system.

Next, I put my driver's seat right back, boy racer style. I lift each chair part across into the passenger seat and then off I go. On arrival, I repeat the entire thing in reverse. Wheels back on and I'm ready to roll.

I've done it so many times, it probably takes no more than a minute or so. It's not hard to do, just a little awkward. Most of the time I don't think about it, it's just what I need to do. But sometimes, when I'm tired, I may have to sit for a minute and scroll on my phone to delay the inevitable.

Making that first approach to ask for help was hard. I may have been living alone and independent, but it took me a while to appreciate that independence is never about suffering in silence, it's about asking for help sometimes.

Living in the house we're in now, I've learned to accept help. With Chris away training and competing, at times I've felt incredibly lonely and isolated, so when help has been offered, it has been so appreciated.

It can be hard living on my own as a wheelchair user, especially when I'm poorly. Things like putting the bins out, coming home with shopping and bringing it into the house, can be exhausting, but that doesn't mean I don't want to do it, quite the contrary.

I often get asked: "You're in a wheelchair. How did you do that?"

My answer? I just have my way. Maybe I break things into chunks, ie: one shopping bag at a time, whereas Chris will lug them all in, in one go, but I have found ways to do everything I need to.

It helps that I have spent a fortune making my house work for me, and do you know the greatest thing? You could walk into our bungalow and not even notice anything different about it. It's the little things that make all the difference.

For instance, there's a gradual ramp to the front door rather than steps. You'll struggle to see it because Dad and I made sure it was discreet.

Then there's the bathroom layout. I got to build it from scratch. Again, you'd be hard pressed to notice anything unusual about it, thanks to subtle design touches. It's only when you walk up to the sink that you may clock it's just a little lower.

Our Wiltshire home is the second house I've bought. I bought my first in my mid-20s.

I was working really hard and I'm a great saver. Thanks to prize money, I had an income from a young age too. I wanted to find a new way to have some income and invest my money a bit.

I rented out my first house for a while and then bought my current home after just two years of Chris and I being together.

It took quite a while to find the right home for us because of my physical access needs.

When Chris came into the picture, it changed things again.

Before we got together, I'd envisaged having a house in the middle of nowhere. More countryside because I'm a country girl through and through.

I saw Chris being around forever so I needed to make the house hunting work for both of us.

Chris was so incredible during this time. I'd always set my heart and dreams on buying a home to live in. I'd set myself a goal, and I just had to achieve it. He understood this completely and wanted to contribute to make this happen, but recognised I had to do this part independently, as I'd always planned.

One of the many things I respected about Chris was that he recognised this meant the world to me and that it was a financial goal I wanted to achieve for myself.

He didn't let classic masculinity or his ego get in the way. He got that part of me from day one and understood that I have to have something to aspire to. He got it so much that he bought me a necklace which never leaves my neck. It says: 'Abnormally ambitious.' That's what he's always called me. He'll say: "There's ambitious, then there's you!"

Chris knew that this had been a dream and ambition of mine since before he came into my life, so now it was ours. This was us, and that meant everything to me.

Today, we are just days away from being a 'full-time' living together couple as Chris retires from competitive Judo.

By the time this happens, I will have lived here, semi-alone, for five-and-a-half years.

I can't wait to welcome Chris home.

Chapter 38:

Ableism: Why It Needs to Stop

Ever heard the term ableism? Know what it means?

Ableism refers to discrimination or prejudice against individuals with disabilities. It often stems from societal norms that prioritise certain abilities over others.

This form of bias can manifest in various ways - from exclusion and stereotyping, to systemic barriers hindering access to education, employment, or public spaces.

It can perpetuate harmful stereotypes and undermines the diverse strengths and capabilities of people with disabilities, limiting their full participation in society.

Here's an example of ableism. Someone assumes a wheelchair user is incapable of certain tasks without considering their unique skills and abilities.

The assumption is based solely on physical appearance, perpetuates stereotypes and reflects a lack of understanding about the diverse capabilities of someone with a disability.

A personal example in a social setting is when I am shopping. So often, if I ask a staff member a question or go to pay, that person then ignores me and speaks to who I am with, handing them my money/bags. Why? Trust me, shopping is something I am more than capable of without help, just ask my husband!

Education plays a crucial role in dispelling misconceptions and generating understanding about different abilities.

So, much of my work going forward will be educating others about this. By helping to promote inclusivity and accessibility, communities can create environments where individuals with disabilities feel valued and respected - most importantly, places where they can thrive.

Chapter 39:

A Life of Contrasts...Still

I was at the community radio station I speak on today and it was really nice. I haven't been there for a couple of months because I've been so busy with Wimbledon, mentoring and delivering a tournament, so it was lovely to return.

Afterwards, I wanted to quickly grab some food from the supermarket before I went to work in the afternoon.

I was just getting stuff off the shelf when a woman approached me and said: "Oh, that's a really nice one of those." She was referring to my wheelchair. I thought, 'You can say the word wheelchair, it's okay.'

When I have these weird encounters, believe it or not, it's the only time I'm speechless because I just don't know what to say in response.

The woman followed up with: "I haven't seen any of those around. They're really good, aren't they? You'd be lost without it."

...and then she got to her point: "Oh, because most of them are really clunky and a bit big, and yours looks a lot easier to get around with."

Right. That was what you were trying to get to, but in trying to get there, you've just wasted five minutes of my life. Why are we talking about this? I just want to buy my sandwich. I just want to get on with my day.

Then I was on my way to the till. To be fair, I had piled up too much stuff, so I was pushing with one hand, which means I have to navigate the space. I timed it beautifully so the customer in front of me walked off, I was rolling into the vacated space and was going to end up at the till. But then the customer stopped dead in front of me and said: "You're going a bit fast, aren't you?" Suddenly, I was dropping stuff, had to grab my wheel and stop.

I replied politely, as I always do: "After you", only for her to reply: "No, after *you*." This went on for a few seconds until I had to firmly respond: "Please carry on and I'll go." This was said because I had now messed up my rhythm when all I wanted to do was pop into the shop and buy a meal deal.

Then I got to the till. Chris was in the paper that day for being selected for the Paralympic GB squad. I thought I'd buy a couple of copies so I could send one to his mum.

As I grabbed two papers, the conversation went something like this:

Man behind till: "Oh, I think you picked up two accidentally."

Me: "Yep, I deliberately picked up two copies."

Man behind till: "Are you sure?"

Me: "Yes, I'm sure."

As I left the shop, I just felt a tad annoyed.

Why is everybody talking to me like this? Questioning me, treating me like a child.

Situations like this happen all the time. None of the people mentioned here had ill intent. Granted, it was unlucky to have three of these encounters in a super short space of time, but I just don't understand why people feel the need to mention the fact that I'm in a wheelchair.

It reminds me of that scene in Notting Hill when a character says to Gina McKee's character: "Hello! You're in a wheelchair" to which she replies: "Yeah, I know."

Why do we have to mention someone's wheelchair, why are we still talking about this?

Now, if someone gets chatting to me and they say, for example: "I've got a friend in a wheelchair. I hope you don't mind, but I've seen you out and about and I'd love to tell my friend about your chair. Where could they purchase this?" This is a beautiful conversation that I so welcome and one that we can bond about. My approach in this situation is to see how I can help, but there's a big difference between this, and just randomly pointing out that I use wheels to get around.

I often say that these strange conversations always seem to happen in supermarkets and car parks.

I remember buying broccoli in a supermarket one day when a woman approached me and said: "It's so good to see you here."

Not sure what was going on, I replied: "Thanks, but I don't know what you mean."

The woman responded: "You know... seeing you out."

My reply? "Where do you think I should be?"

That response completely shut her down. I did it nicely, but to me, the horrible inference was people like you, out like me. It was certainly a cringe moment.

I remember thinking, 'I've just been praised for basically buying a bit of broccoli. Bizarre.'

Then there are the car park conversations that happen fairly frequently and sometimes lead to awkward interventions.

I always think it's really sweet when someone offers to help when I'm putting my chair in the car. Now and again, I've taken them up on their offer and I've really appreciated it.

But there have been occasions when I've had to virtually wrestle people trying to put my chair in the car. Offering help anytime is nice, but 'no' always means 'no'. More often than not, I'm alright and I know what I'm doing.

One time, a person offered to help me and then kept offering, despite me assuring them I was fine. In the end, I had to wrestle with the frame of my chair because the person was trying to take it off me.

All the while I was thinking, 'What are you going to do with this thing? You don't know where I put this and you don't even know how to take a wheel off, when I do.'

In this situation, the person was trying to help, but because they didn't know what they were doing, they were making things harder.

These situations occur regularly and it can really get my back up. I'm an independent, 33-year-old woman, so please don't assume I need saving or rescuing. I'm okay.

It's very kind to offer to help. I don't mind that, I really don't, because I would offer to help somebody too. But just because you're not in a wheelchair does not make you more able and capable than me. My chair doesn't instantly make me less of a person and less capable.

Things like this would happen repeatedly after I'd flown home from a tournament. There I'd be, returning from a successful trip - a Paralympic athlete at the top of my game - and then I'd become someone perceived to be in need of help to do the simplest of tasks like popping into a shop to buy a sandwich. Sometimes days like today, when I had three incidents in a row, can feel like a real struggle.

It's just a massive slap in the face reminder that not everyone is totally cool with disability yet. There is still pity, ignorance, confusion, and ableism out there and it makes me feel sad. However, I do feel it's heading in the right direction, so I am determined to remain positive and change those perceptions when I have the energy and time to do so.

Chapter 40:
PEEP Show

Christmas 2023, New Year 2024. Chris and I were enjoying a much needed break.

Being given your own emergency evacuation plan may not sound like a cause for celebration, but in this case it really was.

Do you know what a PEEP is?

PEEP is short for a "Personal Emergency Evacuation Plan for a person who may need assistance in evacuating a building or reaching a place of safety in the event of an emergency".

Feeling safe in a hotel is, of course, crucial for all guests, but it holds particular significance for me and others with disabilities.

When Chris and I arrived at the beautiful Celtic Manor Hotel in Newport, a staff member immediately asked us if I'd need help in case of an emergency.

Please note, they asked and did NOT assume. I wish more hotels would take this approach.

Our room was on the seventh floor so, of course, my answer was 'yes'. This attentive staff member then took me through my own PEEP.

The professionalism and thoroughness demonstrated, which involved showing me the emergency lift and exit and explaining where staff would meet me, was exemplary.

They asked how many people I'd need to help me. Such attention to detail created an environment where, regardless of my disability, I felt valued, safe and cared for during my stay. Most importantly, I didn't feel like a burden, which I so often do.

It was the best experience I've ever had when it comes to creating a PEEP. Thank you, Celtic Manor. We'll be back.

I urge other establishments to take this approach. I'll say it again, please just ask and don't assume. Everyone's access needs are different, so checking in with us is the best step forward. So often I don't even need a PEEP, so taking this approach often saves them a lot of work for all concerned.

Chapter 41:

Choose Your Words with Kindness

Yesterday, I went to a business exhibition where I was to present one of my talks. I couldn't find an accessible entrance or anyone to help me. I was feeling a little under the weather. Today, I feel really sad thinking about what happened. If I'm having a bad day, I'm the person that comes home to somebody and they'll drag me out of it eventually. I'm one of the lucky ones.

What about the people who don't have that? You must understand the power of your words. Wrongly chosen ones can set someone back. I know, because it's been done to me multiple times. For many years I thought I was unlovable, simply because of a comment from a boy who said he couldn't date anyone in a wheelchair. This response led to me believing that if you were in a wheelchair, you couldn't be loved. Those words taught me that narrative.

Now, talking with people around me, I understand that this belief is not true, but not everyone has a support network. So, before saying something, take a breath and think about the words you're going to use. Be kind always.

Chapter 42:

Language Lessons for Us All

I just want to take a moment to talk about language around disability. Language is a really challenging subject because it's ever evolving.

I know I probably used words when I was younger that I wouldn't use now.

If you're worried about what words to use or struggling to find the right words, try not to panic, just check and ask.

My go-to is always to ask people what language they prefer, and what they're comfortable with.

A really good example of this is the term 'able-bodied'. It's a term I've used my whole life and it's never bothered me; I still use it today. However, I'm very conscious that other people really do not like the term. Instead 'non-disabled' is the preferred go-to for a lot of people, which makes a lot more sense.

I mean, of course it makes more sense because we are still 'able'; disability doesn't automatically make you less able.

Another example when looking at people's preferences, is terms such as 'people with disabilities' and 'disabled people'. Again, personally, both these terms sit comfortably with me. However, I am incredibly conscious that's not the same for everybody, and I totally get it.

Instead of saying, 'disabled person', many people prefer 'person with a disability'. This emphasises the person's identity first, rather than first describing a disability. Although some terms are more widely preferred than others, it's all personal.

Of course, there are words that are generically accepted like 'disabled', but we're all different, so always check with anyone you are chatting with.

Then there are lots of old-fashioned words like 'handicapped', 'cripple' – words that, unfortunately, I still hear occasionally, but are, thankfully, a thing of the past. One day I hope these words will disappear permanently from our language.

None of us are perfect with the language we use. I'm not perfect. Sometimes I get it wrong. I think it's really good to try and keep on top of this by always checking and asking. We all have our own preferences, so let's build our awareness around this and be mindful.

Please never assume how someone would prefer to be referred to. I personally hate labels, but sometimes we do need terms to refer to ourselves and others, just to put things into context.

So, always check, ask someone what they prefer and abide by their wishes. Above all, let's always be kind and thoughtful.

Chapter 43:

Boobgate, Blunders and Sporting Heroes

Who says tennis has to be serious or that everything goes according to plan?

I've certainly had a few funny and challenging moments on court over the years.

Let me tell you about Boobgate.

I was at the World Team Cup in Holland and we were playing on clay.

It had been raining heavily so, as I wheeled myself out for a training session, my front wheels got stuck in the clay surface.

I fell forward and straight down.

As the coaches pulled me up, there were two perfect mammarial mounds in the clay.

Oh, how we laughed, and laughed...and laughed.

My GB team mate, Lucy, was there to laugh with me.

She was also with me in Korea when facetime took on a whole new meaning. We were playing doubles at the time.

As she put her hand up for a ball from the ball boy, he threw and it hit me straight in the face. Lucy's face was a picture. Mine just a little red, but good to smile another day.

There have been a few kit breaking moments at key moments too. We're always breaking strings on rackets, but the big one is popping tyres.

Tennis chairs have to be inflated with air as opposed to solid tyres on my everyday chair.

They have to be inflated this way as you need to be able to play around with the pressure.

I've lost count of the times tyres have gone pop, and when it happens, the noise they make certainly takes you by surprise. Luckily, there's always repair guys on hand to help when it happens, and to be fair, I can do most repair jobs myself.

I was asked recently who my sporting hero is. I find that quite a hard question as there are so many people who I know and have had the privilege to meet over the years.

Obviously, Chris is certainly one of them.

I know he seems like an obvious choice, but I say this with nothing to do with him being my husband. I say this because he is the most dedicated, hard working athlete I have ever known, yet he remains kind and humble - a tough and rare balance to find. He is the ultimate sporting role model in my eyes.

Tanni Grey-Thompson also comes to mind as she was the first person I met who had a disability like mine, and who was smashing it.

As well as her incredible sporting achievements (16 Paralympic medals, including 11 golds and 6x London Marathon winner), what I love about her now is that she's gone on to have an amazing career in the House Of Lords.

I love that she's shown, not only that it's possible to break down barriers as a woman with a disability, but that she's gone on to have a career outside of athletics.

She demonstrates perfectly that athletes do have brains and have so much more to offer after retirement from competitive sport.

I love this because this is the kind of mark in the world I want to leave. I want people to see that tennis players can do more than just hit a fluffy yellow thing over a net.

Growing up, I never really idolised sports people, but Tanni is such a great example of what is possible to achieve post sporting retirement.

Chapter 44:

Loving Lockdown, And Then Not So Much

Before the world locked down, I was in a pretty good head space. I was in a crazy and busy routine of balancing work with tournaments, but things were under control.

My coach and I had finalised exactly what I was going to do for the end of the 12 month qualification period for the Tokyo Paralympics. We decided I was going to Malaysia for a couple of weeks, America and then some European competitions.

We went back and forth quite a lot on which tournaments I should play. It's quite a tough decision sometimes because it's about chasing points, but trying to dodge people (who are trying to achieve the same things as you) while equally needing to beat them in competition. So, it's a bit of a mathematical thing that you have to try and work out, to the best of your ability, what's good for you. I also had to factor in balancing work alongside all this too.

There's always an element of risk because you have no idea where other players are going to play. Also, at this time, more than ever before, we had to be super smart when looking at the cost of everything as I was funding myself for these trips.

Anyway, we had just decided what I was going to do, so I had a good bit of peace of mind in terms of my tennis. I was nervous, but okay because I'd got a plan. I was going to stick to it and give it my all.

So, it was all about going to work, in terms of finishing that part of my tennis career, while aiming to retire from sport after the Tokyo Paralympics.

Then all changed. I was at a training session with my tennis coach at an indoor centre when a doctor friend messaged me to say: "I'm not really supposed to be telling you this, but I know it's going to affect you, so I need to give you a heads up. It looks like the country is going into lockdown, most likely from tomorrow."

In my head, I thought, 'they're not going to stop things like tennis where we're so far apart on the court', which was quite a weird reaction, given I'm a realist normally.

I told my coach about the message.

"But we'll be here tomorrow, won't we?" I asked him.

Coach: "I think you should take your tennis gear." (Note: I used to leave all my kit/tennis chair at the centre to make life easier as I was there every day).

Me: "Why? We'll be training tomorrow."

Coach: "Read that message again."

On his advice, I packed up my tennis gear and my chair and took them home.

The next day we went into lockdown.

The centre stayed closed for over a year. It didn't even open up again between lockdowns.

If I hadn't taken that advice, I wouldn't have had any of my kit. Thanks Ali, you were right.... as usual!

At the time of the first lockdown, Chris and I were sharing our home with our friend, Claire.

As Covid cases soared, the three of us came up with a plan.

Claire made it her mission to do everything she could to stop us from being put at risk. She did the shopping and went out to get anything we needed. She is more like a sister to us both now, a true diamond of a friend.

I was scared, but we had this plan and it felt okay. And then, like so many of us, I got the letter from my GP saying I was 'clinically vulnerable'. I hate labels and it did feel like it was being shoved in my face. For a while I felt really weak.

I'm a very strong, resilient person, physically and mentally. The stuff I've been through, I don't know many people that could have coped with it as well, so I just really hated having that finger pointed at me. It was hard.

Letters and text messages stating my 'highly vulnerable' status increased to weekly and I found this difficult too.

On one hand, all this felt really intrusive. My immediate reaction was, 'I know I'm vulnerable, thanks for reminding me.'

But on the other hand, I know it happened for the right reason and I have to really credit the system in place.

On the positive side of things, I got text messages asking if I needed help picking up any medication or help with my shopping.

I was lucky in many ways during lockdown. I didn't get COVID. To my knowledge, I've never had it. I've tested and had symptoms, but somehow, for a person that tends to get everything, I seem to have dodged it, which is bizarre.

I wasn't alone. I had my wonderful husband, friend, Claire, and dog, Milo in the house, and my family not too far away.

For me, lockdown began as one of the most beautiful times of my life, but it was also one of the hardest.

As I'm sure it was for many, seeing the hastily built Nightingale Hospital, in London, on TV for the first time, had a huge impact. It sent me into total meltdown.

I was absolutely convinced I was going to end up there and potentially die there too. With anxiety through the roof, it took a lot of support from Chris and Claire to get me back on a level playing field.

From that moment on we decided we would only watch the news for Government updates as anything else simply wasn't helpful.

At the start of lockdown, I think we all got addicted to the news, but it didn't do me any good. I've always had a certain stance on the news. I literally never watch it as it always feels so negative and biased, and I hate opening myself to that.

During the first lockdown, I couldn't get hold of a lot of the medical supplies I needed. When I was down to my last few catheters, I was terrified. I felt really sick. It was a tough thing to deal with.

It was always Claire or Chris going off to pick up medical supplies/shopping and I found it really hard not being independent. The two of them went above and beyond in supporting and protecting me. I've never felt more loved and cared for than I did in those moments.

Another tough discovery was finding out I wasn't eligible for self-employment financial support from the government, nor funding from the International Tennis Federation as I had just dropped out of the ranking needed. Financially, I was screwed.

The same day, I discovered that the 2020 Paralympic Games in Tokyo, the one that was to be my Paralympic finale, was to be postponed for a year.

Two athletes in one house responded in polar opposite ways. Chris was devastated, but his approach was: "I've got another year to get better and stronger."

Me: "I can't do this for another year."

I had my heart set on finishing those few months later, after Tokyo, and everything had changed.

In this moment, in true Chris style, he gave me some great advice:

"Now is not the time to make a big decision," he said. "We need to get through this, you need to go back to tennis, play some tournaments, and then see how you feel."

Once I got through that really tough wave at the start, things started to shift and improve.

I think that physically and mentally, I was potentially the healthiest I've ever been. I felt incredible because I spent my days fulfilling the things that bring me so much joy.

Doing things to the house, being creative, making things, recording videos with Claire (which we often roped Chris into as well) would entail us making up songs, creating videos with Milo, making music, documenting our goings on and organising online quizzes with our loved ones during that unique time. All the things that I love mentally, I threw myself into. All with our best friend in the world, my fur baby, and my husband. I felt like the luckiest girl on earth.

When I was struggling, Claire would bring things for us to do. She always had the best ideas for distraction, and this wasn't isolated to lockdown - this could be any day of the week, any time.

On one occasion, she turned up with two, one quid garden gnomes, for us to sit and paint. Today, every time, when we create something, it's unbelievable what that does for me. Post lockdown, we now call our creative get togethers 'craft and chat'. I know what you're thinking, aren't we the coolest 30-somethings you know? But I can't tell you how much I enjoy these little pockets of time together.

It was such a special time and I'm reminded of the memories we created to this day. Every time Claire visits, she reminds me there's something around every corner that we made, painted, re-decorated or tweaked. It's like we almost built our home through it, and that was magical.

I feel bad saying this in some ways because I know for far too many it was a horrendous time.

Physically, I hadn't been that fit in a long time because Chris and I would train together every day. We would combine the things that we did in our own training - teaching each other and learning about each other's sports training regimes. I also enjoyed being back in a routine where my physical fitness/sport was a priority again, and wasn't dominated by having to work too.

We'd have music on and we'd work out outside our home. We'd call it our driveway workouts, and then we'd go for bike rides. We kept really fit and healthy.

The thing I learned from all this, is how important it is for me to be creative and, something which I've actually stuck to, is to make sure I always have space for the things that bring me happiness and joy.

The third, and most beautiful thing, was I learned I wanted to marry Chris at this time, and he felt the same for me. He always says it was when he realised he had to propose.

Chris and I had been solid since day one and lockdown was a really magical time for our relationship.

In the busy life we were living as Paralympic athletes, where we were both travelling all over the world a lot, we were so grateful for the time lockdown gave us together. Up until this point, we could be apart up to six weeks at a time, so lockdown provided us with a new level of togetherness.

How lucky were we that we got months of quality time with no distractions? We're probably never going to have that again, at least not until we both retire, and even then there's other distractions and responsibilities.

We always like to see the positives in things, but it was really hard going back to normal. After lockdown and then after getting married, being apart became so much more painful.

We've always had a really open, honest relationship. There's no topic off bounds. There's nothing to be embarrassed about. So, I think we just really cemented ourselves as the ultimate team.

One of the things I love about Chris and I, and another thing I loved about lockdown, is that we had a relatively spacious house so we could do things apart, but in the same space, and still have a nice time. There'd be days when I'd be outside with Claire doing something creative, like mindful colouring, and Chris would be doing his workout or sitting in front of the TV. We'd talk for a couple of hours, and that was fine. It wasn't that we'd spend every second of every day together, but the parts when we did were beautiful. I think that's a sign of a really good relationship, even if I am a little biased.

Chris and I loved lockdown, we never fell out and found joy in every day. We love each other's company so much, and that's what Chris says was one of the reasons why he wanted to marry me. He would often say: "I went through lockdown with you, had all that quality time and loved every moment, and I hate going back to normality."

The highs, but more the lows during lockdown, were a steep learning curve and led to a tip I always share with people, which I can't really take credit for, as it was my incredible sports psychologist, Karl, who taught me this: "When you're struggling with something, feel all of those emotions - shout, cry, let it out - then really decompress and take a moment to look at the reality of it. It's unrealistic to think we can just suppress those emotions entirely; they'll come back to haunt you eventually, we're human aren't we? So learning to have them and then move forward afterwards really helps."

My reality sucked in lockdown, when it came to work and tennis, but I did get furloughed for a part-time job I had at a local charity. Although it brought in next to nothing, with Chris and Claire's income, the three of us kept the house running.

We were a team.

Chris and I were a team.

When I first met Chris, I had this real struggle of not being an independent woman all the time. I was so used to doing everything and being completely independent but, as time went on, I needed him and had to lean on him emotionally and financially.

I had to let go my high horse of independence, and that was a really, really big growing moment.

Throughout our lives, our roles have switched. We've had moments where I've earned a bit more money and he's leaned on me, and I've learned that that's okay too. It's actually a sign of a really beautiful, strong relationship, and that feels good.

I'm not interested in being in a relationship that's got yours and mine. I've grown up with really good role models, in a family of healthy marriages where everything is ours. So, never be afraid to be in a team with your partner, it actually feels pretty amazing.

In stark contrast to the first lockdown, the winter lockdowns were horrific for me.

As part of the rules, elite athletes were allowed to train so Chris was away training and Claire was back at work in childcare.

I was allowed to go and train too, but that was my only break every day, for a couple of hours. I loved it, but it wasn't enough for me. I just felt so flat. Very little of my work stuff was happening so I felt so alone. The whole experience was very isolating. In retrospect, I think I was really depressed.

Throughout this, Claire was doing her best to be the best friend ever, keeping her distance to keep me safe from the virus. We were both in the house, but we weren't eating together. I would make dinner and then leave it for her. We'd talk across the kitchen, but it was difficult to remain positive. I so often just wanted to hug her, but knew it wasn't the smartest idea as she was in contact with people every day.

With Chris gone in the week for training, it was difficult with him coming back and forth to home. During that time I was effectively housebound, bar going out for one tennis hit a day.

At the time, I had this habit of really retreating when I was struggling. For someone like me, who really bounces off people, it's the worst coping mechanism. In fact, it's no coping mechanism at all. It just doesn't work.

I like to describe myself as an extroverted introvert. I need my own time to recharge, but I also thrive off other people and value the energy they bring, so this balance was hard to find during this time.

Ali, during my training sessions, and my sports psychologist, Karl, were my rocks throughout, making sure I reached out to Chris and spoke to Claire every day. I tried my best to do simple things around the house like tidy a cupboard, rearrange something, be creative. These things really helped, but those winter lockdowns were a real test of my resilience.

Nowadays, I have a raft of coping strategies up my sleeve and enjoy doing a lot of things on my own. A huge contrast to the me that was just lonely all the time.

Chapter 45:

Travelling Trickstar

Just because I'm sat in a wheelchair, why shouldn't I be able to use them? I just have to make that judgement and, to be honest, decide whether I can get away with it. Can I do this without sending the security guard into an absolute frenzy?

If I'm seen near one of these, there's very often someone telling me: "You shouldn't go on there. It's not safe."

Escalators. They're used by millions of people every day and as I was taught how to use them at wheelchair training school (yes, that's a thing), I use them all the time. People freak out about it, but it makes me chuckle.

When I was taught to go down steps in my chair, I was shown how to hold a handrail and go down slowly, and it's the same principle as going onto an escalator.

I just have to wheel onto it and time it right to make sure my front wheels are cleanly on the step. As an escalator is flat and turns into steps, I then get myself into a wheelie position. As long as I'm holding on tight, all's good. I love it because the handrails go a bit quicker than the stairs, so it's an amazing back stretch, which feels fabulous.

I always laugh about this because a couple of my friends absolutely hate it when I say we're getting on an escalator. One in particular (Hannah) hates it so much because she's just scared I'm going to fall off, but my training kicks in and I'm completely safe… ish haha!

It's a really important life skill being in a chair, and if you're able to learn how to use an escalator safely, why wouldn't you?

How often is a lift out of order? All the time, so it's a case of, if there's an escalator, I'll use that instead.

I've collected some good stories with escalators over the years. The most ridiculous one was when I was in The Louvre museum in Paris, with one of my best friends, Becky.

The escalators there are so high and steep, with signs everywhere saying I can't go on them. I told Becky I wanted to get on it.

At The Louvre, the escalators are in the middle of the venue so you can enjoy the building more by going on them as you can take everything in. By contrast, if you go up in the lift, everything seems hidden away.

So, on this day, I decided to go for it. Becky was really chilled about the whole thing as she always is with any unexpected idea I bring to the table. She's very much used to my crazy ideas, and this was mild compared to many so, as I saw the security guard eyeing me up, I said it's "now or never". As I wheeled myself on, the security guy was shouting at me to get off, but it was a case of 'I'm on here now - there's literally only one direction this is going to go for me'.

At times like this, I've seen people take photos of me and do a double take, but I just go ahead. I must confess to getting caught out once when I was in a famous sports store, although I learned something really cool.

The lift was out of order, so I went up the escalator, but I hadn't noticed there wasn't a down escalator. So, when I asked staff: "Can you help me?" they replied: "How did you get here?" When I explained that I used the escalator, it turned into quite a conversation.

I was pretty stressed in that situation, but I learned something amazing. The store manager explained they could reverse the escalator - in other words, they could change the direction so I could go down on the same escalator I'd come up on. Since finding this out I feel even more safe taking the escalator.

It is funny. Becky's got a video of us in Vegas, and I'm wheeling toward this place, while there's a massive sign. There's a wheelchair with a cross on it saying: "Don't go." And I just wheel past it, flash the middle finger and go on up. I don't want to go the long way and have to find the lift all the time. If the escalator is right there, and I know how to use it safely, I'm going to use it.

However, there is one note of caution to this story. On another visit to France, a guy had come up the escalator in his chair, but they had those barriers/poles at the top which were only so far apart and he couldn't get through them and out. There was no warning sign about this and so he was stuck.

I asked him if he was okay and he explained what had happened. Neither of us had experienced anything like this before, but I helped him out a bit. He got on the floor, moved through the gap on his bottom. I helped him dismantle his chair and put it back together the other side of the poles. I didn't even know him and I just happened to be there and understood how to help him, but that could've been tricky for him otherwise. Luckily, that's not happened to me... yet.

Chapter 46:

Gold! Living The Pie Life

GOLD!

Live on Channel 4 for the Tokyo Paralympics and millions must have heard my cheers.

Chris had just won Gold in the Judo, B2, -100kg category.

I'd been commentating on the tennis while watching Chris' progress via iPad all day, so when he clinched victory, I just couldn't contain my joy.

In judo, competition is all over in one day for competing athletes, so the tension had been building by the hour while I tried to focus on my commentary job.

I was watching each of Chris' fights, one by one, so when he was declared Paralympic gold medallist, the emotion was unreal. It was such a surreal moment.

Tokyo was my first experience of commentating for a Paralympic Games, but due to Covid restrictions, we were based in London.

I was working alongside the fantastic Gigi Salmon for the very first time. We had bonded straight away and were having so much fun together.

When Chris won, I cheered so loudly that Gigi had to let viewers know what I was screaming about. She was the only person with me in that moment and I appreciated her so much. She handled things so beautifully, so supportive.

I only commentated for the first half of the tennis event because I wanted to ensure I was home when Chris got back to the UK.

I'm so glad I was able to pick him up from the airport. It was a magic moment, as was our arrival home.

When we got back, our neighbours and friends had decorated the driveway and filled our house with pork pies! Why pork pies?

One of Chris' first TV interviews after his win, had something to do with that.

Looking into the camera, he announced: "Louise, get the pork pies in, I'm coming home!"

Chris' lifelong love of pork pies is well documented, so it was the perfect way to celebrate.

Pork Pies have ruled Chris's life for a long time so, when we got engaged, he said he wanted a Pork Pie Wedding Cake, which he duly sorted. It was his pride and joy on the big day.

The Pork Pies interview clip has become synonymous with the Paralympics. It's been used recently for the Paris Games - something that makes me chuckle every time I see it as that was all that was on his mind, despite winning the ultimate sports prize.

Chris's TV appearance resulted in countless pork pie deliveries to our home. We had so many! We now have this running joke that pork pie overload before and during the wedding led to Chris' Celiac disease diagnosis.

Although he can't eat his beloved pies like he used to, we have since found a few Gluten Free versions.

Having announced my retirement from elite sport a few months before Tokyo, I had been contacted by Whisper TV to see if I'd like to commentate for Channel 4 on the Tokyo Games.

Talk about when one door closes, another one opens. I had taken a minute to contemplate this decision as I'd wondered how I'd feel being a commentator at Tokyo when I'd been aiming to end my tennis playing career there. I'm so glad I took the opportunity. What an incredible experience for me and for Chris, with or without pork pies.

Chapter 47:
Rollercoaster

2022. A rollercoaster year which started in the most incredible way.

Day 1 and finally our big secret was out. Chris, my wonderful husband-to-be, had been awarded an MBE for his achievements and services to Judo.

It was the perfect follow on from his gold at the Tokyo Olympics the year before.

We were given the good news just before Christmas 2021, but were sworn to secrecy.

We were itching to get to January so we could tell the world. So, when the announcement came, boy were we ready to celebrate.

We were on such a high. Not only had Chris won gold in his beloved sport, but he'd been recognised for it.

All this and I was going to marry an incredible man, with a honeymoon in The Maldives to follow.

Life was so good. My best friends were planning the ultimate Hen do of the century (more on this later). Chris and I were both working hard. Me mentoring and speaking, Chris was in normal training, and I'd run another successful tennis tournament in Bolton.

Wedding planning was going well, lots of fun stuff was happening. We'd started to look at bridesmaid dresses, and suits for Chris.

We were on a real high. What more could I want of my life? My future husband was achieving every dream possible. He'd attained a new level of respect and achievement which he so deserved. Amazing.

The first five months of 2022 were truly lovely, but then in May...

It started with a poorly Milo who had been struggling with a sickness bug.

Taking Milo to the vet's on my own is a little tricky, so with Chris away, I'd asked Mum to accompany us. As a thank you I'd planned to cook dinner for the two of us that night.

Then, as I drove home from work, I received a call. It was Mum: "Louise, I can't come and help you. Lorna's collapsed. You'll have to go on your own."

Mum was speaking at a gazillion miles an hour and I could hear the concern in her voice.

Lorna: best friend to Mum, second Mum to me. I'd grown up with her my whole life. We'd lived side by side for many years - my parents were hers and Dennis' (Lorna's husband's) children's guardians. We were family.

"What's happened?" I asked.

Mum: "I don't know, but I have to go now. Your dad's off to get the defibrillator with Hannah."

It was those last few words that hit home the hardest.

Only days later did I discover that when Lorna had collapsed on the patio, Dad had run to the village and ripped the defib machine off the wall in his bid to help.

Over time, I'd find out lots of things about how that day unfolded for all those involved, and it still makes me cry.

But back to *the* day. I rang my friend, Bethan, when I got home - the friend that is a paramedic and superwoman in her many achievements. She was often not free due to her busy workload, yet here she was, instantly picking up my call. Meant to be!

I asked her to come to the vet's and she agreed to meet me there. It was a big relief.

Then a second call came. This time from Elizabeth - a close family friend whose daughter went to school with me. She lives next door to my parents still. She checked to see how I was and, on discovering I had Bethan with me, told me to call if I needed anything.

As we got Milo treated, it was hard to focus. I couldn't help my mind wandering, wondering what might be going on for Lorna and my parents.

I sat outside the vet's with Bethan, and then Elizabeth, who is a nurse, called again to check on me.

Both being in the medical profession, they were able to chat through what had happened and explain exactly what might be going on.

Elizabeth gently broke it to me that Lorna was very poorly. She used more technical terms when speaking to Bethan, but when I saw the look on her face, I threw up. I was so worried.

Bethan followed me home in her car and was there throughout to answer my many questions.

It soon became clear that Lorna, the woman who I had never known my life without, had been airlifted to hospital after suffering a Spontaneous IntraCerebral Haemorrhage.

In a strange twist of fate, on the same day Lorna had collapsed, I'd been announced as an ambassador for Wiltshire Air Ambulance.

Earlier in the year, they'd asked me to take on the role, but I'd been unsure. I knew how amazing they were. I was blown away by what they do, but one thing stuck with me – a stat that said most people would know someone who's relied on the service. That wasn't me, so I was worried I'd be seen as a fraud as I had no personal connection.

In retrospect, I know that it was immaculate timing. In the days that followed, I would become their ambassador and take on the role with gratitude and pride.

Back at home, Bethan sat with me, explaining things and offering her support.

She did it with the utmost kindness and professionalism. The way that she spoke to me and held my hand, she was the perfect person to have with me in that moment.

She knew what to say, what not to say, and between her and Elizabeth, they prepared me for the news no-one wanted to hear.

As we waited, I spoke to Chris on the phone.

"I'm coming home," he said. At that point I needed him more than anything, but I knew he couldn't just leave a talk he had been booked for.

"No, you're not," I replied.

It was unprofessional. He'd been booked for this event for so long and he needed to stay.

We had been busting our asses for two years, taking every job so we could have the wedding we wanted. We were relying on his fee to cover a big part of our wedding costs.

After talking things through, we agreed Chris would come home the next day.

At hospital, machines were keeping Lorna with us. What followed was a long and worrying night for all.

The next day, as Chris made his way home, I called Dad.

We agreed to go to the bluebell woods with Milo. It's a place that means a lot to my family and holds so many beautiful memories for us.

We'd spent a lot of time with Lorna there and have some amazing photos of us at the woods when we were kids. Years later, we went back as adults and recreated the same photos (look out for one in the book) which always makes me think of Lorna.

On the day of Lorna's collapse, with one eye on our phones, Dad and I explored this familiar space again. To this day, I don't think either of us can remember what we said to each other. Our minds and our hearts were elsewhere.

The whole time, as I stared at my phone because we knew what was coming, it still felt special to be at the woods; it felt like the right thing.

Still awaiting news, we eventually made our way home. We arrived to a classic Dad response in challenging moments.

"We're going to make something," he said. You can see where I get my creative side from.

So, there we were, worried beyond belief, with Dad carving out a table in the shape of a flower with a wine bottle holder in it, while I varnished our new piece of furniture.

So random, but so perfect, and I see Lorna every time I look at that table.

It was a little thing, but at the same time, such a big moment. Dad and I together again, keeping busy as we battled with our emotions. It had been the same at other key moments in our lives, like Gramp's death. I felt awful for Rob when Lorna passed away, as his son William was unwell so he kept his distance from us, to avoid the risk of passing anything on. When Gramp died, he was at work on his own.

Earlier that day, Mum had taken the call when Lorna's youngest daughter, Hannah (friend and part of my bride squad), rang for help. Mum immediately went to their aid. In any life changing moments, Mum has always been the one being the glue holding everything and everyone together.

Lorna was rushed to hospital on May 3rd. On the evening of May 4th, the machines supporting her were switched off. She died in the early hours of May 5th.

When she died, it hit me in a way I've never experienced before. It felt like someone had physically beaten me to within an inch of my life. My body, my mind, every part of me hurt. I felt battered and cried all the time, for days and weeks.

It had been a waiting game and a shock in a very short space of time, I was devastated.

Our beloved Lorna had been my mum's rock and she hers - they were the best support for one another.

As dear friends, they would message every day. There was so much synergy between them. Their lives were so in sync.

Lorna had three children, who have always felt like siblings to me, as we grew up closely together – Amy, Hannah and Alex. Hannah is one of my best friends.

My mum's best friend, my best friend's mum, had died. It was so intertwined and so unbearably painful.

Lorna had a huge influence on my life. After her death, her eldest daughter, Ami told me to never forget I'd been like a daughter to Lorna. It meant the world because I saw Lorna as my second mum. Every WhatsApp she sent me would start with 'darling daughter' and end with 'love you!' I miss receiving those so much. I'll never forget how comforting Ami's words were in that moment. I don't know why it helped so immensely, but it did.

There are so many reasons why I loved Lorna so much, far too many to write here, but let me share a handful.

Lorna was colourful, vibrant, unique, with an ability to make you happy and laugh, whatever the scenario. Oh the irony, that we could have really done with her at a time like this.

Lorna's randomness was legendary. The way she would turn up with a bag of items, like one potato, half a beetroot, a flower out of the garden. If you saw the random ingredients she'd rock up with, you wouldn't believe it.

She'd arrive, present her random gifts, to which I'd reply: "Thanks. I'm not sure what to do with this," but somehow she/we'd manage to cobble something together. The irony is that Lorna was actually a really good cook.

She made a killer Lasagne. Thank goodness, Hannah has carried on that tradition. It's as close to Lorna standards as you could ever get.

Lorna was also trained in massage. She gave the best massages. It may sound a bit weird, but she would look at me, stand behind me, sense how I was, and massage my shoulders. I would always feel better afterwards.

It wasn't just about how good she was at massage, it was the calm she brought.

I can still remember helping her in one of her massage exams. She had to massage different types of people and different parts of the body, so I ticked a lot of boxes.

I was in one of her exams when she had to massage my stomach. We were both in stitches because I was so ticklish. We just couldn't get through it as we could not stop laughing.

Goodness knows how she passed her course with what I brought to the table that day.

Lorna loved to socialise and hang out with friends and family with nice wine and food, but had her own mental health struggles. Even in her darkest times, she still had this magical way of making you feel safe and full of joy, and I so miss her.

On the day Lorna collapsed, one of the many difficult tasks for Mum and Hannah was to take Lorna's beloved dog, Tia to be put to sleep. She was already booked in that day to be put down, and Lorna had spent the day spoiling her and saying goodbye.

Tia had had a long and happy life, but she was getting really old. Lorna and the rest of the family knew it was time to say their farewells.

I have never met a person and a dog with a bond like theirs. Tia was literally glued to Lorna, going everywhere with her, their emotions always in sync.

I find it so telling that both lives ended so closely together; that on the day that Lorna collapsed, Tia was going to be taking her last breath.

I know science probably won't agree with me, but I don't think they were meant to live without each other. So close in death, as in life.

Lorna's funeral took place just over two weeks later, and it was perfect.

There was no black, just everyone in rainbow colours.

When Lorna got married, her bridesmaids were in every colour of the rainbow and she was a rainbow, a glorious rainbow within herself. A beautiful soul.

If anyone could have had a body and blood full of rainbow colours, it would have been her.

Lorna's dress sense was unique. She could put all colours together, all different patterns and somehow, on her, it always looked absolutely gorgeous. I would often wonder, 'how are you pulling that off?' I could never work that one out.

On the day of the funeral, Chris was going through a horrendous time in Kazakhstan, dealing with classification issues. Yes, sadly the classification issues in 2024 were not isolated. As a paralympic athlete you have to be classified to compete, which in short means grouping athletes together based on their abilities/impairments. This is to ensure fair competition by balancing the impact of their disabilities on performance.

The classification really dragged up a lot of difficult stuff for Chris surrounding his diagnosis. Things were very tough for him and it really affected his mental health. It was so difficult to see him like that.

"I'm so sorry, but I just don't know how to be there for you right now. I don't know how I can support you." I told him as we talked things through at home. I was just beside myself with grief and felt incredible guilt as I could barely function.

His response was beautiful. "You don't need to be," he reassured me. "Lorna's death is the most important thing right now."

A week before all this, Chris' uncle had died too, so we had a massive decision to make about attending both funerals, as they clashed with the Kazakhstan trip. We went back and forth so much on it.

With Chris going through this awful classification scenario, I felt terrible because he just couldn't be a priority in that moment.

I also wanted Chris there with me for Lorna's funeral. I felt so broken, but I acknowledged that nothing he said or did would make me feel better amid my grief.

"Lorna would not want you to miss out on this trip. This is so important for your career," I said, urging him to carry on with his plans.

I knew that I would not be alone, that I would have so many people at the funeral who would love and support me.

So, Chris stayed put and the night before the funeral, Bethan, once again, was right there by my side, sitting with me all night.

Everything about the funeral was perfect and reflected Lorna completely.

The wake was at Lorna's family home overlooking the beautiful hills of the Ridgeway in Liddington - the same views we will be looking at when I launch this book.

As I drove in, there were so many people. Marquees and so much food and drink. It felt like a mini festival, party atmosphere, and Lorna loved a good party.

It's really hard that Lorna's not here, but she knew Chris had got his MBE and that we were getting married, so that makes me really happy.

She was so happy for us and Hannah revealed that Lorna had already 'put money in the pot' for my hen do and bought drinks to celebrate with.

Chris and I still find it weird that Lorna wasn't at the wedding. I still have so many messages from her saying just how much she loved both of us and how she couldn't wait to see us tie the knot.

As we struggled to come to terms with Lorna's death, in contrast, there was the sheer joy of Chris' MBE presentation in July.

There we were in the grounds of Windsor Castle, dressed up to the nines, excitedly awaiting the nod for Chris to receive his MBE from Prince Charles.

As an interesting aside, this award ceremony was the last one carried out by the Prince before he became King Charles III.

To see Chris receive his MBE was like being in a fairy tale; it was magical. I've never felt so proud of anything or anyone in my life. It was just so beautiful.

This incredible experience lasted for about two hours. It began with champagne and chat with our fellow guests, all in our finery.

We were then taken gradually, room by room, through the castle until it was time for Chris to receive his Member of the British Empire honour.

Talk about proud. In the weeks leading up to the ceremony, Chris went through a 'What did I do to deserve this?' moment or two.

As we always do, we talked things through. I explained that though the wording for his award was for 'Services to Judo' it wasn't just about his amazing gold winning achievement, it was also about everything he'd given back to the sport: his mentorship, his incredible kindness and generosity with his time, and the fact he's an incredible role model for Paralympic sport in general.

This is what had led to this honour; it was so much more than that gold.

As his MBE was pinned to his chest, I couldn't have been happier.

And then something that still makes us laugh to this day... In a random co-incidence, or divine timing - I'm not sure which - our attention was drawn to the pianist who had been providing beautiful music throughout the ceremony.

It's no secret that I am the biggest musicals fan, and one of our family favourites is The Sound Of Music. Guess what tune was playing? Cue, "the hills are alive..... with the sound of music."

I started crying, Chris started crying. Beautiful.

It was a magical moment, amongst many magical moments that day.

After the ceremony, I took so many pictures and video in the castle grounds. I even took a little bit of video of Chris jumping for joy. It's my favourite thing to look back on from that day.

I love remembering this moment and looking at the pics and video. It was extra special because it was just us, Chris and I.

We share so much with so many people, because we love the people in our lives and want to spend time with them. But, there is something about getting pockets of time to ourselves that we both value so much, and this was one of them.

As Chris was only allowed to bring one guest with him to the ceremony, our two families joined us for a meal that evening. It was a lovely way to celebrate as Chris showed everybody his MBE.

There was so much speculation about who had nominated Chris for his award. We had absolutely no clue, and still don't.

But, if you're reading this, thank you. Whoever you are, it was a wonderful way to reward Chris for his incredible achievements and his dedication to the sport that he has loved since he was a child. It means everything to us both.

As we began to return to our routines - Chris training and me undertaking my various work activities - July soon turned to August, and with it came more excitement. My hen do!

Hannah took full control of arrangements. As an experienced event planner, she knew her stuff. Celebrations were to take part over a whole weekend, with the nickname of 'Lou Fest'.

It was really special. Fourteen of us, including Mum, family friends, my bridal squad which, of course, included Hannah. We had our own mini bus.

Hannah had so many wonderful surprises up her sleeve, and the first one was delivered movingly as we travelled on the bus to Oxford.

We'd talked a lot about Lorna, how much she would have loved our celebrations, and of how we would miss her presence.

As Lorna's daughter, Hannah had written a beautiful speech about how her mum would have loved to have been there with us. It was the perfect thing to do on a day already filled with so much emotion.

We arrived in Oxford and enjoyed a wonderful, rooftop meal overlooking the city, surrounded by beautiful flowers.

After that, we split into two teams and took on a pirate themed escape room. I live for escape rooms, so it was spot on. It was a really special day and one that included family friends from Canada, as well as Dana who flew in just for my hen do all the way from America.

Of course we found time for a spot of shopping, before returning home when Hannah hosted a party at Mum and Dad's house.

On arrival, it felt like I was being dragged through the house, into the lounge. The curtains were shut and I was wondering what was going on.

On the TV screen was a Mr and Mrs game, tailor made to test Chris and I's knowledge of one another.

It was really fun, but quite scary how well we did. I got every question right.

Hannah also surprised me with personalised Lou Fest t-shirts, all in our favourite colours, names on the back, with a specially designed Hen Do logo.

When we went outside to get some fresh air, I discovered big Indian garden tents and a band playing my favourite tunes.

We tucked into fish and chips and partied the night away on the patio.

Hannah had invited many friends and my dear Nan was there dancing with me. It was a very special night.

Nan's health had been declining for some time and she needed support, so that year, following an operation, unexpectedly she moved in with Mum and Dad. As per usual, my parents were completely selfless and prioritised my nan's needs over their own.

Watching someone you love dearly lose their memory is one of the hardest experiences imaginable. I don't think any of us were really prepared to see this decline in my nan.

It was a big life change for all of us, alongside everything else happening that year. However, on the night of my hen do, and like so many other get togethers at Mum and Dad's since, the plus side was that Nan was there with us, creating memories.

With everyone staying over for the party, the next day Hannah had invited male guests, so it meant I could celebrate again, this time with friends' partners, Chris, Dad, Rob and William (Rob's son) too.

I wanted everyone to be included in the celebrations at some point, so Hannah had nailed it.

All teetotal and I had the best time ever.

Chris had two stag dos. One with his mates in Hull, the other with his Judo mates.

What was done for both of us was perfect for our personalities and what we like. It was so good, amazing.

With all this happening, you can probably understand why I still refer to this time as our Wedding Season. I'd love to say I came up with this great title, but it was actually the lovely Jordy (bride squad member) who came up with it.

This wasn't all. A few days before the wedding, Dad organised a party for lots of people we love and care about, but who couldn't be invited to the ceremony. It was in our home village. Can you tell that I come from a party family?

Our celebrations were wonderful, but exhausting. Chris's mum's gift of a day at our favourite spa was just the recharge we needed two days before the wedding.

Great massages, a good swim. We laid out on the sun beds and I went to sleep, as I always do.

Having a day just for us, before the big day, is something I'd recommend to any wedding couples. It's wonderful celebrating and chatting with guests, but it can be so easy to forget this time is about the two of you. Keeping time for you both is so precious.

With our 'wedding season' coming to an end, on the Friday we drove to our wedding venue - Holbrook Manor in Somerset. We were one of the last couples to marry there and we felt really lucky to be in this position because it ticked all the right boxes for us.

We wanted an exclusive venue that was solely ours where we could just be us, and that's what we got.

I arrived at the venue the night before our wedding and had dinner with all my bride squad. I was under strict, but supportive instructions, to have an early night.

In my room by 9.30pm for a good night's sleep. They knew from experience that if I was tired and run down, I'd be ill. They would do everything to ensure nothing was going to ruin my big day.

That night I had no sleep whatsoever. No nerves, not one. The only thing I felt was excitement and love.

In the morning, my bride squad left me alone for ages. They were trying to get me to rest as much as possible. No chance of that. I just could not wait to see Chris.

I'll never understand why someone would get nervous on their wedding day.

In my head I was thinking, 'If food arrangements go wrong, we order a takeaway. If the band don't turn up, we plug in an iPod'.

I couldn't see anything that would happen that would ruin my day, other than Chris not turning up, and I knew, in my heart, he would be there.

I just wanted to see Chris and to be his wife; that's all I thought about all morning.

Our wedding was at 1.30pm. Apparently, I was the only bride that had ever turned up early. Typical behaviour, with the Louise tradition of being on time, every time.

Getting ready that morning with everybody was so much fun. My hairdresser had been styling my hair all my life so is more like a friend, my make-up artist had done my brows and lashes for a long time too and was also a dear pal.

And then there was Mum helping me into *the dress.*

Months/weeks before, I'd been speaking to family friend, Maggie about designing a dress, but I just couldn't decide what I wanted.

Instead, she suggested I go dress hunting and she would make adjustments from there.

Finally, I tried a dress on with so many components I liked. Her instruction? "Buy it, and we'll just play with it." So, that's what I did.

To say she played with it downplays the incredible adjustments she made to turn it into my dream gown.

She changed it completely. Altered, tweaked it, those words seem inadequate. She did so many things to make it just right for me. She took out a lot of the skirt to accommodate me sitting in a chair. I needed the front shorter than the back and the bodice to be shortened so it would sit perfectly in my seated position.

With a beautiful scallop back, she brought the scallop shoulders up to match. Maggie put so much work into my dress and it was so fun working with her.

I felt a million dollars!

Of course, I was expecting to pay Maggie for her incredible work, but then she delivered the biggest surprise of all.

"I don't know what to buy you for your wedding, so I'd like you to have your dress as a gift," she said.

I couldn't believe it.

The best wedding gift I could have ever received, because she gave it to me.

With my dream dress on, it was time for our ceremony.

As Dad walked me down the aisle to Elton John's Your Song, I was so chilled and happy.

Not bad given that I'd managed to get my dress dirty before the ceremony even started.

Somehow, I'd managed to pick up a dirty mark from under the table where we sat to take our vows, literally as I got to it, but as I said to our photographer, Neil: "Whatever. I really don't care. I just want to marry Chris." Neil reassured me: "Don't worry, it won't appear in any photos", and it didn't; he erased it beautifully.

When I got to Chris, I was filled with so much love, joy and relief because I was just so desperate to see him, and gosh, did he look gorgeous in his suit.

We made the whole thing a really personal ceremony. Firstly, we wrote our own vows, with help from my bridesmaid, Becky. Both vows ended with the same line at the end: "I love you to infinity and beyond."

I'm guessing most of you reading this will recognise the reference. The words chosen date back to the start of my relationship with Chris.

Both of us love anything Disney related, so I bought Chris a mini Buzz Lightyear, which became his lucky charm. He still carries it everywhere now - it goes with him all around the world.

After time, 'I love you to infinity and beyond' became our thing.

We had readings from Josh, my Bridesman, and Chris' sister, Hannah. We asked both of them to write something about us and their interpretation of our love.

What we heard was a total surprise and so special.

The celebrant announced us 'Husband and Wife' and we kissed, but then something I wasn't expecting... Chris ran me out of the room. He was so fast, I didn't even hear our exit music -Crazy Little Thing Called Love.

Off we went into a side room and he told me: "I just wanted to be alone with you."

Having a moment like this on our big day was so precious, and so needed.

"We're together and we're so good. It's beautiful," said an emotional Chris as we stole some more alone time later in the day, away from our guests.

We knew how important it was to have these moments throughout the celebrations.

Several people had advised us to book in time for just the two of us, and it was such good advice. So good in fact, I'd urge any couples to do the same at their weddings.

Then came the confetti arch, all our friends and family lining up to shower us in happiness.

And the music. Music runs in my blood and has been the only thing that could have saved me many times in my life.

I really wanted to give Chris something super special for our wedding day. We'd agreed we weren't going to do traditional presents and that helped me because it meant he wasn't expecting anything. Chatting with Claire, she and I came up with an amazing idea. "Chris' favourite thing in the world is when you play the piano, so why don't you write him a song, record it and play it at the wedding?" It was perfect. When I play piano, Chris always stops what he's doing and listens; he just loves it. It's so sweet. So, that's what I did.

I knew I couldn't do it live because I would just cry my whole way through it, so I made him a music video. I played the piano using some of our favourite songs, but with changed lyrics. We included Your Song and at the end was Sweet Caroline. The latter one was a little in-joke. When we went on an 80s cruise, every corner we turned, we heard it and it drove us crazy. I changed the words to Sweet Christopher and then got everyone in the room joining in. It was really cool and a lovely moment which added to the whole musical vibe.

Then there was our band who were incredible. A friend from New Zealand wrote us a wonderful song and played it on the venue's grand piano. He handed out lyrics so that all our guests could join in. Everyone sang, and on the grand piano was a treasured photo of me with Lorna. Always with us.

Our first dance was so special. Yes, you read that right. Our first dance.

Fancy that? Chris and I dancing at our wedding?

I'm amazed when others are amazed about us dancing together on our big day.

Nobody in my life is surprised because they know I love parties and a dance, but in an interview I gave recently the interviewer was stunned that we had a first dance.

I remember thinking, 'Why is that so surprising? It's only my legs that don't work. The rest of me can party hard.'

I'm shocked at how many people act surprised when they find out I like to dance. I think people forget I'm a human and not some alien species.

Chris thinks it's another great example of how people underestimate what I can do.

"It's annoying because Louise is more able than anyone I've ever known." I love that he said this about me one Sunday as we were baby sitting my nephew and enjoying the summer sunshine.

The song for our first dance was Frank Sinatra's I Love You Baby.

We chose it because Chris would always sing it to me, especially in the shower during the early days of our relationship. I loved it because he didn't know the words so he would make up different ones about me every time.

We thought it was a perfect song because not only is it sentimental, it's slow at the start. It meant we got our little moment together, but then everyone could join in with us when it got more lively.

It was a beautiful moment. The truly wonderful thing was that no-one was shocked by us dancing. We were just Chris and Louise. The way it should always be.

We had an incredible day, summed up beautifully by my friend, Karen: "Your wedding was like being in a musical," she enthused.

For me, the biggest musical nerd, it was the greatest compliment.

Sunday was an equally beautiful day. Hotel breakfast and then back to our Wiltshire home. Two loved up newlyweds, cosied up together, surrounded by so many gifts and cards.

We'd agreed that we'd open some of our presents before we went on honeymoon and some after. Well, that was never going to happen.

Instead we ordered takeaway and just opened everything.

The love we felt from all our messages and presents was overwhelming. Sweet things like our Canadian friends clubbing together to pay for a trip to Canada - that's on the plans for 2025, and we can't wait.

But first, our honeymoon. 10 Days in the beautiful Maldives.

My airmiles and Chris' gold card - that he was given after winning gold in Tokyo - gave us first class tickets there and back. Magic. I actually enjoyed those flights. Shocking, I know.

Our honeymoon is the happiest and most well I've felt my whole life.

I've never seen beauty like it, I've never felt peace like it, before or since.

The Maldives is my dream place and I'd go back in a heartbeat.

It averaged 30 degrees every day, with the sea only one degree cooler than the air. When you get into the water, it's like a bath.

I love being warm. My body felt incredible. I wasn't having to deal with hot, then cold, as we do in the UK. There were no moments of my body freaking out.

Chris said he'd never known me be so well for 10 days straight. I felt great.

I loved the remoteness of The Maldives, I loved the feeling that we were in the middle of nowhere and no-one could find us.

Just the two of us on this tiny island, surrounded by crystal clear, warm, beautiful sea, teeming with tropical fish, sharks, sting rays.

I just felt amazing. I did every single activity I wanted to, and loved it.

Jet skis, underwater propellors, parasailing, coral reef swims, swimming with sharks, we did it all.

The food was amazing and so were the people.

We wanted to try all these different activities, but as I always am, I was prepared to argue my case in order to do them.

Any adventure I want to do, I'm always ready to give the big speech explaining how independent and capable I am. The 'I'm really strong, I know I'm in a wheelchair, but I can do this,' blah, blah, blah statement.

On numerous occasions in the UK and around the world, I've been refused at this point. From not letting me ride roller-coasters, to sitting in certain theatre seats, and not being allowed to partake in adrenalin activities, this speech had been well prepared and used.

Not this time. As I assured staff I could swim, there was no problem at all.

"Oh no, we've seen you swimming around the resort. Please don't worry. That's fine."

I was stunned. Never had anybody reacted so positively in this kind of situation.

Then they turned to Chris: "However, sir, we've noticed you're not so confident in the water. Is that right?"

Initially, Chris's initial reaction was one of frustration and embarrassment, but he knew how much this moment meant to me, so we just burst out laughing at the unexpected irony.

Chris isn't a naturally confident swimmer, like me, but during the honeymoon, and since, his water confidence has grown.

We had some amazing adventures together and the staff's approach was wonderful. There were never any weird conversations about my disability. They offered help when it was needed and did what needed to be done.

On our shark swim, for instance, I found it really hard to get back on the boat as it was quite high out of the water.

So, with my butt on Chris' shoulder and another guy pulling me up onto the boat, we made it work. The staff just pitched in and helped. They weren't scared, they just listened to what was needed.

Throughout our trip, it was never a case of 'should we?'; we just found a way to do things, supported by the island team.

This approach led to one of the most beautiful moments during our stay.

Parasailing over two schools of dolphins. Around 80 in two pods, it was the most beautiful thing I'd ever seen.

Islanders told us they'd only ever seen this a couple of times so we were really lucky.

We had wanted to parasail, so they pushed our session back later to bring in another staff member to make it easier for me to land.

Dinner at a Thai restaurant on a rock. We were picked up in a speedboat, but there were steps, so Chris carried me. There was someone to pick up my chair so we could enjoy this incredible moment.

Being out on our coral reef and shark swims. Our guide was so aware of my strong swimming ability and was happy for me to take point on Chris' safety. Someone saw my genuine ability. I was the one saving us in the water if something were to happen. It felt so empowering and such a refreshing change to have such a positive experience.

Always thinking of me, asking what I needed, never questioning my ability. Everything was so easy throughout our stay. The way it should be.

Enjoying a massage, with a glass floor. Watching Nemo and Dory and a huge tuna fish swimming below me. Bliss. I'd go back to The Maldives in a heartbeat.

Coming home from this incredible honeymoon was hard. Not because we were going back to our 'normal' things, as we love what we do, but hard in the sense that we found it so difficult being apart.

Chris and I felt so different after we got married, in that we didn't want to have so much time away from each other.

Coming away from our honeymoon, we realised being apart felt just as bad as it had done after our lockdown time together ended. We knew we had to find a way forward that built in far more time for us.

As we continued discussions around this, there was some wonderful family news. I had a new nephew. Benji was born in November 2022. Mum and baby were home and doing well.

My brother, Rob, and wife, Abby, felt complete. A baby brother for William.

All seemed good, until it wasn't. Benji started getting really poorly. He had developed a rare heart condition which left medics puzzled. Rushed to hospital in Bristol, we were repeatedly told to prepare for the worst; terrifying and heart breaking.

I'll always remember holding him at the hospital. So small, so fragile. He was rigged up to so many tubes and wires. I wondered whether this would be the first and last time I'd be able to do this.

Seeing Benji, my brother, sister-in-law and parents all go through this was awful.

At the same time, Grandad (Dad's Dad) was really sick and my parents were having to shoulder it all alongside other difficult family issues.

With all this going on, I was happy to spread some much needed happiness for my nephew, William, on his birthday.

With Rob and Abby at the hospital every day, William's celebrations were down to me, so I was determined to make it a day to remember.

Going into full Aunty mode, I bought the world, including a bubble gun, which William adored.

William played with it repeatedly and loved it so much that taking it away from him brought a lot of stress and tears. Weeks later, said bubble gun mysteriously 'disappeared'.

Anyone else smell BS here? I certainly did. ;-)

It was one light moment among weeks of uncertainty and worry.

As Benji fought to remain with us, my grandad, Jack, passed away.

Grandad had the sweetest personality. He worked on the railway his whole life and was very content.

He loved his garden and grew so many vegetables. Grandad would grow all year as he understood the seasons and knew exactly what to plant, and when, for the best results.

Those home grown vegetables were his pride and joy. One of my favourite things was going to Grandad's house for a tour of the garden. He'd tell me about all the things he was growing and Nana would cook everything fresh that he had harvested.

The food was delicious. Combined with Nana's home baked cookies, I was in food heaven.

The week before Grandad died, I went to see him one last time. He was unresponsive, but as I opened the wedding photos and pics of baby Benji on my iPad, he opened his eyes again. I looked at him, he looked at me; it was a precious moment.

When Chris and I married a few months before, Grandad had been too poorly to join our celebrations, so this was my way of sharing our joy with him.

I'd spent so many joyful moments with him over the years. Grandad had been the ultimate party animal when he was younger. At my 18th birthday party, he sang Delilah - his favourite song - and was the last one on the dance floor.

While everyone else was recovering from a late night, he would be the first one up the next morning. An unbelievable man and sweet to the very core of him. I loved him to bits.

Just months before his death he'd confessed to me that he was done suffering and that he didn't want to be here anymore. Though it was hard to hear, it was his truth.

Although he was bright as a button mentally, physically his body was failing. For someone that swam in the sea, had been so independent throughout his life, this seemed like torture.

So, when Grandad passed away, though devastated for us as a family, I was relieved for him.

It was the right time and I felt at peace because this was what he wanted.

Grandad had been in hospital a lot during his last months and died in early December, aged 92. His funeral took place on December 30th, 2022.

At the time, little Benji was still battling in hospital. So, we agreed to livestream the service so Abby could be part of it while caring for him.

It may seem strange, but I still chuckle when I think about this. There was Chris, sitting in the corner of this little pew, with my Nana sat in the row in front, as she talked her way through the whole thing.

Blah, blah, blah, on she whittled, making us smile with her comments.

I looked at Rob to my right, and he was laughing, as we tried so hard to hear what Dad and my aunty were saying about Grandad. I saw Abby on the screen and she was laughing too. A little merriment at such a sad time, somehow it just felt right. Nana chatting her way through Grandad's moment - she was always the boss in that marriage; it was oddly fitting.

Nana's such a quirky soul and I love her. I wouldn't want her to be any other way.

She loves Chris and I so much and has always been so supportive.

In the weeks following Grandad's funeral, there were too many times when we thought my little nephew may not make it.

2022 was truly a rollercoaster year, for me and Chris, for my family, but some way, somehow, we had made it through together.

Preparing to welcome in 2023, my thoughts turned to my little nephew, with a perfect smile and the most beautiful red hair you've ever seen.

Ginger hair that wasn't expected as it was blonde until he received emergency treatment.

The Bristol Infectious Diseases team told Rob and Abby they weren't completely sure why my nephew's hair changed colour, but that it may have been the result of one of the drugs he was prescribed, or a combination of drugs.

All I knew was that as I looked into Benji's eyes (Boy, is he going to be a real heartbreaker), I felt so much gratitude, love and hope.

A new year, a new journey ahead, so many more adventures to come...for all of us. I felt so lucky.

Chapter 48:

Introducing The Bride Squad

I'm the luckiest girl in the world. I have a lot of amazing friends and I have my amazing bride squad. I had seven bridesmaids and one bridesman at my wedding to Chris in 2022 – Josh, Hannah, Abby, Becky, Claire, Jordy, Bethan and Dana.

Sadly Dana couldn't be there in person as she was too busy being a legend at the US Open. Gosh, I'm so proud of her, but more on our friendship later.

I very easily could have ended up with more, but I made the right call. I'd lay down my life for every single one and love them dearly.

Let me tell you about each of these beautiful souls I get to call my friends, and how they truly have shaped my life and continue to do so.

Josh

We met at college and he's been my constant. Everyone needs a friend who will tell you straight what you need to hear, not what you want to hear.

Josh's tough love has been invaluable in my life and has been the reason I have managed to get through many a dark period of time.

His mutual love of musicals and BUSTED means we have so much in common, resulting in our days out always being magical, and the best part? He arranges them all and never gets it wrong when it comes to access and what I need.

As the person who often has to arrange most things and think about all access relatable obstacles which may occur, I cannot explain the gratitude I have for this man, for knowing me and giving me stress free days out which I can just show up to.

Hannah

My sister, my longest friend. Our families grew up in sync together (literally next door) and she is the one friend who I have never been without. She's been by my side through every phase of my life and, trust me, there's been a lot. She's supported me all the way, judgement free.

From fighting off those primary school bullies to fiercely supporting me in my ventures now, she's always been there. She makes me laugh hysterically and always knows how to make me smile even when times are tough. She has the most brilliant immature sense of humour, just like me which, when combined, turns us back into children.

The ups and downs we have shared are endless and will continue to be, but one thing remains, and that's that we are always there for each other.

Abby

The friend who became family. Abby married my brother, which in my mind then made her my sister. She is so much more than a sister-in-law to me. She is a friend I would choose any day, and I just got lucky that she's now officially a family member.

Having a true friend within your family is priceless, especially for those eye roll moments when we think the same thing, or when times have been really hard, and she just understands on a different level because she's in that same circle as you. Her sense of humour is wonderful and, along with my brother, has given me the most beautiful nephews imaginable.

Becky

My soul sister. Becky and I have a compatibility that's so special, that began when we met at secondary school. The way she can read my mind in any scenario and work out how I'm feeling is next level. I always feel safe and secure with her. A look alone will communicate so much between us. It was with her that I had my American adventure down the west of the country, undertaking the ultimate US road trip, with the Double's Masters thrown into the middle, as you do.

It was on this trip where I fell in love with Chris, and we told each other we loved each other for the first time. Becky was driving and we were on route to Vegas for the final stop of our trip. It was like a movie moment that I love replaying with her.

She's been fiercely by my side through many other adventures, highs and lows, and even helped Chris and I with our wedding vows, ensuring they perfectly synced without us even knowing. She cares deeper than anyone I know, and I thank my lucky stars that I get to be someone she gives time to in her life. When we're together, it's like a puzzle finally being finished, I feel complete.

Claire

Our family, my safe space. Claire is our family and I have known her since I was 11 years old. We met at secondary school. Living with her (in particular through lockdown) bonded us forever in a magical way. The four of us (me, Chris, Milo and Claire) became the most beautiful, unconventional family and I wouldn't trade those memories for a thing. Living with a friend was something I always wanted to do, and to have done this with Claire brings me so much joy and gratitude.

We had endless fun, and it was in that time that she helped me learn so much about myself. Claire is so brilliant at reminding me what I need to do when times are hard. From showing up with a craft to coming up with video/music ideas, she's the one and only person who truly understands how creativity can bring me out of the darkest places. Our WhatsApp conversations never contain hellos or goodbyes because it's just an ongoing narrative that never ends, because we are just there for each other, forever and always.

Jordy

My sister, my opposite. I have known her since I was 5 years old, and it was tennis which brought us together. We even retired from sport within a year of each other. So, our whole playing carers were in sync.

The thing that makes us chuckle about our friendship though, and that I love that we are so honest about, is that we couldn't be more different.

Have you ever seen the film Elemental? If you haven't, have a watch, and basically those two lead characters are us. We contrast beautifully, mainly in terms of our personalities. I have always been bubbly, happy go lucky and upbeat, and Jordy, let's just say, is a little quieter and more reserved. This is what makes our friendship super special though because we bring out different sides to each other, which others don't. Our lifetime of friendship means we know every single, tiny thing there is to know about one another.

We bond over our cherished memories and adventures which happened all over the world throughout our lives, and the fact that we are similar in terms of our ambition, sense of humour and views on various topics.

The greatest gift she ever gave me was asking me to be present at the birth of her gorgeous son Jackson. I've never been so flattered or felt more trusted than in that moment.

Bethan

My rock and real-life hero. This woman is indescribably brilliant in every single way. She has supported me through so many moments, but in particular when the hard times have hit, she has sat by my side and got me through.

Her honesty and kindness makes her super special, and she is just gold in human form. She's smart, talented and bloody hard working, and I cannot believe I am lucky enough to call her my friend.

We share a love of travel and love hearing about each other's adventures and future plans. I'm so happy I got onto that college course (BTECH Sports science) because that's how we met. Without her at college, my lessons would have been very dull indeed and it was worth every second to gain our lifetime friendship.

Dana

My brain twin. Where to start with Dana, or D-Dawg as I named her many years ago, and it seems to have stuck? Tennis brought us together, but our mutual love and respect for one another *keeps* us together.

We call each other our brain twins because that's how we are. I cannot believe how much in sync we are, how we think so similarly and react and respond in similar ways too.

She makes me laugh until I'm in physical pain, because she finds things as funny as I do. It breaks my heart every time we say goodbye and I always wish the sea between us was smaller.

We have been in tandem with so many moments in our lives - from studying to personal life things (like getting married) which has bonded us in such a unique way, that it feels like one of us always knows exactly how the other is feeling. We've always understood and supported one another in what we are going through and show up no matter what, despite the miles that separate us.

Do you know what makes me so lucky? That all of these friends could not care less what I did in tennis. Most have no idea.

A group of them came to watch when I qualified for Wimbledon and a couple came to tournaments with me, but they kept me balanced and my feet on the ground outside of the tennis world.

What I have always loved about them is that I could be anywhere in the world competing, I'd have a call with any one of them and we wouldn't talk much about the tennis; instead they'd ask: "How are you?"

It would never be a question of: "Did you win?" Instead they would ask: "Are you okay, are you homesick?" They weren't bothered by the results, only if it really bothered me. All they ever really cared about was me and my wellbeing, and that's why my friendships are so strong.

I've got a group of friends that really care and know me well, and I'm so grateful for them.

My bride squad all come from very different parts of my life. Each one is so different in their unique ways. They all have different jobs, interests, beliefs, yet, don't ask me how, when we all get together, it works. There's no judgement, just total love and acceptance.

Some of us have made some silly mistakes, done some stupid things, but we can always talk about it and work through things together.

These are the kind of people I want to surround myself with. Throughout my life I've experienced quite a few one-sided relationships, but my lifer friendships are completely two-sided. These friends are my family.

Over the years they've made loads of loving Louise interventions. When my Gramp died, I later found out that one of my friends had created a group chat so they could all be there for me. They all showed up at his funeral too.

There's been lots of moments like this where they have been looking out for me, where they've been united in that and for each other too. They all genuinely care and ask about one another, and that is priceless.

Chapter 49:

Positive Progress: A Family Affair

I am so like my dad, through and through. It's why we butt heads occasionally, but I appreciate that.

We have a real zest for adventure.

Today I say that Mum and Chris are the rocks, and Dad and I are the butterflies. Maybe it's something to do with our star signs. Mum and Chris are Cancerians, Dad and I Geminis.

Whatever it is, the family dynamic works really well.

As I started going on tour with tennis when I was so young, quality family time together was extra precious when I was growing up.

I always wanted to spend more time with my family, but I just didn't have the time, and then when I did have the time – full disclosure here - I was too knackered and just wanted to hibernate at home.

It's why it was so nice when I was able to spend a block of time with Mum and Dad in Laugharne, Wales in 2022. No distractions, just us together.

We spent five days there in Mum and Dad's time share - a long overdue trip as I had missed so many of these opportunities in previous years due to tennis commitments and work.

I had the best week and it was really sweet when Dad said he'd missed spending time with me. The truth is, I had too.

Although life is still very busy, there are things that we enjoy doing every now and then. Mum and Dad are so generous with sharing their timeshares around the country with us.

On one of these timeshare visits with family members, it was really nostalgic because it was somewhere Mum and Dad used to take my brother and I as children.

It was the year after I'd retired from competitive sport and came at a time when I was trying to work out what to do with my career and my life in general.

I had this dream of becoming self-employed, but I had also been offered two other jobs. One was a senior role for a sport charity and another was in employment helping people with mental health issues. Both were interesting roles, but my heart wanted to just go out on my own.

I can still recall the chat I had with Mum, Dad and my brother, Rob. All three of them thought of something completely different and offered advice and support. This is why I love my family so much.

I didn't know what to do, but these conversations came at just the right time. I'm very passion led and Mum gets that. She was very much about going in the direction of what I wanted and that it wasn't just about the money. She reminded me that, over time, I would earn good money, but that I just had to be a bit patient.

My brother has always been more money oriented so his advice came from that perspective, of financial security. Dad was a bit more neutral. His advice was: "Make sure you're safe, you've got stability and it'd be really cool to say you've been in a top role of a charity/organisation, even if you just do it for a year." All good advice.

It was the most wonderful chat and provided lots to think about. It really helped. The next day I declined the two roles and then wrote my action plan for self-employment.

The irony is, I never needed it because everything started to align.

It was the weirdest moment of my life and the greatest reminder that if you're brave and go for it, the world will reward you.

Prior to this chat, I'd spent the whole year going back and forth. I'd been chatting with Chris, mulling over the self-employment dream which I'd had in my head since before my sports retirement.

But it was the stopping with no distractions and taking the time to sit and really think about things that was the key to moving forward.

I talked about it, and it gave me the space I needed to make the decision.

One important thing I've learned about self-employment is that when you work for yourself, you run the risk of saying 'yes' to everything, and this, I tell you now, can be a very dangerous path to fall down for your mental and physical health. I definitely took on too much in those early days and certainly have had my moments since. It's hard because I genuinely want to do it all, but not at the sacrifice of my health and quality time with those I love.

So, always stop and think. Give yourself the same time and space as I gave myself. You have to stop, you have to have breaks from your usual work routine because that will give you the headspace you need to work out exactly what you want. Then get all your ducks in a row so you can move towards that goal and create the future you dream of.

On reflection, COVID and lockdowns also helped me do this. It aligned for me in that I didn't have tournaments so I could sit and have those important conversations.

Don't wait for these moments to come along, these opportunities to dig deep, as I did. Make space in your year to have time to get your shit together.

There's something about giving yourself space, making the effort for it and really understanding its benefit.

Now I make an effort to do this every week, but a word of caution, you have to be really strong with this if you want it to work for you.

I put those stop moments in my diary. Sunday is usually a stop day for Chris and I. It's our day, our time to relax and just be together. What I've found over the years is that quite a lot of people don't get it, so you need to be clear on this.

Sunday is our day when we lock down, we see nobody, we stay in our village and enjoy some quality time together with Milo.

Think about how you can do something similar. What does your stop look like and when will it be?

Just bear in mind that some people around you may just not get it, but that's okay. Try taking my approach.

I've realised that the old Louise, in my competitive tennis days, might have succumbed to pressure to let go of that stop day or she might have been really annoyed about it.

But today I'm very comfortable with saying 'no', with telling people that Sunday is my day to do nothing, and have quality time with my husband, who I only see two days a week, if I'm lucky. (It fills my heart with joy that this will no longer be the case very soon as he will be home for the entire week, every week).

This is a really big thing for someone who was once a people pleaser, who didn't prioritise myself and my mental health.

In the past, I may have made something up to get out of something because I wouldn't want to upset the person I was talking to.

Of course, it wasn't about this person. I loved them and wanted to be with them, it's just that I needed the space.

Even now, if I don't have a reset button in the week, I can't function, so I've learned from experience, that it's better to be honest, have those conversations and say 'no'. You know what I love? The people closest to me get it.

Some of my friends are good at reminding me of my stop days too. They'll say: "I'm not even going to ask to you to do something on Sunday because that's your day with Chris and you're doing nothing."

This response, this understanding, shows me they are the right friends to have around me.

And there it is again - the importance of your tribe and surrounding yourself with those who put you first and empower you to make the best decisions, for you, when you may have lost your way.

Quality time is so important. If people around you don't get it, then tough. When I was writing this book, I realised that in one month, Chris and I only got one night together.

It was at the Europeans and we were asked to come out for dinner. Again, I stuck to our stop time and turned down the invitation, explaining that we were planning a quiet meal and some precious time together.

For me, there's nothing that makes us feel more connected than just taking Milo out. It's the best feeling. It's something I've come to really appreciate since the family trip that helped me plan for the future.

Just like that trip, our dog walks are wonderful reminders of how much we miss each other when we're not together. It's very easy to go from one thing to another and be busy, but this stop time is precious.

Now I always make space for this time, whether it's with Chris or with other members of the family. It can be hard as we're all really busy, but we're the Hunts and that's how we roll.

Chapter 50:

Find Curiosity and Joy in Others' Success

Jealousy. Bitterness. Try replacing them with curiosity and learning.

As soon as we tell ourselves something is unattainable, we can leave the door open to a negative mindset.

Chris and I were wandering around our village one day and there's a house that we love. There were two lush cars parked outside. Our reaction wasn't one of bitterness or jealousy, it was curiosity.

"I wonder what they do?" I said to Chris. "Should we ask?"

"That's going to be us one day," I added.

I want us to be happy, so why would I not be happy for others around us?

This 'knock 'em down', 'it's alright for them' attitude seems to be all too common, and I just don't get it. Not having a good approach to life can hold us back in so many ways.

My success has come from adopting the attitude of learning from others. I want to reach the highest levels in my field, so every opportunity to learn from someone is such a gift. My Gramp embedded this in me, and it's worked well so far.

Whenever I get the chance to meet somebody, I want to talk to them because I want to know how they got where they are in life and, if it feels right for me, how I can achieve that.

Curiosity gives me the steps needed to get to a point where I can have that lovely car, that house, or both.

Holding this attitude will help me get there. How's your attitude right now?

Chapter 51:

The Smallest Room, But the Biggest Comfort

If you really want to see someone every day, put them on the wall of your toilet. Yes, really.

We have a massive picture of our wedding day with all our guests in it, in the main bathroom of our house, and I love that whenever people come over, they can spot themselves. It's like Where's Wally!

Sometimes it also acts as a sad reminder of those who couldn't be with us on our special day. Lorna, my dear second mum. Guess where I have my favourite photo of the two of us? In our ensuite bathroom because I get to see her face every day. Put the people you love in the loo, guys. There's some advice for you, for free.

Joking aside, having the right people around me, people I can lean on, can learn from, has helped me battle through so many tough moments.

It's why I talk to others, all the time, about the importance of building a tribe around you and having balance in that tribe.

If you have a disability, I cannot encourage you enough to surround yourself with at least a small group of people where you're exposed to them on a semi-regular basis, where you can just be you and they'll get it, with no explanation.

The only thing I miss about being on the tennis tour is that trusted tribe of people. It's the way that things like a broken spoke on the chair or having a UTI is common language and conversation, requiring no explanation.

In these moments I feel like I can start breathing again because the people around me all get it, I don't have to explain.

It's really good to expose yourself to that. So, if you are struggling, but have no-one to help pull you out of that space, go and join something where there'll be people, maybe just one person, who gets it - who gets you - with little or no explanation.

That understanding is something that I took for granted growing up because my parents did an unreal job of placing me at Stoke Mandeville and Tennis camps, from the age of five – an amazingly supportive environment. I've only ever had this in my life, and it wasn't until I left sport that I realised just how that environment had really helped me. It was a refreshing place to be. It's nice to dip into that place when I'm commentating on, or organising tournaments now.

Chapter 52:

Limitless Future

I always describe it as one of the weirdest jobs I've ever been given because no-one teaches you how to do it. I just got on with it, learning by doing. A classic Louise move, really.

Wimbledon. Every tennis player's dream. I was still playing the first time I was asked to commentate for the BBC.

When I was asked to do it, it was really exciting. My first commentary job.

Here I was in the commentary booth, sitting alongside the lead commentator, and, quite frankly, with no clue what I was doing. It was a case of: "Here's your headset, off you go."

At the time, the BBC had only just begun covering wheelchair tennis fully, i.e.: having commentary on every match possible, and all being available to watch online/via the red button. It was a brilliant, exciting step forward, but it meant they were trying to cover all courts, all matches, with a relatively small commentary team.

At first, I didn't understand when to comment during a match. When I've watched tennis on TV, I've never thought of the particulars of when a commentator should be talking. Why would I? One of the first rules of commentating is never to talk over a point.

I didn't know that if I was asked a question by the lead commentator and a player was about to serve, the right thing to do would be to give a short, snappy answer and continue the answer after the point was played. Instead, I just carried on talking.

I didn't know that I couldn't talk over any graphics showing the score either, and that you had to wait for the graphic to come down.

This virgin tennis commentator was as green as the perfectly manicured courts. It makes me cringe beyond belief, but I didn't even understand how to mute myself so viewers couldn't hear me. No-one had told me how to turn myself 'off'!

Instead, I'd be trying to eat or drink without making too much noise and holding out for a loo break that never came. It was a long time ago and I was still young, but a positive thing about all this is how it shows the development of commentary for wheelchair tennis at Wimbledon; how the BBC went from having me and one other wheelchair tennis pundit/expert having to cover four or five matches back-to-back, to showcasing the sport on court 1, on prime time TV, with a broad team covering each match. It's amazing and I'm honoured to have been a part of that movement.

Some may say that TV sports commentary is a pretty dog eat dog world. It's really competitive with quite a small pool of commentators for specific sports.

To put things in context, when I first saw wheelchair tennis at Wimbledon, I was 14 years old. It was in its infancy, with just a handful of men's double pairs competing for no prize money; I believe they were given about £1,500 each to play a demo.

It was very much about exhibition matches rather than a full blown competition.

Nowadays, in 2024, the wheelchair tennis prize money pot sits at 1 million with the singles winners taking £66k each.

As more and more players got involved in those early days, interest grew until the Wimbledon organising team contacted the LTA (Lawn Tennis Association) and put my name forward as a potential commentator, alongside Pete Norfolk, a GB wheelchair tennis legend.

It was pretty cool, although not without some challenges, particularly around scheduling. In those first couple of years, I'd be in the commentary booth from 10.45am up until 8pm, trying to eat my lunch silently. I felt like there was no time to go to the toilet, to the point where I'd have to speak to a lead commentator and they'd say: "You're in here the whole day. Please go."

It's how I built good bonds with a couple of commentators, including Paul Hand, who I really adore. Paul took me under his wing and gave me this invaluable piece of advice: "Remember, you can press mute."

Back in those early days, when I was still learning, he was also the one that told me to take 20 minutes when I needed it and helped us create a schedule that worked for everyone on the team.

In that first year of wheelchair tennis on the BBC, we were all learning.

We covered every match, which was brutal as they were all on two outside courts, hence the long days. Not like it is now where the wheelchair matches are on show courts too and integrated with the non-disabled matches.

Its progression has been interesting to watch. One thing that's really changed is that wheelchair tennis experts like me are not needed on every match. Today you'll see a wheelchair match with a regular lead commentator on their own. They know their stuff.

What they tend to do now is put me/other pundits on the big matches, or ones where there is British interest, so I'll do, on average, two in a day, with a little break in between.

It's a far cry from those early days.

We're now also on mainstream TV and not just the red button, which is really exciting.

It's amazing to think that I've learned all my commentary skills on a pretty big stage. Between Wimbledons, I've commented on The Masters, Paralympics, European Championships and the British Open, which I've also helped to organise and run.

It certainly keeps my organisational skills on top form, balancing so many different roles.

In 2023 I was asked to join the commentary booth for The Europeans in Rotterdam and, for the first time, as lead commentator.

While admitting that I'd not taken on the lead role before, I knew I'd be more than capable, but when I was asked to commentate for the whole thing alone, I said 'no'.

It meant nine days of commentary from 9am until at least early evening, and my reply was: "It's not going to happen. That's too much to ask of me."

It was a seminal moment which showed me how far I'd come. At Wimbledon it had taken me three years to speak up about the scheduling.

For the first time, I said 'no' and asked for us to look at other options. I was asked who I would recommend for the commentary booth, and I suggested a suitable colleague. I was put in charge of the schedule and created a roster, so we were able to break up the days a bit and ensure there was balance.

This felt like a really big step in my commentary career because I was lead for the first time and in charge of a great team. This led to the Masters where I flew solo as lead commentator. Then I was contacted by Whisper/Channel 4 again to see if I wanted to work on the Paris 2024 Paralympics.

As we move through 2024, it feels like this year the commentary side of my career has really taken off because I've gone from being a pundit to a lead commentator, and I've shown I can do both roles.

Now I have the experience, I don't mind being on my own in the commentary booth, I don't mind teaming up, which gives you options. I really like commentating and enjoy it for the spot of time I'm doing it, but I don't want to sit in a room looking at a screen for my full time job - I like people interaction too much.

I really care about helping to grow wheelchair tennis and people getting it right. There's nothing worse than hearing a commentator say stuff that just isn't correct. This is happening less and less now but, at times, I have sat with my head in my hands, so I want to take that responsibility on because I know I'll get it right.

One of the big mistakes I see relates to explaining classification, or categories, for competitors. To be fair, these confuse *me* so I understand how hard it can be to get it right sometimes.

For example, I've heard the quad division described as being for athletes who have impairments in their arms, when it's actually far more complex. Many other factors are taken into account to classify someone into this category, and it's decided on a points system. In one sense the commentator wasn't wrong. They might have disabilities in their arms, but it's more than that. It's honestly a minefield, so there's no judgement here, but I feel more equipped to explain these things.

This really opens up the debate about how to best prepare commentators for their roles so they can fully inform their audiences.

Commentary is such an interesting role as no commentators sit in a room and learn the rules of the sport, whether it's tennis, football, golf or something else. It really is a case of learning as you go.

What I've learned from speaking to fellow commentators is they got into the work after having worked in the sport, either as an ex athlete like me, or in another role. Alternatively, they have a real interest in the sport.

Once you're on the commentating team it's down to us, as individuals, to keep up to date with the latest talking points in our sports so we can pass on that knowledge to our viewers and listeners.

I regularly top up my knowledge by following the tour and checking in on results. It also helps when I have organised tournaments as I am present to see the results happen.

I love the excitement of being part of a team going live on the air and the challenges it can bring.

Unexpectedly, in 2023, I experienced my first solo commentary spell when a rain delay led to a scheduling blip.

Producer to me: "Where's X, our lead commentator?"

Me: "I don't know where he is, but I'm here."

Producer: "Right, Louise, you're flying solo."

Me (To myself): 'I've got this.'

Deep breath, unmuted mic and I went for it.

"And welcome back to a very wet and windy day here at ..."

It may have only been for five minutes, but I saw it as my warm up. A little sign that I am ready to take my commentating even further in the future.

My passion and drive is having an impact in the male dominated commentary world. The same way I love being with a young person and seeing them smash their goal - that is my oxygen. It's about breaking down barriers and showing change can happen, that we don't have to do it a certain way 'just because that's how it's always been done'.

I still want to carry on commentating at the big tennis events, but three or four a year for me is great. I think this approach helps show people I'm no threat as I don't want to do this all the time.

I'm in a really nice position now where I know where I'm at with my commentary level and I feel confident to go it alone. I don't want to sound arrogant, but I've put the time in and I'm really excited to be in Paris for the Paralympics in 2024 - as a commentator, both as a lead and pundit.

Beyond Paris, I want to run an 'able-bodied' tennis tournament. I was given the chance to do this in 2023, but I just couldn't make it work with my diary.

The scheduling didn't work out and it clashed with other work commitments I already had in place, such as school visits.

When it comes to wheelchair tennis, I live and breathe it, basically, which makes my job easier as I have an extensive knowledge bank to call upon and share with audiences.

It's why I'm passionate about ensuring we have the right voices behind the scenes; those with the latest information ready to share with tennis fans. It's how we are going to help the sport grow.

Things like getting classifications wrong, lack of knowledge, using the wrong terminology to explain disability, can be so detrimental to our sport at a time when we're keen to see bigger draw sizes at Grand Slams and other events. It is happening - for example, they upped the draw size at Wimbledon in 2024 to align with the other Grand Slams, which is great. We're getting there, but we still have further to go. Draws have now grown to 16, rather than 8, like it was when I was playing. Change is happening and I am so here for it!

Chapter 53:

Welcome to the World of Celebrity

I love how I really bonded with my Nana over something I never expected - our mutual love for Cliff Richard.

As I mentioned earlier in the book, Cliff and I met when he presented me with my first tennis chair at Wimbledon.

Nana has music on all day, every day, a lot of it from the swinging 60s. Cliff is one of her favourite singers. If she's ever got his music on when we're chatting, she'll say: "I'm listening to your friend," which always makes me smile.

My journey with Cliff is really beautiful. From that first meeting at Wimbledon when I was five, we met again when I qualified for the Championships for the first time in 2015.

He was a part of that very special time in my life.

I began thinking that I would really like him to know the little girl he inspired that day (me!) made it to Wimbledon - his favourite tournament on the planet.

So, I went on a bit of a social media rampage. I shared the picture of him presenting me with my tennis chair and asked if anyone could help me tell Cliff I qualified. The message got to him!

Shortly afterwards, I received a message from his PA saying he was delighted, and he was really grateful I had made the effort to get in touch. I was so pleased.

Some people don't realise the positive impact they can have on someone's journey, especially celebrities. With such hectic diaries, they come in, have an impact and then go.

So, this is my chance to say: "Thanks, Cliff, for being part of my tennis journey."

Included with my first time player experience at Wimbledon, I was given a theatre ticket of my choice. I went to the theatre box office in the grounds and, on someone's recommendation, opted for American singer songwriter, Carole King's musical.

A week or two later, I was sat in the theatre audience and in front of me, about four rows ahead, was Cliff.

I grabbed a napkin, as that's all I had, wrote, 'I'm not a stalker. I'm sitting behind you and I'm the little girl you presented with her first tennis chair all those years ago.' I asked one of the ushers to pass my note onto Cliff.

I didn't think any more of it. Then as I came out of the theatre, I heard "Louise! Louise!" and there was Cliff with his head out of the car window.

He stopped, got out of the vehicle, and came to give me the biggest hug.

He thanked me for my note and explained he had a link to Carole King. He said the show was really important to him so he was there supporting his friend.

Cliff asked if I had enjoyed the show and, as people started crowding round us, he apologised and said he had to go.

Luckily, I was able to grab a quick photo of us together before he disappeared into the night.

The connection with Cliff has continued. Bizarrely, someone I worked with at Phoenix had a link to Cliff and then a couple of months later I received a video from him telling me how much he loved all the work I was doing.

I also received a birthday card in 2024. I'm so happy that he stays in touch as I'm grateful for his part in my journey.

One of the coolest things about my life in tennis, and my travels around the world, has been the incredible opportunities I've had to meet some amazing people, including Cliff, various members of the royal family and other celebrities.

Over the years, I've had the honour of meeting our late Queen twice. The first time was during my teens when she opened the National Tennis Centre. The second meeting was at Buckingham Palace when I was invited to a Garden Party along with other Paralympians after London 2012. I took my mum and it was magic. We got all glammed up and had the best time ever. I'm super lucky. I've also met Prince Charles, now King Charles, on three occasions and Kate Middleton, Princess of Wales, plus a variety of celebrities such as Drake, Bradley Cooper and Scott Mills. I'm so grateful for these opportunities as I wouldn't have had them if it wasn't for tennis.

Chapter 54:

Ever Evolving Relationships

The Lawn Tennis Association. It's built my skill set, my confidence, my prospects and profile.

What the LTA means to me now is something I never anticipated. Visiting the national tennis centre is very different now too.

As a young player, I was filled with anxiety and dread. At the time, my self-worth and stress levels were sky high. I felt like I was under immense pressure and was being compared relentlessly - that is elite sport after all - but it really affected my confidence.

Today, my relationship with the LTA is something I'm really proud of.

When the LTA first offered me an opportunity to run a tournament, I trusted my gut. I knew I had to give things a try. Different people, different environment, different role. How would I know if it was for me if I didn't give it a go?

There were plenty of discussions, and after lots of going back and forth, Kirsty - an events manager there - convinced me to take up the new challenge.

I have known Kirsty a long time and we have always got on really well. She directed many tournaments I played in, so we've spent a lot of time together. Kirsty believed in me and saw something I didn't see in myself. When someone shows a bit of belief in you, it can transform your life and your opportunities. This was one of those moments for me.

I like to pass on this bit of life advice whenever I get the chance: When you see something in someone, go tell them.

Kirsty is a brilliant mentor for me because she did exactly this and has taught me so much about running a successful tennis tournament.

She has never made me feel stupid whenever I've asked questions. She only ever makes me feel empowered and I feel really proud to be associated with her and the LTA events team.

So far, I've organised five tournaments as a tournament director and supported Kirsty at others too, with one more to do in 2024 and hopefully more in 2025.

Building this relationship has helped in so many ways, not least in allowing me to change the narrative of what being at the National Tennis Centre means. I love visiting there now and feel empowered and confident in the work I do.

It's only 10 years ago that I would sit in my room at the National Tennis Centre, trembling and sobbing uncontrollably because I was so anxious and felt so intimidated. I felt like I stood out in the worst ways and felt horrendous. Now things are so different.

It just shows that it is possible to change your view and relationships, and I am so grateful for that.

Chapter 55:

Time For Equal Play, Equal Opportunity

Just 1 in 4 disabled children are included in PE lessons in the UK.

Equal opportunity is a basic human right and it is crucial that disabled children have the same access to sport and physical education (PE) as their non-disabled peers.

So often, disabled children are left out of PE at school. Paralympics GB ran a brilliant campaign around this during the Paris Paralympics, calling for equal access to PE and school sport for disabled pupils. The latest statistics shared here are not only heartbreaking, they're a disgrace.

It's about so much more than ticking the box of inclusion and equality. Sport and exercise can transform a young person's life in terms of personal development and physical health, but also create a space for social integration, which are all essential for the wellbeing and growth of all children.

Ensuring equal access to being active, empowers disabled youngsters, helping to break down societal barriers and stereotypes, while giving them the same opportunities to enjoy the physical, mental and emotional benefits of active play and exercise.

In one of my roles with Wheelpower (the national charity for wheelchair sport – *wheelpower.org.uk*), I love delivering an online course all around how to include wheelchair users, specifically in exercise sessions. It's brilliant as it creates a safe space for people from all walks of life, but often teachers come and ask questions and share their fears and concerns around including disabled people or wheelchair users in their PE classes. It's okay to be unsure, so this is a great space to ask those questions. The only thing that not's okay is to exclude for no valid reason. A lot of the time it's fear of safety, worrying about the non-disabled students in that session, but the reason WheelPower do such a good job with these courses is it's breaking down those fears and finding ways to make sure every child, in every lesson, feels included, seen and is getting the best experience they can out of their sport and exercise sessions.

I strongly encourage schools to ensure all students are included in every lesson and to be brave enough to adapt and try new ways to ensure every child is getting the most they can from that lesson.

The best thing you can ever do is ask that young person how they feel they could be included in the session, ask what would they like to do, and give them the same opportunity as their peers.

Sports shouldn't be an excuse to exclude, just because somebody is different.

The thing I love most about sport is that it can bring people together. One of the things that made me love Wheelchair Tennis so much was the way I could play with such a variety of people. You can have a tennis court with people playing in wheelchairs, on their feet, with visual impairments, hearing impairments, the list goes on, and we can all play together.

Why can't PE be like that?

If you work in a school, please don't be afraid to think outside the box and try something different; remember that the disabled child you may have in your lessons just wants to be included like everybody else.

This is another area where Commonweal School really supported me and learned alongside me. When I first started, they insisted on me having a teaching assistant in those sessions, but through listening and having conversations, they soon realised I didn't need that support.

With my PE teachers, I worked out which PE sessions I could join in with my classmates, and when it was something not ideal, such as an activity on the field, we worked together on a great alternative - something I could do with my friends alongside me.

I never missed a PE session and always remained active. I really appreciated being included.

Sometimes inclusion can mean treating somebody differently to make sure they have the same opportunities and experiences, and that's okay.

Every child has the right to partake in sport and activity and this should never be defined by a label or the fact they have disability. It's about what they can do and enabling that, so they are included like everyone else.

Chapter 56:

What's A Winning Mentality for You?

A winning mentality can look different to everybody. For me, it's adventure driven, opportunity driven, money driven, but what is it for you? Be honest with yourself.

If you're reading this and you're over 30, like me, or older, please always remember that age is nothing.

I love sharing my story and journey. What seems to resonate with people is understanding that a winning mentality is an individual thing. Your idea of this can look completely different to your colleague, your partner, your friend, a family member, a stranger.

I really wanted to own my own house one day and that pushed me to work hard. I'm not as bothered about travelling as I used to be; the things that drive and motivate me change, and that's exciting. To me, this is a winning mentality right here because I've got my goal and I'm going to set my sights on that.

So, allow your definition of a winning mentality to be unique, to develop, to be different. It doesn't have to be wrapped up in the same way that it serves me.

Strive to achieve and then enjoy the feeling of achieving. I think pride is something that's really underestimated. It's okay to be proud of yourself. I personally find that quite attractive in somebody else. I'm always attracted to someone that owns what they do. It's a great thing. I just feel so much joy when I see someone reach their goals, and the happiness it brings them - it's infectious!

My Gramp always said: "I work hard because I want my family to have a nice life. I want to go on nice holidays, I want to do nice things and leave a legacy."

That was his driving force. This is certainly something I would love to do in the future too, as I have seen my parents live this way, and it's a truly joyful way to live. Life is so much fun when you share what you have with those you love. I hope that, one day, I can take my family on magical Christmas holidays like my Grandparents used to, providing that precious family time together, or be in the position my parents worked so hard for, so they can support and be there for me and my brother at every opportunity.

Leaving a legacy is also important to me. That's partly why I wanted to write this book, as I hope this will leave a little bit of me in the world when I'm no longer here. The way Gramp and Lorna's names come up so often shows the legacy they left in our hearts and, if I leave even a fraction of what they left, I'll be so content.

Gramp, Dad, Chris. Their level of ambition, their drive. Being abnormally ambitious (the way Chris describes me) that's me too. I put us all in that category. Every day, it's about how can I make my life better, what can I do better? What am I striving for?

I have to give Mum and Dad credit for instilling this approach in me too. My character means that when the highs are so high, the lows are low.

Karl, my sports psychologist, helped by saying this: "The best thing you can ever do is live in that moment, as much as that's hard."

I used to run away from that, but now I know that doesn't help. It makes the low moments even lower. So, now it's all about recognising that you can't have the high without the low sometimes. The important thing in these moments - your priority - must always be to work through them, and remember to take care of yourself, because they will pass. One day these same moments will not be such a weight on your shoulders as they once were.

Chapter 57:

Some Louise-isms For You to Ponder

These may refer to my life, but try applying them to yours.

What does 'normal' actually mean? I struggle with this word a lot. I challenge you to think of one person you can define as 'normal'; I bet you can't!

How different would my life have been if I had been born into a different family or had different opportunities presented to me?

You are solely responsible for your behaviours and efforts in life, so take ownership of that and realise how impactful this can be.

Raising awareness of what makes people different doesn't have to be a negative thing. It can become your greatest strength.

Showing up is everything! Do this and you'll have no regrets.

Life can and will be hard at times, but it's the effort in overcoming those hard times which builds strength and makes you feel proud of what you've achieved.

The lows are there to ensure we can enjoy the ride when we hit those highs.

Never let your pride get in the way of you living a fulfilled life.

Your mind is the best thing you'll ever have, take care of it and, if you want something enough, you will find a way to do it.

Half my body doesn't work, so I want to keep using the other half. If I ever get to a point where it doesn't, I'll be getting an electric wheelchair because I'm not staying indoors.

Understand the power of your words. Use them wisely, with love and kindness. Think before you speak.

Drop me a line on any of my socials and tell me what your favourite Louis-ism is, and why.

Chapter 58:

76 Reasons to Believe in Myself

7 London Mini Wheelchair Marathon Wins

13 World Team Cup appearances

2 Paralympics

13 Senior Singles titles

41 Senior Doubles titles

What are your reasons to believe in yourself?

Write them down. Put them somewhere you can see them every day.

Chapter 59:

C'est La Vie: Paris and Beyond

As I near the end of writing this book, my mind is on the Paris Paralympics.

In a few days' time I'll head across the English Channel to commentate on this incredible event for Channel 4.

I'll also be supporting Chris as he competes for Paralympics GB in what will be his third Paralympics and sporting swansong before retirement from his beloved sport.

I expect emotion, lots of emotion, so many highs and probably a few challenges along the way.

It will, undoubtedly, be another magical time for the Hunt Skellcys as we connect with fellow athletes on a world stage, at the greatest show on earth; making friends and connecting with familiar faces from our ever growing and developing global family.

It's a huge privilege.

Chris and I have been preparing for this moment, and all the other moments around it, for a long time, but suddenly it's knocking on our door. Ready to welcome us in and then spit us out into a bold new future together.

I'm sure Chris won't mind me saying that it's been a rollercoaster of emotions these past few months and years as we've prepared ourselves for what's to come.

Unyielding training schedules, qualifying for Paris and, most challenging of all, dealing with a traumatic classification process, which re-surfaced a lot of dark emotions for Chris. There have been tears, there have been triumphs and everything in between.

Living the life of an elite athlete is never easy. We both know that because we have lived it, are living it right now. But some way, somehow, we have found a way through...together.

When Paris is written into the sporting history books, I'm sure Chris and I will look back on this time as a defining moment in our shift from professional sports to entrepreneurship.

I may have a bit of a head start when it comes to shifting to self-employment, but we have both already begun putting the building blocks in place to secure our future as successful business owners, mentors and thought leaders.

One of our first projects together is Enable Rise – a groundbreaking business dedicated to promoting inclusivity, empowerment and positive change within companies, organisations and through entrepreneurs.

I launched the business in 2024 with fellow wheelchair tennis player, dear friend and disability advocacy pioneer, Samanta Bullock.

Samanta, former Brazilian wheelchair tennis number 1 and often my doubles partner, is someone I looked up to from a young age, and now have the privilege to call my friend and business partner.

Since her accident at a young age, she has achieved so much, and with husband, Mark Bullock, has created Bullock Inclusion – a business that promotes inclusive fashion and sport.

Samanta, who lives in London, performed in the 2012 Paralympic Games Opening Ceremony and has been named as one of the 100 most influential disabled people in the UK, five times. I've only made that list once so far so I have some catching up to do!

Despite coming from very different backgrounds, our shared passion for wheelchair tennis and our advocacy for the disabled community has helped create a strong bond for nearly 20 years.

We worked on Enable Rise for months in the background so it's so good to see it all coming together.

Chris, and Sam's husband, Mark, who has 30 plus years' experience in Paralympic and disability sport and sports development, have joined Enable Rise as consultants and speakers. Mark is also someone who I have known for most of my life as he was a national coach when I was just starting out in tennis. He has always believed in me and continued to open doors of opportunity for me, and for that I am so grateful. They say it's not what you know, it's who you know and, in this case, it couldn't be more true.

Enable Rise launched at the National Tennis Centre in London in June 2024 with a host of VIP guests. They included multiple grand slam tennis champion and Paralympic medallist, Jordanne Whiley MBE (that's my bestie, otherwise known as Jordy, who you've already heard about), Joao Alfredo dos Anjos, Brazil's Consul General and Ambassador to the UK and Lily Mills, Special Olympics GB team member and gold medallist at the Learning Disability National Championships.

We received such incredible support from all those there and it's heart-warming to see so many passionate individuals come together to champion inclusivity and empowerment.

I can't wait to see how we all work together to change perceptions around disability and ability and help others to embrace what diversity really means.

As Sam so eloquently puts it: "Our mission is to break down stigmas and motivate others to help us create a world where everyone is valued and represented."

It's exciting to see how Enable Rise develops into the future.

At a young age, Sam became a true role model for me, showing that beauty knows no boundaries, especially for wheelchair users like us.

She has taught me that elegance and style are accessible to everyone, regardless of physical differences.

Sam's belief in me has had a profound effect on my career path. She instigated my first modelling opportunity – an unforgettable experience that not only introduced me to the fashion world, but also significantly boosted my self-confidence.

Thanks to her, I've wheeled the catwalk of London Fashion Week. I know, me? Crazy, isn't it? I would never have dreamed of doing that or even being confident enough if it wasn't for Sam.

I've also worked with fashion students to co-create adaptive clothing as part of an exciting inclusive fashion project. It has created me bespoke, one off pieces which are super comfy and fashionable.

Inclusive fashion goes beyond simply accommodating diverse body types, encompassing various abilities, genders, ages and cultural backgrounds.

Its importance is in its capacity to empower individuals, creating a sense of belonging and self-confidence... something I am so passionate about.

I was thrilled and honoured to host a panel on this important topic during London Fashion Week and hope to be involved in future discussions; again this opportunity was thanks to Sam.

In the past year I've also started a new venture with friend and HR expert, Rachel Weaven, providing advice to businesses on how to build an inclusive culture and work environment.

We're both passionate about helping companies create an inclusive workplace where people of all abilities and backgrounds can thrive. There are so many benefits to this approach. It enables a business to ensure they get the best out of every employee by creating an understanding, safe and happy work environment.

If we look at the most obvious group of people based on the themes of this book, disabled people are twice as likely to not be employed in the UK.

I see that as an incredible waste, so that's where Rachel and I come in.

We're different, which is why we're so effective. We're definitely not part of your usual tickbox EDI exercise. Our sessions are fun, interactive and, most importantly, honest.

We like to share our lived and professional experiences to help businesses feel more confident, and excited about EDI. We use positive, inspiring, real life stories to show what can be achieved by taking the time to understand someone and how that, in turn, benefits the business.

Since retiring from competitive sport, I have loved growing the mentorship area of my career; something I intend to expand further in the months and years to come.

I frequently speak and mentor young people in schools, helping them to develop life and employability skills through sports.

Part of my mentoring work is in collaboration with The Tim Henman Foundation.

Its mission is to transform the lives of disadvantaged young people by creating sporting and educational opportunities and improving mental and physical health. This is achieved through sports and education programmes, mentorship and grants.

In summer 2024, the foundation arranged a great visit to an RAF airbase with 200 Year 8 and 9 female students. I was part of a team of military, reservist, veteran and civilian women sharing their experiences to inspire and motivate these young women.

With a theme of If You Can See It, Then You Can Be It, the event aimed to challenge the Dream Gap - a project created by

Barbie which looks at the space between young girls' imaginative ambition, and their full potential, and the way these can be hindered by society.

I loved how the day inspired students to believe they could pursue careers in any field.

It showed them that through hard work, resilience and determination, they could overcome physical and mental challenges, and achieve any goals they set their mind to.

It was an amazing and unique opportunity for them to see who they could be, through the stories shared by a diverse group of female role models.

They learned about the variety of career opportunities available to them which then led to some meaningful conversations about the world of work.

I am so grateful to have played a part in this incredible day.

Days like this truly light me up, so here's to many more.

I love being an athlete mentor too, which is my role for the Youth Sport Trust. It's incredibly rewarding to witness the growth and achievements of the students I work with.

Seeing their hard work, dedication and determination pay off is a testament to their character and potential.

Being a part of their journey and offering guidance along the way fills me with pride and joy, and I have no doubt they will all continue to succeed in the future.

Sharing my knowledge of wheelchair tennis is equally enjoyable. Sometimes I'll go into tennis clubs to talk to their coaches about the sport and invite them to try out sports wheelchairs for themselves.

It's a wonderful way to help them understand the difference between the standing and wheelchair game so they can take this new knowledge into their own work.

These practical sessions, where they learn the basics and fundamentals of the sport, show them exactly what to look for and think about when adapting their own coaching sessions.

It's always eye opening to anyone when they try our sport for the first time, but what I love to see is when coaches play in a chair for the first time. So many light bulb moments happen because they suddenly experience the feeling for themselves. What's exciting is that I then know this is going to change a wheelchair player's coaching session for the better because their perspective and understanding has changed.

Talks for schools will continue to be a big part of my role going forward. I adore connecting with young audiences and answering the thought provoking questions they ask.

At one in Oxford recently - part of a week of workshops, talks and tailored lessons - the theme was The World Of Water.

How does that fit in with my story, you may ask? Well, it came off the back of a social media post I'd written about my trip to the Bahamas.

It was an amazing visit because I was able to enjoy the same experiences as non-disabled holiday makers.

I cruised around the islands, did endless swimming and had the privilege to use an adapted beach wheelchair.

To swim and be out of that seated position in the chair is the most soothing feeling I ever experience.

Ever wonder how someone unable to walk swims in the sea?

Aside from the indignity of crawling or being carried across the sand (which can often be dangerous), if you're unable to walk, like me, the only answer to this question is the beach wheelchair.

They are expensive and rare to find. So, as I came off the ship, the discovery of a line of beach wheelchairs filled me with uncontainable excitement.

This was the answer to allowing me to partake in everything the beautiful destination had to offer. The most important activity for me being swimming in the sea.

This adaptive chair not only gave me easy access to those sandy shores, but it symbolised a commitment to ensuring people with varying mobility needs could fully enjoy and engage in island activities, like everyone else.

With a beach wheelchair I could explore the coastline, sit on the beach with a good book and swim freely in the beautiful, crystal clear ocean. Lush.

I've always loved being in the water, so this was one of the easiest topics to talk about.

Water sports, such as jet skiing and kayaking, travelling by sea (I love cruises) and swimming have always played a key role in my life. Being in or on the water is a favourite hobby and a wonderful way to relax. Every holiday I've been on has always revolved around the sea as it truly feels like my safe space.

I love telling audiences about some of my watery adventures and sharing an important message about how we can adapt things to ensure people with disabilities enjoy the same experiences as non-disabled people.

As I've mentioned earlier, there are a lot of misunderstandings about wheelchairs. It's one of the reasons why I think it's good to draw attention to International Wheelchair Day on March 1. It's an opportunity for wheelchair users to celebrate the positive impact of their mobility aid, so celebrate it I do!

Whilst my wheelchair is seamlessly just a part of my daily life, taking a moment to recognise its true purpose is so important.

It's an incredible piece of technology, has evolved over the years and, as a result, granted me endless possibilities. It provides me with absolute independence, enabling a life that I always wanted.

I'm so grateful for my wheelchair and the daily freedom it gives me. I will never understand why so many people see using a wheelchair to get around as a drawback.

It's something I'll keep talking about because changing that awful stereotype that it's something to be pitied or 'a worst case scenario' matters so much. They are bloody awesome!

Remember that chat I had with my nan that smashed stereotypes? That mattered and so do all the other conversations that challenge misconceptions about these incredible mobility aids.

Every year, when National Girls and Women in Sports Day comes around in early February, I'm inspired to continue my work encouraging and supporting women of all ages to get active in the sports industry.

It's wonderful to celebrate the achievements and contributions of females in sport who, all too often, have had to fight all kinds of prejudices to leave an indelible mark on the world.

Everything in me is driven towards helping people be the best versions of themselves.

One of the kids I worked with recently asked me: "Why do you do talks?"

My answer was simple: "Because I just want to help."

I love working with young people. When they're at an inquisitive age they will ask me anything.

At one of my talks I asked a group of them: "Have any of you ever been really excited about something when someone's made you feel crap about it and tried to squash your joy?"

All the girls in the room nodded. "How does that make you feel?," I asked.

What followed next was a sea of shoulders dropping. The atmosphere in the room was rubbish.

So, I challenged them and asked: "Why are you surrounding yourself with people like that?"

It certainly opened up some good conversations and gave me an opportunity to show them how important it is to surround yourself with the right crowd, people who truly have your back and will support you, warts and all.

I have been so lucky that the people I have met on my journey have given me little nuggets of wisdom that have stayed with me. They have helped me see that I *can* achieve, that being different is a good thing.

It's something I always pass onto people I work with now.

When we're younger, I think jealousy can exist a lot more because we don't have as much control over our lives and the things we're doing. It's easier to become jealous of a family situation, an opportunity or something else.

I see too many young people squashing their joy without even realising they're doing it. Often, it's because they don't know how to deal with things or respond in a healthy way. Maybe they've never been in an environment where they've been lifted up or celebrated.

I love talking about the importance of surrounding yourself with positive people, those that can support you.

When you're young, you can feel really alone. I certainly did at times. So, I hope that by talking things through in a safe space, it can help someone to believe they're going to be okay.

Seeing those light bulb moments in others is what motivates me. It's amazing when you can see the change in their eyes, their body posture. I love it so much when people I'm working with say: "I never thought I could do that, but I can, I have." It's such a privilege to have that sort of impact.

By the way, I don't think I'm some amazing, life changing person. I just feel lucky that someone did that for me. This is what inspires me to do the work I do. If I positively impact just one person, then that's always enough.

I love being reminded of just how sport has shaped me into the woman I am today. Of how the rebel, warrior, leader in me has been inspired by the rebels, warriors, leaders, who came before.

As an athlete, sport has played a transformative role in my life, shaping my character, teaching me discipline and allowing me to meet some amazing people during my travels across the world. It has built my confidence and resilience.

Even in retirement, my connection with sports continues, holding a very special place in my heart, albeit in a different way.

In some ways I am still that five-year-old who wheeled herself into Wimbledon history; staring wide-eyed in wonder as she discovered the joys of wheelchair tennis in the theatre of tennis dreams. I hope that never changes.

In love with a sport that ran through my veins from the start. It will always be part of me.

But now I have new dreams. Dreams to fulfil in my roles as athlete mentor, business owner, commentator, tournament director, disability advocate, diversity and inclusion consultant.

Dreams with my family. With Chris, with Mum, with Dad, with Milo and all those who love me and I them. The people who have stood by me, held me, supported me and empowered me. Who have never seen me as 'different', as 'special', as 'other'... just Louise.

Rebel, Warrior, Leader.

Paralympian. Speaker and mentor. International sports commentator.

Tennis Player. World Traveller. Conversationalist.

Businesswoman. Partner to Chris. (The ultimate team). Mum to Milo (my canine companion) for always.

And finally...

I had an interesting conversation recently with someone I really admire.

They told me they had been surprised by so many things I had posted about what it is to live and thrive with a disability in 21st Century Britain.

They said they felt embarrassed and guilty for never considering the points I'd raised. They weren't the first person to admit this to me.

If you're sharing some of these feelings, then listen up.

It's completely understandable if you haven't been aware of the challenges related to living life with a disability, until now.

Empathy and understanding often arise from personal experiences, and not everyone has had the opportunity to gain insights into different perspectives.

Learning and growing in awareness is a continual process, and the important thing is that if you didn't know much before reading this book or my social posts, I'd simply ask that you engage with these important topics now. Just retain the information ready for a scenario where it may be relevant.

For example, if you enter a building with no wheelchair access, mention it to a relevant person. If you hear inappropriate language/behaviour talking around the topic of disability, please challenge it.

The important thing is willingness to understand and support. This is what creates a more inclusive and empathetic world for individuals facing unique challenges.

Embracing newfound knowledge about living with a disability is a positive step forward. Openness to learning and acknowledging diverse experiences contributes to creating a more inclusive society.

It's okay to not have been aware initially; what matters is ongoing effort to educate yourself and promote understanding for a more compassionate and supportive world.

So, please take it from me. Never feel guilty or embarrassed for not knowing something beforehand. We can't all know everything, but there is always space to learn.

As an athlete, sport played a transformative role in my life, shaping my character, teaching me discipline. It has allowed me to meet some amazing people, travel the world and build my confidence and resilience.

Even in retirement, my connection with sports continues and holds a special place in my heart, but now in a different way. Taking on roles like commentary, being a tournament director and athlete mentor, these roles allow me to share my passion and experiences. I'm so happy I have ways in which I can continue to contribute to the growth and empowerment of women, of people with disabilities, in sports, in all capacities.

I'm so happy that my journey in sport didn't end with retirement - it just evolved, and continues to evolve, into new avenues, helping me create a legacy beyond being an athlete. I am so excited for the future. I am just Louise, I am proud and I am so ready for whatever life throws at me next. Are you?

PS: A FAIRYTALE FINALE

My aim and hope when I was writing this book was always that I could end it with a fairy tale finale to this chapter of our lives. I'm writing this in my hotel room as I'm about to leave Paris. Chris won a bronze medal yesterday, and I couldn't be more proud. In his words, six months ago: "If someone said I could even step on the mat in Paris, I'd snatch their hand off." I felt the same. Chris just being here was enough of an achievement to be proud of for the rest of his life.

This has been such a tough year; it's been a whirlwind rollercoaster of emotions, with Chris having to deal with classification issues and challenges that left him in one of the darkest places he'd ever experienced. The way in which he was treated by classifiers, and the uncertainty that caused, was utterly devastating for him.

However, getting through this and him winning bronze here, we've both agreed, feels even sweeter than that gold medal a few years ago, because this one actually signifies so much more. It's a beautiful end to this chapter of our lives, and it's absolute proof that people can try and throw you down as much as possible, but you can still get back up and achieve your goals.

The night before Chris's fight, I was asked by Whisper if I were happy for them to follow me around with the camera crew all day to follow our journey together once again, just like they did in Tokyo. My day began with an 8am filming session in my hotel room and ended in the most magnificent way ever (side note, Chris had no idea I was doing any of this). What they also asked me to do was conduct Chris's final ever Mixed Zone interview. If you haven't heard of a Mixed Zone, that's the area where all the press sit and athletes go to immediately after competition to get those exciting initial reactions. Chris had no idea it was going to be me doing this interview. When he sat down, we were both overwhelmed with emotion. We literally cried and giggled our way through.

I can honestly say that conducting that interview for Chris is the biggest highlight of my professional media career so far. I was truly honoured that Channel 4 trusted me to take hold of that magic moment, and for Chris and I to share that moment in our respective careers felt like something dreams were made of. It was like 'look how far we've come, together'. Apart from asking the obvious questions, I left with the most important one. I checked in with, how much do you want some gluten-free pork pies right now? And his response naturally was: "I hope you've got some at home love, because we're going home." - the same words he muttered three years ago in Tokyo and that have made all the Paralympic adverts this year. After a hectic day, we were whisked off to Channel 4's late night show, The Last Leg, where we could celebrate with other athletes and enjoy that magic moment a little bit longer.

I've never felt such joy, pride and love in my life. Chris repeatedly makes me proud. Every time I think he's made me feel every emotion that could ever possibly exist, he tops it yet again. There are two moments that stood out from yesterday. One, when he had his opponent in the bronze medal fight pinned. He just smiled. He eked out that moment. He milked it for all its worth, that winning moment. He knew it was his last one and he wanted to soak up every second. Seeing him smile, making it last as long as possible, was incredible because I just got to sit for a little bit longer realising, he's going to win this. The other moment was when Chris leapt into my arms straight after he'd won. The first thing he said was: "We're done, let's go and live our lives." That's what we're about to do, and I can't wait.

GET IN TOUCH WITH ME

Thank you so much for reading and, if you've loved this book, please leave me a review on Amazon and share your comments across social media. Thanks so much, it is so incredibly appreciated.

Follow me on my social channels:

@louisehunt1 – Instagram and X

Louise Hunt Skelley PLY on LinkedIn

www.louisehunt.co.uk

WITH LOVE AND THANKS

I actually can't believe I've done it. Finally, I have my very own book telling the story of my whirlwind life and adventures... so far.

To create this has been an ambition of mine since I can remember, and for it to be a reality is incredibly surreal.

It feels like I need another whole book to thank every person that's had an impact on my life and made this happen, but I'll try and keep it as short and sweet as possible.

To Liz McDermott for helping me begin my book writing journey. Thank you for making me believe I had a story to tell and helping me get on my way.

To my incredibly selfless, beautiful, kind and caring parents and brother Rob, thank you for being by my side my entire life and ensuring I always believed in myself and for supporting any crazy idea I may have had. I would have never got to where I am today without you.

To the Bride Squad, each and every one of you holds an incredibly special place in my heart and make me who I am today. I adore you and want to thank you for your unwavering support, unconditional love and friendship, and for being by my side through every weird and wonderful phase of my life, judgement free. I love you all deeply.

To Chris and Milo, my boys. My family, my core, my beating heart. Everything I do is with you two in mind and there is no safer or happier place in my world than by both of your sides. I love you both more than words can ever explain.

My dear husband, thank you for believing in me and being my biggest cheerleader in any goal I set myself. Never forget I'm your biggest fan too and together, I can't wait to see what the future holds for us.

And last, but by no means least, a super special thanks must go to the wonderful Asha Clearwater, without whom, this book wouldn't have been possible. I'm absolutely delighted that you were willing to go on this journey with me. I'm so proud of what we have achieved and I'm truly honoured to have created this with you by my side. Thank you for believing in me, helping me to tell my story and for making me feel remotely interesting. You're a legend, an incredible talent, beautiful soul, and I appreciate you so much.

It took me a while to think about who I wanted to dedicate my book to. Truthfully, it's dedicated to every single person who's been by my side and helped me get to where I am today. But actually, if I could dedicate this book to anyone, it would be my younger self, my younger teenage self, my younger childhood self, who often didn't quite know where she was going, had moments in wavering confidence, felt lonely at times and different, and not always for the better. I dedicate this to you.

I wish I could have been there for you. But now I hope you see that being different and unique were your greatest strengths and the most interesting parts about you; that it's okay not to be okay, but most importantly, it's really okay to be quirky and different. 'Normal' (whatever that means), is overrated and boring, my dear!

The people that love you the very most will embrace you for every one of those unique characteristics. So, to the younger me, you are loved, you are capable, and the only limits that exist in this world are those you set yourself.

Printed in Great Britain
by Amazon